THE NIGHT OF WENCESLAS
and
THE ROSE OF TIBET

Lionel Davidson is a three-times winner of the Gold
Dagger Award (for *The Night of Wenceslas*, *A Long
Way to Shiloh* and *The Chelsea Murders*). His thrillers
and adventure novels, most recently *Kolymsky
Heights*, have won him enormous international
acclaim. He has travelled widely, spent some time in
Israel, but now lives in North London.

LIONEL DAVIDSON

THE NIGHT
OF WENCESLAS

and

THE ROSE
OF TIBET

Mandarin

A Mandarin Paperback
THE NIGHT OF WENCESLAS and THE ROSE OF TIBET

The Night of Wenceslas first published in Great Britain 1960
by Gollancz
The Rose of Tibet first published in Great Britain 1962
by Gollancz
This combined edition published 1995
by Mandarin Paperbacks
an imprint of Reed International Books Ltd
Michelin House, 81 Fulham Road, London sw3 6rb
and Auckland, Melbourne, Singapore and Toronto

Copyright © Lionel Davidson 1960,1962
This combined edition copyright © Lionel Davidson 1995
The author has asserted his moral rights

A CIP catalogue record for this title
is available from the British Library
ISBN 07493 2340 X

Printed and bound in Great Britain
by Cox & Wyman, Reading

THE NIGHT
OF WENCESLAS

Chapter 1

1

THE little swine had his head well down in the books when I went in, so it was clear Miss Vosper had forestalled me after all. I had been popping up and down half the day to peer through the frosted glass panel of his door, and she wouldn't miss a thing like that.

He kept his head down religiously – usually he'd have a quick blink up to see who it was – and after a couple of minutes I shuffled my feet and coughed somewhat aggressively.

He looked up then, pretending his rather charming 'tired' double-take and said, 'Yes, Nicolas?' He kept his finger ostentatiously on the line.

'I'd like a word with you if you're not too busy.' I'd promised myself I wouldn't say the last bit, and to salve my pride added loudly, 'It's important.'

'If it's important it won't wait,' said the Little Swine humorously, and he carefully jotted down his last figure and pushed the ledger back an inch. 'What can I do for you, Nicolas?'

'It's about money,' I said, taking the seat he hadn't offered. I used to sit in it as a little boy waiting for my father. The Little Swine had been junior partner then. 'I just can't manage on seven quid a week.'

The Little Swine stared at me disbelievingly. 'A young man with no responsibilites can't make seven pounds last seven days? What are you telling me, Nicolas? A postman with a family manages on very little more.'

7

'Well, I can't. When I've paid for my digs and fares I've got about fifty bob left. I've got to buy clothes and – and entertainment, taking a girl out occasionally. . . .'

The Little Swine was shaking his head. 'What new clothes, Nicolas? You got yourself a fine rig-out when you left the army. I myself buy a new suit only once in three years. It's the car, Nicolas. At the time I told you – a certain liability, unjustifiable extravagance. Do I have a car?'

He waited for me to speak, smiling, knowing in his swinish little way that he'd cobbled me, and when I didn't, said, 'Nicolas, be a good boy and try just for once to follow my advice. You're a boy twenty-four – all right, a man then! When you've learned the business thoroughly you'll take up your full duties as a partner. This talk of jobs and rises is undignified in your position. You're getting spending money – a very handsome allowance – while you learn the business. Do you think you're worth even seven pounds a week to the business at the moment?'

He paused again with his hands outstretched and a whimsical smile on his face. I knew he'd tell me all this and Maura had told me what to reply, but for the life of me I couldn't sort the answers out. The Little Swine had known me all my life. His younger sister had been my nanny. He'd come into this room one day when I'd wet the chair. I even used to call him Uncle Karel – it still slipped out sometimes.

I said glumly, 'All I know is I can't manage. I'm borrowing all the time and I'm in debt.'

'Debts? Who are you in debt to?'

There was a bill for £7 16s. outstanding at the garage for the past four months.

'Various poeple,' I said. 'I even had to borrow a fiver from my mother a few weeks ago.'

'You should not borrow from your mother,' the Little Swine said reproachfully. 'You know I would always lend you the money. It is too bad to worry her. How is the sweet lady?'

'She's all right,' Maminka lived in Bournemouth, and I knew I had really borrowed the money from old Imre, who lived in the same private hotel; she would merely ask him for a loan until I had repaid it.

'It is so long since I have seen her,' the Little Swine said sadly. 'With business so hard to find I have not had a moment for years to go and pay her a visit. Is she still so beautiful?'

'Yes,' I said truthfully. She was.

'And Mr Gabriel? His lungs?' The Little Swine inquired delicately.

'Imre's all right.' There was nothing wrong with Imre's lungs. He had been in love with my mother for years and his supposed enfeeblement gave him an excuse to live in Bournemouth, too. He ran a small stamp business from the hotel.

'I must go down to see them. I will try next month after the audit.'

He looked as if he meant it, so I said hastily, 'She lives in the past a great deal, you know.' She had always treated the Little Swine in a very condescending manner (his first job had been sweeping the floor in her father's glassworks) and had got it into her head that he was merely superintending the business until I wished to take it over.

The Little Swine took the point, but he said, 'And what a past! You would hardly remember Prague, of course, but your mother was the uncrowned queen, I assure you. An enchanting lady. It is no wonder she prefers to think of those days.'

He sat there with a rather lingering smile on his face, no doubt well satisfied at the changes in their respective fortunes, until he recollected himself and drew the ledger back. 'Well, Nicolas, we must not think of the past, but of the present and the future. There is a good one waiting for you as soon as you settle down and take an interest. Meanwhile, get rid of the car, my boy, and you will find you have money to spare.'

He gave me a little nod, and automatically I stood up. I was outside his office before I realized I'd got nothing out of him. Nothing at all. No promises. No half promises. Nothing I could tax him with, even in my own mind. I didn't know what I was going to tell Maura.

My face must have been so glum that Miss Vosper, drawing

her own conclusions, tried hard to suppress her hideous delight and began sticking stamps with her enormous gargoyle tongue.

'I've stamped all yours,' she said with her unique leprous smile, 'and checked the stamp book. It was only out ninepence this week.'

'Right.' The single word must have sounded so bitter that she turned her head to conceal a smile. The suppression seemed to release a gust of her special odour, and a cloud of it wafted towards me. I blew my nose hard.

'Is Mr Nimek free now?' she asked, almost giggling.

'Yes.'

She stood up with her notebook and paused over my desk for a moment so that I was almost choked and had to turn my head away. 'He's been a thorough tartar all the week.'

The idea of the Little Swine as a tartar was so singular that when she went I stared after her. Miss Vosper had been with him seventeen years; ample time to see him as he was. This new vision of him rivalled in lunacy only her demoniac hatred of me, the interloper, the young toff, the threat from the past.

My father had started this business, an Englishman who had worked for years in Prague where he had met and married my mother. He had set up the English end as a selling outlet for the Bohemian glassworks just before I was born, and had sent Karel Nimek, the Little Swine, over to look after it. The Germans took over the glassworks in 1938 and the London importing firm became the main business.

My father had died of cancer in 1941, having made over most of his shares to the Little Swine. He had not got much for them, for the main assets of the business consisted in a claim for compensation after the war. But he had left me thirty per cent, and had come to an agreement with the Little Swine that I was to be allowed to establish parity with him in our respective shareholdings when I left university and had received a grounding in the business. He had then bought my mother an annuity, settled a sum for my education, and had died confident the agreement would be honoured.

Why he expected the Little Swine to honour so vague an undertaking I had never known. In effect he had put the Little Swine on his honour. A chancy thing to do. Since coming out of the army nearly a year before, I had been the general dogsbody of the office. My shares meant nothing, since he had never distributed any profits. Seven quid a week.

It was just on five – another hour to go before the office closed. I didn't think I could stand it a moment longer. I picked up my mac and the letters and walked out.

The liftman hated to come up two floors to take down-passengers, so I leaned on the bell till he did so. He came up white and shaking and silent with rage and, cheered a little by this, I rode down and walked out into the street and as far as the Princess May before realizing I had forgotten to post the letters. I slipped them into my pocket and went into the saloon instead.

'Bitter?' Jack said.

I had been going to say Scotch, but thought better of it and nodded.

Jack pulled it. 'What's up with you?' he said. 'Lost your granny?'

I said, 'Aa-ach,' and took an enormous swallow of beer. 'It's a bloody life,' I said.

He stood leaning against the bar, amused. 'Got the sack?'

'No such luck.'

'Women?'

'No.'

'Car broke down again?'

'It's the only thing that hasn't.'

'Here,' he said, 'that reminds me.' He groped in a cubby hole behind the till and brought out the back of a cigarette packet with markings on it. 'A customer wants to buy an old M.G. You thinking of selling?'

I started to say no, automatically, and changed my mind. 'How much is he prepared to pay?'

'He'd go up to two hundred for what he wants.'

'Cash?'

Jack scrutinized the card. 'He didn't say. He looked as if he could afford it. You interested?'

'I might be. You'd better take my phone number in case he looks in again.'

I wrote it for him on the cigarette packet and he returned it to the cubby hole.

I couldn't afford another, so I left, feeling more dolorous than ever at the idea of giving up the car.

I thought about the car all the way home. I thought I might as well pick it up from the lock-up in case the chap did want to come and see it over the weekend. This was not such a simple operation, for the rat-faced proprietor of the garage had been growing definitely old-fashioned towards me of recent weeks, demanding payment in full before I took the car out again. I still had the key however.

It was now just after six and the garage would be shut. I thought it was worth a try. My spirits rose a little when I saw the drive-in deserted, for the proprietor sometimes monkeyed around for half an hour at the front. They fell again when I turned in to the alley and the lock-ups. His daughter, a solitary child of ten or eleven, was dancing about in some hop-scotch squares. She ran off the moment she saw me.

I unlocked the door, pulled out the M.G. and was just relocking when Ratface appeared.

'Good evening,' I said.

'Were you thinking of paying off your bill?'

'I'm afraid I've not brought very much money out with me.'

'Well, you can just push that car back and give me the key. I'm not interested in promises or excuses. There's ten hours' work gone into that car in addition to the petrol feed, the carburettor, and the gaskets. I don't mind letting you run on a bit with your lock-up rent, but I've come to the end of my patience. Pay up or the car stays here.'

Silently I reached for my wallet and scrutinized the contents. Six pounds ten in notes; pay-day. 'I could let you have a couple on account,' I said.

'I've told you. I want the lot.'

'I'm very sorry, Mr Rickett. I just haven't got it. I've been trying to get the money for you.'

'Well, try a bit harder,' he said. His face had gone pale with passion and his little pointed head was down dangerously as though he meant to savage me. 'I don't want to be hard,' he said after a moment, relaxing a little, and no doubt realizing that some was better than none. 'You can take it if you pay half now and your word that I get the rest by the end of next week.'

Half was nearly four pounds. That meant no rent for Mrs Nolan. Or no lunches for me, and no dates with Maura. I suddenly remembered that I was supposed to be seeing her tonight. The thought momentarily distracted me so much that I gave him the four pounds. I made one last stand. 'Would you mind shoving a couple of gallons in? I think I'm rather low.'

He looked at me and something that could have been a smile crossed his rat face. 'Well, you're cool, I must say,' he said. But he seemed so taken with the coolness that he actually unlocked the pump and let me have a gallon. 'There's one,' he said, 'to get you off the premises.'

He stood and watched me with the same smile on his face as I backed down the alley, and this tribute to my coolness, added to the pleasure of taking over the wheel, raised my spirits instantly. I backed into the road, pulled her round in two cool, snappy movements, and actually waved to him as I shot up the road. He did not return the wave.

2

This aged, red, strap-bound M.G. was my most important possession and if not, in fact, actually priceless, certainly represented to me more than it could possibly fetch. The week before I had bought it I had been unable to think of anything else. There were many things I should have thought of, like getting a flat and some furniture.

One of the troubles was that I had not known what I wanted to do. If the vague haven of the business had not been awaiting me for several years, maybe I would have exerted myself in some direction. As it was I was lazy, unable to project any alternative to Maminka's vision of the glorious future that awaited me.

Maminka's idea of the business was so grotesque that it embarrassed me to hear her talk about it. In my father's day, certainly, it had been a little more attractive – the office had occupied the whole floor, and somewhere in the East End there had been a large warehouse. Since then the Czech glass imports had dried up and the Little Swine had gone in for sidelines. He was now running a rudimentary two-room organization that suited him perfectly.

All through university and the army, on the infrequent trips I had made to see the Little Swine, the business had grown smaller and tattier, and his increasing joviality – 'Well, Nicolas, we will soon be ordering your desk' – had depressed me more and more. In the event he hadn't even done that; I took over the desk of a clerk he sacked.

I had never known if this was all part of some deep-rooted scheme of the Little Swine's to make the future so unattractive that I would opt out of it, or if his affairs had not merely become with the years a more faithful expression of his personality; whatever it was, the prospect of settling in for life with him held no enchantment.

It was in this frame of mind that I first clapped eyes on the car, pointing her nose out of a second-hand lot. £130. Nippy. Snip, the whitewash said. I had £170. I was going to see a flat whose tenant wanted £120 for his furniture. I walked up to the corner and round it and stopped to light a cigarette, and then I walked slowly back.

A man in a dirty white coat nodded at me and smiled. 'Saw you looking at her. Knew you'd be back. A beaut, ain't she? Cock your leg over and sit in her.'

I cocked my leg over the low door and sat behind the wheel. 'Grab hold. Tight as a drum.'

The steering was beautifully tight. (It did not, alas, remain so.)

'There,' he said. 'Buzz off to China if you want now.' He walked away and left me with the car, and I sat there looking along the bonnet, and I was hooked. That tremulous moment before I was committed, when I knew I could afford the car or the flat but not both, was the most poignant of my life. I saw myself travelling light, sun-dappled roads, sea glitter, free, free as a bird; no young man of affairs with a valise as Maminka saw me; no young chair-wetter to be schooled in a little, dreary, bloody business; quite a new vision I had never seen before; another, pleasanter, very agreeable identity.

'She's taxed to the end of the year,' the man said, coming back. 'Souped up, of course. Take a decko if you like.' He opened up the bonnet. A lethal-looking supercharger winked in the sun. 'Goes like a bomb and steady as a train.'

I walked back to Paddington in a trance without looking at the flat, and took the train to Bournemouth, and leaned out of the window seeing the car all the way.

I bought it a week later, sick with relief at finding it still there.

In terms of hard cash it might not have been the keenest bargain of my life; in all other terms it was certainly so. It was still the chink in the grimy barriers building up round me; still, in a way, my defence against Maura. The thought of selling it made me feel sick.

I slowed at the corner and tooled along to number seventy-four rather slowly, listening to a peculiar sort of rattle from the clutch every time I changed gear. This was something new. I wondered if Ratface had been tinkering with it, whether he'd been tinkering with it all along so that he'd have to repair it, but after a moment of viciousness dismissed the idea. He wasn't a bad Ratface at heart; this last was only one of a series of bills he had let me run up. By the sound of the clutch – a fiver's worth, I thought – I'd be owing him a bit more soon.

I drew into the kerb, let myself into the house, walked up the three flights. There was a note stuck under the plant on the plush tablecloth. It was in Mrs Nolan's indelible pencil and read:

Mr Whistler. Your young lady phoned. She said she phoned your office at 5.30. Will you ring her at home when you get in. L. Nolan.

I thought Maura could wait a bit. I hung up my mac and went out to the bathroom for a wash and came back and smoked a cigarette, sitting on the divan with my feet up on the edge of the coverlet. I wondered what I was going to tell Maura.

I had known her only for six months, but already, it seemed, for a lifetime. She was Irish, red-headed, and she had digs in a square off Gloucester Road, not far away. It was Maura who had given the Little Swine his soubriquet, and she who had manoeuvred me into today's confrontation. Maura said the position was ridiculous. She said I was either a partner or I wasn't. She said anyone with thirty per cent of the firm's shares should count for something. She said the business must be making *some* profits, and where were they?

I had not even got round to that one with the Little Swine.

Even worse than her constant preoccupation with the Little Swine was her mania about my Uncle Bela. Bela was my mother's brother. He had emigrated to Canada several years before the war and now lived in Vancouver. He had never married and on a trip to England to see Maminka after we had arrived from Czechoslovakia, he had told her I would be his heir.

Any family such as mine with European connections and relatives who have emigrated have figures such as Bela. I had a hazy recollection of a large asthmatic man always supposed by my father to be excessively mean. It was a fact that he had never helped Maminka in any way, and the only present he had ever given her was a rather flashy zircon brooch which she never wore.

Bela's name was seldom absent for long from my mother's lips; she took it for granted that he would leave me at least a dollar millionaire, and her only hinted criticism was that he had not already settled the money on me.

It was probably because he had entered Maminka's mythology more than anything else that made me regard Uncle Bela as a somewhat dubious prop. She wrote to him regularly and I knew that she managed to contrive some mention of me in every letter. As he seemed to take equal pains never to refer to me in his infrequent and curiously uninformative replies, it seemed obvious he had regretted his earlier impulse. He operated a cannery and the only reference he ever made to his financial affairs was his annual comment that the fruit was very poor and very expensive.

Although Maura had never met my mother, she seemed equally credulous about Bela, and infinitely more annoying. She, moreover, knew the true state of my affairs, and regarded my reluctance to solicit his help as the sheerest idiocy. In self-defence I had had to turn Uncle Bela into a joke – the ship that was going to come in, the treble chance that was going to turn up one day. I had built him up into such an unlikely shadow that, maddeningly, I was beginning to share their superstitious belief in him.

The cigarette burned down and I stubbed it out and reluctantly left the divan and went downstairs to the phone. Maura answered instantly.

'It's Nicolas,' I said.

'Well?'

'Well, what?' I said irritated.

She made a little kiss down the phone and said, 'What happened this afternoon? Did you see him?'

'Yes.'

'You left early. I wondered if you'd had a row.'

'No row.' Mrs Nolan came out of her lair behind me, and I thought I might as well put across the same news item to both parties, so I said quickly, 'Look, Maura, I've had to pay a bill on the car and I haven't a sausage left this week. I can't afford to buy a bottle for tonight.'

'Oh, Nicolas. You can bring a bottle of beer. They brought one to my party –'

'I can't even afford a bottle of beer,' I said loudly. 'I'm flat broke. I'll have to do without lunches for a couple of days. I'd better not come tonight.'

Maura seemed to latch on that this was intended for another, for she said without concern, 'Do you want me to leave five bob at the off-licence?'

'No.'

'All right. I'll see you there. What did he say?'

'All right, then. Goodbye.' I hung up quickly. You had to be quick.

Mrs Nolan was standing behind me, listening.

'I wonder that young lady wants to go out with you the way you treat her so sharply on the phone,' she said.

I smiled at her wanly. 'I'm worried about money, Mrs Nolan.'

'No rent for me this week, I suppose,' she said with her own curious tone of winsome aggressiveness.

I said stoutly, 'You know I wouldn't dream of letting you down with the rent, Mrs Nolan. I'll just have to borrow it elsewhere.'

'Oh, I don't mind you, ducky,' she said. 'It's the others. Don't you mention it or they'll all be going off to buy cars.' She gave my arm a little push to show she meant no harm. 'And you go off to that party tonight or someone else'll be after your young lady, and then we shall be sad. I've got a bottle of port you can take.'

I followed her into the kitchen and accepted the bottle of British port she handed me from the fridge. She always kept one in this curious place.

'Don't you run off now,' she said. 'Dinner's in ten minutes. A nice bit of fish for Friday, same as your mother'd give you.'

She said this every Friday. I had never understood what she meant by it.

3

I walked to the party to save petrol, still wondering what to tell Maura. I was twenty-four and she twenty-one; we had no claim on each other but increasingly in recent weeks the feeling had grown that if only I exerted myself with the Little Swine, or with Bela, or with the economic world at large – in a word began to make something of myself – we could have some claim on each other.

This had induced a feeling of profound inadequacy. To make up for it I pressed home my somewhat decorous and well-signalled advances with great desperation. I seemed to be making some progress here.

I heard the gramophone thumping out and turned in at the gate. The chap who was giving the party opened the door to me and cried, 'It's Nicky. Come in, you terror of the City.' Nobody else called me Nicky, and I disliked it and him. His name was Val and he worked in a film publicity business and lived with an ageing model girl called Audrey. It always embarrassed me to be with them.

'What's this?' he said, breaking into laughter as he examined the bottle I had been clutching grimly. 'Port type wine, for God's sake. You City barons! Can't let it alone, can you? Bung it in the bowl, there's a good lad. It'll help out with the cup. In the kitchen,' he said as the door bell rang again.

I did as he bade and returned to the drawing room as he was introducing the two newcomers. He stopped to call attention to me. 'And this type slipped in while I wasn't looking. Cheer up, Nicky. Boris Karloff will kick the bucket soon.' He always called Uncle Bela by this name, and it was always good for a laugh. I had encouraged this, and did so now by crying in a cracked voice, 'You'll be glad you knew me yet.'

I could see Maura frowning at the other end of the room — she did not care for jokes about Uncle Bela — and I kept out of her way. By judicious shifting of position I was able to do so for most of the evening, and when we at last stood in the hall making our farewells she seemed needled.

Her lips were tight as I took her arm and cut through the dark squares to her digs.

'So you didn't get the rise?' she said at last.

'I'm seeing him again next week.'

'That seems satisfactory to you, does it?'

The dark seat under the tree where, all being well, I should make continued progress, was fifty yards away. I said sombrely, 'He wants to consider it. He agrees I'm in a special position. You've got to admit the prospects are good.'

'Did you mention about the profits?'

'Yes,' I said doggedly.

The pale blur of her face turned to me in the dark, but she said nothing.

We were at the seat now. 'Like to take the weight off?' I said heavily.

'Do you mind if we don't, Nicolas. I'm terribly tired tonight.'

'Oh.'

'I've had rather a headache all day – worrying about you. You don't mind if I just go to bed?'

'No. Yes,' I said dully.

Her hand touched my face for a moment. 'I'll sit and smoke a cigarette with you if you like.'

'No, you'd better go off to bed. I thought you were looking a bit washed out,' I said.

'Well, I am,' she said tartly.

'Right. I'll see you to the gate.'

We walked the rest of the way in silence.

'Good night, Nicolas,' she said, when we got there.

'Good night.'

'On Sunday, then.'

'Yes.' If you're lucky, I thought bravely, walking off right away. But I knew I'd be seeing her on Sunday.

I shoved the covers over the car when I got back and let myself in and went up the three flights and undressed and crawled in, more inadequate than I'd felt for weeks. I tried to imagine myself at the wheel of the car, sun-dappled roads, sea glitter, free as a bird, but it seemed to be a different person I was watching.

Uncle Bela, I mouthed silently at the ceiling. *Why don't you just quietly die?* And presently he died on the ceiling in his big bed in Vancouver. The noisy asthmatic room grew silent, the smooth white sheets were still over the dome of his stomach. I bent over Uncle Bela and his pale jowl was slack in the moonlight, the mouth open like the fish on the draining board because it was Friday, and on Friday I had to see the Little Swine. The Little Swine's face was calm on the pillow in the moonlight, but always dangerous and now pallid and rat-like as he said I couldn't have it unless I paid half. So I paid him half, and there were thousands more in the wallet because I'd filled it from the dome, and I sat in the seat and backed down the alley and turned in two cool and snappy movements and then I was there, there in long-breathing rhythmical movements, there on the sun-dappled road, caressing the wheel, so warm and smooth, so warm and smooth where the stocking ended.

When I awoke in the morning the first thing I thought of was how I'd willed Uncle Bela to die and I lay there, slightly sick. Not much lower now, I thought. I'd have to do something about myself; frittering away the weeks and the months and the years. I rolled out of bed and into a dressing gown and into the bathroom.

I couldn't get it out of my head, however, about Uncle Bela, and my haunted look in the mirror frightened me. I had never been to Vancouver. I had never seen anyone die. And yet the details were horribly clear; the sudden cessation of the asthmatic breathing, the shape of the white sheets draped round his stomach; an entity of stillness and death. My eyes stared back at me superstitiously, and to banish the vision I began to scrub and towel with great vigour.

Saturday was eggs, and by saying 'Eggs, *eggs*!' to myself in varying tones of wonder as I dressed I was able to cry, 'Ready, Mrs Nolan!' with a fair counterfeit of enthusiasm as I filed briskly into the dining room.

I nodded briefly to the three others already eating, sorted out my newspaper and mail from the pile on the sideboard and took my seat, which was just as well.

The moment I clapped eyes on the long white envelope, a pang went through me. The postmark was sw1. I turned it this way and that, extraordinarily reluctant to open it. I had a desire to run with it into the kitchen and stuff it unopened in Mrs Nolan's boiler.

All in all, such a course might have saved me a great deal of trouble. No night for me then on the Vaclavske Namesti; no dalliance by the terraces of Barrandov; no knowledge of the poor morals of Vlasta Simenova, the girl with the bomb-shaped breasts.

Some current of pre-knowledge must have vibrated through my frame. But I suppressed the urge to run to Mrs Nolan's boiler. I opened the envelope and read the letter and watched my hands begin to tremble.

It was a short letter and I read it four times. It said:

Dear Sir,

With regard to the estate of the late Mr Bela Janda, I should be glad if you would telephone this office to arrange an early appointment.

Yours faithfully
Stephen Cunliffe

Chapter 2

I

'Two for you 'cos you sound hungry,' Mrs Nolan said, coming in with the eggs at this moment. She gazed at me and began shuffling about with her wig in some confusion. 'Something the matter with me?'

I must have been gaping at her with rigid eyes, and now hastily averted them.

'Bad news?' Mrs Nolan asked.

I licked my lips.

'Is it your mother?'

'No, no.'

'Lost your job?'

'It's my late uncle. He's dead.'

Mrs Nolan pulled out a chair and sat down beside me. To prevent her embarrassing condolences I quickly handed her the letter, which she read at a distance.

'I'm very sorry indeed, Mr Whistler. This'll be from the solicitor, I suppose?'

I looked at the letter again. The stationery was severely plain with the name Cunliffe & Co. in small black type in the left hand corner. 'I suppose so.'

'Did you know him very well?'

'I hardly knew him at all. He lived in Canada.'

'Well,' said Mrs Nolan sensibly, after a pause, 'it's a bit upsetting all the same, I suppose. I'll get you a cup of strong tea.'

She did so and I took the scalding draught down in one enormous mouthful that brought tears streaming down my cheeks. Mrs Nolan blew her nose and asked the others who had been gazing at me with religious respect to leave the room. They trooped out with embarrassed alacrity muttering furtive condolences.

The moment they had gone, unable to contain myself, I sprang up and executed a brief, lunatic dance of joy around the table. Bad news? *Bad* news? Even Mrs Nolan, that splendid creature, who could read between the lines of a lawyer's letter like anybody, had felt compelled to treat it with sad respect.

I dropped into a chair and read the letter again, very soberly. There was something so exactly right about the 'late Mr Bela Janda' that I was surprised I had not thought of him in this way before. The late Mr Bela Janda was all right; he had spent the long years well and prudently, consolidating his assets and preparing to be late, and I told him so now, in a low mutter, nodding to his name on the letter.

Mrs Nolan popped her head in as I sat muttering to the letter and quickly popped out again, and presently I ate my two eggs, taking only the yolks and leaving the whites with luxurious abandon.

This state of controlled hysteria lasted till I was up in my room again. There I could only bounce up and down on the divan, smoking one cigarette after another and waiting until it was time to phone this Stephen Cunliffe.

It was an address in Francis Street, Victoria, and I went bounding up the steep and narrow stairs like the long-lost heir coming to claim his inheritance, a proper way to bound in the circumstances.

I had spoken to Cunliffe's secretary on the phone and had learnt he would not be in till half past eleven. Mrs Nolan had lent me another bottle of British port to while· away the time and had seemed to find my request perfectly in order.

There had been some difficulty in starting the car, for in addition to its other ills, the battery had gone flat; but by almost kicking it to pieces in my excitement I had found a spark of life.

Cunliffe's secretary, a rather severe-sounding female with a slight foreign accent, had asked me to bring along the letter and my birth certificate, passport and any other documents to establish identity, and I had these in my hand as I knocked on the frosted glass door marked Inquiries and went in.

It was a small, very tidy room with a big ticking clock on the mantelpiece, a desk and a few files. Nobody was in the room. I closed the door behind me and shuffled my feet. An inner door opened a few inches and a woman whose middle-parting gave her face the appearance of a hot cross bun said severely, 'In just one moment.' She left the door open and I heard a mutter of voices for half a minute before she came out.

'My name is Nicolas Whistler. Mr Cunliffe –'

'Yes, yes. I spoke to you on the telephone. You have the letter and other papers?'

I handed them over and she glanced at the letter before disappearing in the other room again. 'Please sit down one moment, Mr Whistler,' she said over her shoulder. 'Mr Cunliffe will see you right away.'

If not a damned sight quicker, I thought, somewhat irritated by this middle-parting popping in and out, and suppressing a gust of gaseous British port. Bunface, it seemed to me, was treating the young master in far too officious a manner. A little servile bowing and scraping would have been perfectly in order here.

I was still brooding over this when a chair scraped in the next room and Bunface came out, her face now wearing something like a smile. 'It was necessary to establish ...' she murmured before I was in the room and facing Cunliffe.

I had to look twice to see if he was not hiding himself somewhere, for the Cunliffe I had imagined was a huge, lantern-jawed, gimlet-eyed character who might or might not have worn his hanging-judge wig during our interview. This one was practically a midget, a little dolly of a man who walked forward with quick, perfect miniature steps to take my hand in his two.

'Mr Whistler?' he said, in a voice so deep and gravelly that I looked down at him in astonishment. 'I am pleased to make your acquaintance. Take a seat.'

I sat down, still unable to take my eyes off him.

'Cigarette?'

I took one from his full-sized gold case and watched with fascination as he lit one for himself and blew out a stream of smoke. There was an extra-large emphatic quality in every gesture and for a moment I had the uncanny feeling I was watching a performance by some master ventriloquist who would shortly reveal himself.

'I should like to express my condolences on your bereavement,' he said. 'You didn't know your uncle very well, I understand?'

'No. I only met him once, actually.' I was suddenly aware of his foreign accent; the shock of his appearance and voice hadn't made it register.

'I knew him very well indeed. A fine man. He had a heart attack on Wednesday afternoon and died the same evening.'

'I never knew.'

'No,' he said dryly, and blinked. 'You couldn't have.' The eyes when you looked at them were exceptionally grey and large and intelligent. 'You are the first member of the family I have informed. I believe he was very close to your mother? Perhaps there is some older person you would wish to break the news to her ...'

'Yes, there's a Mr Gabriel who lives in the same hotel in Bournemouth. He's a great friend. That's a good idea,' I said, ashamed that I had not thought of this aspect.

'Yes,' Cunliffe said, and fiddled with some papers on his desk, and in the pause I could hear my heart going. 'You know, I suppose,' he said at length, 'that you figure prominently in Mr Janda's will?'

I licked my lips. 'I'd heard he was thinking of leaving me something.'

'He has. The lot,' said Cunliffe, the skin crinkling round his eyes.

He sat smiling at me, the little mannikin, in a rather worldly wise, sardonic manner, while the British port rose gaseously in my throat.

'Apparently he has made no alterations to the will in the possession of my Canadian associates which is the one I drew up for him in 1938. I am not able to give you a complete figure, of course, but I can give you a general idea of the size of the estate if you would like?'

Correctly interpreting my semi-paralytic jerk as an affirmative, he went on, 'In cash and securities – the lesser part of the estate, it is thought that he left something in the region of fifty thousand dollars – about seventeen or eighteen thousand pounds. The greater part of the estate consists of the cannery, transport and so forth, together with a fair-sized fruit farm which he bought in 1952 and which is, I understand, quite a valuable property.'

'Supposing – supposing I wanted to dispose of it. Is that possible?'

'Certainly. You are the absolute legatee.' He looked down at his papers again. 'The last valuation was taken in 1951 before he bought the fruit farm. It is surmise only but I would say the whole estate now would realize roughly four hundred thousand dollars. Of course it is subject to death duties –'

'Four hundred thousand –'

'About a hundred and forty thousand pounds,' he said. He blew his nose and began sniffing quickly.

He nipped off his chair. He seemed to be picking up a cigarette that was burning a hole in the carpet. I was staring rather closely at the back of his neck. I remember only leaning over with a sense of gratitude to kiss this little neck, and then I was in his chair sipping a glass of water and a woman was whispering, 'He has had too much to drink. I smelt the brandy on his breath. Perhaps you should not have told him just now —'

'Better now?' Cunliffe asked, smiling. 'The news was too much for you.'

'I'm afraid it was. What was that figure again?'

'A hundred and forty thousand pounds. Thank you, Miss Vogler,' he said to Bunface who was hovering, and waited till she had gone.

In the next few minutes he gave me a brief, smiling lecture on the best way to hang on to a legacy, and himself proposed that I might like a little on account. I had been wondering how to frame this question and accepted eagerly.

'A hundred or two, perhaps?'

'Two hundred would do fine.'

'I expect you would like to take cash now,' he said, looking at his watch. 'I had better ask Miss Vogler to slip out for you. The banks will be shut in just five minutes. Five-pound notes?'

Bunface returned at length with the money and Cunliffe produced two documents which he folded over for me to sign. 'I had a suspicion you might like something on account,' he said, smiling wryly. 'They are already prepared. Just sign your name here and here. You see, I have filled in the exact amount — it is intuition.'

I signed jerkily, moved by the impressive words 'two hundred pounds' spelt on each form and slightly hypnotized by the fivers fluttering around me as he counted. The efficient Bunface whipped away the papers with two sheets of blotting paper and I watched as Cunliffe came to his final 'Thirty-eight, thirty-nine, forty.'

'There. Are you satisfied with my count?'

'Perfectly.' I could hardly keep my hands off them.

A couple of minutes later he was telling me that he would communicate with me as soon as he had more news, and was taking my hand in his two again.

'Think,' he said, his large, intelligent eyes twinkling. 'Mr Janda left certain funds with me. But think before you spend. A little splash would be understandable, but don't throw it all away.'

I don't remember going down the stairs. I found myself in the M.G. wondering what I should do first. For some reason, despite the British port, I felt wonderfully clear-headed for the first time that day, perhaps for the first time that week, possibly for the first time in my life.

There was a clear necessity to take myself swiftly off to some place of solitude with this miraculous two hundred quid and work out a few first principles. With this thought in mind I pressed the starter, and at once fell to swearing with great power and obscenity and leapt out like a madman with the starting handle. There was something that would have to come even before first principles and I drove round to the squalid enterprise of Ratface Rickett, pulling up in the forecourt with a scream of brakes.

Ratface was not about his usual task of gloating over his petrol pumps, and I walked round to the back to find him at work in a pit inspecting the underside of a lorry with a wandering lamp.

'Mr Rickett.'

From his crouched position he looked round quickly and turned away without speaking. This familiar and expected action filled me with such pleasurable fury that I crouched like a frog, inserted my head carefully between the two front wheels and, inflating my lungs, roared: 'Rickett! Rickett! Rickett!' like some maniac baritone on a cracked record. Ratface straightened up as though shot, catching his head a stupefying blow, and began a sub-human, wordless moaning as he clutched his head. One word of apology would have had him swarming at me with a six-inch spanner and so, suppressing a desire to run and pretending not to notice what had happened, I called urgently,

'Come on, Rickett, surely you can finish that later – I'm in a hurry, man!'

This attitude so surprised him that he actually crawled out after a moment or two, but his eyes were still so bloodshot and murderous that I said loudly, 'Damn it, I've been yelling my head off. Didn't you hear me down there? I'm in a hell of a hurry and I want a new battery and to settle my bill.'

I had meant to play with him a little over the question of payment, but since the encounter had provided such reasonable value and there was, anyway, the matter of getting off the premises without his savaging me, I reluctantly paid up and took off in triumph at the first touch on the starter.

I drove to Henley, and by a quarter past one was sitting slowly sipping a pint of beer and watching the swans.

The young master had come into his own with a vengeance. I could almost feel the gigantic sack of loot on my shoulder like some unimaginably heavy piece of nuclear material darkly awaiting conversion into other and more useful forms. Millions of miles of dappled roads, a big house for Maminka to queen it in, an island, a pub, a boat, a small group of harlots. Or one could acquire and slowly pulverize the entire affairs of the Little Swine, selling Miss Vosper into white slavery.

The swelling wonder of these reflections occupied the first pint, and it was as I was sipping the second that I approached cautiously the problem of Maura. I had been aware all morning of a strong resistance to the idea of reasoned thinking on this subject. I hadn't wanted to tell her about the letter. I didn't want to tell her just yet about the money. There was bound to be a reason for this, I thought, nodding sagely to a swan who had come to stare at me.

It was not a difficult one to find. The presence of the money meant (a) that it was time for positive action with regard to our relationship, and (b) that Maura would have ideas on what should be done with the money. Take a certain line with regard to (a) and (b) as a personal problem would cease to exist. And yet it went deeper than this. So long as I hadn't been in a position to marry the girl she had seemed, no doubt about it, a very desirable one. Desiring her had indeed been a major preoccupation for these past months. But there had been many months before Maura, and there would be many months after her. Was this, in short, the girl for me?

I blew out my cheeks and considered. Marriage, it was a fact, was a serious business, and Maura had many defects. She was too damned bossy for one thing. She looked on me as something less than heroic for another.

All in all, it seemed to me, I needed to give this more thought; which, in its turn, meant keeping the news to myself for a while. For the time being I had two hundred pounds to spend, less Ratface's bite, and all the time in the world to decide what should be done with the remainder.

It was now getting on for two o'clock and people were strolling out to enjoy the river after their luncheon. I could not be bothered to eat and instead stayed slowly disposing of two further pints before the bar closed and I tooled gently back to town, listening with only mild interest to the noise from the gearbox. I thought I might buy Maminka a present, might run down to Bournemouth with it this evening; might even run down now.

At this point I recalled Cunliffe's advice to pass the tidings through Imre, and pulled up at the first phone box to put through a call.

He came to the phone right away, and I said, 'Hello, Uncle, it's Nicolas. How are you?' grinning to think of him standing there big and shapeless in his alpaca jacket, with the hairs of his nose waving in his powerful breath. He was a gentle, flabby, elephantine man.

'Nicolas,' he said breathily. 'It is good to hear from you, my boy. How are things with you?' His voice sounded a shade muted, as if he had just undersold another stamp. Well, there'd be enough for Imre, too, I thought with a wave of regard for the old boy, and I said cheerfully:

'Couldn't be better. I'll tell you all about it. But first how's Maminka?'

This was a mistake, but it had to be gone through. There was never anything wrong with Maminka, but the old hypochondriac could usually find something; it gave him an added reason for living with her.

'Well, my boy, I will tell you,' he said confidentially, with a return to something like his usual form, 'she is not so well today. There is a touch of fibrositis in the shoulder and I think she is starting a cold. I am keeping her in bed today.'

'I'm sorry to hear that, Uncle. How is your own health?' I said, blowing out my cheeks and nodding to the phone.

'Me, me – you know how it is with me, Nicolas,' he said, pleased, giving his little deprecatory laugh. 'I need a new pair of lungs. Things are never quite right with me.'

'I was thinking of running down to see you. I've got great news. Uncle Bela has died and left me all his money.' This could have been expressed in other ways, and I was thinking of the words, when he said:

'What is this? What is this you say? Just a minute, Nicolas. The door is open. I cannot hear very ...' He put the phone down and came back in a moment. 'You say Bela ...' he said breathily. 'What is this, Nicolas?'

'I'm afraid Uncle Bela has died,' I said. 'He died on Wednesday after a heart attack. I heard from the lawyer today.'

'Oh, this is bad,' he said. I heard his noisy breathing for a few seconds. 'It will distress her terribly.'

'Yes,' I said, somewhat irritably. 'Not too good, is it? But I saw the lawyer today. It seems he left a considerable fortune. He left it to me.'

'Well, this we knew he would do,' he said. 'It is no surprise. I do not know how to – I can't tell her today, Nicolas. She is not well enough for such news today.'

'Well, that's rather the point. I hoped you would break the news to her before I got down.'

He breathed into the phone for a while. 'Nicolas,' he said at last, 'I think it would be better if you didn't come down this weekend. You understand, a shock like this, her only brother ... I wouldn't like to say ...'

'All right,' I said, a little put out. 'Uncle Bela left quite a lot of money.'

'Of course. He was a rich man. You will tell me about it later. I must think what I should say.'

'I hope Maminka's not too upset about it.'

'She is bound to be upset. She will be terribly distressed. I can't prevent it.'

'Well, I'll call you in a couple of days.'

'In two or three days, yes. Goodbye, Nicolas.' He put the phone down before I did.

I got back into the car with a feeling of let-down. It seemed there was nobody I could tell about the money. The weight of the hundred and forty thousand pounds was suddenly heavy on me. The beer had left a sour taste.

I drove slowly back home, aware I shouldn't be driving at all. By a stroke of luck, Mrs Nolan was not prowling in the hall. I went up to my room and fell on to the divan and was asleep immediately.

Only one other thing of note happened that day. I awoke at half past eight in the evening. Mrs Nolan had gone to the pictures and one of the lodgers was knocking on the door to call me to the phone. I took myself frowstily down the three flights. It was the man Jack had mentioned who was interested in buying the car. I told him rather shortly that it was not for sale, and hung up.

I didn't take his name or number.

3

I called for Maura next morning, and watched her in my new role of scale-weigher. What I saw went solidly on the plus side. Nothing wrong there, I thought, as she hopped nimbly into the car. Her red hair was cut short. She was wearing a gaily coloured cotton frock and a shoulder bag. Her lopsided smile could take your breath away in that sedate Sunday-morning square.

She said, 'Nicolas, I was so mean the other night. I've been depressed about it.'

I said, 'Well,' with a tremendous lift. 'I've not been feeling so hot, either.'

'Then let's forget it and have a wonderful day, I've got something to tell you.'

'What is it?'

Her lopsided smile came on briefly. 'I'll tell you later. Can we afford a run in the country?'

'I've got a secret, too,' I said, and dug into my wallet for the twenty-five pounds I had brought with me. 'Look. I won it.'

'Nicolas, you never did!'

'At the dogs.' I'd rehearsed this in the bathroom mirror, but it was coming out a bit too quickly.

'Was this last night?'

'Yes.'

'You never told me you were going. You've never been before, Nicolas, you're fibbing . . .' A thought struck her and she looked at me, blinking quickly. 'There wasn't anything more about the Little Swine? You weren't keeping anything back?'

'No,' I said irritably. It had started to go a bit funny.

'Well, it's wonderful anyway,' she said. It didn't sound so wonderful now. 'Let's have a picnic. We can buy food. I was dreaming about the country. I was dreaming about Ireland.'

So that seemed all right again, and I shoved in the clutch and took off like a jet through Chiswick, through Datchet, through Taplow, and we sang like little larks, not knowing what would befall.

That was a perfect July day, the best of that wild summer.

We ate in a clearing in the woods beyond Cliveden and afterwards lay back and smoked. Maura said, 'Nicolas.'

'What?'

'I've been thinking of going back to Ireland.'

'I know. In August.'

'I mean for good.'

I sat up and stared at her. 'Why, for God's sake?'

Her eyes, which had been closed, now opened, grey-green, and regarded me mournfully. 'You know why, Nicolas.'

This could only be an obscure reference to the Little Swine, it seemed to me, and I bent to kiss her to obliterate the thought. She twisted away, lifting her fingertips to my face.

'All my family are in Ireland,' she said mournfully. 'I've got nobody here.'

'How about me?'

'How about you?'

'You know how I feel about you, Maura.'

'I know you want to go to bed with me.'

'Damn it,' I said with fright. It was the first time she had said anything like that. 'There's more to it than that, Maura.'

'What?'

'I love you,' I said, awkwardly. The scale-weighing, it seemed to me, was not going too scientifically.

'I love you, too, Nicolas,' she said. 'But there doesn't seem much chance of our ever being able to do much about it, does there? Oh, I can see,' she said mournfully, beginning to enjoy it, 'I can see it's not going to be any use. You'll be a lifelong poor relative. The Little Swine won't do a thing unless you push him, and your uncle in Canada won't either because you don't show a spark of interest. I've tried hard to believe some miracle will happen to change you . . .'

'Well, try a bit harder,' I said, echoing Ratface, and suddenly invigorated by the recollection, took her head firmly in my hands. 'Look, Maura, I've had more than enough of this conversation. The time has come to settle a few simple points. (a) My formative years are long past and nothing now is going to alter my character. (b) Changes of circumstance, of which there could be many, should not affect our relationship, viewed as a long-term proposition. If in your mind they do, well, you're perfectly right – it's no go. And now,' I said, 'let's forget it.'

She wriggled her head round fast before I could get down to her. 'Nicolas, what's happened to you?'

'You've happened to me,' I said. She returned my kiss with

enthusiasm. Her eyes were lively and alert and sparkling when we drew apart.

'If you knew how worried I've been,' she said. 'Is everything going to be all right now, Nicolas?'

'Yes,' I said reluctantly.

'He agreed to your becoming a full partner?'

My mental defences had shaken themselves wearily into life like a big tired bulldog. 'Well, it's difficult to explain.'

'All right,' she said, lightly. 'I've got no right to know.'

'Maura, you have. I'm just not able to tell you at the moment. Believe me, Maura,' I said, with a desperate attempt at her own line of dramatics, 'I've thought about this and thought about it, and I know you've got a right to be told, but you've just got to trust me.'

'No right at all,' she said, but only the words were cold. Her eyes were warm and curious. 'When will you be able to tell me?'

'Soon,' I said, wondering how the hell I'd placed myself in this insane position. The idea had been merely to keep from her for the moment the fact that there was now no bar or impediment to marrying her. She now understood (a) that I could, and (b) that her prompting to approach the Little Swine had paid off. The fact that the latter was untrue was not only irrelevant. It was damned inconvenient. My firm intention had been to see the Little Swine for just one further and rewarding session. I would now have to create a detailed day-to-day fantasy for her.

The prospect was so enervating that all thought of smooching swiftly dispersed. I lit a cigarette and lay down beside her. Our heads were together, but she did not say anything further. For a long time I could see her eyelashes from the corner of my eye, blinking rapidly and intelligently at the sky.

4

The next three days passed deliriously. I had a short, perfect interview with the Little Swine and with Miss Vosper, which was not so much a burning of boats as the entire disintegration of a familiar shore. I had not meant to let it go so far as this; I was drunk with good fortune.

I ordered two new suits; bought one off the peg; three silk shirts, two pairs of shoes, three motor car tyres and a gear-box, and paid off Mrs Nolan. Her curiosity about the lawyer's letter was now warm, and, anxious that she should not let drop anything to Maura on the telephone, I told her there was a legacy but that the legal situation was complicated by other claimants and that I had pledged myself to remain silent.

This rage of spending kept me busy during the day, and I saw Maura each evening. Our relationship had now developed a curious, somewhat uncertain, but not unpleasant character. She was quieter, rather quizzical, scrupulously uninquisitive. It was as though we were meeting for the first time. Titillated but uneasy, I felt myself compelled to invent complete and detailed days in the Little Swine's service.

On the Wednesday I rang Imre again.

'Nicolas, my boy,' he said breathily, 'you must be patient. I have not told her yet. She has not been at all well.'

'Damn it, Uncle – I must see her.'

'I know, my boy, I know,' he said unhappily. 'She has been asking why you have not been. Perhaps if you could leave your visit till the weekend.'

'Well, if you think so,' I said.

'Say Saturday. It will give me more time. She is improving a little now. Saturday would be the best. We can have a little talk downstairs first.'

'All right.'

'Goodbye,' he said abruptly. Maminka must have wandered into hearing.

'Goodbye,' I said, after the click, and nearly smashed the phone in fury.

It seemed to me that my mother would show a rather more rugged fortitude over Bela's death than Imre gave her credit for; my interests came first with her. I felt safe, therefore, in taking her some rather grand present. With this in mind, I went up to my room and inspected the state of my finances.

I took out my wallet and emptied my pockets in a small pile on the divan and began counting. There were eight fivers, two one-pound notes and a handful of silver. I stared at it appalled. Over a hundred and forty quid gone in half a week. And I'd only paid a deposit on the two suits; that meant another eighty pounds to lay out. I wondered how I was going to explain this to little Cunliffe.

I found myself trying a few specimen interviews with him in my mind, and after a while I lit another cigarette and went downstairs to phone him. Mrs Nolan came out of her lair as I picked up the receiver, so I dialled TIM instead, checking ostentatiously with my watch, and went out to telephone from the public box farther up the street.

Bunface put me through to Cunliffe right away.

'Yes, Mr Whistler, what can I do for you?'

'I was just wondering if you'd heard anything further.' I caught my reflection smiling in a rather sickly fashion in the small round mirror.

'Nothing at all. I am not expecting to for a while. Have you any particular problem?'

'Not exactly a *problem*. I was wondering if we couldn't arrange something a little more definite about money – perhaps a regular remittance.'

He didn't say anything.

'There might be one or two things I want to buy,' I said, sweating. 'It would be useful to know the money was available.'

'I don't quite understand,' he said at last. 'You mean you have spent the two hundred pounds?'

'Oh, no! Not at all. Rather not, Mr Cunliffe,' I said. 'I merely thought – if one could fix up something *definite*. Perhaps starting this weekend.'

His gravelly laugh came over the phone. 'How much of the money have you got left?'

'Well, about forty or fifty, actually,' I said, relieved that the little buffer was taking it so well. 'But that includes . . .'

'You don't need to explain,' he said, still laughing heartily. 'A certain amount of celebration is understandable, but I must

say – a hundred and fifty pounds in four days is something outside my experience. We will have to have a little chat about it.'

'Well, that's rather the point. I'd like to do that, Mr Cunliffe.
You see, I've sort of given up my job, and tend to be without
visible means of support. There was quite a bit we didn't go
into when we met . . .'

'Of course, of course,' he said. 'Come and see me in the
morning about eleven o'clock.'

'It'll be O.K., will it, to draw a bit more?'

'I am sure we can arrange something.'

'Well, fine. See you tomorrow then.'

'At eleven. Goodbye, Mr Whistler.'

I stepped out of the box smiling vacuously with relief. The
strain of keeping the news to myself and the nerve-racking
mystery that had developed with Maura had conspired to start
in my mind a terrifying suspicion that the whole thing was some
immense practical joke. Little Cunliffe's encouraging attitude –
he had not struck me as the type to laugh off the disintegration
of a hundred and fifty pounds in rather less than that number
of hours – filled me with such elation that I walked back feeling
about ten feet tall. For the first time I could really believe that
Uncle Bela had left me a hundred and forty thousand pounds.

5

'Mr Cunliffe is expecting you,' Bunface said with a brisk bob
and a smile the moment I opened the door. She hustled me in
and bobbed out and little Cunliffe had slipped off his seat and
was shaking me by the hand before I had properly adjusted my
eyes to his level. All this was very satisfactory and I gave him a
kindly good morning.

'I didn't think I would be seeing you again quite so soon,' he
said jovially.

'No – ah – well,' I said, not knowing quite whether I was the
sheepish young gentleman or the mad young rip, but prepared
to oblige with either.

'Sit down, sit down. Cigarette?'

Again he produced the massive case with one of his emphatic semaphore gestures and again I watched with fascination as he lit one himself and blew out a stream of smoke. He sat himself on the desk and crossed his little legs and looked at me quizzically.

'This is a very high rate of spending, Mr Whistler. Don't think I am criticizing – in my profession I have always found it impossible to predict or to judge other people's appetites. But how exactly have you managed to get rid of it so soon? I thought at least a week, possibly two.'

He was smiling, but not actually laughing. There was still no cue for the two characters waiting at my elbow so I said neutrally, 'There were a few things I had to buy.' I then told him exactly what I had spent.

He made a note of it. 'Yes, I think I have a fair idea,' he said slowly, stubbing out his cigarette. 'And you say you have given up your job, too. Without ill-feeling, I hope?'

I told him about it and he laughed heartily.

'Yes, I can appreciate the situation. It is clear that you need money. I am sure we can come to some arrangement.'

'I was thinking,' I said tentatively, 'of a regular weekly sum until I've sorted myself out a bit.'

'Yes?'

'I thought about twenty-five pounds a week would be reasonable – just until the legacy comes through.'

He slipped off the desk and seated himself in the swivel chair. 'Possibly,' he said, judiciously. 'I'm afraid I have a little shock for you, Mr Whistler. There is no legacy.'

For a moment I had a wild idea that the ventriloquist had gone and that the doll had seized the opportunity to say all the terrible, lunatic things it could think of.

I actually said, in a music-hall voice, 'No legacy?'

'I'm afraid not.'

'But Uncle Bela . . .'

'Is thriving, I dare say.'

'But – but . . .' I gazed at the little madman, practically speechless. 'What about the money? You gave me two hundred pounds.'

'I lent it to you.' He pressed a buzzer and, as Bunface popped in, said pleasantly, 'Ask Mr Pavelka to step in, please. And Miss Vogler – you might bring in the receipts relating to Mr Whistler.'

I was still gaping at him. 'What the hell . . . You *are* a solicitor?'

He inclined his head. 'Once, alas. I am now a humble money-lender.'

'But you know damned well I didn't borrow money . . . What exactly is this . . .'

Cunliffe got up, smiling, with his hand outstretched. An enormous gorilla of a man with the ugliest face I had ever seen had entered the room.

'This is Mr Pavelka,' Cunliffe said. 'He will explain why we want you to go to Prague.'

Chapter 3

I

PAVELKA, whose face, on closer inspection, was like a St Bernard's rather than a gorilla's, shambled forward and extended his hand.

'*Dobry den*,' he said.

'*Dobry den*.' I was still so shaken that I was unaware for the moment of the lapse into Czech.

Pavelka folded my hand in his massive paw and slowly shook it, gazing earnestly at me like some champion of his breed trying to catch the judge's eye.

'I am very glad to make your acquaintance,' he said in Czech.

'This is a wonderful task you have undertaken. I only hope you prove worthy of it.'

'Task?' I said in Czech through dry lips – it was uncanny how natural the Czech tongue sounded; even Maminka had not spoken it to me for years – 'Task?' I looked helplessly from one to the other of them, and for an instant my sole thought was escape; perhaps to throw Cunliffe at Pavelka and, clutching Bunface as a shield, bound down the stairs four at a time and rush screaming into the street.

Cunliffe smiled dryly. 'Mr Pavelka is going a little too fast. Please sit down both of you. Ah, thank you, Miss Vogler,' he said as Bunface bobbed in with the papers.

He waited until she had gone before continuing. 'Very briefly, Mr Whistler, we have been looking for some time for a young gentleman like yourself to go on a small mission for us. It is completely without danger but so unusual that we realized some inducement would be necessary. In your case we thought – I thought, as a matter of fact – that it might be best to place you in our debt in some way and then offer you the opportunity of cancelling the debt and, at the same time, earning yourself a handsome fee. I took the precaution of securing your signature to this standard loan certificate. Perhaps Mr Pavelka will hold one side of it while you read it.'

He handed the paper over the desk and Pavelka, with a murmured *'Prosim'* to me, took it, inclining towards me like a slightly animated Tower of Pisa.

It was a printed document. My eye went dizzily over the close columns of *pursuant to the Acts* and *hereinafters*. It was folded horizontally. Below the fold was Cunliffe's TWO HUNDRED POUNDS and below that my own jerky signature.

'You will see,' Cunliffe said, at the same moment that I saw the paragraph, 'that your motor car is down as part security. At a rather low figure, I am afraid.'

I think it was the sight of the car quoted at fifty pounds that, more than anything else in the last stupefying five minutes, maddened me into sudden action. With a wordless snarl, I tore the paper from Pavelka's grip, and at once found myself on the floor with my head nearly knocked off. Without moving an inch he had caught me a paralysing clout on the ear.

'No, please!' he said in English, looking down at me with embarrassed alarm. 'Why do you do this?'

I looked up at him, horribly shocked. It was the first time anybody had ever hit me. His head, the entire room, was expanding and contracting with an agonizing boiler-house roar.

'It is perfectly all right, Mr Pavelka,' I heard Cunliffe's voice grating. 'I have another copy of the document, also signed. Ah, just a little torn is it? Two are better than one. I hope you are not hurt, Mr Whistler?'

Pavelka, after handing the form back, was helping me to my feet like a troubled elderly uncle. My ear felt as if it had been hit with a hammer.

'I'm sorry I forgot to mention about Mr Pavelka,' Cunliffe said. 'He used to be quite a well-known amateur wrestler. Wrestling champion of Bohemia – I think I am right, Mr Pavelka?'

'Western Bohemia,' Pavelka said.

I sat down and gazed at him through a mist of pain as he slowly took his seat. The shocked, aggrieved expression was still on his face.

'Mr Pavelka is startled by your behaviour,' Cunliffe said, with an I-thought-it-would-be-so shake of his head. 'The young man has been greatly upset by money troubles,' he said in Czech to Pavelka. 'He is not yet aware of our offer.'

'And I'm not bloody well going to be,' I said. 'You let me out of here and I'm going straight to the police.'

It was not the most inviting of offers, but I heard my voice with amazement, astonished at my own courage. Cunliffe diplomatically produced his cigarette case and passed it round.

'You are at perfect liberty to go whenever you like,' he said mildly. 'I don't know what exactly it is you want to tell the police. I don't think you have any letters from me?' (This had occurred to me as he was speaking; I had brought back the only letter he had sent me.) 'You will find that I am a fairly well-known money-lender. To any sensible person it would be obvious that, having accepted a loan, you have rashly squandered it and are now displaying reluctance to meet your obligations. Moreover, you would force me to take the motor car from you right away, as I am fully entitled to do.'

I inhaled an enormous lungful of smoke, and it seemed to ease my ear a little. The room had ceased its painful contractions. The situation was no less mad. I leaned forward, groping for some strand of understanding.

'If all this about Bela is just – just invention, how did you get to hear about him in the first place?'

Cunliffe's eyelids drooped wryly. 'You have not exactly made a secret of your expectations.'

I gazed at him, appalled. Someone had been watching me, taking careful note of the absurd little jokes. . . .

'But why me? You don't know me,' I said urgently. 'I'm not cut out for this sort of thing.'

'You are exactly cut out for it. As I say we have been looking for someone with just your qualifications.'

'I haven't any qualifications, Mr Cunliffe,' I told him slowly and desperately. 'Before you go any further, you've got to understand that. I am not qualified to do anything. I am also a coward. I don't know what it is you want me to do, and I don't want to know. I'd be less than useless to you.'

As I spoke I was frightening myself and the words came in a gabble at the end. I didn't seem to be frightening Cunliffe who was holding Pavelka with his eye as though to ensure that he heard every word. He gave a little nod and Pavelka, who seemed to have reassured himself about me, at once sat forward and grasped my knee.

'I like you,' he said simply. 'You look like your father. You have no recollection, I suppose, of Pavelka ware?'

'I know nothing at all about Czechoslovakia –'

'Nobody has today,' he said bitterly. 'It was excellent glass. I had the finest factory in Bohemia. Since 1934 I employed a research staff of twenty-seven – *yoh*, twenty-seven !' he repeated, wrongly interpreting as astonishment the look of despair I threw at Cunliffe. 'Twenty-seven men uneconomically employed who did nothing but experiment to try and produce unbreakable

43

glass. Not oven-proof glass, not plastic. Beautiful table glass, as delicate as the finest in my complete range. Since 1934! Now they have found it, and you are going to Prague to bring it to me.'

His inhumanly large hand was gripping my knee tightly, his great creased dog's face not a foot away.

'Mr Pavelka!' I cried. 'This is incredible! The very idea –'

'*Yoh*, incredible! But it is so. Since 1934 twenty-seven men working at nothing else, and now they have it. And they will flood the world with it. You know what it means.'

'I don't, Mr Pavelka,' I said. 'I don't know anything about glass. I only worked in the office.' His big dog eyes were looking seriously at me, but it was plain he didn't understand me, or didn't believe me, or didn't care. I glanced desperately at little Cunliffe. He gazed blandly back.

'You need have no fears, Mr Whistler,' Cunliffe said after a moment of silence. 'It is the simplest job in the world. I could do it, or Mr Pavelka here or a reasonably intelligent boy scout. It is all a matter of finding someone with a legitimate reason for visiting glass factories – someone the Czechoslovak authorities would not suspect. Your father was a well-known glass importer. It is entirely natural that you should wish to start up trade again. You will go as a buyer, of course.'

'They're not going to sell me this unbreakable glass!'

'No. It's not in production yet. And I gather a specimen of the glass wouldn't be very useful for our purposes. One can't hope to duplicate it after analysis because of the fusion process in glass – you'll know more about that than I would. You're bringing back the formula.'

His reasonable tone had been bringing the project down to earth; the word 'formula' although casually dropped in put it back on a new mad plane. Cunliffe saw my expression and smiled. 'A bit of paper with a few figures on – you won't know anything about it. I assure you unless I told you where it was you wouldn't know you were carrying it. The whole thing has been arranged so that there is not the slightest danger to you. After all, we're going to quite a bit of trouble and expense to get that formula, and Mr Pavelka, as you can see, has thought about scarcely anything else since 1934.'

'That's just it,' I said eagerly, and turned to Pavelka who was staring moodily at a drinking glass on the desk. 'There's so much trouble and money involved here that I'd be a definite weak link. I'd be frightened out of my life. They couldn't help but suspect me. You've waited years for this. For God's sake, Mr Pavelka,' I cried, 'put someone you can trust on the job. I'd wreck your chances for life.'

'It is very pleasing, is it not?' Cunliffe said to Pavelka, his head held a little to one side as he listened to me. 'I thought I was not mistaken the first time. Modesty, circumspection, reserve, a little childish cunning. . . . I won't conceal from you, Mr Whistler,' he said to me, 'that I am more and more taken with your manner. I am sure the Czechoslovak authorities will expect you to be a little – well, a little as you are. Your family was there in the old days, the former capitalist class. . . . It would be difficult to make a better choice for the job. And now to business,' he said as my mouth opened.

'The moment you return with the – the bit of paper, I hand you the loan certificate. Both copies!' he said, smiling. 'And on top of that we will pay you a further two hundred pounds. Moreover, if you do not feel inclined to return to your job, I dare say Mr Pavelka will be prepared to offer you something. He has the highest hopes for the new process.'

'It will be colossal,' Pavelka said. 'Of course you will work for me.'

'There,' said Cunliffe. 'The prospects are unlimited and you've got to admit the pay is princely for a few days' pleasant sightseeing with all expenses paid.'

'How many days?' I asked reluctantly.

'That is not entirely clear yet. Perhaps only four or five. They will want to give you a good time. It is all a matter of how quickly you can tear yourself away.'

'And when do I pick up this – this formula?'

'Probably the day after you arrive. If so, of course, you must try and cut short your stay. It is really something you must decide when you are there. They will make a programme for you and one of the items will be a visit to Mr Pavelka's factory. We have asked for that – in your name of course. Incidentally, your visa application is going through – we applied for it as soon as you brought your passport along – and we have been assured it will come through almost immediately. I expect we will have it tomorrow.'

There was a long pause while I thought this over.

Pavelka said moodily, 'They have changed the name, the robbers. It is the Zapotocky Works now.'

'Of course.'

'Somebody will give me this formula?' I asked at length.

'It will be given to you. You won't know anything about it.'

'How?'

'You must leave that to us. I will explain everything before you go. It is remarkably simple and you need not have the slightest fear.'

'Well,' I said, and stood up. 'I'll think it over.'

'Of course,' Cunliffe said. 'You have several days. You will be leaving by plane at ten o'clock on Tuesday morning.'

Pavelka unfolded himself and grasped my hand in his again. 'I am relying on you,' he said with his great St Bernard face. 'I only wish I could go myself.'

I wished he could, too. I was too full of worried care to speak.

'You might telephone me on Sunday,' Cunliffe said, slipping out of his seat to come to the door with me.

'I'll be in Bournemouth on Sunday.' I had forgotten that I would be staying overnight until this moment.

'Bournemouth?' he said sharply. 'Bournemouth? Ah, your mother. I'm not sure,' he said slowly, 'if that is a very good idea.'

'Well, that's too bad,' I said, with a sudden idiot pleasure in crossing him. 'She's expecting me and I'm going.'

He looked at me consideringly. 'You understand, don't you, that the only possible danger to you is if you mention any of this to anyone? *Anyone at all*. I advise you to forget everything that has been said here. Put it out of your mind.'

'Right away,' I said, allowing my face to lengthen in a sardonic leer. God knows what I'd got to leer about. It seemed to worry little Cunliffe. He looked at me pensively.

'Well, ring me when you get back. You can get me at this number,' he said, writing it on a sheet of his diary. 'You must be back on Sunday night. Ring me however late it is.'

2

When I was back in my room and lying on the divan, the situation was so awful I couldn't think about it. I tried for a while, smoking one cigarette after another, but the entire scene, the extraordinary proposal, was so grotesque it didn't seem to concern me at all. I was conscious only of three sharp impressions. One, there was no fortune; two, I couldn't propose to Maura; three, the car didn't belong to me. The crazy flow of incident in the last few days had anaesthetized me against the first two; most of the time they had seemed fantasies anyway. Number three, however, left me in such desolation that I looked distractedly round the room for something to break.

I thought of my session with Ratface, of the three new tyres, the new gearbox, the new battery, of the man on the phone I had put off so brusquely. I addressed myself to each wall of the room with savagely waving arms and voiceless imprecation. This bout of silent declamatory passion slipped me into a higher gear and with a mindless sense of action I went out, got into the car and drove decisively to town.

It was after one and Jack was busy serving sandwiches and beer. I ordered a Scotch and inquired if they still had the name of the man who wanted to buy a car.

'I think we threw the bit of paper away,' Jack said. 'I'll find out.'

The place was filling up. I finished the whisky slowly and the warmth of it and the buzz all round me and the masticating City jaws began to draw a veil of sanity over the bomb-lit areas of my mind left by the interview with Cunliffe. The idea of going to Prague to steal a secret formula seemed more grotesque than ever. Looking around me I decided suddenly, no nonsense and once and for all, I wouldn't do it. Enough was enough. What could Cunliffe do about it? I had the car and the log-book. If I sold it quickly and handed over the money he could have no legal claim on me.

Thinking thus, I ordered another double and with some excitement began to plot out my moves. First there was the business of getting hold of Jack's man – or, for God's sake, anyone who wanted to buy a car. There must be thousands of them. One way or another I could have a hundred and fifty quid plus within twenty-four hours. . . .

This escaped-convict-like scenting of the new landscape took me through the second whisky, and I was just beginning to perceive with a sinking heart that by working flat out I might be able to get back where I started, minus the car, minus my Little Swine prospects, probably minus Maura, when Jack came over.

'Phyllis says she threw it away. He'll probably be in again. I'll keep an eye open.'

'Thanks, Jack.'

'Having your ups and downs like the rest of us?'

'Like the rest of us,' I said faintly. 'I'll have another of these.'

With the third whisky, I *knew* I was back where I started, but the prospect was not so cheerless as it might have been. Nodding dolorously to the whisky, I felt the presence of old friends here. Here was indecision and sloth and confusion. . . .

One thought seemed to be drawing clear of all the rest, it seemed to me after a while. Indecision argues an alternative. Somewhere in that blind country of the mind one of me had accepted Prague *as* an alternative.

3

I was waiting across the road with a splitting headache when Maura left the office at half past five. I waved limply and she came across, surprised.

'What are you doing here? Is anything wrong?'

I had arranged to meet her at half past seven. Since three,

when I had left the Princess May, I had been dozing on a seat in Lincoln's Inn Fields wondering what the hell I ought to tell her. I seemed to spend half my life doing that. When five had struck, the prospect of waiting around for another couple of hours had become suddenly unbearable. My head was throbbing. If I went back home and crawled on the divan the chances were I wouldn't get off it. I had taken myself queasily to wait opposite her office.

'I got away early,' I said, slipping automatically into the daily fantasy of life with the Little Swine. 'I thought I might as well pick you up.'

She stared at me. 'Have you been drinking, Nicolas?'

'I had a couple.'

'Spirits?'

'Look, can we go and sit down somewhere?' People were streaming home all round us. I felt ramshackle enough to topple over and over if one of them bumped into me.

She looked at me in a decidedly odd manner, but made no comment. We walked meditatively to a Lyons' tea shop.

Over the tea she said quietly, 'What's up, Nicolas?'

I'd been beating my tired brain to find the words for this one. I said, 'It's damned awkward but something's cropped up that might interfere with my – my plans.'

She didn't say anything.

'I might have to go away for a bit, Maura.'

'How long for?'

'I'm not sure.'

She looked at me without speaking for a long time. 'I see,' she said quietly. 'We won't be seeing so much of each other in the future – have I got the drift right?'

'No, you haven't.' I took her hand over the table. 'You haven't got it right at all. I love you, Maura,' I said, groaning inwardly and savagely cursing Cunliffe, Pavelka, the entire Czechoslovak Republic, and my two hours of fuddled gloom. 'I love you and I meant to ask you to marry me, but now a lot's happened unexpectedly. ... I'm going to Prague,' I said, listening to my own voice with a certain unearthly fascination, and knowing as I said the words that I must have made the decision hours before.

'Prague?' She stared at me and her mouth dropped open. 'Did you know about this at the weekend?'

'No.'

'But there was something. ... It's the glass business, isn't it?'

'Yes,' I said truthfully. 'But for God's sake, keep it to yourself. I shouldn't have told you at all, really. I've never done anything like this before. ...'

'And I'm sure you'll make a success of it,' she said, pressing my hand. Her eyes were shining. 'Oh, Nicolas, you fool you – you don't have to pretend to me. And you don't have to prove anything to me. You're trying, and you've got him to give you this chance. That's what counts – your attitude to it. Can't you see that, Nicolas?'

I gazed at her with the shocked but dull resignation of some elderly beast after an unsuccessful attempt with the humane killer.

'It's not quite like that, Maura. Don't bank on anything concrete coming out of it. ...'

'I'm not banking on anyone but you, Nicolas, dearest. I've got complete faith in you, my darling.'

There was rather more than the normal quota of endearments here and embarrassment was added to my ruined condition. I pressed her hand silently.

'Your mother will be delighted to hear the news.' She knew I was going to Bournemouth over the weekend. 'I'll see you on Monday, I suppose?'

This seemed doubtful. If I did go off on Tuesday there would doubtless be many essential preliminaries to tie me up on the Monday. My head, which had eased a little when I sat down, now began to throb again. I said wearily, 'I'm not dead sure when I'm going off on – on this thing. It could be Monday or Tuesday. I'll have to get in touch with you.'

'Monday or Tuesday!' Her eyes opened wide. 'Is it so urgent? So silly little Nicolas had to go out and get tight to tell me. ...'

Silly little Nicolas,' she said softly, with love, brushing my mouth with her hand.

Too wrecked by the events of the day to fall in with this sort of talk easily, I could only smile like a silly little Nicolas. The attempt cannot have been successful. Maura showed immediate concern.

'Oh, Nicolas, you're looking terrible. You'd better get off to bed.'

The car was where I had left it in the side street next to the Princess May. I drove Maura home and made to kiss her briefly. She grasped me in a close, love-communicating hug that jarred my head and made me grit my teeth.

I drove home slowly and left the car without covers and walked upstairs, holding my head. The divan waited solidly in the darkening room, and I embraced it with a muted groan. Almost at once, sleep, like some rhythmical, snoring vacuum cleaner, consumed the awful day.

4

Saturday was hot, and I was up early and unrested with that glazed efficiency of movement that often follows a drinking session. I ate breakfast, and shortly regretted it, and by nine o'clock was on the road, trembling all over with a nerveless and unidentifiable feeling of apprehension.

Somewhere around Winchester with its chain groceries and post office vans, however, the apprehension began to diminish and I even felt a slight accession of confidence. The events of the past few days, it was a fact, were no more insane than the previous reality of life with the Little Swine. Through the New Forest the road was sun-dappled, and I sang a little, cautiously.

In my mother's presence, I thought, I would see the proposition for the grotesque and unthinkable nonsense that it was. Maminka, faery of vision though she might be, was at least a constant in my life. The young man of affairs I knew about and could cope with. The young secret agent, never. Let him, this Cunliffe, just try and take the car, I thought. Let him just try.

In the freshness of the morning, with the tree shadows falling hypnotically across the bonnet, I abandoned Cunliffe; abandoned Maura, too, and every other complication, and felt free as any bird. Who was Maura? I thought. And who the, who the, who the, I sang as the tree shadows fell rhythmically across the bonnet, who the hell was Cunliffe?

Somewhat dazed by the rush of sun and shade and with only the mildest groundswell of despair, I drew up at the Pleasance Hotel at eleven-thirty.

Imre, who had evidently been lurking in the foyer, came out at once, and stood rather helplessly like some huge, embarrassed baby in his black alpaca jacket.

'Nicolas, my boy! It is good to see you. There is so much to talk about.' The hairs of his nose were waving in his powerful breath. 'We will walk in the garden, it is such a pleasant day.'

He was gripping my arm tightly as I walked with him. 'How are you, Uncle?'

'Thank you, thank you.'

'And mother?'

'She is a remarkable woman. Today she is in excellent health. Of course, she expects you. This, naturally, must be taken into account. But Nicolas, I must tell you . . .'

He was labouring under some powerful anxiety, the hairs of his nose billowing.

'You have not told her about Bela?'

'I could not. This was an impossibility. Her health . . . I would like you to understand, Nicolas . . .'

He was in the throes of some large agitation. I said kindly, 'No harm done. There are plenty of complications anyway . . .'

'Complications,' he said. 'Yoh, complications!' He stopped in the path and faced me, breathing stormily. 'You will not be angry, my boy? Promise me you will not be angry.'

'What is it?'

'How to explain?' he said, looking at the sky. 'I decided – it seemed a sensible thing to do – that while she was not well enough to hear the sad news about Bela, she could hear the

52

good news about you. After all, good news. ... Your mother has wonderful recuperative powers.'

'What is it you've told her?'

'It is not what I have told her,' he said with some heat. 'It is what she has made of it. She is a wonderfully imaginative woman. ... I merely said,' he went on hastily, noting my expression, 'that you had had a success in business and might be travelling abroad. I wanted to work round to Canada – I suppose you will have to make a trip there – so that in a week or two perhaps we could come round to the subject of Bela. ... And right away she took it you would be starting your father's business again in Europe. In Prague,' he said nervously.

He was gazing at me apprehensively, but I said nothing.

'Your mother does not keep up with the news,' he said anxiously. 'She thinks Prague is as she left it. It is not possible to tell her of the changes. ... You are very angry?' he said at length.

I was not angry. I was merely enfeebled. Short of jumping on his shoulders and tattooing with my fists on his head or driving endlessly there and back through the New Forest to resurrect my mood of nihilistic freedom, there was nothing to be done.

'I think we should go in,' he said, looking round. 'She will have seen your car. We must cheer up, she will expect it. You don't know what it is, my boy,' he went on aggrievedly as we walked back, 'when an imaginative woman gets an idea in her head.'

I do, I thought with melancholy. Better than you. Better than anyone. There was a weird and lowering feeling of inevitability in my vitals as I walked up the steps to the hotel. I knew I would be going to Prague on Tuesday.

Maminka was smoking a cigarette and writing a letter at her little escritoire when we went in.

'Nicolas, *bobitchka*! But you are so thin. You are working so hard. Why have you not been to see me? Let me look at you. Come, kiss me.' It was seldom necessary to speak for the first five minutes in my mother's company, and I made no attempt to

53

do so, merely smiling at her with melancholy affection. My mother demands much affection and can always claim it. She is tall, with large, beautiful almond eyes. Her hair is grey, rinsed with blue. She has the complexion of a young girl and has enjoyed, all her life, perfect health.

She engulfed me now in kisses and caresses, speaking rapidly as Imre, only slightly subdued by our conversation, watched with somewhat proprietorial pride.

'Stephanie,' he said at length, reproachfully, noticing her cigarette for the first time. 'It is the second cigarette you have smoked this morning. You promised me. Your throat . . .'

'I have been writing letters,' she said loudly. 'I must smoke when I am writing letters. Of course,' she said confidentially to me, 'it is not my throat that worries him. It is the price of the cigarettes. Oh, you will be repaid!' she told him scornfully. 'I know you keep an account of the small loans. Be so kind as to let me have a list. My son will attend to it very shortly now. Really,' she said, drawing me to her again, 'the creatures one has to rely on these days.'

'Stephanie,' said Imre, with pain, 'you know this is not the case . . .'

'But you, Nicolas,' said Maminka, disregarding him entirely. 'I cannot tell you how delighted I am at the news. Of course, I had not the slightest doubt that you would open the offices again. Your father often spoke of it. Can you get the same building, do you think, on the Prikopy? I used to look in every day on my way to Wartski's in the Vaclavske Namesti. There was a little lift with golden gates, and such a darling old man who worked it. He had a fresh flower for me every day. Ah, those days! Will they ever return? Now sit down and tell me all.'

I sat down with acute enervation. 'It isn't anything important, Maminka. Just an exploratory visit. Nothing might come of it, you know. Things have changed greatly.'

'Of course. Nothing stands still,' said my mother with great energy, looking swiftly at Imre. 'Men of affairs have to be up and about. Are you thinking of taking Nimek with you?'

'No.'

'Your father had a high opinion of his shrewdness. He is a, low creature and I could never see the need for taking him into partnership, but he is undeniably shrewd. Would it not be safest to take him?' she asked wisely.

I regarded her with helpless affection. 'Maminka,' I said, 'Nimek is running the business now. Don't you remember, I told you?'

'Certainly. Of course,' she said impatiently. 'It was merely a suggestion. Not that it matters. I have written you several letters of introduction to the people who count. And, of course, to Hana Simkova – you remember old Baba who used to nurse you? And now,' she said briskly, seating herself beside me and taking my hand, 'if Mr Gabriel could only be persuaded to respect the privacy of other people's rooms, we have much to talk about.'

Poor Imre went presently. My mother's high clear voice went on and on.

Imre got me on one side before I left, on Sunday. 'Those letters,' he said, 'I couldn't prevent her writing them. What was I to do? It made her happy.'

'That's all right, Uncle.'

'Even to your old nanny, Hana Hana is dead. She died two or three years ago. Of course, I didn't tell her. Even the husband moved away somewhere. . . . She is very much behind the times, your mother,' he said sadly. 'You are very angry with me, Nicolas?'

'No, Uncle. I'm not angry.'

'Here, give me the letters. I'll throw them away. I'll burn them.'

He was so contrite and anxious to please that I did so.

I left after tea, and tooled back to Fitzwalter Square at half past eight. It was growing dark and quiet in the square. I sat in the car for a while in a mood of profound melancholy. I had no wish to see Maura. I had no wish to go up to my room. I sat and brooded, on Cunliffe, on Pavelka, on the trip to Prague. I wondered where I would be next week at this time.

Presently a few lights began to come on about the square and I got out of the car and walked to the Musketeers in the High Road. I had a drink there every Sunday. Mrs Nolan was in the saloon bar with a friend, transfixed by the television. I ordered a pint and drank it. She did not take her eyes off the screen.

I went into the other bar from which sounds of livelier activity were emanating and saw Val and Audrey, the couple who had given the party during the week. The ageing model girl waved at me, and I waved back, but I didn't go across. I watched this group with some curiosity, noticing other familiar faces and wondering which, if any of them, had been spying on me. It was a profitless speculation. I left and walked slowly back to the car and put the covers on and let myself into the house.

It was a quarter to ten. The hall was dark. From an upstairs room there was the soft mutter of a wireless. Somebody listening to a Sunday night play. But nothing so strange as this play, I thought, as, with a feeling of the strangest detachment, I dropped the coppers in the box and dialled Cunliffe's number.

He answered at once, and I said, 'This is Nicolas Whistler.'

'Yes, Mr Whistler.'

'You asked me to ring.'

'Yes. It is good of you to do so. I wished to be sure you had returned from Bournemouth. But I have already been informed of that.'

My scalp began a slow and unpleasant crawl. I said, somewhat breathily, 'Are you still having me watched?'

'One must exercise a little prudence. It is an important assignment you have undertaken. You are holding yourself ready to leave at ten on Tuesday?'

I did not answer, thinking of the noisy group in the Musketeers. Any one of them could have slipped out after I had left. Mrs Nolan, even, I thought, recalling suddenly the small, transfixed figure by the television. But Mrs Nolan had not known of the jokes about Bela. Only friends had known about Bela – friends of Maura's and mine. Maura. Could it posssibly be. . . . But not Maura. How Maura? Maura did not know I was back.

56

Shamed and confused by this thought, I said loudly into the telephone, 'I'm not sure yet. I haven't made up my mind.'

'I understand perfectly,' Cunliffe's wry voice grated in my ear. 'Perhaps you could come and see me at eleven in the morning. Your visa has come through.'

'I'll see.'

'It's rather important,' he said, and rang off at once. I replaced the phone and walked upstairs slowly in the darkness.

On the second landing I began to have an unpleasant suspicion. The muttering of the wireless had grown louder, but it had not come from the first floor, and it was not coming from the second. The only room on the third floor was mine.

I climbed the next flight softly and stood outside the room with my heart thudding. There was a crack of light under the door. The wireless was unmistakably on inside. I put my ear to the door. There was a small creaking from the divan and the rustle of paper.

I was not feeling heroic. I wondered if I should sneak just as softly right down the stairs again to get a poker or a policeman or a fire engine. I did none of these things. Reckless suddenly in the dark, I bent and took off my shoe and, holding it as a weapon, flung open the door, shouting gruffly at the same time, 'Who's there?'

'I am,' said Maura. She was sitting on the divan unwrapping a toffee. 'I wondered how much longer you'd be.'

5

Her lopsided smile had acquired a faint roguishness of late. She said, 'Who did you expect to find in your room?'

I licked my lips. 'How did you get in?'

'I rang the bell.'

'Mrs Nolan's out.'

'An old man on the first floor let me in. He seemed a bit annoyed.'

'How did you know I was back?'

'Your car was outside the door.'

'When was that?'

'Well, really,' she said, the roguishness departing swiftly. 'I don't know. About half an hour ago, I suppose. Aren't you ever going to come in?' she asked impatiently. 'And why have you taken your shoe off?'

The return to her old asperity was some faint comfort, but there was still rather too much to take in here. I gazed at the shoe and at her, and licked my lips again. If she had telephoned Cunliffe would she have come up and waited for me in my room? I didn't know. I didn't know about anything. It was the first time she had done this. I bent down and put on the shoe and gazed at her in some bewilderment.

She said, 'Would you like to stop looking like one o'clock struck and tell me what's happening?'

'You caught me by surprise. I didn't expect to find you.'

'I thought I'd look in and say hello. I might not see you before you go off. You don't mind, do you?'

'No. No. Not a bit.'

She looked at me shrewdly. 'The trip is still on, is it?'

'Yes. Absolutely.'

'I expect your mother was pretty pleased.'

'Yes. Delighted.'

'Well, good.'

'Yes.'

A pistol shot suddenly went off on the wireless, and I jumped about a foot. Maura turned the wireless off and said, 'Look here, Nicolas, what's up?'

'Nothing. I'm a bit tired, Maura. It was the drive back, I expect.'

She looked at me consideringly for a moment, and said slowly, 'Well, I'll leave you to get some sleep.'

I didn't say anything.

'No idea when you'll be back?'

'In a week or two, I expect. I don't know for sure.' I wondered if she did.

'Right.' She stood up and stuffed her sweets in her handbag

and slipped on a jacket. 'Perhaps you'll look me up when you come back.' Her lopsided smile came on briefly.

I wanted to take her hand then, but desisted. 'I'm sorry about this, Maura. I'm terribly tired.'

'That's all right. I can see myself down.'

I saw her down, but I made no offer to accompany her home. In the dark hall I felt closer to her than I had been in the light, felt suddenly that I should take her in my arms and get rid of the suspicion once and for all. But I knew it wouldn't get rid of the suspicion. She said good night and went down the path without looking back.

I walked slowly back upstairs and smoked a cigarette on the divan and undressed and got into bed. Just for a moment as I swam light-headedly into sleep, it all seemed believable.

Chapter 4

I

As we filed into the airport bus at Cromwell Road on Tuesday morning, I could see Cunliffe watching me from his car parked across the road, so to give him a little early-morning pick-me-up, I dropped the guide book I was carrying. It was a gesture of the merest bravado. I felt acutely frail, boneless, bodiless almost without the book.

The man behind me picked it up and gave it back to me and I thanked him, marvelling that I was not sick with hysteria all over it. This book – it now seemed to me unbelievably obvious – was the nub of my mission. Beneath its flyleaf when I returned would be Pavelka's formula.

Cunliffe had explained the operation to me in endless and sickening detail. I must carry the book everywhere. I must allow it to leave my hand only once – in Pavelka's factory where I had to 'forget' it on the desk in the manager's office. It would be returned to me before I left.

'That is really all you need to know,' Cunliffe had said. 'One may claim without immodesty that it is quite a neat little scheme. It is entirely natural for you to carry a Norstrund about – indeed, it is the only up-to-date guide book on Czechoslovakia. You will find it invaluable. Prague is a beautiful city with many ancient monuments. Relax. Enjoy yourself. I am only sorry you have to know you will be carrying the – the bit of paper.'

I was sorry, too.

I got in the bus and it shortly moved off and I turned my head to see if Cunliffe was following. His car stayed where it was. I was glad of this. I had stayed awake half the previous night toying with expedients that might prevent my departure. These included throwing an epileptic fit at the airport, or locking myself in the lavatory until the plane had gone.

At the airport, although I could not quite screw up the gall to throw the epileptic fit, I did lock myself in the lavatory, staying there for longer than seemed humanly or technically feasible. The party was still there when I emerged. A minute or so later, the loudspeaker boomed an announcement and I found myself flowing nervelessly across the tarmac.

In four hours I was in Prague.

2

When you have left a town at the age of six and return eighteen years later, there is a certain quality of enchantment. The streets, the monuments, the church spires, set up a whispering in the mind. You know, with dream-like certainty, what is coming round the next corner, and the sensation of finding you are right is inexpressibly poignant.

All this was totally unexpected, and despite the terror in which I had stepped out of the aircraft and negotiated Passport

Control and Customs, I arrived at my hotel, the Slovenska, in a mood of swollen, if highly unstable, elation.

The Hotel Slovenska stands three-quarters of the way up the Vaclavske Namesti – Wenceslas Square. This thoroughfare, despite its name, is not a square but a broad avenue. At one end is a large grey Victorian museum standing in its own gardens. At the other end, crossing it like the top bar of a T, run the town's main business streets, the Narodni Trida to the left, the Prikopy to the right.

I stood outside the hotel and gazed about me, remembering it all. It was a scene of vitality in the hot sun, the pavements crowded, the little one-decker trams clanging up and down the wide cobbled street. At the far end, Wenceslas, beloved figure of my childhood, glittered from his iron horse in the middle of the road. Even the hotel itself, I thought, was familiar, and after a moment realized why. Here, under another name, was the Wartski's where my mother used to take tea, the big sash windows open now to the pavement in the heat.

I was grinning at all this in a somewhat loose-jawed way, recollecting intimately the plushy darkness of the interior, the racks of newspapers, the heavy velvet curtains, the old ladies dabbing their mouths with little handkerchiefs. It was inconceivable that I should be back.

There were, however, no old ladies present when I went inside. The place was abustle with open-shirted men in sandals. At the reception desk a centre-parted woman, not at all unlike Bunface, was engaged in some intense calculation over a ledger. I waited two minutes and said in English, 'I have a reservation.'

She looked up sharply and flicked quickly through a pile of cards.

'Pan Whistler, Nicolas?'

'That's it.'

'There is a letter for you. Your room is quite ready. One-forty,' she said in Czech to the porter who had come to stand by my bag.

I took the letter and followed the porter into the lift. He was a bent little ancient with an immense adam's apple and a prominent stud in his collarless shirt. He gazed at me with interest, grinning and shaking his head.

'The *pane* has been to Praha before?' he asked in Czech.

'Not for a long time.'

'Many changes,' he said, and hawked politely behind his hand. 'Once we used to be full of business men. Not so many now.'

'No, well. Times have changed.'

He hawked again. 'Still, Praha is the same city, very beautiful. I'll bet you haven't seen many cities as beautiful as Praha.'

I was no longer listening to him. I had been examining the envelope and, as we came out into the corridor, had seen the small inscription, *State Glass Board*. It was evidently my programme. My stomach turned rapidly to water again, and I was thus not able at first glimpse to appreciate the magnificence of room one-forty.

When the porter had deposited my bag, however, and departed, grinning, I stood in the middle of the room and gazed about me. It was, no doubt about it, a handsome apartment. It was tricked out in green and gold. A large bed, curtained all round, stood in an alcove. There was an adjoining bathroom with a shower compartment. There were easy chairs and a chaise longue and a writing desk. Double french windows stood open to a broad balcony. Cunliffe was doing me proud.

I sat down on the chaise longue and opened the envelope. There was a booklet and a two-page letter. The letter, signed *L. V. Svoboda, general manager, State Glass Board*, read:

Dear Pan Whistler,

It is a privilege to welcome you to Prague. I enclose you a booklet relating to our glass industry and also a programme planned for your visit. The programme, as you will see, is brief but quite comprehensive, and it will be a convenience if you will telephone the undersigned on your arrival to indicate if any changes should be required. Believe me, dear Pan Whistler . . .

The second page of the letter, headed *Visit of N. Whistler, representative of Bohemian Glass and Bijouterie Limited*, read:

Wednesday 10.00. Discussions with L. V. Svoboda, State Glass Board offices, Ujezd 23. Followed by luncheon at showrooms, Vaclavske Namesti 48. Afternoon, Discussions with departmental managers, S. N. Czernin, P. Stein, B. R. Vlcek, and tour round departments.

Thursday 10.00. Automobile to Zapotocky Glassworks (Kralovsk, 15 km.). Full day. Luncheon at works.

Friday 10.00. Automobile to Tseblic Glassworks (Tseblic, 23 km.). Full day. Luncheon at works.

Saturday. Free Day. Return visits or further Discussions as necessary.

As L.V. Svoboda had said, brief but quite comprehensive. The visit to Pavelka's old plant was on Thursday. That meant, all being well, that I would have the formula within forty-eight hours. It also meant I would have to carry the bloody thing around for a further forty-eight. Unless, as Cunliffe had suggested, I could cut short my stay.

I had read the programme rapidly. Now, lighting a cigarette to try and control the shaking of my hands, I went through it again. No point in arousing suspicion by asking to leave immediately after visiting Pavelka's factory; especially since they had only laid on two glassworks to be visited. The Saturday free day, then.

I inhaled deeply, pondering this. A terrifying thought had struck me in the aeroplane that there might be some mess-up on the actual day. Cunliffe had not allowed for this. I was to 'forget' the Norstrund; someone would pick it up; it would be returned to me. Fine. But what if some ill-starred maniac refused to allow me to 'forget' it? What if it somehow weren't returned to me? I might be very glad of that free day with its wise provision for *Return Visits*.

As Cunliffe had said, it was natural enough for a visitor to carry a Norstrund around with him. So long as I put it promptly into service and carried on that way, all might be well. All things considered, the programme was best left as it was. L. V. Svoboda should be advised of this. I should also book my return flight for Sunday.

I put down the programme and realized I was still clutching the Norstrund. It had not left my hand all day and was now sticky from the perspiration that had flowed freely. I thought I might have a shower first, and also a bottle of beer. I went to the telephone and ordered the beer, and then stood under the shower for ten minutes.

I seemed to be washing off more than the grime of travel.

When I emerged, refreshed and relaxed, the room was in green semi-darkness. A striped awning had been lowered on the balcony. The beer was waiting on a tray. I had heard no one come in.

I took the beer out on the balcony, and drank it, looking down on the Vaclavske Namesti. The street was a-crawl with people. In the hot sun, a queue waited outside an Automat cafeteria opposite. The little trams clanged up and down. Far down the street, Wenceslas glittered in the hard light, and at the top end, by the Prikopy junction, an enormous picture of Lenin looked down, inscribed with the words, 'Every hand, every brain for the building of socialism.'

It seemed suddenly a very long way from London, from the Little Swine and the Princess May and Maura.

Far down the street, the trees began to move in the museum gardens and a moment later the awning above my head fluttered as a small breeze swept the street. I finished my beer and lit a cigarette and went in to phone Svoboda.

3

I took the Norstrund out for a walk that night. There had been a few spots of rain but the Vaclavske Namesti was warm still and noisy. The lamps were lit, the trams clanging. I crossed the cobbled street at the Prikopy junction and cut through into the old part of the town and could remember as clearly as if it had happened yesterday holding my mother's hand as I had made this same journey.

There had been no home for me since leaving here, no real security. All this was bedded firmly in my childhood, and as I walked in somewhat emotive silence, a loose smile twisted my mouth from time to time.

I walked round the dark bulk of the Karolinum and across the Staromest square to the lovely grey sleeping Klementinum. I crossed the long, stone-figured Charles bridge with the Vltava liquid and winking below, and up, by the steep Mostecka, to the palaces on the Heights: the Czerninsky and the Loreta, the Schwarzenberg and the great pinnacled Hradcany.

There was a little desultory singing and the hum of talk as I passed the lighted entrances of the kavarnas in the narrow medieval streets, and the loose smile tugged at my lips. I could never have seen this in the dark before and yet I seemed to know it in my bones, and my feet found their own path.

It was cooler on the Heights. Below, through the trees, Prague glittered in the dark. I stood and looked down and remembered the shape of it and the smell of it and the places where I had played and was extraordinarily moved. Presently I walked down again and crossed the river by the three islands at the Smetanov bridge.

There was dance music coming across the water and I recognized, twinkling with lights, the old stone tower by the Manes café where often I had gone with my parents to have tea on Sunday and to bathe from the large rafts moored alongside.

I had meant to look down the Prikopy to find the office Maminka remembered with the little lift with the golden gates, but I found myself suddenly tired and lost. A policeman was walking along the embankment, alien in high boots and broad flat shoulder tabs. But his face as he passed was young and boyish with that peculiar steadfastness of the Slavs.

He put me right for the Vaclavske Namesti, and I found myself back in the broad, brightly lit street in an exceedingly curious state of mind. The crowds were still there, noisier, more vivacious than London crowds. Open necks, open faces, a new breed. They seemed to be streaming down the road together, millions of them. At the end of the street the monstrous picture of Lenin looked down, illuminated now. 'Every hand, every brain for the building of socialism.'

I felt oppressed and bruised by these hardy hands and brains. The town of my childhood had been taken over. It lay asleep beneath their vigorous sandals.

I badly wanted a drink, but the lounge was full of them, open necks, open faces, forward together. I went upstairs instead.

The floor-waiter, a plump, immaculately tail-coated character, whom I had already encountered, was prowling about the corridors. He saw me coming and stopped to wait. He had glossy black hair, a blue chin and a gold-toothed smile.

'You have been out to take the air, *pane*?'

'Yes.'

'It's cooler now. We'll have a storm, I think. I have closed the shutters but left the windows open in your room.'

'Thank you.'

He seemed disposed for a chat, smiling with darkling fervour and rubbing pale, plump hands. 'You plan to make a long stay?'

'Just till the end of the week, I think.'

'I hope you make good business. We need the business men back here.'

'You seem pretty full already.'

He shrugged and shook his head sadly. 'Delegations. A different class of business. It's not like the old days.'

'No, well. Times change.' I felt I was repeating myself, tired as hell suddenly in the airless corridor. I put my key in the door.

'Perhaps you would like something?' he said wistfully. 'A glass of beer?'

'No thanks.' I wanted only my bed now.

'Well then.' His gold tooth winked. 'If you should require me, I am Josef.'

'Right. Good night, Josef.'

'Good night, *pane*.'

4

By six o'clock the following evening, my apprehension was dispersing fast. Svoboda and his acolytes, Czernin, Stein, and Vlcek, seemed to be business men like any other business men, if somewhat overgiven to Discussions. Svoboda himself, a kindly old character with spaniel eyes and a Mikoyan moustache, remembered my father, and this was certainly all to the good. In my service with the Little Swine I had picked up a little glass lore, but by no means enough to be a young master out buying. Any bona fides that came my way were more than welcome, and as he called huskily into the telephone for glasses of tea, I assiduously searched my memory for the names of old retainers who had worked in the warehouse. I actually recalled one or two.

There had been more tea in the glass showrooms, and an enormous meal with several toasts to trade and peace, and by mid-afternoon I was comatose, my face stiff with intelligence and my hand cramped from writing in a notebook. This book was now half full with largely indecipherable nonsense about delivery dates and output over which I had nodded so vigorously that as I finally emerged into the sunlight I had a splitting headache.

I seemed to have collected a genie, a strapping young woman who had been driving me about all day, and as I came out on the pavement, I saw with some nervousness that she was waiting for me. She was, no doubt about it, a hand and brain. She was massive and tanned. She wore a white shirt and swept-back hair. She had a splendid bust and sturdy, though shapely, legs. She was studying English and had practised on me conscientiously.

She hopped out of the car when she saw me.

'You will want the automobile again today?'

'No, thanks. I'm only going back to the hotel.'

'Ah, I have wait for you.'

'I'm very sorry. I didn't know.'

'It is no trouble. You will require the automobile tomorrow?'

'I'm going to Kralovsk. Will you be driving me?'

'No. For longer distances is another service.'

'Right. Well,' I said, teetering in the hot, vigorous street. 'Like a drink?' This seemed only right after the immense creature had sweltered all afternoon in the car, but I made the offer diffidently and without enthusiasm.

'Oh, thank you.' Her teeth glinted. 'I would like it.'

'Fine. Let's go to the hotel.'

She did not speak on the way, walking massive and solemn beside me. My head thumped abominably.

We found a place in the open-necked throng and she sat down, gazing about her with interest. 'I do not come here often for myself,' she said. 'Here is very expensive.'

'Yes, well. On business one travels on expenses.'

'Ah, so. You travel to many places?'

'Around and about.'

'The work of a merchant must be very interesting.'

'Very. What will you have?'

'Tea, please. I should like to do such work myself.'

'Ah.' Her bust seemed to be on a level with my eyes. I removed my gaze and said in some desperation, 'You've got a very nice tan. Been on your holidays?'

'Yes. I have worked on a farm.'

'Was it nice?'

'It was very interesting. It must be interesting to see many different places.'

'Ah, well, Prague is very interesting.'

'You like Prague?'

'It's very pleasant.'

'I hate it.'

I had been urging her mentally to stow it, to lap up her tea and leave the merchants in peace. But at this curious statement I stared at her with interest. She had high cheekbones, long grey eyes, a straight nose, no lipstick. Her shirt was clinging to her and her magnificent breasts stood out like bombs. It suddenly occurred to me that she could not be very much more than twenty.

I said, 'What don't you like about Prague?'

'Oh, it is so dull here. The people are dull. It is very boring.'

'Where would you sooner be?'

'Anywhere. London, Paris, New York. Vienna even,' she said glumly. 'In Vienna also is the rock and roll.'

This statement from such an unlikely source struck me as so

grotesque that my eyes swivelled. 'Are you keen on rock and roll?'

'Not just the rock and roll. Everything.'

She had dropped her voice and was beginning to look about her in some embarrassment. My headache lifted quite suddenly. I wondered if I dare take this giant girl out. I said faintly, 'Would you like to have dinner with me?'

'Oh, that would be nice.' Her teeth glinted again. 'I would like it. Thank you.'

'About seven-thirty, here?'

'Ah, tonight is not possible. I go to evening classes for the English studies. Tomorrow I could come.'

'All right.'

'And it would be better if we did not meet here again. Somewhere else, perhaps.'

'You say where.'

'You know the Slavia kavarna? It is on the corner of the Narodni Trida, by the river.'

'Slavia kavarna, seven-thirty tomorrow. Right. Well,' I said. 'You know my name. What's yours?'

'Vlasta. Vlasta Simenova,' she said and stood up to go. I watched her leave with a somewhat mixed and fearful anticipation. She was certainly a lot of girl.

On the way up in the lift I suddenly remembered what else was going to happen tomorrow and my stomach turned over in a single paralysing movement. I had forgotten about that. I went in the room and tossed the Norstrund on the desk and flaked out on the chaise longue.

I had put off thinking seriously about this since my arrival, but now gave myself over to it in a daydream of much detailed terror. This was no time to be thinking of taking big girls out. I wondered if, by tomorrow evening, I would be free to take myself out. I thought of all the terrifying slip-ups that could occur.

Presently I dozed off into a confused and nightmarish dream and awoke to find the room in darkness. I thought someone was there, and lay in panic for a minute, listening. But it was only the outer window rattling. It was raining outside. I got up and switched on the light and looked at my watch. It was a quarter to ten. There was a sour taste in my mouth.

I had a shower and went down for my dinner, but when it came I couldn't eat it, and went back to my room again, sick with foreboding. I slept badly.

5

The foreboding was still there next morning. I ate no breakfast but drank two cups of coffee and had smoked three cigarettes by the time the car turned into the gates of the Zapotocky glassworks.

Vlcek, a small vulpine character with receding hair and a mania for statistics, accompanied me, pouring into my ear for the entire fifteen kilometres a ceaseless stream of data. He was still at it when we got out of the car.

'Of course,' he said, as we entered the office block, 'I have given you the merest outline. Pan Galushka, the director will tell us much more. Pan Galushka is a brilliant man. He is the architect of the plan for our industry. He is not, perhaps,' he said, and smiled uncertainly, 'the easiest man to get on with.'

I stared at him uneasily.

Pan Galushka awaited us in his office, and the moment we entered I thought I should be sick on the spot. The desk upon which I was discreetly to forget the Norstrund was one of the largest I had ever seen. It was also, except for an ashtray and a diary, totally bare.

Galushka walked over from his desk, hand outstretched. He was a spare man with small uneven eyes and a rather odd twisted smile. He said, '*Dobry den*, Pan Whistler.'

I shook hands numbly.

'Pan Whistler has asked especially from England to see the Zapotocky works,' Vlcek said in a rather ingratiating way. 'I have explained a little of what you are doing, but naturally not in detail.'

70

Galushka had still retained my hand and was looking at me rather carefully. He suddenly revealed a line of uneven and discoloured teeth. 'We are complimented,' he said. 'They still remember our lines in England, then, Pan Whistler?'

'Very well,' I said. I licked my lips. 'They were very popular.'

He let go my hand. 'I am glad to hear it. Sit down, sit down, Vlcek. Pan Whistler, a chair for you.'

There was a certain amount of kefuffle here while we were seated and while Galushka handed round cigarettes, and in the course of it, without any plan or intention to do so, I simply placed the Norstrund on the desk. I looked at it with cold fright.

'Well,' Galushka said, 'I think I can assure you – Pan Vlcek will correct me if I do not speak the truth – the glass we turn out is as good as it ever was.'

'It is so,' said Vlcek, speaking to me behind his hand and clowning gruesomely. 'But we will not give them swollen heads. Now we have to see,' he said, smiling at Galushka, 'if they can fulfil the plan for the year.'

'Is our increase not enough for you in Prague?'

'It is useful for a start,' said Vlcek, winking at me and screwing his cigarette into a holder. 'An increase of two hundred and thirty per cent in four years is certainly a useful start.'

This hearty joshing about percentages and output had gone on yesterday and seemed to be the form for commencing Discussions. Vlcek, however, appeared to be working overtime to show that it was all in fun. Galushka sat relaxed, smiling with his uneven eyes and his curious mouth. He wore a lightweight grey summer suit, sandals, and a dark blue celanese shirt, buttoned but tieless. This seemed to be the form for bosses; Svoboda, too, had worn sandals and a tieless shirt – although, it had seemed to me, somewhat apologetically. The acolytes were more formally attired.

Galushka was looking me over carefully. He said, 'At any rate, you will find no change from the old Pavelka ware, except for the better. I sometimes have to remind myself that it's not called that now. I worked in this factory for many years with the old Pavelka, you know. I doubt if he would recognize the place now. We have grown. Of course it could have happened in his time if he had put the interests of the industry first.'

'He was a good employer, quite a progressive manufacturer according to his lights,' Vlcek said, screwing his cigarette in some embarrassment and glancing at me.

'A paternalist,' said Galushka.

The conversation seemed to be taking a decidedly odd turn, and I sat frightened out of my life. I had no wish to discuss Pavelka. It was as much as I could do to keep my eyes away from the Norstrund. I had a sudden horrible suspicion that Galushka knew all about it, and was playing with me.

He was still smiling, however, as he said slowly, 'I only raise the point to bring to your attention, Pan Whistler, that to make Pavelka ware one does not need a Pavelka. Many of the men who made it are still making it – a great deal more of it and the quality has not suffered. It is important to realize this and for us to understand each other in a friendly way.'

His eyes had been wandering over the Norstrund, but as he said the last words he looked up at me. There was nothing particularly friendly about his smile.

The Discussions then formally began. Cunliffe had supplied me with a list of questions and I asked them, shoving in a supplementary from time to time on information gleaned from yesterday's Discussions. Galushka, fortunately, was a man obsessed with his subject, and the moment he began to talk about glass in its technical aspects appeared to undergo a personality change distinctly for the better.

He seemed to have some minor bee in his bonnet on the subject of plate glass – not included in my queries – and made frequent and fairly flattering references to a British factory which specialized in it, apparently at St Helens, Lancs. This seemed to please little Vlcek, who nodded encouragingly.

For myself I was obsessed only with the Norstrund lying screaming on the desk, and with Galushka's roving eye. When once, to illustrate some obscure point of pliability, he picked the book up with both hands and began vigorously to bend it this way and that, I thought my heart had stopped. But he threw the book casually down on the desk again.

After what seemed several hours, Vlcek became mildly restive, and Galushka, looking at his watch, apologized. 'Pan Whistler asks questions, I must answer. But we've almost missed our lunch, my friends. Come, we can continue at table. I hope, at least, Pan Whistler, that you begin to have an idea now of how we work here.'

I said I had.

He stood up. We all stood up. The Norstrund remained screaming on the desk. We left the room. I thought, *Now go to it, whoever you are. Go to it as quick as you like.*

We ate with three of the departmental managers who had been waiting for us at a round table in a secluded corner of the canteen. There were small crossed flags, British and Czech, as a decoration in the middle of the table. I found myself drinking even more than the previous day. It did nothing for my nerves but seemed, at least, to assist the food down my throat. I felt sick and light-headed. My legs were trembling under the table. Galushka dominated the conversation, returning again and again to his preoccupation with plate glass, no doubt as some obscure compliment to me.

It emerged that the firm in St Helens had recently installed new continuous rolling machinery which had excited lively admiration in the glass world. One of the departmental managers wanted to know if I had yet had the opportunity to inspect it.

I said, wistfully, that I hadn't.

Galushka laid his hand jovially on my shoulder. 'My friend,' he said, 'you should come and work with us. Here few things are secret. Here an aspirant can see and learn any process he wishes to master. I think,' he said, looking joshingly at me, 'you are not yourself interested so much in hollow ware. I could tell it as we talked. I'm right?'.

I didn't know how to answer this. Vlcek, who had been drinking cautiously, came to my assistance. 'We are embarrassing Pan

Whistler. Hollow ware, after all, is his subject. Can a man claim he isn't interested in his own subject?'

Galushka nodded round the table. 'Isn't it a criticism of a form of society that a man is forced to specialize in a subject that doesn't interest him? I think, Pan Whistler,' he said to me shrewdly, 'that if you worked here with us in Kralovsk, even though you are a specialist in hollow ware, you would not miss an opportunity to inspect the continuous rolling process with plate glass. Ah!' he said, as I broke obediently into a sheepish smile and his delighted managers chortled round the table. 'Ah! We'll say no more about it. We won't talk any more of plate glass, comrades. It's a forbidden subject.'

I was very glad to hear it. It seemed to have put the company into the best of humours, however. When, later, the party broke up, there were hearty handshakes all round. The managers returned to their life's work. Vlcek, Galushka, and I went round the factory.

6

Of this tour round Mr Pavelka's old works very little remains in the mind. Glass-making is a noisy business. A great deal of the finished product manages to get itself broken. It is also conducted in enormous sheds, very hard on the feet, and in a variety of temperatures ranging from the merely tropical to the oven-like. It is enough to say that by half past four we had finished.

Galushka said he had some papers he wished me to take. I was very glad to hear this, having been distracted half out of my mind over the problem of manoeuvring a return to his office. We went back there.

'Of course,' he said, as we entered the office block, 'your programme is impossibly limited – you have seen only the merest outline. Have you the possibility to return before you go?'

'Saturday is a free day,' Vlcek said. 'Perhaps Pan Whistler will be able to use the opportunity.'

I said I fervently hoped so, and followed Galushka in. I was feeling physically ill. I thought the Norstrund wouldn't be there and I would have to ask for it. I had the clearest vision of myself tottering about making conversation while it came back through the channels. Maybe it wouldn't come back at all. Maybe whoever was fiddling with it had not had enough time; had been disturbed. ... I could see a variety of cock-ups looming, and, as I entered the office closed my eyes in a brief wordless prayer. When I opened them I looked at the desk. The Norstrund had gone.

'If you'll just wait one moment,' Galushka was saying, pressing a key on his intercom, 'I'll get the report on tensile strength that interested you so much. I think also you should see our papers on heat treatment and annealing. Miss Bironova,' he said into the intercom, 'please bring me in the reports on ...'

'Aren't you well, Pan Whistler?' Vlcek said in alarm. 'Sit down a moment. It's the heat – you're not used to it. Here, let me help you.'

I sat down, sick and shaking. Galushka got me a glass of water. While they were both staring at me in some concern, his girl came in with a sheaf of papers and the Norstrund.

One of the messengers had brought it in to her, she said. Perhaps it belonged to the *anglicke pane*. I said yes, yes, it was indeed mine; I must have mislaid it ... and sat there a few minutes longer listening to Galushka, and my own voice responding very civilly to his remarks.

Just a little while later I was on the way back to Prague.

I locked the door of the room very carefully behind me and flaked out on the chaise longue. I was not excited or even nervous. I felt merely exhausted, as if I'd been shovelling for several hours or had gone a few rounds with some nimble-footed flyweight, not a heavy puncher, but fast.

I sat up presently and opened the Norstrund and examined the flyleaf. It was crinkled a little in one corner. I didn't think the mark had been there before. I couldn't see any other sign of tampering. As Cunliffe had said, unless you knew about it you couldn't tell.

It was not yet half past five. I thought I'd take a warm bath and soak, and presently got up and went in the bathroom.

75

Despite the magnificence of the apartment, the tub was an ancient instrument standing on four claw-like legs about eighteen inches out from the wall. It lacked a soap dish. It also lacked a plug. I looked underneath and around for the plug. There was a loose bit of lead piping on the floor near the wall, and that was all. I thought it was time I made use of Josef and rang for him.

Josef brought me a plug and I drew the bath and got in, lowering myself gently horizontal. I felt extraordinarily calm. I thought of all the heart-thudding, bowel-loosening hours I had gone through. Well, it was all over now. I'd got it. All I had to do was get back with it.

I think I dozed off.

I came to at a quarter past six and got out and dried myself. I put on clean underwear and went through to the room and lay down again on the chaise longue, relaxed and pleasantly ruminative. The day wasn't over yet. I wondered what else was in store. At seven o'clock I dressed and rang for a beer and went out on the balcony.

I stayed there, sipping slowly, until the clocks began to chime the quarter past, and then went in and picked up the Norstrund and left.

Seven-thirty, she had said, at the Slavia.

Chapter 5

I

THE effect of a bath and a rest and a beer had wrought some miraculous change in me as I stepped out of the hotel and into the still-crowded Vaclavske Namesti. I felt excessively clean-limbed and English, and in the mood for Adventures.

Prague, it is a fact, is still the most Ruritanian of the capitals of Europe. Despite the hands and brains, an aura of romance lingers over the city. At sunset lamps are lit in the linden trees on the embankment. A hundred points of saffron reflect the last light of day from the pinnacled Hradcany on the Heights. As the neon slogans begin to flash in the Vaclavske Namesti, so the turreted grey buildings and the cobbled courtyards of the old town come into their own. One feels the presence of Black Michael and enigmatic young countesses; one is no more than a stone's throw from Zenda.

All this was very satisfactory and I lingered as I cut through the old town. The clocks began to boom the half past as I came out on the embankment, and I put on a spurt. Even so I was ten minutes late.

The Slavia was a big corner café with huge windows, half open to the river. It was a hive of activity in the warm evening, waiters and waitresses shuttling there and back between the crowded tables. She was sitting with a glass of tea near the window reading a newspaper in a cane rack. She was wearing an embroidered blouse and had done something to her hair. It was now coiled on top, giving her a long and rather luscious neck.

She hadn't seen me come in and I approached from behind and said, smiling, into her ear, 'Dobry vecer.'

She started and looked round. 'Uh. Dobrý vecer.'

'I'm sorry I'm late. I didn't realize how long it would take me to walk here.'

'Oh, don't think . . . It isn't any matter . . .' She had flushed rather stunningly, and seemed to have run out of English in her surprise. I took the seat opposite and gazed at her with frank admiration. 'You're looking very attractive. I like your hair.'

'Thank you. You are gallant.'

'What have you been doing today?'

She told me in a rather solemn and child-like way. I continued to gaze at her with this same frank admiration. She had a thin gold chain and a cameo suspended from her neck. The embroidered blouse did nothing to cramp her wondrous figure.

There was just a touch of wildness about the high Slav cheek-bones. I felt myself begin to tingle with pleasant anticipation. Whistler Nicolas, no doubt about it, could have done a great deal worse for himself.

I had taken the only available seat at the table, and the curious attentions of the other patrons seemed to be inhibiting her. When I suggested that we move elsewhere she sprang up immediately. The punched bill was on the table. I paid it and we left.

Out in the street my misgivings returned. She stood almost a head taller, and walked with a powerful loping gait. I found myself beginning to sweat with embarrassment. It didn't seem to affect the girl. She talked slowly and studiously, grappling her way through the syntax and gazing down at me with long grey candid eyes.

We ate at the Zlaty Kohoutek, the Golden Cockerel, a nightspot across the river. It looked a little gimcrack place from the outside with a flashing sign of a cockerel and musical notes in several garish colours. Inside it was rather romantic, a long room, darkish, with lamps on the tables and much gleaming napery. A five-piece band played softly and cornily during dinner.

The girl ate and drank with healthy enjoyment. I had left the choice to her. She ordered carp, roast goose, sour cream, something called Soufflé Milord, and a water ice. She also ordered powerful cocktails, a half bottle of Hungarian white and a bottle of Hungarian red wine, and Rumanian brandy with the coffee.

All this had a profound effect on me. The band at the end of the long room showed a tendency to float gently up and down. The effect on the girl seemed equally beneficial. A certain primness in her manner departed. She put her elbows on the table and smiled across at me like the Mona Lisa with her chin cupped in her hands.

She told me she was twenty, and lived with her father, a musician and a widower, at Barrondov a few miles down the river. She had been a driver for two years.

I said, 'What was all this about rock and roll? Are you very keen on dancing?'

'Not the dancing. I wouldn't call it dancing. It is the gayness. Gayness?' she said, recollecting her studies.

'Gaiety.'

'Yes, gaiety. It is the gaiety and youth. But I love dancing, that is true. I would have been a dancer with the ballet. My father wished it, but it was not possible. I growed too much.'

'Like Topsy.'

'Topsy?'

'She was a girl who growed too much. It's a joke,' I said, noticing the bafflement in her eyes. 'The word should be grew really.'

'Ah, a joke. Thank you. I am glad when you correct me. This is the only way to learn the language, don't you think it is so?'

The band had begun its slow upward levitation. I said daringly, 'They say pillow English is very effective.'

'Pillow English?'

'It's just another method. Forget it,' I said, alarmed suddenly at the large, brooding face.

She didn't forget it, frowning .over it. 'Pillow English. A pillow is for the head?'

'That's it.'

Enlightenment dawned. 'Ah, you mean when people are in bed together.'

'I'm sorry. I shouldn't have said it.'

'Oh, it's nothing. Don't be shy,' she said surprisingly, smiling at me. 'There is such a phrase in French. I forget it. You mean people in love learn the language quicker?'

'Sort of. It was just another joke.'

She was regarding me with interest, teasing a wisp of hair that had come loose. 'As a merchant you travel a great deal?'

'Here and there.'

'You have many mistresses?'

I goggled at her. 'Not really. Not many.'

'How many?'

'I don't know. You know I was only really . . .'

'Have you a wife?'

'No.'

There was an odd flicker in the wine-bright eyes as she smiled curiously at me. 'It is so interesting to learn how other people live. I would like to learn so much more.'

'Maybe I can teach you.'

'Maybe you can.' She laughed, rather huskily, very promisingly indeed, and leaned towards me. I took her hand.

'You'd like to dance?' she said.

I had been dreading this for some time. The band had stopped playing softly and cornily and was now playing loudly and cornily. Several people were on the floor. I wedged the Norstrund in my pocket and stood up.

It was not nearly so bad as I had expected. On the dance floor, she was limber and light on her pins, responding to the merest touch. We swung tipsily round for a couple of numbers. Nobody seemed to find anything remarkable in the performance. Several small men were dancing with large, well-found women, and wine was flowing all round the shadowy room. Her bust, all the same, was rather too near my chin for absolute comfort, and she seemed to be leaning on it fairly freely. All this opened up certain vistas, but I was glad when the music stopped.

We left at ten o'clock and went for a walk, crossing the river and strolling along the embankment in the greenish light under the linden trees. I thought I might put my arm round her waist, and did so, meeting with no objection. Indeed, she snuggled up very amiably. I was content to await events.

Presently we cut through to the Vaclavske Namesti, seething and noisy as ever and brilliantly lit. A number of stalls had opened up at the kerbside, selling *parkys* – hot sausages – and pickled cucumbers.

'You'd like to eat a *parky*?' she asked.

'No, thanks.'

'I think I would like to eat a *parky*.'

I queued up and bought her one, marvelling at her appetite. The *parky* came on a slice of black bread with a smear of mustard. She disposed of it rapidly as we strolled along.

The clocks began to boom a quarter to eleven.

'I have so enjoyed myself,' she said. 'Thank you very much for this evening.'

'I've enjoyed it, too. Thank you for coming.'

'I think I should go home now.'

I said, 'Right,' supporting this move entirely. In the crowded street I'd had to take my arm from her waist. Barrandov, down the river, sounded pleasantly secluded. 'Where do we get the tram?'

'Oh, there is no need for you to come.'

'That's all right. I'd like to.'

'No, please. See, we are at the tram stop. It is no trouble for me. You have work tomorrow.'

'But I must take you home,' I said in dismay. It seemed impossible that I had misread the signs.

'No, please. It's late. And my father waits for me. I will go alone.'

She had rooted herself solidly to the pavement, and seemed to have made her mind up. I was suddenly conscious again of her massive physique. She was holding out her hand to me.

I took it drearily. 'Well, if you insist,' I said, cursing the missed opportunities. We had passed several useful-looking courtyards off the embankment.

'We can meet again, if you wish it.'

'Does your father wait for you every night?'

'Most nights,' she said, dryly.

There was something about her that I couldn't quite fathom, a certain off-beat humour lurking in the long eyes. I'd seen it in the restaurant. I said, 'How about tomorrow?'

'Tomorrow is not possible. I have to help my father with his practice. Truly,' she said, smiling apologetically. 'I play the piano for him.'

'Saturday, then?'

'Saturday would be very nice. Must you work in the afternoon?'

'No. I'm finished then.'

'I also. If you wish, we could swim in the river. I go every

Saturday to the bathing station at Zluta Plovarna if the weather is good. Later, we could eat at Barrandov?'

'At Barrandov?'

'The *Terasy*.'

It seemed there was a kind of lido there, a pool scooped out of rock, flanked by terraces cut into the stone. In the evening one could dine and dance on the terraces.

I thought it would fill in the time, if not in hoped-for pursuits, and gave the programme somewhat grudging approval. She gave me her telephone number, which I noted in my diary.

'Perhaps I will say one thing more,' she said, stepping from one leg to the other, and watching my face. The flicker was back in her eyes. 'My father will not wait for me on Saturday.'

'Oh.'

'You understand me?'

'Yes. Certainly. Rather.'

I wondered if I did.

'Good night, and thank you again,' she said warmly.

I said good night, and walked back to the hotel, slightly punch drunk.

2

Vlcek picked me up again in the morning and we drove to Tseblic (23 km.). This proved to be more or less a repetition of the marathon at Kralovsk, except that the manager, a keen technical type, was clearly not in Galushka's class as a force to be reckoned with. Vlcek didn't reckon with him much. After lunch, at which he drank more freely than on the previous day, he quietly faded away – for a snooze in the car, I suspected.

It was swelteringly hot, and the red dye from the Norstrund stained my hands as we trudged for endless hours round the works. Vlcek joined us again, very perky, soon after four, and by five we were driving back.

'Well, Pan Whistler, I hope the visits have left you with some favourable impressions?'

'Yes, indeed.'

'I think Kralovsk interested you more. I have arranged the automobile in case you should wish to return there tomorrow.'

'No, thanks. It won't be necessary. I've got everything I need.'

'Ah, you prefer then further Discussions with Pan Svoboda?'

'No. No. I don't think I do. I shan't want anything more at all. Everything's been beautifully planned,' I said, noting his disappointment. 'I wouldn't have thought it possible to work in so much in the time.'

Vlcek smiled with sad pleasure. 'We try to do our best in Prague. It isn't always obvious to – to some people. Perhaps if you are satisfied you would not mind saying so in a letter when you return to England?'

'Of course.'

'And when shall we see you back again?'

'Back again?'

'We understood this was an exploratory trip for Discussions and Visits. Pan Svoboda hoped you would return soon. With your order book,' he said gaily.

'Ah, yes. Well, that's up to my directors.'

'Your report will be favourable? Excuse me,' he said hastily. 'I do not wish to pry. In the old days I was a salesman. I booked orders from England, France, Germany, Belgium ... One knew how to handle this one with discounts, that one with long credit ... It's different now. Today one thinks very much more on industrial lines. Output, work flow ... It is very interesting,' he said sadly.

'Ah, well, you'll get the foreign trade back.'

'Undoubtedly. It must come,' Vlcek said excitedly. 'We are, after all, a trading nation. Once the industry has been firmly re-established, salesmanship will be required again. Salesmanship, salesmanship, and yet more salesmanship.' His vulpine little face was alight with prophetic fervour.

He dropped me at the Slovenska. I went up in the lift. Josef was prowling in the corridor.

'Ah, Pan Whistler. You have made good business.' He was rubbing his hands, smiling the darkling smile.

'Yes, thanks. A full day, anyway.'

'You look hot. It is the humidity. The big storm has not come yet.'

'I wish it would soon.'

'Never fear. Tonight or tomorrow perhaps. I should say a glass of Pilsener would suit you.'

'I'd say the same.'

'Right away,' he said, with pleasure.

I went in and through to the bathrom and stripped off and stood under the shower. I hoped the big storm wasn't going to wreck tomorrow's planned events. I pondered over them for ten minutes.

The beer was waiting for me when I came out.

3

'In England the girls wear two pieces or one?'

'I think one-piece at the moment.'

'Yes,' she said sadly. 'I thought it was so. I saw recently a German magazine. They are quicker in Germany with the fashion.'

She was wearing two pieces herself, in black sharkskin. I could hardly keep my eyes off either of them. Below the top-piece there wasn't an ounce of surplus flesh on her magnificent body, the waist flat and golden, legs long and smooth. She was leaning over on one elbow, moodily nibbling a blade of grass, gorgeous breasts pendant.

We were lying in a river meadow, a long tram ride from town, at the bathing station of Zluta Plovarna. Willows hung limply in the heat. It was somewhat overcast. Josef's storm had not come yet. The river was narrower here and gurgled between green banks. I longed to lie about in it, but desisted. The Norstrund was wrapped in my towel; I had hired the towel and a pair of somewhat skimpy shorts at the kiosk.

The girl had seemed rather moody when we met and had been severely rationing her conversation since we came out on the grass. I wondered uneasily if some physical deficiency of mine had upset her.

I said, after a lengthy silence, 'You seem sad. Is anything the matter?'

'No. No.'

'Don't you like the heat?'

'I don't mind it.'

'Did you wear yourself out at the piano last night?'

'No,' she said, unsmiling.

I stretched out, baffled.

'You will go tomorrow!' she burst out, glumly.

I looked up at her, flattered and surprised. I had only taken her out once. It was hard to know what to say. 'Oh, I expect I'll come back again.'

'You think so?'

'I might.'

'No, you won't. Ah, I wish I could go, too,' she said passionately. 'How I wish I could leave this country.'

'Haven't you ever been away?'

'Once. To Hungary,' she said scornfully. 'It was just the same.'

'Well, this is a very nice country. I mean,' I said lamely, 'you've got beautiful scenery and everything. The weather in England is terrible.'

'The people are free to travel.'

'Most of them never leave the country.'

'They can if they want to. Anyway, they are free there. There are so many things.'

It seemed to be time to try and edge her out of it. I smiled at her. 'Like knowing whether to wear a one-piece or a two-piece?'

'That's a part of it.'

'And rock and roll?'

'Oh, the rock and roll! You will not forget it . . .' She was smiling all the same, and seemed to have cheered up a bit.

'Did you make good business here?'

'I did what I came to do.'

'What was that?'

'Look round glass works and have discussions.' I looked up at her curiously. 'You know all that.'

'Nothing else?'

85

'What else?'

'I don't know. You're not working for the Americans – to come and see things and tell them?'

'Why should I be?' My heart had started to flutter a bit.

'One hears stories. They say all Westerners are spies for the Americans. Isn't it so?'

'Of course it isn't.'

'I don't mind if you are. You know what I feel.'

'Well, I'm not,' I said shortly. 'You mustn't believe all that rubbish, Vlasta. I'm here on business.'

'Would you tell me if you were working for the Americans?' She was smiling down at me. The nasty patch seemed to be over.

'What do you think?'

'I think I could tell,' she said. She tickled me with the grass stalk. 'I know your face very well now.'

'You haven't seen it very often.'

'I think I know it all the same.' She edged nearer, tickling my nose. 'It is quite – quite a comical face. I can tell what you are thinking, little merchant.'

The twin luscious bombs in black sharkskin hung a few inches from my face. I stared at them hypnotically.

'What am I thinking?'

'I know,' she said, tickling with the grass stalk. 'I know. I know. . . .'

So that seemed all right.

4

The terraces of Barrandov were quite a sight. We had fallen asleep at the bathing station and it was after dusk when we took the tram to the *Terasy*. The little nightspot shimmered like an iridescent shell in the velvety darkness. The rock-pool was a mussel-shaped depression hacked out of the rock, several yards below ground level. Running down to it, and following the same conformation, were the stepped terraces like the galleries of the Roman Colosseum. Floodlights picked out bits of statuary and shrubs in pots. A dance band was playing. Shadowy figures were sitting and strolling around the various levels, and here and there a few couples were dancing; it was early yet.

All this was more than satisfactory, and we swung along to the entrance, arm in arm, full of fresh air and with healthy appetites. The girl had gone into the river for a dip when we awoke in the half light, and had emerged, dripping, laughing, and so athletically radiant that I could scarcely contain myself to see what happened on the nights her father didn't wait for her.

The band was playing from a large building adjoining the pool. A few score people were dining and dancing inside.

'You would like to eat here or outside?'

'As you please.'

'Outside is a cold buffet. It's very good,' she said, smiling.

'All right, outside.'

We walked through to the terraces and found a table near the pool and then walked over to the buffet. This was a large table, supervised by several efficient-looking men in short white jackets, and supporting some dozens of trays of *hors-d'œuvre*. We made a selection and the plates were brought over to us.

It was very pleasant. The dancing reflections on the water gave an illusion of coolness in the warm, humid night. She was wearing a little bolero over a sun-top, and she took it off. I ordered a bottle of wine, and watched in some fascination as she cleared her plate. I was setting to myself, but had still not half finished when she wandered off to the buffet again.

'I am hungry,' she said when she returned.

'So I see.'

'Aren't you hungry?'

'Yes, I am.'

'For the food, I mean,' she said, flickering.

'That's what I mean. How's your father?' I said, responding to her smile with a leer of my own.

'He is well.'

'What's he doing tonight?'

'He plays at a concert at Pilsen.'

'Good show.'

'What is that?'

'I hope he has a good concert. What time will he be back?'

'Very late.'

'Then here's to music and Pilsen,' I said, raising my glass.

She responded to the toast, eyes flickering over her glass. 'I think you are a bad man, little merchant.'

'Don't scream till you're hurt.'

It took her a moment or two to work this out, and seemed to afford her rich amusement. She spilled her wine, fairly glowing at me over her heaped plate.

'I never scream, little merchant.'

Better and better.

At eleven o'clock, I said, 'Like to go now?' We had drunk another bottle of wine and danced a bit.

'If you like.'

She put on her bolero and we left.

The music followed us into the black void. The road was bordered by thickets; it seemed to be almost in the country.

'Do you live far away?'

'Not far.'

'Anywhere to sit down round here? I thought we might smoke a cigarette.'

'There is a seat by the telephone box a little farther along – on the other side of the road.'

We crossed and found this seat, a sturdy rustic piece. The telephone box was unlighted, I was glad to see.

'Cigarette?'

'No, thank you.'

'I don't think I will, either.'

'Wasn't that what you wanted?'

'Not all I wanted.'

In the dizzy, fractional pause, I kissed her.

She responded swiftly, her two arms whipping out like pythons – not, as I momentarily feared, to repel me. I found myself crushed in an embrace of powerful ardour. She wore no perfume or lipstick. She had a curious odour of her own, of tanned skin, fresh air, some kind of spice, a Slav smell, very stimulating.

'*Milacek*,' she murmured a minute or two later when I found strength to draw back for air.

It was a word I had forgotten. *Milacek*. Darling. It came back powerfully over the years. . . . I returned to her in the blackness. And then all hell seemed to be let loose.

There was a single tearing razor flash of lightning, an instant eruption of thunder, and the sky fell in. A sheet of water seemed to drop solidly out of the air.

Josef's storm had begun.

It happened so quickly we were drenched even before we got off the seat. The girl cowered against me, muttering. I swore evilly.

'Quick. Nip in the telephone box,' I said, and led the way. We stood pressed together inside, sodden and dripping. The night sounded suddenly like a river in full flood.

'Maybe it will soon stop,' I said miserably.

She shook her head. 'I think not. We have these storms sometimes. It will last one hour, perhaps two.'

We stood without speaking for some time, our clothes beginning to steam in the hot, close air. One or two people raced past, splashing. The night was now brilliant with lightning, reverberating with thunder. Water streamed like a plastic film down the window.

'Now what?' I said.

'I don't know.'

'Maybe it will ease off after a bit.'

'Maybe. We could try to run to my home.'

'Will your father be back yet?'

'Not yet. Not until twelve or one o'clock.'

'All right.'

We waited in the noisy, flashing darkness.

'I think it is not so bad now,' she said after a few minutes. 'Come, we can try. We will have to be quick. It will start again.'

We pelted out of the box. It seemed suddenly cold outside, the rain still falling heavily, but not flooding down as before. The road was running, fantastically, with water, an inch or two deep already.

We splashed hand in hand for some minutes and turned right up a side road. 'The white house. Look, you can see,' she said, as lightning began to flash overhead again. It stood by itself, a small bungalow. A cluster of others stood near it.

The rain began to belt down fiercely again as we got to the gate. She fumbled for her key and opened the door and we stumbled in, streaming. She put the light on and looked at me and leaned against the wall, laughing. 'To see yourself! You have had your swim, after all.'

I sneezed, not sharing this joke.

'I am sorry. Come in. Take off the wet coat. You will catch an illness.'

I thought I'd caught one already. The unusual exercise through the puddles – she had dragged me along with racing, Olympic strides – in addition to the damp and debilitating session in the box, seemed to have taken their toll.

'Give me it. I will put the electric fire on. So. It will dry a little.'

My trousers were equally sodden. There didn't seem much to be done about them. I stood there, damply uncomfortable, while she brought in towels and we dried our hair.

'Now who is sad?' she said. 'Come, smile for me, little merchant.' The brisk run seemed to have done her good. She was lively and cheerful, eyes sparkling. 'I will make you some coffee, then I will change. Maybe I can find something of my father's for you to wear while your clothes dry.'

She disappeared into the next room and I looked sourly round. There seemed to be three rooms, one of them a kitchen-dining room. A cottage piano stood in the living-room. There was also a divan, made up as a bed. A large round clock was mounted on the wall. It registered a quarter to twelve. Her father would be back soon. A fine night this had turned out to be.

She came back after a minute with her hair down and in a dressing gown, inspecting a suit at arm's length. It was of brown tweed and evidently made for some circus freak. 'My father is bigger than you,' she said unnecessarily. 'Try it anyway.'

I slipped the jacket on, to her excessive merriment.

'I am sorry,' she said. 'Keep it on, anyway. Put on the suit.'

'How about your father.'

'He cannot mind. It is only till yours is dry. Go in the next room. Oh, little merchant, you will have to grow!'

I was beginning to tire of this description, and also of the massive, humorous girl. There didn't seem much else to be done, however. I went in the next room and changed into the enormous trousers, and shuffled back in them, nerving myself for the expected peals of laughter.

They didn't come. She was sitting on the floor near the electric fire, and smiled only sombrely when I appeared. 'So. This is the last time we meet, Nicolas.'

I said, 'Not necessarily,' half-heartedly, and sneezed again.

'You had better have a drink. You are cold. The coffee isn't ready yet.' She got up and fetched a bottle of slivovitz from a cupboard and poured me out a glass. It was fiery stuff with a mule-like though humanizing kick. I took a less jaundiced look round the room. It was quite large and tastefully furnished. There was a balalaika on a small table.

'Is that your father's instrument?'

'No, no. He is a cello. The balalaika is mine.'

'How about a tune?'

'I don't feel for it. I will see to the coffee.'

I didn't feel much like a tune myself. My suit was steaming away on a chair. It was two minutes to twelve. I wondered how the hell I was going to get back. I thought it would have to be a taxi. I had noticed a phone in the hall. I finished the slivovitz and put the glass down and sat down in an easy chair, wishing with all my heart that I was tucked up snugly in the Slovenska awaiting the morning chimes and the ten o'clock plane.

She came in with the coffee, and we drank it rather silently:

'Another glass of slivovitz? Your suit is not yet dry.'

'Thanks.'

She had one herself, and raised the glass. 'To the success of your business, Nicolas.'

I couldn't think of much to say to this, and merely raised mine with a cheerful nod.

'Do you think you will really come back?'

'Well, it's possible. In business you never can tell.'

'When could it be?'

'Hard to say. Quite soon, perhaps. I *would* like to hear you play the balalaika,' I said, to change the noisome conversation.

She smiled moodily and picked up the instrument and sat down on the rug and began to play. It was a Slovak song my mother sometimes hummed, and presently she began to sing. It was something about pine trees and love and death. I listened, at first pleasantly surprised, and then astonished. She sang wonderfully, a husky, thrilling voice, mournful, perfectly attuned to the dolorous rhythm.

She ended with a final twang and let the strings die slowly in the quiet room. It was very effective. I said sincerely, 'Vlasta, that was marvellous. Play another.'

'You like the balalaika?'

'I like the way you do it.'

'The balalaika is for firelight,' she said with a mournful smile. 'Switch off the light.'

I did so, with an anxious look at the clock. It was a quarter past twelve. Outside the rain was still pouring steadily, thunder rumbling distantly. I took my seat again in the easy chair in the red glow of the fire. She had poured out two more drinks and drained hers with a single toss before beginning to pluck the balalaika again.

I don't know how many songs she played. She poured more drinks between them. I sank back in the warm darkness, aware I should be going, unable to go, thinking just one more, and just one more. At some point she moved over to lean against me as she sang. I dropped my hands to her shoulders and played with her damp hair. Its odour came up strongly in the dimly lit room.

She swayed from side to side as she sang, and I swayed with her, head beginning to spin, fire rolling, darkness lurching. I cupped my hands under her chin, and, as the room rolled and the low voice sang, dropped them inside her dressing gown.

She didn't stop singing; bombs rolling warmly, smoothly, heavily in the dark. And then the balalaika had stopped and she had turned round and was nuzzling my face. *'Milacek.'*

'I shouldn't be here.'

'Stay now.'

'Your father.'

'It's too late. He won't come.'

'How do you know? How can you . . .'

'The concert must have ended late. He will come early in the morning. They have a motor bus. It has happened before.'

My heart was thumping, mouth dry, the girl's face swaying in the dim light. I said huskily, 'Vlasta, are you sure?'

She stood up and pulled the sash. Her dressing gown fell open. She had nothing on at all underneath.

'I am sure,' she said.

Chapter 6

I

I WAS rowing this enormous boat with a rope round my neck and the man hitting me over the head with a shovel when it gave a final lurch and I came up out of it. I opened my eyes. A large white face was circling several feet in front of me. It stopped after a while and turned into a clock, which, after much diligent frowning, I calculated to be registering ten minutes to seven.

There was an awful numbness at the back of my neck and my head seemed to have been crammed forward over my eyes. I lay quietly for a while puzzling why this should be and trying to think where the hell I was, and suddenly remembered and sat up in a panic. I was going home today. I was due at the airport at ten. Three hours.

I had been lying on her arm. Her large, beautiful body lay stretched out on top of the coverlet, one massive tanned leg across mine. Her bomb-like breasts rose and fell profoundly. She was fast asleep and moodily magnificent.

She had loved with such ferocity last night that even in my drunken excitement I had been unnerved at the appalling strength of her. In this shattered morning state I was more than unnerved. I felt broken, ruined, and in much physical danger.

Across the chair, in some disarray, lay the inhumanly large clothes of her father. I had no wish to be around when he arrived; still less, a far graver and more urgent contingency, when his insatiable daughter should awake.

She lay sleeping like the mother of the universe. I began trying to manoeuvre my leg from under hers. This was no simple operation, and in the course of it her arm came round in a loose movement batting me numbingly on the ear.

She was turning over.

I waited in palpitating and queasy silence, but apart from a sombre, muttered '*Milacek*,' she did not awake.

I drew myself slowly off the bed, watching her minutely. The Norstrund was on the floor beside the almost-empty slivovitz bottle. I picked it up and tip-toed into the bathroom.

My clothes were still damp and crumpled. I put them on swiftly. The room lurched. I rammed my tie in my pocket and left my shoe laces undone and tip-toed back to the doorway. She had turned half on her side, knees drawn up. She was sleeping soundly with the healthy and magnificent grace of some satisfied jungle beast. I said silently, Goodbye, Vlasta, goodbye *milacek*, and let myself out quietly.

I walked softly up the gravel path to the side road, but once there tied up my shoe laces and began to run. It was a still morning, hot already, the sun glinting everywhere. My mouth was parched, stomach gravely uneasy.

At the main road I stopped and looked up and down. There was nothing in sight, no trucks, no farm wagons, not even a bicycle. The telegraph wires hummed softly in the silence. A tangy smell was coming up off the road in the early heat. I began to panic again. I had a terrifying feeling the girl had woken up and was storming around looking for me and would shortly come bounding up the road in amorous fury. It was a damned long way from the hotel. Too far to walk; two hours at least. And I had to pack and pay and get to the airport.

In a state of mild frenzy, I began to trot up the road, and five minutes later had to slow down, gasping. A couple of minutes after that, I saw a horse and trap pulling out of a side road ahead of me and yelled like a madman for the driver to stop. He did so, staring curiously as I panted up.

'You drive to Prague?' I asked in Czech.

'*Yoh.*'

'*Dobry den,*' I said belatedly as I clambered up.

'*Dobry den.*' He was a little wizened carrot of a man, in shiny gaiters. He still looked curiously at me, but apart from a sly remark of 'How goes the night work, comrade?' made no comment as we trotted down to the shining river.

We crossed the water at the Jiraskuv bridge and he dropped me at the corner of the Mezibranska and I walked past the museum and up the Vaclavske Namesti, quiet for once in the still of this sunny Sunday morning, and got in the hotel by ten past eight. I had a shower and packed and went down for my breakfast and had paid the bill by twenty past nine. And then with nothing to do, but a compulsive need to do it, I called a taxi and left.

I was too early to go through the customs but, with a mindless sense that it might show the innocence of my luggage and of my conscience, I left my case on the inspection table and walked up and down, grateful, in a complex way, for this confusion of stomach and mind that obscured the terrors of the final handicap.

There was no need for worry. The customs officials showed no interest in my luggage. They didn't notice the Norstrund.

Five days after leaving it, only ten hours since parting from the beautiful giantess on the bed at Barrandov, I was back in Fitzwalter Square. I let myself in with my latchkey and paused for a moment in the hall, leaning against the front door, grinning with disbelief.

Mrs Nolan came out of the kitchen with a loaded tray. 'Hello, duck,' she said. 'Back already? You're just in time for tea,' and passed into the dining-room.

2

I had told Mrs Nolan I was visiting my mother in Bournemouth, and having no desire to enlarge on this or indeed to do anything but flake out on the divan and gaze with hilarious relief at the plush tablecloth and the plant and the entire sanity of my familiar surroundings, I remained in my room.

I couldn't believe I was back. I couldn't believe I would not shortly awake to find myself in the bed at Barrandov with the large and brooding Vlasta; or in the green and gold splendour of the Slovenska with the noisy Vaclavske Namesti outside and the Norstrund to be guarded. I couldn't believe I'd got away with it.

I picked up the Norstrund and opened the cover. It was still crinkled a little in one corner. I ran my hand all over it. It was smooth and flat and innocent, a very expert job indeed. Impossible to believe that I had here the secret of a new industry; that I had blarneyed my way past Svoboda and Czernin and Stein and Vlcek and Galushka, had emerged from the muscular embraces of Vlasta Simenova, and had smuggled it out.

I was still somewhat dehydrated from the slivovitz, and presently went down to the bathroom and drank from the toothmug. While I was there I thought I might as well have a wash and took off my jacket and bent over the bowl. This familiar action, in shirt sleeves and braces, and the sight of my own face in the small cracked mirror, convinced me suddenly as nothing else had done that I was back. I towelled myself vigorously in the mirror and showed my teeth and smiled. I even said, 'Well, Pan Whistler, you made it,' and winked at my image, feeling at that moment extraordinarily debonair and alive and also, my nostrils carrying still the sharp odour of the girl at Barrandov, a bit of a young dog.

I went back to my room still smiling vacuously, but once there thought I'd better ring Cunliffe right away and picked up the Norstrund, out of habit, and went downstairs again.

Mrs Nolan had been watching out for me.

'You're surely not going out again before you've had a cup of tea, ducky?'

I had intended phoning from the hall but now thought better of it. 'I won't be a tick, Mrs Nolan. I'm only walking up the street.'

'Brought her a nice book back, have you?' She winked at me. 'She's been ringing up, you know. She hasn't forgotten you.'

I had not spared so much as a moment's thought for Maura, and now, reminded, felt the familiar distractions settling on me. I had no wish to see Maura yet, no wish to think about any of that at all. I said, 'Did she leave any message?'

'Only for you to get in touch with her when you got back. No further news about the other thing yet, I suppose?'

It was so long ago, such a lifetime ago, that I couldn't think for the moment what the devil she was talking about.

'The other thing – your poor uncle.'

'Oh, no. Nothing further. I wasn't expecting to yet.'

'No, well. These things take time, don't they?' She had lowered her voice in referring to the other thing, but now raised it again. 'Well, off you go then. Only don't make a meal of it. And don't you go catching her by surprise – you might get one yourself,' she added with a playful little shove.

I went down the street thoughtfully, several familiar worries returning to mind. They were still in an unresolved and un-coagulated state, however, by the time I reached the telephone box and I took out the torn bit of diary sheet Cunliffe had given me and dialled his number with elation.

'Hello. This is Nicolas Whistler.'

He said, 'Who? Oh. You are back. Excellent. Just one moment,' and went away for a while. 'I am very glad to hear your voice,' he grated warmly when he returned. 'Did everything go as planned?'

'Yes. A few worrying moments, but no hitches. I've got the doings all right.'

'That's wonderful. I don't think we should discuss it on the telephone, you know.'

'No. Do you want me to come round right away?'

'I don't think,' he said slowly, 'I don't think that's absolutely necessary.'

'Later this evening?'

There was a pause. 'I don't think you should come here at all. See me in the office in the morning.'

I said, 'All right,' with some disappointment.

'There isn't anything – nothing went wrong in any way?'

'No. It's just that I've been carrying the bloody thing around for several days. I thought it was urgent.'

'It is indeed. I will see you tomorrow, Mr Whistler. At nine o'clock. Goodbye.' He hung up right away.

My features in the little round mirror were sheepish and disappointed. I replaced the receiver and went outside. It was too early for a drink. I went back for tea, with the Norstrund.

In the night, I woke up, parched again, but couldn't be bothered to get out of bed. For some reason, I felt depressed as hell. A lot of things had come crowding back to mind and I turned over on my back and licked my lips and thought of them.

The night Maura was in this room. Just a week ago. She'd said the fellow on the first floor had let her in. I knew something was wrong with that, but couldn't place it at the time. I could now. He was deaf. Not just hard of hearing; practically stone deaf. You had to dance about like a lunatic in front of him to attract his attention, our Mr Larkin. So he was the one who'd heard the doorbell and let her in.

I thought about Cunliffe then. He'd been surprised, no doubt about it, by my call. He hadn't known I was back. Nor had a lot of people. Nor had Maura. But she'd been ringing up to find out.

I thought, oh no, how could it be? Why should Maura have me sent out on such a dangerous mission? But it hadn't sounded very dangerous the way Cunliffe had explained it. It hadn't, in fact, been very dangerous. It might have sounded a lot better, a lot more useful and enterprising than sticking stamps for the Little Swine.

But how could Maura have met Cunliffe? He was a money-lender. She hadn't been borrowing any money. She had never mentioned any social occasion when she might conceivably have met him. She was a typist in a West End estate agency.

I turned on my side and tried to sleep, but I knew I wouldn't unless I had a drink, so I got up and had one and returned to bed and slept, heavily.

The sun was shining on Mrs Nolan's aspidistra when I awoke and somewhere below that jolly lady sang as she bashed about with the crockery. I felt extraordinarily refreshed and full of beans. And why not? I thought, springing out of bed. I had nipped behind the Iron Curtain and found time to dally on the way. I had returned with a secret worth, say, a king's ransom. I seemed to have swapped for good one way of life and almost any change would be an improvement.

As for Maura – Maura was an imaginative girl with a talent for shoving her nose in. She'd meant for the best. And everything probably was for the best. There would be time to sort out Maura. For the present, there were things to be done this day.

The depression of the night seemed to have been a last poisonous kick out of the slivovitz, and I dressed and breakfasted and picked up the car and wove in and out of the traffic to Francis Street in a very agreeable frame of mind, arriving there sharp on nine.

Bunface had not yet arrived, but Cunliffe had left his inner office door open, and called, 'Is that you, Mr Whistler? Please come right in.'

He was sitting waiting for me, still in his street coat, and I placed the Norstrund modestly on his desk and he took both my hands, smiling whimsically into my eyes without saying a word.

'You see?' he said at last, releasing my hands and picking up the Norstrund. 'I told you how it would be. I never doubted for a minute that you could do it.'

'No. Well,' I said, dropping negligently into a chair, 'there were one or two worrying moments. Is Mr Pavelka coming along?'

'Mr Pavelka is out looking for a factory,' he said, smiling. 'In Ireland at the moment, I believe. As you saw for yourself he has the highest hopes for this – this new process.'

He had opened the Norstrund and was running his fingers as I had done over the flyleaf. I thought: Ireland, looking for a factory, estate agents, Maura; and saw in that moment exactly how it must have been, Pavelka with his great creased dog's face explaining earnestly what he wanted, and Maura saying *Glass, glass – I wonder, Mr Pavelka*, her busy little brain working on it right away.

Everything fell into place then, and I sat there grinning at Cunliffe, and he looked up from the book and caught me grinning and said, 'Yes, he's a very impetuous man, Mr Pavelka, but you should be complimented at the confidence he has in you.'

And I was complimented; really quite touched. *I like you*, he had said. *You look like your father*.

I told Cunliffe everything that had happened to me in Prague then, with some personal exceptions, and he listened quietly, his large grey intelligent eyes unblinking.

'Yes,' he said at the end, 'it's really much as I thought. We've been getting reports out, of course. And now,' he said, slipping the Norstrund in his briefcase, 'I've got to go somewhere with this.'

There was a pause as he fiddled with the straps of his case, and I wondered if I should ask about the money yet. It was, plainly, Pavelka's money, and he hadn't got the formula in his hand yet. There was also the point that I was, so to speak – Pavelka had as good as told me – already in his employ.

Cunliffe looked up, smiling. 'But we still have a little business to transact.' He got up and opened his safe and took out a packet and tossed it lightly on the desk. Inside were four bundles of ten fivers. The full sum, I saw, with elation and astonishment, two hundred pounds.

'And these,' said Cunliffe. He had taken out of the safe also the two copies of the loan agreement. 'One a little bit torn, I am afraid,' he said wryly. 'There are no hard feelings?'

'None at all.'

'You understand it was necessary to manufacture some – some inducement?'

'Absolutely. The trip sounded a lot more frightening than it was. I've no complaints at all. When will Mr Pavelka be back?'

'Within a very few days. He's not the most predictable of men.'

'I'd better keep in touch then.'

'I'll get in touch with you. He'll undoubtedly want to see you as soon as he comes back.'

'Well, fine,' I said, my head fairly singing with relief and good fortune. The danger was all over now. Ahead lay the boundless future with Pavelka.

Cunliffe had picked up his briefcase and was waiting for me to go. I thought there was one thing I might get sorted out, and said, 'There's just one point. This – this person who's been watching me. You don't feel inclined to tell me who it is now?'

'I'm afraid – not yet, Mr Whistler,' he said, smiling broadly. 'There are still some little secrets until everything is fixed up.'

'Not even if I named a name? I've a pretty shrewd idea who it is.'

'I'm sorry.'

'All right,' I said, a bit put out, and went.

Outside in the car, I thought I might have made a more determined effort and decided to wait until he came out. When he didn't appear after a few minutes, however, I began to feel a bit of a fool, and since it might look as if I was waiting to see where he went, I started up and turned round in the road and buzzed back up Francis Street. Outside the Fuller's tea shop on the corner, I saw Bunface standing wrapped in thought, and gave her a honk. She came out of her trance and dropped me a swift bob and walked quickly down the street.

It didn't occur to me until later that she might have been seeing me off the premises.

3

One day's indolence very easily breeds another. It was a beautiful time in London then, fine golden days, cooler than Prague, freer than Prague, and I awaited Pavelka's pleasure. I had a fitting for the suits I had ordered. I messed around with the car. I ran out one day to the river and tried all the pubs from Laleham to Old Windsor and slept under a tree near Runnymede.

It was a brainless time, an undemanding time, and I didn't want it to stop. But on Thursday I woke up with a mild sense of worry that something should be happening and by mid-day all the old apprehensions had returned.

I wanted to ring Cunliffe, but I knew he would have no news for me. I wanted to ring Imre and Maminka, but there was nothing I could tell them. I wanted to ring Maura, but the situation here was still obscure.

I wondered how she had managed to get into my room that night. Had she somehow got hold of my key and had it copied? And why hadn't she come to see me again? She would know I was back. It must have occurred to that busy brain that I might have tumbled her. You would expect her to put out a feeler or two.

Puzzling over this, I thought there was at least one thing I could clear out of the way, and I waited that afternoon for Larkin to come home. He was a queer old man, very reticent and aloof, in a world of his own with his deafness. He took his meals alone and I had not seen him since my return.

I waited in my room and heard him come in and go into the lounge with his paper as he usually did. I went downstairs and opened the lounge door and saw him buried behind his paper in an easy chair and I said, 'Afternoon, Mr Larkin.'

'Afternoon,' he said, without putting the paper down.

I felt a flush starting up from my neck and I closed the door slowly behind me and said, 'Mr Larkin.'

He lowered the paper then and looked irritably and I saw the wire dangling from his ear. Mr Larkin had got himself a natty little hearing aid.

I rang Cunliffe five minutes later from the call box on the corner. He seemed glad to hear my voice but there was no news, and I said, 'Mr Cunliffe, I know how you feel about this, but it's become very important to me just now – it's this person who's watching me.'

'Oh, now, Mr Whistler. You know I can't say anything about that. It's all past and done with, just a prudent step I was bound to take before we knew each other.'

'Yes, I know. I understand perfectly. I don't mind in the least. It's just – I've got to know,' I gabbled rapidly, as he tried to interrupt, 'if it's my girl friend, Maura Regan. I wouldn't let her know, or hold it against her or anything. It's just that I haven't the faintest bloody idea how to talk to her ...'

He had been going to say something else, but choked suddenly on the phone. 'Your – your girl friend! Oh, dear me, no! Oh, my dear Mr Whistler,' he said, laughing heartily, 'I feel perfectly safe in assuring you that it isn't. I'm dreadfully sorry. I wouldn't for anything in the world want to interfere with your love life. I had no idea ...'

So that was that, and I put the phone down, a bit light-headed and with my heart banging, and picked it up again and put more pennies in the box and phoned her office. It was twenty-past five; just in time to catch her.

She said, 'Hello,' and I said, 'Guess who,' and there was a pause for a moment and I could imagine her lopsided smile coming on.

'Is it Nicolas?'

'Who else?' I said and grinned in the mirror, and she hung up.

I couldn't believe it. I rattled the phone. I said, 'Operator.' I hadn't any more pennies. I hopped out of the box, muttering like a madman, and stopped people in the street, and telephoned her again. They said she'd gone.

I got out of the box and stood in the street for a minute, muttering obscenely under my breath and wondering what in God's name this lot was about. But I knew all right; knew in an instant, the trip to Prague and the four golden days vanishing into oblivion as I found myself back in the continuous situation with Maura.

We'd parted in a queer sort of way. Quite enough for her to be miffed about in that alone. And I hadn't written, not a line, not a postcard. And she'd probably seen the car back, had almost certainly seen the car back, had probably tooled round regularly to see when it came back.

I thought, oh Jesus Christ, experiencing the familiar enervation at the course of wooing now called for, and started off to wait outside her digs.

I waited an hour and a half before realizing that she must have gone off somewhere right from the office. She evidently meant me to work at it a bit harder than that.

Next day, Friday, I telephoned her in the morning, and was told by a breathy, giggling girl that she wasn't there. So at lunch time I went to wait outside the office.

She came out at one sharp, in a hell of a hurry, with another girl, and I said, 'Hello, Maura,' and she said, 'Sorry, Nicolas, can't stop. We're off shopping,' and the pair of them jumped on a 25 bus.

I stared after this bus, swearing, and said to myself wearily, Right, well, one more go and that's your lot, and was outside the office again at twenty-past five.

I stood at the opposite side of the street in a deep doorway so that I would see her first, and I told myself that if she came rushing out merrily with another girl, she could continue right on.

But she was alone when she came out, at twenty to six, and she wasn't smiling and she wasn't in a hurry. She looked quickly up and down the street and didn't see me, and began walking slowly to the Tube station, looking so like a little girl, lost and miserable, that my heart began bumping and I crossed the road and fell into step beside her. She looked at me and jumped but said nothing.

I said, 'Hello, Maura.'

'Hello.'

We continued slowly and in silence to the Tube station.

'Like to stop for a cup of tea?'

'No, thanks. I must get back.'

'You've got every right to be angry with me, Maura, but you don't know what's happened.'

'I don't want to know.'

I stopped in the street and said, 'Ah, for God's sake, Maura,' with a haggard look I'd been practising all afternoon. 'I've got so much to tell you. I've been waiting to for so long and couldn't.'

She wasn't really able to resist this, but followed me very coldly as I turned into the tea shop. I found an empty table and we sat down and I told her all that was good for her to know.

I told her the trip to Prague was a brilliant success. I told her I might be leaving the Little Swine and going into an enormous project with a big-time manufacturer. I told her all this was so secret that I had been sworn to silence and had not dared to get in touch with her lest I be tempted to reveal some minute part of it.

She listened in silence, looking down at her tea, completely enchanting in her small girl pride, and when I had finished, said, 'Do you mean it, Nicolas, about wanting to tell me?'

'Of course I do, Maura.'

'And you still can't tell me any more about it?'

'I shouldn't be telling you this.'

She stirred her tea slowly. 'Everything's going to be all right, though, now, is it?'

'I hope so, Maura. I've just got to wait for a man to come back from – from somewhere.'

She looked up and said, 'Well!' and the lopsided smile came on across the table. 'Oh, Nicolas, don't ever do that to me again. Give me some warning. I've been through torture. I couldn't stand that again.'

She was pressing her leg hard against mine under the table, and I groaned inwardly, thinking of all that bottled-up melodrama, all the hours and hours of it, wondering how a girl with such attractions and so much of the right stuff could be at the same time so bloody irritating.

<h1 style="text-align:center">4</h1>

We ate, rather late, in Soho and had a bottle of wine; and later waxed somewhat melodramatic on the seat under the tree. But with that out of the way our relationship blossomed wonderfully, progressing indeed so rapidly on Saturday (in Epping Forest) and on Sunday (in my room while Mrs Nolan graced The Musketeers) and in so enjoyable a fashion that I thought, Pavelka, or no Pavelka, I would soon have to do something about it.

I took her out to lunch on the Monday, and decided that I would definitely ring Cunliffe when I got back to start some action. I didn't have to start any. When I returned there was a note in Mrs Nolan's indelible pencil on the plush tablecloth. It read: *Mr Whistler. Please telephone Victoria 63781*. And underneath, a later addition, *Please ring your mother*.

I went down the stairs two at a time and out whistling into the street. I called Cunliffe first and Bunface answered, and I dropped her a quick bob in the mirror and asked to be put through.

'Oh, Mr Whistler, we have tried to get you. Mr Cunliffe is out just now. He is out with Mr Pavelka. He asks will you come for a meeting at eleven in the morning.'

I let out my breath, grinning stupidly in the mirror. 'Certainly. Absolutely. Tell him yes.'

'Thank you.'

'Thank *you*,' I said, and put the receiver down and went out into the street, still grinning. I was half way back before I remembered about Maminka, and returned to the phone, having no wish for Mrs Nolan to overhear this conversation either.

It was unusual for Maminka to telephone me. I wondered if

Imre, with his talent for doing the wrong thing at the wrong time, had suddenly decided to tell her about Bela, and when he came to the phone, felt a wave of irritation, and said quite brusquely, 'Hello, Uncle. What is it? Maminka rang me?'

'It was I, Nicolas. I called you. How are you, my boy?'

'I'm all right. Is there any trouble?'

'No trouble. Certainly not. I was worried about you. You were so downcast when you were here.'

'You haven't, by any chance, told Maminka about Bela?'

'I haven't. The heat is not good for her. She walks always in the sun without a hat and is naturally fatigued. It is totally impossible to reason with her,' he said, breathing noisily.

'Well, that's all right,' I said. 'I shouldn't bother to tell her just yet, Uncle. I'll explain later.'

'You are not still angry with me?'

'Of course not. Everything's O.K. Don't worry. I'll come and see you soon.'

'Oh, I am glad,' he said, and sounded it. 'I thought maybe you didn't wish to talk with me.'

He sounded so helpless and contrite, the old booby, I wondered for one mad moment if I dare tell him, just a hint; but thought better of it instantly. There'd be time for that after I'd seen Pavelka. Only a few hours more, another night of discretion, and then I would be able to take steps in several directions.

I was not able, however, to exercise this discretion with Maura. Embracing her that night on our trysting seat something seemed, as they say, to snap inside me and I found myself asking her to marry me. I was completely unable to prevent myself; the words seemed to be washed out of me on this swelling tide of good fortune. And after a moment's silence in the dark, Maura clutched me tighter and said, 'Oh, yes, Nicolas, please. I want to. I want to,' and that was that settled.

She asked me no questions, the lovely creature, but when an hour later I said good night at her gate, she said, 'Can I come with you to tell your mother, Nicolas? I'd like to be there then.'

I said, 'Of course, Maura.'

'Perhaps we could pop down on Sunday and stay overnight so that I can get to know her a little. We could come back early on Monday morning.'

'That's a splendid idea, Maura. I'd like that very much.'

And so I left her and walked back through the dark squares rejoicing to Mrs Nolan's, thinking how wonderful Sunday night would be, and how much I wanted to introduce Maura to Maminka; which, of course, I would have done and with much pleasure, if Sunday night had chanced to find me in Bournemouth, instead of, as it did, in Barrandov, in bed, with Vlasta.

Chapter 7

I

'I will come right to the point, Mr Whistler,' Cunliffe said. 'The formula you brought back is incomplete. We don't know how or why this should be but the fact remains – Mr Pavelka, would you mind showing him the – the object – all that it makes is this.'

Pavelka, who had been sitting massive and dejected in his chair, came slowly to life and handed over a piece of glass he had been clutching in his hand. It was part of a hollow blown sphere, cut to show the thickness. It was green and opaque. As a piece of glass, it was of quite exceptional ugliness.

I licked my lips and looked from it to Pavelka. I had known the moment I came in the room that something was wrong. Pavelka looked back at me sombrely, but said nothing.

'Mr Pavelka feels,' Cunliffe said after a moment, 'that the only explanation must be that the formula was written in a hurry. There were several apparent inconsistencies that puzzled our chemist, but one of them – perhaps you would elaborate, Mr Pavelka.'

'Golombek is a bloddy idiot,' Pavelka said heavily.

'I don't think,' Cunliffe cut in smoothly, 'that Mr Whistler needs to know . . .'

'A bloddy idiot!' Pavelka repeated. 'In 1937 once I nearly dismissed him. I should have done it,' he said bitterly. 'He lets me down after all this planning! There is too much iron, *yoh*?' He was pointing one banana-like finger at the glass in my hand.

'Iron, Mr Pavelka?'

'Iron oxide. The green is iron, *yoh*?'

'Ah. *Yoh.* Yes.'

'This proportion cannot be. It is a useful glass but we are not making beer bottles. Perhaps he has transposed it with the dolomite – I wonder,' he said, his great St Bernard's face creasing suddenly. He remained in intense thought for several minutes.

Cunliffe broke the silence. 'What it amounts to, Mr Whistler, is that the formula is very nearly right, but not quite. Mr Pavelka feels it would be possible to go ahead with research here on the basis of it, but this would almost certainly cost a great deal in money and time. . .'

'*Yoh*, money and time!' Pavelka said darkly. 'That bloddy idiot! When you go back you will take him a personal letter . . .'

'If you please, Mr Pavelka,' Cunliffe said sharply. 'Mr Whistler will do nothing of the sort when he returns. We have headaches enough . . .'

'When I what?' I said, the lunatic suggestion suddenly breaking through.

'When you return,' said Cunliffe. 'To Prague. To Mr Pavelka's factory. As I was trying to point out, research here might involve a considerable investment and it would almost certainly be cheaper and quicker for you to return to Prague immediately. You could do this very simply and without bother . . .'

'Oh, I couldn't, Mr Cunliffe,' I said. I had come bounding

out of the chair, still clutching the piece of glass, and was now wringing it urgently. 'I really couldn't. There's nothing simple about it at all. You don't understand ...' As I spoke I had the clearest possible recollection of all the heart-thudding, mouth-drying, sick-making hours I had gone through, of Vlasta, of Galushka. 'There's Galushka,' I said. 'Galushka, for a start, would see through it. You've no idea how dangerous ...'

'Galushka?' said Pavelka. 'What has Galushka to do with it?'

'Oh, dear,' said Cunliffe, and took out his cigarette case. 'I'm afraid I took the liberty of omitting what you told me about Mr Galushka. He annoys Mr Pavelka intensely.'

'Galushka?' said Pavelka again, breathing heavily, his massive brows beetling. 'Galushka isn't anything. I sacked Galushka years ago.'

'Well, he's back now, Mr Pavelka,' I said loudly. 'Times have changed. He runs the factory. He's a very sharp man. We'd never get past him twice with this. You'd much better press on with your researches and later on maybe ...'

Pavelka was staring at me thunderstruck and now began to swear horribly in Czech. 'That agitator runs my factory! What can a man like that ... You told me Golombek!' he said to Cunliffe.

'I assure you Golombek is our man,' said Cunliffe patiently, offering his case. 'This is really very foolish. I thought we had agreed that it was very much better that Mr Whistler should not know any of the arrangements. I really do not share your apprehensions,' he said to me. 'The Czechs are interested only in trade. It is entirely natural that you should return urgently after discussion with your principals. From what you have told me, they expect it.'

'But what in hell am I going to talk about? I was in deep water several times ...'

'You will be adequately briefed, I assure you. But this is really a matter between you and Mr Pavelka,' he said, sitting back and shrugging his shoulders. 'You have done the job you were asked to do — and very well, too, if I may say so. It is certainly not your fault that this has occurred.'

This calming statement and the absence of the previous sort of pressure certainly put the matter in a different perspective. I sat down and looked at Pavelka. He was still smouldering over the revelation of Galushka.

'We'd use the Norstrund again?' I said.

'Why not? Nobody suspected it the first time. They will be used to seeing you with it.'

'And used to my forgetting it on Galushka's desk?'

'Really, Mr Whistler,' said Cunliffe mildly. 'Whoever noticed you leave it last time? But if it would make your mind easier, don't forget it. Merely ask to leave it. Say you don't want to carry it round the factory with you.'

'Why should I want to see round the factory again? They've shown me it once.'

'Yes,' Cunliffe said, and looked at me thoughtfully. 'I'll have to arrange for you to see one of the processes again.' He scribbled on his pad. 'He could be quite a useful young man, this one,' he said to Pavelka without looking up.

'Of course,' said Pavelka. 'I saw right away.'

There was silence for a while after that. The thing was not after all so fantastic. Pavelka had undoubtedly owned and run very successfully an enormous factory. I had seen it. He could do the same thing here. I said, 'You consider it essential for me to go back again for this formula, Mr Pavelka?'

'Certainly. Naturally,' he said. 'It would shorten our work. Come back quickly with it. We have a lot to do.'

'When would I need to go?'

'Well,' Cunliffe said, looking dubiously at the clock. 'I've been trying to expedite matters, but I doubt if you could get away before Friday. I spent a perfectly dreadful day rushing about yesterday.'

'How long would I be away?'

'If you went Friday, you could go to the factory on Saturday and be back on Sunday afternoon. Less than three days in all.'

Less than three days, I thought. I should surely be able to cope with that.

Later on, I saw Maura and told her as much as was necessary. She said, 'Oh; Nicolas! You will try and be back in time on Sunday.'

'Of course I will. I'll be back at tea-time. We can buzz off right away.'

'I'd hate anything to interfere with that. I've been so looking forward to going there and seeing your mother and everything.'

'Well, you will.'

'I'd feel superstitious about us if it didn't come off now.'

'That's because you're a silly little thing.'

'You'll write to me while you're away?'

'I'll only be gone three days.'

'Three whole days.'

'And I'll see you on two of them.'

'Write anyway. Write in the aeroplane, and write when you get there, and write on the way back. And post them. Then I'll know you were thinking of me.'

'Don't you trust me?'

'No. Oh, Nicolas, I do love you. I love you so much. Do you love me?'

'No.'

'Nicolas, truly.'

'Well, a bit.'

'How much?'

'As much as this. And this. And this.'

Quite a lot of this was going on lately.

2

She saw me off on the Friday morning. Cunliffe had not been too taken with this idea, but there wasn't anything I could do to stop her. He sat waiting in his car opposite while we shuffled our feet in the entrance hall. I was carrying in my case a brand new Norstrund that he had given me that morning, and had been mildly troubled in case the flyleaf might be bulky with Pavelka's threatened letter. Cunliffe had laughed me out of that one. 'Have no fears, Mr Whistler. His bark is always much worse than his bite. You'll be carrying nothing at all on the way there – the return cargo is the point of this operation.' And indeed the flyleaf was immaculate. If I hadn't known it had been specially prepared for easy opening and re-sealing it would have been impossible to tell.

Maura had not told them at the office that she was taking time off, and was tending to make a Departure of it. She clung silently to my arm, her face white and dramatic, eyes large and staring. This nerve-racking performance was giving me an acute and unexpected attack of the jim-jams.

We moved at last, mercifully, and in the queue she gave me a quick kiss and dug in her bag. She had brought me a present, wrapped in a brown paper bag.

I said, 'What is it?'

'Something to read. Maybe it will keep you out of mischief,' she said with a feeble smile, and gave me a little nudge up the steps.

I spared a quick glance for Cunliffe and got in the bus, and hoped to God it would move quickly for Maura was rooted to the spot outside like one of the women in a pit disaster.

Presently the bus did move and I turned and waved to her, and saw Cunliffe still sitting in his car. And then all that was over and I sat jolting in the seat with only that curious unease of the stomach that is a part of every departure.

We were at the Chiswick roundabout before I opened the brown paper bag to see what Maura had brought me and I had drawn it half way out of the bag before I was sure. I said quietly, 'Oh, Jesus Christ, no!'

My neighbour on the seat, an immense business man with a blue chin, horn-rimmed glasses and a valise, said, '*Pardon?*'

'I'm sorry. It was nothing.'

But it was something. Maura had bought me a Norstrund. A brand new Norstrund.

The implications of this second Norstrund were borne in on me as the bus turned up the Great West Road. A man who appeared habitually with a Norstrund might or might not arouse suspicion. A man who had another Norstrund tucked away in

113

his case was quite a different proposition. My room at the Slovenska had possibly been searched once. It would possibly be searched again.

There was also the chance of the two copies becoming mixed up. One could always mark one of them. But better, far better, to leave Maura's behind, to deposit it somewhere, lose it.

I tried to do this. I looked out of the window and let the bag bounce off my knee. My blue-chinned neighbour picked it up. I tried kicking it under the seat when we left the bus. The driver came running up with it twenty minutes later as we streamed out on to the tarmac.

It was an ill omen. The trip had started with complications. I stuffed Maura's gift in my raincoat pocket and glanced at the bulge every few minutes.

By the time we touched down at Prague all the butterflies were back in my stomach.

At the Hotel Slovenska I had been given the same room, and on all sides there were welcoming smiles. The intense receptionist nodded quite gaily, the ancient porter grinned and gawked and hawked. On the second floor, Josef awaited me with darkling fervour.

'What pleasure to see you back, Pan Whistler. We didn't hope for such a quick return.'

'No, well. Business, you know.'

'The *pane* thinks trade is beginning to move?'

'I hope so, Josef.'

'That's good news. We miss the business men. I hope you are the first of many. Can I bring you something, *pane*?'

'Beer, please, Josef.'

I went in and had a shower. This familiar action and my re-emergence into the green and gold splendour for my beer had a calming effect on the butterflies in my stomach. I took the beer out on the balcony and looked down on the Vaclavske Namesti. It was hot and steamy and rain had fallen, but nothing had changed. The crowds still streamed in the heat. The queue still waited outside the automat. The trams clanged up and down. Wenceslas strode his iron horse far down the street. And from his perch above the road junction, Lenin still stared down on his disciples. 'Every hand, every brain for the building of socialism.'

It did not seem, as it had a fortnight ago, to be a different world. London no longer seemed so remote. And the task had not the unknown dangers. Even the formidable Galushka, now that I was here, seemed not quite so frightening. There was only the complication of the Norstrunds.

I came in from the balcony, got them both out and compared them. There was no doubt about it; they were alike as two peas. Only when you looked hard could you see slight differences. Maura's was an earlier edition, 1950. Cunliffe's was 1953. I thought I had better mark it up to avoid confusion, and went to get my pen out of the jacket in the wardrobe.

The room phone rang.

I jumped about a foot. The two Norstrunds were spread out on the table. Here was where confusion could start. I swore out loud, let the phone ring, and marked a small dot in the top right hand corner of Cunliffe's copy. Then I stowed both books in my case. The damned phone hadn't stopped ringing. I picked it up with sweating hands.

'Hello.'

It was Svoboda, from the Glass Board, hoping he wasn't disturbing me.

'Not at all.'

'There were things in your telegram we could not grasp, Pan Whistler. Do we understand you are empowered to conclude a deal on this visit?'

'Not exactly. We wanted reassurance on some matters, and my principals desire quick action. We thought it more convenient for me to make another personal call at the Zapotocky works.'

I was tending to shout with nervousness, and Svoboda drew his own conclusions. 'Of course. Naturally. Do not misunderstand me. We are delighted you should return. Please tell me of any way we can help. Perhaps you wish for immediate Discussions? I can send a car right away.'

I had an instant vision of the giantess of Barrandov standing in stormy silence by the car outside the hotel. 'No. No, thank you. It won't be necessary.'

'You wish to deal directly with Kralovsk?'

'That's it. I'd like to go tomorrow. In the morning. It shouldn't need more than an hour or two there. My principals expect me back in time for a conference on Monday morning.'

'Very good,' Svoboda said. 'I will see everything is arranged. A car will call for you at – what? Is nine o'clock too early?'

'Nine o'clock would be fine.' I had no intention of leaving the hotel tonight. A nice, quiet trip, early to bed.

'And you wish for no Discussions today?'

'No, thanks. I've got everything I need for the moment.'

'Excellent,' said Svoboda.

He sounded a shade muted at this dearth of Discussions.

3

Little Vlcek was there with the car in the morning, vulpine and informative as ever.

'I hope you have brought good weather back with you, Pan Whistler. Since you were here last we have had nine and a half centimetres of rain. Perhaps now the sun will shine.'

I said, 'It looks a bit overcast now.' The air was steamy and stifling; I had slept badly.

'Ah, there might be a shower or two. But the meteorological service says all should be well for the parade on Sunday. That is the main thing.'

'What parade is that?'

'You have not heard?' Vlcek was delighted. 'It will be one of the greatest in recent years. See the stands are going up. One hundred and eight contingents are coming from outlying districts alone. The district of Brno, for instance, is sending one thousand seven hundred participants. You will see, the decorations go up today and the town will start filling tonight. There are many interesting problems in coping with such an influx ...'

After a while I stopped listening again, and looked out of the window. Vlcek went on talking ceaselessly. He had not mentioned what the parade was in aid of; I felt far too queasy in mind and stomach to ask him. We were nearing Kralovsk and my palms were sweating on the Norstrund. I was carrying Maura's copy in the pocket of my raincoat. I wondered how I was going to leave the book this time. Knowing definitely now that Galushka was not in the plot did not help. I wondered how I would stumble through the questions I had to ask him, and if he would regard them with suspicion. He had already pointed out everything that could possibly be communicated about his bloody glass. God, I thought. How I hate glass.

Vlcek, as before, was still talking as we got out of the car and went through the front hall to Galushka's office. It was some interminable nonsense about the organizational problems raised by the parade, but none of it required further response than an occasional nod. Which was just as well. I was feeling sick again.

They had buzzed through to Galushka from the front hall, and he was at his door to meet us, his small, uneven eyes roving over me in the unpleasant way I remembered.

'Well, Pan Whistler, so we are honoured again.' He had taken my hand in both of his and was slowly pumping it up and down. 'Comrade Svoboda tells me you are troubled about some of our arrangements.'

'Pan Whistler's principals, you understand,' said little Vlcek, whickering slightly and showing his gold teeth with extreme uneasiness. 'Before concluding a deal naturally they wish to satisfy themselves on all points. Pan Whistler, I understand, merely wished to confirm what he has already seen. I believe you were more than satisfied with Comrade Galushka's systems, Pan Whistler.'

'Quite,' I said. My mouth was dry and my heart pumping very unpleasantly. 'We thought a further visit to the factory would be worth while in view of the impending trade agreement. We wish quick action.'

'I too,' Galushka said. He had released my hand and ushered us into the office. 'This is the essence of our industry. Speed, efficiency and quality. You know, Vlcek,' he said, 'it will take much work from Prague to convince our customers – our Western customers – that our specifications are so high. Article for article our product is both better and cheaper. They are amazed. They wonder what is the drawback. Oh, there is nothing personal in this, I assure you,' he said to me. 'I understand very well the psychology of the Western business man. I had excellent opportunity to observe it for thirty years. It does not surprise me and I do not resent it. We will have to educate them.'

His twisted smile was quite genial. Poor Vlcek was grinning horribly from one to the other of us. 'The glass is very good undoubtedly,' he said in embarrassment. 'Pan Whistler, as I understand it, does not doubt it. It is merely a new market opening. One understands the problems and so forth . . .'

'Well, I am at his service entirely,' Galushka said. 'What exactly is it you wish to see again?'

I told him, exceedingly relieved that he should regard my return in this light. He rang round to two of his departments while Vlcek screwed a cigarette into his long holder and strove to shed amiability. Embarrassment kept him less conversational than usual, however.

'Well,' Galushka said, putting down the phone. 'We can go.' He looked out of the window and picked an umbrella from his stand. 'Rain again. But leave your raincoat here if you wish, Pan Whistler. The one umbrella will do for both of us. There is not much walking between the shops.'

The rain was a godsend. I had been wondering what to do with the raincoat, having no desire to leave the two Norstrunds hanging about in the room. I said, 'No, I'll take it, thanks. It isn't any bother, and it will leave you the umbrella. But I'll tell you what I will do,' I said, marvelling at the way it came out. 'I'll just leave this book here.'

'Of course,' Galushka said. And then, looking at it, 'Ah, you are still attached to your guidebook, I see. We must not let you forget it this time.'

And that was that, the first part over.

The back of my neck was damp with sweat as we left the

office. Little Vlcek came too. Nobody asked if he had a raincoat and Galushka didn't offer to share the umbrella. He got very wet.

It was just after half past nine when I had arrived at the works and it was not yet a quarter to twelve when I finished. Unless you're very keen on it there are few things actually more boring than the mechanical production of glass. A number of dull minerals are melted in a furnace, the resulting fused 'metal' being then rolled or moulded, depending on what you are making with it. The questions I had asked related to the 'metalling' of fine table ware and the annealing of three of the ranges on offer, processes of such total lack of interest that I remembered nothing at all from my last visit.

Galushka proceeded on the principle that I remembered nothing at all and saw to it that I wrote everything down in my notebook. I emerged from the last of the shops with a filled notebook and my face again stiff with painful interest.

The rain had stopped and the ground was steaming in the tropical heat. The sun seemed to be trying to come out.

'You see, Pan Whistler,' Vlcek said. 'I said you have brought the good weather with you.' He was sneezing a little but had kept very cheerful. 'We were all worried in town for the parade on Sunday,' he told Galushka. 'But the meteorological service announced today that the sun would shine. They do not realize Pan Whistler brought it with him,' he said gaily.

'Ah, the parade,' said Galushka. 'You are staying over to see it, Pan Whistler?'

'I'm afraid not. I must fly back tomorrow.'

'You will be missing a worthwhile experience. To see the young people from every region in their national costumes, all dedicating themselves to the state – this is to understand the source of our strength.'

Since I had taken down his every word he seemed kindly disposed towards me, and now showed an inclination to stand and chat. I was in no hurry. Every minute wasted here was a minute gained for whoever was fiddling with the Norstrund. Nothing had been said about staying on to lunch. I wondered if the mysterious Golombek, that bloddy fool, would have had enough time to do his work.

Presently we strolled back to the office block. The car was waiting outside.

'I hope you have now sufficient information,' Vlcek said to me. 'There is nothing else Comrade Galushka can tell you while you are here?'

I couldn't think of anything. It seemed impossible that there could be anything further to tell about glass. I felt the back of my neck beginning to sweat again with the strain of wondering how to draw attention to the Norstrund.

'If there is anything further,' Galushka said, putting one hand on my shoulder and taking my right hand with the other, 'don't hesitate to get in touch. I do not resent it,' he said, his uneven eyes smiling. 'I understand very well the reasons.'

'Yes, well. I think I've got everything . . .'

The sneezing but alert Vlcek came to my assistance. 'Ah! Your guide book, Pan Whistler. We have nearly forgotten it again!'

'Of course,' Galushka said. 'I will get it.'

He seemed to be a hell of a time about it. Vlcek and I made heavy conversation among the steaming puddles. Presently Galushka reappeared. He had the Norstrund in his hand. A minute later we were cruising back to Prague.

As Cunliffe had said, once you stopped worrying there was nothing to it.

4

The car put me down outside the Slovenska and Vlcek took a sneezing farewell. He was a friendly little soul, and I felt sorry for him. If anyone was going to get the chopper when this lot came out, I knew who it would be.

It was half past twelve, too early for lunch. I felt wound up, too excited to go to my room. I thought I would walk up the street towards the museum, and have a drink on the way.

I was light-headed with relief and hilarity. I knew from previous experience that the mood would not last, that very shortly

I would begin to jangle like a piano wire. But just then, at that moment, I had a heady conviction of total success. I knew I'd got it this time. There had been a certain smoothness, a certain inevitability about the whole business. All I had to do now was fill in the hours till ten in the morning.

The Vaclavske Namesti was glittering in the sun, cobbles, pavements, trees, sparkling and steaming from the rain. As Vlcek had said, the decorations were going up and there was a new air of bustle and cheerfulness about the place. Workmen were up ladders attaching banners and streamers. Outside the Zlata Husa restaurant, a group of them were swaying in a cradle fixing a giant triptych of portraits.

Farther along by the Opletala, a banner broke across the street above the little shuttling trams. TO A LASTING PEACE. TO THE PEOPLE'S VICTORY. Young office girls out for the lunch break streamed along the pavements, gossiping and laughing, their splendid Slav bosoms straining in light summer dresses. Even the old black-clad crones, a changeless feature of the place, seemed to be sharing some common joke, toothless gums grinning as they shuffled by with shopping bags.

By the time I reached the statue of Wenceslas I'd decided to amble down to the embankment for a drink, and crossed the road, winking at him on his iron horse, and walked down the Mezibranska by the side of the museum. I walked under the linden trees to the Manes café.

It was chiming one o'clock all round when I got there and the crowds were streaming back to work. I sat at an open-air table and ordered a large beer and drank it, watching, in the hot sun, the bathers diving from the raft into the molten river.

I had no appetite for food. I stayed at the Manes café drinking the light beer till three o'clock. Then the sun went in and clouds came over again. I picked up my mac and left.

With the sun gone, the air was too thick and sticky to walk back. At the tram stop by the Smetanov bridge I caught a number seventeen for the Vaclavske Namesti, and had to stand all the way, jolted and jostled in the throbbing heat. I got off at the Prikopy junction with a violent headache.

They were trying out loudspeakers that had been installed on lamp-posts as I walked the few yards back to the hotel. A military march. My head throbbed, mouth sour with beer, heavy and oppressed again in the suddenly grey, hot afternoon.

Josef was lurking on the second floor.

'You have eaten well, Pan Whistler?'

'No, Josef. It was too hot to eat. I've been drinking at Manes.'

'Ah, so. It's very sensible. A thunderstorm will clear the air.'

'It looks as if we're going to get it.'

'Yes. In an hour or two, I think. Have you further business today?'

'No. I'm going to lie down now on the bed.'

'It's a good idea. You'd like another beer?'

'No, thanks. I've drunk enough.'

'Try an iced Pilsener before you rest. I recommend it.'

I didn't want any more beer, but he seeemed installed for a chat, so I said all right to get him out of the way and went in the room. The canopy was down on the balcony, the room green and dim like the inside of an aquarium. I flaked out on the bed and edged my shoes off and kicked them on the floor.

The row of the military band came in through the open window, but presently stopped. The technicians began testing with numbers. *'Jeden ... dva ... tri ... ctyri ...'*

The throbbing in my temples had begun to ease when Josef reappeared with the Pilsener. He stood and watched me sip it, smiling in his darkling way.

'It's good?'

'Wonderful.' It wasn't wonderful. It was the strong export Pilsener, too tangy for my sour mouth.

'You want to lie here all afternoon or shall I call you for tea?'

I thought I'd better write to Maura, as promised. I said, 'What times does the post go?'

'From the hotel at five o'clock, from the post office until seven. Someone can always go if it is urgent – the post office is just along the street. It's a letter to England?'

'Yes.'

'Better to get it in the six o'clock post. A call at five-thirty then, *pane*?'

'Five-thirty would be fine.'

He went and I put the beer down and lay back again. Just a short block of time to get through now. Rest until five-thirty; write, eat, drink, read until ten. Then bed. Only a few hours.

It suddenly occurred to me that I had not examined the Norstrund. I sat up and picked it up from beside me on the bed. The flyleaf was still immaculate. I hoped the man had had time to do his work. I wondered what the hold-up had been in getting it back from Galushka's office. But if there'd been anything wrong I wouldn't have got it back.

My head had begun to throb again and I felt suddenly dry and sour as hell, my mouth like a birdcage. I took another sip of the Pilsener, but it was too tangy and I got up and went to the bathroom and emptied the glass and took a drink of water. It was hot in the bathroom, the single frosted-glass french window shut. I opened the window and looked out. It was still heavy and grey. A few doors along the balcony, a young blonde was sitting out in a négligé, showing rather a lot of leg. She smiled at me. I went back in.

I took my jacket and shirt off and loosened my belt and flaked out again, kicking the raincoat to the foot of the bed. I shoved the Norstrund under the coverlet where I could feel it by my side, and after a minute got up again and put my passport and wallet there, too. Presently the throbbing in my head stopped again and I dozed.

A soft tapping on the door brought me out of it and I lay still with my eyes closed and let Josef come in and shake me. Josef came in, but he didn't shake me. After a bit I wondered what the hell he was doing and opened my eyes a slit. He was standing by the door, not looking at me. He was looking round the room. After a moment he picked up the glass and sniffed it.

My heart gave a lurch, a single sickening thump. I thought: *there was something in the beer.* I knew this couldn't be, that I was on edge, that there was no reason why anyone should put anything in the beer. If they suspected anything they could haul me off quickly enough. But the beer had tasted queer. It had dried my mouth. My heart began to pump very unpleasantly.

My breath must have come out sharply, and he turned and looked at me. The bed was in shadow and I closed my eyes quickly. I heard him put the glass down. I felt him bending over me; warm, slightly sweaty, the faint tang of shaving lotion. Presently he moved away.

I didn't open my eyes again until I heard him over at the other side of the room. He was closing the french windows, his back broad, much broader than I'd realized in the black morning coat. He turned from the window, rubbing his hands gently, and gazed thoughtfully round the room. Then he began to search it.

Chapter 8

I

My case was over on the slatted luggage rest and he went soundlessly across to it. The case was not locked; he went through it carefully and then moved across to the wardrobe and went through the stuff there. He ran his hands over the top and bent and peered underneath.

When he straightened up, I shut my eyes again. I thought he'd be trying the bed next, under the pillow, the mattress. I didn't know what to do if he looked under the coverlet. The Norstrund was there. I could feel it against my side. I had given no serious thought to the nightmarish contingency of being discovered. I was too appallingly frightened to do so now.

I thought: shall I let him take the Norstrund if he finds it?

God, no. But why not? He wouldn't find anything inside it, unless he was specifically looking. And if he was specifically looking, what chance would I have anyway? The only prospect then would be to try and brazen it out. I wondered where the British Embassy was, if I could somehow get down into the street, jump on a tram, hide.

My heart was going like a steam hammer. I couldn't control my breathing. I heard a rustle of cloth, and opened my eyes again. He was fumbling with something and I couldn't see what it was until he held it up. My mac, at the foot of the bed. He was feeling the pockets. He withdrew something.

Maura's Norstrund. I had forgotten it. I had totally forgotten it. But now with a single flash of inspiration, I saw a chance of salvation, a slim, slim chance. He didn't know about Maura's Norstrund. Nobody did. If he showed any kind of informed interest in it, I'd have to wake up, stall, get him out of the room for a few minutes while I did something about the other one. I didn't know how I would do this. I felt sick with terror at the prospect. It seemed the only chance.

He'd turned half away from me and I couldn't see what he was doing with the damned thing. Presently he dropped the mac and took something out of his own pocket. It was a moment or two before I realized what he was about. A small delicate movement of the elbow: he was cutting. I thought, *Oh, God, he's on to it, this is it,* and, half vomiting with the beer rising in my throat, stretched and groaned and sat up.

I didn't see what he did with the Norstrund. In one movement, he bent, began tidying my shoes where they had fallen beside the bed, and picked up the mac.

'Ah, you've wakened, Pan Whistler. A good sleep?'

'Yes, thanks. God!' I said, holding my head. 'How long have I slept?'

'It's early yet, not quite half past four. I came in to shut the windows. The loudspeakers were making a great noise.'

'Do you have such a thing as an aspirin?'

'Right here,' he said, and changed hands on the mac to fiddle in his inside tailcoat pocket, and I saw how he'd got the Norstrund, in the hand holding the mac. I thought I'd better let him leave the room with it. It would take a few minutes for him to fiddle with it and find nothing there and seal it up again.

I licked dry lips. I said, 'I'd be glad of a cup of tea, Josef.'

'Right away, Pan Whistler. I will just hang up your raincoat.'

He turned with his darkling smile and opened the wardrobe to do this. And then the clumsy oaf dropped the book. There was no possibility of looking away. It bounced off the bottom of the wardrobe on to the floor.

His eye caught mine. He said slowly, 'Ah, *pardon*. There was something in the pocket,' and picked up the book. He didn't know what to do with it, and stared from it to me. I gazed at him in dull horror. He placed the book on the table and left the room.

I moved quickly off the bed, locked the door and got Cunliffe's Norstrund from under the coverlet. I didn't know what the hell to do with it. I looked round the room. No hiding place they wouldn't spot easily enough. I went through to the bathroom. Nowhere here, either. The single french window was open and I looked out on the balcony. There was a flowerbox against the short stretch of wall between the bathroom and bedroom windows. It was an oblong box with a few pots of petunias standing on a gravel base.

I reached out and pulled it towards me. I took two of the pots out, scrabbled up the gravel, pushed the book into it and smoothed the gravel over again before replacing the pots. Then I pushed the box back and washed the gravel and sand off my hands.

I had worked quickly and in extreme panic and not more than half a minute had elapsed since Josef had left the room. I wondered how far he had got with Maura's Norstrund and picked it up. There was no mark on the front flyleaf. No mark on the back, either. I couldn't make out where he'd been cutting and examined the book all round. Something fell out, into my hand, a tiny strip of what looked like red leather. A bit of the binding. I saw then what he'd done. He'd sliced a shaving off the bottom of the bulging spine. I poked my little finger inside the gap. There was a loose slim shield of cambric, and something else. I edged it out. A corner of rice paper showed.

My forehead had gone cold and I felt sick as a dog. I thought, *I've hidden the wrong one. I've got them mixed up somehow.* I couldn't understand how it could have happened. I couldn't understand why the paper was hidden in the spine instead of under the flyleaf. I pulled it out. It was a single sheet, folded over, about four inches long and three wide. It was written in ink with a very fine nib, a mass of figures, letters, equations.

My body seemed to be covered with fine cold sweat all over. I was shaking like a leaf. I thought, *it can't be, it can't be.* I knew I hadn't mixed them up. This book had stayed in my rain-coat pocket all the time at the glassworks. It had been the other one I'd left on the desk. There wasn't any doubt about it, no room at all for error. I'd left it on the desk, and then it had been returned to me, and I had carried it in my hand ever since, had slipped it under the coverlet when I stretched out. It was now in the flower box. Yet the formula was in this one.

I sat down on the bed, my legs shaking, staring stupidly at the book. There was no dot on it. Of course there was no dot on it. I had put the dot on the other one. I had put it on in this very room. I remembered it clearly. I'd got the two books spread out in front of me. But then Svoboda had telephoned. The bloody phone had gone on ringing. Had I put the dot on the wrong one?

Now wait. Think, I told myself. *Work it out.* I had known which one was Maura's because it was an earlier edition, 1950. Cunliffe's had been 1953.

I opened the book. It said 1953.

All right, I said, streams of sweat running down my forehead, and accepting this nightmarish fact. *This one is Cunliffe's. I accidentally switched it. It was Maura's I left on the desk at the glassworks. It is Maura's that is now in the flower box. This one here in my hand is Cunliffe's. It stayed in my pocket all the time.*

Then how the hell, I thought, *does this one come to have the formula in it?* The sweat trickled over into my eyes. The answer was all too clear. There was only one way it could have the formula in it. I had brought it in with me.

There was something very peculiar going on here. I thought again, *Now wait. Think. Be absolutely certain. Check the other book again.*

I got up, went through to the bathroom at a shambling trot, pulled the flower box to me again and got out the Norstrund. I brushed it off in the washbasin, checked the publication date. 1950. It was undoubtedly Maura's. I got out my penknife, ripped open the flyleaf, front and back. I ripped off the bottom of the spine. Nothing. Nothing at all. Yet this was the one I had left at the works. There could now be no doubt at all.

I buried the book in the flower box again and went through to the bedroom. The formula was lying on the table next to Cunliffe's Norstrund. It floated off on to the floor in the draught of my hand as I reached for it. I bent and picked it up. I had examined it briefly before. Now as I held it close in the dim green light, I saw that the top line was in clearer notations and stood slightly away from the rest. I screwed up my eyes and read it. The top line said: *Amend Aldermaston 8, 3rd stage, Banshee.*

I crumpled the paper up in my hands at once. I said aloud, 'Oh, Jesus Christ, no.' My knees began literally to knock. I looked wildly round the room, licking my lips. There was only one place for this. I went through to the bathroom again, somewhat unsteadily, dropped the screw of paper in the w.c. and flushed it down. My face in the mirror was ghastly and shiny with sweat.

I thought I heard the rattle of tea things along the corridor and belted back to the bedroom in a panic. I unlocked the door, closed the Norstrund on the table and lay back on the bed again. Aldermaston had rung a bell in my mind. Something secret. Something atomic. I had just realized what it was. Aldermaston was the place where they developed nuclear weapons. The Banshee was the latest. I turned away from the door, more terrified, and with better cause, than ever before in my life.

Josef came into the room. 'Pan Whistler,' he said. 'Wake up, Pan Whistler. Your tea, Pan Whistler.'

2

In the moment before I sat up, I decided what I had to do. I had to get out of the room in some smooth and plausible fashion. I had to go downstairs, out of the hotel, find the British Embassy. I had noticed a row of telephone directories on the shelf beside the zealous receptionist. There would doubtless be another row in the post office – a few yards up the street, Josef had said.

I turned over, sat up, groaned.

Josef was standing there, relaxed and smiling. He had put the tray down on the table where the Norstrund had been. It wasn't there now.

'You have slept again, Pan Whistler,' he said jovially. 'You have drunk too much beer.'

'I must have.'

'Well now, refresh yourself.' He was pouring out the tea. 'Maybe you'd like to write your letter now. You can catch the earlier post.'

My heart was thumping wildly. 'I think I'll make it a post-card. Are there any picture postcards downstairs?' I knew there were. I had seen a display of them.

'Certainly. I'll send up a selection.'

'Don't bother I need to wake up. I'll go down myself.'

'As you prefer,' he said. I thought he seemed rather pleased at this. It would probably give him an opportunity to nip back in the room again with the Norstrund.

I waited till he had gone, then slipped off the bed, poured the tea out in the washbasin and rinsed my face. I felt cold and sick. I picked up my jacket and went out of the room. There was no one in the corridor. I walked down the stairs, across the hall. It was crowded, open shirts, sandals, perfectly normal. I didn't think anyone noticed me; not even the receptionist looked up. I strolled slowly and thoughtfully to the entrance. Then I was out, in the street.

It was still grey and hot outside. I was shivering, my teeth chattering, limbs rubbery. As I'd told Cunliffe, I was no hero. I was not cut out for this desperate nonsense. If some hand should fall on my shoulder now, I knew quite certainly I would be sick on the spot.

No hand fell on my shoulder. Nipping in and out of the endlessly streaming crowds, I was at the post office in three minutes. It was a big place, crowded, the huge hall full of that curious shifting dreariness that seemed to go with long lines of open collars.

I found the telephone booths, looked up the British Embassy. B. *Britske Velvyslanectvi. Thunovska 14, Malostranske Namesti. 66144.*

I didn't know where the Malostranske was, couldn't place it. I'd never been in such a jittery, knee-knocking, teeth-chattering panic in my life before. I had a sudden overpowering urge to hear a British voice. I went into a booth, rang 66144.

The number went on ringing.

'There is no reply,' said the Czech operator.

The box was terribly airless. My heart was beating dully. I said faintly, 'There must be a reply. Try it again, please.'

The ringing began again, went on. Suddenly the receiver was taken off. A testy Cockney voice said: 'Hello, hello. British Embassy.'

I said, 'Thank Christ for that. Whereabouts are you?'

'Who is that speaking, sir?'

'My name's Whistler. I'm a British citizen. I've got to come round there. Whereabouts are you?'

'Thunovska, just off the Malostranske. Know it?'

'No. How do I get there?'

'Got a car, have you, sir?'

'No. No, I haven't. I'm in the Vaclavske Namesti.'

'Right. Take a number five or nine tram over the river. Then change at the first stop over the other side, that's the Ujezd. You then want a number twelve coming up to Malostranske. It's three stops. All right?'

'Right,' I said, scribbling frantically on a cigarette packet. 'I'll be along right away.'

'Oh, I shouldn't do that, sir. Nobody here now – they've all gone for the night.'

I had felt a warm wave of relief sweeping over me at this splendid, solid, understandable sort of fellow at the other end. My toes now began to curl inside my shoes. I felt my voice dry up in my throat. I actually said in a kind of falsetto, 'All gone for the night?'

'That's right, sir. Open again at ten in the morning.'

'But I've got to get there tonight,' I said. I suddenly found my voice. 'I'm in serious trouble. I'm in deadly danger. I'm a British subject. I've got to have protection.'

'Run into a spot of bother, have you?'

'Bother!' I said. 'Look, the secret police will be after me any minute now. They're probably looking for me right this very moment. You've got to –'

'Well, it's no use telling me about it on this phone, sir,' he broke in tartly. 'It's an open line – follow what I mean?'

I followed what he meant. I found myself idiotically dropping my voice. I whispered into the phone, 'Look, I've simply got to get to the Embassy. I can't explain now . . .'

'All right, sir,' he said, 'I live here. Keep a cool head. Things aren't always as serious as they seem in this country, you know. We'd be called in if you was in any real difficulty. I should sleep on it if I was you, sir. And don't forget to bring your passport. Can't let you in without that.' He hung up right away.

A few minutes later I found myself walking up the Vaclavske Namesti, dazed and shaking. *I live here*, he had said. *Don't forget to bring your passport. Can't let you in without it.* What did he mean? What else but come round right away, I'll let you in and you can stay here. If the line was tapped he couldn't say more. And the business about sleeping on it? Obviously to put off anyone else who might be listening. *Keep a cool head*, he had said. My head was cool enough. It was dripping with icy sweat.

There was a number nine at the tram stop and I got on it, and went swaying and lurching down the Narodni Trida to the river, crammed between two strapping girls and kept upright by their simply enormous busts. This served to distract me for a minute or two from my problems, and presently I began to feel some faint return of confidence. Nobody seemed to be following me. It had all happened very quickly. In twenty minutes or so I could be safe inside the Embassy telling this reassuring Cockney all about it.

By the time the tram ground to a halt at the National Theatre on the river embankment, the reaction from danger had set in, and I was beginning to feel a certain lunatic hilarity. I wondered what the Cockney would make of the crazy rigmarole I had to tell him. He must be an old embassy retainer of some kind, an old soldier, a sergeant probably. Keep a cool head, sir. Don't let the bleeders rattle you. Got your credentials, sir? Don't forget your passport. Can't let you in without it.

The conductress planted herself against me with her ticket machine. I couldn't get to the money in my trouser pocket. I felt in my breast pocket for my wallet. There was a sudden ghastly hollow in the pit of my stomach. I felt the other side, in both jacket pockets to make sure. But I was never surer of anything in my life. My wallet was back at the Slovenska. It was under the coverlet in room one-forty. So was my passport.

3

A few spots of rain were falling and the clocks were chiming six all round as I walked back to the Vaclavske Namesti. I had had two stiff vodkas in the Slavia while pondering my best course of action. I had got off the tram in a panic, but once off had had second thoughts and had wandered about for a few minutes distracted with indecision.

I thought: he'd have let me into the embassy. How could he throw me out after hearing my story? But it wasn't the likeliest of stories. And I'd have to admit that I'd been engaged in smuggling. I would not be too popular at the embassy *with* a passport. Without one they would probably prefer to wash their hands of me.

I saw all this as I teetered, sweating, under the linden trees. I certainly didn't fancy going to the embassy without a passport. I didn't fancy going back to the hotel to get it, either. And time was ticking by.

The vodka had a calming effect. For the first time I thought about the whole mission. It was plain I had been tricked all along. Smooth little Cunliffe who'd fooled me once about the legacy had fooled me again about the formula. It was beyond belief that I could ever have accepted the story. And yet there had been a crazy logic about it at the time. It was easy now to be wise after the event.

They had wanted someone who would have a plausible reason for visiting an Iron Curtain country. Czechoslovakia was the easiest; it traded with the West; had a large glass industry. Find someone with connexions with the industry. Rig up a story to convince him he is bringing something out, some character like myself who wouldn't dare to examine the thing he was supposed to be bringing out.

I could imagine the consternation in the glassworks when they had found nothing in the Norstrund. No wonder there had been some delay in getting it back. They must have stripped the thing. There must have been a quick message to the hotel to search my room; to drug and search me, too, when I got back.

But why drug me? Why not arrest me? Why such finesse?

Because, it seemed to me, after much intensive thought, perhaps they weren't absolutely sure I'd brought anything with me. They might suspect some slip-up, some last-minute change of plan in London. ... Every mission, after all, would not go as smoothly as the first.

I began to see that I might have acted rashly in dashing from the hotel. They would have let me return home. The courier had proved useful once. Why destroy his usefulness for the future?

Once I'd got as far as this, I thought of plenty of small details to support this view. Little Vlcek had dropped me willingly enough at the hotel and had not waited to see me go in. I had not been followed to the Manes café, and there had been no anxious inquiries on my return. Josef had not sought to detain me after the bit of business with the beer. There had been no restraint on my movements since. As far as I could tell, no one was following me now.

I thought it was time to go back.

Although it was only just after six, the lowering clouds had brought premature darkness. The trams were lit up and, as I rounded the corner of the Vaclavske Namesti, the floodlighting suddenly went on all down the street. One by one the banners and portraits sprang to life. There were 'oohs' and 'ahs' from the crowds, people came clustering out of offices and shops to look, and as I arrived at the hotel the entrance filled up with an assortment of hands and brains hurrying out from inside.

It seemed a propitious moment to pop in unnoticed.

I hadn't made up my mind quite what to do. If no further alarms were offered, it seemed to me that my best bet was to remain in the hotel and demonstrate visible unconcern. If anything suspicious should occur I should keep ready to slide swiftly out again. I didn't know what might rank as a reasonable suspicion. I didn't know if I'd be allowed to slide out again. All in all, it seemed safest to use the stairs instead of the lift.

I had taken my room key out with me and had it in my hand as I reached the second floor. Josef was not lurking as usual, but I saw, farther along the corridor, his tailcoated behind as he leaned out of a window overlooking the floodlit street.

He heard me coming and drew in his head.

My heart began to thud again.

'Ah, Pan Whistler. You're feeling better now?'

'Much better, thanks.'

'You've been out?' His smile was perfectly genial.

'Yes. I took a breath of fresh air. The floodlighting is quite a spectacle.'

'They say it's even better on the Heights. You should take a look later.' He was rubbing his hands gently, prepared for a chat. He had searched my room and found nothing. All part of the day's work.

I suddenly realized what a muggins I had been to panic and make a dash for it, but in the same moment knew that I had nothing to worry about. I was the simpleton who thought he was smuggling something out of the country. Any signs of nervousness or eccentricity were perfectly understandable.

I gave Josef a cheerful good evening and opened the room door, my mind at rest and operating a good deal more clearly than at any time since I had left London.

This was just as well. Two things stopped me short like some stricken beast in the doorway. One was the sight of both Norstrunds lying neatly side by side on the table with my passport and wallet. The other was two men out on the balcony. As I stood there stock still they turned and came in the room. Behind me Josef firmly closed the door.

4

They were wearing long pale raincoats, unbuttoned, and both of them had their hats on. They had been chatting on the balcony and were still smiling as they came into the room. One, somewhat shorter than the other, said conversationally, 'Whistler, Nicolas?'

I said, 'Yes,' and licked my lips.

'We must ask you some questions. Please take a seat.'

I said, 'Who are you?'

'S.N.B.'

The taller man withdrew a wallet from his breast pocket and opened it in front of me. The wallet had a glazed window. Inside was a card with his portrait and the words STATNI NARODNI BEZPECNOST. State Security Police.

I seemed to have stopped breathing some time ago. My chest was tight and suffocating. My hands, feet, scalp, lips had begun to throb. I didn't think I could get to the chair he indicated. I sat down heavily on the arm of the easy chair.

'We've been waiting quite a long time for you, Pan Whistler. We wondered where you'd gone.'

'I went out for a walk. I had a drink.' My voice seemed several tones higher than usual.

'Where?'

'Somewhere.' I couldn't think. It had gone out of my mind. I thought, *two Norstrunds. They'd found it then in the flower box. They knew I'd hidden it. They had an idea now what had happened.* 'I don't know the name of the place,' I said.

'Have you been there before?'

'I think so.'

'Was it the Manes café?'

'No, no.'

'You've been to Manes before, haven't you, Pan Whistler? You were there earlier today.'

'It wasn't there. I can't think where it was. Somewhere by the National Theatre. Why do you want to know?'

'Was it the Slavia?'

'The Slavia, that's it.'

'How long were you there?'

'I don't know. I had a couple of drinks.'

'Did you speak to anybody while you were there?'

'No.'

'Not even the waiter?'

'Well, the waiter, of course the waiter.'

'What did he look like?'

'I can't remember. It was a woman,' I gabbled suddenly, as though this feat of memory could help me in any way. 'I can't remember what she looked like. Why should I remember what she looked like?' My breathing was not getting any easier. 'What do you want to know all this for?'

'Did you meet anybody during your walk?'

'No.'

'You walked there and back?'

'Yes. No,' I said, confused. 'I took the tram there.'

'Why did you do that, Pan Whistler?'

'I don't know. I felt like it.'

'But you say you went for a walk.'

'I did. It was too hot to walk when I got outside. I just took the tram.'

'You knew where you wanted to go?'

'I wasn't going anywhere. I thought I'd just get off somewhere on the way.'

'And you got off at the Slavia?'

'Yes.'

'And spoke to nobody there?'

'I've already told you.'

The smaller man looked at his companion, who had replaced his wallet and was now jotting down notes on a pad. The taller man put down his pad and regarded me speculatively.

'You're not frightened of us, Pan Whistler?'

I licked my lips. 'Why should I be?'

'I don't know,' he said.

Suddenly he hit me full in the face.

The force of the blow took me clean off the chair. I tumbled over clumsily backwards and hit my head on the wardrobe. I stared up at them in shock and pain. My nose felt as if it had been squashed over my face. The excruciating pain had filled my eyes with tears. I was too shocked to utter a sound.

'Get up,' the tall man said.

I got up slowly, holding my nose.

He hit me again, very hard, on the side of the face, his knuckles jarring my head and sending me stumbling back against the wardrobe. I bent double, trying desperately to shield my head and face, thinking, *Oh God, oh God, this is going to go on now. This is what happens. It will go on and on.*

But no further blows landed. The other man said conversationally, as though nothing had happened, 'You were telling us where you had been, Pan Whistler. You said you took a tram to the Slavia. What happened there exactly?'

I straightened up slowly, head and face singing with pain. The taller man was still regarding me speculatively, gently rubbing his knuckles. My jaw was trembling.

'Is our friend here inhibiting you?'

I nodded.

'He's only trying to help. If you tell the truth there will be no more work for him. Who was it you saw at the Slavia?'

'Nobody. I'm telling the truth,' I gabbled quickly. 'You can check up. Someone must have seen me there. I'll tell you whatever you want. I'll tell you anything I can. I don't know what it is you want of me.' I thought the bastard would suddenly hit me again. You couldn't tell. I hadn't been able to tell before. He had just hit me very quickly.

'Yes, you do know, Pan Whistler.' The smaller man picked up the two Norstrunds and dropped them. There was a bit of sand on one and he brushed it off slowly. 'You know very well. You're trying to think of some lie that might satisfy us. You'll have to learn that only the truth will do. We know why you came here. We know why you suddenly left the hotel. We know that you were away for an hour and a half. We are sure you met someone and gave them something. We don't know – I am honest about it, you see – just who this person was. But we can find out. We intend to find out. The only question for you is whether you tell us somewhat unwillingly now, or very willingly indeed later on. There isn't any doubt that you *will* tell us. Do you understand?'

A trickle of blood was edging down my lip. My whole face seemed to be swelling outwards like a pig's head. Outside, the loudspeakers suddenly started up again with a jaunty march. The french windows were still open.

I said, 'I swear to you that I gave nothing to anyone.'

'Why did you leave the hotel in such a hurry?'

'I was frightened.'

'What of?'

'I saw the waiter searching the room. I thought he would find the – the thing I was trying to hide.'

'But you found it instead, didn't you?'

'No.'

There was nothing quick about it this time. The tall man put out one hand to steady me and hit me, as hard as he could, with the other. It was in the stomach. I doubled over, gasping and retching, and he stepped back and let me fall on the floor.

I was sick.

Presently the smaller man said, 'Get up now, Pan Whistler.'

I tried and couldn't. He helped me to my feet. 'Sit down if you want.'

I sat on the arm of the chair.

'If only you told the truth right away none of this would be necessary. It is stupid to lie. We will find out the truth, you know. We know you found the paper. Admit it.'

I nodded.

'And you wished to get rid of it quickly in case it was found on you. That is so, isn't it?'

I nodded again, still too sick to speak. And yet curiously, in this moment of physical horror, I found my brain suddenly beginning to function again. They couldn't really know I had found the paper. They had to assume it from my dash from the hotel. But why should they also assume I had given it to someone? I had thought myself a courier of glass secrets from the country, not nuclear secrets into it. If I had seen the paper it was obvious what I would have done with it – destroy it at once in a panic. Then why assume I had passed it on to someone else?

I suddenly saw why, in a flash of inspiration. They didn't know if I'd understood what it was. There was still a possibility that I hadn't rumbled what was going on. That was the point of all these questions. They didn't think I'd given it to anyone. They were giving me the opportunity of saying, *Why the hell should I have given it to anyone? I destroyed it. I flushed it down the lavatory pan.* Then they would know that I knew. Then I'd be cooked.

I said, 'Can I have a drink of water?'

The small man went and got me one in the bathroom. The other man sat down on the bed, still rubbing his knuckles gently, looking at me without hostility, looking me all over as though selecting the next place. The small man came back with the water and gave me it and sat down himself on the bed, side by side with his thoughtful colleague.

He said, after a while, 'So, Pan Whistler, let's try again. I'll give you one last chance. I don't need to tell you what a serious matter this is. We know well what it was that you were carrying. There is still the possibility that it can be stopped from leaving the country. If that should prove to be the case, it might not go so badly with you. If not I can promise you the highest penalty. It is in your own interest to tell us what you did with it.'

I said slowly, 'Can I believe that – that it will be better for me if you get it back?'

'Certainly.'

'Well, I just hope you can,' I said. 'I posted it.' The idea had come to me as he spoke. It sprang to life fully documented, without fumbling or hesitation. It wasn't going to save me. It might give me a few hours' respite.

They were taken utterly by surprise. They looked at each other.

'When did you post it?'

'The minute I left the hotel. I went right out to the post office. It should have caught the five o'clock post.'

'To whom did you send it?'

'To a man called Cunliffe, the man who sent me, in London.'

'You thought it would go through the post without examination?'

'I didn't know what to think. I was in a panic.'

Nobody said anything for a minute. The loudspeakers boomed outside. It had begun to rain heavily. I could hear it splashing down off the awning on the balcony. I began to tingle all over, pain forgotten for the moment. There was just a chance, I thought.

The small man said slowly, 'It didn't occur to you to destroy the paper? That would have been the quickest and safest way.'

Think now. Think. I said, 'I wish to hell I had done. But I'd come all the way to get it. I thought there was just a chance it would go through. There was nothing to connect me with it. I just put it in an envelope and addressed it.'

Silence again for a minute. 'Very well,' he said at last, heavily. 'We will see, Pan Whistler. I hope, for your sake, that you are telling the truth this time. Get your coat.'

I turned to get it from the wardrobe, heart pounding. I knew there was nothing to lose: I thought, *Oh God, I'll never do it.*

I took the raincoat off the hanger and turned round with it. They were both looking at me thoughtfully, side by side on the bed. The raincoat was creased from the morning's rain. I shook it out. I seemed to be shaking it out for about two hours, everything suddenly in slow motion in the last paralysing moment before action. Then I thought, *Here it is. Now. Now,* and did it.

I threw the raincoat over them. I punched both heads together with a crack. I switched off the light, opened the room door, yelled at the top of my voice. Then I hared back across the room, out on to the balcony. The bloody flower box was in the way and I tripped over it. I scrambled up, kicked the flower box slanting in the opposite direction and went in quietly through the bathroom window, pulling it to behind me.

I don't know how many seconds it took. I was shaking all over. I got down behind the bath in the gap between it and the wall. I crouched there, holding my bruised stomach and trying not to be sick again.

There was a confused row from the next room, people stumbling about. The room light went on again. Josef's voice. 'He didn't come this way. I was in the corridor.' Then they were on the balcony. 'This way. See. He tripped over the flower box.'

Footsteps running in the opposite direction. I couldn't hear if they got as far as the fire escape at the opposite end. The loudspeakers drowned everything. But they'd certainly be coming back. I had perhaps half a minute to get out through the bedroom. I couldn't tell if Josef had gone with them.

My stomach was painful as hell. I levered myself up from the floor in the narrow space, found something there at the side of the bath. The bit of piping I'd seen there, weeks, years ago. I picked it up, edged out of the gap, careful to make no sound. I tiptoed over to the half-open door to the bedroom. No one was there and I went in.

Josef stepped in from the balcony.

He stood stock still for a moment, jaw dropping with surprise. I ran across the room with the piping. He said, 'No, no,' caught me by the shoulder and half turned me round. But I managed to lift the thing and hit him once, as hard as I could. It landed above the ear. His eyes turned up, he gave a single, heavily-exhaled breath and fell against me. I stepped back and he folded up on the floor. I didn't know if I'd killed him. It was the first time I'd ever hit anyone.

I said aloud, 'Oh, Christ,' panting, half sobbing. I looked quickly round the room, saw my passport and wallet and stuffed them in my pocket. I didn't know how I was going to get out of the hotel. I was sure they'd have people watching, a full description of me.

The moment I thought of this, and with a mindless sense of inevitability, I began tugging Josef's tailcoat off him. He was like a sack of lead, head banging on the floor. I yanked him round, split the seams at the shoulder as I pulled it off. He had no shirt underneath, just a wide dicky, taped back and front, and a clip-on bow. I got the whole lot off, then his trousers, tugging and jerking in a panic. I thought they'd be running back along the balcony at any moment. I wondered if I should drag Josef into some other room, but dare not risk the corridor.

He was shorter and broader than me. I was in his trousers in less than half a minute; had trouble with the dicky and let it hang loose at the back. There was no time to examine the bow tie in the mirror. I bundled him under the bed, kicked the pile of clothes after him, transferred the money and passport, and went out in the corridor.

Rain was bouncing in at the open window there. I thought I'd better get a raincoat; it would look suspicious going out without one. I couldn't take my own. The raincoats were different here, long, thin, pale-coloured. I knocked on the first door along the corridor. The room was empty, unused. I tried the next without knocking. The blonde I had noticed earlier on the balcony was sitting naked before the dressing table mirror, carefully examining one breast. I said, '*Prosim*,' shut the door quickly and tried the next one.

There were clothes scattered on the bed, a case open on the luggage rack, splashing coming from the bathroom. I opened the wardrobe door, saw a man's raincoat inside, and took it.

I had noticed some back stairs at the other end of the corridor and wondered if these were the service stairs. I walked quickly back again, my feet soundless on the carpet, terrified the men would come suddenly bursting out of the room again. I didn't see a soul. The steps were narrow and badly lit. There was a dark little cubby-hole on the first landing and an old chamber-maid sat on a three-legged stool eating a piece of bread. She looked at me curiously as I passed, but said politely, '*Dobry vecer.*' I wished her the same and went on quickly down the stairs.

They let out into a dim, tiled hall with a concrete floor. There was a green baize notice board and a clock on the wall. Two boys in tailcoats, evidently young trainees, were pushing and shoving each other around, laughing. They froze when they saw me, muttering subdued *Dobry vecers*. There was a swing door at the end, and a double door beyond that. I went out through it. Outside a man in a hat and raincoat stood in the shelter of the doorway out of the rain. He raised his arm to hold me back. 'I'm sorry, no one is to leave.'

I said, 'I know, comrade, I know. They've got him. He's upstairs now. I'm the floor waiter.'

He watched me getting into my raincoat, somewhat sourly. 'Where do you think you're going?'

'To the chemist's,' I said, my stomach turning over and over. 'They need something quickly. Ring up and find out if you want, only for God's sake don't hold me up. He's a delicate little soul liable to pass out any minute. You won't be very popular if he does.'

He said, 'Wait here,' and went in through the double doors.

I heard the swing door going, and ran up the alley. It was unlit, black, black as hell, a canyon between two tall buildings. I wondered if there was any way out into a side street that would bring me into the Prikopy, but it was a cul-de-sac, and I turned and belted back, panting in the dark. Presently the alley curved and I saw the lights at the end.

Nobody stopped me this time. I walked out into the Vaclavske Namesti.

Chapter 9

I

THERE is something about coshing a man for the first time that inspires a certain wild but unstable confidence. One moment you are faced with a powerful and unnerving obstacle; the next, without thought or subtlety, you have overcome it. By disengaging from the habits of a lifetime you have slipped into a new effortless gear in which all things seem possible. Minutes afterwards the adrenalin aftertaste still tickles the roots of the tongue, nauseous, exultant, the unique flavour of rewarded violence.

I had buttoned the raincoat up to my chin, and was clutching the piece of lead piping in my pocket. Despite the rain the street was still thronged with hardy hands and brains. The crowds seemed denser farther down the street where the floodlighting was brightest, and I instinctively moved towards them, shuffling briskly and head down past the hotel entrance.

I knew that my only hope was to get to the Malostranske as quickly as possible, and to effect, as they say, an entrance to the British Embassy. The grotesque picture of myself as a fugitive from the secret police in this crowded and hostile city did not, in those first moments, seem at all incredible. I felt extraordinarily alive and effective, not at all the familiar coward.

The Malostranske lay at the other side of the river, perhaps a mile and a half away. I had suddenly a clear picture of the thoroughfare that I had forgotten so completely in my panic earlier on. It lay at the end of the Mostecka. I must have passed it on my walk to the Heights on my first visit. It would take me half an hour to walk there in the crowded streets. I thought I'd better get the tram.

I walked over to the island in the middle of the road. The little trams were ding-donging by, packed to the steps, but three number nines came in quick succession, and I managed to get on the last. No fares were being taken. It was impossible for the conductress to move. I stood on the step, battered, bruised, my stomach still stiff and aching from the last blow, but wonderfully alive as we swayed and lurched down the brilliant, seething street.

I thought: I've got away with it. Not half an hour ago I was being beaten up by the secret police. I fooled them. I knocked out a man who tried to stop me. Incredible but true. It was wonderful what you could do when you tried.

In my desire to get away from the hotel and make for the thickest crowds, I had walked down the street. The tram now took me back up it, past the hotel, to the huge picture of Lenin at the junction. My cockiness lasted until approximately this point, where the tram ground to a halt. It seemed to be stationary longer than usual. I leaned out to see what was happening. The whole line of trams had stopped at the junction. I felt a premonitory sickness in my stomach again.

The conductress presently struggled off, muttering, and after a minute or two came back. 'Anyone in a hurry had better get off,' she said. 'You'd do better to walk. They're looking for something in front.'

A noisy, larky bunch of teenagers tumbled off the tram. I tumbled off with them, crossed to the pavement, and made my way up to the junction. There was really no need for me to look. The sickness in my stomach had provided accurate forewarning. The passengers were coming off the leading trams singly, each opening his coat as he got off, each showing his papers. Two men in hats and raincoats stood by each of the three leading trams. It was all very businesslike. They'd not wasted a lot of time.

I continued numbly to the corner, saw the same performance taking place on the pavement with pedestrians wishing to debouch into the Narodni Trida and into the Prikopy, and turned and made my way back down the street.

There are nine main roads running off the Vaclavske Namesti, five of them in the direction of the river, four of them away from it. It took me forty minutes in the crowded street to investigate them all. I could have given up after the first. The five streets running to the river were covered; the four running away from it were covered. As I'd seen from the start, it was a businesslike operation. I wasn't going to the British Embassy tonight. I wasn't going to leave the Vaclavske Namesti. I was cobbled.

2

By half past ten the street showed no sign of clearing, but the rain, although it had slowed to a drizzle, had mercifully not stopped. I kept the raincoat buttoned up to my chin and trudged wearily up the street again. I was sick of the sight of it, having gone there and back six times. The loudspeakers, after repeating a medley of marches, were now rendering selections from *The Bartered Bride*. I was dropping with exhaustion.

The future, it seemed to me, was short and brutally unpromising. There were perhaps twenty thousand people in the stretch between Lenin and the museum. They would all have to go to bed at some time – say in an hour, two at the most. There was nothing for the police to do but wait.

In my perambulations up and down the street I had gone endlessly into the problem of how to get rid of the tailcoat. There was no public lavatory in the Vaclavske Namesti – and I wouldn't have dared to enter it if there were – or any enclosed building where men might be waiting. I couldn't get out of the tailcoat in the street. Even if I did manage this contortionist feat, there would still be the question of papers. There was no way out. I was trapped.

I was obsessed with a horrifying vision of the old movie, the one where the character is walking up the empty street and they start coming for him out of doorways and he runs off down a sewer. I didn't know where to look for a sewer in this noisy fairground of a street. I knew it wouldn't end like that for me. I would merely get more and more tired, it would get later and later, and all the people would drift off. Then the police would begin to round up stragglers. 'Open your coat. Where are your papers?' There was nowhere for me to run. There would be no point in struggling. Just a brief ride in a closed van, and then they would start hitting me again.

I thought, Oh Christ, and turned round and started back again, seventh circuit. I thought, if I could just sit down for a minute. If I could just take the weight off, have a drink, think calmly. There was no chance of that. I had to keep moving, one of the crowd. I trudged on, shoes letting in water, stomach sickly empty, mouth parched.

I had counted six *parky* stalls up and down the street, their naphtha flares pale in the floodlighting. My stomach revolted at the thought of the hot, greasy sausages and the coarse black bread. It would make me thirstier than ever. But I knew suddenly that I had to sit down. I didn't think I could keep going five minutes longer without a rest. There was a wooden box outside the next stall, and a woman sitting on it, eating.

I teetered around the stall until she had finished, and then I quickly claimed the box. Four or five people waiting to be served looked at me. The stall-keeper said morosely, 'In the queue, comrade. There are others before you.'

'I'll wait. I'm in no hurry.'

'Maybe someone else wants the seat.'

They said they didn't want the seat. He grunted, turned back to his pan again and served the others. There was a naphtha flare at each end of the stall. Fumes from the pan hung in the harsh yellow glare. I thought I was going to be sick and turned my head.

The man said, 'How many?'

It seemed to be my turn. 'One, please.'

'Mustard? Mustard?' he said and leant over to look at me. 'Is something wrong, comrade?'

It had risen in my throat. I couldn't speak. I said faintly after a moment, 'I feel sick.'

'You want some mineral water?'

'Yes, please.'

I hadn't seen any bottles. He moved away inside somewhere and came out of a side door with a glass. 'I'm sorry, comrade. I didn't see you were ill. People are shoving and pushing their way to the front everywhere tonight. Here, drink.'

A few other people had come up and he went back inside and served them. I sat on the box and drank the mineral water and presently felt well enough to eat the *parky* and black bread he had left on the counter for me. I wondered where he had got the bottle from. I wondered what else he had in there. The stall was about six feet long, four wide, a wooden shack on iron barrow wheels. The counter flap was not more than a yard long. There must be some sort of compartment between it and the side door. I felt the stirrings of something.

'All right now, comrade?'

'Yes, thank you.'

'Maybe you walked too much in the crowds. There are too many of them shoving and pushing tonight.'

'Maybe that was it.'

'Leave the glass there. Don't bother to get up. Rest for a while.

'That's all right,' I said and went round to the side door and handed the glass in to him. You could step right inside and not be seen from the street. Two or three people could step inside. There were a few shelves with bottles, raw sausages, loaves of bread, a dark area about a yard square.

I thanked him and continued slowly along the street, hope beginning to expand again like bubbles in some steamy swamp. I wondered if all the other stalls were the same. I thought they would be. I thought there should be something one could do about this.

I suddenly realized exactly what I could do about it and stood stock still on the pavement, the back of my neck beginning to sweat. It would have to be a very small stall-keeper, I thought.

I couldn't cope with anything bigger than a dwarf in my ruined condition. And it would be better if it were on the other side of the road where the streets ran off to the river.

I had a dim recollection of a gnome-like figure superintending a stall at the corner of the Stepanska, and crossed the road and made my way to it. The naphtha flare was not more than ten yards from the corner. There were four or five people waiting at the counter. The side door was ajar. I went past the front of the stall and came back again. I hadn't been wrong. He was a little skinny fellow with a marked resemblance to Ratface Rickett, only about two hundred years older. He wore a peaked cap and a shiny plastic jacket. It was several sizes too large for him, I was glad to see.

I got in the queue and had another *parky* and looked carefully inside. It semed identical with the other stall. I waited till there was a lull in trade and went round to the side door, trembling. I pushed the door open and went in.

He saw me right away and said irritably, 'Round at the front, round at the front.'

I said, 'I've got something for you.'

'What is it? What do you want?'

He came over with a string of sausages and a knife in his hand and he was so damned old and bent I could hardly bring myself to do it. I hit him quite gently on the head with the piping. His cap fell off and he clutched his head, staring at me in horrified silence. I thought, *Oh Christ, Oh Christ,* and hit him again in a panic, and he fell down. I said silently, *I'm sorry. I'm sorry, old man,* getting quickly out of my coat and the damned tailcoat. I ripped off the bow and the dicky, and bundled the lot on a shelf, and pulled his jacket off and got into it myself.

I hadn't realized there was no floor to the stall. The road was directly underneath, and his cap had rolled in the gutter. I picked it up quickly and put it on, and in the same moment someone began rapping on the counter and calling, '*Prosim, prosim. Parky, prosim,*' and a man leaned over and saw me as I was straightening up.

I said, 'Coming, coming.'

'I should hope so, comrade,' he said jovially. 'The customers are waiting.'

I went over to the counter, sweating. There were half a dozen of them there. They'd materialized suddenly. I didn't think I could have been more than a minute or two.

'Three,' the man said. 'With mustard.'

A pan of *parkys* was stinking away on the stove. I fiddled about with them, my heart beating dully, and wondered how I was going to cope with this. I didn't think the old man could possibly be seen, but shoved him over with my foot nearer the backboard, just in case. The bread was sliced and I forked three *parkys* out of the pan and handed them over.

I had never seen more than half a dozen people at a stall all night, but now for some ill-starred and damnable reason this one became suddenly popular. In no time there was a queue of a dozen or so, and I shambled there and back, emptying and replenishing the *parky* pan in the yellow malodorous glare until I was faint with nausea and fatigue.

I heard eleven o'clock strike and then a quarter past, and shortly after that the loudspeakers stopped and the stream of customers dried up. I thought it was time I got the hell out of it. I bent and looked at the old man. He had not stirred, but he was breathing. I couldn't see any blood. I thought he'd gone off to sleep. I went back to the counter again and looked out into the street. The crowds had definitely thinned. On the corner of the Stepanska, a few yards away, a couple of rain-coated S.N.B. men were on duty, big solid fellows. They were stopping everyone who entered the street. Open your coat. Show your papers. Well, I thought; I could show mine. I looked swiftly in the pocket of the plastic jacket and found the old man's wallet. His papers said he was Vaclav Borsky, seventy-four, one hundred and sixty-one centimetres, born Kutna Hora. I was not too bothered about this discrepancy in age. They weren't really looking at the papers, just seeing that everyone had them. They knew Whistler Nicolas, the well-known spy, hadn't.

I left the counter and walked out of the side door and went

haring back in again faster than I'd ever moved in my life. One of the S.N.B. men was walking over.

He said gruffly, 'You're packing up early.'

I said, 'No. No.'

'Do us a couple quick, comrade, and the same for my friend. We're dropping there.'

I said, 'Certainly. Of course.'

He watched while I fiddled with the *parkys*. I kept my head down, terrified he would have some minute description of my face. He was looking hungrily at the *parkys*, however, and stuffed his in his mouth as soon as I handed it over. I felt some comment might be called for, and said in a kind of soprano, 'What's all the excitement been, comrade?'

'Ah, don't bother your head. It's an enemy of the people at large.'

'What's he done?'

'Nothing to what we'll do when we get him. He's a famous American criminal, an expert in disguise. He escaped dressed as a waiter.'

'I hope you catch him.'

'We will,' he said, walking off with his colleague's *parkys*. He had not paid.

I remained inside the stall, quivering like a leaf. I sat down on a box. I poured myself a glass of mineral water. The stall was in plain view of the men on the corner. Now that the streets had thinned they could see me perfectly. There seemed no prospect of walking away. In a matter of minutes the street had gone quiet, and I was suddenly aware the trams had stopped. An ominous silence set in. There was presently a subdued rumbling, and after a few moments the two men on the corner turned to stare at me. One of them walked over.

I almost fell off the box in my haste to be up.

'Are you staying here all night, comrade?'

I said, 'What? No. I must have dropped off. Time to be off, eh?'

'Your friends are all going. Better get that rattle trap off the street now. There might be some shooting soon.'

I came out of the side door. The floodlighting went off suddenly. Up and down the street the naphtha flares were moving, iron barrow wheels rumbling over the cobbles.

'Look sharp now. The inspector will be round any minute. He wants to find the street empty.'

I said, 'Right away,' and went numbly back inside wondering where the hell to start. I picked up the frying pan and then thought of something else and nearly collapsed in panic. The inspector wouldn't be finding the street empty. Vaclav Borsky was lying about in it, at present under the stall and snoring rhythmically.

The other policeman stepped over to join his mate, saying irritably, 'Come on, come on now. What's the trouble? Smirtov will be here any moment. Here, give him a hand.'

I came out of the side door at a rush, crying, 'No. Wait. Don't trouble yourself, comrades. I've just got to go somewhere a minute. Watch the stall for me, please. I'm bursting,' and hurried off, making motions indicative of a violent need to urinate.

I don't know if they believed me. I was beyond caring if they believed me. I thought it would take a minute or two for them to suspect, a little longer for them to know definitely. I had about three minutes.

I went round the corner of the Stepanska like a whippet. The street looked long and hideously straight. A few yards round the corner the huge bulk of an hotel glimmered dimly, but after that it was black as hell. My footsteps rang back from the high walls at both sides. I stopped and wrenched my shoes off, panting and sobbing, and hared on again in my socks.

I thought there must be an alley or an entry. I couldn't see anything. Tall buildings; blank walls. I'd picked the wrong street. After a minute or two I was winded, stomach hurting like hell, and had to slow down to a trot, breathing heavily. Suddenly I heard a single enraged shout at the other end of the street and took off again like a rocket. Almost immediately, I fell over. The pavement had ended. I went sprawling on cobbles.

I got up, lost one of the damned shoes, scrambled frantically for it on the wet cobbles, found it. There was a light somewhere, a tiny glimmer. I couldn't make it out, took a second or two to contact. I'd found my alley.

I went up the alley slowly, puzzled by the light. A hospital, police station, cul-de-sac of some sort? I suddenly heard my breathing echoing back, realized I was in a roofed place, and stopped and held my breath, trying to work it out. It seemed to be an archway. In the silence the gutters gurgled steadily outside. The rain had stopped. A still close night. My elbow was throbbing. I must have fallen on it. Suddenly a car revved up and came whooshing down the street. Men shouting. Another car starting up. I couldn't stay here, would either have to take my chance on it being a cul-de-sac or get out in the street again and find another alley.

I went on through the archway.

After a few paces I saw what the light was. A statue. A madonna, with a little oil lamp over her head. A few flowers showed whitely in an urn at the base. A cobbled, medieval courtyard; not, evidently, a churchyard; no obvious church; big blank buildings all round. There might be an alley running off at the other side. I ran across the cobbles in my socks and suddenly stopped, quite still.

There was someone there.

I stepped back to the wall, unable to place the direction. A girl laughed, over to the right, and I saw them, a single shape that became two, then one again. A man and a girl scuffling and laughing softly in the angle of two walls. A bicycle showed dully nearby.

The muttering went on; giggling again. The man's voice, gruff and wheedling, 'Ah, why not? You said you would.'

I thought I could safely leave them to it, and edged round, keeping close to the wall. The courtyard was a rectangle. Railings; basements; everything in darkness. The backs of business premises, I thought. From somewhere close by a clock chimed half past eleven, and all round other clocks began to strike.

There was an opening at the next corner, a cobbled path not a yard wide. I couldn't see where it went, everything pitch black. Another car went by in the street, and men running. I was in no position to choose. I went swiftly into the opening, feeling my way with my right hand outstretched. The wall curved right, left, right again. No chance to escape if anyone came in after me in either direction.

My outstretched hand suddenly fetched up against a blank wall. Dead end. Panic. *Wait. Wait*, I thought. How dead end? Why dead end? The path must go somewhere. There had been no doors or gates opening off it. I felt all round, found that it turned sharply at ninety degrees to the left, hurried on, sobbing with relief. From all round now there seemed to be a fair amount of activity. Car doors banging, men shouting. I'd lost all sense of direction. I knew I mustn't be caught up this alley. I began to run.

Immediately I tripped, stumbled, went floundering down a flight of steps, and landed heavily on my backside. There was something underneath me, something alive and shrieking. A cat. A bloody cat. It tore out from under me, clawing and spitting, and a dustbin lid clanged a yard away. I scrabbled to my feet, terrified of the row, and at the same moment a light came on from an upstairs room in front of me. I was outside a gate, the end of the path, railings at both sides. Really dead end now.

A woman's voice called, 'Franti?'

I couldn't somehow move, stiff from my fall and hypnotized by the light. There was a group of buildings beyond the gate. The woman came out on to a balcony and stood silhouetted against the light.

She said, 'Frantisek? See you put the bicycle away tonight. It will rain again.'

I tried to edge into the shadow. She was leaning over a small coping, peering at me. A flight of steps ran up to the balcony. 'What, lost your tongue? Ah, there's no need to sneak in, you fornicating beast. I've been waiting for you. What was it tonight?'

I couldn't understand the layout of the buildings. Not houses. Not warehouses. A large formal structure, many windowed, a gothic arch.

'All right. Stay dumb. You can stay out, too. Maybe she'll give you a bed. Or see if you can find a girl again in the gymnasium. You filthy beast!' she said bitterly, and went in and slammed and bolted the door.

I thought, gymnasium. A school, perhaps. The caretaker's lodge. I tried the gate. There was a simple iron latch. It opened easily, but I didn't go in. There would be a front entrance on a street, a naked public street. My instinct was to remain in the dark alleys. I couldn't somehow think. I was aching all over, desperately tired. I suddenly realized I'd been on my feet for the best part of seven hours. I felt behind me for the steps and sat down, holding my head and trying to work it out. In the silence I could hears the cars still, a confused distant row. I couldn't tell how far I'd gone. But I knew I couldn't stay here. The fornicating Frantisek would be along any minute with his bike. No point in going back down the alley for the same reason. Nothing else but the gate.

I got up and pushed it and went in.

A wide quadrangle, dark, no visible features except the bulk of the buildings. I skirted them on the left, found a high wall and followed it round. I followed it for several hundred yards and came up against a building. Dead end. I cut back across the quadrangle to try the other way, and suddenly a finger of light swung across and I froze. A bicycle lamp. I heard the faint clang of the gate latch and then the light went off. I remained quite still in the ocean of darkness, listening for him. The faint hiss of tyres on the wet surface. I couldn't place the direction, wondered if he wasn't coming towards me to put the bicycle away in some shed, and backed quickly to the wall.

I lost him completely then. Total silence. Suddenly a light came on, an institutional blister lamp under the balcony where the woman had appeared. The pool of light spread all the way to the gate. I saw him leaning the bike against the wall. He seemed in no hurry. He wiped his face and collar carefully with a handkerchief, fumbled around in his pocket, and I saw the weak spurt of a match. The flame leapt. He was lighting a pipe.

I told him silently, *Go, damn you, go.* He didn't go. He began to walk up and down smoking the pipe, breathing deeply. I leaned against the wall, sick and aching. My feet were cold and wet in the socks. I wondered if I might sit on the ground, and lowered myself painfully but surely right into a bloody puddle. I was so dead beat I couldn't bear to move and sat there, watching him.

A quarter to twelve struck.

He knocked out the pipe and walked back to the bike and the light suddenly went off. I levered myself to my feet again. I heard the faint sound of him going up the stairs, and started moving. He'd be down again pretty soon, I thought. I knew one fornicator who wouldn't be entering the conjugal home tonight.

I actually managed to trot on my maltreated feet past the gate and away over to the other side of the quadrangle, but after a few seconds slowed to a painful walk again. The sky seemed to be lightening a bit. The clouds were breaking up, a dim radiance appearing. I saw the outline of the wall now, and then the main gates.

Beyond the gates, the street seemed deserted. I peered through them in both directions. I had no idea at all where I was. I felt it couldn't be far from the river. I didn't know what I was going to do when I got there. They would have the approaches to the Embassy well covered by now. It seemed pointless to try and get there. But what was the point of trying to get anywhere? I couldn't hide indefinitely in Prague. I couldn't spend the rest of my life running up and down alleys. They were going to catch me some time. My only hope lay in trying to get to the Embassy. If I failed then it meant failing earlier instead of later. This meant I had to cross the river. I would have to boat or swim across, both prospects so grimly unattractive that I groaned faintly in the dark.

I wondered at which point of the river embankment the street led out. There was only one way to find out, and I turned the handle of the gate and pulled gently. Nothing happened. I tried the other way, pushed, pulled, wrenched, swore obscenely. The gate was locked. It seemed about a mile high; straight vertical bars, too difficult to climb, too risky to climb, exposing me against the skyline to anyone who might be patrolling in the street.

The sky was brightening rapidly, tattered, luminous-edged clouds scudding across now. A breeze fluttered over the quadrangle, cold against my wet trousers. I looked round the school walls, saw a cluster of buildings beyond the wall on my left, and, farther along, an unexpected godsend, a builder's ladder. I made for the ladder, planted it firmly against the wall and climbed up. At the other side of the wall there was a collection of lorries and handcarts; a big building with hangar doors; a warehouse of some kind. Away to the right the street wall continued. I could see over it now. It was dark and quiet out there. There was a faint yellow light perhaps fifty yards along; evidently the corner, the river embankment.

The lorries were parked in line at the side of the warehouse. I thought there must be a gate or door at the far end that would open directly on to the embankment. Perhaps there would be a gap or a keyhole through which I could check my position.

There was a handcart directly below at the other side of the wall. I pulled myself on the wall, dropped the shoes on the handcart and went cautiously after them. A cobbled yard, faint stink of diesel oil, and something else – polish, wood, shavings? I went carefully down the line of lorries, found blank double doors, padlocked, no gap, no keyhole.

I went back again, round the warehouse, to the hangar doors, and suddenly stopped. A glimpse of light, a crack in the door. I see-sawed my head from side to side to catch it again, couldn't, and stepped back a pace. It wasn't a crack in the door. The door was open, not quite pulled to, a gap of an inch or so.

I pushed gently, waiting for the creak, but there was no creak. It opened ponderously, but quite smoothly.

The light was coming from big plate glass windows at the other end, faint yellow lighting from street lamps on the main road. I went slowly in, and stood for a moment just inside, sizing it up.

Furniture. Chairs, dressing tables, beds, standard lamps. Towards the window the stuff was laid out in suites. A clock suddenly struck and I dropped one of the shoes in panic, and picked it up, sweating, swearing, nervy as hell. The other clocks chimed in then. Twelve o'clock. Three-quarters of an hour since I'd left the *parky* stall. Only five hours since I'd coshed Josef and run for it. It seemed a lifetime. But I was free still. I'd got away with it so far. I'd got to the river.

With a faint resurgence of hope I moved in to the wall in the shadow of a line of wardrobes and went slowly up to the windows. As I got there the moon came out. A silvery luminescence swam over the street like a filmy curtain going up at a theatre. There was someone out there. It only needed one look to see who.

Silent and alone in the moonlit street he bestrode his great horse, sword raised, iron eyes staring sightlessly along his broad imperial way. Like some homing pigeon I had come back to him again. Like some demented rat I had run back into my trap. Like a bloody fool I sat down and wept.

3

I must have been about twelve when I wept last. I didn't know why I was weeping now. I hadn't wept when the policeman had knocked me about in the bedroom. I sat on a little coffee table and felt the tears streaming uncontrollably down my face, and thought what a right Charlie I had been. It had been such a hellishly long day, such a nerve-shatteringly long night, I thought I'd got away with it. I thought I was miles away.

I snapped out of it presently and, edging back into the shadow, sat down on something more comfortable to take stock of the situation. The river was obviously in the opposite direction. I'd come round in a half circle. There was nothing to be gained by going back up the alley. It led only to the Stepanska.

The alternative seemed to be to get into the side street. I went drearily over the operations necessary to achieve this. Then what? It would be best to keep off the street. Nip in and out of alleys, work my way round to a point below the bridges, and cross the water as best I could. That would take – how long? An hour? Two? I thought it wouldn't hurt to have a rest first.

I sat down on a settee, the seat and back wrapped with brown paper, and then slowly and luxuriously lifted up my legs and stretched out. It was warm in the room and stuffy with the smell of furniture. I could feel the seat of my pants wet from the puddle, my feet damp and throbbing in the soggy socks.

The street was bathed now in brilliant moonlight, the cold ghostly figure of Wenceslas leaping as clouds went swiftly over. It was utterly still out there, no cars racing now, no men running. I wondered where they were searching for me. Obviously along the river; they would know where I had to get. They would be at it for hours yet; plenty of river front to search.

It suddenly occurred to me in the warm musty darkness that one of the few places where they wouldn't think of looking was on a settee in a showroom on the Vaclavske Namesti.

I lay there, blinking rapidly at Wenceslas, working out the implications of this one.

It was stupid. I couldn't stay here all night. How would I get out in the morning? Where could I hide in daylight?

But why should I have to hide in daylight? Why should I have to creep down alleys when the streets were crowded with people? I could get out early when the first trams started, join the streaming workers in the streets. They would be unlikely to carry out further checks in the Vaclavske Namesti. But how to cross the river in daylight? There might still be checks on the bridges. . . .

The blissful, spreading comfort of the settee was overpowering. If tonight had taught me anything, it was not to think too much, not to plan too far ahead. I shifted the piece of piping out of my pocket and moved over in a new marvellous position. A crumpled dustsheet was lying at the end of the settee, and I pulled it over me. I didn't think I was visible from the street. The settee was in shadow. But the moon would slip round.

I thought I'd better will myself to get up every time the hour struck so that I wouldn't drift off into a deep sleep. I thought the first trams would be along about six o'clock. Six hours.

I got up when one struck, and again at two, and walked about stretching myself in the shadow at the back of the showroom. I was stiff as hell. After that I stayed where I was. I knew I wasn't going to sleep. I thought I might be too exhausted for sleep, too nervous, brain going busily back and forth over it all.

I must have watched Wenceslas for longer than anyone in the world. I can still see him when I close my eyes, leaping on his iron horse in the ragged moonlight. Soon after the chorus of clocks struck five, my eyes closed and I dozed off for a bit.

It didn't seem more than five minutes, but next time I opened them it was broad daylight, a tram was ding-donging by, and a man was looking down at me. He had the piece of piping in his hand and he said, 'Don't move. Stay where you are, or I'll brain you.'

Chapter 10

1

THE piece of piping was a couple of feet from my head. He must have picked it up from the side of the settee. He was an elderly man, broad, grizzled, wearing an alpaca jacket and carpet slippers. His eyes were intensely blue and Slav, and, at that moment, very hostile.

He said, 'How did you get in here?'

I licked my lips, shaken as hell. I said, 'The door was open.'

'It was locked. I locked it myself last thing at night. You must have forced it.'

The alpaca jacket and carpet slippers registered then. He was the caretaker. Not a very careful caretaker. I sat up, felt the seat of my pants still warmly damp, each individual bone aching and unrested. I said, 'It was open, comrade. Just a crack. Maybe you locked it later.' I knew he couldn't have done, unless he made a practice of locking up some time after five o'clock in the morning. It seemed a useful loophole to offer him. 'I must have been drunk. I had nowhere to sleep. I hope it won't get you into trouble, comrade.'

He had taken this latter point, of course, long before it had occurred to me. He still held the piece of piping at a workmanlike angle, however. 'How did you get into the yard?'

'I came over the wall. I was out drinking with a fellow – Frantisek something. He said he would put me up, but his slut of a wife kicked us both out. He told me you had a kind heart. He said you would fix me up. He brought me a ladder to climb the wall.'

This inspired lie, delivered in whining and wheedling tones, sprang to life ready made like some work of art. I listened to it with astonishment. It seemed to be registering with the caretaker. The hand holding the pipe dropped. 'I should hand you over to the police,' he said without much conviction. 'You ought to have come and seen me first.'

'I tried to, comrade. I looked all round for you, but it was dark, I thought I would just rest a minute until you came on your rounds. Frantisek said you never missed your rounds. He told me what a kind heart you had.'

He grunted and looked me over, not unfriendly. 'That Frantisek – he takes too many liberties. You're just up for the parade, I suppose?'

'The parade, that's it entirely, the parade,' I said eagerly.

'And what about this? What did you mean to do with this?' he said, raising the lead piping.

'That. Well, that, now,' I said, thinking rapidly. 'I took it off a fellow. There was this big brute came at Frantisek when he'd had a few too many. That's how we came together. Ah, you don't get that where I come from,' I said, my wheedling tone leading me effortlessly into the accusing burr of some Czech village idiot. 'Where I come from they don't go around coshing

161

people when they've had a few too many. They see a chap home to his bed. They're glad to give him a bed – and his breakfast in the morning,' I added, shaking my head reproachfully as I recalled suddenly that the automats might not be open on Sunday morning.

The grizzled caretaker seemed somewhat taken aback by this rustic rebuke. He made no attempt to prevent me getting off the settee. He said, rather uncertainly, 'Well, no harm done, I suppose. Whereabouts are you from, comrade?'

'Round Brno way. You wouldn't know it. Just a little village. Ah, you can keep your big towns,' I said, carried away by my performance, and improving every minute. 'Folks aren't friendly here. Just tell me where a fellow can get his breakfast and a wash-up in a town like this, comrade, and I won't trouble you any longer.'

The caretaker scratched his head. He watched me stretching myself. He said, 'Where's your national costume, then? Don't you country fellows dress up in national costume when you come to town?'

I said, 'National costume,' and licked my lips. 'Don't talk to me about national costume. You can have one, Jiri, they said to me, if you join the Party. Otherwise you can go up to Prague looking the tramp you are. We're a bit short of national costumes, Jiri, they said. Party members only, see? So I told them what they could do with their national costume, I did. A fellow's got to do too many things already these days. He's got to know all the reasons why he was ever born these days. No, comrade,' I said, shaking my head with wooden defiance at the little caretaker, 'you won't get me to do that, so it's no use your trying. I've got no time for it, and I won't waste any more of yours if you'll just put me on my way.'

The caretaker had brightened considerably during this rebellious speech, and now took my arm warmly. 'Not so fast, countryman, not so fast,' he said, dropping the 'comrade' and smiling indulgently. 'Get your boots on first. I dare say I can fix you up with a bit of breakfast and a wash. It's just that a fellow's got to be so careful these days. I'm here on my own, see? It's hard to know who's an enemy of the people and who isn't. This way now. No harm done. Just follow me.'

He gave me an excellent breakfast in his small and shipshape flat above the warehouse, which I repaid with a detailed fantasy of life in the small village near Brno. Despite the horrors of the previous night, I felt full of a wild and febrile confidence. I could hear my own voice and was in that lightheaded state when nothing about my own body or immediate surroundings seemed at all real.

The caretaker's steadfast Slav eyes hung on my words. He said at length regretfully, 'Well, countryman, time for you to be off, I suppppose. It's getting on for nine. The rest of your party will be up at the camp, eh?'

'The camp?'

'Isn't that where they bed them out? The camp at the other side of the Charles bridge, just before the Mostecka.'

The Mostecka, I thought. Surely that was near the Malostranske, the British Embassy. . . . I felt the beginnings of something and said slowly, 'The Mostecka, is it? Yes, yes. That's it, of course. The Mostecka. Now what's the name of the square near the Mostecka? They said we had to rally there.'

'A square near the Mostecka? Let me see, that must be the Malostranske.'

'Malostranske!-' I said. 'That's the one. How's a fellow to find that now?'

'Why,' said the caretaker, jumping up promptly, 'I'll take you there myself, countryman. In just one moment.'

He hurried out, and I executed a brief bob to his departing back, and considered how well things went when you left them alone. What I needed was a spot of cover while reconnoitring the Malostranske, and here was this grizzled ancient, heaven-sent and tailor-made to provide it.

I walked over to the window and looked out. As little Vlcek and his meteorological friends had promised, it was a magnificent day with that shining, pristine quality that mornings sometimes have in very old cities. Already the street crawled; splashes of colour from wandering groups in national costume; queues

163

inevitably forming at stands and tram stops. The caretaker had told me the parade would begin at eleven and that trams would stop at ten. There would be a good deal of shifting movement all over the town, particularly over the bridges. There couldn't be much attempt at searching in these conditions.

The old man reappeared, very spruce in a blue serge suit and brown shoes, and we went out, down the side street and past the school gates towards the embankment. As we walked I began to realize how damned lucky I'd been. The warehouse was miles from the river. The street led into a broad thoroughfare, the Zitna, which ran through botanical gardens to another street, the Myslikova, before reaching the embankment. The Stepanska, down which I had originally fled, also ran into this complex: I could imagine the activity there while I had lain quietly in the stuffy darkness watching Wenceslas.

We walked under the linden trees past the bathing platform and the three islands to the Charles bridge. There seemed to be no check of any kind but my rising spirits were damped somewhat by the old man's growing suspicion that we were going the wrong way. There were now increasing numbers of national costumes, all moving in the opposite direction.

'They're coming away from the Malostranske, countryman. Are you sure you got the instructions right?'

'Yes, yes. I'm sure. A square near the Mostecka is what they told me.'

'Couldn't it have been the Mezibranska? That would be back by the museum, you see. That would be at the beginning of the parade, countryman. It sounds more likely.'

'No, no,' I said doggedly. 'Malostranske is what they said.'

'What about all these people then? Don't you recognize any of them? Over there, look – isn't that a Moravian costume? That'll be from somewhere near Brno. Shouldn't I stop and ask them, countryman?'

'You must do what you want,' I said, suppressing a powerful urge to stuff his cap in his mouth and bundle him briskly along in my arms. 'I know what my instructions are. Just put me on my road, countryman, and I'll be obliged to you.'

This sort of thing went on until we reached the Malostranske, where the caretaker held my arm, gasping and wheezing – I had walked at a swift pace up the steep Mostecka. 'There, countryman, there! Not a sign of a rally, look. You must have mistaken it. Let's get back quickly now.'

'I can't understand it,' I said, shaking my head stubbornly and gazing rapidly about the square. 'What about the other side of the square?'

'Nothing, countryman, nothing at all there. Come quickly now. We'll never get back in time.'

'And that little street?' I said, my heart suddenly leaping. I had glimpsed the Union Jack fluttering limply in the morning breeze. 'Doesn't that lead anywhere?'

'Ah, that's only the Thunovska. It's a cul-de-sac. There's just one of the foreign embassies there. Come, countryman, everybody's leaving.'

But everybody wasn't leaving. I had looked for them, and now I saw them. Four men, two on each corner, stood by the entrance to the Thunovska. Even at this distance one could discern the characteristic poe-faced look of the S.N.B. They turned to stare at us as we stood wrangling in the square. I was suddenly sharply aware that I was wearing the cap and jacket of Vaclav Borsky. I said, 'Perhaps you're right, countryman, let's go,' and we turned and went back down the Mostecka.

Even though I had expected the Embassy to be covered my spirits had swiftly sunk. With four men commanding the entrance to the narrow cul-de-sac it had been obvious at a glance that I wasn't going to get in by merely walking in. But at least I had spied out the lay of the land. At some point I would have to return. The journey had not been wasted.

The problem of my return to the Malostranske, nerve-racking as it was, was not, however, so immediately urgent as two others that now sprang to mind. There was the question of Vaclav Borsky's clothes. Excellent cover on a weekday, they constituted on this day of high festival an all too obvious solecism. Like the caretaker, everyone in the street was got up in his best.

Once the parade started I would be jammed stationary in the crowd, an easy mark in my cap and plastic jacket for roving eyes.

The second problem was the caretaker, now deeply intent on handing me over as soon as possible to my compatriots from Brno. It seemed only a matter of time before he encountered the right group. I would have to give him the slip.

The opportunity came at the next cross-roads, a busy intersection jammed with people. I clapped the caretaker on the back, and, with a rustic cackle of 'I see them, countryman, I see them – wait here for me,' at once crossed the road, waving my hand and walking very fast for a hundred yards. I cut across the intersection, re-crossed the road, and looked back. The caretaker was patiently watching, staring in the wrong direction. I continued down the street, found that it ran into the Narodni Trida, and here took stock of the situation.

It was now a quarter past ten and the parade was due to start at eleven. It was plain that I must stay with the crowds, just as plain that I should not be trapped immovably in the Vaclavske Namesti. A single stand farther down the street indicated that the parade would come down here, the fact that it was only a single stand that less dense crowds were expected. The Narodni Trida seemed to be the place for me.

There were two or three automats down the street, only one, the largest, open. I hovered near it. There was bound to be a rush for food after the parade. I thought I'd better be among the first.

It was already growing warm and my feet had begun to ache again. I padded there and back in front of the automat. The street was filling up, the fatigue of jostling crowds coming on me again like toothache. I was sick to death with them. I wished they would get the damned thing over. I wondered when I was going to be able to sit down again and how I would fill up the rest of the day. It stretched before me, hours and hours of it, hot and complicated and dangerous.

It was forty-five minutes before the first contingents came marching round from the Vaclavske Namesti. The loud-speakers had been announcing their progress for the last fifteen of them, and excitement had been building up steadily in the cavernous Narodni Trida. Between the steep and sombre buildings the red banners hung. Garlands and slogans criss-crossed the road; the pavements seethed. As the first line of bob-bobbing flags turned the corner, the whole street seemed to ignite and roar like a forest fire.

There were a hundred thousand marchers, peasants in costume, hearty girls in gym slips, factory workers in overalls, sokols in white vests swinging their gymnastic clubs. They chanted as they marched, a dozen different jingles roaring in the seething street.

> *Ceskoslovensko is our land,*
> *We want no other,*
> *Socialism is our creed,*
> *Every man our brother.*
> *NAZDAR!*

Nazdar! cried the hysterical announcer over the loud-speakers every half minute. *Nazdar!* cried the marchers. *Nazdar!* echoed the crowds.

> *Fight for peace and down with war,*
> *Goodwill to all nations,*
> *Marx and Lenin show the way,*
> *Comrades, Action Stations!*
> *NAZDAR!*

There was an appalling row going on, the street roaring and baying rhythmically as the river of marchers flowed on; garlands flying through the air, flags waving, an occasional hand and brain rushing out into the street to embrace the marchers. The girl assistants from the automat had come rushing out to watch. I kept on the move, never straying far from them.

A large float came trundling down presently, decked with flowers and paper doves. A battalion of laughing amazons on board were tossing the cargo to the crowds, who enthusiastically flung it back. The parade seemed to be nearing its end. The assistants went back into the automat. I took my station outside, stepping from one aching foot to the other and watching for the first sign of a movement of customers. When it came, I was in like a trivet.

I took my seat with a gasp of relief. It was painfully obvious I wouldn't be able to stay on my feet all day. I was weary all over, every bone aching, my stomach still stiff from the beating-up in the hotel. I would have to find somewhere to lie out, the botanical gardens or a park, perhaps. The sun was beating down fiercely outside. It might be possible to divest myself of Vaclav Borsky's cap and jacket and acquire others.

I had a cup of coffee and a sandwich, and over it was smitten by inspiration. My eyes had been attracted to a poster on the wall. Below a picture of a serious looking man in a bathing cap was the legend *Swimming is Healthy*, and under that *Visit Zluta Plovarna*. Zluta Plovarna! I was amazed I hadn't thought of it before. With one stretched-out body looking like another, it was the ideal place to stay anonymous. There would also be a large variety of unattached clothing.

I tried to remember how they ordered the disposal of clothing at Zluta Plovarna. There was a bit of business with an arm-band....

I finished my coffee and left.

It was twenty past one, the white and glaring deadspot of the afternoon. The street was like an oven even in the shade of the shops. The sun blinds flapped and rattled dryly in the hot breeze from the river. There were few people about. It might not have been such a good idea to leave so early. I wondered if the watchers were out in the street.

I walked slowly down to the embankment, stiffer than ever but keeping a wary eye open. I didn't think I would be able to run very far or very fast if they came for me now. Some vital damage seemed to have been done to my stomach. It caught me every time I breathed. Not, I thought, that this would be anything to what would happen if they laid hands on me again.

The thought was so peculiarly horrible in the hot afternoon that I actually managed to hobble a bit faster, and got down to the tram stop just as half past one was striking.

Despite the emptiness of the streets, there was the usual queue for the tram. I elbowed my way on to a number twenty-one and stood all the way, emerging so dazed and weak at the other end that I had stumbled almost to the entrance of the bathing station before I pulled myself together a bit and looked the place over.

It looked safe enough. It was hard to tell. I remembered it clearly from my last visit. Two old women, heads protected by newspaper cones, sat at turnstiles in a wicket fence. Farther back, grass sloped down to the river. It was early yet, too soon after the parade for large crowds to be here. A bit of picnicking was going on. A few young men and girls were splashing about at the river's edge. A few children were in the water. There seemed to be nobody standing around watching.

The gritty street was swooning in the heat. I took my place in the queue of people from the tram, went through the clicking turnstile and over to the changing huts. There was a sweaty shed with piles of wire baskets. I hired a pair of drawers and a towel, was given a basket by the old crone in charge, and went off to one of the huts to change.

In the hut, I locked the door and painfully undressed, saying goodbye, one by one, to Vaclav Borsky's cap and jacket and Josef's trousers. I took everything out of the pockets and wrapped them in the towel. I got into the shorts and examined my stomach. There was nothing to see, no discoloration even. A little cracked mirror was hanging on the door and I inspected my face in it. The nose was slightly reddened, as if by the sun. Not a lot to show for a beating-up by the S.N.B. I wondered if anyone would believe me. I wondered if I'd ever have the opportunity to try and make anyone believe me, and sighing to my reflection, loaded the wire basket and went out to the sweaty shed.

The old crone took the basket and handed me a red rubber tag with a number on it. I slipped it on my wrist and went out on to the grass. It was long and green and luxuriant from the rain and I found a spot under half shade and sank down in it.

In the heat of the early afternoon there was a slow-motion dream-like quality about the bathing station. Willows waved gently against the sky. The river glooped and gurgled between its banks. Voices droned like bees on the air, and over the grass the sound of gramophone music wafted thinly.

All this was so exactly what was called for that I lay back with a faint moan and closed my eyes and floated away in the bland honey light, stomach easing, limbs twitching remotely, nothing at all in the world but the cool lushness of grass and the drifting sibilance of water.

There was something else in the world, of course; but no hurry yet, I thought, coming back after a little while. Rest. Recuperate. Restore the tissues for the lunatic business at the Malostranske tonight....

When I woke up, the sweat was pouring off me and I was in full sun. The place had filled up. I sat up, licking my lips, and gazed about me. I was hemmed in on all sides. Thousands of them, chattering, knitting, eating, drying off children, thumping about with balls. I looked at my watch. Five o'clock. I had slept nearly three hours. I was dry as hell. There were tables outside the café now, and people sitting with drinks. I picked up the towel and went over there.

I bought myself an ice-cold Pilsener and drank it right off in the café and then bought another and took the long misted glass out to one of the tables and sat down. I ran a hand over my stomach. A slight soreness; nothing to bother about. The sleep in the open air had done me good. I felt fine, relaxed, a new man.

I lit a cigarette and smoked it, gazing around at the animated scene. One of these characters must be around my size. Before

170

I had dozed off, I had the germ of an idea how to switch arm bands. It came back to me now, ready-made.

Dusk would be coming on at around seven o'clock. I thought I'd better be at the Malostranske then to watch anyone who might be popping in or out of the Embassy for dinner. I didn't know who actually lived at the Embassy or if this kind of activity took place on Sunday night. There was a lot to be found out.

I finished off the cigarette, marvelling how even a type so essentially unheroic as myself could attune himself so swiftly to danger. I had no idea where I would sleep tonight. The chances were rather better than average that I would be picked up, beaten up, maimed, killed even; certainly not allowed to leave the country. I seemed to have ingested all this murderous data like some electronic brain and to have made the necessary compensations to restore equilibrium. I thought I must have become warier, better organized mentally. Certainly my planning, such as it was, was now all fore-shortened: I had to prepare only for the hour or two ahead.

I thought I'd better get on with it.

I stubbed out my cigarette and went and bought an essential bottle of sun lotion at the shop. I then strolled back over the grass, weaving in and out between the groups, stepping over recumbent figures, and suddenly almost dropped with shock and turned and made swiftly in the opposite direction.

I had seen Vlasta.

There was no possible doubt about it. She was lying on the grass, leaning on one elbow facing me. She was in her black sharkskin two-piece, talking moodily to a man whose back was to me. Her magnificent breasts alone would have been unmistakable in any crowd.

I loped quickly away, nerves jangling. The one person in the whole of Prague who could identify me as easily undressed as dressed! I tripped over an old man smoking a calabash pipe and went full length on the grass and picked myself up, swearing with nervousness, and scrambled on again to the other side of the bathing station.

The people were as thick on the ground here as at the opposite end, and I stepped slowly among them, nerves still jumpy, looking for the right type. This was not an operation that could be hurried. Feet and neck size were at least as important as any other dimension. In addition I wanted someone who was on his own, and not too quick on the uptake.

It took me a few minutes to find him, a young stringy character with a forehead so narrow it was hardly there. He was lying flat on his back and sleeping soundly with his mouth wide open. I stretched out beside him. There was not fraction of an inch difference in height. His legs were apart, toes pointing upwards, and I carefully measured my feet against his. We might have been twins.

There was a thin film of sweat all over his face and body and he was sleeping so soundly he might have been dead. The open mouth and rudimentary forehead suggested promising qualities. His armband was a few inches up his wrist. I thought I'd better get it over with quickly.

I took off my own armband, lit a cigarette and pressed it unhurriedly against his wrist. He came right up off the grass like a leaping salmon, and with a single profound oath began hopping about staring at his wrist in consternation.

I said, 'What is it? What's the trouble, comrade?'

'I been shot,' he said. 'I been blank blank well shot.'

'Let me see. Give it here, comrade.'

He was hissing slightly, hugging the wrist to his chest like an only child. I prised it away. A fleck of white ash showed immediately below the armband. I said, 'Ah, it's just a burn. I must have done it with my cigarette. Here, we'll soon fix it up. I've got some lotion. We'll just get this off,' I said, quickly stripping off his armband and dropping it on the grass. I poured some of the lotion on to my handkerchief, dabbed his wrist and gave him the wrong armband back, all with some speed and talking incessantly before he had gathered his scattered wits.

'There. That'll be all right now, comrade. It's only a little burn. You won't feel it in a minute.'

'I can bloody well feel it now,' he said truculently.

'I'm sorry, comrade. I didn't even notice.'

'I thought I been shot. I was fast asleep! You want to watch what you're doing,' he said. There was a lowering look about him. It seemed tactless to offer him a cigarette. There didn't seem to be anything else I could offer him. I apologized again, picked up my things and walked off with his armband.

I worked cautiously round to the shed, watching out for Vlasta. She was lying in the same position on one elbow. I wondered if the man was her father. He looked big enough.

There was a queue in the shed, and the old crone was shuffling about in a temper. She snatched the armband from me. I waited with some interest to inspect my new wardrobe. She was unaccountably smiling when she returned.

'Had a good day?'

'Very nice, thanks.'

She dumped the wire basket on the counter. 'We ordered the right weather for you, anyway.'

'Yes. Yes, you did,' I said, wondering what all this was about; and suddenly caught sight of what was in the basket and felt my toes curling up.

'What's up? It's the right one, isn't it? Nine three eight,' she said, shuffling about with the basket, and examined the armband again. 'There's no mistake, is there?'

'No, no mistake,' I said and picked up the basket and moved off in a trance.

'Wait. There's your hat. I hung it up,' she said, bringing the thing over. 'We don't want to spoil the lovely feather, do we?'

It was a little cockeyed green thing like a demented midget bowler. There was an enormous peacock feather hanging from the side. She put it on my head, and I said, 'Thank you,' bloodlessly, and walked off to the changing huts.

I thought the caretaker, at least, would be satisfied. I'd won myself a national costume.

3

I stepped off the tram like a cripple in the gigantic jackboots. Each seemed to weigh about a ton. I was wearing baggy trousers, an embroidered blouse, a little red bolero with brass buttons and a large rosette. I had scrambled into this lunatic assortment as quickly as possible, terrified its owner would soon be claiming it. I didn't know if I'd got any of it on properly, but it seemed to be effective. In the tram there had been kindly smiles. A woman had even got up to give me her seat.

I clumped along the embankment numb with horror, wondering what I should do if I met a party in the same get-up. Luckily, dusk was falling.

I was bang on schedule, anyway.

It was a quarter to seven. Across the river the floodlit palaces on the Heights winked in the uncertain light. Below the linden trees the crowds shuffled, murmuring. The lights in the branches cast a greenish aura. As I crossed the bridge the loud-speakers came on suddenly, Smetana's *My Homeland*, liquid and mournful across the darkling, flowing Vltava.

There was a shifting mass of people in the Malostranske. I dawdled nearer the entrance. A church – St Mikulase, I remembered suddenly from childhood – had its cupola levitating in floodlighting, as though trying to cast off from its centuries-old but now ungrateful anchorage. I dawdled near the entrance to the Thunovska and saw them still there, two on each corner, not talking, just looking. I slowly gravitated nearer. No one seemed to be coming in or out of the Thunovska. A single light shone in the cul-de-sac. The buildings were in darkness.

After half an hour an open-necked man wheeling a bicycle came out of the Thunovska. He was stopped for his papers. Ten minutes later, he went back again. He was again stopped for his papers. My heart sank. It seemed almost utterly hopeless.

I stepped from one foot to another, wondering what the hell I should do. My mind was made up for me almost immediately. One of the S.N.B. men walked over.

'Waiting for someone?'

My lips seemed to be stuck together. I mumbled, 'Yes. Yes. My comrades.'

'Where are you from?'

'Banska Bystrica.' That's what it said in the papers in the pocket of the bolero.

'Your papers.'

I handed them over.

The S.N.B. man glanced at them and handed them back. His nod was not unfriendly, but he had a good look at me. He sauntered away.

I stood there for a further few minutes, trembling all over, but afraid to attract attention by moving too soon. I waited till the clocks struck eight, then ambled across the square and got to hell out of it as quickly as possible.

I had no idea what to do. I knew I had to keep away now from other national costumes and the police. The peasant and his friends would be looking out for me. I walked aimlessly on and presently found myself in the Ujezd. Svoboda had his offices here. I thought I remembered a kavarna somewhere nearby, and when I saw its lights dimly shining, turned in there, too distracted to think on my feet any longer.

The place was empty. An old woman served me with a large slivovitz, and I tossed it down and ordered another and took it to a small table. As I sat down the landlord appeared.

'Well, countryman,' he said convivially, 'a fine day, eh?'

'Yes. Yes.'

'You won't forget it in a hurry.'

'I won't,' I said sincerely.

'Slipped away from your comrades for a quick drink?'

'That's it.'

He wiped the table and sat down. 'What time do you go?'

'Go?' I said; but understood him entirely in that deliberating moment. Countrymen came. Countrymen would have to go. Trainloads of them. There wouldn't be a national costume in the whole of Prague tomorrow. Except one.

'You all go back tonight, don't you?'

'Yes. Yes. Not for a bit yet.'

'You'll have tramped a few miles today, eh? You look bushed.'

'I think I'd like another slivovitz,' I said bleakly.

He went to get it and I sat, lumpen in my boots and my

bolero, seeing the end of the line close in sight. I couldn't risk another night of dodging up and down alleys. There could be no question of showing myself out of doors tomorrow. I had to go to earth now. I needed a place to rest and eat. I needed a friend now.

I suppose the idea had been there ever since I'd seen her, a last desperate expedient. I felt in my pocket for my wallet. My diary was there, her number still scribbled in it. The landlord came back with the slivovitz and I drank it quickly and left.

There was a telephone box farther along and I went in and rang the number. I wondered if her father was with her. I thought if a man answered I would hang up right away, and waited, heart thudding.

A man didn't answer. Nobody answered. The phone went on ringing for three minutes. I hung up and went out into the street and stood there in the dark with a feeling of sick desolation, trying to think just what there was for me to do. I couldn't hang about here. I couldn't stay in Prague. I would soon be the only peasant left in the place. I thought I'd better get over there to Barrandov, while I was able to, and wait for her.

I set off, walking, keeping to the darker side of the street, the feathered hat in my hand.

It was getting on for half past nine when I approached the terraces, glittering in the dark. There was a dance on, figures twirling on the several levels, dance music beating out. Across the road, a hundred yards or so beyond, was the rustic seat where I had sat with her and just beside it – I had forgotten it – the telephone box. I went in the box and rang her again. There was still no reply.

I left the box and went on to the house, hugging the shrubbery. The side road was in pitch darkness. There was no light in the house. I waited on the corner for a few minutes, but there was no cover here. I wondered if Vlasta herself was being watched, if they had discovered that I had taken her out and spent the night with her, my only contact. It seemed best to get back to the shrubbery again.

There was a thicket near the telephone box. I crawled into it, and sat down on the ground to wait. A few couples came and went from the dance. A bit of hanky panky went on on the seat. I nosed out from time to time when the coast was clear.

I called her twice more from the box. The last time, at a quarter to twelve, she answered.

I said in English, 'Vlasta, it's Nicolas. Nicolas Whistler.'

'Nicolas! What are you doing here?'

'Is anybody with you, Vlasta? Is your father there?'

'No. No. I am all alone. Nicolas, this is wonderful. I don't understand . . .'

'I'll explain everything when I see you. Can I come along now?'

'But, *milacek*, of course. I was just going to bed. Ah, this is wonderful.'

'Well, carry on to bed. Don't wait up for me. Put the lights out.'

'But of course I will wait up for you! How long will you . . .'

'Vlasta, please do as I say. I don't want to attract attention. I don't know how long I'll be.'

'Ah, so. Well, then, I will leave the door open. Just push it. I will be waiting for you, *milacek*.'

I put the phone down, grinning with relief, and went out into the street.

As luck would have it, a couple were lying on the grass at the entrance to the side road. I went back to the shrubbery and waited for them to go.

Thirty minutes later they were still at it.

It was getting on for half past twelve and the moon was well up when I at last went down the side road. I stopped before the gates, watching and listening. The place was in darkness, silent as the grave.

The gate creaked a little as I opened it. I crunched softly up the gravel path.

As she'd said, the door was open. I pushed it and went in.

Chapter 11

1

She had not gone to bed. She was waiting for me in a dressing gown in the living-room. There was a little table lamp on, the curtains securely drawn, and she was lying smoking a cigarette on the divan.

She had her eye on the door, and sat up sharply when I came in.

'Who is it?'

'It's me, Vlasta. Nicolas.'

She sprang up. 'Nicolas. What are you — what clothes have you got on?'

She stretched out her hands to hold me at arm's length, goggling.

'It's a hell of a long story. Vlasta, do you have such a thing as a drink?'

Now I was inside, in safety, in the warm, dimly lit room, the reaction had come on. I felt myself beginning to tremble.

She threw her arms round me, the long, sombre face twisting loosely with a smile at the curious sight I must have presented. '*Milacek*, of course. You look so funny. You're tired, Come, sit down.'

I was sitting even before she'd told me, sinking heavily back on the divan. She looked curiously at me, but asked no further questions and went to get a bottle and two glasses.

She poured me an enormous glass of slivovitz, which I drank immediately.

'Another?'

'Please.'

I took a little of it and sat back again, sighing and uncoiling as the neat spirit exploded wonderfully inside me. She lit a cigarette and placed it in my mouth and I inhaled deeply and closed my eyes, wondering how the hell to begin.

'Vlasta, has anyone been asking you about me?'

'No. No. Why should they?'

'When is your father returning?'

'Wednesday, perhaps. He is giving a concert in Bratislava.'

'You're not expecting anyone to visit you here?'

'No. Nicolas, what is it?'

I said, 'Vlasta, I'm in serious trouble. I need your help.'

She drew the dressing gown more tightly around her. She looked not exactly frightened but a shade reserved. 'What is it you want me to do?'

'I've got to hide, Vlasta. I want you to let me stay here.'

'What is it you've done?'

'It might be better if you knew nothing about it.'

'Is it – something against the State?'

'In a way.'

She said quietly, 'You're not a spy, Nicolas?'

'No, Vlasta. Not really. It's very complicated to explain. I need to get in touch with the British Embassy. I've tried already but the place is covered by S.N.B. men.'

'S.N.B.' She stubbed out her cigarette, gazing at me. 'How serious would it be for us – for my father and me – if they found you had stayed here?'

'It could be very serious indeed. But I've got nowhere else to go, Vlasta. I've just got to have a night's rest. I've been on the run for two days. They'll kill me if they catch me. I'll go to-morrow if you want me to.'

The Slav temperament is built to respond to melodrama. She was deeply touched. She leant over me with her heavy breasts and took my head. '*Milacek*, of course you will stay. Tonight, anyway. You're exhausted. Maybe it isn't so bad. We'll think of something. You will tell me about it.'

I had no intention of telling her about it. It seemed to me the fewer people who knew the better. The whole episode was so grotesque the effort of explaining it once only would be quite enough.

'Have you eaten?'

'I don't want anything.'

She refilled my glass and took one herself, and we sat there on the divan in silence. With the third glass of slivovitz the dim room was showing its remembered tendency to roll. I thought of the S.N.B. men in the hotel bedroom, of the hours spent trudging in the swarming Vaclavske Namesti, of Vaclav Borsky, and the endless alleys. I remembered how I had spent last night, the damp fug, Wenceslas leaping in the moonlight. It was all, I thought, each and every bit of it, totally unbelievable. A series of horrifying hallucinations in the dim, rolling room.

'*Milacek*, come to bed.'

She was leaning over me, sombrely, nuzzling my face.

'In a minute.'

'It's better in bed. Lie out.'

'Yes.'

'It's no use worrying.'

'No.'

'Maybe I can go to the Embassy for you.'

'Yes.' I was not listening to her, rolling warmly in the rolling room; the statuesque creature no more real than Vaclav Borsky or the S.N.B. As I heard this, however, I swivelled round to gaze at her. 'The Embassy? How do you mean the Embassy? Have you been to the Embassy?'

'But of course. Two or three times a month. Even more often lately. There are many messages because of the forthcoming trade agreement.'

'Well, for God's sake!' I said, seeing in the one moment a whole range of new vistas. A letter from me; a car drawing up one night; myself in the back under a rug. Safe. 'Vlásta, do you think you could do it?'

'I don't know. Why not? It's dangerous?'

Suddenly the telephone rang. I was off the divan and practically in her lap with fright. She stared at me, jaw dropping.

'Who could it be? Your father?'

'I don't know.' She went to answer it. I sat palpitating. It was nearly one o'clock. A damned funny time to ring up. Unless he had just arrived back in town. I strained to listen.

'No, no. No trouble. I wasn't in bed yet. Very well indeed, gracious pane,' she said in Czech. 'He is in Bratislava. On Wednesday I expect him. Certainly I will tell him. Please do not concern yourself. It is nothing at all. Thank you. You are very gracious.'

She slammed down the receiver and came back, face stormy. 'One of his musical friends. They ring at all hours.' She paced around the room angrily, and stopped by me, softening.

'Milacek, stop worrying. You're too tired. Come, we'll go to bed now.'

So we did.

She pulled off my boots, whickering slightly at the bizarre collection of clothing decorating my sparse frame. She had nothing on herself underneath the dressing gown, but with some obscure feeling that seriousness was called for, put on a loose nightie before getting into bed.

As she'd said, it was better in bed. The sheer voluptuousness of it, the massive, well-remembered embrace, took me in a breath far from the horror.

'You've stopped thinking about it?' she said in my ear after a moment.

'Trying to.'

'Too tired to think about anything else?'

'Pretty tired.'

She gave me a mournful hug.

I sank into a dreamless doze, and drifted awake, and dozed, and woke again, ear warmly damp with her breath. 'Still too tired?' the husky voice said softly, at some time. The slivovitz, the soft warmth, the rolling curtain of sleep, had destroyed all strain, all knowledge, all identity in the darkness.

I don't know what I said, but in a trice she had whipped off the nightie. Just for a moment, as she came swarming down again, I remembered where I was supposed to be tonight. Bournemouth, my mother, Maura. All a long way away. A world away. Far, far away from the breathy blackness of Barrandov.

I don't know how much later it was when I woke up again. She was sleeping softly with her head in the crook of my neck. The slivovitz had left me gravely parched, and I licked my lips, seeing the situation with sudden clarity in that moment.

Her father was coming back Wednesday. I had two days here. Two days in which the police would have no sign or news of me, no abandoned clothing, no Borskys left lying about.

They would have to face three possibilities: (a) that despite the national costume I was somehow managing to sleep out and to steal food; (b) that I had slipped out of Prague; (c) that someone was sheltering me. Of them all, only the last was a probability. The question would then be who was likely to do so. Cunliffe would have passed on the information that I had no contacts left in Prague – I recalled that he had asked me specifically about this. That meant I had either made some, or had somehow managed to get in touch with the Embassy.

The fact that no questions had been asked of Vlasta indicated that this contact at least was unknown. After all, she'd been circumspect about it. She'd declined to have dinner with me at the hotel that first visit. I was pretty sure I'd not been followed when I went out with her. It was a fact that the S.N.B. men had been genuinely unaware of my movements when I dashed from the hotel. That seemed to indicate that I'd never been followed. They had been pretty sure of me.

All in all, it seemed to me, they would be driven to the conclusion that I was being sheltered by one of the Embassy staff. So they would watch the Embassy staff. They would watch their homes and their cars. All this was going to be a headache at some stage. The snags would have to be indicated in my letter. They would also – it was only fair – have to be indicated to Vlasta.

I had begun to stir about a bit in the bed with this appraisal of the situation. The gorgeous giantess moved murmurously at my side.

'Vlasta.'

'*Milacek.*'

'I've been thinking of. what you said, Vlasta, about going to the Embassy.'

'Yes, *milacek*. Later. We'll talk of it later.'

'I think we should talk of it now. You'll have to get up in a few hours.'

She flung one arm around me in a hug that drove the breath from my body, and sleepily sat up and put the bedside light on. She regarded me sombrely. 'You want to get to the Embassy as soon as possible, little merchant.'

'That's the idea.'

'Then this is the last time we'll be together.' Her wondrous torso stood out in the lamplight. She leaned massively and mournfully against me. 'You'll never come back again. Never. Never.'

'No, well,' I said plaintively. 'Vlasta, there are things I've got to tell you.'

She planted a kiss on each side of my nose. 'Well then, Nicolas,' she said with a sigh, 'tell me.'

This I proceeded to do in a revised, edited, and severely expurgated version. I told her I had come to Prague for Pavelka to learn confidentially of the glass process he had initiated; that I'd had to come back again to learn of a new development, and that this second time the police had learned what I was doing, necessitating flight and several disguises.

She was frowning when I finished. 'It sounds serious, certainly,' she said. 'But they wouldn't kill you for that. You are too nervous, my Nicolas.'

I ground my teeth a little. 'There were a couple of things I didn't mention. There was a *formula*,' I said earnestly. 'You don't need to know about that. The point is they're looking for me, and my only hope is to get to the Embassy.'

'So. And you wish me to go for you. Yes, *milacek*.'

I didn't think she was quite on wavelength. She was looking in a certain way at my nose as though about to return to her main preoccupation. I said, 'I want you to take a letter there, Vlasta. I want them to try and smuggle me in, in a car. I don't want the car to come here, do you understand? I'll have to get out of here.'

'Yes, yes. We can arrange everything. There's plenty of time yet. It's not so serious.'

I ground my teeth again. The girl was proving quite exceptionally tiresome. I seriously considered rolling about with her for a bit to wake her up; but persevered once more. 'It is damnably serious, Vlasta. I'm trying very hard to save my life. I've got to put all this in a rather complicated letter, which I should be writing now. But I had to tell you the main details. Do you think you understand?'

'Yes, I understand. You do not wish to bring danger to this house.'

'You're sure you can get to the Embassy tomorrow – today?'

'Monday is not a busy day. I should be able to manage.'

'You go right inside, do you?'

'To the reception desk.'

'Is it an Englishman at the desk?'

'No. A Czech.'

'Does he open whatever it is you normally take there?'

'I don't think so. I don't know.'

'Could you get hold of a Glass Board envelope and write "Urgent, Personal, For the Ambassador's Attention Only" on it?'

'I think so. Yes, yes, I think so.' She had woken up a bit now, and seemed abreast of the situation. Her mournful eyes were blinking slowly and thoughtfully. She absently scratched one bomb-like breast. She got up presently and put on her dressing gown and loped about gathering writing materials and a suit of her father's. After this she went into the kitchen and made coffee.

I sat up in bed, smoking, and enumerating all the things that could go wrong. I was aware of a feeling of deep but shame-faced gratitude to the immense creature. Apart from her initial reservations at the dangers to her father and herself, she had not stinted her help or her generous affections. She could very easily end up in a concentration camp. I found myself liking her very much indeed. I got out of bed and slipped on the peasant trousers and walked through to the kitchen. She was standing by the gas stove waiting for the coffee to heat, and I took her somewhat awkwardly by the shoulders and kissed her on the neck.

She leaned back against me but did not turn or speak. I kissed her again, gently, and felt her shoulders begin to shake. I realized with alarm that she was crying.

'Vlasta.'

She shook her head.

'What is it, Vlasta?'

'It's nothing. It's the last I'll see of you,' she said.

'Oh, now, Vlasta,' I said awkwardly. 'Maybe we'll meet again. You'll always be in my thoughts.' If only I get to hell out of here, I thought; if only I'm left with any thoughts to think; but touched all the same.

She took a handkerchief out of her dressing gown pocket and blew her nose sadly. 'Write your letter, Nicolas.'

I went to the drawing room and began writing on the divan, and presently she came in with the coffee and sat over me.

'You're copying out your passport number?'

I was, together with every other bit of personal information that would make the crazy rigmarole even faintly believable.

She watched me for a bit. 'And the formula? You're putting that in?'

'No,' I said briefly, not even allowing myself to think of the impossibility of explaining this to her.

'I don't mind taking it, Nicolas. There is no danger to me. Don't think about me.'

'I'm not, Vlasta. There isn't a formula. It doesn't exist.'

'I don't want you to tell me anything you don't want to.'

'Right,' I said; and was presently aware that the divan was shaking slightly. She was crying again. 'Ah, Vlasta, what is it?'

She put her head on my shoulders, sobbing quietly but powerfully. I put my arm awkwardly round her.

'You're thinking only of me. You say they'll kill you if they find this thing.'

'No, no, Vlasta. It isn't like that. I haven't got the damned thing.'

'I love you, *milacek*. I hate myself for not being able to help you more.'

'You can't help me any more than you are doing.'

'I can't bear to think of you in danger in this terrible country, little merchant. Let me share it with you. Let me take this thing for you.'

I rolled my eyes horribly. There was a degree of obtuseness about this otherwise splendid girl that made all normal communications impossible. I said wearily, 'Dearest Vlasta, I haven't got the formula. It isn't of any importance. I'm telling you the truth.'

She looked at me through tear-stained eyes. 'You only say this to comfort me, *milacek*. Who else would you have given it to? There was only the old person your nanny, and she is dead. The husband? Would you trust him more than me because he is a man?'

'No, of course I wouldn't. I can't even remember him. Vlasta . . .' It was useless, of course, but I made the effort. 'That formula, Vlasta. It wasn't the right one. It was something else. I got rid of it. I've forgotten it. All I want to do now is get to the Embassy. You're the only one who can help me do that. You can't do more, Vlasta. Please believe me, *milacek*.'

I had talked myself into a state of some emotion, and now fell to covering her ample, tear-stained face with kisses. I was not sure if she believed me, her mournful eyes indicating only recognition of large areas of nobility in my protestations.

It was now four o'clock and she had to be up at seven. I could finish the letter in the morning. I got back into bed with her.

Between the sheets she was still fearful and massively emotive. I felt suddenly shaken and unsure of myself. There was a lowering keening quality about her murmurous embrace that was unnerving. But it wasn't that, I thought. Something else; some factor that I hadn't bargained for. It hung about, cloud-like, on the fringe of consciousness. I tried to identify it; couldn't. Presently I went off to sleep in her arms, still troubled.

The tall S.N.B. man had got me up against the wardrobe and I couldn't move. I knew he was going to hit me again. He'd got hold of my chin with one hand, and he was going to smash it with the other. He was looking at me thoughtfully, without malice, and I could hear myself grunting with the effort to shift my head. The sweat was pouring down my face. I was bleeding and sick, and it was going on and on, with the other one, the little one, waiting quietly to go on with his interrogation. But I couldn't stand any more. I couldn't stand being hit again. My neck felt stiff and half broken against the wardrobe, but I thought I'll break it, I don't care, he mustn't hit me again, and I wrenched my neck sideways and broke it and got away, swam away, threshed away out of the room and into the blackness of Barrandov.

Her elbow was under my chin. I had somehow kicked away from her in my nightmare. She was sleeping heavily in the perspiring bed, and I lay there for a moment thinking, *Oh God, still night time. Which night?* the interrogation still going on and on in my mind. *Who did you give it to? You'll have to tell us. Now or later, as you please. We know you gave it to someone. Who is it you trust more than us? Did you give it to the husband of the old person, your nanny?*

But no, I thought, heart sickly beating, that was Vlasta, not the interrogators; the obtuse girl going on and on about it. Everybody going on and on about the bloody formula. And I didn't care about the formula. It should be obvious I didn't care about the formula. Why should I care about it with my life at stake? There was some great mass delusion in this insane country. They all thought alike. Maybe this was how their own nationals would behave. Hanging on at all costs to the formula, the slogan, the message, the chant.

The big uncomplicated creature slept heavily beside me, unknowable, Slav, wanting to get away from the country but part of it, her reactions the same. Wanting to suffer, to have her steadfastness tested; with some new element added, some hand-

and-brain element that thirsted to be trusted as a comrade. Would I not trust her as much as the husband of the old person my nanny, because he was a man?

But wait, wait, I thought, heart still sickly beating. Who said anything about this old person my nanny? Who the hell so much as mentioned this old person?

I thought back frenziedly over each and every conversation with the girl. No nannies. No occasion when nannies might have arisen. With sudden sinking recognition, I realized what had troubled me before I went off to sleep.

This girl knew something about me that I had never told her.

I thought, Oh, God, no. Something gravely wrong here; and in the same moment saw a whole series of other wrong things. This spacious bungalow just for her father and herself in a town where space was at a premium. The telephone call at one o'clock in the morning. Her insistence on the bloody formula.

I sat wildly up in the bed. In an instant she was wide awake beside me. She had not moved. The quality of her breathing had merely changed. I saw now that it must have been like this the other time. I felt my teeth begin to chatter. I put one foot out of bed.

'What is it, *milacek*?'

'Toilet.'

'You know where the light is.'

I knew where the light was. I went in, trembling, but didn't switch it on, imagining the police camped out there. A hell of a lot of things had come flashing to mind. Her tears; the old Slav keening quality that had come into her voice. She had become fond of me in her way, I thought, but it wouldn't stop her doing whatever she had to do. I had walked right into it.

I sat nervelessly on the lavatory seat, shivering in the draught from the open window, and wondered what the hell to do now. It was growing light outside. I had taken off my watch and left it on the bedside table. Five, six o'clock? She'd be getting up soon. No prospect of escape this time. The instant she was out they'd be in to nab me. That mysterious telephone call ... checking up that all was well. And all had been well; *milacek* installed and ready to perform and spill the beans. But what beans? What had I been expected to spill to the girl that they couldn't knock out of me in half an hour?

I held my head in my hands and racked my weary brain.

'Are you all right, *milacek*?'

I came off the lavatory seat as if it had caught fire.

'Quite all right.'

I washed my hands and went back in the room. She had the bedside light on and was sitting up moodily rubbing her breasts in the draught from the open door.

'You're so restless, *milacek*. You're worrying still.'

'Just a bit.'

'Was it anything else you wanted to tell me?'

'No,' I said, getting into bed; but in the same moment saw that indeed there was.

The formula! The unspeakable, unmentionable, thrice-cursed formula! That was it. They genuinely didn't know what had happened to it. There had been a fatal gap in the reconnaissance system when I had dashed from the hotel. There was just a possibility – it could be no more than a possibility – that I had hidden it somewhere, passed it on to someone. They could knock me about and find out. But I had proved slippery enough already. Here was an easier way. One night with the insatiable giantess, with the illusion of safety, and I would tell her everything.

The tireless creature had thrown her arms round me again and was nibbling my cheek. '*Milacek*, why are you so worried? You don't trust me enough.'

'I do, Vlasta, I do,' I said, and sighed. 'It's just that – I'm beginning to doubt if the Embassy will believe that letter. They'll think it a trick.'

'What else is there?'

'Just one thing . . . I daren't ask you to do it.'

'Nicolas, Nicolas. I've told you a thousand times, I'll do anything.'

I paused, heart beating in a sick sort of way. I thought she must feel it thumping there under her supercharged superstructure. 'It's that formula, Vlasta. I didn't destroy it. It's a lot more important than I am. And it could just save me. That's something they would have to believe. If only you could take it with the letter.'

'*Milacek*, I've been pleading with you to let me take it.'

'You don't understand, Vlasta. I haven't got it. I told you the truth about that at least. It's hidden.'

She was silent. I wondered if I'd ladled it on a bit too thick. She said after a moment, 'You want me to go and get it?'

'No, Vlasta. There are other people involved. You wouldn't get it. I would have to get it myself and meet you in town. And that's why I daren't ask you to do it. If I'm spotted, it would be the end for you, too.'

Again she was silent. She released me, blinking thoughtfully. She said slowly, 'Is this the truth, Nicolas? Is this all that's worrying you?'

'It's enough.'

'It's nothing at all. Oh, I know the police. And the S.N.B.,' she said scornfully. 'I live here, little merchant. Do you think we don't all of us know what they look like!'

'Vlasta, it's dreadful asking you to do this. It's so terribly dangerous.'

'*Milacek*, stop worrying now.'

'But of course,' I said, just in time as she fell on me again, 'if I'm followed anywhere, I'll cancel the plan. I daren't compromise you or my – my colleagues. I'll die before I give anything away.'

This improbable statement gave her fractional pause. She shivered suddenly. 'Forget it now,' she said in my ear. 'Don't worry about anything more, *milacek*,' and returned to her more fundamental preoccupation.

The milkman shattered the last of the night at ten minutes to seven. I had been lying in a sleepless daze for the past half hour listening to him exclaiming to his horse and turning over in my mind a succession of increasingly lunatic plans.

I felt time-worn rather than tired. An enormous number of

things seemed to have happened to me; a roar of events like water over some crumbling fall. Now, I thought, as the milkman holloahed and yoicked, the water had exposed bedrock, gleaming calcified strata to be identified as the essential particulars of Whistler Nicolas. Here were the layers of fraud and deception; here the unsuspected cat-like qualities of survival. Here too, I thought, as the vast slumbrous thing beside me yawned to life, stamina of an even more unsuspected and, in happier times, more useful order.

I shut my eyes as she woke up.

'Nicolas. Time to get up, Nicolas.'

She was clear-eyed, relaxed, a little gay even. It hadn't been a bad night for her, I supposed. She gave me an affectionate buss on the chin and sprang out of bed. I turned out more slowly.

'It's late. I forgot I have an early job this morning. I'll have to make a telephone call,' she said, when she had washed and dressed.

I had been wondering how she would cope with the change of arrangements, and listened with interest as she went to the phone. *'Agnes, I'm afraid I will be late this morning. The early job will have to be put off. No, no, nothing wrong. I'll alter the schedule myself when I come in. There is no need for you to do anything, Agnes dear, nothing at all.'*

I finished the letter in the kitchen while she ate her breakfast, and watched with some fascination her magnificent jungle appetite.

'You know what you've got to do, Vlasta.'

'I am to put this in a Glass Board envelope and mark it "Urgent, Personal, For the Attention of the Ambassador Only".'

'In English, remember. You want me to write it out for you?'

'No, no. I can remember it.'

'And you meet me where?'

'At the Slavia at twelve. If you're not there by ten minutes past, I go away.'

'And then?'

'I am to telephone you here from a call box at two o'clock.

If there is no reply I go back to the Slavia again at five. If you are not there I take the letter as it is to the Embassy without the formula.'

'That's it,' I said. A bit of elaboration had seemed worthwhile. I took both of her hands and looked sincerely into her eyes. She looked sincerely back, champing her jaws. 'I won't try to thank you, Vlasta. You know how I feel. But for both our sakes, keep exactly to the instructions. If I don't keep any of the arrangements, it means the police are on to me. Don't take any chances. Don't hang about. Go right to the Embassy. It means the formula won't exist any longer.'

'You won't let them take it?'

I shook my head slowly. 'They'll never do that, Vlasta. It's on rice paper. I'll eat it.'

Her jaws paused fractionally.

She went ten minutes later. I sat on, smoking a cigarette and staring at her empty plate. She had eaten three slices of cold veal, half a loaf of bread, a dish of sour cream and a large bowl of coffee. Even after everything that had happened this feat still had the power to surprise me. Even after everything that was still to happen, it is the thing I remember best about her. That and a certain smell and a bomb-like shadow on a wall in lamplight.

4

I left the house at half past ten, and realized as I came out into the side street that I had forgotten my watch on the bedside table. I didn't go back for it. It was hot already with the tangy smell coming up off the road. Men were hosing down the *terasy*, and the sun glinted back hard and white off the wet rock. I felt light-headed and momentous, a convict on parole, far from home and blindingly exposed.

I thought I had four or five hours of relative freedom of movement. Over three cups of coffee and four cigarettes I had considered how to use them. I thought I had better find out first how relative the freedom was.

I caught a juddering Skoda bus into town, and changed there to a tram which took me north of the river to the Stromovka district. There was a park here that I had seen advertised, the Julius Fucik Park of Culture and Rest. I went through the park gates and along the main path to the opposite entrance. There were a few gardeners hoeing and hosing; no one else. I paused outside the gates, lit a cigarette, went trudging back. The gardeners did not look up. Nobody had followed me. I left the park and returned to town.

All this took time and was hard on the feet. I had bulked out her father's enormous shoes with two pairs of thick socks. They still slopped up and down, rubbing at my heels. The heat enabled me to carry the jacket over my arm, which was just as well; it fitted me like an overcoat. The trousers had needed turning up four inches and I had secured them with a pair of bicycle clips I had found in a drawer. There had also been a hammer in the drawer. It now weighed down my right hand jacket pocket. I thought I might need it.

I got off the tram before it reached the river and changed to another that would bring me out on the Embassy side. I had given much thought to my movements, and alighted when the conductress shouted, 'For the Hradcany.'

I was on the Heights. The molten river glinted through the trees, and over the old town the air shimmered in the heat. I could see the little trams shuttling like toys along the embankment, and hear the distant sound of them, coming up in waves. A number of workmen, stripped to the waist, were laying cables on the hill. A warm breeze swayed the foliage.

I stood for a while getting my bearings. It was nearly twelve o'clock. The cluster of glistening palaces swam in the air currents. Below, a few hundred yards beyond the wavering pinnacles of the Hradcany, I could see a familiar cupola and steeple. I thought this would be the church of St Mikulase in the Malostranske. This was where I wanted to be.

It was hot as hell, a dry incinerator heat disturbed only slightly by the breeze rattling the foliage. I held my jacket by its hanger over my shoulder and mopped my forehead. Suddenly a factory hooter went and from the old town below the clocks began to dong and boom. Twelve o'clock. Vlasta would be at the Slavia. The workmen had stopped on the instant, and were now squatting on the hillside drinking from bottles. I thought I needed a drink myself.

A steep path ran down through the greenery. I followed it, coming out to a street which skirted the Hradcany, and crossed over to the Schwarzenberg Palace square. I had walked here on the first night of my first visit. It was still familiar, hauntingly familiar as childhood. There were a number of kavarnas. I stopped in one and had a glass of ice-cold Pilsener, and continued on down. Not a lot of time for what I had to do.

I entered the Malostranske from the far side, where I had not been formerly and found the square as I expected crowded in the white lunch-time heat. The shops and offices were still letting out, girls arm in arm, chattering, gesticulating, bicycles weaving in and out, bells jangling.

I passed the Thunovska, saw the men still there, two on each corner, and went down the next street, running parallel with it. It was a narrow street of tall buildings, reeling in the heat. There were a number of small kavarnas and bars, all crowded; each, I hoped, with its quota of caretakers wetting their whistles. I didn't want to meet any caretakers.

I went in the first big building, saw a lift shaft, stairs going up and down. I went down. There were broad stone steps, a green-tiled wall, a half landing. I continued on down. At the bottom of the stairs was a little glass-enclosed cubby hole of the kind one finds in public lavatories. The electric light was on. I waited for a moment, listening. No one was there. Beyond the cubby hole was a door, half-opened and leading to a boiler room and small urinal. A naked light bulb shone in the boiler room. A strong smell of fuel oil. I looked all round. No windows. No back way out. A little ventilation grating high up in the urinal; not, evidently, very effective.

I inspected all these features at speed, and went back up the stairs and out into the street again. A man was sitting on a camp stool eating bread and sausage in the next building. After that a kavarna; four small shops; another office building – deserted. I went inside, found the same arrangement as in the first building, and went down the stairs again. Landing. Cubby hole. Door to boiler room.

It was in rather better shape than the first, a strong smell of carbolic predominating. The boiler was a large cylindrical affair with, beside it, a large heap of coke. I had seen no coke in the other building, and now looked around for a chute. There was no chute. There was a round iron ceiling hatch with a hinged iron ladder, folded back and clipped to a hook on the wall.

I unclipped the ladder, drew it into position and climbed up. I waited for a moment under the hatch, listening for sounds of movement on top. None were discernible. I raised my arms and pushed.

The hatch was jammed.

I pushed, shoved, thumped, swore, sweated. The hatch remained jammed. I went up a rung, bent my head, got the back of my neck and shoulders to it, strained, heaved on the ladder. There was a slight sucking, glooping noise. The hatch gave. I went down a rung, paused, sweat running in my eyes, and tried again with my hands. It was heavy as hell, a slab of apparently solid iron, but it went up quite easily. I shifted it to one side, climbed up into the open air and found myself in an enclosed yard. There were a number of dustbins, a builder's cart, an assorted pile of lumber. There was also a pair of double doors, bolted and padlocked. The lock looked rusty, but the key turned without trouble. I took off the lock, undid the bolts and stepped out into an alley. I drew the doors carefully behind me and went quickly up the alley. It ran back into the side street.

With something of the elation of Columbus catching his first sight of that good old stuff, dry land, I nipped back down the alley, locked and bolted the doors, hurried down the coal tip, pulled the hatch back in position and replaced the ladder. All that was called for now was some hours of the deepest and most impregnable seclusion. I was through with running away now.

I meant to walk directly into the Embassy. Give it eighteen hours, I thought, and I'd either be in there astounding all with my ingenuity; or I'd be in quite a different establishment, hoping, rather urgently, for death in some quick and hygienic form.

Chapter 12

I

BOILER rooms in Czech commercial premises tend to be spacious and rambling apartments. For six months of the year the country is frozen; a powerful heating unit and a comprehensive system of plumbing are the minimal requirements for all centres of human congress.

The building I had chosen did not fall below the norm in this respect. The boiler room measured some forty feet square. There were enough cocks, taps, levers, dials, and asbestos-covered piping for the control room of a submarine. There were also two small cupboard-like rooms letting off it. One contained a broken chair, a camp-bed, a bag of soot, and numerous stoking implements; the other logs – no doubt an emergency fuel supply. There were not locks or bolts to either door. I took to the timber.

After a couple of hours I was beginning to regret it. I had scooped a hole for myself in the logs in one of the corners farthest from the door and lay there painfully uncomfortable and half stupefied in the musty heat.

I had learned to identify the sounds of the building; the sucking whine of the lift shaft, chairs scraping, the distant patter of typewriters. From time to time the caretaker came into the boiler room. I heard him lighting his pipe once. He hawked and spat. But he didn't come to the log cupboard. I lay in blackness, watching the crack of light under the door. Once when I moved there was a petrifying rumble of falling logs. After that I remained where I was, sweat trickling incessantly and itchingly all over my body.

I dozed and woke and dozed and woke, three or four times, I think. The last time when I blearily came to, the crack of light had vanished. I lay silently for a while, listening. The whine of the lift shaft had stopped. There was no movement of feet above; merely the shift and creak of an old building.

I clambered drunkenly out of the log pile, felt for the door and went into the boiler room. It was dark, but with a welcome sense of space. I waited in the centre of the room for a minute, listening. There was just the creak and rustle; distant sounds of traffic. I lit a match and went to the door. It was locked.

I'd forgotten to check where the light switch was, and spent several minutes fumbling around with matches before it occurred to me that it was probably on the other side of the door. I swore a bit at that. I had four matches left – and four cigarettes that I had brought with me from Barrandov. It would be a long night.

I thought I might as well make myself as comfortable as possible and got the camp bed out of the other cupboard. It was a telescopic affair of metal tubes and somewhat smelly canvas, and collapsed twice before I got the hang of it. I found myself operating with preternaturally delicate movements, afraid of the sound in the dark. I took my shoes off and lay out flat in the cavernous blackness and let my bruised and aching limbs throb back to life. The air was still warm and stuffy. I lay listening to my breathing and the dull churning of my heart.

I think I went off to sleep like that. I was tired as hell, sluggish and dazed with the crazy sequence of events. I came to after a bit with one leg lying numb on a metal support and my neck stiff. I wondered what time it was, and regretted the watch left on the bedside table at Barrandov. I sat up and lit a cigarette and went round the room with the match looking for a clock among the dials. There was no clock. It was very silent. My body seemed heavy but rested. I thought I must have lain there for an hour or two. That would be, what – seven, eight o'clock? It might be dark outside. I thought I might risk opening the hatch.

I finished the cigarette and put my shoes back on and released the ladder. I went up slowly and listened at the top, and pushed the hatch up and listened again before sliding it to one side. Sky dark blue; welcome cool wetness. It was raining out there. I went up a couple of rungs and poked my head out. Gurgle of drains; wonderfully pleasant splashing – rainwater running out of loose guttering. Distantly clocks began chiming. Half past. Half past what?

I left the hatch off and went back down again and sat on the camp bed, listening. There were quite a lot of sounds. Trams, cars, bicycle bells; even a train hooting somewhere. The moon was not up yet; even so the night sky was surprisingly light; a circle of indigo in the black ceiling.

Another quarter struck. I thought I'd better leave the hatch off all night. There was little chance of anyone poking around in the yard. I thought over the plan I had conceived while lying in bed at Barrandov. Crazy. Wild. As crazy and wild as all the other things that had happened to me. But they had happened.

I lay back on the bed, but found it so uncomfortable now that I got up and fetched a log and draped my jacket round it as a neck rest. I smoked another cigarette like that. Two left.

The clocks began to chime. I counted. Seven, eight, nine, ten. Ten o'clock. About another eight hours to go, I thought. I ought to try and get some more sleep.

I was suddenly aware that I was hungry and felt in the jacket pocket for the packet of bread and sausage I had brought with me from Barrandov, and ate a hunk, lying back and watching the hatch and the rain glancing in.

They would be looking all over the town for me again in the rain, I thought. The Thunovska covered; all the approaches covered; standing there dripping in the rain. I wondered what Vlasta was doing. I wondered if they had taken in Baba's husband for questioning, if they were knocking the poor devil about. I couldn't remember him; could hardly remember Baba; a vague impression of a stout woman, a broad, warm lap, a wart near her eyebrow. She couldn't have been very old; the Little Swine was her elder brother. He was — what? Fifty-five? Maminka was fifty-three. She would be about Maminka's age. I wondered what she had died of.

I slept presently.

2

The boiler room was chill and grey when I awoke, and I sat up in a panic, thinking I'd overslept. But I hadn't overslept. The clocks were chiming the preliminaries, and I heard the first hour-stroke sound. It was five o'clock. I counted, shivering with cold and fear. I'd remembered what I had to do the instant I sat up and my stomach had turned over.

My teeth were chattering. I got off the camp bed and put on the jacket and moved around stretching my body. I could see no possibility of going through with the plan. I felt acutely ill, stiff and clumsy, physically incapable of the effort required. I thought the minute I got out in the street the S.N.B. men would be on me like a shot, and would march me away numb and speechless.

I wondered if I should make provision to kill myself in the event of failure: to get in first and make it quicker. I had the hammer. But how the hell did you kill yourself with a hammer?

The door of the wood cupboard was open. There was a strong temptation to go back in there again, to bury myself and warm up, to live through another drugged and drowsy day.

I didn't go back in the wood cupboard. I walked about the boiler room, circling the ladder. I lit another cigarette — one left — and smoked it in quick, nervous drags. The quarter past sounded. The half past. I was empty and hungry. But when, presently, I opened the packet of bread and sausage and tried to eat, I was sick. This physical misery, distracting me from the immediate problem, left me feeling a good deal calmer, and after it I sat quietly on the camp bed beneath the hatch, waiting.

Small, distant sounds of activity were coming from the waking world above. A train hooted, a car changed gear. There was no sound yet of the trams, or of that other special noise that I awaited.

Just before six o'clock I lit my last cigarette and smoked it lingeringly down to a small stub, and stamped it out.

It was time to be off.

I went up the ladder.

It was a still, grey morning, misty. I crossed the yard and unlocked the padlock and went out into the alley. The street was grey and damp from last night's rain. It was quite deserted, the buildings sober and silent.

I made my way up to the top where it ran out to the Malostranske, and withdrew into a deep doorway. A few hundred yards away in the parallel Thunovska, the watchers would be waiting, too. We seemed to have the damp, silent world to ourselves.

It seemed a hell of a long time between the quarter and the half past. But at last the first stroke sounded. Immediately after – so close to the stroke that I wondered if I'd been mistaken – there was the sound I was expecting. I came out of the doorway, moved as near to the corner as I dared and waited there for a moment, straining my ears. I had not been mistaken. Between the strokes it came again, quite clearly. It was a milkman.

3

The cart came trundling round from behind St Mikulase, a blob of blue and white in the mist. I could hear the milkman exclaiming freely to his horse, boots ringing on the cobbles and bottles clanking, but I couldn't see him. The horse drew the cart a few yards into the square and stopped, shaking its head up and down.

The milkman came then, a big, red, beefy fellow in a dark blue overall and a white peaked cap. He replenished his wire basket at the cart, roaring endearments at the horse, and went off clanking across the square to serve the far side. Each time he returned to the horse he roared something that sounded like '*Whuyill! Whuyill!*' in response to which the horse slopped forward a few yards and stopped again.

I thought *oh, Jesus Christ*, and withdrew again into the doorway to practise a few silent *whuyills* to myself. The milkman was working round from the right; the Thunovska was on my left. I watched him for ten minutes until the cart had drawn level with my corner, and then with mindless action stepped out from the doorway, gesticulating.

The milkman looked at me.

I beckoned frantically.

Head forward in inquiry, he walked over with his empty basket. 'What is it, comrade?'

He was sweating slightly; a smell of horses; an open, country face; a deep bass voice that awoke echoes from the early morning buildings. I wondered if it was arousing any interest on the corner of the Thunovska. It was certainly arousing the interest of the horse which had begun to look across in the most pointed way.

I whispered, 'Quick, quick,' in panic. 'In here a minute.'

He followed me wonderingly into the doorway. 'What's the trouble, comrade? What is it?'

'You go to the British Embassy?'

'*Yoh, yoh*, the Embassy. Why do you want to know?'

'It's this,' I said. 'Look at this.'

Just at the last moment it was painfully hard to do it, the big sweating face so innocent.

'A hammer, comrade – what of it?'

I hit him on the head with it, hard. He seemed to put out his hand and lean on me just as I did it. The wire basket crashed to the ground. He looked at me with eyes wide open in mystified inquiry and puffed and fell down.

I unbuttoned his overall, shaking with panic, and tore it getting it off him and on to me. I put on his peaked cap, picked up the wire basket and walked out of the doorway, out of the street, out into the Malostranske. I felt as if I were walking out to my execution. I was trembling violently in every limb.

The horse, which had not turned its head away since the milkman had walked over, regarded me curiously. I said, *'Whuyill!'* It came out in a strangled bleat. The horse merely stared. *Oh, damn and blast you, bloody well whuyill*, I urged it, putting out my hand to pat the large, dangerous head.

The horse bit me. It was not a sharp bite, more in the nature of a nip by a pair of nutcrackers, but painful. I stepped back and swore in its ear, softly but with great obscenity. I felt myself under acute observation. I had not dared turn round to the Thunovska. I doubted if they could have seen clearly in the mist my contretemps with the knowing animal. But the horse had not moved.

I went back to the cart and filled the basket with milk and cartons of sour cream, and turned blindly to walk to my goal.

I seemed to be walking for about two hours, on cotton wool, with my legs turned all to jelly. There were just two of them, one at each corner, buttoned-up and pinched in the grey mist.

I said, *'Dobry den,'* gruffly, peaked cap slanted over my eyes. *'Dobry den.'*

'More rain again, I shouldn't wonder.'

'Shouldn't wonder.'

I was past. Unbelievably, I was past!

I walked up the Thunovska with my legs nearly collapsing under me. I turned in at the Embassy opening. The Union Jack, limp in the damp grey morning . . . a courtyard . . . steps. . . .

There were big double doors, ornamental knockers, a bell push. I pressed it and heard the mad jangling inside somewhere. I was choked almost now, wits all away, nothing but the thumping of my heart, toes curled up hard inside my shoes.

There was no answer to the bell. I rang again, again, kept my finger on it. I didn't dare slam the knockers, had no idea at all what to do. The S.N.B. men would grow suspicious soon. The milkman would come to shortly. I'd not hit him all that hard.

I stepped back from the door. Away to the left of the courtyard was another door: CONSULATE. There was also an archway. Maybe somewhere at the back, in some domestic bits of the building, retainers would be stirring. I couldn't waste time investigating the possibilities of the archway. I thought, *Oh, God, I've had it,* and pressed, pressed the bell again. *Open up, get up, wake up, damn you!*

'You! Milkman! What are you doing?'

I turned. One of the buttoned-up men was standing at the entrance to the courtyard. My throat seemed to seize up. I opened my mouth speechlessly.

'Leave your milk and come away.'

I said, 'They told me – they told me to call.'

'Put it down and leave.'

'They want cream. The housekeeper said to call with sour cream. There's a reception.'

He regarded me sourly. He seemed nonplussed. He did not venture into the courtyard, but remained there watching me.

I turned in panic, grasped the knockers and began slamming furiously. The noise echoed thunderously in the courtyard. No answer.

'Right. Leave it now then. Come down here. I want to talk to you.'

I didn't answer him. I turned blindly to thump the door, the knockers, the bell, lost now, no hope at all now, the end close in sight, in such a panic I could scarcely see or breathe. A commotion began in the street. A yell. The milkman. Another yell, another voice, shouting. Steps running. The S.N.B. man watching me turned away, exchanged a few sharp words and called, 'Hi! You! Come here. Come here at once!' He had taken something out of his pocket. A pistol. There was no cover on the doorstep; nothing at all but the stone pediment, the big immovable doors.

I was so completely terrorized that all processes of thought seemed at that moment to stop. I remember that I bent and took a bottle of milk out of the basket. I don't know what I intended to do with this bottle – throw it at him, perhaps, defend myself in some way. I had not stopped pounding on the door, but I had given up in my heart. Now, as the other man turned in to the courtyard, there was a shuffling within the house, the clank of bolts.

I don't know, looking back, if the S.N.B. men would have dared to shoot me on the steps of the Embassy. Certainly I would not have gone with them otherwise. Perhaps, as they walked slowly up the courtyard in the misty morning, the two buttoned-up men were aware of this, were trying, in their chilled and worried state, to see some way out of the dilemma. In fact, the agony of decision never came.

While they were still several yards from the steps, one of the doors opened. I fell into the shadowy darkness, bumping into and knocking over the aged, black-clad crone who had opened it; not stopping, indeed, till one foot encountered a bucket of warm water and the other a bar of soap and my ill-used backside came to rest, jarred, numb but indubitably secure, twenty-five feet inside British territory. The bottle of milk, quite undamaged, was still in my hand.

Chapter 13

I

'Hullo. Feeling a bit more rested now?'

'Yes, thanks.'

'You're looking rather more human. I'd like another session with you.'

'Of course. Sit down.'

He had already sat down. He was a tall, pale man called

Roddinghead with a bulging, child-like forehead and small reptilian eyes. He had taken no pains to hide the fact that I had been causing him much trouble. I felt able to bear this. I was in bed in a small room in the Embassy. I had had two lots of sedative and two lots of sleep. I was feeling slightly mad with joy and relief.

Roddinghead said curtly, 'It's that bit of paper. I've just had another cable from London telling me to get my finger out. I'll have to know a lot more about it.'

'I'm afraid I've told you all I know.'

'It isn't enough. Try closing your eyes again.'

I closed my eyes.

'Now then, how big is it?'

'About the size of a packet of twenty cigarettes. Maybe a bit narrower.'

'Very thin rice paper, you said.'

'Yes.'

'And curling at the edges.'

'That's right.'

'I want you to tell *me*. See it clearly. What's on the top?'

'The thing about Aldermaston. Banshee and Third Stage, I think.'

'Right. Now the bottom.'

'I'm sorry. I really didn't look at it.'

'Well, have a look at it now.'

I gritted my teeth. It was the fourth time we had examined this lunatic cigarette-packet sized bit of paper. I suppose it was part of some half-forgotten course. I could hear Roddinghead irritably tapping his pencil on his notebook.

'I'm afraid I can't remember.'

'Try running your eye over it quickly. Anything stand out?'

'This isn't going to work, you know. I only saw the thing for a couple of seconds.'

He made a savage note in his book. 'All right. Now this old nanny, Hana Simkova. You say you're absolutely certain you never mentioned her to the girl?'

'I'm positive I didn't.'

'Couldn't have dropped a reference when you were under the weather, say?'

'No. It never cropped up at all.'

'So you reckon she must have got it from this fellow Cunliffe?'

'Yes.'

'Who got it from whoever was watching you?'

'Well, he must have. I never told him myself.'

'Right. Who else knew this nanny?'

'That's very hard to say. I've been thinking about it. There's her brother, of course – the Mr Nimek I told you about.'

'Yes, yes. They've taken him in for a going-over. .... I'm glad you're amused by all this,' he said malevolently. 'I can assure you nobody else is.'

'I'm sorry,' I said, trying hard to control my delight at this marvellous thing that was happening to the Little Swine. 'I was trying to think who else could know of Baba. Both my mother and Mr Gabriel have quite a large circle of émigré friends in England with whom they correspond frequently. Quite a lot of people could have known about her.'

'I'd like a list of the names of these friends if you can remember them.'

'I'll try.'

'The point being, of course, that we want to find out who was watching you.'

'I'd like to find that out myself.'

He gave me another malevolent look with his reptilian eyes. 'Not that anyone could care terribly about you. The idea is to pick up all the network.'

'Yes. Right. I'll try and think what names I've heard mentioned.'

'You say your mother gave you a letter to this Hana Simkova. She evidently didn't know she was dead.'

'Evidently not.'

'How do you account for the fact that Mr Gabriel knew and she didn't?'

'He is very devoted to her. He keeps unpleasant news from her.'

'I wish someone would do the same for me. Now then, this man Pavelka . . .'

That was the fourth interrogation. There were many more.

2

I stayed at the British Embassy in Prague for ten weeks. I occupied a small room on the third floor. I was not the most welcome of guests. Apart from Roddinghead, whose exact function I never discovered, and two younger and rather more civil colleagues, I had no contact with the staff. Nobody quite knew what to do with me; the policy appeared to be to pretend that I didn't exist.

I was confined to my room. I received no letters and could write none. I listened to the wireless for hours on end. I read numerous books. In the evening I was escorted down the back stairs by Roddinghead or one of his colleagues to walk about in a small walled yard.

The summer passed. The days shortened. I had no complaints. It was better than running up and down alleys. And I had plenty of time to think. I thought about Maminka, and hoped that Inne was devising suitable explanations for my absence. The old booby himself, I thought, must be distracted half out of his mind at not hearing from me. I thought of Maura, and wondered sickly what she must be making of my silence.

I thought of the Little Swine, and to what extent he had been involved in this mad and now half-forgotten nightmare of the third stage of the Banshee. And of Mrs Nolan, and how long she would wait before clearing out my things and installing someone else in my room.

But mainly, I thought of my future, such as it was. That it would not be spent with Pavelka was one thing at least that I had gathered from Roddinghead. Pavelka had not paid for my trips. He hadn't any money. He lived in a single room in Bayswater and, like myself, had been a dupe.

On the question of the Little Swine, Roddinghead was curiously evasive. Mr Nimek was being 'looked into'. A 'bit of research' was going on. One way or the other it looked as if I was finished there, anyway.

So I thought of Bela and Canada. But after a few weeks I didn't even think of this. To live in a single room, waited on, one's immediate needs satisfied, neither prisoner nor free man is a curiously anaesthetizing experience. I slept, woke, ate, listened, read, slept again. Over and over again, day after day. A dream-like time. Dream-like still in the memory.

After the third or fourth week, the interrogation tailed off. I saw Roddinghead less frequently. His manner towards me had ripened slightly. I thought they were no longer bothering him from London. The reptilian eyes ceased to regard me with loathing. They were wry, sardonic, affable even.

He was absent for a week or so towards the end of the summer, and reappeared one day bronzed, the bulging forehead peeling.

He said, 'Hello. How's the prisoner of Zenda?'

'Fine, thanks. Been away?'

'Yes. To the Tatras. Managed to snatch a few days. Things are a bit slack now.'

'They're a bit slack for me, too. Heard anything about me going yet?'

'No. Still a few ends to be tied up. Getting fed up with us, are you?'

'I'd like to go home.'

'So would I, cock.' He ambled about the room, picking up a book, a magazine.

'What's happening exactly?'

'Nothing much.'

'Do you think they've forgotten about me?'

'I doubt it.'

'Have they managed to pick up all the members of the – of the espionage network?' Even at this distance it seemed a ludicrous thing to be discussing.

'I believe so. All they know about, anyway. I shan't be requiring your further thoughts on the subject.'

'Was there anybody I didn't know about?'

'As to that,' he said, reptilian eyes smiling, 'we don't know quite how much you know, do we?'

'Do you mean they're keeping me here because they're still not sure of me?'

'Might be. Might not. I don't know. I don't care very much, either. You got yourself into this. Maybe you won't be in such a hurry next time. There's no future in it, cock, no future at all,' he said moving to the door.

I said quickly, 'Just a minute.' I'd hoped he was in the mood for a chat. He dropped things from time to time. 'What about Cunliffe? Is he in the bag?'

'So I believe.'

'And the person who was watching me?'

'No information. They don't keep sending me postcards, you know.'

'How about Nimek?'

'Nimek?'

'The one I told you about who ran the little glass firm I used to work for. The brother of my old nanny.'

'Oh, him. He's a funny fellow, Nimek. He still writes to his sister, you know.'

'Still writes to Baba? But she's dead.'

'Yes. So you said. Maybe nobody told him. Come to that,' he said, opening the door, 'maybe nobody told her, either. She was looking remarkably lifelike last week. We sent somebody round to see her.'

I stared at the door as it closed behind him, thunderstruck.

The sting-in-the-tail rapidly became his speciality after that. Perhaps the job bored him. Maybe I helped to break the tedium. I can't remember all the discussions. I remember very clearly one other. I had been wondering in a bemused sort of way why I had been involved in the operation at all. I said to Roddinghead, 'It was surely a bit of a Heath-Robinsonish way of passing valuable secrets.'

'Yes, wasn't it?'

'Couldn't they have put it through the diplomatic bag?'

'I don't know, old cock. Maybe it had to be a very independent operation. There's still quite a bit of it going on.'

'Were they a bunch of amateurs?'

'That isn't my information.'

'You mean Cunliffe was a regular spy?'

'That's what I mean. It wasn't his only name, you won't be surprised to hear.'

'Would I have heard of him by any other name?'

'Oh, yes. You gave me one of them. It was on the list of émigrés.'

'Which one was it?'

'Can't remember off-hand. But he had quite a nice lot of addresses, too, one in Ireland. He'd lived there apparently for a long time once – had a wife and daughter with him there.'

'Whereabouts in Ireland?'

'I've forgotten. He separated from his wife some years ago, and the daughter lives in London.'

'Was she in it – in this plot, too, the daughter?'

'Oh, yes. Quite a family affair.'

'I see.'

'Don't worry,' he said, smiling and reptilian at the door. 'We've nobbled her, too. You'll really have to take up another profession. You don't get much of a run these days.'

I didn't listen to the wireless that afternoon. I didn't read, either. I sat looking out at the trees and the grey sky. I felt sad and sick. The last piece of the jig-saw had fallen into place. I saw exactly how it must have happened.

3

The leaves fell in the Embassy gardens. The wind rose. A light but incessant drizzle set in. I had to put the light on several mornings when I got up. One day after breakfast there was a knock at the door and Roddinghead came in. His two colleagues were with him. He had a scroll of paper in his hand.

He said coldly, 'Mr Whistler, I am directed to read you the

following.' He unrolled the paper and read it out, at speed. It was the Official Secrets Act, 1911. When he had finished he handed me the paper. 'Please read it over for yourself.'

'What is it? What's happening?'

'Go ahead and read it.'

I read over the Act in a state of some nervousness. The three of them watched me. I handed it back to Roddinghead.

'Have you understood what you've read?'

'I think so.'

'Stamp, please,' Roddinghead said. One of them gave him a rubber stamp and an inked pad. He impressed it on the paper and produced a fountain pen. 'Sign it.'

'Why?'

'I'm telling you to. Go ahead.'

I signed where he pointed. 'Look, what the hell's happening? What's going on here?'

Roddinghead briskly rolled up the paper, and, his official business evidently then over, relaxed. 'You're going home, cock,' he said amiably.

'Home! When?'

'Today. In about a couple of hours, I should think.'

'Today? But I – why didn't you let me know?'

'Sorry. Only got the wire a few minutes ago.'

I was so stunned I could merely gape at him.

'They're sending a plane in from Germany for you. Cunliffe and his daughter are flying off from the other side.'

It seemed that an exchange had been arranged; that Cunliffe's plane would fly east as mine flew west, both aircraft leaving together.

'Sorry I couldn't give you a little more warning that it was coming off. Still, you didn't bring much luggage, did you? Just the single bottle of milk, as I recall.'

'You mean I'll be free?'

'Within limits. The limits being as defined in the paper you've just signed. You're bloody lucky. You could have got a few years for what you've been up to. Evidently nothing is to be said about it. By you or anyone else. No heroic little dining-out stories. No sensational adventures in the newspapers. And I'm bound to point out that the Act means exactly what it says on that point. You so much as whisper a word to anyone, with or without *mens rea* – i.e. guilty intent – and you'll find yourself inside. O.K.?'

I said O.K.

I left before lunch. An Embassy car drove me to the airport, Roddinghead sitting beside me in the back. We waited in the car until the plane landed, and then drove out to where it stood on the apron. There were several buttoned-up characters standing around as I walked up the aircraft steps with Roddinghead. He looked straight ahead. He had said practically nothing to me in the car.

In the aircraft he held out his hand. 'Well, cheerio, then, cock.'

'Cheerio.'

'I hope we made your stay a pleasant one.'

I felt too bloodless for wisecracks. I said, 'Thank you. Thank you very much for everything.'

'Don't come back.'

He went.

The plane took off almost immediately. Four hours later I was in London.

4

When you have imagined a homecoming for so long and in circumstances so diverse and apparently hopeless, the real thing tends to be something of an anti-climax. I got off the Tube at Gloucester Road and walked slowly to Fitzwalter Square in a mood of profound melancholy. It was six o'clock, a chill and darkening afternoon. The wind scurried leaves along the pavements. I felt like one of them myself, blown by any wind that came along.

From the airport a car had taken me to an office in Queen Anne's Gate. A man whose name I never learned had inquired if I had understood the provisions of the Official Secrets Act. I said I had. I had signed an undertaking to repay all moneys that had been laid out on my account. These appeared to have been for ten weeks' rent at Mrs Nolan's, and seven weeks' lock-up at Ratface's. As the man said, this had been necessary to forestall inquiries. Everything had been taken care of in my absence; all interested parties had been informed that I was abroad on important business in which the government had a commercial interest, and that I had been asked not to correspond. He had then lent me a pound and wished me a very good afternoon.

I had had a cup of tea and an Osborne biscuit at Queen Anne's Gate. This was the only food I had consumed since breakfast. I was not so much hungry as devitalized. An enormous number of things had happened to me since I had walked these streets last. I felt I should have returned exhilarated, bouncing with joy, everything changed in some large and mysterious way. Nothing had changed. The grey buildings were as they had always been. The buses trundled drably along. The people walked by intent on their business. The wind whipped the leaves. I had been away and now I had come back. The summer was gone. I was three months older.

As I came to number seventy-four, I got out my latchkey – miraculously retained through all my changes of clothing – and opened the door. I don't know what I expected to happen. Nothing did.

The hall was in darkness, the wireless on in Mrs Nolan's lair. I stood there for a moment, listening and taking in the familiar odours. I didn't think I could bear to face her. I closed the door quietly behind me and walked slowly up the stairs.

On the third floor, I opened my door and switched on the light. Everything in its accustomed place, neat, tidy, dusted. I might never have left it. Beside the plant pot on the plush table-cloth, however, was a large pile of letters. I flipped over them. Library reminders, football pools, circulars, two letters from my mother, three from Maura. . . . I didn't look any further. I took off the mac presented to me at the Embassy and sat down on the divan and lit a cigarette, looking round.

All this was far from being in the spirit of the returning traveller. I thought what I needed was a sleep. I stubbed out the cigarette presently and flaked out on the divan and went off almost immediately.

I must have slept for three hours. It was quite dark when I came to. I knew where I was before I opened my eyes, and lay there for a few moments feeling the sudden warm rush of relief and satisfaction flowing over me. The old batteries were charging up again, I thought. I was home, anyway.

I went down to Bournemouth next morning. Mrs Nolan had been in a considerable twitter when I had poked my head round her door the previous evening. She had been sitting toasting her legs at the first fire of autumn, but had bustled about in high excitement getting me something to eat and priming me on all that had gone.

It seemed that an exquisite man from the government had called to tell her about me, what an important job I was doing, and the arrangements I had made for paying the rent. My young lady had phoned very often at the beginning, but not for some weeks now. Mr Gabriel had been phoning regularly from Bournemouth. And another foreign gentleman had been phoning, too, a Mr Nimek, and very angry he had been.

All this, together with the familiar food and the well-remembered brown-boot-polish tea had proved highly revivifying. Imperceptibly, as she shaded in the ten missing weeks, I had felt a curious internal reconstitution taking place, as though ribs and organs were being replaced after a period of disuse.

I didn't ring up Bournemouth. I wasn't sure what I wanted to say. I thought I'd better think of that on the way down, and immediately after breakfast went round to the enterprise of Ratface Rickett to claim my car. It was a new and refined version of the Ratface I had known, a most mannerly little Ratface, who gave me a kindly salutation and actually shoved in four gallons without cash or cavil before waving me off the premises. By eleven o'clock I was half way there.

At this time yesterday, I thought, slowing down through Winchester, I was sitting by the window on the third floor of the Embassy in Prague. Just twenty-four hours before I had been a prisoner in the middle of Europe, staring out at bare branches and grey skies. It seemed unbelievable. The whole episode was unbelievable: the night on the Vaclavske Namesti, the hours in the arms of the perfidious giantess of Barrandov, the alleys, the furniture store, the boiler room. No longer even a nightmare; too remote and impersonal for a nightmare; something I had read somewhere at some time and had remembered, names and all. Vlasta, Svoboda, Borsky, Vlcek, Galushka, Josef, fornicating Frantisek, Roddinghead.

Of them all, only Roddinghead, detached and derisive, lingered as a flesh and blood reality. Only Roddinghead could inspire belief that these other phantoms had actually ever existed; that they still existed, going about their business far away in grey and steepled Prague.

No future in it, cock, Roddinghead had said. No future indeed. Not even a very meaningful or profitable past. My only legacy of three dangerous and demented months was a bill for rent and a certain facility with a blunt instrument. Someone had steered me into all this. Someone should pay for it, I thought, swinging on to the A35. But I doubted if anybody would.

5

The old booby was examining a sheet of stamps when I went into his room. The glass fell out of his eye and his mouth dropped open with shock.

'Nicolas! Nicolas, my boy! Oh, thank God! It is wonderful to see you.'

'Hello, Uncle. How've you been?'

'She has been worrying dreadfully. I just haven't known what to tell her. Have you been to see her yet?'

'I've just arrived. I thought I'd better have a word with you first. How is she?'

'Let me look at you, my boy.' He stood up, shaking a bit. It was none too warm in the room. He had a muffler on and a cardigan underneath the alpaca jacket. He looked distinctly older, folds of skin hanging from his face and his eyes a bit glazed. His breath was whistling out with its accustomed vigour, however. 'Oh, thank God you are here. Since the man from the Foreign Office came her head has been full of nothing else. She worries me from morning to night. She is a remarkable woman your mother when she gets a single idea in her head.'

I smiled back with exasperated affection. Some people have a permanent claim on one's affections, whatever they do, however they behave. It was impossible to think of him merely as a man, subject to the same pressures and temptations as other men. He was neuter, a huge, flabby, permanent old booby with a single preoccupation.

He sat down again, shaking, and pulled the muffler tighter round his neck. 'She asked him,' he said, 'she asked him how long you would be in Prague. I didn't know where to put myself.'

'What did he say?'

'He was astounded. He asked why she should think you were in Prague. So of course – you know your mother – she told him. She told him you had gone to start up the family business again. She told him your entire history from a baby. I couldn't make out what was happening. I didn't understand this business with the government. I didn't know what to think, Nicolas. And she sees I am worried,' he said, tapping a finger against his forehead intensely. 'She has a wonderful intuition, your mother. All the time she asks questions. She makes herself ill. She doesn't give me a moment's peace. And I'm ill myself, Nicolas. I am not a healthy man. But enough,' he said. 'Enough about me. Tell me what's been happening to you. Tell me everything.'

I had meant to do this. I had meant to tell him each single and minute detail of it, the beatings-up, the running up and down alleys, the constant terror; the whole of the three awful months. I had been thinking about it as I parked the car and walked into the hotel and up to his room. I had been thinking of the expression on his face when he knew that I knew. I had thought of it a lot since that afternoon on the third floor of the Embassy in Prague. Now that it came to the point I couldn't do it.

I said instead, 'Why did you do it, Uncle?'

'What, Nicolas? What do you mean?'

'Why did you spy on me for this man Cunliffe? Why did you send me out there?'

'I send you? Cunliffe?' He looked at me wildly. 'I don't know what you say, Nicolas. I don't understand you.'

'You'd better try. I don't know what you called him. I mean the man who asked you for all the details of me. The one you telephoned when I left Bournemouth last time. The one who made up the story about Uncle Bela dying.'

The room went perfectly still. The hairs at his nose stopped waving for a moment. Then they began again, very fast. He breathed heavily. He leaned forward. 'I should like you to understand, Nicolas,' he said, and cleared his throat, breathing noisily – 'I should like you to understand, my boy, that all was intended for the best. I love you. You are like my own son to me. Not only for the sake of your dear mother. Do you think I could do a bad thing to you?'

'Why did you?'

'Why did I? It's a bad thing? It's not better than working for Nimek?'

I opened my mouth, but he held out his hand, breathing loudly. 'Sometimes, Nicolas, it is necessary to give a little push. I wasn't happy at your progress with Nimek. I could see there would be nothing with him. I had to consider the effect on your mother. She wants you to be a success.'

I goggled at him. It was hard to know where the hell to start. I said, 'Do you know why I went out there? Do you mean to say you've got no idea what I was supposed to do?'

'I didn't want to know. I didn't ask. It was enough that you were working for Mr Pavelka!'

He told me about it then. How Cunliffe had written to him saying he was looking for a smart young man to be an assistant to one of his clients. How he had gone up to see him and learned the client was Pavelka.

'Pavelka! You wouldn't have remembered Pavelka from the olden days. He was a big man, colossal! It would have been your father's dearest wish that Mr Pavelka would take an interest in you.'

Cunliffe had told him the job was confidential; that Pavelka had grown a little eccentric and wished to investigate my capabilities in his own way, and that I must know nothing about it. So Imre had told Cunliffe everything about me; about my expectations from Bela; about how I worked and how I lived; that I earned very little and spent that little on the car. . . .

I said, 'Did you know he was going to make up the story about Uncle Bela dying?'

He looked at the floor, breathing noisily. He said, 'That I couldn't understand. I tell you frankly, Nicolas, I was uneasy. But he told me Mr Pavelka positively insisted. He said he wanted to see how you would react to the news. Nicolas, I am no great business man! I don't pretend I have made a success of my life. Pavelka, to me, is a colossus. If I understood how his mind works maybe I would be as successful as Pavelka.'

'Haven't you met him?'

'Only once, in Prague, many years ago.'

'You didn't meet him here in London?'

'No, no,' he said smiling. 'Pavelka isn't interested in me. Pavelka is still a very big man. I thought I was acting for the best for you, Nicolas. If he wanted that kind of peculiar investigation, I didn't want to stand in your way. I was worried only for your mother. I knew you would want to run down and tell her this news about Bela. I would have to put you off. I didn't feel good about that. What was I to do? Tell me, Nicolas. Tell me if you think I did wrong.'

'I don't know, Uncle,' I said, gazing helplessly at the old booby. 'I don't know about anything. Didn't he tell you he meant to send me to Prague?'

'No,' he said uneasily. He didn't look at me.

'But you knew it. You guessed it.'

He said in Czech, 'No, no, it wasn't so.' He was breathing like an express train.

'What made you tell him Baba was dead then?'

He didn't answer, clenching and unclenching his hands.

'Why didn't you tell *me* she was dead?'

He said, 'Nicolas . . .' and stopped. The heavy folds of flesh on his face began suddenly to shake. The puckered mottled flesh round his eyes screwed up. He was crying. I said with shock and horror, 'Oh, no, Uncle. Uncle, please don't. I'm sorry. I'm terribly sorry. Please stop it. It isn't anything.'

He bent forward so that I shouldn't see his face. I put my arm round his shoulders. They shook tumultuously. He got out his handkerchief and buried his face in it. His shuddering neck was fat, creased and badly in need of a haircut; and so bloody pathetic I practically joined him with the hanky. I felt full of shame and self-disgust.

He blew his nose presently and sat up, mopping his eyes. They were watery and discoloured. I looked away. He said thickly, 'I must tell you all, my boy.'

'I don't want to know. I don't want to hear anything more about it. It's forgotten.'

'It isn't forgotten. I can't forget it.' He shook his big, stupid old head. 'I am ashamed! I am ashamed before you, Nicolas! Of course I guessed it. Ah, I'm not such an old fool as that. He started asking me if you knew anyone in Prague, if anyone was there still. Oh, this was later after I'd had time to think about it. He asked me if you'd had a nanny or a governess who might still be there. Of course I remembered Hana. I didn't want any trouble for you or for her. I told him she was dead. He asked if she'd been married, if you knew her husband. I said you wouldn't remember him. . . .

'Of course, when your mother gave you the letter to Hana, I had to tell you the same thing. But I was already very nervous. I couldn't understand this business. I was beginning to wonder what they wanted you to do. I thought you'd found out and didn't want to speak to me again. You remember, I telephoned you. I asked if you were offended with me about anything.'

'Yes, Uncle, I remember.' I did remember, just at that moment. It seemed a lifetime ago.

'And I began to wonder if Pavelka was really involved, or if this man was just tricking me – he was always sly, that one, even in the old days. He used to be a lawyer. It really was for Pavelka?'

'Not really, Uncle. Pavelka was fooled, too.'

'He fooled Pavelka also?' he said, and sat nodding his head for a bit, comforted in a melancholy sort of way, and then looked at me and looked away again. 'But still this is not all, Nicolas. It is still not the worst. There is the money.'

'What money?'

'He gave me fifty pounds. He said it was an introduction fee if you proved suitable for the job. I spent it. I couldn't give it back again. We would have had to move out of here if he wanted it back again.'

There wasn't anything to be said to this, and a rather miserable silence fell.

After a moment he burst out, 'Nicolas, understand! For myself, I would sooner beg in the gutter! It is your dear mother I think about. She has no idea what things cost. She thinks her annuity covers everything. It doesn't even pay the hotel bill! I must buy her clothes, cigarettes, the little extras she likes ... I am not complaining, my boy. Don't think I complain. It is my whole pleasure to do these things for her. But lately, I don't know, business isn't so good ... I think I'm getting old. Too old,' he said, nodding to the sheet of stamps he had dropped when I came in.

All this was, in its way, rather more hideous than all the primitive things that had been happening to me for the past three months. We sat staring at each other in dismal silence. Something came to mind, after a while. Throughout his recital, Imre had been calling Cunliffe by another name.

I said, 'This man you went to see in London. What do you call him?'

'Vogler. It wasn't Vogler you saw?'

I said, wearily, that I supposed it was. Vogler; and Vogler on the list of half-remembered émigré names I had handed to Roddinghead. I said, 'He called himself Cunliffe. He had an office in Francis Street and a secretary with glasses and her hair parted in the middle.'

'*Yoh, yoh*. That is Anna, his daughter.'

Bunface. Miss Vogler. Cunliffe's daughter. I had rumbled that one, too, that afternoon when Roddinghead had told me about it. It was nice to get it confirmed. It didn't seem to help the present situation a great deal.

Imre sighed presently. 'Well, Nicolas, I have now told you all. You think badly of me?'

'No, Uncle.'

'I am bitterly ashamed, my boy. I apologize to you.'

'You don't need to feel ashamed. I understand.'

'Maybe in the long run you won't feel so badly. After all, if the government is really interested, it can't be . . .'

'It isn't. That was just a lot of hokum, too.'

'Oh, I am sorry. I am sorry, Nicolas.'

We sat again in turgid silence. After a while, sighing gustily, he said, 'So one door closes, another opens. It isn't the end of the world. At least you can go to Canada with a clear mind.'

I said, 'Yes,' returning to the familiar lunacy.

'After all, you're an intelligent boy. You can learn the business quickly. And you've got to admit the prospects with Bela are magnificent.'

'Yes. If he'll do anything for me.'

He was looking at me in an odd sort of way. 'If he'll do anything for you! You mean you don't know? You haven't heard?'

'Heard what? What about?'

He was gazing at me in astonishment, the hairs of his nose waving in his powerful breath. I said, 'What?' in a kind of squeak, practically leaping up and down in front of him. 'What is it, Uncle? What are you trying to say? What in God's name is it I'm supposed to have heard?'

'About Bela,' he said.

Typically, he'd left it to the last. Bela had written. He had written saying specifically that I was his heir. He had written to say that he had sent me a one-way ticket. He wanted me in the business right away.

'Naturally,' Maminka said, 'I told him you would have to consider it. After all, does he suppose you can drop all your important business to fly to him the minute he remembers his responsibilities? He was always thoughtless, even as a boy. I told him perhaps you wouldn't care for the business, perhaps you would wish to act merely as a kind of consultant. I told him . . .'

I said, 'Yes, Maminka. If you could just please try to remember when you wrote him. If you could try to think again.'

'My dear child, I've told you – a month, two months ago. What does it matter? Let me look at you again.'

'And he hasn't replied?'

'But of course he wouldn't, at this time of the year. This is the time they are so busy. I know Bela.'

I only hoped she was right. Her clear almond eyes were smiling gaily at me. A large number of undigested items had recently come my way. I said, 'And Maura was here? Maura was actually here three times?'

'*Bobitchka*, I've already told you. You are like a little puppy dog. Try to stand still for a minute.'

'And you can't remember when she was here last? Do you think it was when Bela's letter came? Was it when she heard about Bela?'

'Nicolas, I'm not a calendar. Imre might know. Maybe I would think better with a cigarette. Do you know that ogre has tried to stop me smoking for good! He says it is my throat. Oh, I understand very well his reasons! Darling boy,' she said, catching my arm, 'I implore you to stay still for a minute. You are making me quite giddy. Here, come and sit with me. Now tell me everything from Prague. Whom did you see? Where did you go? Did Baba weep to see you again?'

I told her presently. It was a very detailed story, containing everything she wanted to hear. She sat and held my hands, her lovely eyes alive with recollection, exclaiming from time to time. It is always a pleasure to tell Maminka a story, and this one certainly had many merits. It didn't contravene the Official Secrets Act, 1911.

I went back that night after borrowing a quid from Imre. I had meant to ask for five but, remembering what he had told me, desisted. I had only twelve and six left from the other pound. I didn't know how I was going to manage. I thought God would provide. I thought Maura might, at a pinch. I felt slightly drunk.

I thought of Maura, speeding after my headlights through the dark New Forest. I was pretty sure why she'd stayed away from Bournemouth. Bela's letter; the big time. She hadn't wanted to push herself. She hadn't wished to give the appearance of getting her foot in the door. The young master might have other ideas now. If she had only known; that I had been through all this before. There was a lot Maura didn't know. There was a lot she was going to know. I shoved my foot down and fairly let rip.

Just before Lyndhurst the road bends sharply right. I took it at sixty and suddenly was ramming the brake pedal practically through the floor. A pony was standing in the middle of the road looking into the headlights. I don't know if I touched him. I skidded right, left, tyres shrieking, tree trunks rearing into the beam both sides. Car going over, over ... not quite. Steady. Stopped. Silence. Light beams staring calmly into shrubbery. I had stalled.

I got out after a moment, heart still in my throat. The car was slanted into the shrubbery, nose buried in a bush. The registration plate was bent. That seemed to be the only damage. I got back in and started and reversed slowly. She came out quite easily and I pulled into the side of the road and switched off again and lit a cigarette and watched my hands still shaking. I thought it was the sort of Charleyish move I could always expect of myself : to come through the three dangerous and fantastic months in Prague and end by piling myself up against a tree in the New Forest. I started off again presently. I didn't go at more than forty after that.

I had left Bournemouth just after seven o'clock. It was a quarter to ten before I drew up outside her house.

She had been washing her hair. It hung straight and damply gleaming and pleasantly scented. She was in a dressing gown and had no make-up on and seemed so small and finely-drawn, after some I had known, that I wanted nothing so much as simply to gaze at her. We were sitting on the floor in front of the gas fire, holding hands.

She said, 'Oh, Nicolas, if only I'd known. If only you could have given me some hint.'

'I couldn't. I shouldn't be telling you about it now. They could still put me in prison.'

'And you only guessed when this man asked about your nanny?'

I nodded. Some slight amendments had been needed to the official version. Vlasta had undergone a change of sex. 'Yes. I knew I had never mentioned Baba. And later on, of course, when I heard that Baba was not in fact dead, I realized where the information must have come from. It could only have come from Imre, because he was the only person who said Baba was dead.'

She was silent for a long time. I withdrew one hand and put my arm round her and kissed her neck. It smelled of shampoo.

She said, 'You're quite sure about us, are you?'

'Never surer of anything in my life.'

'And you want to go to Canada right away?'

'Don't you want me to?'

'Because I've been thinking.' Her eyes were blinking rapidly and intelligently at the gas fire. 'I want to go with you. We could get married first. I mean, if you're really sure you want to. If you're absolutely certain of it. We could get a special licence.'

I looked at her and felt the faintest pang. She was a wonderful girl, a splendid girl in so many ways. If she didn't just have this thing about working everything out. Her eyes flickered at me and I realized I had been too long in answering.

I said, 'Why, Maura, that's *just* what I want. That's a marvellous thing.' And it probably was.

'It would only take a few days. And there are lots of things you need to clear up first – your car and other bits and pieces. And the Little Swine – we must have a clear understanding about your shares. He'll have to buy you out. Oh, Nicolas,' she said, taking my head in her two hands and kissing me gently on the lips. 'You're a lovely old idiot. I should have been looking after you long ago, do you know that?'

And again she was probably right.

'If only you'd told me about all this business. If only you could have dropped a word right at the beginning.'

'Well. It's over now, and there's nothing you could have done about it. And anyway,' I said, a bit irritably, 'I got away with it. That's something in the circumstances.'

'Oh, Nicolas, of course it is. You've been tremendously clever and terribly brave, and I love you. But you ought to have been a bit more careful about that man Cunliffe. You could have looked him up in the Law List right away.'

'Why should I have looked him up in the Law List?'

'Well, why not? He didn't have anything about being a solicitor on his notepaper. And he was telling you about this legacy. I'd have looked him up. I'd have looked him up right away. It's the first thing I would have done. And then none of this need have happened.'

And she probably would; and it probably needn't, I thought with a sudden grave and lowering feeling in my vitals.

'Oh, Nicolas, I've upset you.'

'No, you haven't, silly.'

'Yes, I have. And I didn't mean to. And I bet I wouldn't have looked up the list, that's only a thing you think of afterwards. Oh, Nicolas, you silly old silly, I do love you, and I wanted to make up to you for everything.' She was kissing me in a certain kind of way between her words, and presently my spirits recovered. And she did make up for it.

It was after one when I left. I tiptoed down the stairs and out into the dark square in some confusion of mind; excited, perturbed, not knowing, as they say, whether I was on my knee or my elbow.

I drove home slowly and put the covers on the car and went in and up the three flights and switched the light on. The letters were lying as I had left them on the plush tablecloth. I went through them again, standing there in my raincoat. It was there, of course; a franked envelope I had mistaken for a circular.

My dear Nicolas,

Excuse the short note. I am busy and not well. Do not tell this to your mother. I have been thinking for some time to make a trip to England and to get an idea of you. This is not possible. I have a slight paralysis of the right side. I repeat, do not tell this to your mother. I want you, Nicolas, to come out to see me right away. I enclose you your ticket. You will understand me.

Your loving uncle
Bela

It was dated 23rd August, five weeks ago. The ticket was inside.

I took off my raincoat. I went and brushed my teeth in the bathroom and undressed and switched off the light. Mrs Nolan had drawn the curtains. I knew I wouldn't sleep for a bit, and I didn't want to lie in the dark. So I opened the curtains and got into bed and lay there with my arms behind my head, looking out at the night sky.

I had been shuttling about a bit lately. I wasn't sure that I knew myself. Too many things happening, a surplus of experience still to be absorbed. I thought maybe none of it had happened. Maybe it was a dream and I would shortly awake to face another day in the service of the Little Swine. But I knew it was not a dream. There was that inner disturbance, the sickness of events; a sensation of distances having been covered. It was not unpleasant. It was not particularly pleasant. I had been living it up, after a fashion.

An aeroplane drifted slowly across the window, winking like a firefly. Long ranges of cloud stood coldly corrugated in the moonlight. The sky was still now; not racing as on that other night, when the iron king had leapt with his iron horse in the moonlight.

None of it had been necessary, Maura had said. None of it

need have happened. I didn't know about that. The pony in the New Forest need not have happened. It had happened. A part of oneself went out to meet the event. A part of oneself remained involved with it; one was diminished by it. It took time to recover what had been lost.

The aeroplane vanished slowly off the edge of the pane. I thought there was rather more Thinking going on here than was strictly called for. Events were mainly incalculable, their significance always dubious. If experience taught anything, it was not to think too much, but to sharpen up the responses. It was a lesson I had learnt on the night that Wenceslas leapt in the moonlight. I thought I'd got it now. I thought my responses had sharpened up a bit, and closed my eyes and went to sleep, not dissatisfied.

THE ROSE
OF TIBET

Prologue

THE decision to call this book *The Rose of Tibet* was made at a fairly late date and at the behest of our managing director, Mr Theodore Links. I write 'our' not in the editorial plural, but because I happen to work for the firm. I am an editor of it. I have been an editor, with this and other publishing firms, for eight years. My name is Lionel Davidson.

It seems necessary to establish all this with crystal clarity because what follows is, as one of the manuscript readers had written, '. . . a bit on the weird side'. It is, however, mostly true: it is because it is only mostly true that a few introductory words are called for.

Charles Duguid Houston left England for India on 25 January 1950, and returned on 16 June 1951. Interested students can find a report of the latter event in the 17th June issues of the *Sunday Graphic* and the *Empire News*, the only two organs who noticed it. (They will have to go to the British Museum Newspaper Library at Colindale, London NW9, to do so, however, since both of these papers, like many of the prinicpals in this story, are now defunct.)

He returned on a stretcher, with a sensational story to tell if anybody had been able to get him to tell it. The fact that nobody did is due less, perhaps, to his own discretion than to the interesting state of the world that month.

In the month of June 1951, the abbreviated newspapers of the time were trying to cover the Korean war, the sinking of the submarine *Affray*, the search for Burgess and Maclean, and the iniquities of Dr Mossadeq, whose government was busy nationalizing the oil refineries of Abadan. In England King George VI was convalescing after an operation, in Capri King Farouk honeymooning with Narriman, in Westminster the Minister of Food cautiously forecasting an increase in the meat ration to 2s. 4d., and everywhere a large concern being expressed at the future of Yasmin and who would control it, Aly or Rita. Several murders were committed. The Festival of Britain shone bravely in the rain. The Marquis of Blandford got himself engaged.

With such an embarrassement of riches, the newspapers had little space to spare for Houston, and so far as can be ascertained no single follow-up was made as a result of the item published in the two Sundays. It was not an uninteresting item. (It showed 29-year-old Charles Houston, former art teacher and resident of Baron's Court, London W, being carried on a stretcher from the Calcutta plane with injuries sustained during the recent fighting in Tibet.) And yet it was not a very unusual one either. Former residents of London W, and Glasgow S, and Manchester C, were being flown in pretty regularly at the time, and from the same general direction, with injuries sustained in far more recent and newsworthy circumstances.

Not even the *West London Gazette* thought to send a representative to the London Clinic (where Houston was taken directly from the airport) to inquire after the health of this former resident.

He was thus left quite alone at a time when as a result of shock he might have been prevailed upon to tell his story; a quirk of fate that would benefit an increasing number of classically minded youths from about 1966 onwards.

While his restless contemporaries were thus holding the stage, Houston was able to pass the month fairly quietly. He had his right arm off. He sought release with morphia drugs from painful memories. Only occasionally did he worry about the disposition of his half million pounds.

The fact of the half million pounds was later, however, to worry a great many other people: it is one of the reasons why this book must be only mostly true.

*

232

'*Why so touchy?*' reads the memo in Mr Theodore Links's handwriting, which lies before me. '*I have said I liked it, and I still do. But it will satisfy R.B. if we can in some way "treat" the passages underlined. Also I feel strongly we shd go out for a fictional kind of title for the same reason. What is wrong with (d)? It is immensely more attractive than the factual ones. Also who is over-riding O's wishes? I seem to remember only one over-riding wish! But if you feel so strongly do a little foreword explg the book and its backgd. . . .*'

Taking the abbreviations in order, R.B. is Rosenthal Brown, our lawyers, who have needed on the whole a good deal of satisfying about this manuscript; (d) the present title – *The Rose of Tibet*; and O . . . O is Mr Oliphant. Without Mr Oliphant there would not be a book. It is Mr Oliphant indeed who constitues the *backgd*.

I do not know when Mr Oliphant first took to writing his Latin primer, but in the first of the two letters I have from him in my file he says, 'It is the result of many years of careful work, and incorporates, as you will see, most of the useful suggestions you so kindly made some time ago.'

This letter reached me, with the primer, in May 1959.

I said to my secretary, 'Miss Marks, who is F. Neil Oliphant and when did I make him some suggestions about a Latin primer?'

Miss Marks looked up from her typewriter and began to pat her face with both hands (a habit of hers when labouring under some anxiety which she will not mind my mentioning).

She said, 'Oh. Yes. That wasn't you. That was Mr — ' (a predeccesor of mine).

'Have we ever published any Latin primers?'

'No. He thought we might like to – Mr Oliphant did. He has a new way of teaching Latin.'

'Who is Mr Oliphant?'

'He is a Latin teacher.'

Miss Marks's face had turned a shade of pink at this unexceptional statement.

I said, 'Where does he teach?'

'He used to at the Edith Road Girls' Secondary in Fulham.'

'At the *which*?'

'The Edith Road... It's an excellent school,' Miss Marks said. 'It's one of the best girls' day schools in the country. The academic record is quite outstanding.'

I began to see possible reasons for Miss Marks's staunch championship of this school, and also for her anxiety.

'I was there myself, actually,' she said, confirming them.

'Oh, really?'

'Yes... Look, I'm sorry about this,' said Miss Marks with a rush, becoming, with every moment, pinker. 'I've sort of kept up with him. He's a nice old man. He happened to mention once that he was writing this book, and he didn't know anything about publishing or anything... I mean, I told him, naturally, that I wasn't in a position to guarantee –'

'That's all right, Miss Marks. Do we have a copy of the correspondence?'

'Mr Links would have it. He took it over when Mr — left.'

'Oh. Why did he do that?'

'Because it was all his fault, really,' Miss Marks said.

She explained why.

It seemed that Mr Oliphant's primer had come in first in 1955. Mr — had promptly rejected it, and that would have been the end if T.L. had not happened to come into the room while it was still lying in his out-tray. T.L. had been having at the time one of his not uncommon raves; on this occasion for the mental-disciplinary benefits of a classical language. He thought that Mr Oliphant's book had something. The book had gone out to a specialist reader, who thought otherwise. None the less, T.L. had suggested a number of amendments to Mr Oliphant. The amended book had reappeared in 1957. By this time, T.L. had lost his earlier enthusiasm, but he felt a certain uneasy responsibility for Mr Oliphant's two years of additional work. Had the book been then even remotely publishable, he would have published it. But it was not. It had gone back with further suggestions.

These were the suggestions now incorporated in Mr Oliphant's latest work.

I said, 'Well, that's easily settled. Let's just bung it through to T.L.'

'I don't think that would be a very good idea,' Miss Marks said. 'He was in a bit of temper with it last time.'

'But I don't know anything about it.'

'No,' Miss Marks said, patting unhappily.

It was at this point that I spotted a fortunate flaw. Three consecutive chapters of Mr Oliphant's book were headed *What the Science University Entrant Needs to Know,* (I), (II), and (III). Even with my own limited knowledge of the subject I was aware that Science University Entrants did not now need to know any Latin; there had lately been a considerable discussion about it in the Press with some fierce broadsides from Mr Oliphant's Latin-teaching colleagues.

I said, 'Your Mr Oliphant doesn't keep up with the news much, does he?' and told her why.

'Oh, dear,' Miss Marks said sadly. 'That poor old man.'

'How old is he?'

'He must be getting on for 80 now.'

'H'm.'

On form, it seemed to take Mr Oliphant two years to rewrite. In the natural order of things it was unlikely that he would be doing so many times more ... Any solution that would not involve dashing, once and for all, an old man's hopes, would be a charitable one.

I said, 'Look, Miss Marks, write him a letter,' and told her what to put in it. 'Make it a nice one. I'll sign it.'

I didn't, however, have to. That very afternoon, Mr Oliphant telephoned. Perhaps somebody had put him right about Science University Entrants. He asked for his book back. Miss Marks and I exchanged a look of relief as she replaced the telephone. I had been listening on the other one.

Our relief was short-lived. For with only three chapters to attend to instead of a whole book, and perhaps with some intimations of mortality rustling in his ears, Mr Oliphant went into top gear. Just four months later, in October 1959, the familiar primer came homing in once more.

It came at a time when I was inclined to view the problems of authorship with a certain kindly sympathy. My first book *The Night of Wenceslas* (Gollancz, 13s. 6d.) was awaiting publication. I had been shown the various niggles of the manuscript readers. I hated the manuscript readers. Manuscript readers, non-creative people generally, it seemed to me, should try and create something – anything – some tiny thing; then we could hear further from them. It was iniquitous, it seemed to me, that such people should sit in judgement on the works of creative people. To spin something out of nothing, to put something together, to make something quite new in the world – this was an admirable, a laborious task. The people who did it, it seemed to me, should be given votes of thanks, slapped on the back, not subjected to a barrage of vile criticism for their pains.

In this frame of mind, Mr Oliphant became my brother. I regarded his work with the warmest admiration. He had had it all typed out again, which was certainly a point in its favour. His hand-written corrections were neat and unobtrusive. He had fussed about with colons and semi-colons in a way which made my heart go out to him. And moreover, so long as the reader brought a little effort to the job – a millionth part perhaps of that lavished by Mr Oliphant on his – he could very easily pick up a little Latin from it. Why, after all, should we not publish such a book? We published 124 books a year. Why not Mr Oliphant's?

I did not, however, as the heart dictated, send the manuscript directly to the printer's. I sent it out to the reader again.

The reader was not waiting to have a book published.

He regarded Mr Oliphant's work with something less than my own admiration.

He said it was written in a style of pedantic facetiousness that had gone out at the turn of the century. He said the exposition was pitched far above the comprehension of a modern schoolboy, and the wit far below. So far as he was able to judge it was aimed at an audience of unsophisticated cryptologists aged about seventy.

I took this report in to Mr Links. I couldn't see what else was to be done with it.

He gnawed his lip as he read it. He turned to the manuscript. 'There was something here,' he muttered, leafing through. 'I remember I got quite a flash from it.... I told him *adult* education – the discipline of classical language for adults...'

'Well, that's what he seems to have done,' I said. 'You'll see here in —'s report, he says the book is aimed at – at quite mature people.'

'It won't do,' he said. 'No, no... Oh, my God! ... You know, this is my fault, not his. I thought he could do it... *My* mistake.'

'Well, what's to be done about it,' I said, in the silence.

'I don't know.'

'We can't publish it as it is.'

'We can't publish it whatever he does.'

'Who does publish primers?'

'Macmillan, Longman... The snag, is it isn't a primer now.'

'Would an agent take him on?'

'With this? ... Look, see if he's still got his first version. There was *something* there. I saw it. *Help* him with it. I don't think it's anything for us – I'm sure it isn't now. But after all ... Give him the right outline. See if someone in the office can rough it in for him. I'll look at it myself if you like. And then we'll see. We'll get it in a publishable state for him, anyway.'

This assignment – to tell my brother Oliphant that his four years of work had been wasted and that all we could do now was to show him how to write a book that we didn't intend to publish – seemed to me a highly unpleasant one. I said as much.

'I don't see how I can possibly put all this in a letter,' I ended.

'No. No. I don't think you should. I wasn't suggesting it. As I remember, he's quite an old man. Go and see him. It will be a nice gesture.'

I said, with extreme reluctance, 'Of course, if you think I should . . .'

'Certainly. It will be much easier face to face. You know,' he said, returning the manuscript, 'there's not a bad lesson in publishing here. It's fatally easy to encourage the wrong people. You've got to be on guard all the time. Kindness,' he said, seeing my hesitations, 'is no help – to the author or to the publisher. It can be a very cruel thing.'

'You don't think,' I said, fumbling, 'we should let him have another go, off his own bat. I hear he's getting on for eighty now . . .'

T.L. blew down his pipe a bit and shook his head. He said slowly, 'We can't do that. We can't do it . . . You know, I wasn't wrong to begin with. There was something there, a tiny kernel. Someone could publish it. Let him have that pleasure before he dies.'

'All right,' I said.

Mr Oliphant lived in Fitzmaurice Mansions, Fitzmaurice Crescent, Baron's Court. I rang him up that afternoon and drove out the following one.

Fitzmaurice Mansions turned out to be a vast ornamented Edwardian pile in reddish-orange stone. I went up very slowly to the second floor in a little dark lift with a highly complicated arrangement of folding doors. There was no window on the landing, and the light wouldn't work. I fumbled around looking for number 62a.

Two half-pint bottles of milk stood outside the door, and the morning paper was still jammed in the letter-box. I rang the bell, and a minute or two later had to do so again.

There was presently a shuffling noise inside. I braced myself as the door opened. A tall, thin, bent man in a dressing-gown looked out.

'Is it Mr Davidson?'

'That's right.'

'Come in. I hope you haven't been waiting long. I dozed off.'

I had my hand outstretched, but he didn't seem to see it. He reached beyond me for the milk and newspaper. There was a peculiar smell inside, the smell of old people who live in close places.

He closed the door behind me. 'I've not been too well lately I was having a little nap.'

'I'm sorry to have disturbed you.'

'Not a bit. Not the least little bit. Through here. I've been looking forward to it. I don't know how I happened to go off like that.'

In the light it was possible to see that Mr Oliphant was exceptionally grimy. He looked ill and unkempt. His face was immensely long and thin like a greyhound's; and at the moment much in need of a shave. He put the milk and the newspaper down, pulled his grey stuff dressing-gown more closely round him and slicked down his sparse hairs.

'I'm sorry you have to find me like this. I meant to clear up a bit,' he said, looking round at the terrible confusion of clothes and bedding and old meals. We seemed to be in his bedroom. 'I thought I would just rest for a minute or two after lunch. I had no sleep last night.'

'I'm sorry to hear that,' I said, somewhat nasally, for I was trying to breathe through my mouth in the appalling stench of the room. 'What's the trouble?'

'Bronchial. I get it every year about this time. Hard to breathe, you know,' he said, tapping his throat.

His breath did seem to be whistling a bit. There was a faint, soft suggestion of Ireland in his voice. I said, 'If you would like to put this off to another day, Mr Oliphant – there's quiet a lot to talk about.'

'No, no. I wouldn't hear of it, my dear fellow. I'm only sorry for all this. Let me get you something. What can I get you? We haven't shaken hands or anything ...' he said, holding out with embarrassment his own skeletal and by no means clean one.

I shook it. I refused refreshment. He pulled up a couple of chairs to an electric fire, and we began to talk.

There was not, after all, very much to talk about. For despite his apparent senility, Mr Oliphant had kept his marbles in very fair trim: he summed up the situation in a trice and at once

239

with an old-fashioned and perhaps racial courtesy began to ease it for me.

'Your Mr Links is a man of enthusiasms,' he said. 'I like that in a man. He sent me a splendid letter when I first completed the book. I'm sorry he's not so keen on this version.'

'Yes. Well. That's one of the things – '

'Oh, not that I blame him. I couldn't get very enthusiastic about it myself. I'm sorry about the science students. I put that material in to try and broaden it... But the first version wasn't bad, you know, and he spotted it. I didn't think anybody would. It wasn't the normal run of Latin reader. Just as a matter of interest, Mr Davidson, why was he so interested?'

I said, in a bit of a panic, because just at the moment I'd forgotten, 'Why, because he appreciated the basic idea – the idea of a dead-language becoming, what shall I say ...'

Mr Oliphant told me gently what I should say. 'A kind of mental discipline for adults ...?'

'Precisely,' I said, and elaborated gratefully on this type of discipline.

'Yes,' Mr Oliphant said. 'I ask because naturally after a lifetime of dealing with Latin works of one sort or another I do not recall ever seeing your imprint on one of them. It was entirely because of Doris Marks – how is that dear girl, by the way?'

'Fine. Fine. She sends her warm regards. That leads us to a point, Mr Oliphant. It's a fact that we don't publish Latin works. It isn't really our preserve at all. What Mr Links now feels – what we all feel,' I said, with acute embarrassment, and went on to tell him.

The old man sat and breathed heavily.

'We would like to give you every kind of assistance with it – secretarial, technical, anything you might need. There have been a lot of changes in the educational field in the past few years – changes that you wouldn't perhaps know about – but I haven't the slightest doubt – '

'Yes. Yes. It's uncommonly good of you. I'm very grateful. I really am,' he said, smiling at me. 'I'll think about it very seriously. But I doubt if I can get any work done this winter. I'm going to have a rest this winter. I'll look at it again in the spring. All the same,' he said, laughing, 'I have a feeling I might be too old a dog to learn new tricks. If I had any of my own teeth, I would say I was getting too long – '

He stopped. His expression changed. He began to cough. It was the most extraordinary cough I had ever heard in my life, and for a moment I couldn't believe it was coming from him. It sounded like a klaxon, and from the way he bounced up and down in the chair, as if he were setting it on and off.

I got up in alarm and patted him on the back. He began waving his hands towards the bed presently, and I looked around and saw bottles on his bedside table, and brought them all to him with a spoon. He pointed one out with a shaking hand, and I uncorked it and poured him a spoonful – and one for the carpet in my excitement – and got it in his mouth. He managed to control himself for a moment, and presently began pointing silently under the bed.

With some horror, I got down on my knees and poked about there. There was a plastic bowl covered with a cloth. I got it out and gave him it – I have to admit with the cloth still on – and he uncovered it and spat.

'I'm very sorry about this,' he said feebly after a few minutes. 'I shouldn't have laughed. No, leave it out. Leave it here, I might need it again.'

'Is there anything I can do for you?'

'Nothing. Someone is coming to see me later with some things I need. Please don't worry. Sit down. It goes off quite soon.'

I sat down, very gingerly.

'I think on reflection, you know,' he said presently, as if he'd been thinking about it all the time, 'that I won't take advantage of your very kind offer. I'll let sleeping dogs lie. At my time of life, after all . . .' he said, beginning a dangerous smile.

'I'm sure you'll decide differently when you've thought about it,' I said, watching him nervously. 'Perhaps you'll let me come and talk to you about it again in a few weeks.'

'Of course, my dear fellow. It's very good of you. But I don't think you'll get me to change my mind. You see, you won't want to publish the book yourselves – for reasons I quite understand – and that would rather take the gilt off it for me. I'm going to tell you a secret,' he said, his smile becoming a little sheepish. 'I started the book out of vanity.'

'Vanity, Mr Oliphant?'

'Vanity. I met Doris – Miss Marks – at a school get-together and for some reason I told her I was writing it. I wasn't, actually. It had occurred to me just at that moment. I suppose I wanted to impress her. Living alone, one's tongue tends to run away in company . . . I meant to tell her, when it was published, how she had inspired it . . . Well, it isn't a very serious loss.'

'There's no reason why it should be a loss at all.'

He wasn't really attending to me. He was still looking at me and smiling, but his smile had become somehow – sly. His tongue moved round his lips.

'I expect you would very much sooner publish works in a living tongue,' he said.

'Well, that's our business, Mr Oliphant.'

'I expect you would very much sooner publish a story like Houston's,' he said in the same tone.

I didn't know what he was talking about. He didn't seem to be talking to me at all.

He got up and began rummaging in the bed. Two shiny red exercise books were buried in the eiderdown, and two more were under the pillow.

'I've just been re-reading it,' he said. 'I had the idea some years ago of writing it myself, but I was busy with my Latin reader. I doubt if I ever will now. Would you like to read it?'

'What is it?'

'It's Houston's account of what happened to him in Tibet.'

He was handing me the exercise books, so I took them, Mr Theodore Links's words ringing ominously in my ears. '*Kindness is no help to the author or to the publisher. It can be a very cruel thing.*'

I said, 'You know, I'm not sure if this is our kind of thing at all, Mr Oliphant. We do very little travel.'

'I wouldn't call it a traveller's tale,' he said. 'I don't know what I'd call it. It's certainly very odd.'

I was racking my brains as I leafed through, trying to think who the mysterious Houston was. Phrases came up at me – in what looked suspiciously like Mr Oliphant's own neat handwriting – from the ruled lines.

'... doss house like an enormous catacomb, a great cliff of a place with little stone rooms flickering in the light of butter lamps. ...'

'... simply took off all his clothes and jewels and gave them away ...'

'... kept out of the way all day and biked on to Kanchenjunga ...'

'... to Darjeeling left luggage office, where so far as I know ...'

'... so badly beaten-up I knew I was crippled, but I had to ...'

I said, 'Mr Oliphant – if you could just refresh me – who actually was Houston?'

'He is a very dear friend of mine. We used to teach at the same school.'

'He went to Tibet on – am I right? – a bicycle?'

'Yes. Well. Mainly,' Mr Oliphant said.

'I wonder why nothing has been published about it.'

Mr Oliphant offered several possible reasons for this omission. He watched the effect of them on me, still smiling rather slyly.

'I thought you'd like it,' he said.

'It certainly sounds a remarkable story.'

'More stimulating than those of ancient Rome, say.'

'Well. Different.'

'Yes,' he said, enjoying himself. 'Yes, I thought you'd take that view.'

'Who wrote it?'

'I did,' said Mr Oliphant. 'He dictated it to me. He hadn't learned to use his left hand then, of course.'

'I see.'

'But there wouldn't be any difficulty about publication. He gave me it. If you're interested.'

I said cautiously, 'We might be. Whereabouts is Mr Houston now?'

'He is in Barbados.'

'You're in touch with him, are you?'

'Oh, yes. This is his flat. He still pays the rent. I went out to see him a few years ago – three years ago. He was in Jamaica then. I had just had another go of this bronchitis, and he invited me out, at his expense... Of course, he is a very wealthy man now.'

'Is he?'

'Oh, yes. He left Tibet with about half a million pounds. I expect he could have had very much more if he'd been able to carry it. He knows where the rest is.'

'I see,' I said again.

I didn't, of course. But presently, as Mr Oliphant explained further, a few items did seem to fall into place. It is easier now to remember than to describe the dry gusto of his manner – perhaps if the reader will imagine a beardless version of Bernard Shaw sitting in a grey stuff dressing-gown over an electric fire in a darkening October afternoon he will come somehwere near it – as he recalled these items. But even in reflection his gusto is odd. Mr Oliphant had led, I suppose, up to that time a blameless enough life, chaste, continent, fairly legal; one, at all events, far removed from rapine and murder, abortion and sacred prostitution. Perhaps he had encountered worse in his classical readings; perhaps he was merely amused that I should find this story alive and those in his favourite literature dead. Or perhaps there was quite another reason. I have thought about it often since.

It must have been a little after four when I had arrived, and it was getting on for six when I left. Mr Oliphant had another attack of coughing in between.

I said anxiously, 'You're quite sure someone is coming to see you? I could very easily – '

'Not at all. I assure you . . .' he said weakly.

'Well. I'll leave you, then.'

'Yes. Yes. Just take the first two exercise books, won't you? I wanted to read the others. And come again.'

'Certainly, I'd like to.'

He didn't really want to talk any more, but just before I left I felt constrained to ask one more question.

I said, 'Mr Oliphant, I suppose he didn't, Houston, ever believe any of this business himself, did he – the supernatural business?'

He had closed his eyes but he opened them again, very pale blue and somehow – how does one describe it? – again sly.

'Oh, no. No, he didn't believe it. At least, I don't think he did. He's a very ordinary sort of chap, you know. Very ordinary ... Odd, though, how it came about, wasn't it?'

'Very,' I said.

I called on Mr Oliphant several times more in succeeding weeks – as will be narrated in the proper place – and on some other people also. But it was not till the following May, after much had passed, that we commissioned from Professor Felix Bourgès-Vallerin of the Department of Oriental Studies of the Sorbonne his account of the significance of the years 1949-51 in Tibetan affairs.

Because this account must also be considered an indispensable part of the *backgd*, I give it, however, not in its chronological place, but here.

BY PROF. BOURGÈS-VALLERIN (Abridged.) ... The year 1949, corresponding with that of Earth-Bull in its Sixteenth cycle, was for Tibet one of long-predicted ill-omen. The events associated with it had indeed been foretold for more than two and a half centuries; latterly with such elaboration of detail that four of the largest monasteries had seriously advocated changing the calendar in an attempt to avert them.

The Tibetan calendar, derived from the Indian and the Chinese, relies upon a combination of elements and animals to designate individual years. Thus, 1948, was Earth-Mouse, 1949 Earth-Bull, 1950 Iron-Tiger, and 1951 Iron-Hare. There are five elements (earth, iron, water, wood, fire) and twelve animals (hare, dragon, serpent, horse, sheep, monkey, bird, dog, pig, mouse, bull, tiger). Each element appears in sequence twice, first to designate a 'male' year and then a 'female' one. The calendar makes a complete cycle every sixty years.

Because certain combinations (wood-dragon, earth-bull, fire-tiger) have traditionally been considered inauspicious, they have attracted over the centuries a considerable body of predicition. Most of the forecast events have come off, notably the Nepalese invasion of 1791, the British Younghusband expedition of 1904 and the Chinese invasion of 1910. Those that have not come off are said to have been 'averted'.

No single year had ever produced so ominous a body of prediction, however, as that of Earth-Bull in its present cycle.

The events would be heralded, it was said, by a comet clearly visible from the three principal cities of Lhasa, Shigatse and Gyantse. Four catastrophes would then follow in strict order: a mountain would move; the Tsangpo river would be hurled from its course; the country would be overrun by terror; and the line of the Dalai Lamas would end.

While all these prediction were of some antiquity, that concerning the Dalai Lama was the most venerable. A succession of oracles had foretold that the line would end with the Thirteenth. In fact, the Thirteenth had died in 1935, and his successor, a 4-year-old boy had been recognized in 1939. By 1949, however, the year of Earth-Bull, he would still be under age and legally incapable of assuming full powers as spiritual and temporal head of the country.

Because of the alarming nature of these predictions, corroboration was sought from the oracles attached to the most important provincial monasteries. Their findings were entirely in line with those of the State Oracle; indeed they were able to provide considerable elaboration.

Thus, the female oracle of Yamdring could state with precision that for her monastery the tribulations would begin in the sixth month of Earth-Bull (August 1949); and that between then and the 'terror', the monastery would have a visitation, 'from beyond the sunset', of a past conqueror of the country who would carry away the abbess together with the monastery treasure.

(The visitor was expected to be an incarnation of the Tartar prince Hu-Tzung, who in 1717 had invaded from the north-east, sacked the province of Hodzo and only withdrawn when the abbess of Yamdring had given herself to him. Because he had accepted the abbess's favours, this prince was subsequently struck dead by Chen-Rezi, the God-Protector of Tibet. For according to tradition, the abbess was divine − a benevolent she-devil who had been the original inhabitant of the Himalayan plateau, before a wandering monkey from India had lured her from her cave, coupled with her on an island in the Yamdring lake, and thus fathered the Tibetan people.)

Other monasteries produced equally gloomy predictions, one of them (the country's second largest, at Sera) providing, however, an important variant. This was that the 'terror' mentioned in the forecast would not take place actually in Earth-Bull, but in the following year, Iron-Tiger, and would begin in the first week of the eighth month (October 1950).

Faced with these lowering and increasingly refined predictions, the Regent convened a cabinet of five ministers. It met in April 1948, and by midsummer had drawn up a number of provisions.

To placate the devils who lived in the mountains, a national spiritual effort would be made: this would take the form of prayers and offerings throughout the country. In addition, so that the devils might be offered no provocation, nomads would be forbidden their traditional right to winter at the foot of the mountains.

In the event of the devils refusing placation (that is, if a mountain *did* move or the Tsangopo *were* hurled from its course) further measures would have to be taken to avert the remaining predictions.

Since by 'terror' it was assumed a new Chinese invasion was meant, it would be necessary to examine all circumstances that might give the Chinese a reason to invade. All contacts with the Western world should be reduced, and all foreigners who could be regarded as 'Western imperialists' dismissed.

Since at the time only five Europeans were living on a permanent basis in Tibet, all of them in day-to-day contact with the government, the cabinet could see no reason for immediate action in this respect.

The five Europeans were: Hugh Richardson, Reginald Fox, Robert Ford, Heinrich Harrer and Peter Aufschneiter.

Richardson was the head of the newly created Indian Government Mission; although an Englishman he was acting for another Asian power, and one moreover that had just thrown off the imperialist yoke: he thus enjoyed the highest diplomatic status.

Fox and Ford were radio operators on contract; it would be enough merely to let their contracts expire. Harrer and Aufschneiter were ex-prisoners of war who had escaped from a British war-time camp in India; they had no official standing and could be turned out at a moment's notice.

For the moment, therefore, all was under control. However, if despite everything, the Chinese did invade, one last and rather more awesome step would be necessary. Seven hundred years of tradition would have to be flouted and the Dalai Lama installed while still under age, to ensure the succession.

This was not a step that any of the ministers cared to plan in detail; but since they had done everything that could be expected of them, the weeks-long meeting adjourned. The Regent set himself to watch the course that events would take.

It is a matter of historical record that they took exactly the one predicted.

In October 1948, the comet appeared, causing widespread alarm and disorders in Lhasa, Shigatse and Gyantse. In July and August 1949 the 'mountain moved', an enormous seismic disturbance that affected the entire Himalayan region and diverted the Tsangpo eight miles from its course. (It 'moved' again even more formidably the following August.) And in October 1950 (in the 'first week of the eighth month of Iron-

Tiger' as the oracle of Sera had predicted) the Chinese duly invaded.

Faced with this final disaster, the Regent took his 'last step'. On 12 November the under-age Dalai Lama was formally installed as Head of State – and three weeks later, on 9 December, fled.

Such the predictions and such the record for the year of Earth-Bull.

Whether the many regional predictions were similarly fulfilled must remain a matter for speculation. Among refugees on Indian-controlled border territory, however, there appeared to be a substantial belief, early in 1951, that some at least of the predicted events had taken place; in particular those forecast for the Yamdring monastery.

A report in the Calcutta *Amrita Bazar Patrika* of 3 February that year quotes one refugee: 'Certainly the troubles at Yamdring began in the sixth month of Earth-Bull. . . . As everyone knows the abbess was abducted and with her treasure to the value of four crores of rupees' (three million pounds sterling).

The story was taken up by other newspapers and caused a good deal of speculation (and some political upsets) over the meaning of the phrase in the prediction 'a visitation from beyond the sunset'. Some editorialists felt it could only mean 'from the west', and that since the Chinese had indisputably attacked from the north and the east, the oracle must have foreseen depredations from Ladakh on Tibet's western border.

This was bitterly denied (9 February) by a partisan member of the *Lok Sabha*, the Indian Lower House, who rejected the 'foul insinuations of certain people in Calcutta who can only ascribe to Ladakhis the base motives that would actuate them in similar circumstances. It is beyond question that any Ladakhi or Kashmiri could have lent himself to the looting of monasteries. . . .'

Despite this and other denials, the Indian Press kept the story alive for several weeks, titillated, even in the midst of such tragic horrors, by the strange tale of an abducted abbess and of four crores of rupees.

As the weather in the border territory grew warmer, however, and the refugees began to drift back to their own devil-haunted mountains, the reports tailed off. By June of 1951 they had quite finished.

F. B.-V. PARIS
1960

That was the month Charles Houston arrived back in London on his stretcher. He had been away seventeen months. It felt, he said, like as many years.

Chapter 1

I

In the summer of 1949, when he was 27, Houston found himself having an affair with a married woman. She was 30, and he was not in love with her, and he had gone into it only because he was bored and lonely. He didn't think that the affair would outlast the summer, but it did, and by the autumn, when he started school again, he was wondering how to end it. He was a bit disgusted with himself.

Houston was living at this time at Baron's Court in the flat which he shared with his half-brother Hugh, who was two years younger and a good deal noisier and rather inclined to take his shirts and his handkerchieves when he was home. Hugh was not at home. He was in India. He had gone in June, with a film unit, had gone very hurriedly, for permission had come through at the last moment; and one effect had been that Houston's holiday plans had had to be altered. He had been going to spend a month with his half-brother walking in France.

As it was he had decided to stay at home and have a look round the galleries and do a bit of painting; and he would have done this if it had not happened to be the hottest summer in London for ten years. Instead, his days began to follow a familiar indolent pattern.

He got up every morning and let the char in, and ate his breakfast and read the paper. After this he fiddled with a sketch and then he went out and had a drink.

From time to time he went to parties. He even held one

himself in the flat. But the people bored him; they were Hugh's friends rather than his own. He felt himself very much older than his brother.

At two of the parties in a single week however, he encountered Glynis, and on both occasions found himself wondering about her and about her small and quarrelsome and very drunk husband.

She was tall and somewhat self-conscious about her height; she stooped a little and wore flat shoes. But her face had about it a fey and unprotected character that appealed to Houston most strongly.

She lived with her husband at Fulham, quite close to Baron's Court, and after debating with himself for a couple of days, Houston had telephoned her.

It was an afternoon in July a high blue day of reeling heat. Houston told her he was going to Roehampton.

'Lucky you.'

'Why don't you come?'

A pause. 'Oh, I think not.'

'Can't you swim?'

'Yes, I can swim.'

'I'll pick you up, then.'

That was how it started. Years later the whole of that curious and aimless summer seemed to crystallize for him in the single moment; the moment of replacing the receiver in the hot empty flat and of feeling the first faint lurch: of excitement, disgust, apprehension.

He remembered very well the heart-searchings of that summer, the times he had taken stock of the position.

He had four hundred pounds in the bank, the lease of the flat, and his job as an art teacher at the Edith Road Girls' Secondary School in Fulham; it was because of the job that he had taken the near-by flat.

He had got in the habit over the years of looking after his brother. When he had come out of the navy in 1946 he had thought of staking himself for a year with his gratuity and the money his mother had left him, and setting up as a full-time artist. If the worst came to the worst he knew he could always teach. But then Hugh had in turn been released from the service and had got himself a job with the film company at five pounds a week, and Houston had had to postpone setting up as an artist; he had gone instead to the Edith Road Girls' Secondary, had signed for the flat, and kept Hugh for a couple of years.

His brother, of course, no longer needed keeping. He was earning more than double Houston's income, and cheerfully spending it. Houston didn't blame him. He knew that if he wanted, Hugh would stop frittering his money and keep him in turn. He could give the sailor's farewell to the Head of the Edith Road Girls' Secondary, a woman he deplored, and on any propitious day set up as an artist.

Why then, he wondered, didn't he? Houston didn't know why. He felt lax. He had a lowering feeling that he had somehow missed the bus, that some of the virtue had gone out of him in the past year. He didn't want to paint quite as much as he used to. He was obscurely disinclined to have his brother keep him. He didn't know what he wanted.

In the middle of July, he thought it might be a woman; but by the middle of August knew that it wasn't that, either.

2

It wasn't till the middle of September that he began to worry consciously about his brother; but once he started he knew that he must have been worrying for some time. He knew that location work would have finished in Calcutta and that the unit would have moved up into the foothills of Everest. The film was of an attempt to climb the mountain. Mail would be carried by a runner and was bound to be irregular. By the middle of September, however, he had not had any for a month. He didn't know what to do about it. He didn't want to ring up the film company, which seemed to him a fussy thing to do. He thought he would wait a bit.

He waited a week, and then didn't care whether it was fussy or not.

The girl on the switchboard put him through to a secretary. The secretary put him through to Mr Stahl.

Houston had heard of this Mr Stahl; he thought he was one of the chiefs of the company. He was somewhat taken about to be connected so instantly with the great man.

'Who is this?' said a quiet voice.

'Mr Houston – about Hugh Whittington,' he heard the secretary's voice say on the line.

'Oh, yes. Mr Houston. I am spending the day on the telephone,' the American voice said dryly to somebody in the background. 'We have received a cable, Mr Houston. I thought you would care to hear it.' He began to read the cable in soft, uninflected tones before Houston was properly aware of the sense of it. It seemed that a party of sixty-six people had been sighted below the west face of a mountain; they were on a rough trail that connected with a trade route. It was not yet known if this route was blocked.

'It's signed Lister-Lawrence,' Stahl said. 'He's the British representative in Calcutta, and our only source of information at the moment. Of course, we are sending a man to the frontier as soon as possible, but it will be a day or two before we hear anything. The earthquake destroyed all the telegraph lines.'

'The earthquake did,' Houston said, dazed, and felt the telephone begin to tremble against his ear.

'Apparently it was quite a severe one. We surmise it blocked their route back and they're going round the mountain. However, we're very optimisitc. With the local people hired out there, our party should come to sixty-six . . .'

The conversation went on for perhaps a minute or two more, and Houston made the necessary reponses, but could not afterwards recall what else had been said. He put the phone down presently and stared at it in stupefaction.

This was the first that he head of the earthquake.

*

Hugh had been 8 and he 10 when they had first realized there was something a bit different about them. That was when he had gone away to boarding school and Hugh had been too young to follow. He had been sick all the term, and Hugh had been sick too, and he had been taken away from that school and the experiment never repeated. He had thought himself over it during the war when they had been parted once for fifteen months without ill effects. But neither had been in any real danger during the war. He had a sensation of danger now.

By the end of September he had heard a good deal more about his brother. He had heard that he was safe, that the film party was resting in a village, but that their return might be held up by three casualties, none of them, however, very serious.

He had heard all this in three conversations with Stahl's secretary, a young woman called Lesley Sellers, with whom he was now on the best of telephone terms.

She rang him again on a Monday at the beginning of October, at school, and asked how he was sustaining himself. Houston said very well and inquired what news she had.

'The best, wonder boy,' said the young woman. 'They're on the way back. The boss heard from Lister-Lawrence last night, and he's expecting a call from Radkewicz some time tomorrow.'

Houston let out his breath; for Radkewicz was the director of the unit and this was news indeed.

He said, 'Where will he be calling from.'

'From Calcutta. A plane has been laid on for them there, so they should be home very soon. I thought you'd like to know.'

'Well, thanks. Thanks very much.'

'Is that all the bearer of glad tidings gets – thanks?'

'What else had you in mind?'

'Oh, I'd leave that to you. You could tell me when we met. We haven't yet, have we?'

Her voice was uncomfortably audible in the listening common room. Houston said quietly, 'Perhaps the first thing would be to organize that. When do you suggest?'

She had told him her suggestion, and a couple of nights later, for the first time, he had met her.

She was waiting on the corner of Wardour Street, a little, pretty, lively thing, shivering in her fur collar in the gusty evening. She put her arm through his without self-consciousness and they walked into Soho.

'So you're the artist?'

'That's right.'

'You're not much like Hugh, are you?'

'We're only half-brothers.'

'I wonder who got the best of the bargain.'

Houston liked her. She had a sideways look that was provocative without being challenging; a small elfin mobile face. They turned into Gennaro's, and examining her more clearly in the light he wondered why he had never met her. He had met most of the people Hugh worked with. He asked her about it.

'Oh, well.' she said. 'I'm not a girl who likes to compete.'

'Who would you be competing with?'

'Sheila, wouldn't you say?'

'Sheila?'

'Sheila Wolferston.' She glanced at him. 'You know about her.'

He could dimly remember a Sheila at a party, but he didn't know what there was, particularly, to know about her.

He said, 'You mean they're very friendly?'

'That's what I mean.'

'Does she work at the office?'

'Yes. Well. Not just now. She's out there with the unit – the broken leg. Didn't you really know?' she asked, looking at him curiously.

'No,' Houston said lightly; but he was oddly disturbed. He wondered why Hugh hadn't mentioned the girl.

But he enjoyed the evening; and he thought he liked her better than most of Hugh's friends. He took her home, to

Maida Vale, and loitered for a while in the hall of the block of flats.

'Perhaps we'll see a bit more of each other now,' she said.

'Yes. I'd like that.'

'The only thing is, my life is a tiny bit complicated at the moment.'

'Mine, too.'

They looked at each other, smiling.

Houston leaned over and kissed her. He expected a cool and light-hearted response; and got rather more.

'Perhaps we'd better start uncomplicating,' she said after a moment.

'Perhaps we'd better.'

She had told him that a reception was being held for the unit if it returned, as expected, on the Saturday, and they agreed to meet there.

'Back to your complication, then, wonder boy,' she said lightly. 'I expect I'll ring you on Thursday.'

But she rang before that.

She rang on the Wednesday, and she asked if he could call that afternoon to see Stahl.

He said, 'I don't know. I suppose so,' confused for the moment. 'Do you know what it's about?'

'I think he'd better tell you himself. Would three o'clock be all right?'

'Yes. Yes. All right.'

He saw by her face that the news was not good, but asked no questions. She showed him in immediately to see Stahl.

He had not met him before, and was surprised by what he saw. Despite the authority of his voice, the director was a small man, almost a midget; a little spare bag of bones. He had a beaky nose with a red ridge across it, and a curious condition of the eyes that kept them moving ceaselessly behind their gold-rimmed spectacles. He came round the large desk to shake Houston's hand.

'Sit down. Cigarette. I have some disappointing news for you, I'm afraid,' he said directly.

Houston took the cigarette without speaking, and tried to keep it still as Stahl lit it for him with a big desk lighter.

'There's been a slight hold-up. Your brother won't be coming back this week.'

Houston stared at him, licking his lips. He said, 'He's not ill, or injured or anything . . .'

'Oh, no. On the contrary. He's staying to look after the ones who are. Mr Radkewicz, our director, was in a hurry to move on. The passes out there start getting snowed up early, and he had bulky equipment to shift. He felt it would take another two or three weeks for the casualties to mend satisfactorily, so they're remaining till they do. Your brother opted to remain with them.'

'I see,' Houston said. He found himself considerably diconcerted by the restless eyes. 'I wonder why he should do that?'

Stahl smiled fractionally. 'There isn't any danger, if that's worrying you. They'll have adequate transport and guides and so forth and the passes are negotiable for ordinary purposes for most of the year. He thought they would appreciate a friendly face and someone who could speak English – although a few people in the monastery do speak a little, apparently.'

'Monastery,' Houston said. 'What monastery?'

'The one they're staying in. In Tibet. You know this, of course,' he said, watching Houston's face.

Since it was obvious Houston didn't, he took the cigarette from his mouth, coughing anxiously. 'Oh, pardon me. I thought I told you. Didn't I mention the route was blocked so they had to go round the mountain?'

'Well, yes,' Houston sasid. 'Yes, you did mention that.'

'Why,' Stahl said, smiling again slightly, 'you go round a mountain anywhere in those parts, you're liable to find yourself in Tibet. That's what they did.'

Silence fell in the room. Houston observed his lengthening cigarette ash slowly curl and drop on the carpet.

'Now really, Mr Houston,' Stahl said, getting him an ashtray,

'I wouldn't worry about this. Sure, Tibet sounds very strange, very remote. But where is remote these days? Last night I talked with Radkewicz in Calcutta. And in forty-eight hours Radkewicz will be right here with me in this room. Believe me, nowhere today is remote.'

'Quite,' Houston said. He wasn't sure he'd got it yet. 'Do you happen to know whereabouts this monastery is?'

'Certainly. I have it right here,' Stahl said, rummaging on his desk. 'I understand it's a fine place. They're very comfortable there. They have good food, doctors, everything. It's actually,' he said, adjusting his glasses to examine the unfamiliar words on the paper, 'a monastery for women.'

But the name when he read it out meant nothing at all to Houston.

'What they call it,' Stahl said, 'is Yamdring.'

3

The reception for the returned members of the unit took place at the Savoy Hotel on Saturday, 8 October 1949. It was a lively party, with relatives and Press, and even though his brother wouldn't be at it, Houston went. He spoke to Radkewicz and to a cameraman called Kelly, a friend of his brother's, and to some others, and what they told him should have satisfied him. As Stahl had said, the monastery for women was an excellent place. They had been well looked after, the food was good, there were doctors, everything. Tibet was not at all as expected; in the valleys, in the summer, it had been lush, with crops in the fields, and people tending the crops, pleasant, friendly people. For the members of the unit it had been just another place; a rather more welcoming place, in the circumstances, than the one they had left, but one that was physically not unlike it.

Kelly had greatly taken to the inhabitants.

'Very fine wogs,' he said. 'I wish we could have stayed longer, but there was stuff to be humped. Several of our own wogs refused to come. They stayed on for a festival there.'

Kelly was not sure what kind of a festival; but it was to have taken place in the middle of September.

'They were getting worked up for it when we left — prayer wheels going like the clappers and everything getting a scrubout. Ah, a wonderful place entirely,' Kelly said.

And indeed it sounded wonderful as he described it. The village of Yamdring lay at the bottom of a valley. The monastery was built into the hillside, terraced on seven rising levels. They had seen it first from a hill half a mile above, and the sun had glinted on its seven golden roofs. An oval lake, emerald green, lay below it with an island in the middle. On the island was a small shrine with a green roof; a bridge of skin boats connected the island with the mainland. They had looked down on it in the late afternoon, and a procession had been passing over the bridge.

'Always having processions,' Kelly said. 'Lovely people. Childish really.'

It had been after nine when they left, too late to go anywhere, too early to make their separate ways. Houston took the girl home.

'Come in and have a drink.'

'All right,' Houston said, and went up with her.

It was a bright, modern little flat, unlike his own somewhat rambling apartment; and more cluttered.

'Don't mind the mixture of styles,' she told him, removing his coat. 'There are three of us here, each with our bits of junk.'

'Friends or relations?'

'Oh, friends. Bachelor girls, as they say. Gin and something?'

'And tonic.'

'Sit down and brood. You've been brooding on your feet all evening.'

Houston sat down and brooded.

'Your drink's on the arm of the sofa,' the girl said presently.

'Thanks.'

'All right now?'

'Fine.' He felt very far from fine. He had begun to tremble

260

inexplicably in every limb. But he realized from the girl's question and earlier quiet hints that he might be demonstrating rather more concern than the situation called for, so he smiled wryly and said, 'You've got to look after young brothers.'

'You two are fairly close, aren't you?'

'Fairly.'

'Well, everything seems all right. He should be home quite soon, shouldn't he?'

'Oh, sure. Sure.'

'Are you cold in here? You're shivering a bit.'

'I must have taken a chill,' Houston said. He didn't know what had come over him, but he knew it was not a chill. He had an urge to get out and walk about in the street; he felt restless and suffocated in the flat.

'Any warmer now?' she asked some time later.

'Yes,' Houston said, and he was, for the young woman was lying in his arms. 'When are your co-bachelors coming back?'

'Oh, later.'

Something in her voice made him deduce that they would not be coming back at all that night. He had a suspicion also that he was meant to deduce this. He didn't think he wanted to do anything about it at the moment. He left quite early.

The girl went with him to the door, somewhat nonplussed.

'I think you'd better take care of that cold.'

'I will.'

'Bed's the place for you,' she said, tentatively.

Houston smiled. 'I'm going right to it,' he said.

But he didn't. He went for a long walk instead. It amused him that he had got along without women for quite a long time and now suddenly found himself with two. It had been like this for him on some occasions during the war. He wondered if he was the sort of man who turned to women at moments of crisis; and he wondered what the crisis was now. Hugh was coming back. He was coming back at the end of the month. All he had to do was get through the month.

4

When he looked back on it later, Houston remembered October chiefly as the month when he tried to get rid of Glynis. It was not a successful attempt. There were tears and recriminations, and also threats, for the girl said she couldn't live without him. Houston, like many artists far from being a romantic, thought that she very easily could if she put her mind to it; but when he saw the pain in her eyes could not bring himself to take the final step.

He had told Lesley Sellers that he was now uncomplicated; for, as she said, she was a girl who didn't like competition; and accordingly found his life more complicated than ever. His encounters with the Head grew no less acrimonious; he was permanently behind with a series of art appreciation classes that he had to prepare for an evening school; and ideas had run out on him permanently for his freelance work. He seemed to be scrambling about on an increasingly slippery slope. Everything about his life had become suddenly insecure and uncertain. He couldn't understand how it had happened.

He found himself beginning to lean heavily on Oliphant, the classics master, a bachelor like himself, whose astringency of manner he found refreshing.

'Do you find yourself able to make any plans these days, Oliphant?'

'I never make plans.'

'Something curious seems to be happening to me. I don't know where the hell I am lately.'

'Maybe you're in love.'

'Maybe I am. I wish I could think of something I particularly wanted to do.'

'I should like to move to a bigger flat and to spend Christmas in Rome.'

And suddenly everybody was talking about Christmas.

'Where are you jingling your bells this year, wonder boy?'

'I've not really got round to that.'

'I rather see myself in Paris. Any interest?'

'It sounds very attractive.'

'Let me know soon. I need to fix my family early.'

And only hours later, it seemed, 'Charles, I've been thinking. Roy wants to go to Bournemouth for Christmas. We go to the same hotel every year. Do you think you could turn up there accidentally, too?'

'I don't know, Glynis. It depends on Hugh a bit. I'd have to see what he wanted.'

'Well, naturally. I see that. Do you think he might like to come, too?'

'He might,' Houston said, doubting it very strongly.

'When do you think you would know about him?'

'I'm not really sure. I've not heard much lately.'

He had not heard anything. It was now the third week of October and there had been no news whatever. Lesley said that Lister-Lawrence was not expecting any special news. There was no question now of a missing party. The group would merely arrive on Indian territory. They would probably arrive between the 25th and 30th when a trade caravan was expected.

The 25th came without news; and the 30th went, without news. Lesley said that Lister-Lawrence was away investigating a riot. In all probability the group was now on the way to Calcutta. They would very likely hear from them before they heard from Lister-Lawrence.

This, however, did not prove to be the case. On the 2nd November a cable arrived from Lister-Lawrence. He said the expected caravan had arrived on the 29th. No British subjects had arrived with it. He was making enquiries.

Houston entered upon the nightmarish month of November 1949.

It was during this month, he realized later, that the abbot and the Dukes of Ganzing and the Governor of Hodzo, had found themselves in their most delicate situation. The governor had felt earlier that he could handle the matter locally and had not thought fit to communicate with the central government. In this he had shown an error of judgement, and he was not anxious to have it revealed. He had therefore concurred with the abbot's plan, which was merely to say nothing until requests for information came from Lhasa; and then to announce the party was missing.

By the middle of November he was wishing most earnestly that he had not concurred. The governor was an elderly man, and he had the clearest possible recollection of the British who had come with Colonel Younghusband forty-five years before. They were inquisitive men, who never stopped asking questions. They believed there was a reason for everything, and they were restless until they had found it. That four people were missing for some weeks on an ice-bound mountain would not seem to such men an adequate reason for giving up either the search or the inquiry into the party's disappearance.

Above all, as the governor well knew, it was essential that foreigners should be discouraged from taking an interest in his country in this ominous year. So long as there was a possibility of any of the group being alive, interest would be taken. He had therefore, towards the middle of the month, come to a worrying decision.

The news went to Lhasa on 19 November and was radioed to Kalimpong on the 24th. Lister-Lawrence had it in Calcutta on the 25th, and passed it on to Stahl in London the same day.

But of all this at the time, of course, Houston knew nothing.

All he did know as November wore on was that his days were filled with activities which were becoming increasingly meaningless. He found himself going through the weeks like an automaton. He taught and corrected and lectured; and in the evenings he did the same. Sometimes he made love. He had started making love with Lesley Sellers, but once in the course of twenty-four hours found himself doing the same with Glynis also. He regarded this performance with a somewhat weary hilarity.

He didn't know what was the matter with him. He couldn't bear to be by himself. His limbs seemed always to be tense, and he caught himself holding his breath. He couldn't sit and he couldn't lie. He couldn't read and he couldn't eat. Above all, he couldn't sleep.

He knew that Stahl was in constant touch with Calcutta; and that Lister-Lawrence was in touch with Kalimpong; and that the Tibetan representative there was in touch with his government. Everybody was in touch with everybody else, but nobody knew what had happened to this missing party.

He went to see Stahl again. He asked whether it wasn't time now for inquiries to be handled officially by the Foreign Office. Stahl said inquiries were being handled officially; Lister-Lawrence was an offical. But the Foreign Office couldn't be involved because the film party had no right to be in Tibet at all. They had gone in – certainly through no fault of their own – without authorization and hence at their own peril. The situation was difficult and obscure. It was causing him a great deal of worry, but he had no doubt they would have news soon.

This interview had taken place on 18 November; and the news had come one week later to the day: 25 November 1949, a Friday. Houston went out and got drunk. He remained drunk all the week-end.

He thought Glynis came in at some time on the Saturday; the flat was certainly tidy when he awoke on Sunday morning. She came again later, and he found her cleaning him up, and was presently aware that Lesley Sellers was there, too. He was in something of a stupor at the time, but he remembered thinking that it was very improper for the two young women to be there together. He realized he should have asked Glynis for the return of her key weeks ago; and that something must have gone sadly wrong with his planning. He heard snatches of their conversation.

'I guessed it must have been that. When did it happen?'

'Two or three weeks ago, apparently, but we only heard on Friday. The avalanche buried them all.'

'They found the – they found them, did they?'

'Oh, yes. They were all dead.'

'Poor Charles. They were so terribly close.'

'Yes.'

He had no recollection of the next week at all. He thought he went to school. Perhaps he attended his evening classes, too. He seemed to be out a good deal. He vaguely remembered having a fight with a man in a public house in Tottenham Court Road, and waking up one night in the tube terminus at Morden. He had confused impressions of both girls wanting him to go away somewhere.

And then it was December, and half a year had gone since he had seen his brother last; and everyone was telling him to pull himself together; and at length he had done this. He had gone in to see the Head and told her he would not be returning next term. And he had written to the L.C.C. Further Education authorities, telling them the same.

Then Lesley was asking finally and once and for all if he wouldn't come to Paris because it would take him out of himself; and Glynis was asking in the same terms if he wouldn't come to Bournemouth. And he thanked them both for their charity and forbearance and said that he wouldn't; he meant to spend Christmas by himself.

And this was just as well; for on the afternoon before Christmas Eve, another Friday, when he was only mildly drunk, he had received a visitor. Stahl had telephoned first, at about a quarter to four; and at a quarter past his black chauffeur-driven Bentley had pulled up outside in the rain.

He had refused a drink, his restless eyes jerking spasmodically over Houston's dishevelled figure, but had accepted a cigarette, and sat down looking round the room.

'What I've got to say,' he said flatly, 'might not strike you as being particularly seasonal. I thought you might like to ponder it over the holiday.'

Houston said nothing. He wanted another drink, but he had caught the disapproving look in the roving eyes and thought he had better wait.

'We've run into a rather curious financial problem. I don't know if your brother ever mentioned it, but we take out an insurance policy for our unit members. Of course we now have four claims pending. For ten thousand pounds each. It's a lot of money.'

'It is,' Houston said. Hugh hadn't mentioned it.

'The snag is, I've now heard there's going to be some difficulty in collecting. The terms of the policy are that the company must pay out for death anywhere in the world from any cause except act of war. The only qualification is that a death certificate has to be produced. This is something we don't have.'

'I see,' Houston said dully, in the pause that developed. He didn't think that he wanted now to discuss the question of indemnity for his brother's death.

'It seems the certificate can only be issued by a British consul or some other accredited official. And he can only issue it if he has evidence – a doctor's certificate or a signed report. Lister-Lawrence can't get this. Apparently no local functionary can sign anything at all in Tibet without the authority of the central government. And the central government doesn't seem to be very interested.'

Stahl took off his glasses and rubbed his eyes wearily. 'I don't think there's anything malicious in it,' he said after a moment. 'Lister-Lawrence takes the view that they're merely nervous of any kind of foreign interest. He thinks they may be frightened of having to pay indemnity or of having to get into negotiations. Whatever it is, they're not answering any inquiries, and the way it looks now no death certificate will be forthcoming.'

'Of course,' he went on, replacing his glasses and allowing his eyes to get busily back into orbit, 'this doesn't mean that the insurance company won't eventually pay up. After a period, death will have to be presumed. But this might be a matter of years, and meanwhile there could be many difficulties for the dependants. Wister's wife has two young children. Meiklejohn and Miss Wolferston both leave widowed mothers. There are complications about pensions, a whole lot of things. Naturally, we have a responsibility in this. We are trying to ease the burden. But I've been wondering the past few days if there mightn't be another way that is worth trying.'

267

He was silent for a few moments, watching Houston.

'I was wondering,' he said, 'if it wouldn't be an idea for someone to go over there and see Lister-Lawrence. He's a very busy man and he's not been able to give this much of his time. If someone could have a talk with him, examine all the documents, perhaps get in touch with the Tibetan representative out there, it might be possible to build up a dossier that could, at the least, hasten the presumption of death. I was wondering,' he said slowly, 'if you'd like to do it.'

Houston looked quickly down at his burning cigarette.

'You'd be acting as a kind of plenipotentiary or agent for all of the dependants,' Stahl said. 'Naturally, they'd contribute to your expenses. I don't know that they'd have anything very much to contribute at the moment – '

'I don't know that I have myself,' Houston said. 'I'd better say right away, Mr Stahl, I'm not very – interested in indemnity for my brother's death.'

'Why,' Stahl said mildly, 'I was thinking more of the other claimants than of you. Pardon me. I appreciate your feelings, of course. I merely thought you were in the best position – a healthy young fellow with no ties. But it was just an idea.'

Houston gazed at him and his mouth dropped open. He had not thought of this aspect of it.

'And as to money, I don't think you need worry there. Your brother had salary coming from June. We'd be prepared to extend that to the end of March next, and to contribute to your expenses. Think it over, anyway.'

'I will,' Houston said, taken aback by this new view of the situation.

He thought it over for the next three days. He had made the decision by the time the office workers were streaming back after the holiday, and had telephoned Stahl to tell him so.

'Of course,' Stahl said. 'I knew you would. When do you want to go?'

'As soon as possible. I've nothing to keep me here.'

*

268

Which was how, that winter, after many unsettling months, Houston came to embark upon his adventure. He had not visited any swamis. He knew nothing of Tibetan prophecies. He was a very ordinary young man who at the time, certainly, claimed no pre-knowledge of the extraordinary thing that was going to happen to him.

He said goodbye to the two young women who had served to distract him during the restless months and promised each of them that he would mend his ways with regard to the other. He offered the use of his flat to Oliphant for he knew the older man was uncomfortable in his own. And as the beneficiary of an eventual ten thousand pounds, he made a will.

He did all these things before 24 January 1950; and early in the morning of 25 January he walked out with his bag into Fitzmaurice Crescent and whistled for a taxi to take him to the air terminal in Kensington High Street. He thought he would be taking one back again within two months.

Chapter 2

I

JANUARY is the first month of the cold season in Calcutta, and though the temperature, in the low seventies, was brisk by local standards, Houston found it spring-like after the damp chill of London. He walked tirelessly about the town, and by his fourth day reckoned to have covered the major part of it. He had ample time to do this. Lister-Lawrence was away. Nobody knew when he would return.

Twice a day, morning and afternoon, Houston walked from his hotel, the Great Eastern, to Chowringhee where Lister-Lawrence had his office in the offices of the Commissioner for the United Kingdom, and stated his business to an eager succession of Bengali clerks. Although each seemed to be called Mukherjee or Ghosh, he had never somehow managed to strike the same one twice.

'Yes, sir. How can I help you, please?'

'You might remember I called yesterday. To see Mr Lister-Lawrence.'

'Ah, you would have seen a colleague of mine. I am Mr Mukherjee, sir. If you will tell me your name I will make a note for Mr Lister-Lawrence. He is away at the moment.'

'Is he going to be away much longer?'

'Oh, no. This afternoon, perhaps, he will return. What is your business, please, sir?'

Houston was at first mildly amused by the appetite of the Bengali clerks for information about himself, but by the fifth day, found himself becoming a little impatient of the delay. After breakfast that morning, he strode up Chowringhee determined to wrest some information from Mr Mukherjee or Mr Ghosh himself.

He said, 'I've been waiting for the last four days, and I can't wait much longer. Can't you tell me where I can get in touch with Mr Lister-Lawrence?'

'Ah, you must have seen one of my colleagues, sir. I am Mr Ghosh. What is your name, please?'

Houston gave it, but he declined to provide the basis for another note, pointing out that eight were already awaiting Lister-Lawrence.

'Excuse me, sir. I must know your business – '

Houston said, pleasantly, that he wasn't going to state it, and after a somewhat rambling argument had begun to turn away, when Mr Ghosh caught his sleeve.

'Oh, wait, sir!' he cried. 'Mr Lister-Lawrence is here. He returned last night. He is very busy but if you will only tell me your business – It is a most strict rule – '

A few minutes later he was shaking hands with Lister-Lawrence.

He was a tall, thin man in a dark suit, with heavy shadows

270

under his eyes and nicotine stains on his fingers. He looked as if he had not had a good night's sleep for some time, and his grasp was brief and limp.

'I'm sorry you've had to keep calling. I've been away for a few days. It's really very hard to know,' he said, waving Houston to a chair and sitting down himself, 'what we can do for you here. I'm sure we sent every scrap of information as it came in to your Mr Stahl.'

Houston told him what he thought might be done.

'Yes. Well, you can try. I'm sorry about the death certificates. I'd stretch a point if I could, but my hands are tied. I don't know if I've quite got it,' he said, offering his cigarettes, 'about the corroboration. There's not very much to corroborate, is there? We've only got the single signal from Lhasa.'

'I wondered if I could borrow that, and the rest of the correspondence, to copy.'

'I expect you could do that.'

'And see any Press reports there might have been about the avalanche.'

Lister-Lawrence pursed his lips. 'I doubt if you'll get much joy there. There must be dozens of avalanches every day in that part of the world. Still, you never know.'

'Also this business of the caravan they were supposed to join – I thought it might be an idea to get a signed statement from someone who was with it.'

'What about?'

'About conditions on the way. It seems a possible avenue.'

'Oh, quite. The difficulty there would be to find the people. It's really something for the Tibetan trade man in Kalimpong – he issues the licences and personal chitties for everyone who goes in and out. I could drop him a line, if you want,' he said without enthusiasm. 'Or better still you could go up there.'

'To Kalimpong?' Houston said.

'Why not?'

'Isn't it a long way to go?'

'You've come a long way already,' Lister-Lawrence said reasonably. 'And I think you'd find Sangrab a very decent old chap. Mind you, I should point out that they've all gone a bit funny up there this year. They've fallen out with the devils and are holding prayer meetings all over the country. They're not too keen on answering foreigners' questions.'

'They'd save themselves, and us, too,' Houston said diffidently, 'a lot of trouble if they'd just answer one simple one. For instance, they must have some register of foreigners who die there. A burial record of some kind, say.'

'Yes, well, they don't actually bury people.'

'Whatever they do. Cremate them, then. Someone's got to keep score,' Houston said lightly, fighting down the deep revulsion for his task that swept over him again.

'I'm afraid they don't cremate them, either.'

'What do they do?'

'Oh, well they have their own sort of customs, you know,' Lister-Lawrence said, energetically tapping his cigarette ash. 'I doubt if this is a very profitable field.'

'What do they do?' Houston said again after a few silent moments.

'Well. Vultures, actually,' said Lister-Lawrence, apologetically. 'I'm frightfully sorry, old chap. We all have our own customs, though, you know. They say it's really very hygenic and all that . . . There isn't much point in pursuing it, is there? But there's absolutely no reason why you shouldn't trot up and see old Sangrab. And you could certainly ask around in Kalimpong about the caravan. They make up all the teams there. It's rather a jolly place, Kalimpong,' he ended, somewhat out of breath.

Houston felt suddenly very sick. He stubbed out his cigarette. He said presently, 'Supposing I don't get very far in Kalimpong, is there any other Tibetan representative in that area I might see?'

'There's a chap up in Gangtok. But that's in Sikkim, and you'll need a chitty to get in there. It's a protected State. I'll get off a line to Hopkinson for you – he's our man there.'

'Would there be any point in having one more try at Tibet? At the British representative there?'

'We haven't got one, old boy. That's the trouble. Old Hugh Richardson is in Lhasa, of course, but he's acting on behalf of the Indian goverment, and we mustn't embarrass him. The snag is, these Tibetans are rather a suspicious shower. They don't get the point about insurance policies. They think we're trying to manoeuvre them into an admission of liability. However, I'll do what I can,' he said, jotting down a few notes on a scrap of paper. 'Meanwhile you have quite a few avenues to explore. Drop in whenever you feel like it.'

2

Houston remained a further three weeks in Calcutta, awaiting his 'chitty' and exploring avenues. He went through the files of the English language newspapers and extracted several items relating to Tibet and avalanches in the Himalayas. These appeared to have been numerous in October, but no details were given of individual ones. The astrological correspondent of the *Hindustan Standard* warned of grave trouble impending for 'a Buddhist land in the north' and suggested that a major spiritual effort would be required to avert it; and from the same authority Houston learned that according to occult information for his birthday his sexual powers would be vigorously tested during the next year. Although aware that the solid columns of rejuvenator advertising on the same page might have had something to do with this forecast, Houston, mindful also of the fact that he had not yet written a line to Glynis or Lesley, pondered somewhat gloomily over it.

Lister-Lawrence had left instructions with his Bengali clerks to give him all the assistance he needed, and he kept the Messrs Mukherjee and Ghosh fully extended looking out all the correspondence that had passed between Lhasa, Kalimpong, Calcutta, Katmandu and London. The sheer weight of the correspondence and the dearth of information it had produced were highly dispiriting; but he plodded on, copying and compiling all the material in his hotel bedroom with the aid of a hired typewriter.

273

By the end of February, however, it was obvious he could do little more in Calcutta. Lister-Lawrence was away most of the time, and there seemed to be no answer from Gangtok or Lhasa. He decided to go to Kalimpong.

The journey to Kalimpong is a somewhat complicated one, but one of the Mr Mukherjees had made all arrangements for him, and Houston found the change welcome. The first stage was from Calcutta to Siliguri in the north of Bengal, and he made it in reasonable comfort on the main line railway. At Siliguri he had to change to a little local wood-burning train which ran through village and jungle as though on tram-lines, swaying and panting and stopping every now and again to raise enough steam to tackle the increasingly sharp inclines.

It was still warm and sunny, but there was a certain feeling in the air of mountains and of a keener and more bracing atmosphere. In the jungle, monkeys had dropped from the trees on to the roof of the train and had swung head down before the open windows, snatching the bits of chocolate and biscuit that Houston offered. By the time he reached his final train-halt, the village of Gielle-Khola, the monkeys had gone. It was noticeably cooler; he could feel the sharp air in his lungs; and the people on the platform seemed to be of a different shape. They were wearing capes and padded jackets, and the facial features to which he had become accustomed in the past few weeks had subtly altered. He was approaching the Himalayas.

The arrangement was for a car to pick him up at Gielle-Khola and take him to Kalimpong; but when after a couple of hours no car appeared, he realized he must have over-extended Mr Mukherjee, and took a bus instead. He had spent one and a half days getting to Gielle-Khola, and it was afternoon when he embarked upon the last leg of the journey.

He got to Kalimpong at dusk on 27 February; the bus set him down in a busy market place as the lamps on the stalls were being lit. Several boys rushed to take possession of his luggage, and he distributed it among three of them. The smallest of the boys had secured only his raincoat, but he could speak a little English, and he trotted importantly beside

Houston, chattering, as they pushed their way through the crowded market to the hotel.

Houston had noticed here and there small groups of men in fur caps, warmly clad except for their arms which were left bare, and he inquired who they were.

'Tibet men,' the boy said, gesturing upwards to the darkening sky; and Houston who had been gazing up at the curiously massive cloud formations, gazed again. The clouds were mountains.

Tibet men and mountains. He thought he was near his journey's end.

3

As Lister-Lawrence had said, Kalimpong was a rather jolly place. Houston like it. He had dined well at the hotel and had slept soundly between clean sheets, and he was up and out early in the morning. The air had the kind of snap and brillancy that he associated with the Vosges mountains in France, and the surrounding landscape, although on a more massive scale, had the same nature: great green hills that crept towards the sky, and a feeling of high places beyond. The peaks that had closed in with nightfall were far away.

He went to the offices of the Tibetan representative, and found a substantial building with a courtyard that was thronged with people. A few mules and horses stood blinking in the bright sun, and groups of men squatted on the ground, chattering and smoking. The small porter of the preceding evening had been waiting for him as he left the hotel and had attached himself again. He ran into the building before Houston and came out again, grinning.

'No room in there, sahib,' he said. 'Many men there today.'

Houston inspected the interior himself and found that this was the case.

'Is it always like this?'

'No, sahib. Caravan comes today. All caravan men here.'

'Will they be here all day?'

'Two, three days, maybe. They get chitty,' the boy said, pounding an imaginary rubber stamp with his small brown hands.

Houston was somewhat at a loss. He could see nobody who was obviously an official. He wondered whom to consult.

The boy had the answer for him. 'You come to see Michaelson Sahib, sahib,' he said. 'I take you.'

They returned through the market square and down a maze of busy streets to a part of the town that seemed to be occupied by warehouses. Lines of mules were being unloaded and their burdens swung up on ropes to first-floor lofts. Directing operations outside the largest warehouse was Michaelson Sahib, who proved to be an enormously fat, elderly man in a bushwacker's hat; he was checking off invoices and smoking a small black cheroot.

Houston introduced himself.

'Glad to know you, sport. You've caught me at a busy moment.'

'So I see. I've been trying to get in to see the Tibetan consul. There seems a bit of a crowd there.'

'A caravan's just arrived. I'd give it away for today, sport, if I were you.'

'I hear it's going to be like this for two or three days.'

'You don't have to bother about that. Look, I'll drop by for a quick one with you this evening. I'm just too tied up now.'

'All right,' Houston said, a bit put-out, and wandered away with the boy.

His feeling of offence did not persist; for the more he saw of the town the more he liked it. There was a smell of woodsmoke and spices in the clean air, and a sensation of heights. He found himself smiling, with the heady feeling he had felt before in mountains.

There was a number of small teashops in the town; ramshackle sheds with trestle tables containing tea urns and trays of sweetmeats; and he had several cups of sweet, frothy tea as he loitered about the streets with the boy. Caravan teamsters strolled everywhere; but although many different races seemed to be represented, he noticed no Tibetans. He asked the boy why.

'They sleep, maybe, sahib. Tibet men no like it down here. They like Tibet.' He raised his eyes again to the sky as he spoke, and Houston was amused and yet vaguely disturbed at this suggestion, even in the northernmost point of India, of a still more remote land, almost a mythical land, towering in the sky.

He said, smiling, 'Is that where Tibet is – in the sky?'

'In the mountains, sahib.'

'Have you ever been there?'

'No. Too young, sahib. I go with my brother in five, six years.'

'With the caravans?'

'With the caravans, sahib.'

'Is your brother away now?'

'Yes, sahib. Ten days away. He work for Michaelson Sahib.'

'What do they call your brother?'

'Ringling. My name is Bozeling, sahib,' the boy said, grinning.

'All right, Bozeling. Let's move on.'

Michaelson Sahib looked in that evening, as promised. He had changed into a white suit, and he came in briskly, rubbing his hands and nodding to the barman who mixed him what was evidently a familiar drink. Houston had waited for some time in the empty bar; he seemed to have the hotel to himself.

'Nippy in the evenings,' Michaelson said. 'Sorry I was a bit abrupt this morning. There's a big load in and the boys get things arsey-turvey if you take your eyes off for a minute. No offence, sport?'

'No offence,' Houston said, and shook hands again.

'It's the first caravan we've had in for some time. Everything's overdue because of the bloody weather. What brings you here?'

Houston told him.

'Yes. I saw the others a few months ago. I doubt if you'll get any change out of the Tibetans, though. They don't want to know about foreigners this year.'

'I heard they'd fallen out with the devils.'

'That's it, Michaelson said, seriously. 'There's a lot of bad omens for this year. Still, you'd better have a go now you're here. I sent a note across half an hour ago asking if he'd see us tonight. I expect he will. He thinks I'm offended,' he said, baring a set of long, yellow dog-like teeth. 'The old sod has crossed me up on a shipment of black tails I've been expecting for six months.'

'Black tails?'

'Best yak. Long hair,' Michaelson said, drinking.

'What is it you do exactly?'

'Trader. Been here thirty years. I'm the institution here. There are a few other European traders, but they flit off during the winter. I practically keep the place going,' he said, showing his teeth again.

'You import yak hair from Tibet?'

'Wool staples of all sorts. Black tails give the best staple. It makes a very hard, tough cloth.'

'And you send goods in?'

'Manufactured goods, food, cloth, anything. There's not much doing now. Caravans are in and out all summer, but it's not too profitable this time of year. The teams sit around eating you out of house and home. I've got one now, been gone ten days and still holed up in Sikkim in a blizzard.'

'You'll have a young man called Ringling on that one. I was talking to his brother.'

'That's right. I took him on when his father was killed on a trip a couple of years ago. I keep him going steadily right through the winter so they've got something coming in at home. He's a good kid, Ringling.'

'I was wondering,' Houston said, 'if I could find the team my brother and his party were supposed to meet in October.'

'I wouldn't know, sport. That kind of arrangement they make themselves. It gives them a few extra ackers. It couldn't have been one of my teams, though.'

'Why not?'

'I had no caravan in October or November. The weather was too bad. I think it's the earthquake that shook everything up. I've never known conditions like it. You having another of these?' he said, looking into Houston's glass.

'Thanks. You mean,' Houston said, 'conditions were so bad that no caravans were running?'

'I don't know. I think Da Costa ran one – he's a Portugese. Sangrab would know.'

Michaelson stayed for dinner at the hotel; but no messenger arrived from the Tibetan consul. Michaelson was irritated by this, but more, it seemed to Houston, because of the rebuff to his reputation as an institution than on Houston's own account.

He said, 'Let me know if you don't hear tomorrow. I'll do something about it.'

'Right. And thanks very much.'

'Don't thank me yet.'

Houston heard nothing the next day. He walked about the town again with the boy, and made half a dozen charcoal sketches. The boy was delighted. But there was still no word from the mysterious Sangrab when he returned to the hotel.

Michaelson appeared angrily at six-thirty.

'I hear that little sodling hasn't condescended to see you yet.'

'I'm afraid that's right.'

'Well, let's have one and get over there. I don't know what he thinks he's playing at.'

'I don't want to do anything that's unwise. I need his help.'

'It's not very wise of him to overlook a note of mine. I'll have that old bastard shifted back home so fast he won't know what's happening.'

'Did you mention in your note what I wanted to see him about?'

'Certainly not. That's your business. And anyway, he'd know. He knows everything that goes on in this town. Bloody sauce!' Michaelson said. His face was red and his tie somewhat ill-adjusted. 'Let's get on over there before he starts dinner. They eat at seven. He'll never leave that once he's begun.'

Houston had some doubts as to the wisdom of confronting the Tibetan representative with Michaelson in his present mood of injured pride; and he suspected that the trader was using him to settle some scores of his own. But he couldn't get out of it without giving offence. He finished his drink and accompanied Michaelson pensively across the square.

The crowds had gone from the courtyard of Sangrab's establishment; the double doors were locked and the building shuttered and silent. Michaelson rapped loudly, and a few moments later a robed Tibetan appeared.

Michaelson spoke curtly, and they were admitted. The door was closed behind them. The servant disappeared. Houston heard Michaelson breathing noisily beside him in the dark hall. Presently the servant appeared again, with a small lantern which he hung on a wall bracket. He murmured a few words to Michaelson.

'As I thought,' Michaelson said. 'He's at his prayers now. We'll catch him just before he eats.'

And indeed, after some moments Houston could distinguish a faint chanting from somewhere in the house, a throaty ululation that was strange but not unpleasant in the flickering lamplight.

The servant returned some minutes later, and they followed him down a dim corridor to a pair of double doors that he threw open for them. Inside, in a blaze of light from some dozens of candles, stood two old men. Houston had never in his life seen such gorgeous figures. They were dressed in robes of richly-embroidered silk, shaped and buttoned across the chest like cossack uniforms. Each wore a jewelled silk choker loosely tied under a stand-up mandarin collar, and hair dressed on top in a glossy black jewelled bun. Each also wore a single pendant ear-ring, and had a little goatee beard.

For an instant, Houston had the impression the two figures were household idols, so still were they; but presently they bowed, and he found himself bowing in return.

He was consideraly impressed to see that Michaelson was in no way put out by all this magnificence. He sat himself easily in a chair and motioned Houston to do the same, and the two old men sat down also.

Houston had been wondering which one of them was Sangrab, and now, as Michaelson addressed him, he saw. The other old man had moved a little apart; he sat beside a small table and rested his hands on it as he watched. There was something of a tortoise-shell cat about him. Tortoise-shell combs gleamed in his hair; bits of tortoise-shell stood out on his hands – little hands place one on top of the other, which fixed and contracted like a cat's. There was something of the cat, too, about his thin upturned mouth and the narrow drowsy eyes. These eyes were, however, turned quite unblinkingly on Houston; he did not see them move throughout the interview.

Sangrab had been playing with his beard, studying Houston from time to time as Michaelson talked, and interpolating a few words himself.

'Well,' Michaelson said in English, at length, 'he's not optimistic about the death certificates – I told you that. But he'll try again, if you want. Meanwhile he's promised to sort out the names of the teamsters you want. The snag is that the October caravan *was* run by Da Costa, as I thought, and he's gone off to Goa for the winter. He thinks the teamsters have dispersed, too. Some of them go and hump tea in Darjeeling and a lot go home to Nepal – they're mainly Sherpas or Gurkhas. Still, you might find some of them here. It will take a few days to get the list – he's got a lot of work on at the moment. Does that satisfy you for now?'

Houston said it did, and they left soon after.

'I must say,' Michaelson said with satisfaction as they turned into the hotel for a drink, 'the little sodling was quite ingratiating. He feels badly about my black tails, of course. And then, the other fellow was listening.'

'Who was the other fellow?'

'He's an official he's got staying with him. He arrived last night – that's why he couldn't see us. They send someone down to check up on him from time to time – he's nicely placed to take a bit of bribery. He'll sit in with him for a few days and then hop it. You never see the same one twice.'

There seemed no reason at the time to doubt it.

4

Houston had not thought to spend more than a week in Kalimpong. It was, in all, several weeks before he left, including a trip to Calcutta in between. He had overlooked the timeless qualities of all transactions in India.

It took him a week to find a single named teamster. He knew the man's address and his usual haunts and the odd jobs he was engaged upon; none the less, and despite the boy's assistance, it was seven days before he ran him to earth in a small and slightly illegal drinking shop.

The result was hardly fruitful.

Yes, the man said cheerfully, he had been a member of the October caravan. Certainly they had been joined by other travellers — by perhaps twelve or so at different points of the journey. He didn't know if any of the travellers had failed to meet them after arranging to do so. This was a matter for the caravan sirdar or his deputy who alone made such arrangements. Where was the sirdar? Why, in Sikkim. He returned home each winter as everybody knew. And his deputy? In Darjeeling, possibly.

Houston still had no chitty for Sikkim, but he could go to Darjeeling without one, and he went. He found the deputy sirdar and several other members of the October caravan humping tea, as Michaelson had suggested.

This visit was not very fruitful, either.

The nearest the caravan had passed to Yamdring was Gysung, sixty odd miles away. Was it likely they would pick up travellers then from Yamdring? Yes, indeed. Why not?

Had they picked any up in October?

In October? No . . . No, not in October.

Had they perhaps *arranged* to pick any up then?

That was possible. It was hard to recall exactly. There were always cases of broken arrangements on every trip. One paid no particular attention.

At what date had the caravan reached Gysung?

It had reached Gysung (this two trips and several discussion later) on 21 October.

So if a party had meant to meet the caravan there, when would they have had to leave Yamdring?

Five days earlier. One allowed twelve miles a day in that part of the country.

Five days earlier . . . 16 October.

Supposing the party had run into an avalanche – where would be the most likely place for this to happen?

Undoubtedly on the Portha-la pass. This was the only place on the Yamdring-Gysung route that one would expect an avalanche.

Whereabouts was that?

Three days' march from Yamdring.

Three days from 16 October . . . It was all very thin, very circumstanial. But still, Houston thought, he might have narrowed down the details a bit.

He wrote in his notebook: '*In view of all the above, the logical deduction must be that the party was overwhelmed on or about 19 October on the Porth-lu pass, some thirty-six miles from Yamdring on the road to Gysung.*' He appended the names of his informants and got them to make their marks.

He returned to Kalimpong tired and depressed. He had been away just over two months now, and had spent in all nearly six hundred pounds. He thought he had got as far as he was going to get; and that unless the Tibetan government showed some rapid signs of cooperation he might as well go home.

He asked at the reception desk if there was anything for him.

'Nothing, sahib.'

All *right*, Houston said to himself. Enough was enough. He would have a bath and a drink and pay one final call on the Tibetan representative. Then away on the morning bus.

He had the bath, and the drink, and a few more after it, and went reluctantly out into the square. He had left it a bit late for the Tibetans. No use after seven o'clock, Michaelson had said. It was getting on for that, the lamps going on above the stalls. He was sick of the place suddenly, sick of all the places, sick of himself. But he walked across the square, and continued walking stolidly even when a small brown bombshell erupted at his side.

'Oh, sahib, you are back!'

'Hello, me lad,' Houston said, glad at least in a melancholy way that someone cared whether he was in this place or that.

'When you come back, sahib?'

'An hour or two ago.'

'I look for you. My brother is back, sahib. You come and see him now.'

'Not just now. Later, Bozeling.'

'Now, sahib, now! Ringling has seen them, the ones you seek.'

'Which ones?'

'The dead ones, sahib.'

Houston felt the hairs on the back of his neck rise.

He said, 'Which dead ones?'

'The English ones, sahib. They marched one day with the caravan.'

'When was this?'

'In December, sahib.'

Houston stopped. He felt himself rooted to the spot in the bustling, draughty square. He said stupidly, 'In December? he couldn't have. They died in October.'

'Yes, sahib, he did. Come now. You come with me.'

Houston remembered the moment with peculiar clarity in later years. The clock on the Scottish mission church had boomed seven as he stood there, and he remembered thinking, Well, I've had the little sodling for tonight, anyway. Then he walked with the boy to his home.

Chapter 3

I

IT was a dark and malodorous shack, lit by oil lamps and with a dung fire burning in a rudimentary grate. Bozeling vanished as soon as they were inside, and Houston found himself alone in the smoky fug of the room, until the boy's mother appeared suddenly, a small plump woman with gold ear-rings, a glossy middle-parting and a long skirt and bodice, and fussed around him, talking half in English and half in Sherpali, as she fetched him a chair and a cup of tea and sat him as far from the reeking fire as was possible.

Her elder son was sleeping, she said; he usually slept for two whole days on returning from a trip. The sahib would forgive her English; her son's, on the other hand, was excellent; he had climbed often with the British. Soon the sahib would be able to enjoy a fine conversation with him.

Houston sat and smiled and nodded to her, afraid almost to open his mouth for the sickness rising in his throat. A terrible nausea had come sweeping over him in the last few minutes, whether from the shock or the airless hovel he could not tell. But he managed to get the tea down; and presently there were sounds-off and Bozeling appeared with his brother.

Sherpa Ringling was a youth of 17, slim, small and with the agreeable monkey face of his young brother. Houston saw the lines of fatigue in the thin features and apologized for disturbing him.

'It's nothing, sahib. Tomorrow I'll be fine.'

'You say you saw some English people in Tibet.'

'That's right. I met them, sahib. They walked one day with the caravan.'

'Which trip was that?'

That had been December. Yes, he was quite sure it was

December. There was no possibility of his confusing it with an earlier trip. Why was this? Why, because the trip before that had been in September – there had been no caravan in October or November – and in September they had gone by a different route, to Norgku. It was only in December that they had travelled via the Portha-la pass. And it was on the Portha-la that they had met the English party.

Houston sat blinking in the smoky room, trying to comprehend this. He said at last, 'They travelled a whole day with you?'

'Most of one day. Four or five hours.'

'Could you try and remember everything that happened that day.'

There was very little to remember. The weather had been very bad, the youth said; a blizzard was blowing. The four people had joined the caravan while it was on the move. They appeared some time during the ascent of Porth-la. They had caught up with the caravan with difficulty, for one was ill and had to be supported by the others. He thought one of the party had been a woman. They had managed to keep up with the caravan, however, and had bedded down with it when it had stopped for the night. Later they had left.

Left? Where had they left?

The boy had no idea. He remembered that guides had turned up for them – either during the night or early in the morning. He had woken to see two of the guides carrying away the sick man, and the rest of the party following. He had been awakened by shouting, in English. He thought the sahibs were angry with their guides. Perhaps they had arrived late. Yes, it had struck him as strange that a foreign party should be travelling in Tibet without guides. He had wondered about that.

But where had they gone to? Where could they have gone?

To a monastery, perhaps, to take shelter; the blizzard had continued for a futher two days.

To the Yamdring monastery? Was that anywhere near?

Yes, it was not far, two, three days, not more.

And there had been no comment among the caravan team?

Could a party suddenly disappear without arousing curiousity even?

But certainly. Parties were joining and leaving the caravan all the time; and this party had not even paid to join. Nobody had objected to this, of course. In winter wandering groups often took shelter with passing caravans. One would expect a foreign party to do this if they had missed their own guides. He had forgotten all about it himself. To tell the truth, it had only come to mind again when Bozeling had told him the sahib was interested. He hoped he had been of assistance. He would try and remember what else he could of the incident; but he didn't think there was anything else to remember.

Houston thanked him, and refused more tea, and also Bozeling's offer to see him back to the hotel, and said good night all round, and left.

He felt very ill. He thought he was going to be sick. He walked slowly, breathing in the crisp night air, and stopped once or twice to lean against the wall. He could see the glow in the sky over the square, and made towards it through the dark alleys. There was nobody about, and he thought after a while he had lost himself; the glow was getting no nearer. But presently he saw a familiar feature, an upended cart he had passed on the way, and a moment afterwards a white shape glimmering in the dark.

He saw as he came closer that it was two men sitting smoking on a low earth wall, and he made towards them to ask the direction. He slowed down a bit as he approached. He didn't know what it was about them. They were sitting perfectly still, not looking towards him though his footsteps were loud in the alley. He felt the hairs on the back of his neck beginning to bristle again, and he had an instinct to turn round and go back.

He couldn't quite bring himself to do that, and continued walking, and that was the last opportunity he had. He saw, without quite believing it, that they had got up and were coming towards him. He saw the clubs in their hands. He stopped and watched them, too petrified to turn and run, still trying to convince himself that they were watchmen. They came quite slowly, without any sound, and he saw their feet were bare. He put out his hand and tried to speak, and they leapt at him.

He caught a numbing crack on the elbow and another on the side of his head and staggered, grunting. He tried to protect his head with one hand, but one of them had got behind him, and he felt another stunning blow. He found himself stumbling forwards and clutching at the man in front of him, and he grabbed at his white garment, still falling, and saw a bare foot beneath him, and stamped on it as hard as he could.

He heard the thin soft cry of pain, 'Aaaah....' and thought the fellow went over, too. He was down himself, scrambling in the dirt, and then his ear exploded and, as he moved his hands, his eye also, a single great pink blossom of pain unfolding above his right eye as he slipped and slithered and tried to stop himself but finally fell into a lurching, bruised blackness.

His unconsciousness was short and they were still there as he came to, bending over him and going through his pockets. He heard someone grunting and coughing and realized it was himself, and they dropped the wallet quickly and looked at him, muttering. They straightened up, and he saw by the way they held the clubs what was coming and tried to twist away but failed and got them both in the pit of the stomach and heard the single drawn-out animal sound as the air went out of his body.

He was over on his side, retching. He had not eaten for hours and only tea and gin and sour bile came up. He had to get his head out of it, and he struggled up on to his hands and knees, trembling. His forehead was icy with sweat and his arms would not support him properly. A dog came to sniff at him, and was soon joined by two others, and they found the patch of vomit, and he had to get away from that, and he was up, somehow, reeling and tottering in the alley.

He must have turned into another alley, for at the end were lights, and he saw it was the square, and he stopped, leaning against the wall before going in to it. He found his wallet in his hand and he dusted himself down with it. He straightened his tie and buttoned his jacket and smoothed his hair, and found it wet with vomit.

He walked across the square as steadily as he could, and went into the hotel and up to his room.

He ran the tap and plunged his head in the bowl several times till he thought he had got rid of the vomit. Then he changed out of his suit and put on a dressing-gown and had a look in his wallet and lay down on the bed.

He heard eight o'clock strike from the Scottish mission church. Only an hour since the boy had first told him. Then nine o'clock struck, and ten. He lay there all night. The servant found him like that, still awake and in his dressing-gown in the morning.

2

He thought that if they had taken all his money, he could explain it to himself. But they hadn't done that; they had taken only the small notes; more in the nature of recompensing themselves for their trouble. He shied away for quite a long time from the explanation that seemed to make most sense.

There were so many new problems here that he though he ought to proceed on the assumption that, right from the beginning, someone had made a mistake. He assumed first that it was the Tibetans.

A party of four people had been found dead after an avalanche. The party had been wrongly identified as a party of missing British people. A message to that effect had gone off to Lhasa. When the error had been discovered, it had taken time to rectify. Communications were bad. Everything had to be checked and double-checked by Lhasa before the error could be admitted. And in the meantime they would give no information.

Well. It was one explanation, as reasonable as any other. More reasonable, in a way. For here were human error and bureaucracy and procrastination. He had met them all in India, and he supposed you could find the same in Tibet. But what, in that case, had happened to the British party? Five months had passed since December. Why had they not come out of the country?

There was no answer to that, so he began assuming on another track. He assumed that the boy Ringling had made the mistake. Ringling had observed a party of four people join his caravan, and thought he had heard them talking English. He had been half asleep when he heard them. They had gone off with their guides. Then, according to this assumption, the people he had seen must have been four other people. They were three other men and one other woman, and they had not been talking English.

Houston didn't like this assumption. The boy would know if they had spoken English. He had no reason to lie. And Houston had given no details himself. The boy had supplied them: the three men, the woman, one of them sick.

So the Tibetans had reported the party dead in October, and Ringling had seen them alive in December. And after he had been to see Ringling to hear this story, he had been attacked. The men had been waiting for him; they had been more intent on beating him up than on robbing him. And in fact they had robbed him of very little.

Houston thought he could see a pattern in this. He was still trying to think where it got him when a voice said softly in his ear, 'Sahib, your tea. You have not drunk your tea, sahib. It is nine o'clock.'

Houston looked about him and saw daylight in the room, and thanked the servant and got up. The walls lurched a bit. His head was still pounding vilely and his stomach felt badly bruised. He took off his dressing-gown and examined it. There was only slight reddening; but his eye, in the mirror, was more spectacular. An angry purple contusion rose between eyelid and temple. He thought he had better wear dark glasses today.

He washed and shaved and dressed and sat down for a moment to recover from these exertions and to allow the furniture to get back in place. He thought he had better eat something. He had had nothing since lunchtime in Darjeeling the day before. He went rather carefully down the stairs and into the dining-room and had fruit juice and warm rolls and coffee, and managed to get back to his room just in time to bring them up again.

He sat in a cane chair, trembling and faint and wiped his sweating forehead. He didn't know what he was going to do about this. He thought he had better not stay in Kalimpong today. He had to go somewhere and think.

He went downstairs and out on to the hotel steps and looked out over the brilliant, bustling square and tried to make a plan that would get him through the day.

'Hello, sahib. Where we go today?'

He saw that here was a problem even more urgent than how he would occupy his time all day; and to get rid of the boy said the first thing that came in his head.

'Sorry, me lad. I'm going to Darjeeling.'

'Oh, sahib, you've just come back.'

'Well, I'm going again.'

'Well. I keep the bus for you, sahib. I see you catch it.'

Houston cursed dully, head thumping in the sharp sunlight as he followed Bozeling across the square. It would have to be Darjeeling, then. But one place as good as another today, he thought; and perhaps he could think on the bus.

It was a magnificent day, high cloudless sky, the great round hills lush and plump with spring. The bus stopped frequently at villages on the way, passengers got in and out, jostling, chattering, joking, the whole world delighted to be about its business on such a day. Houston sat leaden in his seat, counting the swinging hammer blows in his head and trying to control the nausea in his stomach.

They were alive. They had been alive in December. They had travelled without guides in December. And then guides had appeared for them, and they had left the caravan. But why leave it? They had walked all day with it in a blizzard. Why leave it when guides were available to carry the sick man?

Because the guides not guides; because the guides men sent to bring them back. . . .

He thought he could go on indefinitely with this preposterous daydream, and suddenly realized how preposterous it was, and pulled himself together. The situation, from a certain point of view, was not without humour: himself fed up, frigged up and far from home, taking an unnecessary journey to Darjeeling to escape the attention of one single small Sherpa.

And with regard to the robbers: why shouldn't they take only his small notes? They were only small robbers. They were robbers without shoes. Large notes would be an embarrassment to such robbers. And with regard to Ringling's story – he must at some time have mentioned himself what he was looking for, and his brother had been happy to provide the right answers.

This explanation in the clear light of day seemed so very much more convincing than any of his cockeyed assumptions of the night before that he felt himself smiling suddenly with a sense of jubilant release.

'It is very amusing, sir, isn't it, to see the goats playing?'

He had been addressed by a slender young Bengali; he wore a European shirt and trousers and his eyes glistened gaily behind steel-rimmed spectacles.

'The goats?'

'On the hills.'

The bus was groaning up an incline, along the steep green sides of which a flock of goats bucked and kicked skittishly.

Houston said hastily, 'Oh, very. Very amusing indeed.'

'I saw you smiling at the spectacle. It always makes me smile also. But they are very useful animals, most essential to our economy, sir.'

'Really?'

'Oh, yes. I am studying the goat at the moment.'

'You're a vet, are you?'

'Oh, no, sir, I am not a vet,' the young Bengali said, politely covering his amusement with a thin brown hand. 'I am a teacher.'

'Are you?' Houston said, glad to be taken out of himself. 'So am I.'

'Oh, indeed. This is a pleasant meeting, sir. My name is Mr Pannikar,' the Bengali said, extending his hand.

Houston said his name was Houston, and shook it.

'And what business brings you here, Mr Houston, if I may ask?'

Suddenly, Houston wanted to tell him; all of it. He didn't quite do that, but he heard his own voice, with some surprise, explaining that his brother and three friends had gone to Tibet last year and had not yet returned, and that he had come to find out why.

'Ah, yes. I see. There are many difficulties with the Tibetans these days.'

'All these omens, you mean?'

'Oh, the omens and prophecies. I don't listen to such childish things myself. The key to the situation is the Chinese. They feel that Tibet belongs to them. Of course this makes the Tibetans very nervous. They feel they must bend over backwards not to offend the Chinese. I expect this is what your brother has found, Mr Houston?'

'How do you mean?'

'They are regarding him as a spy, are they?'

'A spy?' Houston said, taken aback. 'Why should they?'

'Oh, forgive me, sir. I do not know the facts of the case. I merely thought, if they won't allow him to go just now.... I don't know if you read Chinese, Mr Houston?'

Houston said he didn't.

'I am studying the language. I sometimes see the *People's Daily* from Peking. They are very suspicious people the Chinese, and they think every European in Tibet is a spy. They quite often print names of people. This is what makes the Tibetans so nervous.'

'You think that's why they won't let him out?'

'I have no idea at all, Mr Houston. It was only a suggestion. Have they told you anything?'

'Nothing at all.'

'Ah. That is understandable. And they would naturally try to discourage you from making inquiries. They certainly don't want any international incident or bad publicity this year. But it's possible they might be holding them for an inquiry to convince the Chinese... What exactly was your brother doing in Tibet, Mr Houston?'

Houston told him; and presently went on to tell him what subjects he taught in school, and heard what subjects Mr Pannikar taught, and learned a good deal more about the Indian goat; and he realized the situation had turned upside down again. He realized something else also. Every bit of staw-clutching, every bit of hope that Hugh might be alive was followed instantly by a reaction of dismay, of reluctance to pursue it. And as he sat and chatted with Mr Pannikar he came suddenly upon the reason.

If Hugh was dead, there was nothing he could do about it. If Hugh was alive, there was still nothing he could do about it. He dare not produce evidence that he was alive; for then, whoever had said he was dead would be forced to prove it. There was only one effective way of doing that. He didn't think they wanted to take that step. He thought last night's little encounter might have been designed to dissuade him from pushing them into taking such a step.

So to keep Hugh alive he must pretend he was dead. And to pretend he was dead, he would have to go home. But how could he go home, believing Hugh to be alive? And how could he stay, knowing that he might contribute to his death?

He couldn't go, he couldn't stay. He wondered in that case where in God's name he *could* go to escape from this limbo, and suddenly realized where he would go, and paused in mid-flow.

Mr Pannikar looked at him inquiringly. 'You were telling me about a greetings card you had done.'

'There was a border on it. I copied it from a tile in the British Museum, an Indian tile. It attracted more interest than anything else I did last year,' Houston said, staring at him in shock and amazement.

'Oh, that is very interesting,' Mr Pannikar said, smiling a little uncertainly at the strange expression on his face. 'It is most interesting indeed. What a pity we have arrived in Darjeeling. Speaking for myself, I have found the conversation most stimulating.'

'Very stimulating indeed,' Houston said.

'I wonder if you would care to enter into a correspondence when you return to England. I have my card here.'

Houston did not have a card, but he wrote his name and address in Mr Pannikar's notebook, and shook hands with him and wandered away from the bus station in a daze.

He saw a bookshop in the Mall and walked over to it, telling himself that there was no harm whatever in playing with the idea, and bought a twenty-five miles to the inch map, and turned into the Mount Everest Hotel with it. He wondered if he could keep a gin and tonic down, and ordered one and opened out the map.

Yamdring was a few inches across the Tibet frontier, not more than six inches from Darjeeling, from where he sat in the Mount Everest Hotel with his gin and tonic. A hundred and fifty miles as the crow flew; under an hour in a plane.

He felt his heart beginning to thud. He took a cautious sip at his gin and tonic. He lit a cigarette.

He wondered how many miles it really was, and how long, going deviously, it would take. Ten days, a fortnight. There and back in a month. He had been away nearly two months already.

He finished his gin and tonic without ill effects, and an hour later tackled a light lunch, and managed to retain that also. He went back to Kalimpong on the afternoon bus.

He found his way back to the house that night, and took a large monkey wrench with him, against contingencies; he had bought it in a garage in the town before dinner.

He took the youth through his story again, and could find no variation. There were also no additions, which seemed to him satisfactory; he had offered various bits of information which could have been embellished if the boy were lying or merely anxious to please.

He said at last, 'Ringling, you know the way to Yamdring?'

'Yes, sahib. I've been there many times.'

'Could you take me there?'

'If you get a chitty, sahib, yes. I need to mention it to Michaelson Sahib.'

'Without a chitty. Without mentioning it to Michaelson Sahib.'

The boy grinned at him uncertainly.

'We both need chitties, sahib. You can't get into Tibet without one.'

'Across the border, secretly. The two of us. No chitties.'

'I don't understand, sahib.'

Houston made it clearer.

The boy was sweating slightly when he had finished, and his smile was a pale shadow of itself. He went out and brought a bottle of arak and poured two glasses, and drank off his own right away.

'It's very dangerous, sahib,' he said at last.

'I'd pay you well for the risk.'

'Dangerous for you. Have you ever climbed high?'

'Not very high.'

'Maybe we have to go over twenty thousand feet. I don't know if you could manage it, sahib.'

'It would be a good time to learn,' Houston said, smiling faintly.

The boy shook his head. He drank another glass of arak. He said, 'Could you get a chitty for Sikkim, sahib?'

'I could try. Why?'

'There are mountains there. If you stay a few days at ten thousand feet, maybe we could tell.'

'All right,' Houston said. 'I'll try.'

He kept the monkey wrench in his hand all the way back. But nobody was waiting for him this time.

Houston went to Calcutta a few days later. He went to his bank, Barclay's Peninsular, and drew out three hundred and fifty pounds in fifty-rupee notes, and changed two hundred pounds' worth of these at other banks for two-and five-rupee notes. He booked in again at the Great Eastern and had a shower and left his suitcase there; and then he went to see Lister-Lawrence.

He had telephoned him already from Kalimpong, and had explained what he wanted. The official had not sounded very encouraging; and was scarcely more so now.

'Sorry, old chap. No joy.'

'Why not?'

'No reason. They just don't want you. I did explain that Hopkinson can't hand out the chitties himself. If Tibet doesn't want you, then Sikkim won't, either. They work in very closely with each other.'

'But what trouble would I give? All I want is to see the sirdar of this caravan in Gangtok and hear his deposition and get him to make his mark. I've told you all this.'

'And I told Hopkinson. And I expect he told the visa authorities. They just don't seem to want to know you, old boy. Of course there's nothing to stop you writing to this man in Gangtok.'

'I want to see him.'

'Yes. Well,' Lister-Lawrence said, standing up. 'I've got rather a lot on just now . . . If you'll take a word of advice you'll pack up and go home. You've done all anyone could expect.'

'I'll think about it.'

'Do that. And look in to see me before you go, won't you?'

'Before I go,' Houston said.

Five days after leaving Kalimpong, he was back. Ringling met him as he got off the bus in the square.

'All well, sahib?'

'All well, Ringling.'

'You have the chitty?'

'I'll tell you about it later.'

'And the money, in small notes.'

'Everything. I shouldn't hang about too much here. I'll come and see you tonight.'

He had started packing when they rang up to tell him Michaelson was below. He went down, cursing.

'Hello, sport. Why didn't you say you were going to Calcutta?'

'Something cropped up in a hurry.'

'Something cropped up here, too,' Michaelson said gloomily. 'Come and have a drink.'

Michaelson had had another interview with Sangrab over the matter of his black tails; but this time the consul had not set himself out to ingratiate. He had merely pointed out that he could not discuss his government's methods of allocating licences, and had made a somewhat oblique reference to Michaelson's own methods as being perhaps out of date.

'Out of date,' Michaelson said gustily, signalling for another round. 'You know what he means by that? My face doesn't fit round here any more. Maybe none of our white faces will fit soon. The bloody Indians have their own government now....'

Houston said nothing, waiting for Michaelson to take himself off.

'There's no government behind me, sport. I'm just bloody old Michaelson who's been giving them a living for thirty years. Even my teamsters are leaving. Your friend Ringling – a bloody family I've kept for years.'

'Where's he going?'

'Christ knows. Climbing, he says. Won't be able to oblige me for the next two trips. My oath!'

'You'd take him on again, would you?'

'You've got it wrong, sport,' Michaelson said with morbid hilarity. 'I don't take people on any more. They take me on. Ah, it's time I left this sodding place... Just let me get my hands on a bit of money, and watch me!'

'Well . . . I should be packing myself.'

'One for the road,' Michaelson said.

It was after nine before he was rid of him, and his head was swimming. He went up to his room, collected his papers, passport and flight return ticket and tied them with string and brown paper. He addressed the parcel to himself at the Great Eastern in Calcutta, and wrote 'registered post' on top, and paused.

It looked a bit on the slim side. More bulk was needed to provide a reason why he should not be carrying it with him; so he untied the parcel and included a suit and odds and ends until he was satisfied. He wondered what else he might have overlooked, and cursed Michaelson for befuddling his wits when he needed them most.

He had promised Ringling a hundred pounds for the trip. He thought in view of the changed circumstances he had better make it a hundred and fifty, and unlocked the case and took out the larger notes. He went downstairs with the parcel and the suitcase of money, and told them to lock up the case overnight. He sealed the parcel with hot wax at the reception desk and left it there for posting next day.

'I'm going back to Calcutta tomorrow,' he told the clerk. 'I'd like the bill made up tonight.'

'Yes, sahib.'

'And an early shake in the morning. I want to catch the seven-thirty bus for Gielle-Khola.'

His voice was showing a tendency to boom, and he thought he might be overdoing it, but the clerk seemed to notice nothing out of the ordinary.

'Seven-thirty, sahib. Gielle-Khola.'

'That's it,' Houston said; and went out to tell the boy.

Chapter 4

I

THE first stop from Kalimpong to Gielle-Khola is at the village of Gelong, some six and a half miles away. It is a small, pleasant spot on the east bank of the Teesta river, less hilly than Kalimpong and for that reason the site of the polo ground and country club of the former European Sporting Society. There is a comfortable rest house and a smattering of summer bunga-lows. Houston got off here.

He sat on the seat by the bus stop and smoked a cigarette until the bus had gone. He had slept badly, and he felt weary and hopeless. The idea of walking into Tibet struck him, as he sat with his suitcase and raincoat in the warm and brilliant morning, as more preposterous than ever. He waited till the alighting passengers had dispersed, and threw away his cigarette and followed in the direction the bus had taken.

He walked across the river bridge to where the main road forked, left for Gielle-Khola and right for Darjeeling. He turned right. After twenty minutes he was sweating in the hot and spicy morning. A few people in the fields looked curiously at him as he passed with his suitcase and raincoat. He looked sombrely back.

He spotted the line of telegraph poles marchng off over the hills to Sikkim on the right, and presently the rough track that ran alongside. He turned up this and a few hundred yards farther spied the hut. It was built of logs and had a corrugated tin roof; a little rusting enamelled plate said it belonged to the Department of Posts and Telegraphs. He sat down beside the hut in the shade of a tree and waited.

Ringling appeared after about an hour, riding one bicycle and propelling another. He had a haversack on his back and a large bundle tied to one of the bicycles.

'All well, sahib?' he said, grinning as he dismounted.

'Yes. You're quick,' Houston said.

'The market was empty.'

'Did you manage to get everything?'

'Everything,' Ringling said, and leaned the bicycles against the hut and opened the padlock.

Once, months before, Ringling had come upon a telegraph linesman lying in the road; he had a broken leg. The man had given Ringling his key and asked him to run to the hut to telephone for help. Ringling had done this, and had also seen the man safely to hospital. The linesman had forgotten to ask him for the key back, and Ringling for his part had not offered it. He had since experimented with several huts belonging to the Department of Posts and Telegraphs and had found that the key opened them all.

Houston followed him into the hut and watched as Ringling untied the bundle. There were several sets of clothes inside. The boy took out a pair of khaki shorts and a dirty olive bush jacket, and shut the door for Houston to change into them. He undressed awkwardly, stumbling about between coils of wire and crates of insulators in the cramped and airless space. Before dressing, he opened his suitcase and distributed the money between them; there were a hundred pounds each in small rupee notes. He stuffed his own share in a body belt.

The boy repacked the bundle and retied it on the back of the bicycle, while Houston walked cautiously up and down the track in his new footwear; a pair of old brown oficer's boots that were, Ringling said, in common use among the Sherpas. They returned to the hut together to tidy up; and both were thus aware at the same moment of the next, and quite unforeseen, problem. They stared at each other. There had been no provision for the disposal of the suitcase or the discarded clothing.

Houston cursed Michaelson again. He said, 'Now what?'

The problem was not an easy one. They could not bury the suitcase and clothing; for as Ringling pointed out someone might find the place and alert the police. They could not burn them, for the smoke would be seen, and the operation would in any case take too long.

They decided in the end on a slight change of plan. Ringling knew of another track that would take them in the desired direction; it branched off the main road half-way to Darjeeling. He would leave Houston to wait at this point while he rode into town and deposited the suitcase in the Left Luggage Office at the station. Although the diversion would cost them the best part of two hours, it had certain advantages, for the new track was less hilly and they might even be able to gain something in terms of mileage on the day.

This, accordingly, is what they did.

(Houston never reclaimed his case, which sat quietly awaiting him in the Darjeeling Left Luggage Office for the next four years; it ultimately fetched, with its contents, fifty-five rupees in a sale of lost property in May 1954.)

They reached the Sikkim border soon after one o'clock, and dismounted and walked along parallel with it for some time. Apart from an occasional sign in two languages there was no indication that this was the frontier. The boy was somewhat nervous, however; he said observers were stationed in the hills. Houston thought he saw an occasional flash of glasses from high up in the green mounds, and was prepared to believe him. He had begun, depsite his trepidation, to enjoy himself. They were wheeling the bicycles through a lush and rolling pasture; the fields sparkled with little wild flowers and their scent hung heavily on the air. They had cycled slowly, for Ringling had warned him not to extend himself too much. All the same he could feel the effect of the unusual exercise. He was sweating slightly, and glad of the liberating shorts and the light, short-sleeved bush jacket. He was also very hungry, with an appetite he had not had for weeks; the boy had said they would stop to eat in Sikkim.

Ringling had been picking a large posy of flowers, for the benefit of any observer, but when they came to the timber he got rid of them. He did this in a curious and touching way that

Houston was later to recall in very different circumstances. A little stream bisected the wood, and the boy knelt by it and cupped his hand in the water and sprinkled a few drops on his head and on the flowers; then he cast them into the stream. They were carried quickly away.

Houston did not ask the reason for this performance, and the boy did not offer one. He merely got on his bicycle and rode across the stream.

'We can eat now, sahib,' he said at the other side.

'Is this Sikkim?'

'Yes. No more India, sahib.'

Houston looked at his watch and saw it was a quarter to two. So with only the smallest of ceremonies he had crossed his first frontier. The date was 18 April 1950, and he was not due to recross it again for a long time.

2

The wood extended quite deeply into Sikkim territory, and the boy stopped several times to consult his compass. They rode slowly and silently on pine cones. But presently the ground began to climb steeply and the trees grew denser. They got off and pushed, in single file.

'Do you know where you're going?' Houston asked after half an hour of this. He was breathing heavily and the sweat was smarting in the creases of his arms and legs.

'Everything OK, sahib,' the boy said, grinning back over his shoulder. 'Only a small hill. We come to the top soon and ride down. Very nice. You like it.'

It was nearly another half an hour before they reached the top; but as Ringling said, it was very nice and Houston liked it. The wood ended abruptly and a broad, smooth hill ran into a river valley. The river was quite two miles away; the turf sloped gently all the way. They coasted down to it, and Houston felt the sweat drying on his body in the cool breeze.

They passed a flock of goats, but no sign of human habitation.

'Aren't there any people here?'

'Yes, people.'

'Where are they?'

'Plenty of people, sahib. Even in the wood. We don't stay long in Sikkim. How you feel now?'

Houston had been aware earlier of the boy's nervousness; it made him nervous too.

'I'm all right. Why?'

'We must cross the river. There are two ways. There is a bridge, but we might meet people, or there is a rope bridge. It's much quicker, sahib, but the water is high and you are heavier than me. You think you're strong enough?'

'I don't know,' Houston said, perplexed by these technical considerations. 'What does it involve?'

'There are two ropes. You walk along one and hang on to the other with your hands. You hold the bicycle also.'

'Whatever you think. I'll give it a try.'

The valley, he saw when they were more than half-way down, was in effect a vast saucer; it sloped longitudinally as well as laterally. The river ran downhill fast. It was surprisingly wide, fifty yards at least across, the water white and foaming. They rode uphill along the bank for a mile or two until the river curved and narrowed sharply; the rope bridge spanned it at this point.

They stopped and dismounted. The boy had to shout in his ear above the roar of the water. 'Watch me, sahib. If you can't manage, wave and I'll come back.'

'All right.'

'I'll take your bundle. It will lighten the weight.'

Houston watched as the boy tied the bundle to his back and picked up the bicycle by the crossbar. With palms still open he grasped the upper rope, shaking it to demonstrate the hold, and then, feeling for the lower one with his feet, began edging sideways across. A few yards from the bank, he seemed to learn forward sharply on the upper rope, and turned to Houston, mouthing and grinning. His feet were lost in the white foam.

Houston did not very much like the look of it, but he nodded and the boy continued across. Half-way, Houston lost him in

304

the boiling spray; but he saw the outline emerging again at the other side, and presently the boy was on the bank, grinning and waving.

Houston took a deep breath and picked up the bike and got moving. The roar of water battering against the rock, and the flying spray, confused him. He felt for the lower rope with his feet and kicked both heels hard against it, and edged away.

A few yards out the rope sagged with his weight and his feet were in the water. He hung grimly on to the slimy upper rope, feeling the current strong against his boots, and the next moment was clutching for his life as his legs were rushed from under him. He tilted sharply forward, jack-knifing so violently against the crossbar that the breath was knocked out of his body. He couldn't feel his legs in the maelstrom. He thought he had lost the lower rope. He kicked frantically, and found it, and hung there for a moment, gasping, at an angle of forty-five degrees between the quivering ropes.

He could see the bicycle wheels directly beneath him, and feel his legs numbing in the icy water. He thought he had better move quickly while he could still hold on to both, and inched his way sideways. A few moments later, he was utterly alone, both banks lost to sight in the white, rushing tumult. He saw then what Ringling had meant about his weight; he seemed to be entirely in the river. The solid wall of water blinded and half drowned him as he lay spreadeagled on the ropes. All his weight was on his arms, and he thought he had better let the bicycle go or he would go himself; but he managed to hang on and presently, in a mindless vacuum, to begin moving again.

Ringling dragged him out at the other side, limp and exhausted, and he collapsed on the turf gasping like a spent fish.

'I'm sorry, sahib. The river is swollen with snow.'

'Are there any more of them to cross?'

'Not today ... We should move on quickly, sahib. We can't stay here.'

Houston got back on his bicycle and they set off again. Having coasted down one side of the valley, they now had to ascend the other. The boy steered a diagonal path to keep the gradient gentle; even so by the time they reached the top Houston felt himself completely done in.

They came out of the valley to an extraordinary spectacle. Beyond, the green hills rose in tiers; gigantic folds of land that dipped and fell as far as the eye could see like some petrified ocean. Houston's heart sank. It was now five o'clock and they had been going, with only a short break, for six hours. He said, 'How much farther are we riding today?'

'A few miles more, sahib.'

'Because I'm bloody tired. Do you think it's a good idea to go so hard the first day?'

'We are still near the frontier, sahib. There are people who could see us and tell the police.'

'I haven't seen any all day.'

'Maybe they see us,' the boy said, still grinning but shaking his head obstinately. 'No sense in getting sent back now, sahib.'

'All right,' Houston said. There wasn't much sense in it. He wished the boy would take the grin off his face all the same. He was sick of his continuous cheer and the sight of the small muscular legs pedalling so tirelessly in front of him all day.

The few miles more took another three hours; it was eight o'clock, dark and chill, when they stopped for the night beside a small river. Houston practically fell off the bicycle. He sat sullenly on the turf, every bone in his body aching, while the boy went busily about his tasks. He fetched water for tea from the river, and boiled it on a small spirit stove. He opened a tin of meat and laid out the sleeping bags. He brought more water in a collapsible rubber bucket and offered it to Houston.

'You wash now, sahib. You'll feel better.'

'I couldn't feel any worse.'

'Tomorrow will be easier. We go slowly.'

'Whereabouts are we?'

'Thirty miles across the border. Well into Sikkim. It's been a good day, sahib. Tomorrow we go into Nepal.'

Houston washed and ate and smoked a cigarette and presently did feel very much better. He got into his sleeping bag and looked up at the diamond bright stars and an extraordinary sense of well-being came over him. He smiled in the darkness, astonished at his achievement. Riding a bicycle, he had made measurable progress on the map of the Himalayas. When he closed his eyes he could see every mile of it, the great green valley that they had gone down and up; the rivers; the tiers of rolling hills they had pedalled so slowly across. A good day, the boy had said; not so bad for a man who was in no condition for this sort of thing.

He had a conviction at that moment that he was going to manage it, and breathed deeply of the sharp air, intoxicated with the vision of himself lying there in the enormous emptiness of the hills with the universe swinging all around, and of the further, mysterious places he could reach by going on like this, spending himself a little bit at a time.

He heard a soft snore from the other sleeping bag, and eased himself more blissfully into his own. His arms still twitched from the strain of the rope across the river, and the bones of his backside were bruised from the saddle. Houston moved gently on them; honourable scars, he thought.

That was the first night.

3

Ringling roused him at five the next morning, and he got up immediately. He had already been half awake; despite his intense fatigue he had slept only fitfully. It was grey and misty, the grass wet, the water, fifty yards away, invisible. He washed in the bucket and rinsed out his mouth, and they breakfasted on the remainder of the meat and a few rings of dried apple.

The boy packed everything while Houston attended to the needs of nature and by half past five they were awheel again. His backside was acutely tender and every inch of his frame seemed to creak, but once he had settled himself in position, he got on well enough. There was a certain fascination in bicycling through the mist at this hour in this high place; as last night, he was keenly aware of his geographical location and hungry to pile on mileage. He was also eager to see what kind of country they were in. They had climbed steadily since leaving the river valley, and he thought they were climbing now; he had become so accustomed to the pressure on the pedals that he could not tell precisely.

'How high up are we, Ringling?'

'About eight thousand feet, sahib. How did you sleep?'

'Not too well. Why?'

He thought the boy looked a shade moody, but he only said, 'We don't go so far today. When the mist rises you'll see mountains, sahib. Arnalang on the right and Kanchenjunga ahead.'

'Kanchenjunga,' Houston said with satisfaction. 'How far into Nepal are we going?'

'Only ten miles today.'

'You're not bothered about being seen so near the border?'

'Not up here, sahib. People come and go from Sikkim to Nepal. Getting in from India is the problem.'

The mist began lifting at nine o'clock, but so slowly that Houston was disappointed by what he saw. The mountains were a vague jumble of hazy white peaks, with the slightly higher peak of Kanchenjunga. By eleven, however, the mist had lifted entirely. The sun shone from a high blue sky, and the hazy teeth of the mountains became sharp; first white, then pink, then gold, then white again. Houston's heart sang, watching these fantastic ramparts, as they cycled slowly towards them.

They were riding uphill on springy turf, but frequently dismounted when the going became too steep. They crossed four small rivers, all by log bridge, and stopped to eat in the small valley of the last of them. It was covered with rhododendron, just breaking into flower, pink, red and yellow, and the air was drowsy with flying insects. Houston lay on his back, aching but profoundly satisfied with his situation. They had climbed another thousand feet. They must have put on easily twenty miles. He lit a cigarette, but felt somewhat sick from his exertions and threw it away half smoked.

He saw the boy look at him rather carefully.

'You want to rest long, sahib?'

'No. I'm ready when you are.'

'Right.'

They joined up with a beaten track after an hour or two, and continued along it, passing occasional men with mules, until a few miles from the Nepal frontier, when the boy again cautiously turned off. They entered Nepal by way of two enormous hills, the last of which again broke Houston's zest for the journey. He was exhausted and irritable when they made camp, but again soon recovered after washing and eating.

'How high now, Ringling?'

'It's hard to say, sahib,' the boy said, studying the map. 'We've gone up and down. Over ten thousand feet.'

'And how many miles for the day?'

'About thirty-five.'

'It's surely more than that. We were going at it for nearly twelve hours.'

'We walked a lot of hills, sahib. I didn't want to tire you.'

He had caught the boy looking at him a bit closely once or twice, so he had said nothing and got on with his meal. He hadn't much of an appetite and he didn't feel like a cigarette tonight. He thought he had probably done a bit too much and that they had gone farther than the boy calculated. He turned in as soon as they had eaten.

Again, he slept very badly, tossing and turning most of the night, and he was glad to be up in the morning.

'How far today?' he said heavily, when they had started again.

'Oh, just Walungchung, sahib – fifteen miles.'

'Walungchung. Is that the place where we get the mule?'

'Yes, sahib. We change clothes there also. It's colder.'

'Does that mean we climb to get at it?'

'An easy climb, sahib. There is only one bad bit.'

They walked steadily uphill along the track for most of the morning, passing an occasional group of men with mules, and arrived at the 'bad bit' at midday.

They had entered a rocky defile, and went along it for half a mile until it ended in a steep incline of loose shale. Beyond the shale was a rock wall, forty or fifty feet high, almost vertical and with rough steps cut in it.

A small caravan was there before them, and they waited in the narrow, hot defile, until men and mules had gone up. The mules went slowly, slipping and halting on the shifting slope. Two men climbed the rock wall with ropes; these were attached to the mules' packs, and the animals went up the wall half pulled and half shoved, one at a time.

Ringling had told him to keep quiet when people were around, and he did so, watching the operation with misgiving. They waited nearly an hour before they could begin themselves. The sun was almost overhead and hot on the shale. Every two steps Houston took he slipped back one. He stopped frequently, sweating and panting, aching in every limb.

It took him half an hour to negotiate the slope and he was almost all in when they came to the rock wall. Ringling had a rope in his pack and he lashed the two bicycles together and went up first. Houston followed, holding the machines away from the wall. The steps were steep, and the muscles in his legs jumping, and once or twice he had to stop, half fainting, to hang on to the bicycles.

It was after two when they finished, and they had not yet eaten. They went off the track into a patch of scrub and Houston lay on the ground.

'Eat something, sahib.'

'I don't want anything.'

'You've done very well. Drink some tea, at least. You'll need it.'

'How much farther have we go to ho?'

'Two, three hours. It's up a small hill all the way. We can rest here for a while.'

They rested an hour and got moving again. Ringling's small hill turned out to be a slogging, preciptous hell that lasted all of three hours. It was beginning to get dark when they got to the top, but far below, in a valley, they could see the village. They coasted down to it.

They reached Walungchung Ghola in fifteen minutes, and rode through the village to make camp a mile or two outside. The long freewheeling ride and the excitement of seeing a human settlement again restored Houston's spirits; his tiredness fell away and he quite gaily helped the boy to fetch water. The plan was to sell the bicycles and buy a mule, a tent and food, and as Ringling was anxious to transact this business while the market was still active they merely washed and had a mug of tea before he set off.

Houston took leave of his own bicycle with pleasure. He had conceived a violent dislike for it. He hated its shape and smell and feel. There was something brutish and unpleasant about the broad flat pedals. He detested the handlegrips and even more the merciless saddle. Most of all he resented its weight. He didn't think he had ever in his life loathed an inanimate object more than this one, and the idea of being free of it, of being able to walk on his own and to stop when he felt like it, was so liberating that he began to whistle quite chirpily.

The camp, all the same, was somewhat rudimentary without the bicycles; the two bundles and the haversack lay in a disconsolate small heap. He unpacked the sleeping bags and fetched more water for tea and opened the last tin of meat.

Walungchung Ghola is at an altitude of 10,500 feet, well within the tree-line, but the last sizeable village before the lifeless rock barrier of the Himalayan plateau. The air was brisk and Houton was cold in his shorts and a bush jacket. He got out one of the padded jerkins and a pair of the long woollen stockings that Ringling had brought, and put them on, and sat on his sleeping bag, looking about him.

They had passed Kanchenjunga on their right during the day, and now ahead lay an unbroken line of mountains. In the darkening evening they had moved closer, and he felt he could almost touch them; the solid, bluish ramparts of Tibet.

He smiled in the half light, not at all weary or aching now but conscious only of a feeling of utter astonishment. On foot

311

and on bicycle he had dragged himself to within the shadow of these ramparts. In two days more, he would be over them and into the mythical land. He didn't doubt now that he could do it, or that he would. One did not have to be an explorer or a mountaineer, or very strong, or even very brave. One went each day as far as one could, and recovered, and went on again the next day. He thought he had got the hang of it now, and that he could cope with whatever might befall; and he wondered what would befall him beyond the blue mountains.

He thought of Lister-Lawrence in his office in Calcutta, and wondered how he would deal with his non-appearance; and of Lesley Sellers, coping no doubt with new and pleasurable complications in her flat in Maida Vale, and of Glynis with her little drunk husband in Fulham. He thought also of Stahl in Wardour Street, and of Oliphant, moving about now in the familiar sanity of his flat in Baron's Court, and he shook his head in the dusk. They had all played a part in bringing him to this place; he could feel them quite close to him in the dusk.

He thought he had a sudden lightning flash of the pattern beneath this affair, and of his place in it at the moment, and of its continuation, but it went before he could grasp it; he sat for quite a long time in the lingering half-light trying to find the warm disturbed place in his mind.

Of all the moments of his journey, this was the one that Houston later remembered the best: the vision of himself sitting there on his sleeping bag beneath the ramparts of Tibet, with, all around him, the world disappearing into darkness, and the impression that he had glimpsed a destiny that was neither pleasant nor unpleasant, but merely inevitable.

He was already sick then from the altitude but did not know it.

They spent the next night twelve miles away in a cave at the foot of the mountains, and were up in the darkness at four o'clock to begin the ascent. By three o'clock they had climbed 2,500 feet, and were in Tibet.

That was 22 April 1950.

A study of the relevant map section today (General Staff Geographical Section, Series 4646, Sheets NG and NG 45) shows clearly enough the route taken by Houston on his outward journey.

It was not a route Ringling had ever taken before, but it seemed to him to have many attractions. It was short (only seventy-eight miles from Darjeeling to Walungchung Ghola), it neatly shaved off a corner of protected Sikkim, and it placed them at a point in Nepal where they had little to fear from border police. Also it led in a direct line to Yamdring.

It was not until they had crossed the Tibetan border that he had any doubts about it.

They had crossed the border at a point twelve miles north-east of Walungchung Ghola (that is, fifteen miles west of the 88th meridian); this route as GSGS 4646 NG indicates leads directly to the series of impassable ridges shown as Contour 18. Ringling, however, did not have GSGS 4646 NG. He had the map Houston had bought in Darjeeling. This was a section of an earlier survey (Hind 5000 TBT 14) and instead of Contour 18 it showed merely rising ground broken by an unnamed pass at 15,000 feet.

This was the pass they were making for.

Houston realized something was wrong with him at eight o'clock. They had pitched the tent on a bit of level ground between boulders at 14,000 feet. Ringling had turned in as soon as they had eaten, and had gone to sleep immediately. Houston lay listening to him. He was numb with cold and his head ached. His chest ached also. It had been giving him trouble since early afternoon. He thought he had strained it during the climb, and presently tried to sit up to get into a more comfortable position.

He found he couldn't move.

He lay wincing in the darkness, alarmed at the fire that leapt in his chest. There didn't seem to be anything wrong with his breathing. He waited for the pain to subside before cautiously trying again.

This time he gasped out loud, and lay back, breathing very quickly. His chest was tight and constricted as if someone was sitting on it.

He managed to work his arm out of the bag after a minute or two, and shook Ringling beside him. The boy came awake immediately.

'What is it, sahib?'

'Get me up, will you? I can't move.'

The boy came out of the bag fast and switched on a torch and hoisted him up. 'Where is the pain, sahib?'

'In my chest.'

The boy studied him silently in the torchlight.

'I think I wrenched it,' Houston said with difficulty. 'During the climb.'

'It's the altitude, sahib.'

'No, it isn't that . . . It just came on me.'

'You've been sick for days. It's your heart,' the boy said moodily.

'What the hell do you mean?'

'It won't let you sleep or eat. It's going too fast. It's getting tired.'

The moment he said it, Houston knew it was so. He could feel it now, unpleasantly swollen, and pumping heavily. It seemed to fill his chest.

'I've been watching you, sahib,' the boy said. 'There was nothing to be done. There is a pass ahead of us, and then we go down to eleven thousand feet. I thought we could stay there till you got well.'

Houston looked at him with his hand on his heart, and licked his lips.

'It means we have to climb another thousand feet to get to the pass, shaib, but you can ride on the mule.'

'Will my heart stand up to that?'

'I don't know. We'd better see how you are in the morning, sahib. Sit up for tonight. Like this.'

314

He arranged the bundles at Houston's back, and Houston sat up for the night. He dozed off one or twice, and woke up, and called for Ringling to rub his back and arms in the numbing cold, and somehow got through it.

At five o'clock Ringling boiled a pan of snow for tea, and fed the mule, and they had a mess of tsampa (barley flour) in the tea that he had bought in the village. Houston was sick as soon as he had eaten and lay with his back against a boulder while Ringling packed the tent. But he did not feel as badly as he expected when he was levered to his feet.

The boy hoisted him on the mule, and Houston leaned back against his arm, breathing quickly in the freezing blackness.

'What do you think, then sahib?'

Houston said, 'I don't know. How far is it to this pass?'

'About three hours. It should be light when we get there. We could be down to eleven thousand feet by midday, sahib. How is the heart?'

'Not so bad,' Houston said. He could feel it labouring away in his chest. He didn't know what difference an extra thousand feet would make, but there was little effort in sitting on the mule.

'You want to try, then?'

'All right.'

The boy slapped the mule gently. They set off in the darkness for the pass.

Chapter 5

I

IT had not snowed during the night, and it had still not begun at daybreak. At half past eight Ringling stopped to get his bearings while he could. There was a mildness in the air that he did not like. He thought that when the snow came there would be a lot of it.

He was by no means happy at the position. He knew his compass was a few points out, but he had made a rough correction and nothing that he could see tallied with the map. They had been trudging for three hours, and he thought they must have climbed well beyond fifteen thousand feet. There was still no sign of the pass. Even in the dark, the white, featureless hills had glimmered quite steeply on both sides. In the light he could see that one of them towered still thousands of feet above them.

He didn't like the feel of the ground underfoot – he had gone up to his waist several times – and he didn't like the look of Houston. He was slumped over the mule's neck in a semi-stupor and his face was bluish. Above all, Ringling did not like the map.

He swore softly to himself, looking about him.

He heard Houston grunting, and levered him up again on the mule's back. He said in his ear, 'Not long now, sahib.' Houston closed his eyes, but the boy saw he was still conscious.

He swore again. All would be well when they had lost a few thousand feet; but it was plain that for the moment he could not safely go up very much farther. He didn't know what was for the best: to go on or to go back.

But since they had come so far, he thought they should try for another hour. Then if there was still no sign of the pass – back down again, quickly.

He slapped the mule, and they set off once more.

By half past nine, the summit was in sight, so they kept on till they reached it. It was after ten when they came out of the valley, and when he looked slowly behind him his heart sank like a stone. The ground sloped steeply, and went up again just as steeply: a series of ridges extended as far as he could see. He thought there might be a way along the valley floor, but he did not like the look of the floor. There would be crevasses: it might even be one huge snow-bridged ravine.

He turned the mule round and they went back again right away. They went quickly, keeping to their own tracks, and by half past eleven had come to their camp of the previous night. Ringling did not stop. He ate a handful of dry tsampa, and butted the mule threateningly with his elbow when it turned its head to look at him. But presently he relented and gave the animal a handful, too, for it had carried the deadweight of Houston unprotestingly.

Houston himself did not need anything. He was unconscious.

They stopped for the day on a rock ledge at twelve thousand feet. Ringling thought they must have left Tibet, but did not know precisely or even care. He was exhausted and worried, and he hurried to get the tent up. Houston had fallen off the mule when they stopped, and was lying on his side, back and front already thickly encrusted with snow. It had started to snow at midday, and despite the rising wind and the cold had continued.

The tough black yak-hide tent bellied like a sail in the freezing wind and it took him over ten minutes to erect. There was ice under the snow on the ledge, and he hammered in the metal pegs with the back of the axe, using the axe itself as a final retainer.

He dragged Houston inside and sat him up against his knee while he unpacked the bedding. His breathing was dry and rustling, and he thought he had better try to get some liquid into him. He put his own rolled sleeping bag and the bundles at his back and collected a pan of snow and set it to heat on the spirit stove. He had bought tea bricks in Walungchung Ghola and a large cake of yak butter, and he pared off half a handful of each and stirred them in the water. He poured tsampa in his own mug and a drop of arak in Houston's, and took him in his arms and tried to get him to drink.

He thought he took some of it and that his breathing and colour improved a bit, but the failing light and rising wind made it hard to tell. There was a pinched look about the nose and lips that he did not like.

He took off Houston's boots and rubbed his feet and put him in his sleeping bag and tied it up. He felt half frozen himself, and his tea was cold. He heated it again on the stove, and lit a lamp, and sat crouched on his bag, drinking the tea and watching Houston. The pitch of the wind outside threatened something more than a quick blow. He doubted if they would be moving again for two or three days. He wondered what he had let himself in for.

2

Houston's coma lasted (Ringling told him) for two days. He was aware from time to time of the boy lifting him and rubbing him and of his mouth and throat protesting as hot liquid flowed into him, and of a creaking, aching constriction in his chest. And then quite suddenly he was aware of many things more: a small yellow lamp flickering on swaying black walls, a blast of cold air coming in from the grey-black slit in the wall, a thin monkey face with an anxious grin bending over him.

'How you feel now, sahib?'

'What's happening?'

'You've been ill a couple of day. We rested up in a blizzard.'

The boy turned away and reappeared with a mug and crouched down beside him.

'Here, sahib, drink.'

There was tsampa in the tea, and he chewed it and began to feel sick immediately. The boy watched him.

'How you feel, sahib?'

'Not good.'

'Try and swallow it. You'll feel better soon.'

He knew he wouldn't feel better soon, but he tried to swallow. The nausea seemed to come sweeping up from his boots, and he turned his head just in time. The vomit shot out in a warm stream and he heard the boy hissing anxiously as he held his heaving body. He fell back again weakly and wished it would all recede once more.

He said, 'I'm sorry,' with eyes closed.

The boy said nothing, but he felt the arm withdrawn. He opened his eyes presently. The boy was looking at him.

'Where are we?'

'I don't know, sahib. The map was wrong.'

'In Tibet?'

'Maybe.'

He remembered wishing once before that the boy would take the grin off his face, and wondered again what in hell he found so funny. But then he saw that the boy grinned when he did not know what else to do, so he said, 'Is the blizzard off now?'

'Just finishing now, sahib.'

'What time is it?'

'Three o'clock. It's the afternoon. You've got to eat something, sahib. You don't eat, we can't move. You're very weak.'

'All right.'

Houston closed his eyes, and when he opened them again the boy was bending over him with another mug of tea. He could feel the tsampa thick inside and forced himself to take it. He drank the lot and lay back again quickly, willing himself to keep it down. It turned and rumbled inside him, the rancid taste of the greasy butter rising in his throat. He kept his eyes tight shut and his mouth tight shut and imagined himself out in the wind and the snow wanting nothing so much as to be in a sleeping bag with a mug of tea and tsampa and a fine big piece of stinking yak butter, and it worked for the best part of half an hour, until his stomach suddenly gave a single diabolical turn that seemed to squirt it at pressure out of his nose as well as his mouth before he had time to get his head up out of the bag.

The boy had been hovering, however, and almost jerked his head off getting the rubber bucket in position in time.

Houston opened his eyes again after a minute or two and found the boy carefully studying the contents of the bucket.

'Very good, sahib. You kept some back.'

'For a rainy day,' Houston said.

He thought he was on the mend.

When he got back to England again in 1951, Houston found he was ten days 'slow': he had kept a sort of check while he was away and he had in some way lost these days. He could account for three of them in the hospital at Chumbi, and for perhaps six more during the time he lived under the ground with the girl; but he thought he had probably lost one also on the outward journey. It seemed to him likely that while he was in a coma, Ringling, too, had gone to sleep for a complete day and had forgotten about it. (He saw him do this later.)

At all events he subsequently altered from 27 to 28 April the date when they set off again, allowing two clear weeks in the mountains before the next verifiable date (12 May).

He did not take a very active part in events for most of these two weeks. He lay on the mule by day and wherever he was put at night, and just at the time when he recovered himself and could have taken his share of the chores, they ran out of food. This was not an important setback, but it was one that Ringling had to cope with alone. Houston stayed by himself in a cave for two days.

Having lost faith entirely in the map, Ringling was proceeding by instinct and his own mountain lore. They had gone back down the track to Walungchung Ghola until they had found another, branching off to the west. This took them parallel with the frontier and around the Kang-la massif. They had Kangala in sight for four days until they went high again themselves and lost it in the jungle of white peaks.

They went up to nineteen thousand feet, and although Houston felt dazed and headachy and was as weak as a child, he was able to retain most of his food and was not prostrated again.

Ringling had reckoned a week to get through the mountains (he could have done it in four days himself), and even though Houston was not eating his share, it was obvious that the food would not last.

They went off the track in a wild and desolate region to look for a cave (for the boy was nervous of showing the tent during the day), and when they found one, he installed Houston as comfortably as he could, and slept there the night himself and went off with the mule in the morning.

They had been travelling in a thick mist all the previous day, and it was still thick when he left. There was nothing to identify this bit of mountain from any other, and Houston wondered if he would ever see him again. But the boy turned up on the second day, at dusk, grinning, with the mule and food and news.

Below the mountain was a village called Shonyang, and he had been able to get his bearings there. By taking a lower road they could reach Yamdring in four days; it would take them six if they kept to the mountains. It was summer down below. The sun shone. The sky was blue, the barley stood green in the fields. There was also considerable excitement there. The governor of the province had himself just visited on a tour of inspection. He had inspected the police force, and had augmented it, and had in addition left a runner from his own staff with orders to return at once to Hodzo Dzong (Fort Hodzo, the capital of the province) if any strangers from the outside world should appear. Ringling had found considerable difficulty in buying food, for the governor's direction had been taken as a general warning against all strangers.

'Does that mean,' Houston said, 'we're going to have trouble at Yamdring?'

'I don't know, sahib. Yamdring is a big place. There are always pilgrims and beggars there.'

'Do you think they know I'm in the country?'

Ringling shrugged. 'It's a year of bad omen, sahib. They don't want any strangers here. The next pass is Kotchin-la – a bad mountain. There are devils there and people are afraid.'

Houston saw the boy was not too happy himself at being so close to this bad mountain, for he enlarged once more on the felicities of the lower route. Houston thought they had better keep to the mountains all the same.

The boy accepted his decision with the most muted of grins,

and turned in sombrely after he had eaten. Houston stayed awake quite a long time himself. His sickness and the days of wandering high above the clouds had made the warm world he had left behind him curiously remote. That the boy should have climbed down into it and returned again all in the space of three of four meals while he had lain with his thoughts in the bare and self-contained world of sleeping bag and spirit stove moved him strangely.

It was all going on down there still, another plane of existence, like a continuous film in some lower hall; he could almost feel the muffled vibrations coming up through the miles of rock to his stretched-out body lying solidly on the roof of this other world where the sun still shone and skies were blue and fields green, and the human termites went warmly and ceaselessly about their activities.

He went down after a while for a closer look himself, and found himself in Fitzmaurice Crescent, at night. He let himself into the flat and walked familiarly round it, opening doors and switching on lights. He remembered every corner to it. He remembered the smell of it. It made him restless again, the old lonely restlessness of summer, and he went out again, closing the door behind him, and walked down to the Kensington High Street. Crowds teemed on the pavements and he walked with them past the lighted windows of John Barker's and Derry and Tom's and Pontings. The Belisha beacons were winking, a long double line of them, not quite in phase. He saw it had been raining, for the road glistened. It was crowded with traffic. He didn't know where he was walking and he didn't want it to be night, so he made an effort and it was day.

He was in a boat, on a lake, and he thought it must be in Regent's Park, for he had not been rowing with her anywhere else, and she was laughing at something he had said. He was laughing himself and he shipped the oars and took a breather, looking at her. She was very brown. She had been very brown at Roehampton, the day before. She wore a halter neck. She was wearing a new kind of lipstick, orangy. He could smell the sun on the water and on the boat and the not-unpleasant odour of his own sweat. The sky was high and blue and it was going to continue for days, and he had an idea she would be coming back to the flat with him. It was greenish, her dress, linen, with a freshly washed, ironed look, and he made up the colours in his mind that were needed to produce this shade, and at the same time imagined her ironing it, for some reason in a sunny room, early in the morning, standing very tall in a pair of slippers and her basic underwear, long-legged, girlish. His shoe-lace was undone, on the thwart, and she bent to tie it up for him, and he saw the division of her breasts down her dress, and felt the first breathless, needle-like stab; and from his frozen upper world savoured it again. But he knew how it continued and felt sad guilt and went away.

He went to a door and opened it, and switched on the light. She said, behind him, Who did you expect to find in your bedroom? He said Fairies, and led her into the living-room. He made to take her coat, but she was huddling into the fur collar, and he said, You're the chilliest person I know. And she said, That's why I need so much warming up, wonder boy. He thought this was the fist time she had come to the flat. She said, You lured me up for coffee – I suppose I have to make it. He said, If you're able, and she looked at him sideways in that curious way. Oh, I'm able, wonder boy. Able and willing

He remembered with certainty that this was the first time, because of his excitement. He was a little tight and the girl, too, and he went up behind her in the kitchen, and put his arms round her. She said, Hey, what about this coffee. And he said, What about it. And she said, as his hands moved, Yes, what about it, but more as a comment than a question, and they went into the living-room. He had switched the light off as he came out, but he had put on the electric fire. There was an area of soft radiance before the fire, and he went exploring there in it. He explored her thoroughly, and her teeth glinted up at him as she smiled in the rosy light of the fire, the pair of them breathless and writhing through the long thrilling minutes. And here surely was nothing but pleasure, each of them dilated in passionate enjoyment of the other, a limited relationship that gave only pleasure.

But he knew that it didn't and that it wasn't, for he was betraying and probably she was betraying, and beyond the firelight there was bitterness and pain; so he left them to it and came back. He thought you couldn't isolate pleasant bits of the jigsaw, for the pleasure was relative and none of the pieces particularly meaningful or worthwhile unless the pattern was worthwhile. He didn't think he had managed to find a worthwhile pattern; and he didn't know now that he wanted one.

Lying on the roof, he had the clearest sensation of the trampling confusion in the hall below; the milling specks darting this way and that on forgotten errands, stopping to make love, to build structures and take them down, to make rules and change them, creating new devices to make the errand easier, and trying at each performance to discover what the errand was.

He saw how easy it was in this high place to find objectivity, and he knew he didn't want to get lost again in the stifling confusion below. He thought: to remain in this high world of calm mist and freezing stillness; and was presently aware that it was neither calm nor still. Ringling was shaking him violently in the bag.

'The wind is coming up, sahib. We better move now.'

He turned out, bleakly. It was four o'clock in the morning. The wind sucked and moaned like a vacuum cleaner at the mouth of the cave. The small lamp was lit and the boy had the spirit stove going. Houston was shrivelled in the sudden deathly cold, and he pulled on his boots and his quilted jacket, stumbling about in the dim light of the cave. He rinsed out his mouth with melted snow and rolled up his bedding and sat huddled on it while he drank his tea and tsampa.

The boy had kicked the mule into life and was feeding it. He went silently about his tasks, serious and unsmiling. He scoured out the mugs with snow and packed them, and the cooking utensils, and the bedding, and strapped everything on the reluctant animal.

He said, 'We have to move fast, sahib, or we get stuck on Kotchin-la. It's better if you walk.'

'All right.'

'You feel strong enough to walk?'

'I said all right.'

The boy looked so small and pinched and harrassed that he wanted to apologize for his curtness, but Ringling merely turned away, tight-lipped, and began pummelling the mule with hatred, crying 'Hoya! Hoya!' until it moved, and the opportunity was gone.

Houston put on his goggles and followed, into howling blackness.

4

Apart from the blizzard, when he had lain unconscious, there had been no high winds since they had entered Tibet. Houston had no idea what to expect. It hit him like the sea, a terrific icy buffet that knocked him instantly off his feet. He was not sure if he was on his back or his front, the blackness in the first moments so intense, the ocean of pressure so solid all around that he seemed to be in another element. He couldn't breathe and the freezing current, rushing past his muffled ears, was like the sound of trombones. He floundered and was on his knees, and off them again, two or three times, before he felt the arm pulling him. He was gasping, his mouth full of the suffocating wind, and he bored into the wind and the steady vibration of sound, and found he was boring into the mule, his face pressed hard into its hairy stomach. The boy was holding him there, roaring in his ear.

'Head down, sahib. Keep double. It will be easier soon.'

He nodded his head, too shocked to speak.

'Easier when we get to the track.... Head down into it....'

He nodded again and the boy shook his arm and they turned and went head down into it.

He had scarcely used his legs for days; they felt like a marionette's. But he leaned into the wind, and found the way to breathe, head tucked into his chin, and one leg followed the other, and he supposed they were moving.

He lost all idea of time and direction, concentrating grimly on the reciprocating machine-like movements of his legs and the unbelievable roar of sound; and presently fell into a fantasy in which he was part of the sound, the essential time-keeping part, and it became important that he should not stop, for if he stopped the sound would stop and all would stop.

He had an idea after a while that it was trying to pull away from him, and he worked hard to control it. But it went, strugging and wrenching, streaming into a higher key as it worked first a quarter, and a half, and then a full turn behind him, so that he had to lean backwards with all his weight against it; and he emerged from the fantasy and saw that they were on the track and that it was the track and not the wind that had turned, and that day was dawning.

They were in a wide gorge between rock walls and the funnelled sound had risen higher in pitch like fifes and trumpets. The air was full of flying particles, snow and ice torn from rock, that broke ceaselessly against their heads and backs. Below the knee, all was lost in spray, the whole snow floor of the gorge shifting before the wind so that everything, the glimpsed boulders, the laden mule, themselves, seemed to be bobbing and dipping frantically in a river of ice. It was a scene of such desolation in the dirty grey light that all vitality left him. He thought they must have been going four or five hours. He was deathly tired.

He caught Ringling's arm, but the boy merely looked at him and away. Houston saw that beneath the big goggles the boy's face had become smaller and more pointed, shrivelled by hours of wind into the semblance of a fox's mask. It looked somehow wild and self-protecting.

It had been their custom to stop every hour or two for tea and tsampa, but it didn't look now as if they would stop at all.

Houston saw that the boy's mouth was working as he walked, and thought he might be praying.

He knew that prayer could not sutain *him*, and, suddenly, that he was unable to take another step, and stopped to tell him so; but as he stopped felt a sudden diminution of all his energy and found himself falling backwards, into the wind. He seemd to be falling for some moments, quite gently, but quite powerless to stop himself, and lay there in the shifting spray of snow hearing the wind scream past his ears and feeling only blessed relief at the rest. The boy was bending over him, lips still moving, and he could hear the words now. '*Om mani padme hum ... Om mani padme hum ...*' over and over again, the invocation against evil, 'Hail jewel in the lotus'.

The boy was trying to pull him up, and he was not ready yet to get up, and the praying stopped and Ringling was shouting urgently in his ear. 'Sahib, not here ... We mustn't stop here.'

'I've got to rest,' he said, and heard the words come in a soft, drunken mumble. 'I've got to rest here.'

'Not here, sahib. It will snow. We get stuck on the pass. Come, sahib. Come, now.'

'I can't. I can't move.'

'On the mule.'

He was upright again, enormously bulky and clumsy, the boy pulling and the wind pushing, and he leaned backwards into it again, and found he was leaning against the mule while the boy shifted the load. He had a leg up, and was lifted, and felt himself coming off the other side, slipping, clutching feebly, till the boy wrestled and held him there, and they were moving again. His head rocked up and down, face sunk in the stiff icicled hair at the mule's neck, and presently the chant began again, in his ear.

'Om *mani padme hum*.

'*Om* mani *padme hum*.

'*Om mani* padme *hum*.

'*Om mani padme* hum.'

The emphasis was shifting rhythmically, and his head rocking all the time, and he tried to say the words himself, but found the effort too great and let them slip away. An enormous wave of fatigue was sweeping over him, and he let it take him, and went away, rock-rocking into a deep and soft and finally furry ocean.

The waves had stopped and all was still, and he knew he had been dreaming and lay listening to a curious low-pitched moaning that was neither human nor animal. It was a minute or two before he had it. The wind was coming up in the mouth of the cave, and they had to be off. He stirred himself, and in the same moment the mule tossed its head, so that he clutched instinctively, and so saved himself from falling.

He sat up, on the mule's back.

He was alone, in an enormous cave, a great bowl of ice coated rock. The wind was moaning. He could see no entrance to the cave. He looked up, and saw sky. Something was moving there, and he peered, and it was Ringling, coming down fast, scrambling from one boulder to another. They were in a cleft of the mountain; he saw that this must be the pass, and deduced that the boy had been shouting defiance and throwing the obligatory stones at the devils who lived there.

He was mumbling as he scrambled down, and his face, beneath the big goggles, was skeletal and grey with fear and fatigue. He showed no surprise that Houston had wakened, but merely thumped the mule, and walked instantly ahead, so that Houston again had to clutch to save himself as the animal jerked into movement.

The rock bowl ended in scattered boulders, ice-covered but with a surface of hard snow. The mule slipped on the first, and Houston fell off.

The boy turned and looked at him a moment without ceasing his chat, and motioned him to walk, and helped him. The snow began to fall, almost immediately. It fell solidly, not in flakes but as though sacks were being emptied above, and Houston saw the reason for urgency in negotiating this trap. In the space of minutes the jagged jumble of boulders was obliterated and a deceptive slope of clean snow swept smoothly upwards.

The boy went first, falling between the rocks and picking himself up and climbing steadily. The mule followed in his tracks, and Houston followed the mule.

He had to find the strength to keep up, and for the first minutes he did, husbanding his resources and using himself with care. But the hellish day had gone on too long, his exhuasted sleep had been insufficient, and the limp muscles stretched and sagged on him. He had to stop, just for a moment, to recover, and did so, bent double and panting into the blank white wall that increased freshly like a gigantic mound of flour; and he knew right away that it was a mistake, for all the strength seemed to drain out of him, and he hung on, willing his trembling thighs to keep their hold, and seeing with despair the shuffling fastidious hind legs of the mule recede from view.

The boy had not once turned to watch him, but suddenly he was beside him, with an encircling arm, and they were going up to where the mule waited, head down and already almost invisible in a robe of snow. He leaned on the mule, but there could be no further rest; the snow fell incredibly through the cleft in the mountain. He hung on, making the motions with his feet while the uncomplaining animal dragged him slowly upwards; and in this fashion they left the pass.

This was the last ascent of the outward journey. From Kotchin-la the track fell – slowly at first, and then very rapidly. They turned in at three o'clock in the afternoon, under a rock overhang, too exhausted even to put up the tent. Houston dozed and woke, in his sleeping bag, several times, coming to so feebly that he had to ride the mule all day.

He remembered sitting on his rolled bedding that evening waiting for the tea to boil, but had no recollection of drinking it, and next came to find himself in the sleeping bag with the feeling that weights had been removed from his chest and that he had slept a long time. Daylight was coming in through the tent flap and he looked at his watch and saw it was ten o'clock; he had slept eighteen hours.

He felt wonderfully refreshed. He had an enormous desire

329

to eat. He could hear the boy outside, and he put on his boots and crawled out to him.

Ringling had not been up long himself, and was still gathering snow. Houston saw that he was singing.

He said, 'Hello. We've slept in.'

'Yes, sahib,' the boy said, grinning. 'Good sleep here. Come and see.'

Houston went with him to the edge of the track and looked down to where he pointed; and that was the best thing of all this splendid morning. It was a bush. It was not much of a bush. It was a little grey stunted thing that seemed to be part of the rock itself. But it was not part of the rock. It was a bit of spiny, leathery life, and it was growing there.

They had come out of the lifeless land.

5

They got to the tree-line in the evening, the track dropping steeply, and walked over the little cones of a sparse pine wood, and had energy enough to talk and smoke for an hour before turning in.

The boy had been teaching him a few words of Tibetan at the start of the trip three weeks before – for though they had agreed that he should act as a dumb man it seemed common prudence that he should arm himself again necessity – and he took up the lesson again over a final cigarette in their sleeping bags.

'Very good,' the boy said. 'You've not forgotten. You speak like a Tibetan, sahib.'

'Hadn't you better stop calling me sahib, then?' Houston said.

'What shall I call you?'

'Try Houtson.'

'Houston.'

'Not Houtson. Houston. Hoo-ston.'

'Yes, sir, Houtson. Hoo-tson. Hoo-tson,' Ringling said, trying.

Houston had noticed before the boy's inability to get his tongue round certain words, so he merely smiled and let it go for the moment.

He extended his vocabulary to something like a hundred words in the next couple of days as they dropped down through the delicious summer drifts of pine and rhododendron and maple; and he felt better than he had ever felt in his life. The woods were loud with the sound of birds and falling water, and there was an effervescence in the air that made him want to sing. The weeks on the mountains seemed like some ghastly nightmare, and he recalled with astonishment his desire to remain there, neither dead nor fully alive, his recollections of the beautiful world below so sadly awry.

They came to a valley, alive with flights of multi-coloured birds and aflame with rhododendrons, and he laughed aloud with pure delight.

The boy laughed back at him.

'It's good, Houtson, sir?'

'Very good.'

'Only one day more. You need to shave your face tonight, Houtson.'

The boy's own face was as smooth as when they had started, but Houston's was thick with black beard; he had worried in case it should be pale underneath. But when that evening he shaved, painfully, and with the boy's assistance, the skin beneath was almost as darkened by wind and exposure as the rest of him.

The boy examined him critically, and passed him, but he was mildly troubled at the need for Houston to keep shaving – a rare necessity in Tibet.

'Well,' Houston said, aware that this was one among so many problems. 'Let's face that when we come to it. Turn in now.'

'Yes, Houtson.'

'Houston.'

'Yes, sir. Houtson. Good night, Houtson.'

*

Houston awoke the next morning with a slight breathlessness that had nothing to do with the altitude, and they washed and breakfasted briefly, and got started on the last lap. The boy took him again through his few bits of Tibetan as they talked, and he even managed to add to his modest store. But he did not manage to improve Ringling's pronounciation. The boy was still calling him Houtson, and he was still extracting mild amusement out of it when they came out of a little grove of rhododendron and found themselves on a smooth turf cliff that dropped steeply into the emerald waters of a lake. Just one hour later they were looking down on the seven golden roofs of Yamdring. That was early in the afternoon of 12 May 1950.

Chapter 6

I

IT had been only seven months since he had first heard of this place, and only four since he had left London to hear more; but it was as familiar to him as if he had know it all his life.

Just so the film party must have come on it for the first time, nearly a year before; and just so the acute camera eye of Kelly had recorded it for him. Two thousand feet below the fluted gold canopies swam in the rising currents of air; the monastery glistened on its seven toy terraces like the layers of a wedding cake. Multi-coloured specks seethed in the lower courtyard, and a line of them weaved and swayed across the bridge of boats to the little island. There was a building on the island, a flattened obelisk with glittering white walls inclining inwards to a green roof which sloped steeply away into a thread-like gold spire. The narrow lake lay like a green cheval glass in the cleft of the alley, a score of boats drawing thin insect trails across its perfect surface. At the far side, the village began, and straggled, winking, along the shore to the monastery, and lost itself in the green hills behind.

In the warm afternoon a rich and spicy smell came up out of the valley, and with it, a thin tintinnabulation of sound: the distant clink of metal on stone, snatches of music from some curious, tinkling instrument, an occasional high, disembodied cry, and, from the monastery, enclosing all the sound and regulating it, it seemed, the wafted dong and boom of a gong.

'Yamdring,' the boy said.

They sat and watched it in silence for some time. The boy had estimated it would take three hours to get down, and was in no hurry to move. Evening was the best time to arrive; they could then turn immediately, and without attracting attention, to finding themselves a place to sleep in the crowded doss-houses of the village.

Houston smoked a cigarette and gazed down at the extra-ordinary spectacle, wonderfully at peace and most keenly aware of himself sitting in this place in the golden glow of the May afternoon.

He had made it, then. By mule and bicycle and his own two feet he had crossed the impossible mountains to find this prize in its hidden place. He knew that he couldn't have done it by himself, and that he nearly hadn't done it at all. All the same it had happened.

He breathed deeply, experiencing again the feeling he had had weeks before when he had sat on his sleeping bag and watched the blue mountains lean in towards him in the sunset: the strange feeling that he was both actor and observer in the events that were happening, and that with a little effort he could see what was still to come. And again the glimpse vanished as swiftly as it appeared, leaving him only with the sure knowledge that his brother was here somewhere, not half a mile below him.

The boy had stretched himself out full length on the turf and was peering over the edge with satisfaction.

'It's very good for us, Houtson, sir. Plenty of people here today.'

'Yes.'

'It must be the spring festival. They come to pray to the monkey.'

Houston threw his cigarette over the edge and came reluctantly out of his reverie. He said, 'What monkey is that?'

The boy told him then, the legend of how the monkey had come over the mountains from India, and had found the benevolent she-devil in her cave, and had tempted her; and of how in the spring he had carried her to the island in Yamdring lake, and in the autumn had coupled with her.

'They did it there,' the boy said, pointing. 'Just there where the shrine is now.'

'I see. So that's how Tibetans were made.'

'Yes, sir. By the monkey. He is my father,' the boy said simply.

'Mine, too,' Houston said wryly. 'Or maybe that was another monkey.'

'Yes, sir, another monkey. This one is still here.'

'He must be a very old monkey now.'

'Ah, it's not the real monkey. It's only the body of the monkey. The real monkey died,' the boy said with regret.

'And the she-devil?'

'She wept and her tears turned the lake green in his memory. Then she built the shrine as another memory. She went to live there,' he said, pointing to the lowest level of the monastery. 'She lived there nine hundred years.'

'What happened to her then?'

'She went away.'

'She didn't die?'

'The she-devil can't die. She just comes and goes.'

'And she's just gone again now, is she?'

'No, sir, no, Houtson,' the boy said keenly. 'She's here.'

'In the monastery?'

'In the monastery. In the top one. She's the abbess – the

abbess and the she-devil. She goes away and comes back. She is in her eighteenth body now.'

'I see,' Houston said cautiously. 'How about the monkey — does he come back?'

'Oh, Houtson, no,' the boy said, swiftly covering a smile with a charming gesture of his slender hand. 'The monkey can't come back. Not the real monkey. What a surprise for the abbess if the monkey came back for her.'

'H'm,' Houston said, bemused by the complexities of this legend, and squinted at the sun. 'Isn't it time we were moving?'

'Yes, sir. We can go now,' the boy said, and got up and punched the mule lightly in the ribs, still chuckling at the nature of the abbess's predicament.

They started down, for Yamdring.

The mani wall began after half an hour, and continued, with intervals, almost all the way. The boy bowed to the inscribed tiles, with their regular invocation of the jewel in the lotus, and chanted a little as they walked. He was still in excellent spirits at the thought of the monkey returning, and inclined to be somewhat ribald.

The track left the cliff to skirt a long field of barley in which women were at work, and Houston saw that many of them had dropped the tops of their orange cloaks, exposing copper breasts in the hot sun. The boy whistled and waved enthusiastically, and one or two of them turned, teeth glinting in the sun, and waved back.

'Yamdring women, sir. Lovely women,' Ringling said, grinning cheerfully at them. 'From the monastery,' he added.

Houston looked again and saw that each of the splendid young creatures had her head shaved, and he said in astonishment, 'You mean they're nuns?'

'Nuns, sir? I don't know.'

'Holy women?'

'Oh, yes, sir, holy. Priestesses. They live in the monastery, one thousand of them. Very holy women, Houtson, sir.'

'H'm,' Houston said. The bare-breasted young women did

335

not look particularly holy. Even allowing for the customs of the country, he thought there was a certain liveliness of glance and gesture that he would not have associated with nuns.

The boy caught something in his tone, and he glanced at him, grinning. He said, 'You mean – do they do it, Houtson, sir?'

'Is that what I meant?'

'Oh, they do it, sir. My God, they do it. They do it like rattlesnakes! They do it whenever they can!' the boy said joyously.

Houston looked again at the lively young priestesses in the barley, and he didn't for a moment doubt it. He said, 'Are they allowed to do that?'

The boy laughed aloud. 'No, sir, not allowed. But they do it. They can't help themselves, sir. All the young ones do it.'

'You seem to know a hell of a lot about it.'

'Oh, everyone knows, sir. It's the only pleasure they have. They live in stone cells. They sleep on stone shelves. They have a hard life, sir. It's no wonder they love to do it so much.'

'When do they get the opportunity?'

'In their cells, at night-time, sir. They're locked in, but the monks unlock the doors. There are only one hundred monks for all those women.'

'That must keep the monks very busy.'

'Yes, sir, very busy. But sometimes people can get in from outside. Some of the women can do it ten times in one night,' the boy said, running his small pink tongue round his lips with a leer of extreme lasciviousness.

Houston shook his head. 'You're a bad young devil, Ringling,' he said. 'I don't know how you've had time to find all this out.'

But it was not Ringling's badness, or even how he had come by his detailed knowledge, that made him smile as they left the barley field behind. Something else had come to mind; something he had read, weeks before, in a dusty newspaper office in Calcutta, and he pondered over it as they dropped steeply down to the labyrinthine monastery with its thousand stone boudoirs.

The proclivities of the holy women of Yamdring had come, certainly, as a great surprise to him. He didn't think they would surprise the astrological correspondent of the *Hindustan Standard*.

2

They got to the village at dusk and entered a narrow, jostling thoroughfare that became, before they had gone half-way through it, as bright as day. Thousands of butter lamps were being lit: on the ground, on the stalls, and above the stalls on rods stretched across the street. The market was in full cry.

To Houston, after the silent weeks in the mountains, it was as though he had been pushed into a steam organ at a fair. The stupefying blare of sound seemed to batter all the sense out of him. Traders cried, musicians clanged, dogs barked, gramophones ground, and above all, like the amplified noise of a colony of parrots, shrieked the voice of the crowd.

The boy sold the mule before they had gone a hundred yards, for eighty rupees, and they continued, pushing their way through the throng, lumbered with the sleeping kit and their personal bags. It was a scene of such extraordinary animation that Houston found himself unable to stop smiling. On all sides the people gesticulated and laughed, handsome, vivacious, noisy people, fluttering like butterflies in the warm brilliant of the butter lamps. They clustered thickly round the cloth merchants with their lengths of glistening silk; and round the trestle tables piled high with jewellery and mouth organs and hand mirrors. Tight knots of them chattered and shoved outside the booths of fortune tellers and letter-writers, barbers and dentists; and more argued and bantered across the provision stalls with their stocks of yak butter, tsampa, dried fruit, tea bricks, green ginger, purple beans and blocks of melting yellow candy.

Here and there groups squatted and drank in narrow lanes between the stalls. Ringling pushed his way through one of these, and Houston saw that behind lay a terrace of tall houses built of rough stone, several storeys high. People were leaning

337

out of the glassless windows in the warm evening, and behind them, more batteries of butter lamps shone in the crude rooms. From one end to the other, this side of the street seemed to be a single enormous catacomb of flickering stone chambers, and he saw that these must be the doss-houses the boy had mentioned.

A stream of people was being turned away from the first doorway, and they had to hump the baggage up and down the exhausting, noisy street for over an hour before they could find a house with accommodation to offer. The room they were allotted, with two other men and a woman, was on the fifth floor, and they struggled, hunched under their baggage, up a narrow, tunnel-like staircase reeking of hot rancid butter from the lamps lining the walls.

The landings ran off into a bewildering series of narrow corridors, brilliant and choking with the fuming butter; and in each was a warren of tiny stone chambers. The young Tibetan who had led the way showed them into one, and left, and Houston looked at his three new companions. They were little, lithe, gay people who had chattered and laughed all the way up through the building, and they were still at it as they came in the room. They clasped their hands and told their names, and Ringling told his own, and pointed to his mouth and his head as he explained that Houston was dumb, and not quite right in the bargain.

There were five palliasses on the stone floor, and a big leather bucket in the corner; this seemed to be the only furniture. A hide cover was fastened over the window and the tiny room stank even worse than the corridor. One of the men removed the hide and hung out of the window, singing, while the other, with the woman, began preparing a meal on the floor with a small butter burner unpacked from the baggage.

Houston lay back on the palliasse and closed his eyes and mouth while Ringling unpacked their own kit. He had never in his life been assailed by such an overpoweringly evil stench, and his head was swimming with the noise and the glare. The clanging and shrieking in the street seemed if anything to be

338

louder now that they were above it, and the people in the room were shouting to make themselves heard. Ringling was shouting as loudly as any of them, quite happy and quite unaffected by the confusion.

Houston lay back on the palliasse and closed his eyes and tried to shut out the stone box and the yellow smoking glare, and succeeded for some minutes, till the boy shook him and he sat up and saw that the woman had prepared a large bowl of some soup-like substance and all were sitting round eating.

'Eat now,' the boy said loudly in Tibetan, grinning at him. 'Eat. Good to eat.'

Houston looked at the bowl and saw something swimming in it, and in an unwary moment breathed through his nose, and he was struggling to his feet, gagging. He didn't know where to go, and the boy was quickly beside him, and he hung, trembling, over the bucket, and saw that it had not been empty even to begin with, and spewed, and leaned on the greasy rim some time longer, knees trembling and eyes watering into the vile receptacle.

He turned, smiling apologetically, to the people round the bowl, and they smiled back at him, in no way disturbed and still eating heartily.

They went out after that, for he couldn't bear to stay in the same room with the food and the bucket, but out in the street found himself suddenly hungry, and they ate.

They ate at a stall at the far and less noisy end of the village, sitting on boxes and entertained by a single blind musician who played gentle tunes on five small gongs. They ate hard barley cakes with soft cheese and washed it down fairly copiously with a mild malty beer, and with this fare, the finest he had tasted for weeks, and the respite in the cooling night air from the din, Houston felt himself again. They strolled round the village smoking each a coarse but flavoursome cigarillo, and Houston saw how the monastery lay in relation to the main street.

They had come in behind it in the dusk, and had divined only its bulk. But now, half a mile away along the lakeside, and with the moon up and glinting on the overhanging gold eaves, they could see it quite clearly. Thousands of lights glimmered in seven tall columns against the dark hillside. It seemed, from this angle, like some great leaning tower lit up for a celebration.

A breeze was scudding across the lake, and the bridge of boats moved uneasily in the chop; the butter lamps danced like fireflies. Even at this hour, the procession had not ceased, and the ant-like lines went endlessly there and back to where the white walls of the shrine stood pallid in the moonlight, the slender spire shining like a needle.

'You want to go to the shrine, sir?' Ringling asked, watching him.

Houston didn't want to; he thought he had done as much as he wanted for one day. But he recalled that the monkey was the boy's father, so he smiled and nodded, and they turned and walked back along the lakeside. As they neared the monastery, he saw how enormous the complex of buildings was. Even the lowest level reared high above them in the dark sky, peppered with light and pulsing with sound.

A flight of steps led up from the lake to a broad courtyard; and from the courtyard another flight to the monastery's great iron gates. Uniformed men stood outside the gates, with clubs and togas and what looked like Grecian helmets, and a small squad of them patrolled the upper flight, evidently to keep it clear. The courtyard below was crowded with people; they stood quite still and quite silent, listening to the chanting inside.

There was an ululating quality about the chanting that Houston had heard before, and he smiled in the dark, remembering where he had heard it, and who he had heard it with, and he wondered how Michaelson was faring at the other side of the mountains.

The bridge of boats began from a small jetty at the foot of the steps, and they jostled their way on. The boats were of animal skins and very buoyant, and the slatted bridge bobbed and dipped like a cork in the choppy water. The procession was at first somewhat hushed, affected by the silent crowd in the courtyard above, but by midstream had recovered its form, and both queues, coming and going, laughed and clutched quite gaily at each other as they swayed and stumbled above the glittering water.

The island was perhaps a quarter of a mile long, and the shrine stood in the middle. There were no guards here and the queue streamed vivaciously and unreverently into the building. Inside was a single room, stone paved, and with a high pointed ceiling. In the middle crouched the monkey. It was made of gold, twenty feet high. There were indications of great kindliness and affability in the fashioning of the monkey's face and hands; and of high fertility in other of its alert golden features. Houston walked round it with the appreciaiive crowd, and he enjoyed it. There was a series of murals on the walls, their colours somewhat faded, and he would have liked to look longer at these, but the crowd pushed from behind, and he was swept on and round and finally out of the shrine. An orange-robed monk waited with an offertory tray outside and Ringling gave money, for himself and for Houston, and they walked back across the dew-soaked turf to the bridge.

The crowds were dispersing from the courtyard when they came off at the other end, and the lights were going out in the monastery. They would be locking the young priestesses away for the night, Houston thought, and he smiled again in the dark. It was a lively place; livelier, noisier, stranger by far than one would think on hearing of it first in a carpeted office in Wardour Street half the world away.

A chill breeze was coming off the lake and he felt stiff and tired. It seemed more than only a day since he had wakened in his tent high in the hills. They cut across the darkening market and found the tenement again and climbed the five tunnel-like flights, and spent some minutes searching in the choking warren for the right corridor, and let themselves quietly into the room.

It was dim now, all the butter lamps but one extinguished; the three Tibetans lying on their palliasses like waxen dolls.

They undressed in silence and Houston got in his sleeping bag, and just as the lamp went out heard the boy's soft 'Good night' in his ear.

341

He stopped himself in the moment of replying. There was no one to hear, but he thought he might as well get it right, so he grunted; a grunt suitable for a man who was dumb and also not quite right in the head, and lay back licking his lips and wondering what the morrow would bring.

But there were hours before the morrow.

The Tibetans laughed and murmured in their sleep. Houston lay awake and heard them. Both men visited the woman in the night; and all of them visited the bucket. Houston heard this, too. He couldn't shut off his hearing, but he could do something about the sense of smell, and he lay breathing through his mouth, throat parching as hour succeeded hour in foetid fumbling blackness.

It was not the best of nights.

3

There was a pump in the backyard, and Houston washed himself gratefully at it in the early sunlight. Men and women had stripped without inhibition all around and were taking stand-up baths. Mindful of the money belts next to their skin, Houston and the boy washed only their faces and feet, and dried themselves on their sweat-stained clothing. They had breakfasted already, on tea and tsampa, in the foul cell of the night, and had booked the room again so that they could leave the kit. There was no reason for them to return, and they left.

Every day for weeks now, Houston had started out in the morning burdened with baggage and with the discipline of so many miles to cover in so many hours. As they entered the street in the sparkling morning he felt curiously lost and light as air, as though he had forgotten something.

The stalls were opening in the market and the street already filling with people. They cut through to the lake and walked along the shore. The sun was low on the water still, but a few pleasure boats were out already and kites flew in the morning breeze. The monastery courtyard lay in a pool of shadow.

They had planned very thoroughly what had to be done today, but familiarity did not make the idea more believable. Even more than on the previous night it struck him as incredible that he should be walking about in a Tibetan village.

'We go inside first, then,' the boy said in his ear. 'All right, sir?'

'All right.'

'How you feel?'

'Fine.'

He felt very far from fine. From somewhere inside the monastery a gong was booming steadily, and his heart had begun to boom in time with it. The gates were open now, guards patrolling with their clubs outside. A thin line of people was being admitted at one gate, and from the other orange-robed priestesses came and went.

The boy said nothing more as they mounted the steps and crossed the courtyard. They joined the queue and shuffled slowly up the second flight. On the terrace at the top, a line of heavy prayer wheels had been set up; they turned, propelled by the hands of all who passed, the greased wooden spindles rumbling softly like a slow train over a bridge. A guard stood on the top step, in helmet and toga, looking over the queue, looking into each pair of eyes as he stolidly swung his club; and Houston felt his heart begin to thud very unpleasantly. From the corner of his eye he saw that Ringling too, was nervous; grinning again with the wild and rigid gaiety that he had come to expect at moments of crisis.

But they edged up to the guard, and past him; and up to the rumbling prayer wheels, and past them; and they were inside.

Houston didn't know what he'd expected to find in there; the result was certainly a let-down. It was like, he thought, nothing so much as St Pancras station: a vast, vaulted place echoing with metallic noise and the sound of scurrying feet. Butter lamps hung in festoons, and in their dim light stood old gilt idols like neglected advertisements. A group of priestesses lugged a trestle table decked with monastery merchandise, and here and there about the hall pilgrims trooped into gated chapels like conducted parties on to railway platforms.

They paused and looked about them, and Houston saw that there was rather more than this. A number of people crawled forward on the stone floor of the monastery on their faces. A little skeletal old wretch sat beating his head quite savagely against an idol, and here and there groups squatted cross-legged holding smoking incense sticks and chanting while monks beat small gongs. Several small gongs were going off all around; he couldn't see the big one. The boy touched his arm and they moved off.

There were perhaps fifteen of the chapels around the hall, some merely cubby-holes with an idol and a tray of flowers. In each people sat in smoky candle-light clutching their incense sticks. The smell of incense was heavy on the air. But there was another smell above the incense, and Houston sniffed and identified it instantly across the months: the veritable odour of the Edith Road Girls' Secondary. It was borne in on him suddenly that this was indeed an institution for females, and that beneath the robes they were sisters, all of them; and he looked through a pair of gates and saw why the smell was so strong here. In a long stone hall, some hundreds of the shaven priestesses were sitting in rows on the floor, chanting. They were swaying as they chanted, like a bed of marigolds.

A guard wandered by as they looked in, and spoke to them, and the boy led him away. He saw then that several of the guards were circulating; the butter lamps caught an occasional gleam from their helmets.

He couldn't get the hang of the place. There seemed to be many smaller halls leading off the main one, and a number of doors and passages: it was an ancient building that had grown with the years in all directions. But there was little hope of investigating now, for the guards were everywhere.

The boy had been questing about like a terrier, and he drew Houston into the wall, and said in his ear, 'It will have to be the other thing, Houtson sir. No beggars here.'

344

Houston had seen this for himself, and he merely nodded and they walked back again down the hall.

The shadow was shifting from the courtyard when they came out of the monastery, and the sun was higher over the lake. It was just on eight o'clock, and their first job was over.

4

It occurred to Houston to wonder later what would have happened if he had enjoyed the benefit of an accurate map when he had started out on the journey from Kalimpong. Certainly he would have arrived two weeks earlier. But would he then have shared the bed of a she-devil, or have had his hands awash in the blood of murdered men, or have suffered his own mutilations? He could never tell; but he rather doubted it.

As it was, owing to the limitations of Hind 4,000 they had arrived in Yamdring on the first day of the spring festival, and this seemed to Ringling nothing but the very best of good fortune, for it lasted in all for seven days, and on each one of them the crowds in the village increased. He could thus snoop to his heart's content, without attracting undue attention, and he did so. For each of the first three days, he settled Houston in the line of beggars in the courtyard, and went busily about his inquiries, returning only to see that Houston got his free issue of tsampa at noon.

There were horrible monstrosities in the mendicant line, and Houston was at first hard put to it to show himself a deserving case. He met with much hostility from the amputees on either side, but by persistent gurgling and grunting, and occasional frothing, at last won acceptance — from the professionals if not from the patrons: his collection was meagre.

For eight hours a day he sat and sunned himself on the hard flags of the courtyard, and only his backside, already ill-used, suffered from the treatment. For himself he was enchanted. His deepest instincts told him his brother was here, only yards away. He felt himself a spy in an enemy's open city. He thought

345

he had never known such satisfaciion: of observing a scene that few had seen before, and of finding that it appealed most strongly to his tastes and his talents.

There was a bizarreness to the spectacle that engrossed him. Frequent masses were held, for the monkey's children to remember him, and their kinship, and notable visitors arrived daily. Once the steps were cleared for the approach of a well-known flagellant, an emaciated wretch who had hobbled forty miles on his knees over a mountain pass, flogging his face and neck and shoulders at every stop with a thong of yak-hide. He crawled moaning like a dog up the two flights, raw from top to toe and still flogging himself, to the respectful hissing of the crowds.

Once, too, the beggars were moved to make way for a magnificent retinue: the hundreds of caparisoned horses and their attendants quite filled the courtyard. At their centre was a palanquin borne by eight gigantic spearsmen, and out of it stepped a young man clad entirely in turquoise brocade. His long black hair was braided over his head and caught at the back in a jewelled bun, and from one ear dangled a long turquoise ear-ring: he sparkled all over with pearls and precious stones. The beggars saluted him respectfully, hissing and poking out their tongues, and Houston did the same, and watched with astonishment as the young man, bowing to them, stripped himself down to his shift and gave away his clothes and his jewels and turned and went into the monastery. He emerged after the mass, still in his shift, and was again borne away, the palanquin, the equipage, the horses, descending the steps with a slow measured pace.

For three days Houston sat and sketched continuously in his head; but by the fourth felt impatience and a need for action growing in him, and he shook himself out of the dream-like state that sun and idleness and the rich visual experiences had induced, and saw that it was time that he took control himself.

He had walked for miles by the lakeside each evening with the boy, to shave himself and hear his news, and the news had not been particularly encouraging. It was not that Ringling was idle, but rather that he was by nature credulous and a lover of mystery for its own sake, and he had fallen into a line of inquiry that was becoming steadily more oblique. In addition, he was having to drink to pursue it; Houston found his hiccuping gaiety a continuing annoyance.

He walked with him again on the fourth evening and listened to the latest budget with a sinking heart. It was of the same kind: a record of petty detail that supported a rumour that a party of Europeans was living in the monastery. But the boy had not found anyone who had actually seen the party, and none of the stories seemed particularly relevant.

He said at last, 'Well, Ringling, what are we going to do about this? We're getting absolutely nowhere.'

'There's the half-crown, Houtson, sir,' Ringling said reproachfully: this had been the very latest item. 'Don't forget the half-crown, sir.'

'I haven't forgotten it,' Houston said, and ground his teeth a little. 'It's very interesting. I was very glad to hear it. But it isn't very useful as proof. There were twenty or thirty English people here last year. Any number of English half-crowns might be circulating in the village as curiosities.'

'Ah,' the boy said; he had not thought of this.

Houston looked away across the lake. It had occurred to him earlier what might be done; he didn't know quite how to put it.

After some moments, silent but for the boy's hiccuping, he said, 'Well, been catching the eye of any of these priestesses on your travels?'

'No, sir, not this time,' the boy said, grinning broadly.

'Have you ever?'

'Oh, yes, sir. Many times. Many times in the past. They like me.'

'In what way?'

Ringling told him in what way, giggling a little in the dusk.

'How did you get in there?'

'Oh, there are ways, Houtson.'

'I'd have thought – you were too young for that.'

347

'No, sir. Not too young. They like young men.'

'Even boys of 17?'

'Better than old monks of 70,' the boy said scornfully, and listed some of the limitations of this age-group.

'H'm,' Houston said.

'It's true, sir. I don't tell you lies.'

'How old was she?'

'I don't know. Thirty. Thirty-five. She loved it.'

Houston took a breath. 'How about trying her again, then?' he said.

'Trying her again?' The boy hiccuped faintly in the dusk.

'This time.'

'During the festival?'

'Why not?'

'During the festival . . .' the boy said, sobering rapidly. 'It's very difficult during the festival. I don't know if I can. They're not supposed to do it during the festival.'

'They're not supposed to do it any time.'

'There are so many guards now.'

'I see,' Houston said.

'But any other time I could. I could do it easily!'

'All right,' Houston said. 'You'll have to do it another time, then, won't you? When you're a bit older,' he added.

Ringling helped with the issue of tsampa next day. The young priestess came round with a mule doling out the tsampa from panniers on the mule's back. She gave to each beggar and blessed him as he ate, and heard his thanks to the monkey for sustaining him at this season.

She waited some time with each one, and the mule waited with her. Ringling waited with the mule. He held open the panniers for her to get the scoop in, and when one set of panniers was finished, staggered out with fresh ones. The priestess was a tall young woman, broader than Ringling and stronger than him, but she let him do these jobs for her, and at the end gravely blessed him. Ringling clasped his hands while she did this, but Houston saw that despite his humility and the woman's priestly calm, both of them were regarding each other with a certain interest.

The boy went off to pursue his inquiries in the village without returning to tke mendicant line. But he returned in the afternoon, and Houston caught his eye. The boy winked.

He woke up in the night to hear someone using the bucket, and thought it was Ringling, back already. But it was not Ringling. It was the woman and she settled back again with a little sigh. Houston sighed himself, and prepared to wait.

He had to wait a long time.

He heard a dog bark in the street, and was instantly alert. A couple of minutes later the latch clinked and the boy shuffled into the room.

He said softly, 'Ringling,' and heard the boy coming across. He sat up on the palliasse. 'Did you get in?'

'Of course. She loved it!' the boy said in his ear.

'Well?'

'They're there, Houtson. They're in the monastery, all four of them. One is mad. I tell you in the morning.'

5

They had cooked the story up between them, and it had worked. Ringling had told her that Houston was his uncle and that he had given up work to bring him here to beg, as a penance. He had also told her that he had been a porter with the European party of last year, and that one of the Europeans owed him money, and that he had heard this man was still here.

'She believed it?'

'She believed it. She will take me to see him.'

'How can she do that?'

'I don't know, sir, but she will. It's a secret between us. You are not supposed to claim money for work while on a penance, so she won't tell anybody, sir. She likes me,' he said proudly.

'You're quite sure she's actually seen them. She's seen them herself, not just heard about them?'

'Seen them, sir. She sees them every day. They are in the third monastery. They play with a ball in a courtyard there all except the one who is mad.'

'Which one is mad?'

'I don't know.'

'How do you mean mad? What way mad?'

'She didn't say, sir.'

'All right,' Houston said. 'Let's just hope you're lucky tonight. You can find out then.'

'Luck,' the boy said scornfully. 'It's not a matter of luck, Houtson. She will do whatever I say. She will do anything for me.'

But it was a matter of luck; for the priestess didn't do what he said. She came up instead with another idea, that had the merit of not involving her in any infraction of the rules, and she presented it to Ringling as an alternative.

The following day was the last of the festival and would be celebrated with a Benediction. The abbess herself would be pronouncing this, and every soul in the monastery, and as many as could manage from outside it, would be crowding into the lower hall to hear her. It was the one day of the year when an outsider could slip in and roam at will in the upper monasteries.

'What do you say, sir?' Ringling said, smiling. 'She'll take me tonight if I want, but this way we could both go. We could go right up there and have half an hour alone with them. What you think, Houtson, sir?'

Houston paused before replying. It had been a long time. It had been the best part of a year. And there had been difficulties and complications almost every day of it. But he couldn't for the life of him see any insuperable complications now. There was a certain inevitability about the way everything was shaping that seemed to augur only success.

He said quietly, 'All right. We'll do that.'

'Yes, sir,' the boy said, grinning. 'So tonight I don't need to worry.'

'Only about your health,' Houston said.

That was how matters stood on the last day of the spring festival at Yamdring; which was also the last day that Houston could have saved himself.

Chapter 7

I

THE Spring Festival of the Monkey at Yamdring has a recorded history of 850 years; the Second Festival rather less – it was initiated only by the Third Body, an abbess of legendary high spirits, in her sixtieth year. Since both festivals were prophesied to come to an end in 1960 (a doom almost certainly accomplished by the Chinese under the Obscene Rites article of their Rectification Laws, 1959) increasing numbers of people had taken to participating in them; a fact which accounted for the large crowds while Houston was there.

Allowing for the way of life and the happy ambivalence of the people with regard to their priests and their religion, Houston was not able to find anything shockingly obscene about the spring rites himself, although some features of the later ones upset him a bit. By that time, of course, he was rather more intimately involved.

The twin ceremonies that ended the spring festival, the Courtship and the Benediction, took place before nine o'clock in the morning (the Courtship, by tradition, 'before the sun has found the shrine'). Because it was important for them to be among the first in the courtyard, Houston and the boy turned out at half past five, but even at this hour found the tenement ominously abustle. In the narrow corridors, doors were opening and shutting as the sleepy inmates tumbled irritably out. In the

351

backyard, a half-naked crowd of them besieged the pump, splashing and scrubbing briskly in the chilly morning.

Houston had slept badly and was sick in the stomach with excitement. The boy had not slept at all; he had barely had time to get in, and was whey-faced with exhaustion. Houston looked at him, and nodded. They left right away, without washing.

It was grey and somewhat misty in the street, and there was a curious hollow moaning in the air that Houston had heard in his room; he saw the reason when they arrived at the lakeside. A number of monks stood on a balcony of the topmost monastery blowing horns in the direction of the shrine.

'What the hell is that?'

'They call to the monkey,' the boy said softly. 'The abbess will go to him later.'

There was an extraordinary eeriness and solemnity about the calling of the horns in the valley that was disturbing and oppressive in the leaden morning, and Houston did not inquire further. He saw that none of the groups of people now streaming to the monastery looked across to the shrine or even up at the monks: they hurried head-down like harried wraiths along tke lakeside.

The guards were out in strength in the courtyard, but executing their duties, Houston noticed, not only in a manner more gentle than he had ever seen, but also in almost total silence. The monastery gates were locked, and the area round them kept clear. The people assembled quietly where they were bidden. The beggars were not being allowed to take up station today: they had been shepherded into a line on the upper flight of steps, and Houston and the boy took up their places and waited in silence.

Within half an hour, the courtyard, the two flights of steps, the little jetty, were entirely filled, except for a central aisle that had been kept open, and Houston looked down upon a remarkable spectacle. Below him, some fifty or sixty thousand people stood and waited. They waited with their backs to the lake, gazing up at the monastery and listening in awed silence to the horns invoking their ancient ancestor on his mist-bound island. There were some hundreds of children in the crowd, babies even; all as unnaturally hushed and immobile as their elders.

It was now a little after half past six, and the mist had begun to lift off the water. Suddenly, with a final concerted blast, the horns stopped. In the same moment the chanting began in the monastery. From the crowd arose a vast sigh like a single exhaled breath, and all at once the people seemed to come alive. They smiled, they craned; a slow creep forward began. Houston turned to the monastery and saw that the gates were being opened.

They were opened from the inside, very slowly, and a man stepped out. He was a tall, lean man, a monk, with a ravaged, wasted face and glittering eyes.

(This was the Lama Rine, Abbot of Yamdring, and his face was wasted because he had fasted a full seven days to sharpen his perception and enable him to identify the more readily an incarnation he was expecting. But Houston did not, of course, at the time, know this.)

He stepped out on to the terrace above the steps and stood breathing deeply for a few moments, gazing about him with violent and affronted eyes. Then he clasped his hands to the crowd and addressed them with a single incantation,

The crowd chanted a reply to the incantation.

He incanted again.

The crowd replied again.

The lama glanced about him for a moment and began to walk down the steps. He walked slowly, enunciating loudly and clearly a four-word chant, which swelled presently as the procession emerged behind him.

Houston had never in his life seen anything like this procession, and despite his preoccupations, found himself lost in the fascination of it. All thousand of the priestesses seemed to be participating. They walked in twos, the first twenty in green robes instead of orange and wearing on their heads tall spires of golden ornaments which tinkled and jangled as they moved. They carried prayer wheels in one hand and silk flags in the other, which, as Houston watched, began to flutter in the breeze that sprang up at that moment from the lake.

The slender column of gold spires flowed down the steps and crossed the courtyard with astonishing grace and beauty; and presently monks followed, forty couples of them, swinging golden censers and deepening the shrill chant of the women. Houston saw that the middle four carried between them, suspended from thin chains, a large salver of beaten gold. There was a sparkling of dull green stones on the salver that he thought must be rough emeralds, and the crowd bowed as the salver passed. But their eyes remained on the monastery, and after the second body of women had passed, he saw why.

A woman came out. She was enormously fat and enormously imposing in green robes and a vast tricorn head-dress. She was also enormously out of breath. She stood on the terrace staring about her, and panting hard.

At sight of her, there was an extraordinary transformation in the crowd; in a twinkling all faces had turned black. With incredulity Houston looked again, and realized he was seeing merely the tops of heads. The crowd had bowed deeply; it was sinking to its feet.

He felt the boy's hand plucking at him, and he sank down himself, and in the presence of the she-devil felt the hairs rising at the back of his neck. But he looked up presently and saw he was mistaken. For the woman in the tricorn was not the she-devil. She had stepped aside; she had sunk, gasping, to her own knees. Another procession was issuing from the monastery.

It was a small procession. There was just a single palanquin, supported on the shoulders of eight monks. A devil sat in the palanquin. She sat up straight in green robes, with her legs crossed and her hands clasped before her, her terrible face staring straight ahead. The devil's face was all of gold, with pointed ears and a leering mouth, and empty slits for eyes, and polished emeralds for eyeballs.

The gooseflesh had come and gone quickly, and Houston looked hard as the palanquin went by him, and saw the white of an eye glimmering from behind the emerald. He saw also that the devil's face was not on securely; it shook slightly with the motion of the palanquin.

The fat priestess in the tricorn laboured to her feet and brought up the rear of the procession; and that for the moment seemed to be the end of it.

A wave of hilarity swept over the crowd as they stumbled to their feet and fell, laughing, against each other. Houston moved gladly from one stiff leg to the other, stamping to restore the circulation in the cool morning.

The mist had quite lifted from the island, and the leaders seemed already to have arrived. He saw the green and gold thread swaying towards the shrine. He had heard something of the procedure: the entire procession would walk round the monkey, and then leave the abbess alone with him. She would commune with her once and only husband, in the terms of their courtship, and then return to give his benediction.

He thought, in the general murmuring, that he might chance a word in the boy's ear, and he whispered, 'How long before they bring her back?'

The boy looked round him nervously, and muttered 'They don't bring her. She comes herself.'

'She walks back?'

The boy shook his head. 'She just appears. She appears in the monastery.'

'How?'

The boy didn't know how, for it was an annual miracle. He was too nervous to say another word with the crowds hemming in on all sides, and merely shook his head.

The she-devil certainly did not seem to be expected again. The crowd chattered and craned quite gaily as the abbot, the priestesses, the monks, and finally the empty palanquin returned and entered the monastery.

Houston was left to ponder.

Two monks came out presently, and called to the officer of the guard, and he saw they were discussing arrangements for the admission of the crowd. It seemed that the beggars were to be allowed in first, and one of the monks came over and shifted

355

them up a step, and was then joined by his colleague, who carried, Houston noticed suddenly, a large wood-bound book in one hand and a writing brush and ink-horn in the other.

There was no reason as yet for his stomach to turn over at sight of these implements; and he could cite it later as a useful instance of the premonitory faculty at work, for it did so. It turned over and over, and every nerve in his body cried out to him to turn and lose himself in the crowd. But he did not do this. For he saw that the boy, far from sharing his apprehension, was actually laughing. He was laughing quite heartily, and the monks were laughing, and the beggars were laughing too.

They were giving their names out to be read in the monastery for what was evidently a part of the benediction, and some of the names seemed traditionally comic ones. One old man announced himself as 'The Lord of the Fleas', and another as 'The Mule's Brother'. The younger ones gave only their family names, and Ringling did this; and when it was Houston's turn gave that too.

'Again?' the monk said, looking up and still smiling.

'Houtson. *Hoo-tsung,*' the boy said helpfully, with a Tibetan inflection.

Houston heard the gasp first, and then the clatter of the falling book, and the sound of his name going through the crowd like wind in a chimney.

That was the last thing he heard, for the club caught him deafeningly on the ear, and then on the side of the head, and he was falling into the crowd, and still being struck, jaw, mouth, nose, ears, all exploding in shellbursts of light and pain, and all so fast he could not cover up or cry out or do anything but flounder on his knees in the forest of legs. A palette of colours spun before his eyes, and he spun with it, from yellow into orange and orange into red and red into blue, that was black, that was blacker than black; that was blackest of all.

He was in a stone cell, and it was dark. There was a little light from a butter lamp high up near the ceiling, and more coming in through a grille in the door; but on the floor it was dark. He could see all this in a blinkered sort of way without moving, and he wondered why, and suddenly realized why. He was lying on the floor. He was lying on his back. His head was tacky with blood and flared with pain as he tugged it loose of the floor. He couldn't sit up. He hurt all over, a savage, bone-grinding hurt that made him gasp and moan in a way that was familiar; he thought he must have heard himself making it in a dream.

There was something wrong with his mouth; an old acrid taste of blood, and he moved his tongue round and found several teeth had gone. In the same moment he realized why he felt blinkered: one eye was entirely closed up. His whole head was like a pumpkin, swollen and racketing with pain.

Something awful had gone wrong. He wondered what it was. He wondered if it had happened to Ringling, and where Ringling was. He didn't think he was very glad to find himself alive. He knew he was crippled, and he didn't want to be alive and crippled.

There was a sound at the door, and he saw the grille swinging away, and a face looking down at him. There was something familiar about the violent eyes and the wasted cheeks, but he couldn't recall what it was. The man spoke his name interrogatively, with a Tibetan inflection, and he tried to nod.

The man spoke further, quite courteously, and he tried to tell him that he could not understand, but remembered suddenly that he was dumb and mad, and gurgled instead.

It came back to him, then, all of it.

A number of other things sprang to mind, too. If the man had spoken to him in Tibetan it could only mean that he did not know the truth yet. Either he had not seen the boy, or Ringling had not told him.

He felt a wave of affection for the boy, and winked with his one eye at the two glittering ones above him, and saw that the effort had been too much, for already the two shining eyes had begun to dance away. They danced to the stone wall, and began to revolve there, and he joined them, watching with relief as the colours began to spin again: red into brown, into blue, into black, into blacker than black, into blackest of all.

The man was still looking at him when he came back, but the perspective had changed, and it bothered him. He tried to work out why the perspective had changed, but the light hurt his eye and he gave it up and went away again.

'Wake up,' the man said.

Houston stayed in the dark. Something worried him.

'Wake up. You are well now,' the man said.

It worried him more. What was it? Why was it?

Hands were wiping and smoothing him, and presently, out of curiosity, he opened his eye to investigate. Two women were cleaning him up. They were doing it on a bed. It was day. The man sat on the bed watching him.

'You are feeling better now,' the man said. 'You are quite able to talk.'

Houston shut his eye again at once. Important issues had been raised here; he could not say precisely what they were. He knew it was less what the man had said than the way he had said it.

He saw what the issues were after a moment, and lay quietly, depressed.

'You must wake up and look at me, Houtson,' the man said. 'You have had an accident. Look at me now.'

Houston looked at him. He was an elderly man, very thin, with a head like a copper billiard ball. He wore an orange robe. His eyes were large and unusually protrusive, the cheekbones stark in the spare face. He spoke English well though pedantically, like an Indian.

'I am the Lama Rine, the abbot of this monastery. You can say my name. Try it.'

Houston looked at him.

'Your own, then. Say your own name. Say Houtson.'

Houston decided he had better gurgle.

'No, no. You must stop this. You do not have to do that any more. We know everything about you, Houtson. You must say your name.'

Houston shook his head.

'Yes. It is important. Very, very important for you. Say it now. Say Houtson.'

'Ringling,' Houston said.

The man looked at him with his glowing eyes and snapped his fingers with irritation.

'Houtson. Houtson,' he said.

'Ringling,' Houston said.

'The boy is quite well. There is nothing the matter with him. You may be able to see him later if you try to speak now. Let me hear you say your name.'

'Ringling,' Houston said.

The man went after a while.

A woman brought him food later, and he saw a man watching through the grille. He refused the food. The man came in the room. It was not Rine but a younger, stout monk – the deputy abbot, he learned later – with not such good English.

'No eat,' he said, worried.

'Ringling,' Houston said.

The man went away. Rine came back.

'It is time to stop this now,' he said. 'You are perfectly well. There is nothing the matter with you. You can eat and talk. If you will not, it is your error. I can do nothing.'

Houston closed his eye.

'You must eat now. If you cannot eat the tsampa I will send you something else. Do you wish milk or fruit or cheese? Tell me what you want.'

'Ringling,' Houston said.

Rine went away. He came back with two monks and a stretcher. Ringling was on the stretcher. Houston tried to sit up in the bed when he saw him, but found he couldn't. He was strapped up in a jacket and his ribs hurt. The boy seemed to be in a bit of a mess. His hands were bandaged, and his face swollen and plastered. He was weeping.

'Sahib, sahib.'

'Ringling,' Houston said, smiling painfully.

'They made me tell, sahib. I couldn't help it. They made me tell them.'

Rine said something to him, quietly, in Tibetan, and the monks carried the stretcher closer to the bed.

'You should tell them everything now, sahib. It is for the best.'

'Aren't you able to walk?'

'My feet are a little burnt. It's nothing, sahib. I'm very sorry,' the boy said, weeping.

'It's all right. Cheer up,' Houston said, his bowels turning to water, as he suddenly saw the feet. They were thickly plastered with ointment.

'Now, Mr Houtson, you must speak to us,' Rine said.

Houston spoke to him. He was not by nature a swearing man, but he swore then, surprising obscenities that he had not heard, let alone used, since his Navy days. Rine did not seem to have heard them at all. He said, 'We can go into this later. I am very angry with you. You see what fearful things have had to be done to the boy because you would not talk to us. He is a very good boy, a most loyal boy. It was very painful to make him suffer in this way for you.'

Houston tried to get out of bed to hit him, but sank back again, sick with pain, and when he came to, they were gone. The butter lamp was lit. A young shaven-headed girl was looking down at him curiously.

'Hello,' Houston said.

She stepped quickly back.

'The lord will eat now?' she said in Tibetan.

'All right,' Houston said, and felt his lips crack as he smiled.

She was staring at him in fascination, and she backed to the door and scuttled quickly out. Houston eased himself in the bed. He wondered how many ribs were broken. He could move his arms and legs. He had an idea someone had told him he was crippled. He didn't seem to be crippled. It had been a fair going-over, all the same. The walls of the cell were waving in and out; he thought he was still concussed. His mouth was raw. He wondered if the lord would be able to eat.

He was waiting for his food with a fair appetite however, when the girl returned, and had tucked into it before she was out of the room even. There was a bowl of tea and tsampa on the tray, with a little dish of soft cheese, a glass of warm milk and a few lichees.

He could see the girl watching him through the grille as he ate. He saw her there until he was on to the lichees, and then she went. Rine's face appeared a few minutes later. He came into the cell.

'Ah, you are finished. We will talk now.'

'With Ringling here,' Houston said.

'He cannot come now. Later he can come.'

'We can talk later then.'

'No. We cannot. The boy is sleeping. The doctor has given him a drug. But I will bring him if you wish it.'

'Wait a minute,' Houston said as he got to the door.

The abbot came back.

'What is the urgency?'

'The urgency is that you have been here three days and the people are very alarmed. They have hurt you once already, and I apologize for it. They had no right at all to do so. Quite the contrary. But they have a right to know who you are, and they are waiting to hear. They are still waiting outside the monastery. They will not go away.'

Houston looked at him. The only sense he could make of it was that he had been here three days. He said, 'I don't understand. You know who I am.'

The lama sat on a stool.

'Let us see if we are right. Your name is Houtson, and you have come to find a brother you suppose to be staying here.'

'That's right.'

'What is your brother's name?'

361

'You know his name. Whittington. Hugh Whittington.'

'How can that be if your family name is Houtson?'

'We are half-brothers. We have the same mother.'

'Yes,' the lama said, looking at him. He looked all over his face. 'What was your mother's before-marriage name?'

'Coulter.'

'Was she English also?'

'Scottish.'

'And her mother – also Scottish?'

'No. She was French,' Houston said. 'What the hell has this got to do with anything?'

He felt suddenly ill. He thought he shouldn't have taken the tea. The yak butter was turning over and over inside him.

'From a part of the French empire, perhaps?'

'I don't know.'

'From Cambodia, Indo-China – some such region?'

'I don't know. Look, could you go away now?'

'Shortly. Whose idea was it that you should come here?'

'My idea.'

'Nobody suggested it to you? The boy, for instance?'

'Nobody. Nobody. I don't feel well.'

'One moment more. What had you heard about this monastery?'

'I need the toilet,' Houston said weakly.

The lama rose reluctantly. 'I will send someone in.'

He sent the young girl in, with a pan. She got it under him, and Houston signalled her to leave. She didn't leave. She stayed, watching him with fascination. Houston tried to be discreet, but he was not in a condition to be discreet.

The abbot returned presently. He had a box with him. 'I would like you to identify some objects.'

Houston looked at him with a strange sinking feeling. 'What do you mean, identify? My brother is here. I know he is here.'

The abbot said nothing further. He tipped the contents of the box out on to the bed. Houston gazed at them in perplexity. They were not Hugh's. He couldn't see how they could possibly be Hugh's. There were three silk jackets. There were three pairs of high boots. There were three daggers with chased hilts, and three rings.

'What are they?'

'You don't remember seeing any of them?'

'No.'

'Many years ago, perhaps, in childhood?'

'I've never seen them before in my life.'

The lama sorted out the silk jackets. 'Which one would you pick for yourself?'

'I have no reason to pick any of them.'

'If you were to have a reason. If I were to make you a gift.'

Houston looked at the jackets. They were of similar cut but different design. One was in a traditional Tibetan block pattern he had seen before, one was Indian, the last, the best, Chinese.

'That one,' he said.

'Why?'

'It's the best design.'

'They are all good designs.'

'All right, whichever you want. What has this got to do with my brother?'

'I would like you to select also from the other groups,' the abbot said. 'One object from each.'

It struck Houston suddenly, while he was doing it, what it was all about. He gazed at the lama blankly. He said, 'You're not by any chance – this isn't a test to see if I'm a reincarnation?'

The lama stared at him for several silent seconds. He said, 'You have felt yourself to be an incarnation?'

'No. Certainly not. Not at all,' Houston said.

'Why do you ask this question?'

'I suddenly tumbled what you were doing.'

'Has it happened to you before?'

'Of course it hasn't. I've read about it.'

'Where have you read?'

'I can't remember. Everybody's read about it. It's common knowledge,' Houston said, losing patience. But he did remember, just at that moment: the rapt, jammy sessions with the works of Arthur Mee before the nursery fire at Highgate; all a long time ago, a long way away from the monastery of Yamdring.

The lama was examining him silently.

'Proceed, then,' he said after a moment.

Houston was not thinking very well, but he could see even with his one eye that the objects fell into three groups, Chinese, Indian, and Tibetan; he thought his best bet would be to spread the load. He chose an Indian dagger, a Chinese ring, and Tibetan boots.

He thought the lama was a bit put out by this selection. The bony fingers drummed on the box.

'I hope I've been of assistance,' Houston said.

'I think you have been playing with me, Houtson.'

'I've only tried to help,' Houston said, smiling innocently. 'I'm sorry if I chose wrong.'

The lama stood up. His eyes glittered in the light of the butter lamp.

'This is the problem,' he said. 'You did not choose wrong, Houtson. Your choice is infallibly right.'

3

He slept very badly that night, and his head ached in the morning. The abbot visited him after breakfast. He was not alone, and Houston observed his companion with some surprise. It was the magnificent young man who had given away his clothes and jewels in the courtyard a few days before. He was dressed now in a different shade of blue, and his jewellery was more modest; but his glossy black hair was still braided over his head in the way that Houston remembered, and the long turquoise ear-ring still dangled from his ear. He was followed into the cell by an attendant who carried a decorated pouffe for him to sit on. The young man did not sit on the pouffe. He stood and examined Houston for several seconds.

'I will leave you now,' the lama said, and went, with the attendant.

The young man continued to examine Houston.

'Well,' he said at length, 'you seem to be on the mend now. Quite a change from when I saw you last, old chep. Ganzing – George Ganzing,' he said, coming over and holding out his hand.

Houston took the hand in some consternation.

'I expect you're a bit surprised. I went to school in India. The abbot thought it would be an idea if I asked you a few questions.'

'I see,' Houston said. Once the shock was over, it was possible to detect undertones in the preposterous accent. 'I've got a few to ask myself.'

'I dare say,' the young man said. He sat down on the pouffe. 'Where are you from, Houtson? What's your first name?'

'Charles. I'm from London.'

'You came in from Kalimpong, I understand?'

'That's it.'

'Tell me the names of a few people in Kalimpong.'

'I don't know anybody there. Only a trader called Michaelson...'

'Michaelson, yerss. What sort of chep is Michaelson?'

'I don't know – an ordinary sort of chap.'

'Thin chep, fet chep, old chep?'

'Oh. Fet chep. Fat chap,' Houston said in some confusion. 'Elderly. What's all this about?'

'Who do you know in London?'

'Nobody you would know. I was a teacher. I taught art at...'

'Know a Colonel Brigginshaw? Ronnie Blake-Winter? Duff Walker?'

'No. I'm telling you. I was just a teacher. I taught at a school in Fulham. I lived at a place called Baron's Court.'

'A place called what?'

'Baron's Court.'

'Baron's Court,' the young man said, pulling at his ear-ring and smiling with polite disbelief.

'It's a part of London. It's a big place. Thousands of people live there...'

'Yerss. How about Scotland? Your mother comes from there, I believe.'

'Yes, but . . .'

'Tell me about Aberdeen. Tell me all you know about Aberdeen.'

'I don't know anything about Aberdeen. I've never been there. Look, what are you trying to prove?'

'I'm not trying to prove anything, old chep.'

'I've told you who I am. Get my brother in here. Get Ringling. They'll tell you who I am.'

'That isn't the idea, old chep.'

'What is the idea? Who are you?'

'I'm the Duke of Ganzing. The monastery happens to be in my parish – so to speak. No need to get hot under the collar, old chep.'

'Then what the hell is happening here? Who do these people think I am?'

'The theory is that you might be a chep who was here once before. Rather a bad chep, called Hu-Tzung. Same name, you see.'

'Look,' Houston said earnestly, 'that isn't my name. The boy got it all wrong. It's Houston. You've all been saying it wrong. Houston, not Houtson. Houston. Do you see?'

'Yerss.'

'It's a very common name in England. Thousands of people are called Houston. Millions, probably.'

'Quite. The thing is, you're the only one who has turned up. And just when expected, you see. Our oracle here warned that you would be coming – oh, many years ago now. The time was fixed fairly spot-on.'

Houston regarded him with silent passion. He had the impression he had fallen among lunatics whom he must convince in their own terms. He said, 'Look – this man Hu-Tzung, he was a Chinaman, was he?'

'A sort of. He was a prince who came with a *horde* about two hundred years ago, and did rather a lot of damage. What is worse, the abbess is reputed to have fallen in love with him.

366

People are still pretty keyed-up about it,' he said, shaking his ear-ring.

'Do I look to you like a Chinaman?'

'Ah, I see your point. Of course, I'm hardly the person to expound this – the abbot is your man – but all that is provided for. The oracle spoke of an incarnation "from beyond the sunset". This would seem to indicate from the west. Of course, nobody took it to mean quite so far to the west. The lama has the feeling he has been bowled rather a fast one. The poor chep is very puzzled,' said the duke, shaking his head. 'All the same, you know, an incarnation knows no frontiers. One could just as easily be born in Timbuctoo as Tibet. Or even in – what was it, Balance Cord?'

'Baron's Court.'

'Quite.'

'Look,' Houston said, trying to sit up. 'This is mad. Any number of people in Tibet know about me. Your man in Kalimpong does. The people in the Foreign Ministry in Lhasa – I've been worrying them for months about my brother. My name is on letters and telegrams. I can show you it on my passport if I had it.'

'Where is your passport?'

'In Calcutta. I sent it to the Great Eastern Hotel there with all my papers when I set out for here.'

'Pity.'

'Don't you believe me?'

'It's not what I believe,' the duke said, picking a fleck of silk from his robe. 'You've got to look at it from the other chep's point of view. A chep comes here and gives his name as Hu-Tzung –'

'I've told you. I never did.'

' – He comes bang on time. He comes from the west. And he picks out all the right objects in the test. Well! What do you expect a chep to think?'

'The test was a joke,' Houston said weakly. 'I picked out one of each, Chinese, Indian, and Tibetan. I didn't pick them out because they meant anything.'

'Oh, quite. Of course, some cheps might think you were therefore meant to pick them out.'

'Do you think that?'

'I'm only giving you the strength of the opposition, old chep. Strange things happen in this country. I've seen them myself.'

Houston looked at him and tried to gather his forces. His head was racketing so much that he could hardly think. He said, 'All right. Look at it this way. This man, Hu-Tzung – what is he supposed to come here for?'

'We can't go into that, old chep.'

'He's not looking for a brother, is he?'

'I really – '

'So if someone comes here who is looking for one, whose only thought is to find him and go away again right away, without bothering anyone – he couldn't be Hu-Tzung.'

The sloe-black eyes, which had been regarding him amiably, blinked a little.

'So it might appear. Unfortunately, one or two things have happened – rather odd things – which tend to connect the two stories.'

'What things?'

'I can't tell you.'

'What's happening to my brother?'

'I'm merely a bystander, old chep. I really can't say anything.'

'Why is he being kept here?'

'I never said he was, old chep.'

'I know he is. He's in the third monastery.'

'Splendid,' the duke said, and stood up.

Houston saw the interview was at an end. He said quickly, 'Can't you at least give me some idea what the hell is to happen to me?'

The young man smoothed his robe and rapped on the door. 'That rather depends on who the hell you are, doesn't it?' he said. 'Only the governor can tell us now.'

'The governor?'

'In order to get the crowds away. The village is still packed. They won't leave. It's all been very tricky. Very tricky indeed,' he said, as the door opened. 'Still, we should know by tomorrow. The old chep is getting here just as quickly as he can.'

'Wait a minute,' Houston said. 'How is he supposed to say who I am when nobody else can?'

'Oh ... he has his methods, you know,' the duke said. He looked unhappy for a moment. 'I shouldn't think about it, old chep. Try and get a bit of rest now.'

Houston did think about it. He thought about nothing else all day. They brought Ringling in to see him in the afternoon. The boy had improved a little, and the burns on his feet were now bandaged; Houston could not take his eyes off them.

He fell asleep, still wondering about the governor's methods.

Chapter 8

I

THE governor of Hodzo, at 67, did not account himself a cruel man. In the course of duty, certainly, he had had to exact some cruel penalties. Several hundred tongues and noses and eyes had been removed at his behest over the years. But these, essentially, were tributes to tradition; the governor had the highest regard for tradition. He was happy to think that he would sooner remove the entire organs of an individual, or of a generation of individuals, than alter one whit or title of the divine corpus of tradition that related their functions in society. In this he considered himself a reasonable man: he wished only to leave things as he found them.

He was not, however, feeling particularly reasonable as he transferred from his horse to his official palanquin two miles from Yamdring. He was feeling old and vengeful and frustrated. He had been in Hodzo for precisely four hours when the message had arrived; long enough to hear of the misdeeds of his youngest wife, but not to beat her for them. He wanted to beat her. She was 17 and beautiful and he had not been able to enjoy her for a long time. He had not been able to enjoy any of his three wives, and he thought he would like to beat them all.

In the past year the governor had been able to exercise only the sketchiest kind of control over his private affairs. It had been one of the worst of his life; an endless succession of worrying problems and uncomfortable journeys and bad smells. The fact that he knew himself partly to blame was merely an additional aggravation.

A devoutly religious man, the governor knew that all action led to suffering: it was the first Law of Karma. He had observed the law at work in his own life. Cause was followed by effect, and the tendency of effect was to become, with the years, increasingly unpleasant.

A year before the governor had wished to retire. He had known very well what he wanted to do in retirement. He had planned it with care. He wanted a pleasant house with a park outside Hodzo; he had bought it. He wanted a library of three thousand volumes and a domestic priest; he had acquired them. He wanted to spend the nights in a manner suitable for an old gentleman of regular but sluggish appetites; he had taken a luscious new wife.

And he had been dissuaded. The Regent had spoken of the threatening years ahead, of the governor's unrivalled knowledge of affairs, of his statesmanlike judgement. And the governor had listened. His vanity had been tickled. He had stayed.

This was Cause, and all the unpleasant effects of the past year could be traced directly to it. For the honeyed words had wound the wheel, and the governor's vanity cocked it; Karma had begun to run it down again at once.

First the Europeans had come. Then four of them had stayed. Then one of them had become curious. And then the governor had felt bound to exercise his statesmanlike judgement...

It was an aberration he had never ceased to regret. For if he had reported the matter at once to Lhasa, as ordinary common sense had demanded, Lhasa would have taken it off his shoulders. (He would, however, have had himself to travel to Lhasa: it had been the thought of ten nights' absence from the tormenting and ingenious new occupant of his bed that had deflected the governor from the course of common sense.)

So, carnal desire had brought about the conspiracy; and the conspiracy another stranger to worry him from half-way round the world; and the stranger a series of events that had set a final term to the governor's desire.

This was the way Karma worked, one wheel turning another to achieve its ultimate refinements.

The governor thought of some of these refinements as he dismounted stiffly from his horse in the chilly evening; in particular of the series that had begun with the conspiracy. They formed a pattern so grimly ironic that he groaned a little to himself as he climbed painfully into his palanquin.

If he had not become involved in the conspiracy, he need not have undertaken his subsequent journeys. If he had not gone on the journeys, he need not have suffered so keenly at the thought of pleasures missed. If he had not missed these pleasures, he need not have hurried home so precipitately on horseback to resume them.

All that the governor's haste on horseback had got him was a hernia. With the hernia he could not enjoy his pleasures.

The hernia was only the latest of the ironies of Karma, but it was the one most on the governor's mind as he eased himself gently on to the air cushion in his palanquin. He had bought the air cushion on a journey to India earlier in the year; it had struck him at the time as the most worthwhile, if not the only, contribution made so far by western science to the art of living, and he had been looking forward for several hours to supporting his hernia on it. He realized instantly, however, that even this comfort was to be denied him. His youngest wife, in an effort to conciliate him and show her love, had blown it up herself. She had blown it up too hard. He could not find the nipple to let the air out, and had to sit down heavily upon it as the palanquin was borne aloft and carried briskly along on the uneven track.

The governor had preserved a stoic silence in the saddle, but in the relative privacy of the palanquin permitted himself to hiss rhythmically with pain. The drum-tight surface of the cushion thrummed against him like a tennis racket, transmitting with perfect fidelity every irregularity of the track direct to his hernia. He was reminded, in the blinding firecracker flashes of pain, of a Chinese torture he had witnessed once in the year 1911. All the same, he could not bring himself to order a reduction of speed, for it was an article of faith with him that the business of the State came before that of the individual; and even now speed was important.

He could see the glare of the butter lamps from Yamdring over the brow of a hill, and shortly afterwards, the village itself – still crowded four days after the festival. A stop would have to be put to this.

The governor was well aware that he was the only official in Tibet who could say for certain whether the latest arrival at the monastery was the person he claimed to be or an impostor. He rather hoped there would be room for doubt. His mind had become centred with peculiar persistence on the Chinese torture. He had never tried it himself, for it was not among the measures listed in the penal code. But he could not see that tradition would be violated by a genuine piece of research into its efficacy.

He thought he might be conducting this research quite shortly, and the prospect gave him some satisfaction. It was the governor's only source of satisfaction as, balancing on his vibrant cushion and hissing with pain, he was borne briskly through the butter-lit streets to the monastery.

Two monks iifted Houston out of his bed and on to a stretcher. Neither of them spoke to him, and he did not bother to ask the reason. He thought he knew the reason; he had not been able to eat any supper through thinking about it.

Despite his mental unease, his physical improvement had continued apace. He could sit up. The chief medical monk – an excellent doctor of a keenly scientific turn of mind, with whom he was now on the best of terms – had told him that his ribs were not broken but only cracked. His bruises were changing from purple to yellow. And he could see through both eyes.

With their aid he was able to observe now that he had been kept in considerable isolation. His cell was at the end of a long and narrow corridor; there were no other cells in the corridor, and two guards were posted at its outlet.

The guards allowed the stretcher through and he was carried across a long stone hall and through a pair of gates into the main hall. He began to get an idea of his bearings then. These were the gates he had looked through days before to see the lines of priestesses sitting on the floor.

The main doors of the monastery were locked, and the lights were being snuffed. Several priestesses were engaged on this task and they gazed curiously round at him as he passed. There was a hushed air about the cavernous place that set his heart thudding more strongly still. He could feel it drumming in his ears with the awful pre-operation dread of childhood. But that operation had been carried out with anaesthetics. He doubted if this one would be.

He passed rapidly through hall and corridor in the shadowy labyrinth of the building in a silence broken only by the scuffing felt boots of the monks; and as they came to the end of a corridor heard a sudden stamping of feet. As they rounded the corner he saw the reason. A body of men was lined up before a doorway. The men were dressed in a uniform he had not seen before. Houston realized this must be the governor's retinue. He had arrived at last.

At first, after the darkness outside he was almost blinded by the glare within. Some hundreds of butter lamps shone; they shone from every nook and cranny of the walls and ceiling, and two enormous candelabra fitments of them were suspended above a long table. Two men sat at the table, in silks and jewels, with braided hair and long turquoise ear-rings; and for a moment, recalling his entry into another brilliant room with other jewelled men, he had the nightmarish impression that on his journey through the monastery he had in some occult way been carried back in time to the house of the Tibetan consul in Kalimpong; an impression so strongly confirmed by the tortoiseshell cat look of one of the men that he looked wildly round from the stretcher to see if Michaelson was not also in the room.

Michaelson was not in the room, and neither had Houston been carried back in time. The abbot was there. The deputy abbot was there. The vast priestess in the tricorn was there. And so, too, was the Duke of Ganzing; he was seated at the table. Also at the table was the man with the face of a tortoiseshell cat.

Houston looked at him more closely. The man's hair bristled with combs. His little slit eyes were creased in a smile that was belied by the tight cat mouth. His diminutive hands were folded one on top of the other like little paws. And he was regarding Houston intently, in just the way that the man in Kalimpong had regarded him. In the same moment, realizing who this man must be, Houston felt an enormous weight lifting from him.

He said with incredulity, 'But – but I've met him before.'

All eyes were upon him in the brilliant room.

'I met him in Kalimpong. I met him in the house of the consul. Ask him,' he said urgently to the abbot. 'Ask him if he doesn't remember me.'

The abbot had already begun to speak, before he had finished, and Houston, watching the cat-like face, saw a shadow cross it – a shadow of disappointment, almost of bitter annoyance. The man was seated, for some reason, on an enormous pile of cushions and he moved on them, hissing slightly, so that it seemed he was going to deny having met him. But after another long and searching look he nodded slowly and spoke a few curt words.

The abbot turned and snapped his fingers. The monks, who had laid the stretcher on a table, picked it up again. Houston saw with confusion that he was being taken back.

He said, 'Just a minute. What's happening? What's been decided?'

'Nothing has been decided,' the abbot said. He walked over and looked down at Houston off the stretcher. 'You should not have come.'

'What do you mean? What's going on here?'

The abbot's eyes glowed sombrely. 'You have brought it on yourself,' he said.

He snapped his fingers once more. The stretcher-bearers turned. Houston said in exasperation from the stretcher, 'Look here, what the devil – I've got a right to know – ' but had to finish his protest in the corridor.

Moments later he was returning at a brisk shuffle through the dark monastery, through the complex of halls and corridors, to his cell, to his bed. The door was closed, the bolt shot, the corridor lamp snuffed, and he was alone, in darkness.

He lay there, bewildered, perturbed; and yet at the same time most powerfully relieved. For he was back at least in one piece, and he had not expected to be. And but for the miracle of the Kalimpong meeting he knew he would not have been. He thought he could see, dimly, how this miracle might have come about; and more dimly still the nature of the predicament in which it had placed the monastery authorities. But he could not see into the peculiar menace of the abbot's last words. They worried him.

It was a long time before he slept that night, and when he did he dreamed that searchlights were turned on him and that his very soul was being investigated, and he awoke just before dawn, chilled and afraid. He seemed to know with complete nightmarish certainty that his future had just then been settled. He wondered how he knew this, and what his future was, but at the same time told himself there was no point in worrying. Someone would tell him soon enough next day what his future was.

In this, Houston was wrong. No one told him anything. He waited all that day, and the next, and the one after, for some official tidings. No tidings came. His only visitor was an old priestess, who, though tending him most solicitously and with the greatest respect, would neither talk nor listen to him. It took him some time to realize why: the old creature was both deaf and dumb. He wondered if she had been chosen for this reason.

During these three days of perfect seclusion, with nothing to occupy him − for they had taken away all his possessions − Houston got to know his cell pretty well. He could recall it in later years with peculiar vividness.

It was twelve feet long by eight wide. It was constructed entirely of eighty-one stone slabs. It contained no furniture of any sort apart from his bed, which was made up on a stone shelf, and the butter lamp fixture on the wall. He had a view of the sky through an outside grille that was too high for him to reach, and one of the corridor through the grille in the door: apart from this his view was circumscribed by the ninety-six square feet of cell.

He got out of bed and measured it. He did this with his forefinger. He also measured his bed; and finding that the snuffer of the butter lamp was operated by a cord, measured that, too; and tied several hundred knots in it, and untied them again. Between times, he exercised his trunk. This was now giving him so little discomfort that he doubted if his ribs were cracked at all; he felt in most respects perfectly fit, eye back to normal, bruises fading fast.

With all this excess of time and fitness, he thought that if somebody did not very soon bring him some news he would go off his head.

But nobody brought him news, and he did not go off his head. He measured, and knotted, and exercised his trunk, instead, and in this way somehow managed to pass the three uneventful days (during which, as it happened, nine masses were held in his honour, nine thousand candles burned to his glory, and his name inscribed in the Golden Book of the Trulkus); speculating continuously, at first with dread, and then anger, and finally only despair, on what was going on.

3

What was going on was an operation of considerable complexity. Houston was being canonized. It had seemed to the abbot and the governor and the duke that there was no other measure even approximately applicable to a problem that was in itself for the moment quite insoluble.

Fifty thousand people had witnessed the arrival of the man announced as Hu-Tzung. They would not believe it if it were stated that he was not Hu-Tzung. From every point of view it was best that he should be handed over to them, thus at one stroke settling the evil disturbance, fulfilling the prophecy, and averting the evil mission – all without stain of blood on the hands of the monastery.

It was a solution the governor would most dearly have wished to approve. But he could not. For he knew very well who the stranger was, and even better, that it was his own errors of judgement that had brought him here. He had gone to Kalimpong to inspect him. He had gone to see if he was the kind of man who would ultimately become discouraged and go away. He had formed the conclusion that he was not of this kind, and had ordered certain preventive measures to be taken.

But the measures had been too few and too late; the governor knew it now. And error had compounded error, until the worst had come about; until in some ghastly and inscrutable way this most damnable of men had become confused with the Incarnation.

The soul of the governor yearned to apply a little of the Chinese torture, to ease his worry, and perhaps the situation. He would most willingly, in the interests of law and order, have turned a blind eye on his special knowledge of this man. But for one thing the man had recognized him, and for another he had come up against religious objections.

As the abbot had pointed out, to agree to such a course would lay them open not only to a charge of illegality, but also to one of blasphemy – and of being accessories to sacrilege. For in acknowledging Houston as the Incarnation, if he were not, they left the abbess, the monastery, and the monastery treasure, unprotected against the real Hu-Tzung, who, in the terms of the prophecy, must certainly come between the sixth month of Earth Bull and the last of Iron Tiger.

From the abbot's point of view it would be dangerously wrong to accept Houston as the Incarnation; from the governor's dangerously wrong not to. Impasse. From out of the impasse, Little Daughter had spoken.

Little Daughter had sat in silence so far, balancing her vast bulk on a tiny stool and nodding her tricorn in occasional agreement. She was a person of some consequence in the monastery, for she was the only one in regular contact with the abbess; but her duties were domestic rather than administrative, and she was somewhat overawed in this masculine and worldly-wise company. She spoke therefore hesitantly.

The issue that Little Daughter raised was one that had vexed scholars for several generations: the question of how it was possible for Hu-Tzung, having once been destroyed by Chen-Rezi, the God-Protector, to return as a man. That he should return in some form to the scene of his crimes was of course expected and perfectly proper; as, perhaps, a mule, a dog, a flea. But that he should do so as a *man* – in the same order of body in which he had transgressed – this was scarcely in aocordance with the divine rule.

What Little Daughter had to suggest, therefore, with the greatest deference to the abbot, was that this man, having passed his tests infallibly, was perhaps a companion spirit of Hu-Tzung; as it might be, an *alter ego*, who had returned either to expiate the transgressions of his pernicious partner, or to avert some further expected ones. Was it possible, she asked, hoping not to be taken for a fool, that they were here dealing with a *trulku*?

'A *trulku*?' said the abbot in astonishment.

'Since he has arrived at the right time,' Little Daughter faltered, screwing her tricorn in confusion, 'and giving the right name – '

'A *trulku*!' said the governor, feeling some miraculous ease-ment come stealing to his hernia at the very suggestion.

The governor knew that he would never himself be a *trulku*; once escaped from the mortal coil nothing whatever, no hope of extra merit, no prospect of early oblivion in nirvana, would ever induce him to return to it. None the less, it was a fact that some did. Through merit they were released from the wheel of existence that Shindje, the monstrous Judge of the Dead, revolved between his teeth; and they gave up the opportunity, to come back, to show the way, to watch and ward. He looked curiously at the abbot to see how he was taking the idea.

The abbot was taking it very cautiously, rubbing his hands and scrutinizing them with extreme care.

'A *trulku* or a *yidag*?' he said at last.

'Are we not bound to believe, my lord, rather in a *trulku* – since he has been sent? An unconscious *trulku*,' said Little Daughter eagerly, 'who has merely felt himself drawn here – '

'With a specific mission?'

'To protect the Mother and all of us,' said Little Daughter. She said it devoutly, but also, the governor thought, a shade plainly, as though to indicate that one hundred monks and an abbot and a duke had not between them so far managed to provide any very effective alternative form of protection.

Although this was unquestionably a theological matter, the governor saw so much sense in it that he felt bound to intervene. 'Bearing in mind the difficulties raised by The Return,' he said, 'and if this suggestion, Abbot, is at all possible – '

'It's possible,' the abbot said briefly, and stood up. 'We must have immediate guidance from the Oracle.'

It was then shortly after three in the morning, and the Oracle, a young woman whose abnormal psychic qualities in no way interfered with her quite normal physical ones, had been in her cell for six hours. Little Daughter went discreetly ahead to see that she was in it alone.

Within minutes, the small procession, now including the Oracle, was making its way through the silent monastery; across the main hall, across the smaller one, up the narrow corridor, to the cell where Houston lay sleeping. The Oracle slipped quietly in; and five minutes later, quietly out again.

'There is an aura,' she announced. 'It is a good one. The soul is perfectly healthy. I cannot say more.'

For the governor, she had said enough.

Half an hour later, having disposed of all objections, and also a stiff nightcap, he sank with a little moan into bed. There were feather cushions at his head, and more at his hernia, and the sheer unimagined bliss after the dreadful day gave him a sensation of floating so marvellously euphoric that, mindful of his irreligious reflections of the day, he made a swift act of contrition.

He forgave his wives. He forgave the English nation. He forgave his fellow conspirators; and even the old vile body whose hungers and weaknesses had brought him to his present indignities; and said good-bye to this old body, to every particle of it, as it slipped away from him into limbo.

Each one of these particles told the governor that his judgement had been right; and as sleep sang in his ears and he drifted down to join them, he felt himself smiling.

Statesmanship, after all, worked. For a year at least there would be no more troubles at Yamdring; for a year no more journeyings. It was a prospect so delightful that he carried it with him into sleep, and as he slept still smiled, this doomed and luckless man.

Later, on a morning when his doom was certain, he was to confess all of this to Houston; all of his hopes and dreams, every small part of what had led up to this moment. He did not spare himself, for he was bent not upon justification but a purging of the soul; he was morally certain what lay before him the next day.

He was drunk at the time, and Houston also; they sat in the governor's library with the governor's wives and the governor's volumes, drinking the last of the governor's arak: he was taking a melancholy farewell of all the pleasures and vanities of his life.

But that was a morning still in the future.

On the morning when the governor could still smile in his sleep, his proclamation was posted. It was posted inside the monastery and out, and all that day runners carried it throughout the province. By noon, when the first of the nine canonical masses began, several thousand people had managed to squeeze in to participate. By evening, thousands more were addressing their prayers through the new *trulka*.

The new *trulka* himself at this time was resting after a long day of measurement and exercise.

During the next two days, while the cycle of masses was completed and the village cleared, he continued with these activities; and on the morning of the fourth day awoke prepared wearily to resume them. He had almost given up wondering what was going on, and he despaired of talking to another human being ever again. On this day, however, one came to see him.

The duke arrived early, with only a small retinue, and by midday was bearing Houston back with him to his mansion at Ganzing. Houston sat beside him in a double palanquin on the journey, deeply bewildered, and for this reason at first mistook the obeisance that was being offered on all sides as respect due to his companion. But he could not mistake it when, in the country, relays of men and women began running beside the palanquin, braving the blows of the outriders for the privilege of kissing his feet.

The duke had hoped to put off all explanation until they had reached the house, but he saw that the hope was a forlorn one.

'A what?' Houston said.

'A *trulku*,' the duke said diffidently. 'It means a sort of saint.'

'I see,' Houston said.

A large number of weird things had happened to him in the past year, but this was certainly the weirdest. He found himself wondering, just for a moment, what two young women in London would make of it.

4

The mansion of Ganzing sat magnificently at the end of a wooded valley, and comprised within its walls a self-supporting feudal community. There was a farrier and a tanner, and a mason and a tailor, and several other craftsmen besides: their little shops and dwellings had been added to two parallel wings of the building, so that the house, with its stables, granary, brewery and working quarters had developed with the years in the shape of an elongated U.

As Houston approached it, by way of a landscaped park and a mile-long mani wall, he saw that the young man's substance was very great. For hour after hour in the fertile Ganzing valley, they had passed vast herds of yaks and rolling fields of barley. All this belonged to the duke. There had even been a couple of sawmills at work, erected by the duke himself – riches indeed in a land where timber fetched almost its weight in butter.

The sawmills were not the duke's only works. In his park he had laid out a golf course and tennis courts; and in his living quarters a central heating system. (The boiler for this system, specially adapted to burn yak dung, had come over the mountains from India, piece by piece, *en route* from Bonny-bridge, Scotland: he later pointed out the trademark to Houston, with particular pride. 'See – a link with your mother,' he said warmly above the roar of the burning dung.)

In the course of the next few days, Houston was able to observe how the quality lived in Tibet. It was on a considerable scale. The duke kept not merely one priest but an entire chapter; not merely three wives but five. ('Just a matter of form, old chep. I only really hit it off with a couple of them.') He had real glass in his windows and electric light (from a petrol engine) in his library. He had the best Scotch whisky in his cellars, and the choicest cigars in his cabinet.

Houston stayed a week sampling these delights. He drank the duke's whisky and smoked his cigars. He rode for miles with him over his estates, and learned a good deal about the agricultural situation of south-western Tibet. He learned very little more about his own. This remained, after four days, as mystifying as ever.

He knew that he was a *trulka*. He knew that he was the *trulka* of the man called Hu-Tzung. He knew that he was expected to avert the evil designs of this man. But he did not know what the designs were; and this the duke refused quite firmly to tell him.

'Why not look on it as a kind of vacation, old chep?' he urged Houston amiably as they sat over their whisky and cigars. 'As a rather unusual kind of vacation.'

'What happens when the vacation is over?'

'You'll go home. I promise you. We've only got to wait for a few prophecies to work themselves out.'

'How am I concerned in the prophecies?'

'I hope not at all, old chep.'

'Will my brother and his friends go home, too?'

'Of course they will. Absolutely.'

'Why can't I see them, then?'

'Ah, now. Now, now, old chep,' said the duke.

In the face of such stonewalling, affable but resolute, Houston was powerless. He felt himself a prisoner in some extraordinary dream. Each morning a young woman came to kiss his feet and wash and dress him, and each night another did the same in reverse. When he went out in the courtyard, the masons and tailors and farriers and tanners and their families ran out to touch him and poke their tongues, and when he stayed in a succession of their objects was brought to him to bless.

A somewhat more disturbing attention was being paid him: a monk had come with the party from Yamdring, and the monk accompanied him everywhere. He walked with him and rode with him and sat with him and all but slept with him, he slept indeed on a rug in the same room. The functions of this monk were so plainly those of a guard rather than an acolyte that Houston lay awake late in the night plotting how to confound them. For a plan had sprung to mind during these days; a somewhat nebulous plan but one that would require complete freedom from supervision.

Its germ had come on his very first night in Ganzing when, still dazed by the mystery of his sudden translation to sainthood, he had thought back over all that had happened, and had come upon another mystery: the miracle of the she-devil's return from the Courtship.

The she-devil had gone to the island in her palanquin, but she had not returned with it. She had returned in some other way. What other way?

She couldn't have boated back, or swum back, or walked back over the bridge, for such a miracle would not have weathered the centuries. For the same reason she couldn't have returned in the procession *in disguise*.

Yet unless there had genuinely been a bit of magic – and after all that had happened he was not prepared to say there wasn't – she had managed by some physical means to shift herself from island to monastery. By what means?

'A tunnel,' Houston said aloud in the darkness.

Of course a tunnel! What else but a tunnel? A tunnel whose one end was buried deep and undiscoverably somewhere in the vast and complex monastery; but a tunnel whose other end was on the island – which was neither vast nor complex; a tunnel, moreover, which since it had to be entered in perfect privacy, must start in the shrine.

Houston's visual memory was very keen, and he could recollect the shrine in intimate detail. A circular room, some thirty feet or so across at the base; a room paved with stone slabs ...

By the end of the week he thought the time had come to find out more about it.

He said, 'I think I'd like to go back now.'

'Go back, old chep? What on earth for? Aren't you enjoying yourself here?'

'Very much. But I'd like to do a bit of painting. I'd like to paint the monastery.'

Paint the monastery! said the duke. Nobody had ever painted the monastery of Yamdring. Why, it was by way of being a sacred, a supernatural building.

Wasn't a *trulku*, Houston asked, smiling, by way of being a sacred, a supernatural person?

Yes, the duke said, unsmiling; he was. Houston was spot-on there. It would have to be looked into.

It was looked into the following day. Houston returned the one after. Two days later, he was painting the monastery.

5

It came about so easily, he found he could use their logic so naturally, that all that happened in the next week or two had about it the bewitched quality of some fable. He explored the possibilities open to him with caution and cunning. He made no requests that he knew might be refused. He ventured no farther than the second monastery. He saw Ringling only once – and this at the abbot's suggestion rather than his own, for he knew he must appear to put the past behind him.

The boy's burns had improved a good deal but he was still unable to walk. Houston, closely supervised, was taken to his cell. He said little to him: there was little he could say yet. But he had fallen into the useful habit of blessing all who came in contact with him, and as he blessed Ringling, managed to wink at him. He doubted if the boy understood: his eyes were still wide with shock and amazement as he left.

Two monks were accompanying him everywhere at this period, artists nominally, who supplied his materials and carried them for him. They were little grinning men, alike as two peas: Houston thought of them as Miny and Mo and grew very fond of them. Neither could speak anything but Tibetan. Houston did not wish it otherwise. He improved his grasp of the language instead.

He mastered other skills also: the use of the writing brush, the mixing of vegetable colours, and became so engrossed in the work that for hours on end he could almost forget why he was doing it.

He didn't forget entirely.

In the second week he asked to go to the island.

He asked so innocently, from motives so obviously artistic, that the abbot, after a thoughtful glance, offered no demur.

The shrine was closed between festivals, but its door, Houston was glad to see, kept unlocked. Twice a day, morning and afternoon, he visited it with his faithful attendants. He sketched it from the banks. He sketched it from the bridge. Then he went to sketch it inside.

He was hard put to it to find expedients for getting rid of both monks together, but when he managed it worked very quickly for minutes at a time. He tested with his hands every stone within reach on floor and walls. He tested in particular the area round the murals and the area round the monkey. In the course of three days he found nothing at all.

He brooded in his cell at night.

Somewhere in that hollow obelisk there was the mouth of a tunnel. It was a mouth that would open freely at a woman's touch It could be a false panel in the wall or a false slab on the floor. It could be worked by a lever or by simple pressure in the right place. He was quite certain it was in there somewhere. He was just as certain he must find it quickly. He had already sketched every angle of possible interest in the shrine. Unless he meant to make a life's work of it he could not stay there very much longer.

The idea of retouching the murals came to him in a moment of inspiration. He tried it tentatively on his artistic companions.

Ah, no, they said, this was not a good idea. It was in fact a most dangerous idea. For the murals, though in a dilapidated state, were none the less of divine origin. No mortal hand could restore them. It would indeed be a sacrilege of the first degree even to try.

Sacrilege for a *trulku* to do so?

Miny and Mo looked at each other. They didn't know. It was a question that had never arisen in the entire history of the monastery. It was a question far above Miny and Mo.

It was a question, in fact, for the she-devil herself.

While it was passed to her, Houston stopped sketching. He wandered about the village instead, accompanied by Miny and Mo. He did a good deal of wandering and a good deal of blessing. He became very popular. He also, feeling that a long enough interval had elapsed, visited Ringling again.

Miny and Mo were somewhat bothered when during this visit he lapsed into English, but he smiled at them so jovially while he did so that they could not think anything was amiss. Houston told the boy to smile, too, which he did, in a sickly and rigid fashion, astonished at the turn the conversation had taken, so that in no time, with Houston and the boy smiling, and Miny and Mo smiling back, the cell was fairly flashing with good humour.

The she-devil's *responsum* (formulated as a matter of course by the abbot after consultation with the Oracle) was two days in coming. Aware of the tide of goodwill washing all about him, Houston was in small doubt as to the result; and was not proved wrong.

Very shortly after, with gold leaf and gum and linseed and vegetable dye, he was installed once more in the shrine. He worked industriously, manipulating wherever he wished – and after several days was brought once more to the point of defeat. It seemed incredible that this bare little building, not thirty feet across, could hide its secret from so persistent a seeker. And yet, he reflected, it must have hidden it for several hundred years. He had noticed that the stones here were very much smaller than in his cell – there were many hundreds of them – and had come to the conclusion that the trapdoor must be worked by multiple pressure on certain of them at the same time or in a given order. He saw he was unlikely to hit on this order except by luck; and at length gave up.

With Miny and Mo he set the shrine to rights. He cleared the debris. He collected his pots. He gave a final lick here and there; and with a last lick to the monkey stumbled on something strange.

The gold in the division of the monkeys buttocks was worn away. There was no reason for any wear at this point. The crease was set in; the fingers of the faithful would scarcely penetrate here.

Houston set down his paint and brush. He took the monkey's buttocks between both hands. He tugged them gently. The buttocks moved.

He sent Miny off to the monastery for more paint. He sent Mo out to brew more tea. He returned to the monkey.

It had been only the slightest of movements, and he tried it again. The gold buttocks moved again. But it was plain they would not move further by harder tugging. There must be a lever here, some outstanding projection within reach of quite a small woman.

Houston walked all round the monkey. There was only one outstanding projection within reach. It was however quite outstanding: the handsome phallic one the crowds had so admired during the festival. Recollecting suddenly the origins of this festival, and the entire ambience of Tibetan society as he had found it, Houston shook his head and swore quite cheerfully to himself. How could he have overlooked it, this symbol of all that was so hilarious, and proud, and somehow benign in the national character, this key to so many Tibetan mysteries?

Reasons of delicacy had prevented him from giving it full attention while Miny and Mo were in attendance. They were not in attendance now.

Houston quite gaily gave the monkey's projection his attention. The gold buttocks sprang open at his third tug.

Houston closed them without looking inside.

Chapter 9

I

IT had been 12 May when Houston had arrived at Yamdring, and 18 June when he had found the tunnel. He went down it thirty-six hours later at about a quarter to twelve on the night of the 19th.

Most of the time in between had been spent in planning how to get out of his cell and back into it again. This was not the simple operation it sounded because the cell was bolted. It was bolted at half past nine at night and not unbolted again until six in the morning. He could see the bolt through the grille in the door, but he couldn't reach it.

The solution, a highly ingenious one, was arrived at with the help of the invaluable snuffer cord. They had given Houston his possessions back by this time, and among them was a little silver knife with his name on it: he had carried it with him since the age of 14. With the knife he took down a length of the cord, unravelled it to provide a longer piece, and with a slip knot lassoed the bolt through the grille. It came out quite easily if somewhat squeakily (a fault he rectified the next day with a lump of butter) but still left him with the problem of locking it again once he was inside.

This one took rather longer to solve, but he was so pleased with the way he did it that he later with his left hand drew a little picture to show the method. The method was to double the cord, run the doubled end through the ring and the shaft and place it round the bolt head (he did all this in the passage). The loose ends he then fed through the grille in the door, and went back inside and pulled. The bolt was pulled into its ring. He then dropped one end of the cord and pulled the other. The whole lot snaked back through the bolt, through the grille and back into the cell.

Two guards were nominally on duty at the end of the passage, but he had seen them both snoring in their cloaks and lost to the world, and so he went in and out of his cell, unlocking and locking it again for most of what was left of the night, until he thought he had got the hang of it.

The following night he went out in earnest.

He went out via a sewage trap which was left unlocked (it was the method used by Ringling on his romantic assignations, and the one the boy had told him about during the conversation that had troubled Miny and Mo). The trap lifted to reveal an open channel, a slippery sewage pipe so disgusting that he was almost sick in it. He held his breath and sloshed through it, however, and presently when it reached a walled cesspit was able to climb out.

He found himself in a small compound, in bright moonlight. There was a wall, the monastery wall, with a herbal border running beside it, and he looked for the rock garden the boy had mentioned that climbed up to the top of the wall, and taking his time, let himself out that way. He dropped gently, on to turf, and worked his way round the side of the monastery to the lake. He had to wait here for some minutes while a guard ambled up and down the bottom step, but as soon as the man turned, he ran – past the steps, past the jetty, and did not stop till he was almost at the village.

A number of boats were tied up at the point where the village lane met the lake, and, after washing his boots in the water, he took one, and, keeping low in the boat cast off and drifted out upon the glittering water. He used the single paddle sparingly, aware that any sudden movement would be visible in the drenching moonlight, and steered himself to the far point of the island. Here, screened by low scrub, he beached and made for the shrine.

Little spectral bushes and white-flowering broom dotted the island, all ashen in the moonlight. He picked his way through them, and came out to the shrine, and waited for a minute or two, watching the monastery, and opened the door and went in.

He found his knees knocking a bit in the paint-smelling blackness, but there was no time for second thoughts, and he fumbled for the tinder in his pocket and lit a lamp and saw the monkey come leaping amiably out of the blackness.

Houston attended to it without formality.

2

He heard the midnight gong go after he had been in the tunnel a quarter of an hour, but couldn't be sure whether it was reaching him from across the water or directly from the onastery. He had gone down into the rock for fifty feet, as near as he could judge, and was now on level ground. He thought he might actually be rising; he was moving with his head bent double and his shoulders brushing the sides and could not tell exactly.

The air was flat and dead and the butter lamp had begun to gutter. There was a strong, stale smell of musk, and realizing from whom it must have come, Houston felt the hairs on the back of his neck bristle. How many times had she been here before him, the ageless she-devil; and how many times in her seventeen former bodies? There was an air of old evil, of cult evil, so oppressive about the narrow stone gallery that he could scarcely nerve himself to continue. He thought that what he needed was a rest, and he stopped to have one.

He stopped with his head bent like an old horse and his breath whistling out like bagpipes. The air seemed to be getting less. He thought there might be more of it nearer the ground, and clumsily lowered himself backwards on to his haunches. Immediately, the lamp brightened. Houston brightened with it.

It was the lack of air – that and his bent posture. With his head upright and his shoulders straight he was as right as rain. There was no call for a fit of the horrors here. He was in a man-made tunnel. It went from A to B. He had very cleverly found the entrance at A and now it was simply a matter of finding where it exited at B. If one thing was more certain than another, it was that no one would bother him on the way.

This reflection was so heartening that after a minute or two he got to his feet again and went on.

The ground was quite certainly rising – and rising steeply. He thought he must by now have emerged from the lake; he would be following the upward slope of the steps. If that were so, the tunnel should presently level out.

The tunnel levelled out.

Houston found this very cheering. He thought he could place himself now with fair accuracy. He was directly below the courtyard. Somewhere upon the rock above him, the guard would be pacing in the cool night air. Very shortly, the tunnel should rise again for the second flight of steps.

The tunnel rose again.

It went on rising. It went on rising for so long that he became utterly bewildered. He saw that he must have mistaken his position. The first gradient had marked only his emergence from the lake. It was this second one that followed the line of the steps – and of both flights at once.

But could even two flights of steps go on so long? Perhaps they could. He was tired and lost; and other factors had to be taken into account. The monastery was built on rising ground: the tunnel would have to rise to meet it. Then, the exit would be placed at the far and less accessible end: that would account for a further rise.

Houston took account of all these factors. He told them over in his mind like so many beads. They did nothing to allay a growing uneasiness. He had been in the tunnel now for half an hour, and it would take him just as long to get back. He had still to face the problems of the boat and of re-entry into the monastery. It would be light in a couple of hours. If he were forced to wait, if he were forced to hide, if one of the guards in the passage should chance to wake . . .

Houston stopped. He stopped because the tunnel had stopped. It had stopped at a flight of steps.

Houston went up the steps.

The lamp suddenly brightened. Air coming in. He could feel it moving gently about his head. He was rising steeply, out of the tunnel, into a kind of pill-box, a structure of such irregular shape that he couldn't for the life of him make out what it was. He raised the lamp above his head. Of course! It was an idol. He was inside another huge idol. The tunnel ended as it began.

The idol was every bit as large as the monkey. He couldn't remember seeing another such monkey in the monastery. He thought he must be in one of the chapels at the rear. He knew that butter lamps burnt night and day in these chapels, and he blew out his own and looked about him for cracks of light in the darkness. He saw one immediately, a long vertical hairline a couple of feet above his head.

He went up two steps and felt it with his hands. It was set in a convex bulge. The bulge did not seem to represent buttocks. He couldn't make out what it represented. There was a little hollow in the middle. He set his ear to it and listened.

Nothing. No snore, no breath, no creak.

Wherever he was, he seemed to be quite alone. He felt with his fingers for the catch and released it. One of the doors jumped open with a small ping. Houston peered through.

Butter lamps burned steadily in a lofty chamber. The room was perfectly still. The lamps stood in a semi-circle around the idol from which he watched. There seemed to be other, smaller lamps glimmering in the background, and when his eyes were accustomed to the light he saw that they burned before a line of smaller idols.

He waited for several minutes, and very cautiously went up two steps more. He opened the doors fully. He stepped out.

There were rugs on the floor, and more hanging from the walls. It was an extraordinarily large and handsome chapel, and he realized presently why he had not been in it before: it was a chapel devoted to the cult of the she-devil herself. The large idol from which he had emerged represented evidently the First Body: he had stepped out of her belly. The later bodies, life-sized, sat cross-legged in a row facing her; devil-headed, unclothed, supporting their breasts with their hands.

In the presence of so many devils, Houston felt his flesh beginning to crawl. He had been holding his breath, and he let

393

it out slowly and tiptoed along the line of devils, looking for the gates.

He counted seventeen she-devils in the row, the seventeen Former Bodies of the Good Mother, and had passed the last of them when he received his first jolt. There were no gates to the chapel. There was a large wooden door. He couldn't recall a chapel in the monastery that had a door instead of gates. He paused uneasily.

But he had come so far, he thought he might as well go a bit farther. He thought he might open the door.

He found he couldn't open the door. The door was locked.

Well; that was to be expected. The chapel was evidently in the nature of a holy of holies. A lock would not make his future attempt at escape any easier, but so long as it was operated by a simple bolt and not a key, it wouldn't make it actually impossible, either. He felt with his hands along the edge of the door; and thus received his second jolt.

The door was not locked with a key. It was locked simply enough with a bolt. The bolt, however, was on the inside.

The implications of this were not slow to strike him; he turned from the door as if it had caught fire; and just as suddenly stopped again. In counting the Former Bodies in the room, he had not included the giant First. The she-devil had occupied only seventeen Former Bodies. Eighteen of them sat watchfully in this room.

Something very peculiar was going on here, and Houston knew suddenly that he had no desire whatever to learn what it was. He wished with all his heart that he had not attempted the lunatic exploration, that he was fast asleep in his cell and snugly awaiting the morning gong; and as abruptly as he had stopped, now moved again, very rapidly, back to the welcome belly of the giant First. He had actually got one foot in it, he could remember later, when the final jolt came.

A voice spoke behind him in the room, a woman's voice speaking in Tibetan.

'Stay, Hu-Tzung,' said the voice.

Houston stayed.

'Did you think I had forgotten? Turn and look at me.'

With his bowels turned all to water, Houston turned and looked.

The eighteenth devil had risen, with her lamp; she was walking towards him.

3

He was so utterly terrorized in that moment that all normal thought processes seemed to stop. He had an idea that the she-devil took him by the hand, that she took him to a bed. He was certainly sitting on a bed with her some minutes later. He remembered thinking that since the bed was still warm she could not have been out of it long; an exercise in deduction that restored him at last to his senses. (But it was some minutes more before he could grasp where he was: he clung stubbornly to the impression that he was in the first monastery when it was obvious that he must have climbed blindly through all seven to the topmost one.)

The abbess had brought her lamp to the bed, for it stood in a dark corner of the room, and was studying him in its light. Behlnd the emerald eyeballs a pair of narrow eyes flickered over him. There was something so blood-chillingly hideous about the devil's mask that Houston looked away. He looked at her body instead; and at first glance found it scarcely less fearful.

There was no hair on the she-devil's body. Her breasts were painted with spirals of green and gold. Her skin was shining and aromatic with ointment. She was a small supple figure of a woman who might have been anything from thirty to fifty. Something in her bearing, in the muffled voice issuing from the mask, and in the talon-like painted fingernails, inclined him to the latter age. He shrank from her in dread.

The abbess set down her lamp.

She said, 'Hu-Tzung, what have you to say to me?'

Houston opened his mouth and found that he had nothing to say.

'I have waited two hundred years for you.'

Houston licked his lips and found his voice then. He said, 'Good Mother, you are mistaken. You have mistaken me.'

'Mistaken you? How could I mistake you, Hu-Tzung?'

'I am the *trulku*, Good Mother – the unconscious *trulku* – '

'No longer unconscious,' the abbess said. She was touching him curiously, his eyebrows, his ears, his forehead. 'And no longer a *trulku*. You have found the way to me and now you must follow your destiny. You cannot deceive me, *yidag*.'

Houston had no thought of deceiving her. Something about her, a certain sanctified quality about her nudity, quite terrified him. He felt he was indeed in the presence of supernatural forces, and in his halting Tibetan found himself confessing his identity and his purpose, and how he had found the tunnel, and why, when the abbess stopped him.

She stopped him with a cold hand on his mouth. Her devil's head was turned to the door; and she rose and listened for a moment; and watching her, Houston experienced a curious pang (that years later he could still remember, and most poignantly), half of relief, half of regret. For he saw that she was indeed only a woman, and that she was not herself free of supervision; and that she did not want him discovered yet.

Something else occurred to him in this short hiatus. He saw that the situation was by no means unsalvageable, and that the crazy logic that had sustained him in the past dream-like weeks could sustain him again if only he made the effort.

He held out his hand to her. He said in a low voice, 'Good Mother, what do you know of me?'

The abbess turned to him again.

'What your lips have told me, Hu-Tzung, and what is written.'

'You have not seen me before.'

'We loved with other bodies, Hu-Tzung.'

'And did you love me truly?'

'Yes, I loved you truly.'

'And do you love me now?'

'Now and always, poor *yidag*. There is no help for me.'

Houston nerved himself to stare into the emerald eyeballs, glinting like a cat's in the lamplight. He said, 'Then tell me my destiny.'

'Only the God knows that, Hu-Tzung.'

'Then tell me why I have come.'

'To love me again and take me away and my treasure with me.'

'And will I do these things?'

'Ah, poor *yidag*, how can you? I have discovered you.'

'And must you betray me?'

The abbess took his face between cold hands. '*Yidag*, *yidag*,' she said. 'I can never betray. I must release you.'

'How release me?'

'By destroying the prison that holds your *yidag* captive.'

Houston had taken the word *yidag* as one of endearment, but he saw now that it might have technical connotations.

He said softly, 'Why do you call me *yidag*?'

'Because this is what you are, poor soul – a suffering ghost in a body that is not yours. It is your host, *yidag*, and your prison, and you must be released from it.'

Houston felt his toes begin to curl inside his boots and his neck to break out in a fine cold sweat.

He said, 'Is it written that you will release me?'

'It is written that you *will* be released.

'Is it written when I will be released?'

The devil's head shook. 'That is not written, *yidag*.'

Houston was very glad to hear it. He was shaking all over like a leaf. But he saw that the situation, dangerously insane though it appeared, was not without loopholes, and that with time he might widen them. Time, however, was something that was now growing very short.

He took the icy hands from his face.

He said, 'Good Mother, I must go.'

The she-devil rose with him and caught his wrists in her thin hands. 'You will come back, *yidag*.'

'I will come back.'

'When will you come?'

'Soon.'

'Come tonight.'

'If I can.'

'Tonight, *yidag*.'

'Tonight,' Houston said.

Something seemed to have happened to the she-devil's breathing. It was coming very thickly through the mask. She said, 'And will you look on my face, *yidag*?'

'I will look on your face.'

'And love me again?'

'And love you,' Houston said sickly.

The abbess's hands were trembling on his wrists.

She said, 'Go then, *yidag*.'

The *yidag* went, as fast as his feet would carry him.

In the tunnel he heard her calling softly.

'*Yidag!*'

'Yes?'

'It must be tonight. Be early.'

He went early. He went at half past ten, reckless of discovery, and half hoping he might be discovered, for he didn't know which was worse, to be apprehended and thrown back on his wits, or to face the pent-up appetites of eighteen generations of she-devil. He saw that to survive he would have to exercise the combined talents of a Scheherazade and a demon lover, and he was not feeling up to it.

He was exhausted. He had slept hardly at all for the past two nights. He thought that at another time and in another place he might see a certain ghastly humour in the situation, but all he could see in it now was horror – and of a peculiarly repellent kind. For the thought of the cold, sinewy body with its sacerdotal ointments and its painted breasts quite nauseated him, and the prospect of seeing her face gave it no added attraction. The women of Tibet aged early: by 50 they were toothless and seamed. The thought of such a face under a shaven head quite unmanned him.

But he forced himself, for he saw that he was acting not only on his own account; and as he entered the shrine and approached the monkey was even able to raise a certain jocular camaraderie in his dealings with it.

But in the tunnel he smelt her ... and his heart failed him again. How could he do it? How had it happened? By what lunatic series of misadventures had it come about that the art master of the Edith Road Girls' Secondary should find himself burrowing beneath the waters of a Tibetan lake to share the bed of a she-devil?

There were no rational answers to these questions, and so Houston shuffled on – in the manner of his earliest predecessor perhaps, with head down and arms shambling, and with fear in his heart and nausea in his stomach – to a dreadful rendezvous with an old cold virgin in a room of seventeen corpses.

But in his assessment of the woman who awaited him, as in so many of his assessments that year, Houston erred. For the abbess was not old, and she was not cold; and she was far from being a virgin.

4

At the time that Houston was shuffling along to his uninviting bed, the governor of Hodzo was just getting out of his. He had been in it alone, for he preferred it so these days, and he had not been in it long; but he turned out with only the mildest expression of annoyance.

The governor was not indeed annoyed at all. He exclaimed a little, for the benefit of his servant; but as the man blew in his slippers and bent to slip them on him, the governor's heart was beating with a pleasurable sick excitement.

He had spent a month of unparalleled tranquillity. His wives had been obedient, his clerks efficient; nobody had bothered him and no outside event had come to disturb him. For an entire splendid month he had strolled about his park and meditated in his library, wholly free of intrusion.

The governor had begun to suspect this tranquillity. It had begun to disturb him. He had begun to lay awake at nights wondering what diabolical trouble could possibly be accumulating for him. For he knew enough of the workings of Karma to know that it was not done with him yet. There had been about the earlier series of events a kind of muscular flexing of forces, a rippling beneath the surface so powerful that even he, a layman, quite without knowledge of the Gift, had been able to sense the presence of the Prime Mover.

The governor was not immodest enough to think that such a concentration of malign energy had been activated solely on his account. He did not believe a stranger had been brought half way round the world merely to give him a hernia. But the mechanism that had – so incidentally! – produced the hernia was turning all about him still. He could feel it. He had the impression that subtle new formations were taking place on the periphery, that fresh series of wheels had been engaged and that movement of an unusual and sinister kind would shortly be imparted to his own quiet sector.

Why, for instance, was his sector so quiet? It should not have been so quiet. As the governor of a province he should have been receiving the normal annoying, but regular, stream of directives from Lhasa. He was not receiving this stream. It had dried up.

After a lifetime in the public service, the governor knew how orninous a sign this was. No news from Lhasa was bad news. In the face of trouble the central government did not work late in the night. It simply closed down. It turned its back on the trouble. It prayed that the trouble would go away.

In the past week the governor had begun to wonder if his own province of Hodzo could possibly be concerned with this trouble, with any of the nationally predicted trouble. It was, it was true, a remote province, far from the eye of Chinese warlords; and indeed owed its comparative immunity from invasion to this fact. But it had not been always, or entirely, immune, for it contained a unique national instituiion – the female monastery of Yamdring – and on two occasions at least an invader had sought to violate it.

On both occasions, the governor of the time had been ordered to regard the monastery as his first charge and to treat personally with the invader for its safety. On the first occasion, in 1717, the invader treated with had been Hu-Tzung. Hu-Tzung had boiled the governor of the time. On the second occasion, in 1911, it had been a General Feng. Feng had merely decapitated the governor. Yet on each occasion the monastery itself had been spared, and the general feeling was that the sacrifices were worthwhile.

The governor considered them worthwhile himself. He knew that in similar circumstances he would be prepared to make a like sacrifice. All the same, he could hardly see the need arising. The Chinese communists, with their many failings, had no interest in violating a monastery of women; and the climate of the time seemed to be against the sacrifice of scapegoats.

And yet he couldn't tell; and it was ruining his tranquillity. He longed for news, for any news, but particularly news from Lhasa; and at a quarter past eleven on the night when Houston shuffled through the tunnel for the second time, his wish was gratified.

He could hear the courier's horse blowing still as it was led away to the stables, and the imperious stamp of official boots in the hall below. The governor thrust impatient arms into his waiting gown, briskly adjusted his truss, and went down the stairs.

Several of the kitchen women had turned out to greet the welcome new male from Lhasa, and were plying him with chang as his boots were pulled off. The courier smelled very strongly of horses and the governor kept upwind of him. But his hands went eagerly enough to the man's equally pungent pouch. He broke the seal and opened it, and at sight of the contents felt his heart begin to bump a little more unevenly. The single dispatch inside did not bear the black wafer of the Department of Home Security; it bore the red one of External Affairs.

The governor took it into his study, and sat himself trembling in a chair while the lamps were lit.

External Affairs? He had a brother-in-law in the Department of External Affairs. What could his brother-in-law be writing to him about under the official wafer? The governor broke the wafer, and was not left long in doubt. His brother-in-law had written in haste and in confidence; he urged the governor to burn the letter as soon as he had read it; he trusted him not to reveal the source of his information.

The governor read on with a sinking heart. There had been in the past six weeks, his brother-in-law wrote, two Notes from Peking. The Notes had not of course been answered. The Ministry had closed down to enable the executive to pray that there would not be a third Note. But Peking had not closed down. Chinese newspapers had arrived in the brother-in-law's office. They contained many grave and menacing items. He enclosed a cutting of one of these items.

The cutting was stuck to the back of the letter, and the governor's eyes went slowly up and down the Chinese characters. It was headed *From People's Tibet*, and as he read the third paragragh he saw the reason for his brother-in-law's alarm.

'*In the west also,*' read the paragraph, '*reactionary lordlings are plundering the people to feather their own nests. In Hodzo, the so-called governor negotiates with an American Kuomintang spy for the sake of the people's assets. By a crude manoeuvre he tries to deceive the people that the spy is a messenger from God! Tsaring Doma* – ' such was the governor's name and his heart almost stopped to see it in cold print – '*be warned! The people are not deceived! The two hundred milliards of yuan can never be yours! Be prepared to give an account of them!*'

The governor's first thought on reading this abominable paragraph was to call for his horse and fly. He had no doubt that this was what his brother-in-law intended him to do. He read it over again, however, and called for a glass of arak instead.

There was about the malicious catalogue of lies just enough semblance of truth for him to realize what it could refer to.

The American Kuomintang spy was evidently the Englishman Houtson. But what possible assets amounting to two hundred milliards of yuan were they accusing him of trying to sell?

The governor pored over the paragraph again and again. The sum quite baffled him. Perhaps if he converted it into its Tibetan equivalent... But the Chinese yuan was in a state of inflation; the rate fluctuated every month. He bethought himself suddenly that Lhasa must have sent him a notice quoting the current rate, and that this notice would certainly be filed in his pigeon-hole board; and he picked up his lamp and went across to the board.

The pigeon-hole board extended fully along one wall of the room and contained several thousand rolled documents. It took him ten minutes to find the right one. *Jen Min Paio – People's Bank Dollar – People's Republic of China*.

The governor blew off the dust and took up a brush and began to jot a number of rapid calculations in the margin.

The current yuan went 330 to the Tibetan sang; the sang six and a half to the rupee... The number was still quite astronomical, and he hurriedly crossed off noughts and converted it to lakhs. It came to four hundred lakhs. That was four crores. Four crores of rupees. What assets to the value of four crores of rupees came within his domain?

The governor did not have to think hard or long over this new figure. It came to him in a shellburst of illumination so blinding that he lowered himself heavily into a chair, gasping at the enormity of the crime of which he had been accused. He was more shocked than he had ever been in his life at the naked malice behind the accusation, at the ravening spite the anonymous writer in Peking must feel for him.

And yet, he reflected, watching his hands begin to tremble again, the writer in Peking had not invented the information; he had not produced it out of his own head. Houtson was indeed in Hodzo province, and so were the assets to the value of four crores of rupees. How could the writer have so accurate an assessment of the value? How could anyone in China make such an assessment? It was known to barely a handful of people

– to no one, indeed, apart from the governor himself, outside the monastery.

Alas, the answer was all too plain. If nobody outside the monastery had told the writer, someone inside had.

This was a conclusion so utterly unthinkable that the governor could not bring himself to consider it. He closed his eyes. He hissed. He tried to think of other things instead.

Why, for instance, he thought instead, had Lhasa not informed him of this attack upon him? And why had his brother-in-law bound him not to reveal the source of his information?

Alas, the answers to these questions sprang just as readily to mind. Why else except that a scapegoat was still needed in the province of Hodzo? Why else except that Lhasa had no wish to frighten him into running away? And that his brother-in-law, at the centre of events and apprehending them perfectly, had precisely this wish – and was seeking to protect them both?

The governor swayed a little in his chair; and yet he knew he was by no means frightened now. He had quite lost the urge to run away. He felt merely old and immensely fatigued. He thought it was time he took himself back to bed.

As he shuffled slowly up the stairs, one hand supporting the lamp and the other his truss, he hissed steadily to himself. There was still work ahead of him ... affairs to be set straight, an inquiry to be instituted. Impossible as it seemed, there was a traitor at Yamdring. One of the easterners, perhaps – a monk or a priestess from the border country, neither fully Tibetan nor fully Chinese, a person of divided loyalties.

He tried to think which of the dignitaries of the monastery came from the east. The abbot didn't. Nor did the deputy abbot, or Little Daughter, or the Mistress of Ceremonies. Perhaps there were one or two others. He couldn't think of any others just now. He could remember them in the morning.

But just as he laid himself back in bed, the governor did think of one other. The discovery shot him bolt upright again. Impossible! Out of the question! Blasphemy even to think of such a thing! And yet – and yet – She came from the east. She came from Yunnan. He could remember the day the Recognition Committee had first brought her – a child of penetrating gaze, eyes classically aslant, ears classically pointed, her hair in a black straight fringe. Her family doubtless still lived in Yunnan. Could she possibly be writing ...

The governor lay back and tried hard to pray for forgiveness. But he could not, as he prayed, invoke the traditional masked image. He saw only a fringe of black hair, and under it, a pair of almond eyes, gazing steadily into his.

5

At the moment that the governor was making his staggering discovery, Houston was making a similar one for himself. He had half expected, as he emerged on the seventh floor of the monastery, to find the devil's head waiting for him on the plinth in the row of Former Bodies. It was not waiting for him on the plinth. It was not waiting for him in bed, either. A Chinese girl was. She was waiting with a lamp, and waiting very patiently.

A good deal of patience was needed for Houston seemed to have taken root in the middle of the room. His mouth had fallen wide open.

'Hu-Tzung,' she said presently.

He said in the ghost of a voice, 'Who are you?'

'Come closer and you will see.'

Houston went closer. He saw that the girl's breasts were painted with spirals of green and gold. He saw that her fingernails were similarly painted. He saw that the body which had seemed so tough and sinewy beneath the top-heavy mask was slim and elongated without it. He saw all this without being able to accept it.

He said, 'Can it be – is it you, Good Mother?'

'Who else could it be, Hu-Tzung?'

'But you are so young!'

'I can never be young, Hu-Tzung.'

She was certainly not old. She was not more than 18. And

she was beautiful. She was the most beautiful thing he had ever seen in his life. A fringe of black hair sat above an oval face, delicate almond eyes above a trim nose, a rosebud mouth above a slender throat. And he could recognize her voice now – slightly throaty, no longer muffled. He was utterly amazed.

The abbess was gazing at him with some anxiety.

She said, 'Am I not as you expect me, Hu-Tzung?'

'No,' Houston said truthfully.

'Am I not as beautiful as my thirteenth body?'

'I don't know.'

'Ah, Hu-Tzung, you do. You must say.'

There was something here so un-devilish, so entirely young womanish that Houston found his wits unscrambling rapidly. He found himself sitting on the bed, gaping at her.

'Am I not beautiful at all, Hu-Tzung?'

He said sincerely, 'Good Mother, you are. You are very beautiful indeed.'

'Am I so, Hu-Tzung?'

'You are the most beautiful woman in the world,' Houston said, simply.

The Good Mother smiled, and the corners of her mouth turned up like a cat's.

'This is what you told me before,' she said.

'Then you haven't changed.'

'And have you not changed, either?'

'How can I say?'

Long arms snaked round his neck.

'That,' said tke Good Mother, 'will be for me to say.'

It was the next night, or perhaps the one after – for he could not be sure of anything in this bemused period – before he learned her name.

He said to her nose, 'Where are you from?'

'From heaven, Hu-Tzung.'

'From heaven, of course,' he agreed gravely. 'From where on earth?'

'From Yunnan on earth.'

'Is Yunnan a town?'

'A province.'

'A province of Tibet?'

'Of China. On the border.'

'And how long did you live there?'

'Until I was 6 and recognized.'

'How did they recognize you?'

'Feel,' she said, and guided his hands.

'They're beautiful,' Houston said.

'They're pointed.'

'Beautifully pointed,' Houston said, kissing the ears. 'What else?'

'My eyes, my hands ... some other things.'

'What other things,' Houston asked, kissing the ones mentioned.

'Oh, the date of my birth, my name.'

'How old are you?'

'Eighteen years in this body.'

'And your name?'

'Mei-Hua. It means in China a rose.'

Mei-Hua, the china rose; and Mei-Hua the name on the thirty sketches in the Kastnerbank of Zurich; Mei-Hua the melting, molten creature he thought he would never forget Delicious and delectable and always unknowable: these were the words that years later he could still apply to her, despite everything.

'Mei-Hua, you must not call me Hu-Tzung.'

'What shall I call you?'

'Try Charles.'

'Cha-wells.'

'Charles.'

'Cha-orles.'

'Try Charlie then.'

'Chao-li.'

'Charlie.'

'Chao-li.'

'All right,' Houston said. 'Chao-li.'

Mei-Hua and Chao-li; names he was to hear so often.

'Mei-Hua, do you understand why I have come?'

'Don't talk about it, Chao-li.'

'The reasons are not those you said.'

'I don't want to know them.'

'There are Europeans here in the monastery.'

'Then we won't talk about them, either,' she said, and lay upon his mouth so that he couldn't. He let her for a while.

'Mei-Hua.'

'No.'

'I must go soon.'

She sighed and sat up and hung over him.

'You don't love me.'

'I love you more than any woman in the world.'

'I am not a woman of the world.'

'Then I worship you.'

'But you don't love me.'

'Love you *and* worship you,' he said. 'Mei-Hua – '

'Well, then?' she said, sombrely.

'Why are they being kept here?'

She shook her fringe. 'Because one of them saw me during the Second Festival.'

'Without your mask?'

'Oh, no. No, no,' she said, shocked. 'How could that be? Only you and Little Daughter see me without my mask.'

'How then?'

'In my tears.'

'Your tears,' Houston said, mystified.

'The tears I wept for the monkey. The green-stone tears,' she said impatiently.

A glimmering of an idea began to dawn on Houston. He said slowly, 'The tears that are like the eyes of your mask?'

'Of course. These tears,' she said, patting the bed. 'And only

408

the monastery council may see them, and then only once a year during the Second Festival.'

Houston sat up in the bed. He said, 'You mean they're here. They're under the bed?'

'Not under it. See,' she said.

They were below the mattress, eight leather bags of them, sealed with green wax; heavy bags of a weight he was to know only too well.

He said incredulously, 'They must be worth a fortune!'

'Four crores of rupees,' said Mei-Hua.

Chapter 10

I

'How much is a crore?' Miss Marks said.

'Seven hundred and fifty thousand pounds.' I had jotted it down from the Statesman's Year Book in my notes. 'Which makes that little lot worth three million. How would you like to sleep in a bed with three million pounds in it, Miss Marks?'

'I wouldn't mind doing anything in that kind of bed,' Miss Marks said.

'Yes. Is anything much happening on that telephone?'

'The operator's ringing it now. I hope she isn't dragging the poor old man out of bed. He sounded quite ill yesterday.'

'He wasn't looking so hot. Hasn't he got anyone who could look after him?'

'Hello,' Miss Marks said.

I got on with my jotting. What had me particularly at sea was the timing. There were hardly any dates in the exercise books. Houston had gone to India in January, and it seemed to be spring when he had arrived in Yamdring. How long had it taken him getting over the mountains, and how long after for all the mad things to begin? There was also the mystifying business with the maps . . . I wrote: *Get time straight*, and under it, *Get maps. Does he know numbers?*

'Mr Davidson,' Miss Marks said. I had been aware of a subdued background of anxiety. 'There's a nursing sister with him. He's been taken ill. She says he can't talk just now.'

'Oh, I'm sorry. I'm very sorry to hear that. What' the matter with him?'

'He had some kind of bronchial spasm.'

'I see . . . I really wanted to pop down to see him today. I wonder if she's got any idea when I'll be able to.'

I watched her as she spoke into the telephone. I hadn't intended seeing Mr Oliphant again so soon. The story had happened, after all, nine years ago; it would certainly keep a bit longer. But it had suddenly occurred to me that the old man might be dying. A certain ghoulishness is endemic to this business. I had so far only half a book, and no right or title to the other half. Also, I couldn't understand the half I'd got.

Miss Marks hung up. 'She couldn't say. She might have some idea if we ring in a day or two.'

'Yes. All right. We'll do that . . . I wonder who called the nurse in.'

Miss Marks shook her head. 'She said her name was Jellicoe,' she said. 'She sounds a bit of an admiral. Poor Mr Oliphant.'

Oliver Gooch of Rosenthal Brown came in in the afternoon, so I stopped brooding over emeralds and monkeys' phalluses and came down to earth. The tricky near-libel he had popped in to discuss didn't detain us long, and then, because I couldn't quite get it off my mind, I said, 'Oliver, I know it's a bit early to bother you with this, but just have a look at it, will you?'

'What is it?'

'It's a book about Tibet. Notes for a book, actually – half the notes.'

He leafed through, nodding as I explained to him, and

skipping freely, and presently put the exercise books back on the desk.

'Yes, well,' he said. 'What about it?'

I said a little sadly, 'Oliver, don't you like any of our books?'

'Try me on some decent ones.'

'You've read half the spring list already. What do you think of this one?'

'It looks a bit tripy to me. Is it supposed to be true?'

'Yes, it's true.'

'Where's the rest of it?'

'The chap I told you about – Oliphant – has the other two exercise books. He's reading them.'

'You're sure he's not writing them?'

'The ink looks a bit old for that.'

'Maybe he's got a bottle of old ink,' Oliver said. 'What is it you want me to say about it exactly?'

'How much do you think we could get away with?'

'Why not all of it? The truth isn't a bad answer to libel, if that's worrying you.'

'That's one of the things. This chap Houston, he's a very rich man now. I understand he got away with a fortune. I don't know whether he was strictly entitled to it.'

'If he's not bothered, why should you be? He'll be signing this himself, will he?'

'I don't know. I don't think so. He's rather lost interest in it.'

'I'm not sure I quite understand. These notebooks belong to him, do they?'

'No. They belong to Oliphant.'

'Oliphant wrote them?'

'Oliphant wrote them, Houston dictated them.'

'Then they don't belong to Oliphant. They belong to Houston. Oliphant was purely an amanuensis.'

'I know all that. I've just told you,' I said irritably. 'Houston *gave* him the stuff. He's not interested in it any more. They're very good friends. He told him he could do what he liked with it.'

'He signed a statement to that effect, did he?'

411

'No. I don't know. Maybe he did. But I'm quite clear in my own mind,' I said, 'that it's Oliphant's property.'

'Are you?' Oliver said. 'Well, I know I wouldn't be.'

Nor, just at that moment, was I. I recalled uneasily that between feeding the old man his medicine and patting him on the back, the question had not somehow arisen.

I said, 'Anyhow, that's just one issue – '

'Yes. Not a bad one for a start, is it? You say this fellow has got a fortune. That should enable him to bring actions against you till Kingdom Come.'

'Let's leave that one for the moment.'

'All right. What have you got, then? You've got a book *about* Houston, not one by him. In that case,' he said, picking up the exercise books again, 'we go through it with garden shears. I mean – these young women in London. They're out for a start.'

'Have they got to be?'

'What else can you do?'

'You can disguise them.'

'How?'

I told him how.

'H'm. And the company his brother worked for? There can't be very many in that line of business.'

'No.'

'And what other line of business could they be engaged in that would take them to Tibet?'

'I don't know. What about a film company?'

'A film company?'

'Why not?'

'Well. You know your own business, of course,' Oliver said, in the tone of a man who strongly doubts it. 'To my simple mind it gives it the last dotty touch. How would a film company get into Tibet?'

'How did this one get in? By accident – that's the whole point.'

'But wasn't it reported in the Press when they came back ... I thought he said here something about a reception,' he said, leafing through.

'That's right. There was a reception, for the first party. And it was reported. Only it so happened that a famous plant collector called Kingdon-Ward was caught up in the same earthquake, and most of the news stories were about him. Anyway, we just change the dates. That's easy.'

'You know,' Oliver said, 'you don't really need me. The only tiny snag – has it occurred to you? – is that once you've finished changing this and disguising that, you're left with something that's neither a true story nor a proper novel. What is it?'

'I don't know,' I said uneasily.

2

I didn't see Mr Oliphant again that week, but early the next managed to secure somewhat grudging permission from his nurse, and drove out there. I parked the car in Fitzmaurice Crescent and went up, looking about me with a rather more curious eye this time. Here was the hall Houston had strode through nine years before to summon his cab to the air terminal, this is the tottering lift he had taken late at night after encounters with his willing females. All very strange, all a way quite haunting.

There was nothing, however, in any way haunting about the woman who opened the door to me. Miss Marks's Nurse Jellicoe turned out to be an enormous Irish nun, very brisk.

'You're the young man from the printer's, are you?'

'From the publisher's.'

'That's it. You mustn't stay very long. And don't let him talk too much. He's still a bit dozy from his sleeping draught.'

This did not sound very promising. I had a number of complicated things to discuss with Mr Oliphant.

I said, 'What's the matter with him?'

'Ach, it's just a nasty turn of bronchitis. He's not as young as he was. Mind what I say, now ... Here's a young man from the printer's for you,' she said cheerfully, showing me in.

Something had happened to Mr Oliphant's room. The air was sweet, surfaces gleamed, no trace of a garment or a meal was visible; the admiral had evidently gone through it like a gale. Mr Oliphant himself lay stiffly in bed as though strapped in it. His teeth were in a glass on the bedside table, and the nun gave them to him, and went. He looked a bit dazed.

He said, 'Well. Well. This is nice.'

'I was very sorry to hear of your attack.'

'Sit down. I've had them before. It's damp, this place. She's turned on all the electric fires. I hate to think what the bill's going to be.'

I sat down, balancing the envelope with the exercise books on my knee.

'You must have taken ill soon after I left.'

'Yes, I think I did. I couldn't go to the door to let Father Harris in. He had to get the porter.'

'He got the nurse for you, did he?'

'Sister Angelica, yes. She's a nice woman. Her Latin's a bit better than her English, you know,' he said, laughing and then stopping nervously as though expecting something to come on again. He saw the packet on my knee.

'Well, you'll have read it, eh? What do you think of it?'

'Very interesting. There were one or two points I wanted to raise. I don't know if you're quite up to it today . . .'

'If I can answer you.'

There was a certain saintly calm about him as he lay on the pillow. I thought I'd better leave the business of the copyright for the moment.

I said, 'One of the things was the timing. I couldn't quite follow when everything happened.'

'Well, he went away in January 1950 and came back in June '51. He was away seventeen months. Isn't that made clear at the end?'

'I haven't read the end. You'll remember I only took the first two notebooks. You were reading the others.'

'Oh, was I? Yes. Yes. They're giving me drugs to make me sleep, you know. It mixes you up a bit. Well, I think you'd better take them away with you. I doubt if I'll want to read them again... I'm not quite sure where she's put them,' he said, trying to sit up.

'Don't bother about it now. I'll ask her.'

'Yes. Do that. She's a nice woman. Her Latin's a bit better than her English, you know,' he said.

I perceived, with a slight sinking of spirits, that I had not picked quite the right day.

I said, 'Mr Oliphant, I don't want to tire you out. I think I'd better come back again.'

'Not a bit. You wanted to ask some questions.'

'They'll keep. It was about the timing of events actually in India and Tibet. It's probably all covered in the other notebooks.'

'Ah, well, no it isn't,' he said, struggling up again with a rather more focused look on his face. 'I see what you mean. That gave me a bit of trouble, actually. I just wrote down what he told me, but when I read through I saw how very confusing it was... He couldn't account for ten days, you know – gave us an awful problem. But we were able to work most things out roughly in relation to other dates. Also I got on to a man at the Sorbonne – I think his name is Bourgès-Vallerin. You ought to get in touch with him if you're interested.'

'I wrote down *Bourgès-Vallerin, Sorbonne* on the envelope. 'What is he – a Tibetan specialist?'

'Yes, Tibet, China. He reads all the papers and so on, a most invaluable man. He put me right on the trouble with the Chinese. Some scholars have a theory about the Chinese invasion. They went in, you know, with eight armies – an enormous force for the kind of opposition they could expect. The feeling is that they merely wanted to get the soldiers out of China for a bit.'

'Houston was there, was he, during the invasion?'

'Oh, my word, yes. They had posters up for him. The Duke of Ganzing had quite an interesting story about the posters. I don't think I ever heard that from Houston,' he said reminiscently.

'How did you hear?'

'He told me.'

'Who did?'

'The duke did.'

'I see,' I said. An old chap in our warehouse had suddenly gone off his head when I was there one day. I experienced the same creepy feeling.

I got up. 'Well, you must tell me about it when I come again. I think I've stayed long enough now.'

'Oh, don't worry about that. She'll tell you when you've got to go,' he said, chuckling. 'Stay and have a cup of tea with me.'

'Oh, really, I don't think ...'

'Nonsense. Just tap on the door ... I think you'd better have the duke's address, incidentally. He could tell you a great deal. He lives in Delhi now. He gave me it when he was here.'

'The Duke of Ganzing was here?'

'Yes, a couple of years ago. He stayed in Abingdon with a friend of his called Blake-Winter. They used to go to school together in India.'

I tapped on the door.

'He was very disappointed to find Houston away,' the old man said. 'He brought one of the posters with him, the ones the Chinese had put up after the murders. That was why the poor fellow had to fly home so quickly. He was in no condition to travel, of course, but the Chinese were putting pressure on the Indians to send him back for trial. Naturally, they didn't want to do that, but he was a bit of an embarrassment to them all the same, so they simply got rid of him.'

My head had begun to spin a bit.

I said, 'This is Houston, is it?'

'Houston, certainly. Of course, you won't have come to that yet.'

'I'm not sure I've quite got it. The Chinese thought he had murdered somebody?'

'Yes. Well, he did.'

I had a swift mental image of Oliver Gooch gravely shaking his head.

I said, 'Was it an accident?'

'An accident?' the old man said. 'No, it wasn't an accident. He had quite a long time to plan it. He did it with a knife. He was quite petrified, of course. Ah, Sister — what about a nice cup of tea? Mr Davidson's tongue is hanging out.'

I thought it probably was.

A few more weird items came my way over tea, none of them conducive to the book's early publication, and when I saw an opening, I said,

'There's just one thing, Mr Oliphant — it would be quite hopeless, would it, to try and get Houston to sign this himself?'

'Oh, I'm afraid so. Quite out of the question. He's simply not interested. He doesn't want to think about it any more.'

'He would have to, rather, when the book came out, wouldn't he? I mean, there would be a good deal of comment. Reporters would descend on him. Does he realize this?'

'I don't know. I'm sure he wouldn't say anything to them,' Mr Oliphant said confidently.

'Reporters are persistent people.'

'They could be as persistent as they liked.'

'And he wouldn't mind what they wrote.'

'Not a bit. All he's got to say he's said here. And he relies on me to publish a true version.'

'In that case why shouldn't he sign this version? You see, what's bothering us is that there is a great deal of actionable material here. There's the question of the money — and now these murders. It's all a little bit illegal, isn't it?'

Mr Oliphant began to grow slightly restive.

He said, 'Look, Mr Davidson, it seems to me this book should be worth quite a sum of money. I don't want to spend the rest of my life quibbling about it... I'd like to get out of this flat. It's damp here, you know. She's turned on all the electric fires. I hate to think what the bill will be...'

I could hear Sister Angelica making warning noises in the next room. The time seemed to be now or never.

I said, 'Mr Oliphant — did Houston even sign a statement to the effect that you could publish the material in these notebooks?'

'Sign a statement? Of course he didn't. There has never been anything like that between us. Certainly not.'

'In the course of a letter, say – '

'We are the best of friends,' the old man said. He had become quite pink in the face and his breath had started to whistle a bit. 'You don't surely expect friends to go about signing statements to each other?'

Sister Angelica came in.

I said, hurriedly, 'Perhaps in one of his letters to you. You might have referred to it in some way, and he might have confirmed – '

'Now then,' Sister Angelica said. 'Didn't you promise me you wouldn't let him talk too much? And just look at you, you poor silly old man. You'll be breathless directly.'

'I'm going now,' I said.

'Yes. You are. This very minute.'

'Just a tick,' Oliphant said. 'You know, I believe you're right. He did write something to me – '

'Well, you can tell him another time. He's going now.'

'I'll look it out for you.'

'Thank you. Thanks very much. Get well.'

Sister Angelica found the other two exercise books, and came to the door with me.

'You know,' she said, 'that wasn't very clever. I told you he wasn't to talk.'

'I'm sorry. There were things that only he could tell me. It might mean a good bit of money for him.'

'He won't need it if he goes on like this. Still – it might help pay the electric bill, eh,' she said, winking very slightly.

'It might,' I said. 'Good-bye, Nurse Jellicoe.'

That seemed to clear the account with the young man from the printer's, at least.

I saw Mr Oliphant three or four times more before Christmas. The letter from Houston, which he managed to turn up, didn't answer all problems, but it showed we could produce a certain kind of book, a rather abbreviated kind of book, based on the notes. I was keen enough, in a modified way, to do so. T.L. was also keen, in an even more modified way. Rosenthal Brown were not keen at all. It became necessary to do a job of research.

A young man called Underwood, an editorial assistant, was put on to this, but for a number of points the only source of information proved to be Mr Oliphant himself. I undertook to handle these.

At the beginning of December, after discussing one of them with him, I found a small, bright-eyed priest waiting for me in the hall.

He said, 'Ah, Mr Davidson. I'm Father Harris. Sister Angelica telephoned me that you were here. I particularly wanted to have a word with you.'

'Of course. I've heard a lot about you.'

'Yes. Just come in here a moment, will you?'

We went into the living-room, chill and dismal in the darkening afternoon. The priest switched on a little table lamp, evidently quite at home in Houston's old flat.

He said, 'Well, he isn't getting any better, is he?'

'No, he isn't.'

'And he can't have Sister Angelica much longer. He should be in hospital, you know, but it's quite hopeless. They don't want old chronic cases. There simply aren't the beds.'

'Can't his professional body do anything for him?'

'I'm trying, naturally. I would very much like him to go to a nursing home. We have one, a Catholic one, at Worplesdon in Surrey. It's a beautiful place, very well run. I visit there. I think I could get him in. Don't you think that would be a very desirable thing, Mr Davidson?'

'Yes. Yes, I think it would be,' I said, suddenly seeing what was coming and thrown off balance by it.

'It would cost eighteen guineas a week,' the priest said.

'Have you tried his friend Houston in the West Indies?'

'Yes. That's why I made up my mind to see you as soon as I could. Nobody seems to know where this Mr Houston has got to. My letter came back from the Barbados stamped "Gone Away – Return to Sender".'

'Oh.'

'He has no other relations, you know.'

'Hasn't he?'

'None.'

'Very unfortunate.'

'Yes,' the priest said, and see-sawed on his heels and coughed a little. 'I wondered if you were prepared to help, Mr Davidson. I wondered if you felt able to make an offer for this book of his.'

'I'm afraid there are complications.'

I told him some of them.

'H'm. But if all went well the book could make quite a lot of money?'

'If all went well. No publisher dare touch it at the moment. It's far too dangerous.'

Father Harris stopped see-sawing. He put his hand on my shoulder. He said very earnestly, 'Don't you think, Mr Davidson, that there's a case here for a sporting offer? After all, it's a very special one.'

'All publishing is made up of special cases, Father. A lot of authors are hard up.'

'They're not all at death's door.'

'No. No.'

'It would lighten my heart a great deal if I felt I could rely on you to do your best.'

I said uneasily, 'Well, you can certainly do that. Of course. Naturally. But you've got to – '

'And may God bless you for it,' said the priest, shaking me very warmly by the hand.

Mr Oliphant moved into Worplesdon the week before Christmas. I went to see him a few days later. I had been to a series of pre-Christmas cocktail parties the night before, and was not at my best. Nor, evidently was Mr Oliphant. They had given him a nice little room and done it up with a lot of gay paper decorations; Mr Oliphant lay in bed in it sunk in profound depression.

'This silly old man thinks he's going to die,' Father Harris said, coming in after a few minutes. He had been having a few glasses of sherry on his round of the patients and was beaming a bit. 'He's gone and made a will.'

Mr Oliphant roused himself from his torpor and began fumbling about at his bedside cabinet.

'I'll get it,' Father Harris said. 'Here we are. He wants us both to witness it.'

It was a somewhat austere will. Mr Oliphant had left all his worldly estate and such chancy assets as might still accrue to it to the foundation of an Exhibition in Latin, to commence five years after his death, at his old university, Oxford. I gathered that this disposition did not meet entirely with Father Harris's approval. He signed it, however, and so did I, and the old man watched us with a certain gloomy satisfaction.

There were four Christmas cards on the cabinet, and I edged round presently and managed to have a look at them while Mr Oliphant's attention was diverted by the priest: it was after all a pitiful enough collection after a lifetime's voyage through the world. I wondered if their paucity might not in some measure have contributed to his gloom.

There was one from Father Harris, and one from Miss Marks, and one from me. The last was inscribed, 'Tight lines in 1960 – and hoping for a good salmon,' and signed 'your old friend Wallie.'

There wasn't one from his old friend Houston.

Chapter 11

I

THE governor of Hodzo was unwell. He was morose. For two whole days after receiving his brother-in-law's letter he remained in his room, listless and sick at heart. His priest read him seven volumes of the Kangyur. His youngest wife played to him on a set of consecrated cymbals. Nothing availed. He remained steeped in melancholy. On the third day, however, despite a continuation of the bowel movements that neither the Kangyur nor the cymbals had been able to arrest, he felt a slight accession of confidence, and after a light breakfast and prayers, he called for his palanquin and set off for Yamdring.

The journey to Yamdring was one of twenty-four hours, and though he knew he would end it in pain and exhaustion, he did not send his servants ahead to prepare for his comfort, for he did not wish in any way to upset the routine of the monastery or arouse suspicion. He planned to examine personally the dossier of every single soul there. He thought he might manage thirty in an hour and two hundred in a day. There were some eleven hundred souls in the monastery.

Because it was essential that none should be regarded as above suspicion he meant to keep the reason for this enterprise strictly to himself, and the last thing that he wanted was to walk into a meeting of the monastery council. This, however, was what he walked into.

The council had been summoned on curious business, and the abbot welcomed him to it, and to the chair most gratefully; for he was sorely puzzled.

The unconscious *trulku* Houtson, he said, had had a dream. He had requested an interview with the abbot that very morning. He had told the abbot his dream.

'There were indications in it,' the abbot said, 'that the *trulku* may be no longer unconscious.'

'What was the dream?'

The dream was that the *trulku* had found himself walking in the monastery. As he walked he had spied a Westerner, a man like himself. He had drawn closer to the man and observed that he was watching a shower of rain falling in the monastery. The rain turned into greenstones and from them emerged suddenly the figure of the Mother. As he watched, a demon appeared behind the Mother with a net and a sack. The demon had made to catch the Mother and the greenstones, but the *trulku* had run towards him, waving his arms and shouting a powerful mantra, and the demon had fled. The Mother had nodded to the *trulku* in gratitude, and he had awakened from the dream.

The governor sat for a moment gazing at his small hands, placed one above the other on the table. He said, 'Who is guarding the *trulku*?'

'Two artist monks, Excellency. They are reliable men.'

'Do they speak his language?'

'No. But he has picked up some Tibetan. Why do you ask ...?' the abbot said, and paused, seeing why the governor had asked.

'Someone has told him of the greenstones,' the governor said, nodding.

There was silence for a moment.

The deputy abbot said, 'But Excellency, even if this were so, who could have told him of the ceremony or the fact that one of the Westerners had witnessed it?'

The governor nodded again and looked down at his hands, for he had seen at once that this was the nub of the problem, and he had not meant to pursue it. If he knew the answer to that, he might also know who had been telling the Chinese ... To give himself time to think, he said, 'And tell me, Abbot, did the *trulku* make any further request of you?'

'Yes, Excellency, he did. He asked permission to see the Westerners.'

'Since the reason for their restraint has now been revealed to him?'

'This is the reason he gave.'

'And what answer did you make him?'

'None. This is why we have met. May I ask what are your Excellency's views with regard to this question?'

The governor drummed his hands on the table. He didn't think he had any views on this question. It did not seem to matter a bean, now that the cat was out of the bag, whether Houtson saw the other Europeans or not. But he thought he should temporize.

'Tell me, Abbot, what was the *trulku's* attitude – confident, assured?'

'No,' the abbot said slowly, 'no, it was not ... A change has come over him lately. He appears dazed. He is like a sleep-walker. There are shadows under his eyes and his step is heavy.'

'It is the burden of knowledge descending upon him,' said the deputy abbot confidently. 'The symptoms are classic, I assure you, Excellency.'

The governor decided to sit back and let others discuss these classic symptoms. They discussed them a good deal. He saw that the abbot and the deputy abbot and the Mistress of Ceremonies were very impressed with them; that Little Daughter was less impressed. Recalling how strongly she had urged *trulku* status for Houtson, he regarded her with some interest; and when the discussion had run its course leaned forward again.

'Are we not,' he said mildly, 'to have the benefit of the views of Little Daughter?'

He saw the flush that came instantly to her round cheeks, and the way her hands went nervously to her tricorn. She said, 'My views, Excellency ... Why, I think – that is, I believe the Mother would think – that there is now no reason why the *trulku* should not see the other Westerners. After all, since he now knows ...'

'Certainly,' said the deputy abbot.

'Of course,' said the Mistress of Ceremonies.

'Yes,' said the governor, neutrally.

The abbot was looking expectantly at him. 'Do we take it, Excellency,' he said, 'that this would be your view also?'

'Why, yes,' the governor said absently. 'You may take it so, Abbot.'

But he was not looking at the abbot. He was looking at Little Daughter. She knew something, he thought. He wondered what it was.

Little Daughter was wondering also. She wondered as she laboured back up the seven flights to the top monastery. She had not meant to give anything away. She hoped she had not given anything away. But she had observed before the uncanny ability of the governor to pick something up out of the air. She was greatly troubled.

It was Little Daughter's belief that she knew the Mother as intimately as it was possible for one soul to know another. She bathed her and shaved her and painted her and anointed her; she had had her in her sole care since the age of 6. She did not merely love the Mother as she was bound in duty to do: she adored her. She regarded her as (and called her sometimes in moments of special tenderness) her little rose. If the Mother had asked her to fly like a bird from the topmost golden roof of the monastery, she would willingly have done so. There was nothing the Mother could ask her that she would not do; and nothing that the Mother could do that would strike her as anything other than perfectly reasonable.

None the less she was troubled.

In her daily ministrations she had observed certain things that indicated that the Mother was not spending her nights alone.

Although herself a virgin and bound to a vow of lifelong chastity (as had been all her predecessors), Little Daughter found nothing shocking in this. Tradition had established that while the Mother was in the world she was entitled, at her will, to the usages of the world; so long as discretion was observed. She could remember all too well the increasing appetites of the

Seventeenth. As she had aged, so she had become more insatiable. It had been a part of Little Daughter's duties to bring men to her, blindfold and with their hands tied behind them; sometimes four or five men in a night. One to whom she had taken a fancy in her old age had indeed become a little deranged by his experiences; and towards the end there had been the minor scandal involving the abbot himself...

It had been the change from this old ravening creature to the delicate flower-like little Eighteenth, and at a time of her life when she was most susceptible to change, that had rooted in Little Daughter her special feelings with regard to the Mother.

That the adored young woman should wish to experiment tentatively with the ways of the world did not, therefore, cause her more than a passing uneasiness; what confounded her was how she was managing to do it.

Little Daughter slept outside the Mother's room. She knew that no one had come in that way. There was only one other way: she had taught it to the Mother herself (as some day, the Mother would teach it to a new Little Daughter: so the secret was preserved, in a straight line). Only two other people in the monastery knew this secret, the abbot and the deputy abbot: they, too, passed it from one to the other. Only one other person had *ever* known the secret. This was Hu-Tzung, and the Thirteenth had told him it while under his spell.

Little Daughter had spent many tormenting hours with the problem. She knew she could discount both the abbot and the deputy abbot. This seemed to leave only the unconscious *trulku* ... But if the unconscious *trulku* had divined the secret then he was no longer unconscious, and moreover no longer a *trulku* but a *yidag*; for such a secret was not proper for a *trulku*; and if by some freak of fate he had been given it then he would most certainly not have used it.

But if he were a *yidag*, the Mother was bound to reveal him. And if she had not revealed him, then he could not be a *yidag*... Little Daughter's poor brain reeled.

'Little Daughter?'

'I am coming, Mother.'

Little Daughter panted into the room and lowered herself, holding her heart, on to a stool.

'Oh, Little Daughter, tell me quickly – what has been decided?'

Little Daughter got her breath back. 'That the *trulku* be allowed to see the Westerners,' she said.

'And what questions were raised?'

Little Daughter told her, observing at the same time the child's fatigue, the droop of her mouth, the anxiety in her eyes. Her heart went out to her.

'Was that all?'

'Yes, that was all,' Little Daughter said; and then, greatly daring, 'Dear Little Mother, if there is something worrying you – some special problem . . .'

'No,' the Mother said. 'No, no. What do you mean? I don't understand you, Little Daughter.'

'You are so tired lately.'

'I am sleeping badly.'

'Then take a little rest now.'

'No. Yes. All right,' said the Mother pettishly. 'If you wish it.'

'It will restore you,' said Little Daughter, quickly helping her off with her robe and turning back the covers.

The Mother got into bed and lay there, her face so like a pale china rose against the pillow that Little Daughter could not refrain from kissing her.

'Try and sleep now.'

'It is too light to sleep.'

'I will close the shutter. Try.'

'Very well.'

She went to the shutter.

'Little Daughter!'

Heart bounding, Little Daughter turned and came quickly back to the bed.

'What is it, little Mother?'

'Nothing . . . Nothing.'

'If there is something you wish to tell me – anything at all . . .'

'It was nothing . . . I am thirsty.'

'Very well,' said Little Daughter quietly, and went out and poured a mug of lime juice in her own apartment. She made it freshly every day. The chief medical monk had advised that it was good for the little rose's complexion.

2

Houston's first meeting with his brother in the monastery of Yamdring took place on 30 June 1950, seven weeks exactly after he had first arrived in the village. It took place in the third monastery, and was between them alone, for this was what he had requested.

(Although he wrote fully of later meetings, when others were present, Houston wrote curiously little of this one: it appears to have been an emotional occasion.)

He found that the party had been able to keep together – all with the exception of Wister who had to be taken away, raving, to the hospital every few days.

Wister was the 'mad' man of the priestess's story, and the 'sick' one of Ringling's. It was he who had wandered into the emerald ceremony during the second festival, still concussed from his earthquake experiences (which was why his cell had been left inadvertently unlocked). In the general confusion he had been able to get back to his own corridor, had managed to unlock and let himself into Hugh's cell, and had even been able to give a rambling account of what he had seen before the guards, hastily summoned by the deputy abbot, had found him. He had been very badly beaten-up, then, and had never recovered from it.

They had escaped in December, after bribing their guards; they had got out at night down a rope-ladder direct from the third monastery, and had managed to put several miles and two days between themselves and Yamdring before the blizzard had caught them on the Portha-la. The caravan had been a godsend, and they had followed its tracks hurriedly, carrying Wister. But the attempt had been a forlorn one. The guards had caught up on their first night with the caravan, and that had been the end of it.

Since then the guards had been changed at weekly intervals, to preclude the possibility of further bribing. But they had been well-treated, with a comfortably furnished cell each, and a common room to themselves during the day, and ample opportunity for exercise in the courtyard of their monastery. They had two pairs of binoculars between them, and were occasionally allowed up to a vantage point from which they could observe the life in the village; and this, since December, had been the nearest they had got to escaping from the monotony of their surroundings.

They had been kept locked up during the ceremonies of the Spring Festival, and had thus not observed the fracas in which Houston had been involved. But they had received hints during the upsets to routine brought about by the canonization ceremonies, and gradually, over the weeks, had learned what was happening. The abbot had himself told Hugh what to expect the previous day; but he still found it perfectly unbelievable.

Houston found it unbelievable himself

He didn't know what to say to his brother. They sat and grinned at each other a good deal.

Houston's days were passing at this time in a curious manner. The weather had grown hot in the valley and he found it hard to stay awake in the afternoons. It was unbearably steamy beside the lake, unbearably odorous in the village. He stayed in his cell and slept. He slept every afternoon, an arrangement which proved entirely satisfactory to Miny and Mo, who brought a couple of rugs into the cell and slept with him.

These were dreamy days. They were intoxicating nights. For he was never wholly free of her now, sleeping or waking. He felt as if he were in a kind of trance, and less and less as the airless days of July drifted into August did he want to come out of it. A number of things were working, however, to bring him out of it.

'Chao-li, Chao-li, you're not listening.
'To every word, little rose.'
'Little Daughter *knows* – she knows something.'
'What does she know?'
'I don't know. And they are worried how you came to hear of the greenstones ... Oh, Chao-li, you're not thinking.'
'I am thinking.'
'You're not thinking hard.'
'I can't think hard when I am wtth you.'
'Then go away from me ... Ah, no, Chao-li, don't go ... Think when you are away from me.'

He thought when he was away from her.
He went to see the abbot.
'Yes, *trulku*, you have asked to see me?'
'I am troubled in my mind, Abbot.'
'You have dreamed again?' said the abbot, loweringly.
'I have dreamed again. I cannot understand my dreams.'
'Tell me them.'
Houston did so. There was a surprising similarity about his dreams, for in each the Mother either nodded to him or beckoned or called. He thought sometimes that he spoke to her, and that she answered; but he couldn't tell, when he awoke, whether it had been a dream or a real meeting, so clear was the apparition. Was it possible, he asked the abbot, for one to project himself physically to another place while he slept?

That such a phenomenon was not only possible, but indeed most comprehensively documented was an elementary part of every young monk's training: the abbot gazed at him searchingly. He wished most keenly that he had the benefit of the governor's advice, but the governor had come and gone.

He decided to employ one of the governor's methods: he changed the subject.

He said, 'Well now, *trulku*, how did you find your – your compatriots?'

'Very well, Abbot, thank you,' Houston said, cautiously. 'They have no complaints.'

'The one who is mad – it was an unfortunate accident.'

'Quite unavoidable.'

'Yes. Yes,' the abbot said, bewildered by this ready understanding. 'And you have quite lost your desire to return home with them?'

'I have not lost it,' Houston said carefully. 'I still have it. It's very strange... I want to go and yet I want to stay. I have a feeling there is something for me to do here.'

The abbot looked at him, and changed his tack.

He said slowly, 'Tell me, *trulku* – you have seen the abbess only once, during the festival.'

'That is so.'

'It was for you a most unusual sight.'

'Most.'

'Perhaps you think of it again sometimes.'

'Frequently. I've even tried to sketch it once or twice from memory.'

'Then isn't it possible,' the abbot said, with an attempt at a smile, 'that you think of it also while you sleep – that your mind goes on making these – these sketches?'

Houston shook his head. He said, 'It's an explanation that has occurred to me, naturally. But the dreams are so real, Abbot... One has the strangest feeling sometimes... And yet, what other explanation is there? Perhaps you are right. You might be.'

'But still – wait. Wait a moment,' the abbot said hastily, as he rose. 'Dreams after all are sent to guide us. Perhaps we should examine other aspects. You think that in your dreams the abbess calls to you and that you go to her.'

'Yes.'

'Where is it that you go?'

Houston frowned. 'To an unearthly place ... a tomb ... a

431

place I have never seen before. There are candles and effigies . . .
I can't describe it.'

'Where do you think it is, this place?'

'I don't know,' Houston said. 'Perhaps, as you say, in my
head. Perhaps in a picture I have seen and remembered. What
other explanation is there?'

The abbot, who could think of several, gazed at him
sombrely. '*Trulku*,' he said at last, 'I must take counsel on these
dreams. It may be that the Mother has need of you. It may be
that she is herself unaware of it. We will talk of it again.'

They talked of it three days later. Houston spent the
intervening nights in his cell. He talked a good deal in his sleep
during these nights; and he knew that Mei-Hua did the same,
for so they had planned it.

And the news the governor brought him at length was not
unexpected.

3

Houston had been granted the free run of the monastery
towards the end of July: it was just over a month before the
Second Festival. He looked back on it later as, literally, the
most marvellous month of his life, for every day brought him
something to marvel at. He had ready access, day or night, to
the abbess, and was utterly and entirely infatuated with her. He
could see his brother and the other members of the party
whenever he wished, and did so every day. And he was
regarded with awe, if not indeed veneration, by all but one of
the monks and priestesses in the monastery. (This one, alas, he
was to encounter later in circumstances rather less marvellous.)

Ringling was better now, too, and accompanied him everywhere. Miny and Mo were no longer in attendance, although
some supervision was maintained over the other Europeans,
and guards were sent out with them on the outings that they
took with Houston.

The outings were frequent. They spent a two-day trip
collecting orchids and herbs in the hills; they spent three days

with the Duke of Ganzing; and many days more working with the priestesses in the fields.

The monastery owned much land, several times as much as could be worked even by its large free labour force, and yet – apart from little prayer wheels and flags – it produced nothing at all for outside consumption. It was, in a sense, a vast hospice, dispensing service. It gave a medical service to half the province; it gave a 'burial' service, a mobile corps of priestesses always out on their dismembering and occult assignments (they stayed some days after the dismemberment to see that the newly freed soul was properly directed to its destination); and it gave a spiritual service. Although it was, in one sense, a government institution, its hierarchy was by no means government-appointed. From the abbess downwards, every departmental head was self-perpetuating; 'recognized', as children, they took over from Former Bodies.

Because of the presence of the she-devil and the establishment's supernatural origin, pure State lamaism was not practised (a dispensation it enjoyed with some half-dozen other major monasteries, Houston learned from the abbot); there were traces of an earlier religion in the dogma and the form of worship, and local deities supplemented the national ones.

Houston was fascinated by these details. He pried at will, and though he came up occasionally against some reserve, no mystery was denied him.

His relations with Ringling and with his brother were less successful. The boy didn't know what to make of him; he was uneasy in himself with a suspicion that someone or something was being made a fool of. He didn't want the fool to be himself, or Houston, or the occult powers of the monastery; he didn't know what to think. But Houston had hired him, and had gone through much with him, and he gave him therefore a certain wistful devotion.

Houston thought he could cope with this, but he didn't know how he was going to cope with his brother. He had the strangest aversion to explaining his relations with Mei-Hua, and when Hugh asked him he gave him guarded replies. It had brought an awkward duality to their relations.

Hugh said to him one day, 'Look here, Charles, what the hell is going on? Why can't we talk together properly?'

'When we get away we'll talk properly. Be patient, Hugh.'

'Why can't your abbess get her finger out and see that we get away? She runs the works here, doesn't she?'

'I don't know.'

'What's come over you? You surely don't believe this bloody *trulku* nonsense, do you?'

'Of course I don't. But they do. We've got to wait until the prophecies work themselves out.'

'What have you got to do with the — prophecies?'

'Not a — thing,' Houston said, using the same term in an attempt at intimacy. 'But they think I have. Just wait till everything works out.'

With Sheila Wolferston and Meiklejohn he was on somewhat easier terms, for here there was no lost intimacy to be regained. Meiklejohn, it was true, regarded him with a certain sardonic amusement and had taken to calling him St Charles, which he found after a time very trying; but with the girl he was able to establish something like a normal relationship. For he had a bond with her; before leaving he had been to see her mother, in a damp little cottage in Godalming, Surrey; and they talked for hours of her mother.

'She does everything herself, you know. It isn't so easy with her leg.'

'What's the matter with her leg?'

'She's lame – didn't you notice?'

'I never did.'

'No, she doesn't like people. She tries to conceal it ... It's so silly. I wanted her to come and live in a flat in town, you know – no stairs – but she wouldn't. She's so obstinate ... It isn't as if she really knows anybody in Godalming. Daddy was the convivial one. She merely *clings*. I suppose it's because she hasn't got very much to cling to.'

He had noticed the somewhat mournful strain in the girl

that he had noticed in the mother; he saw the mother's blunt nose, and the mother's head-shaking ghost of a smile.

They were sitting on his shirt in the stubble of a barley field at the time: a yak with a deep bell round its neck was passing with a sled piled high with tawny stooks, and far below them the green lake and the seven gold roofs swam in the rising air currents... All a long, long way from damp, soft Godalming with its mushy autumnal leaves underfoot and its dark green trains commuting to Waterloo.

She said, shaking her head, 'It's perfectly fantastic, isn't it? We're almost literally out of the world. They think we're dead. And it's all going on there still.'

'I know,' he said for he felt it himself, and, moved by something, took her hand. She had cut her hair short. She wore an orange sun top and skirt, dark glasses, no shoes. Her skin was tanned brown; he thought her very fine and wholesome in a warm, blunt kind of way. He said, quietly, 'I hope all is going well with you and Hugh, Sheila.'

'It's a bit of a strain.'

'Is it?'

'We're on top of each other all the time, and yet not able to be really alone ever.'

'I'm sorry.'

'Some of us are never without company,' she said lightly. 'I understand you're not hampered in that way yourself.'

'No.'

The dark glasses were turned curiously upon him.

'You don't want to talk about it much, do you?'

'Not much.'

'All right. Only you won't forget that our future is in your hands, will you?'

He liked her.

But he liked Mei-Hua more. He liked her more than he had ever liked anyone in the world, and he didn't think that anything could come about that would make him view her differently. That was before the Second Festival, of course.

4

The Second Festival of the Monkey began that year on 1 September, two weeks before it was normally due; this was because, owing to a second earthquake (on 15 August) which caused much damage in Lhasa, the omens had become suddenly more threatening than ever; the Oracle had indeed indicated that if it were not held early it might not be held at all.

Like the Spring Festival, the celebrations lasted seven days. Houston stayed for only four of them, for on the fifth, badly shocked, he left Yamdring and went to stay with the Duke at Ganzing and didn't return for a fortnight.

He left on the day of the emerald ceremony, after participating in it. He had been up very early that day, for the deputy abbot had wakened him at four o'clock to take him to a large chapel in the first monastery where the ceremony was due to take place.

He found the abbot already there, sitting over the emeralds: he had carried the bags down himself from the top monastery, and had watched over them all night. Apart from the abbess, he was the only person who could open and seal these bags.

Houston knew that he was himself to be a supernumerary guardian of the emeralds, but had learned very little more. Mei-Hua had told him that he must not come to her during the week of the festival, for it was to be devoted entirely to remembrances of the monkey; but had refused to tell him anything else. It was not spoken of, she said. He would see for himself.

Houston waited with the keenest interest to do so.

He sat with the two silent men and the eight sacks of emeralds for the best part of an hour, listening to a chanted mass that was going on elsewhere in the monastery. There was a sickly smell of flowers above the incense in the candlelit chapel; it seemed to be coming from a large jade ornament in a far corner. His two companions had fallen into a meditative trance, however, so he did not disturb them with questions but merely sat on his own two sacks and awaited events.

At five o'clock a little handbell was rung, and complete silence fell. In the silence, the abbess was brought down through the seven monasteries. She was brought down on a litter, and deposited outside the gates by four bearers, who left immediately. Little Daughter and the Mistress of Ceremonies had come down with her, and now, with the abbot and the deputy abbot to help, the litter was raised again and brought inside the chapel, and the gates closed.

Houston watched in fascination. She had her devil's mask on. She had been newly anointed: he had smelt it right away. But now as Little Daughter took off her robe, he saw it, too: the abbess stood, quite naked, gleaming all over in the candle-light. She walked to the jade ornament, the small procession following.

The ornament was a large oval urn – three quarters full of rose petals, Houston saw. The abbess stepped into it, and sank deeply in the petals, and kneeled there, with her devil's head bowed slightly so that only the pointed golden ears projected above the rim; and as she did so the abbot began to chant.

All had been done in perfect silence so far, but now, as the abbot took from his robe a long gold knife and bent to break the seals of the emerald sacks, the others took up the chant.

The Mistress of Ceremonies produced a gold ladle, and one after the other, Houston taking his turn, they began to scoop into the urn ladles of emeralds.

The job took a long time to complete. the dull green heap steadily mounting, until at last the abbess was entirely covered, her devil's ears alone sticking out from her lake of 'tears'.

The abbot had not been assisting in the last few ladles, and hearing his chant become suddenly muffled, Houston turned and looked.

The abbot had put on a mask. It was a golden mask. It was the mask of a monkey's head.

He had been fumbling about in another corner of the chapel while he did this, and now as he approached the urn again, the chanting stopped and the deputy abbot and Little Daughter and the Mistress of Ceremonies prostrated themselves on the ground before him. In astonishment, Houston did the same, but, looking up, was able to see what the abbot was doing. The abbot was dipping his hands into the emeralds. The abbess's hand emerged. The abbot took it, and raised her to her feet. She came up very slowly, a few dull stones sticking to her back, and the abbot brushed them carefully into the urn.

His muffled chanting began again as she stepped out of the urn, the two masked figures facing each other and holding hands; and after a moment the worshippers got up from the floor. The Mistress of Ceremonies gently brushed the abbess down, replacing the few adhering emeralds in the urn; and then she covered her again with her robe, and took one of her hands, the abbot retaining the other, and they walked with her out of the chapel.

Houston saw, through the gates, that she took her place again in the litter; and then the handbell was rung and the four bearers appeared, and picked up the litter and carried it away. The Mistress of Ceremonies returned alone to the chapel, and that seemed to be the end of it.

With the others, Houston began ladling the emeralds back in the bags. They were smiling a little, as after a job well done, but not actually talking, and though Houston found himself with many questions he didn't ask them. When he saw the deputy abbot produce a stick of green wax, however, and begin to seal the bags, he whispered in some surprise, 'Doesn't the abbot have to do this?'

'Yes. The abbot,' the deputy abbot said, smiling gently. 'I am now the abbot for three days.'

'What is the abbot?'

'The abbot is the monkey.'

It was all said very genially, with the two women smiling faintly as at some well-established family joke, and for a moment Houston didn't get it, and smiled with them.

He said, 'If you're taking over the abbot's job for three days, what will he be doing?'

The deputy abbot told him what the abbot would be doing for the next three days; and very shortly after, Houston went back to his cell. He stayed there all day, not eating and not sleeping, and the next day he went to Ganzing.

'But my dear chep,' the duke said, 'it's been going on for a long time – for seven hundred years at least. The practice was started by the Third Body. Nobody would dream of stopping it.'

'Doesn't it strike you as particularly horrible?'

'Not a bit. Why should it? You see, you've got it quite wrong, old chep. It isn't just an old monk and a young girl. It's the monkey and the she-devil – we are reminded of our origins. We're very simple people here. You have your cradle-to-grave benefits, and so have we. It's a guarantee that we are still watched-over – that nothing will change for us. It's very touching in a way.'

'It's horrible,' Houston said. 'It's peculiarly, vilely horrible. For three days – '

'And another thing you've got to remember is that our women have rather – rather better constitutions than most. It's, in a way – we shouldn't talk about it, of course – very much harder on the abbot. The old chep isn't getting any younger. He had a perfectly dreadful time with the Former Body – was quite fagged out one year and had to be taken away to hospital, delirious. The chief medical monk had to sit with him for a week. Oh, quite a scandal.'

'And that doesn't disgust and revolt you? The idea of a young girl – '

'The Former Body was 74 at the time,' the duke said, drawing on his cigar.

'Oh, my God!' Houston said faintly.

'And by no means disgusted or revolted, except by the poor old chep's deficencies. The thing is, old chep, you don't *know* us. The act – I'm not embarrassing you? – hasn't the same connotations for us as it has for you. We regard it as, on the whole, a fairly pleasurable and useful occupation. We aren't greatly exercised by problems of legitimacy and so forth, since property can be handed down in the female line, and so the pattern of our social behaviour has tended to develop in – '

'But in a monastery!' Houston said, his distress in no way eased by this rationalization. 'How can you possibly countenance – '

'Ah, well. That does of course lead to certain difficulties. The people there are rather devoted to it – naturally: they have so few alternative pleasures. And of course in *principle* they shouldn't be. It means that three women have to be kept constantly on the go aborting them.'

Such new horrors were evoked by this piece of information that Houston lost all desire to pursue it. He gazed silently at the duke and picked up his whisky and drained it at a gulp. The duke poured him another.

He said, mildly troubled, 'You know, you shouldn't concern yourself particularly with – with anyone here. It could be very dangerous for you. There's such a lot you can never know, old chep.'

But there was something the duke didn't know, either. He said on another day, 'The emeralds? Oh, they're part of the quite beautiful legend. The she-devil is supposed to have wept endlessly for the monkey and so bitterly that finally some of her tears turned to emerald. The monkey comes once a year to dry them up, as it were.'

'She must have wept a long time. There are a lot of emeralds.'

'Are there, old chep? You mustn't tell me, you know. I don't want to know. Nobody's supposed to, except the monastery council and the governor of the province.'

'Where did they actually come from?'

'From a mine. There used to be a very rich vein in the hill the monastery was built on. There was an earthquake several hundred years ago, in the time of the Third Body, and the general view was that the demons were upset at the mine workings. The abbess sealed up the mine and built over it – she was a tremendous builder. She put up the three higher monasteries, and rebuilt the shrine on the island. She was the one who introduced the Second Festival.'

'Whereabouts was the mine?'

'Nobody knows, old chep. There used to be a story – I remember my grandfather telling me it – that it went under the lake and that a lot of cheps were entombed there, but I don't think there's anything in it. You would expect it to go back into the hill. But there's no trace now – none at all.'

Houston didn't bother to tell him otherwise.

He didn't see Mei-Hua for a week after he returned, for he had had a fortnight to reflect and it seemed to him that the duke had spoken nothing but the truth. He didn't know this country or these people, and he didn't think he ever would.

She was a fascinating young Chinese girl, unlike in her features and in her grace any woman he had ever met. But now he had been away from her for a while, he thought he could see her in perspective; and what he saw he didn't like.

She had been picked for a life of sacred prostitution, this was to be the whole of her life, and she could never be removed from it. He had no part to play in this life, and by trying to find one he was, as the duke said, courting danger, not only for himself but for others. He had been infatuated with her and with an image he had constructed of her: of a pale china rose, nurtured in shade, something immensely precious and immensely fragile. But he saw her now as an object lovely but diseased, a rank thing growing unhealthily on top of a dunghill.

He didn't want the rank thing or the dunghill. He wanted very much to get away from both. He saw that to do so he must remain uninvolved and out of trouble for the rest of this dangerous year; and this he proposed to do.

Mei-Hua sent for him twice during that week. He did not respond. The third time, Little Daughter came heavily upon him while he was painting.

She said, '*Trulku*, the Mother has sent me for the last time.'

'It's useless, Little Daughter. You know it is useless.'

'She can force you if she wishes. She begs you not to make her force you.'

'Little Daughter – the Mother has no need of me.'

'She has a need, *trulku*.'

'You know it is unwise.'

'I know it is unwise. But come. I beg you also.'

So he went.

If she had been sulky, or haughty, or petulant, or in any way reserved with him, it would have been easy. But she was none of these things. She clutched him, weeping.

'Oh, Chao-li, Chao-li, you have deserted me.'

'I've been away, Mei-Hua. I've been busy.'

'You could have come. You didn't want to come. What have I done?'

'Mei-Hua – you know we shouldn't see each other. It's silly for us to go on.'

'What do you mean? Why do you say these things to me? You are cruel to say them, Chao-li. You don't mean them.'

He didn't know what else he could say. She had forced herself like a little kitten into his arms and was mewing in his ear.

He had not meant to say it, but he couldn't help himself. He blurted out, 'You didn't tell me about the abbot.'

'The abbot? What about the abbot?'

'That he was to spend three days here with you.'

Her head came up out of his shoulder and her lovely eyes looked at him in bewilderment.

'Not as the abbot, Chao-li. As the monkey. You saw.'

'It was the abbot who was here, not the monkey.'

'In his mask, Chao-li, and I in mine – I can't tell you about that. It is one of my mysteries,' she said, a little horrified. 'I am no longer of this world, then, and nor is he.'

'But you acted with him as people of this world act.'

'Yes, of course. We must,' she said, looking at him, wide-eyed. 'You mean – this worries you, Chao-li?'

He said helplessly, 'Mei-Hua, how often has this happened?'

'Every year since I was 13. It has to happen, Chao-li, as soon as I am able.'

'Oh, Mei-Hua, how can you? How can you bear to?'

'What do you mean? I don't understand you, Chao-li. The monkey loves me. He has always loved me.'

'You mean you don't mind? You like it?'

She said, bewildered, 'I don't know. Why not? It's very nice. Don't you like it? I don't understand you, Chao-li.'

He didn't think that she ever would. He looked for several minutes into eyes that were naïve and yet not naïve, that were young and yet not young, as though another, older intelligence were looking through them. He saw that she was a creature beyond any morality that he could understand.

He said gently, 'Mei-Hua, your life is here. Mine is not.'

'For now it is, Chao-li.'

'But not for always. At some time I must go. We must try not to love each other, or it will hurt too much to part.'

'Ah, Chao-li, there is no help for us. I told you before – it is written.'

He took her two arms. He said, 'Mei-Hua, nothing is written. You know who I am. You know I am not a *yidag*.'

'I know you are not a *yidag*.'

'Then what can be written?'

'That you will love me and help me and leave me. The Oracle has seen it.'

'Mei-Hua, she saw it because I dreamed it. You know where my dreams came from.'

'Nobody knows that, Chao-li.'

'They came from this room. We made them here.'

'If not here, somewhere else. If not this way, another way. You had to come, Chao-li. You cannot escape your destiny.'

He saw that she was a mistress not only of the answers but of the rules, and that she could change them at will. But he tried once more.

'Mei-Hua, you told me once you couldn't tell my destiny.'

'But I know my own, Chao-li, and you are part of it.'

'How can you know it?'

She smiled sadly. 'I have known it two hundred years.'

'Then tell me it.'

She looked him in the eyes and shook her head slowly.

'Not now. One day, perhaps. Do you love me?'

'I don't know.'

'You said once that you did.'

'Then perhaps I did.'

She released her arms and put them round her neck.

'Then for now take what is offered.'

He took what was offered. He did so for three weeks, three strange weeks, in which he couldn't tell if he loved her or hated her, and thought that perhaps he did both; for there was something repulsive to him in the knowledge that she would offer any man what she was offering him.

He saw the unbridgeable gulf between them, and tried to bridge it. And he began to experience then the urge that was later to become obsessional – the urge to know her and to possess her totally.

There was little enough time for him to do it then; for it was 27 September when he went back to her, and 7 October when the Chinese invaded. Houston learned nothing of it till the 20th. That was the day the governor sent for him.

Chapter 12

I

THROUGH July and August and September, the Governor of Hodzo had waited to be informed by Lhasa of the attacks upon him in the Chinese Press. No information on this point came. Some other information did; three items in particular convincing him that his doom was sealed, and a fourth, received on 19 October, formally underlining it.

The first item, sent shortly after the earthquake in August, was a dispatch from the office of the Regent, briefly pointing out that owing to threatening omens, and as a measure of prudence, provincial governors would no longer be informed of military dispositions outside their own areas. The governor had submitted this dispatch to the keenest scrutiny, although its essential feature, left by a careless clerk and plain for all to see, had struck him even before he had read the text. The essential feature was the distribution panel, printed in wood block type on a slip of paper that had become inadvertently stuck to the wafer. Besides the names of the *chef de cabinet* and the Head of Communications, War Office, were those of every provincial governor. Of the latter, only his own had been ticked.

The second item, received in mid-September, from the Head of Communications, War Office, informed him that a new *depon* had been appointed general-officer-commanding for the forces allocated to the defence of Hodzo. The military qualities of this new *depon*, whom the governor had known all his life, were such that at other times he would instantly have inferred that no enemy was expected. But these were not other times; as the third dispatch confirmed.

The third dispatch merely announced that the enemy had arrived: the Chinese had invaded with eight armies on 7 October. The governor would be informed if any special task was required of him.

And the fourth, received five days later, and in the Regent's own hand, had told him of this task. It was a heavy one, it was the traditional one of the governors of Hodzo; he must put himself between the gallant forces of the new *depon* and the Chinese invader; he must seek to parley to secure in any way open to him the safety of the unique treasure in his charge. The Regent expected that the governor would find the Chinese ready enough to parley with him; but gave no reason for this assumption. Without having to dot the i's or cross the t's, however, he enclosed some recent parings from the Dalai

445

Lama's fingernails, and strongly advised the governor to keep them by him in the days ahead.

The governor, a prudent man, did not spurn the parings. He placed them carefully in his charm box; but that same day set in train some other measures that he hoped would prove equally prophylactic for his wives and children.

The measures that the governor had been pondering stemmed from his recollections of the year 1904; in particular those concerning the men who had accompanied Colonel Younghusband to Lhasa. He had formed the opinion at that time that some racial characteristics of these men made them virtually unopposable. They possessed in a rare combination the apparently contradictory qualities of ruthlessness and humanity, unimaginativeness and ingenuity. In addition, an unusual objectivity enabled them to carry out the most complicated plans.

The governor did not have this opinion of his own people. A Lifetime of judging them had given him quite another opinion. He did not think that in time of danger he would trust his personal safety or that of his loved ones to such people. He knew which people he would sooner trust it to.

All this had occurred to the governor quite early in the summer; it had been later after his unsuccessful quest for the traitor at Yamdring that he had begun to toy with an extension of the idea.

The Chinese would come; he never doubted it after the second earthquake. And when they came they would find a friend at Yamdring; one who knew the value of the treasure, and doubtless exactly where it was.

This treasure had to be hidden. That was the governor's starting point. Where should it be hidden? To hide it in the monastery, or to bury it in the grounds would scarcely serve the purpose. For whoever knew where it was now would also know where it would be hidden.

What then?

Then the treasure must be removed from the monastery.

To this there was an immediate objection. The treasure was the personal property of the abbess. It could never be physically removed from her. To remove the treasure would indeed mean removing the abbess also; which was quite unheard of.

Quite unheard of, the governor repeated to himself; surprised, however, by his lack of emphasis.

He sent for his priest.

Under what circumstances could the abbess leave the monastery?

The priest grew very grave. History had so far produced no circumstances that had led the abbess to leave the monastery.

Under what circumstances could the abbess *not* leave the monastery?

The priest grew graver still, for he hadn't an idea. He consulted the Kangyur. He consulted the Tengyur. Then he consulted the principal commentaries on these works. He went back to the governor.

No specific prohibition was laid down restricting the movements of the Good Mother of Yamdring.

Such movements were, however, he assured the governor, quite unheard of.

The governor thanked him. He wrote two letters, one to the abbot of Yamdring, the other to its *trulku*.

Houston had gathered most of the governor's intentions before he was quite drunk; and just at the point when the room began to dance before his eyes, took the precaution of writing himself a memo. He did this on the back of the map the governor had given him.

He had to proceed in the direction of Chumbi; this was the valley that led most directly into Sikkim and India, and the traditional one to which nobles fled in the event of trouble. The Chinese would know this, so speed and secrecy in the matter of route were essential.

He would be making the journey with the abbess, the treasure, Little Daughter, the other Europeans, the governor's three wives and children, and a light escort. The governor could not tell him how much of a start he would have on the Chinese; perhaps as much as a week. At the moment their right flank was thought to be approaching northern Hodzo. How long it would be opposed by the new *depon* with his five twelve-pounders, his collection of ancient Lewis guns and his 1911 strategy, was a matter for speculation. The governor preferred to rely more on his own powers as a negotiator to win time; that it would be won for Houston and his party and not for himself, however, was not in doubt. Of his own personal survival he had no hope whatever.

'Drink up, *trulku*. There is no one to leave it to.'

Houston, already drunk, drank up. The whole household was drunk. The bearers who had brought him were drunk. He could hear them breaking things in another room. The governor's three wives were drunk; they sat in a lugubrious line just out of earshot of the two men who lay on facing couches, a stack of bottles between them.

There had already been a number of scenes concerning the amount of luggage and the number of servants the wives could take with them; and the governor suddenly bethought himself of a fresh source of trouble.

He said, leaning over between the two couches, and carelessly spilling arak into his boots on the floor, '*Trulku* – another matter. Shave their heads. Get it done at the monastery before you leave. And drug them first or it will never be managed.'

Shave heads, Houston wrote. *Drug first*.

'And no finery on the journey. See they wear common travelling robes. Vanity,' said the governor, lying heavily back again, ' – it destroys us all. It is the way of Karma, *trulku*.'

'Of Karma, Excellency?'

'Of Karma. I will tell you a story. Just one year and a half ago, *trulku*, I wished to retire . . .'

It was two o'clock in the morning before he left, a nightmarish, drunken departure in heavy frost, made memorable by a single touching moment; for at the very last, amid a hideous confusion of wailing wives and lurching servants, he had spotted that the governor's youngest wife was not in place, and had himself stormed into the house to seek her out.

It took him some little time to do so, for he passed the room twice, hearing and seeing nothing, so still were they. In all that house, with its butter lamps guttering and doors slamming and servants runnings, there was only one calm spot, the governor's private chapel, and here he found her, holding her husband's hand and looking into his face.

The governor was not aware for a moment of Houston standing over him, for he was kneeling, with his back to the door, but he looked up presently, a smile of rare delight on his face. 'She wishes to stay with me,' he said.

He shook his head. He laboured slowly to his feet, raising his wife with him, and then he kissed her hands, one after the other, and her forehead.

'Go, my child,' he said. 'Go now.'

Houston took her arm. The girl made no resistance. She didn't look back at the governor; but Houston did, just as he left, raising an arm in farewell. The governor raised one back to him. His little thin cat mouth was imperturbably shut and his slit eyes appeared to be smiling, but tears were streaming steadily from them.

2

Houston left Yamdring on the morning of 25 October, in the dark, still with an abominable hangover; setting off from the jetty before the village was astir with a party of twenty-seven people and sixteen horses in four large skin boats. Planks had been laid for the horses, and their hooves muffled; they were hobbled as soon as they embarked, and within half an hour, without noise or confusion, the small fleet was away.

By daylight they had reached the rapids at the foot of the lake. They disembarked here. The abbess was carried ahead in her curtained palanquin, the others followed on horseback or foot, the oarsmen, two to each boat, carrying on their heads the light craft the two miles to clear water.

The lake emptied into a small fast stream which shortly collected a number of tributaries to form a broad racing river. Within an hour they were afloat on it.

The river route had been suggested by the governor, and although more circuitous than by land had the advantage of by-passing all centres of habitation – to the governor's mind a very real one; for mindful of the spy at Yamdring and the likelihood of others in the country, his idea was for the party simply to disappear into the blue. There were many points at which they could leave the river; it would be for Houston to pick one.

Houston thought of this as he studied his scribbled jottings on the back of the map in the late afternoon. They had long since left the snug Yamdring valley and had come into a wild desolate country. The waterfalls on the mountain-sides were frozen, the tracks treacherously glazed, peaks lost in grey fog; it would be snowing up there.

The farther they went, the less he liked it. It was bitterly cold, the horses becoming restive, the governor's shaven wives and two young children, huddled in his own boat, incessantly moaning. He looked about him. The boats were proceeding in single file, his own leading, making excellent if meretricious progress in the fast river. Behind, in the second boat, the abbess's palanquin stood like a hearse, curtains fluttering in the strong breeze. No horses had been embarked on her craft, and insufficiently weighted, it was dancing dangerously on the white water.

Houston was by now stone cold sober and the situation struck him as little short of lunacy. Because the governor had carried in his mind for forty years the mistaken impression that the British were all of them men of action and resource, he had chosen him to lead the party. Because he was drunk he had accepted. But he was not drunk now. It struck him as merely incredible that anyone who knew him – Ringling, his brother – should regard him as a natural leader of men. None the less, they did. They had accepted his role as naturally as their own; and now the experts of the expedition, the boatmen, the guards, were looking to him for orders.

Chilled and worried, he sat over the map in the failing light.

'Ringling.'

'Sahib.'

'Do the boatmen know this country?'

'No, sahib. They have never been here.'

'Do you know it?'

The boy studied the map for some minutes.

'No,' he said at length.

Houston grunted.

The boy said quietly, 'The boatmen are getting tired, sahib. Maybe someone else should take a turn.'

'Maybe,' Houston said, not bothering to consider the suggestion seriously. The oarsmen had been chanting at the beginning of the trip, but they had not chanted for some hours now, requiring all their skill and concentration to keep the boats from overturning. He did not fancy the chances of anyone else at this work.

It had been the governor's suggestion that they should proceed without stopping for the first twenty-four hours of the trip, to put themselves beyond a caravan route that ran laterally from east to west across the river. But the governor had not seen this dangerous water with its submerged rocks and unpredictable currents.

Houston made a decision, his first, and at once felt a curious lightening of his spirits.

'We'll stop for the night,' he said. 'Tell them to keep a lookout for somewhere to pull in.'

The light was going fast. It was quite dark again before the solid black walls rushing past on either side began to show a crumbling of indentations. The bowman reached with his boathook, and eventually caught, and jumped in the icy water and grounded them, manœuvring the boat nimbly so that the others could follow.

They lit lamps and reconnoitred.

They had pulled on to a semi-circular rocky beach. Above, easy toe-holds led to a number of caves.

'A bear has been here,' one of the boatmen said.

A party of guards cautiously investigated several of the caves. They found further evidence of the bear; but no bear.

They lit fires in two of the caves with rhododendron wood (the abbess and Little Daughter with one cave to themselves); and blanketed the horses and staked them behind a boulder on the beach.

Within minutes butter was being churned for tea, the rhododendron flaring in the draught of air, and the party thawing in the orange blaze. Houston, sour and oppressed, ate briefly, and went to turn in.

The corporal of the guard came to him as he got his feet in the bag.

'I have picketed the men, *trulku* – four will watch for two hours at a time.'

'Good.'

'And the Mother will see you now.'

Houston got his feet out of the bag. He put on his fur jacket and went guiltily out into the bitter blackness – for he had given her scarcely a thought all day – and climbed to the upper cave. Two guards with rifles squatted miserably at its mouth. He found the pair of them still eating, on the wool wrapped bales containing the leather sacks.

'Oh, Chao-li, you have been so long. I thought you would never come. Isn't it marvellous?'

'Marvellous,' Houston said.

'It's the most wonderful day of my life. I can't remember anything so wonderful. Chao-li, don't you think I could move about a little in the boat? Must I stay in the palanquin all the time? My veil is secure.'

She had worn the heavy silk veil all day and she was sitting with her back to the cave mouth now so that none could see her.

He caught Little Daughter's warning glance.

'Not yet, Good Mother. Perhaps when we leave the river.'

'Tomorrow?'

'Perhaps,' he said.

He climbed back, chilled and depressed, the arak still in his system, and took off his boots and crawled in again, and slept, heavily.

It was snowing slightly when he turned out; but his spirits were perversely raised. They had made, it was a fact, excellent progress the previous day. Perhaps it was, after all, possible to let someone else have a go at the oars. He decided to try, and after an hour or two, when the early confident chanting had died away, put other men to the task.

He tried one boat at a time, and though they wobbled a bit and progress was slowed, there were no catastrophes. The boatmen chanted again when they took over.

For most of that day (and for years after) their plaintive cries rang in his ears.

> *'Oh, Lord Buddha, lighten our load . . .'*
> *'Oh, Lord Buddha, help with our task . . .'*
> *'Oh, Boundless One, we need your strength . . .'*
> *'Oh, Buddha, Lord, we call to you . . .'*

Perhaps the Boundless One heard; perhaps the expedition was merely easing into a routine. The second day sped past with, for Houston, few of the strains of the first.

They shot the bridge before midday, passing swiftly beneath and seeing not a soul; and with this link with caravan routes and possible pursuers behind him, he began to feel a certain swelling confidence. Someone, after all, had to lead. It was not a duty calling for years of scouting experience; simply one of convenience so that one voice should speak and the rest follow. There was plenty of skilled assistance. Several of the guards had tracking experience, and all twelve of them were well-armed. He had merely to get them to the mountains of the south, and once there to pick a route to the east that would bring them from an unexpected angle into the Chumbi valley.

The snag was, as he realized that evening, that the hurtling river was now taking them in a direction well to the west. The map was a Tibetan one, very detailed in its information as to the location of communities of mountain and water devils, less detailed in purely geographic lore. Towards nightfall, when the river had emerged from its canyon-like tunnel into a broad, rock-strewn tundra, the sunset had lit up distant brick coloured peaks. Ringling thought he recognized one of them as Nanga Parbat, and another as Cho Oyu. The peaks were many miles ahead of them still; but mysteriously to the east. They should have been far to the west.

It seemed to be time to leave the river.

The boatmen remained with them that night, but in the morning collapsed their craft and set off overland to Yamdring. Houston watched them with some uneasiness. It would take them a couple of days to reach the caravan route (where the Chinese might then have reached); and in two days his own party could be well out of sight in the mountains. It was a risk, all the same. He had had to balance it against another, that of taking extra mouths with them into unknown country.

He had made the decision alone, and nobody had questioned it; but Houston questioned it then himself.

'May the Buddha guide your steps!' cried the boatmen as the parties diverged.

'And yours. Go slowly!' replied the guards.

It was the normal formula of leavetaking in Tibet. Houston hoped they would heed it; but had his doubts. It would take them a week, going overland, to get to Yamdring, and he had given them exactly a week's rations.

That was another decision he was questioning as he turned his horse to the distant peaks.

3

From the river bank the stretch of country facing them had appeared flat; but in less than an hour its true bature became plain. It was covered entirely, and very closely, by a series of wearying hillocks of sandy rock. The wind came up at ten o'clock, after they had been going four hours. It was a dry, cold, dust-laden wind, peculiarly hateful, and they took shelter in the lee of boulders and made tea and waited for it to die down.

The wind did not die down. It went on all day (stopping

abruptly at sunset and starting up again punctually at ten the next morning, as though some gigantic machine had been switched on and off in the mountains). They waited an hour, and went on, noses and mouths muffled and eyes goggled against the dry spray, their faces at first raw and then merely numb from the incessant blast. With the hearse-like palanquin in their midst they picked their way through the geological debris like a party of mourners in a valley of bones.

In the late afternoon, with the horses stumbling and sneezing miserably, and the governor's wives and children moaning again, he decided to camp, early. They got the tents up with some difficulty in the shelter of boulders, and Houston crawled into his own and lay there with eyes closed.

Ringling shook him presently.

'Sahib, come and see.'

He went out. The wind had dropped. In the vast uncanny stillness, a great red sun had appeared, arcing swiftly. The barren wilderness was suddenly alive, a glowing bed of fiery red, writhing and vibrating in the fast-changing angle of declension of the huge disc in the sky. He saw the others standing to watch, silent, red-tipped figures, immobile in a spectacle of unearthly stunning beauty.

The boy had not, however, called him out to admire the spectacle; he was pointing to the peaks, visible again, still distant – but to their right now, Nanga Parbat far to the west, Cho Oyu less so. They had passed them both.

On this day, 27 October, despite the dust and the depressing terrain, they had covered nearly forty miles.

'We can go in the mountains now, sahib,' the boy said.

By noon the following day, they were in the foot hills. They camped that night in the shelter of a frozen waterfall. There was no wood to burn, and they cooked with butter lamps. The cold was intense, but Houston felt it less than on the outward trip, for on the governor's advice he was wearing under his clothes a shift of silk.

They were on the move early, before it was light; and it was

455

still not quite light when the first accident occurred. Four horses had passed over the spot when the track suddenly gave; the fifth (with, as it happened, Wister tied to it) simply disappeared. The following horse pulled up sharply, but the preceding one was dragged backwards and fell in a flurry of limbs, hindlegs into the gap.

They had been riding roped together, and the guards were quickly taking the strain. The horse that had fallen completely had broken both forelegs; they dragged it, whinnying and threshing with pain out of the crevasse (Wister, comatose for the past couple of days, no whit the worse) and cut it loose. The other animal, uninjured, climbed out itself.

The injured horse was quickly destroyed, the guards licking their lips as they hacked the carcase into manageable loads. The ropes were retied, and the horses, unmounted, led across a different section.

Horse steaks, somewhat underdone, were on the menu that night.

As near as they could manage they were going due east, but with insufficient altitude and surrounded on all sides by a jumble of mountains, found it hard to get their bearings. From time to time in the first couple of days, Ringling thought he identified peaks; but on the third when the vagaries of the passes had taken them in all directions and rather to the north than to the east, had to confess himself beaten.

He confessed this towards noon as they were proceeding along a broad defile; and shortly afterwards they saw the monastery. It was a tiny place perched like a bird's nest in the angle of two sheer rock faces far above them, approached evidently by a flight of rock steps that began at some point beyond their line of vision.

Houston weighed up the chances as they stopped to eat. Sited so far from any caravan route or village, it was plainly a retreat for mystics. It seemed unlikely that such a remote community would have any frequent or regular business with the outside world. He decided to chance it.

He moved the party back down the defile out of sight of the

monastery. He sent a couple of guards up to it with a request for the loan of guides. He sent Ringling to watch the guards.

By three o'clock the boy had not returned, and Houston found himself in something of a quandary. They were in an unsuitable spot for camping the night. It would be dark in an hour or so. There had been some other spots that he had marked as suitable.

He sent two more guards after Ringling.

They met on the way, and all returned together. The boy was puzzled. The ascent had evidently been more difficult than it looked. He had only been able to see the latter half of it, for an overhang was in the way. One of the guards seemed to have injured himself; the other one had helped him up the steps. He had waved to them, and was sure they must have seen him, but they had not waved back. He had seen the uninjured one come out of the monastery after some time with a couple of-orange-robed monks, and they had been pointing, evidently indicating a route. They had gone back into the monastery, but although, mindful of the coming dark, he had waited as long as he could, no one had emerged again.

'Didn't you call to them?'

'No, sahib, they knew where I was.'

'Maybe they couldn't see you. They might have lost the direction on the way up.'

'Maybe.'

'Yes,' Houston said.

He knew the guards would not have lost their direction, and he knew why the boy had not called. He would not have called himself. After days of hiding, and particularly since sighting the monastery, an oppressive silence had fallen on the party. Even the governor's children had stopped their snuffling.

Houston didn't know quite what to make of this. If the climb were as difficult as it sounded, the guards were unlikely to return in the dark. There was no point in waiting; he must either go on or go back. He turned the party round and went back down the defile.

Although the light was failing with every minute, he let a

couple of suitable spots go by and picked a third because it was protected by a little promontory of rock that commanded the track. Beyond the promontory was a hollow with scattered boulders. He camped there, posting half the guards on the promontory, and the rest back along the track. The cold was so bitter that he knew they would not be falling asleep in it, so he made no arrangement for reliefs.

He didn't think he would be sleeping very much himself that night.

4

There was no point in getting the party out of sleeping bags into the bitter chill until they were ready to move; so though he turned out himself at dawn, he let them sleep on. He had tea, and sent out an urn to the guards on the promontory, and when they had drunk it, swapped round the shifts so that those along the track could warm themselves, too. He sat in his tent, licking the tsampa from the bottom of his mug, and tried to decide what to do.

The dirty grey light was brightening outside. He thought he would give it till eight o'clock, and if nothing happened, move on, leaving two men to wait and to follow them with news.

But soon after seven something did happen; a thin, distant clamour on the air, a gong sounding in the monastery.

Houston walked back along the defile; he found the pickets very nervous, two men watching the monastery from behind a boulder.

'Any movement up there?'

'Some monks have been out for water, *trulku*.'

'No sign of your comrades?'

'Not yet.'

The steps, he realized suddenly, continued above the monastery; he had not seen this in the afternoon light. He realized it now only because an orange-robed figure appeared on the clifftop and began to descend slowly with a pitcher. He watched

458

the figure disappear behind the monastery. It did not appear again.

'Is there another entrance at the back?'

'There must be, *trulku*. That is where the monks have come from. Nobody has come from the front yet.'

Houston watched for some minutes longer, and walked back. He had gone only a few yards when one of the men ran after him. He returned.

Three figures had emerged from the back of the monastery and were climbing the steps; two orange figures, one dun-coloured; one of the guards he had sent up.

'Has he looked down here yet?'

'None of them have.'

The figures mounted slowly.

'Should we call, *trulku*?'

'No,' Houston said. 'No, don't call. Keep out of sight. We're leaving now.'

Something was very seriously wrong. As he walked back along the track, his face carefully scanned by the guards posted along it, he tried frantically to think what to do. The man evidently did not wish to give their position away. They had to move away from this spot, fast. Where? The track backwards led nowhere. They had been lost in it for two days, a twisting, boulder-strewn defile. It occurred to him that it was not a bad position to defend if he had to defend it. But he didn't want to defend it; he wanted to get away from it. It also occurred to him that the Chinese might be moving up in their rear, and that this might explain the reason for the mysterious delay.

'Everybody out, please. We're moving now.'

'They're back, are they?' Hugh said with relief.

'Not yet. We've just spotted them going up the cliff for a better look.'

'Aren't you waiting for them, then?'

'We can get organized meanwhile.'

He didn't want to explain anything. He didn't know what there was to explain; merely a profound feeling in his bones that they must not be caught here in a confusion of tents and bedding, and that he must not himself spread panic.

He thought he would go stark raving mad at the slow motion quality that descended on them suddenly. Endless hours seemed to elapse while the tents were struck and bedding rolled and equipment packed on the horses. But he bethought himself in this hiatus of something else the governor had suggested, and moved over to the palanquin.

He said, 'Little Daughter, the Mother wished to leave her palanquin and ride in the open. She can do so now.'

'She cannot, *trulku*. She cannot ride. She has never ridden a horse.'

'I will help her.'

'No, *trulku*, this is not wise. It is my duty to help her, not yours.'

He said in her ear, 'Little Daughter, *you* must go in the palanquin, and the bags must come out. She will ride your horse. It is for her safety.'

Little Daughter's face went stiff and her mouth trembled. But she dismounted without another word.

The guards turned their heads as the abbess stepped out of the palanquin. She was blind in her heavy veil, and Houston helped her to mount, and adjusted the stirrups and held her gloved hand while the two cloth-bound bales were strapped to the horse.

She said clearly, 'Is there some trouble, *trulku*?'

'No trouble, Good Mother. We are getting guides. It will be an easy ride today. I will be beside you.'

'I know it,' she said, squeezing his hand.

The governor's wives had put up their own veils against the wind, and with fur hats and earmuffs in place were indistinguishable at a few paces from the abbess.

'All right,' Houston said. 'Let's go.'

They had to pass within sight of the monastery; there was no help for that. But nothing moved in the now sinister little eyrie high on its mountain perch.

Hugh came up beside him.

'What about the fellows you sent up to the monastery? Aren't you leaving anyone to tell them?'

'There's only one way we can go. They'll have to follow.'

'There isn't anything wrong, is there?'

'I don't know.'

'What do you mean?'

'I mean I don't bloody well know,' Houston said.

Hugh dropped back.

Ringling moved up.

'You are not leaving anyone to wait for the guards in the monastery, sahib?'

'No.'

The boy rode silently beside him for some minutes. He said softly, 'I have two pistols, sahib. I have them under my cape. One is for you.'

'All right.'

'I will keep close to you, sahib.'

'All right,' Houston said again.

The idea seemed to be catching on.

They had gone for perhaps a quarter of an hour when the voices began calling them from the hills. Because the monastery was on the right, and the guards had gone to the right, they looked to the right; it was a minute or two with the sound ricocheting deceptively from side to side of the defile before they realized the cries were coming from the left.

They halted to listen, and Houston found the procession bunched closely in round him.

It was possible to see that the cries were coming from the two monks and the guard; now far to the left on the opposite side of the defile.

'What are they shouting?'

Nobody could tell what they were shouting, the sound distorted in the hills.

'Should we call to them, sahib?' Ringling said.

'All right,' Houston said, seeing there was no point now in silence. 'Tell them to come down here.'

The party on the hilltop did not come down.

'They are waving, *trulku*. They are waving us to come to them.'

'How? Where is the track?'

Nobody could tell that, either.

He sent a guard trotting ahead to see if he could find a track. They waited, bunched closely together. From behind them, the faint reverberations of the monastery gong began to sound again in the thin air.

Hugh said, 'How the hell did they get up there? There doesn't seem to be any way down from where they were.'

'Maybe there is a wall of rock bridging one side of the valley with the other, sahib,' Ringling said. 'It would be easier than climbing down. We have seen it before.'

They had seen it before. They had seen every kind of geological freak in the past three days.

The guard trotted back.

'There is a kind of track, *trulku*, very rocky. It is a hard climb.'

'Where does this main track go to?'

'There is a rock ridge ahead of us. The track goes on underneath it. There is a bad fall of rock there.'

There seemed to be a kind of sense in this. There would be little point in the guard climbing dangerously down to lead them away from the rock fall when he could do so with ease merely by walking over the rock bridge to a point where he could see them coming.

The party on the hilltop had stopped shouting now. They had stopped waving, too. They must have seen the guard ride out to look for the track, and now they stood and waited; they had shouted enough only to attract attention.

'What about it?' Hugh said.

Houston turned to the guard. 'This rock fall – how bad is it? Can we get past?'

'I don't know, *trulku*. I don't know if it is blocked farther on.'

'Maybe that's what they were shouting about,' Hugh said.

'Maybe.'

462

Maybe it was. He couldn't see very much else for it.

He said with a good deal more cheer than he felt, 'Well, let's have a go.'

5

As the guard had said, it was a hard climb. To spare the horses, only the women remained mounted. The palanquin bearers cursed as they stumbled with the weight of Little Daughter from one ice-glazed rock to the next.

From time to time, with outcrops of rock between them, they lost sight of the three figures silhouetted against the skyline. They lost sight of them once for a quarter of an hour. Houston called a halt for a rest. He found himself alone on a slab with the abbess on horseback beside him and Ringling at his heels.

'It will snow soon, sahib.'

'Yes.'

There was a grey density in the air. He couldn't tell if it had become warmer. He was sweating under his fur jacket, the breeze hissing on the rocky hillside.

'The track is not blocked, sahib.'

'It's hard to see from here.'

'It is not blocked.'

'*Trulku.*'

'I am here, Mother.'

'What time is it?'

'Nine o'clock.'

'I was listening for the third gong. I forgot we must have passed the monastery miles ago.'

He looked at the heavy veil, blinding her, and then across to the monastery, facing him very plainly now, not a mile away across the gorge.

He said, 'When should it have sounded, Good Mother?'

'At eight-thirty, half an hour after the second, of course.'

'What are the first two?'

'The first for waking and prayers, the second for breakfast.

They will be praying again now,' she said, and fell into a little prayer herself, on horseback.

He saw the boy's eyes upon him, wide with alarm; and looked down upon the track that they had come up, and imagined what kind of panic there would be if he turned them round and went back down it.

He said, 'We'd better move on again.'

The watchers were still there, waiting, when they came out from the overhang, some hundreds of feet above them still.

The snow started shortly after; the path began to disappear under the white blanket. The abbess's horse slipped.

'*Trulku*, we should rest again. The horse is tired.'

'Later, Mother. In a few minutes we can rest.'

'The poor animal is sweating. He has the weight of the bags, also. I must protect all animals, *trulku*.'

'When we get to the top, Mother. It is dangerous to stop here.'

'Dangerous for the horse?'

'Very dangerous for the horse.'

'Very well.'

He thought the veil of snow had blanked out the watchers and that they must be waiting there, at the top. But they were not. The party reached the summit, and looked about them, sweating and panting.

'Down below, sahib. See, they are waving.'

From the crest the hill swooped down again; it fell easily into a broad bare saddle of land. Beyond the saddle it fell again, very steeply, a boulder-strewn slope plummeting down to a river, a thin white foaming strand half a mile below.

The two monks and the guard had walked down into the saddle; their tracks were just discernible in the thickly falling snow.

'What the hell are they playing at?' Hugh said.

'Maybe they had to go ahead to show the track before the snow wiped it out, sahib,' Ringling said.

'You think that's what it is?'

'I don't know, sahib.'

Houston didn't know, either. He would have been prepared to bet that the saddle was covered with turf; apart from two massive boulders, one at each end, the land was quite unbroken. It did not look to him as if there had been any particular track. It looked to him very unpleasantly as if men might be waiting behind the boulders and that he had been led into an ambush.

He said, 'We'll take a rest here.'

It was after ten o'clock. The breeze had dropped and the snow fell straight down, thickly and silently. The breath of the party hung in the air.

Hugh said, 'Shouldn't we get on while we can see the tracks?'

'Hugh, come here a minute, will you.'

'What is it?'

He waited till Hugh was beside him. He said softly, 'Something funny is going on.'

'What do you mean?'

'The track below wasn't blocked. And there's something wrong in the monastery. Their normal routine has been interrupted. Apparently there should have been a third gong for prayers. There wasn't.'

'What do you think – '

'I think these jokers have been leading us by the nose all the morning.'

'Why for God's sake?'

Houston didn't answer. He looked down at the boulders.

Hugh licked his lips. 'How about sending someone ahead to see?'

'What would be the point?'

'We could get down again bloody quick.'

'No,' Houston said wearily. 'No, we couldn't. You can't see the track with the snow. It's too dangerous, anyway. They'd half kill themselves in the rush.'

'What do you want to do, then?'

'I don't know.'

'Are you sure of this?'

465

'No, I'm not sure. I've not been sure all the morning,' Houston said. 'That's why we're here.'

'Where are we?'

Ringling had been listening to the quiet conversation in English. He said sombrely, 'We're near the caravan route, sahib. That is the Li-Chu river. I know it. We should be across it and much farther south.'

Hugh said, in the pause, 'Do you think if we just turned quietly round, no panic, and went back down again...'

'You wouldn't do it quietly,' Houston said. 'And who are you supposed to be fooling? If the Chinese are here, you won't be fooling them. If they're not, what's the point of going down again? We've got to get across that river.'

Hugh licked his lips again.

He said, 'Do you think they *are* here?'

'There's only one way to find out,' Houston said. He saw that the others were watching them intently. 'Better get back in place now. There's no point in spreading panic.'

He waited till Hugh had done so, and at once, without allowing himself time for second thoughts, for no alternative seemed to be offered, gave the signal to move. They moved quite silently, in thick snow. Houston found himself shaking in every limb; for despite what he had told his brother, he thought he was by now pretty sure. If his little contretemps in the alley in Kalimpong had taught him anything it was that when all the signs pointed to a certain conclusion it was as well to accept it. The signs had been pointing all morning to a conclusion he had not wished to accept. And they were still pointing now. For the two monks and the guard had stopped waving, and they had stopped moving. They stood quite still and watched, as men whose task was completed.

He had been wearing his goggles, but the snow was falling so thickly that he pushed them up from his eyes. All the same he sensed rather than saw, in the white swirling air, the men who suddenly appeared, the small, stocky apparitions in padded olive uniforms cradling like children in their arms their automatic weapons.

Because he had been watching for them, he thought he was the first to notice; and yet the phantoms seemed to materialize in an incredible kind of slow motion; the bulky figure on horseback moving quite casually forward, loudhailer raised to his lips; the eight boatmen from whom they had parted five days ago, emerging from the steam-coloured landscape like well-remembered wraiths from a dream.

'My friends, we have come to find you!' cried the horseman in Tibetan. 'See, your comrades are here, waiting. We will not harm you. Stop and throw down your guns. We are your friends!'

What happened then, although it happened in the space of seconds, had about it the kind of elaborate spontaneity of some minutely rehearsed ballet. The men holding the palanquin dropped it. Little Daughter tumbled out into the snow. A body of the Chinese, perhaps ten or twelve, moved towards her. One of the guards dropped to one knee and fired. The Chinese brought up their little cradled toys and fired back; a harmless pop-popping in the thin air like the distant sound of a two-stroke motor-cycle. Suddenly, but quite slowly, everybody was firing; the protagonists dropping to their positions in the swirling snow, the little make-believe weapons sneezing dryly, the whole evolution so solemnly unreal that Houston lost all sense of fear, and took up his own cue as if he had been waiting for it all his life.

He swung himself up on the horse behind her. He dug in his heels and bent forward over the girl's back and set the horse's head to the river slope. He looked round once, and saw the horseman with the loudhailer pursuing him, and actually found himself laughing out loud with pure exhilaration. There had been no plan, no plan at all in his mind; he had acted in response to some gay, some irrepressible summons of the blood. But now the drop was approaching, and just at the last, seeing what it had not seen before, the animal jibbed; and Houston, seeing it in the same moment, jibbed also.

There was no kind of slope at all from the edge; the ground simply fell away quite sheer for fifty feet or more, and below, thickly studded with boulders, dropped only slightly less precipitously for another fifty before losing itself in the curtain of snow.

Between his legs, Houston could feel the girl's body rigid with fright, and felt his own arms go stiff as ramrods as he leaned back to slew the animal's head round.

But weight and momentum had done their work. With forelegs raised high like those of a rocking horse, and carrying on its back the abbess of Yamdring, the man from beyond the sunset and a fortune of three million pounds, the animal sailed sickeningly over the edge.

Chapter 13

I

THE horse did not touch for quite sixty feet. It touched and flew, and touched and flew, screaming with every breath; for a hindleg had snapped at the first impact, and a foreleg seconds later. Houston hung on, quite paralysed with fright. Because of the bales, one at each side, he could not get his legs down, he was up high like a jockey, and leaning so far forward against the girl that her head was buried in the animal's mane.

Despite its hideous injuries, the horse managed to remain upright, frantically dodging the enormous boulders that reared on every side; but could not dodge them all. A glancing blow on the breast slewed it round and then they were over, and rolling, the girl leeching to the horse, and Houston to the girl, so that all three, locked together, careered down the mountainside like some ungainly snowball.

The reins had become caught below Houston's elbow, and the animal's long hairy head was twisted round towards him, eyes rolling, yellow teeth snapping, from its mouth issuing a scream so human that Houston could not be sure it was not coming from the girl.

There was another blow, a dull stunning one to the neck, which stopped it screaming, and then a third – a blow so final that it brought a single great belch from the animal as all the air and all the life were driven from its body.

They had brought up on a slope like the side of a house, against a rock so razor-edged that the horse seemed almost to have been cut in two. A great gout of blood washed up out of it and spat back into Houston's face, and he lay in the snow, stupefied with shock, feeling the warm rivulets trickling down his neck. He saw a leg, which was his own, and another, which was not, and tried to kick it away.

He felt her then, the faintest of movements below him.

He had landed on his side with the horse still between his legs, and she was somewhere below. He twisted about and dug frantically, and found her fur hat, and tugged at it; but realized that it was caught below her chin and that he might be strangling her, and made a space for her to breathe instead.

She gasped for air, her veil off, her face deathly pale.

'Mei-Hua, don't struggle. Don't struggle. I'll get you out.'

He bore down, swinging one leg back off the horse and wrenching the other from beneath her, and managed to drag her half out. They lay back, panting in the churned-up snow, and he felt a dreadful lurch of vertigo; for it seemed to him that even lying back they were only a few degrees off the vertical. A good deal of row seemed to be going on above: a dull deadened row, the single-shot cough of rifles, the sneezing pop-pop of the automatic weapons, voices shouting. All about them now, the snow had begun to turn red.

'Mei-Hua, we can't stay here.'

She didn't answer, and he saw her face screwed up in pain.

'Are you hurt?'

'My foot is twisted.'

'Give me your hand.'

469

But when he stood to help her, he felt so like a fly upon a wall that he fell back again abruptly.

'Wait. Wait a minute. Rest fist.'

They rested for several minutes, and he tried again, feet planted deep in the snow and leaning backwards.

'Now.'

She cried out with pain and fright. 'Oh, no. No, Chao-li.'

'Don't look below. Look at me.'

'Chao-li, no, I can't. Please.'

'Mei-Hua, dearest,' he said weakly. 'We must get away from here. They can see the blood. Try again.'

She tried again. He turned her on her back, and on her front, holding first her arms and then her legs. The girl dug herself with terror into the snow.

'Mei-Hua, I am holding you. I won't let you go. Please, please, dearest . . .'

She was sobbing at the last attempt. 'Chao-li leave me alone. Leave me for a minute.'

'If the snow stops they will see us.'

'I can't help it.'

'Try again. We'll find another way.'

'There isn't any other way. I'll do it. Just leave me for a minute . . .'

But there was another way, and the instant he thought of it, he was climbing back the few feet to the horse. He sat in the sticky red mess and heaved at the ropes, and scooped out snow to get at the one underneath, and dragged both bales clear. Each bale was wrapped around with stout ropes which she could easily grasp, and he tied them together again, and spreadeagled her on them to distribute the weight, and lowered the sled to clear snow. It handled with ease, weighty enough to bed down a few inches and prevent it running away, wide enough not to plough in entirely.

Within minutes he had developed the technique to a degree of some proficiency, taking the strain with both arms, and shuffling down on his haunches, a brisk sideways shuffle of the backside giving sufficient lateral motion; and in this manner, with the abbess and her treasure, dropped in a gentle diagonal to the Li-Chu river.

The snow stopped at about midday, and the soldiers came over the edge soon after. Houston watched them from behind a boulder. He had not managed to get down to the river, but had taken cover some minutes earlier, aware that the snow was petering out and that he must allow for their most recent tracks to be covered. He could no longer see the red mess of the horse, but could not be sure that it was not visible from above.

The men were being lowered on ropes. He could see the officer with the loudhailer and several other horsemen directing operations from the clifftop. The shooting had stopped a long time before. The soldiers came down slowly and very cautiously, a dozen or so of them, with their automatic weapons. They began quartering the mountainside.

They found the horse soon after one o'clock, and the officer had himself lowered immediately. Houston saw them digging under the horse, and observed the officer's growing agitation as nothing came to light. The man had himself hauled up again, and seeing soon after the flash of binoculars, Houston had to get his head down. He kept it down for a couple of hours, hearing the occasional boom of the loudhailer, and the strange chattering of the groups of soldiers on the mountainside.

The snow started again at about three o'clock; but aware that a group of Chinese soldiers was no more than fifty yards above him, Houston did not dare to move again. He lay with his arms about the girl on the two bales, listening.

'What are they saying?'

'Some wish to return but the others say they have no orders and will not be pulled up. They are roped together but not from above.'

He thought after a while that the voices had passed to their right, but, afraid that the snow might suddenly stop, he still could not nerve himself to move; which was just as well, for minutes later he heard voices immediately below him, evidently of another party which had come down more directly, and was now traversing.

He lay, feeling the girl trembling in his arms; both of them on their sides facing each other, the snow settling heavily upon them. The voices passed below them. He heard the two groups calling to each other, and then a third group, and slowly all of them receded. Soon after the snow stopped again.

He could see very clearly how near the men below had come – the deep footprints not twenty yards away – and thanked providence for his decision not to move, and lay silently with the girl, waiting.

At four o'clock (breathing on his watch to clear the ice) he heard the loudhailer going again, and chancing another look, saw that ropes were being lowered to draw the men back up the cliff face. By half past, all were up, and there was no further sight or sound of the party. He stayed where he was. It would be dark in half an hour. It must be obvious to the Chinese that they were on the slope somewhere. The bales had been taken from the horse, and there had been insufficient time for them to get down to the river. He thought that if he were the Chinese officer he would himself have called off the search and quietly stationed observers to watch.

He waited till the light was almost gone before cautiously getting to his knees behind the boulder and working his limbs to restore the feeling. In the bitter, creeping cold the girl had gone into a sort of doze and he did not wake her yet. He thought she might as well enjoy what oblivion she could while she could.

He gave it a few minutes more, until he could no longer pick out the division between the clifftop and the sky, and shook her.

'Mei-Hua, we're going to move again now.'

She came to with a little moan, and he took her hands and removed the gloves and worked her fingers with his own.

'Can you feel with them?'

'I don't know. Where are we going?'

'Just down a little farther to the river. The soldiers have gone now. Can you hold on?'

The girl was not too clear what she could do or where she was. Her teeth were chattering violently. He spreadeagled her on the bale again, and waited a few minutes more until even the footprints in the snow were no longer distinguishable, and got moving.

The girl fell off at once.

The snow was freezing into ice now, and she slid gently, quite stiff like a fresh-killed salmon for several yards until she could dig her elbows in. He lowered the sled and got her on again, and thrust her wrists beneath the ropes and tied them there with the bight that he had been holding, and took a turn round his own wrists, and began shuffling down again at once, for the girl, supported by her wrists now, and feeling the pain in them, was protesting weakly, and there was nothing he could do to ease her except to get it over with quickly.

He had the strangest feeling of treading water and of moving quite automatically for there was no sensation in his backside and he could not feel himself touching the ground at all. His knees came up and his heels dug down, and in some way he was descending, diagonally, skirting the boulders and the short vertical drops.

The light went entirely after some minutes, and in the still, freezing evening he heard a distant volley of firing, and took it to be a signal recalling the observers on the clifftop, and soon after heard a series of single shots, two, three, four, and another one seconds later, five, evidently the men replying; and at the same time, feeling some return of sensation in his limbs, an old familiar nagging ache, thought he might take a rest. He dug his heels in, and slewed the sled sideways, and lifted her up off her wrists and kissed her. She was moaning softly into the cloth of the bales, her face icy cold against his lips.

'Oh, Chao-li, Chao-li.'

'You've been very brave, little rose. It won't be long now.'

He didn't know what it would not be long *until*; for even in the dark he could see the pale spuming line of the river and

473

hear its muffled hiss. It was going very fast. Until now it had seemed goal enough merely to get to it.

He felt her shuddering in his arms; and had a sudden vision of the nightmarish day through her eyes – the heart-stopping tumble down the icy mountain, the sudden exposure to hostility after the years of veneration and love and protection. How soon the outside world had ceased to be marvellous!

He had eaten nothing since his mug of tsampa at dawn, and couldn't be sure that the girl had eaten even that. He thought he had better see what steps he could take to cross the river while he still had strength, and in a few minutes, kissing her gloved wrists before tying them once more, set off again.

The hissing of the river swelled into a soft, deepening roar as they dropped slowly down to it. It was evidently not at the full for a little beach was dimly visible, and through the flying spray he saw that large rocks were left uncovered.

He left her to lie on the bales on a gentle slope, and lowered himself down to the beach and stood there in the steady, rushing roar, stamping his feet and beating his gloved hands as he looked about him. He had seen immediately that he was not going to swim across; the far bank was out of sight, and the spray, lashed viciously back from the rocks, gave a discouraging indication of the current. The tops of the uncovered rocks were, however, clearly visible, and a little farther on a line of them seemed to stretch across like stepping stones.

He picked his way along the beach to the line of rocks, but before reaching them thought he heard her calling, and turned back.

He was climbing the slope when he heard the voice again, and went flat on his face and lay there, for the voice was not Mei-Hua's, but a man's.

He prayed that she would not sit up and give away her position, and lay with his heart choking, trying to distinguish, above the roar of the river, which direction the man was coming from. He heard a clink of stone from his right, and got his head up cautiously, and thought he saw something, a vague moving blur against the pale river; and a moment later looked again, and spotted it quite clearly this time; an angular figure, very tall, moving in a curious jogging motion, and he screwed up his eyes and blinked a few times, and saw what it was. It was a man on a horse. He was moving quite slowly along the beach, his head thrown back to look up at the hillside. With his heart thumping, Houston took off his glove and reached inside his clothing and drew out his silver knife and opened the blade.

It didn't seem possible – unless the man had been addressing his horse – that he could be alone, and Houston didn't know how much use his little knife would be to him in the circumstances. He held himself ready to use it, however, and as the horseman passed directly beneath him, turned very gently on his side.

The man called again, then, just as he nerved himself to do it.

'Sahib!' he cried softly. 'Sahib! Are you there, sahib?'

2

The boy had got a little bag of tsampa with him, and they ate it dry as they moved briskly along. He had passed on his journey a stretch of river that he thought might be negotiable, and he led the horse hurriedly towards it along the beach, the abbess and the bales mounted, Houston stumbling beside him.

The shots Houston had heard had not been a code of signals, but the Chinese firing after Ringling and one of the guards who had escaped with him. Ringling had given the man his second pistol (and was now regretting it, for he thought the guard had been hit and recaptured) and they had each shot a horseman and mounted a horse and bolted.

The boy knew this river: he was certain the Chinese would not come down the mountain after them, for there was a bridge a few miles along, and they would cross there and spread out to pick them up at the other side. It was therefore a matter of urgency for them to cross as soon as possible and make what speed they could before the Chinese were in a position to cut them off.

He had a reasonable working knowledge of the country beyond, and thought he would have a better one as soon as they spotted the caravan route; it was along this route that the Chinese had come and picked up the boatmen and taken control of the monastery. They had been waiting in the monastery for two whole days, with pickets on the cliffs above and a mounted squadron out investigating the best site for an ambush; for they had wanted the abbess and the treasure out of the defile; they had wanted them in an open space where the slow-moving palanquin would be within their sights, and there would be no possibility of the abbess and her treasure being spirited away.

The old wily man in Hodzo had thought of that; he had thought of a number of ingenious measures to allow the abbess to escape. But he hadn't, it occurred to Houston as he stumbled miserably along in the spray-drenched darkness, thought of what was to be done after the escape. Something had had to be left to the heir of Colonel Younghusband.

It was getting on for eight o'clock before they found the negotiable stretch of river; the banks widened here, the beach was broader, the water, evidently, shallower. Massive rocks stood out of the bed, and about their tops was wreathed the debris of the spring floods. The boy anchored himself by rope to the horse and waded out. Houston glimpsed him, through the spray pulling down a branch from a rock and trying to plumb the depth. He returned, soaked.

'Is it deep?'

'Very deep, and very fast.'

'What's to be done?'

'I could try with the horse, to get a line across.'

They worked out a system of signals: two pulls for Houston to heave him back, three that he had landed safely at the other side, four that he was ready to heave them across; and four also from Houston that he was ready to be heaved.

The boy tied the rope in a bowline round himself, and

exchanged places with the abbess, averting his eyes as she dismounted.

'Good luck!'

The boy slapped the horse without answering and rode straight into the river. He went in quickly before the horse could express an opinion, and Houston lost him almost at once. The rope jumped and quivered so much in his hands he couldn't tell what frenzied signals might be intended, and, swearing once, began a half-hearted heave back before he felt in his hands three slow, strong tugs, and a minute later four more.

The girl had been sitting on a little rock, huddled in her cloak and shivering violently in the clammy chill. Houston got her to her feet and roped her about the waist, and himself also, and allowing several yards of rope in between so that they would not be dragged down, attached the bales.

'We must cross now, Mei-Hua.'

'I cannot swim Chao-li.'

'The horse will pull us. I will hold you,' he said, and kissed her, and while he was kissing her gave four tugs at the rope, and a moment later felt the drag, and held her as she fell, and then they were in the water.

The spray had been cold, but it had not the deathly bone-searching iciness of the river, and he heard her gasp and cry out at the appalling shock of it, and hung on to her grimly. It was impossible to tread water, the thrumming current carrying away his legs, and his arms, about the girl, powerless to keep him up. The roaring white water blinded and choked him, and he was under, the girl struggling in his arms, the rope about his middle pulling strongly. He felt the pair of them, locked together, turning over and over in the water, and the dull pain of limbs striking rock; and then he was on his feet, and off them again, and on his knees and dragging on the rough bottom, and they had made it. The girl was retching and spluttering and he tried to stand up to help her, but was dragged down again, the rope sawing and pulling at him from two directions, and he realized what had happened and cried

477

out to the boy with all his strength. The boy seemed to realize it himself a moment later, for the pressure from the bank eased, and the boy was beside him in the water, swearing, and going out beyond him, and the rope thrummed and came free, the bales releasing from whatever underwater obstruction had held them.

They took a few minutes, gasping and coughing, to wring out their clothes as best they could, and then the boy retied the bales on the horse, and Houston helped the abbess remount, and they were off again, teeth chattering in the freezing night.

The moon came out from behind mountains as they struck the caravan route, and the boy mounted a small hill for a reconnaissance before tackling it. He was back down again quickly.

'The soldiers are all about here, sahib. I saw their fires. We will have to keep going all night.'

They cut across the track, the boy going surely now, for he had travelled this country before, and went across rough hills before choosing, towards midnight, a secondary track, a mere gutter between high cliffs, but one that went due east.

Houston was by now almost out on his feet, and kept awake solely by the searing agony of fallen arches and wet clothes rubbing against sores. The insides of his thighs seemed to be quite raw. There was a sore across the back of his neck, and when he had leaned forward to ease it, he had raised another under his chin. He had tried walking bow-legged to ease the chafing at his thighs, and had produced two new sores where his boots rubbed his ankles. They seemed to be telegraphing him now from every point of his body, and he no longer tried to evade than, registering the sequence with a kind of ashen stoicism, and keeping, as it were a kind of count, for he had fallen into a belief that if one outpost of pain failed, the rest might fail, and that horrors of some new and less familiar kind would supervene.

The boy had been walking stolidly ahead with the bridle; but when the moon began to go again, he slowed, looking about him. The track had widened quite suddenly. He halted

478

them, and gave the bridle to Houston, and went on by himself with the coiled rope in the darkness.

Houston heard the girl moaning and trying to sit up on the horse, and he knew he must stir himself to catch her if she fell; but she sank back presently, eyes closed and teeth chattering, to the spot she had made warm on the horse's neck.

He was not himself any longer aware of the cold, so obsessed with his interior network of pain and the necessity of keeping it going while he stood still, and that he did not even at first hear the boy calling him, and was only conscious of it when stones began to fall about him. He looked up.

'Sahib! Can you see me, sahib?'

'Where are you?'

'Can you see anything at all?'

'No.'

The boy said nothing more, but he could hear him banging about faintly above, and presently a rope's end fell, and in a shower of ice and snow the boy came down it. He walked up and down in the track, looking upwards.

'There are caves here, sahib. We had better stop now. There is open ground a few miles ahead. We mustn't be caught on it in daylight.'

'How do we get up there?'

'By the rope. The abbess will never manage the other way. I will go up again and pull her.'

Houston didn't know how he would manage himself, but he was beyond further questioning, and merely, in a kind of nightmare, found himself doing as the boy instructed, helping the abbess off the horse, tying the rope round her waist, and hoisting her up while the boy, who had shinned back up again, pulled. He saw her limbs working feebly in the frozen undergrowth, and then lost her in darkness, following her progress only by the shower of snow-clumps and her soft moaning. And then the rope landed at his feet once more, and he tied it about his waist, and went up himself. It was steep but not impossible, with plenty of toe-holds and patches of strongly rooted spiny undergrowth, and only one smooth vertical face

479

below the cave itself, and he got his hands on the ledge, and with the boy pulling, and his own exhausted muscles making a last effort, rolled over and fell inside on his face.

He thought that he was dreaming, and that in the dream he had climbed out of a black and icy hell into some warm and radiant compartment of heaven; for the cave was bathed in a soft rosy light and he felt the breath of heat and aromatic smoke fanning towards him. The abbess was sitting over the fire, staring into its orange heart, her cloak open and steaming gently; and, too exhausted to get to his feet, and fearful that the vision would vanish unless he embraced it at once, he began to hobble towards it on his hands and knees, thrusting aside a clutching obstacle in his way.

'The rope, sahib. I must have the rope. There is the horse to be seen to.'

He felt the fumbling at his waist, but did not stop, and then he was there, and he reached for her and sank back into the marvellous softness of the rock floor, washed by wonderful waves of light, and gliding instantly away into them. Something was happening remotely to his limbs, and he opened his eyes after a moment and in the flickering glow observed the boy stumbling over him, dragging something, two large sacks. Sacks of what? Sacks of something important; sacks that gave him just then a feeling of completion; of knowing that all was right with the warm and gentle world that was drawing him so deliciously into itself once more.

3

Somebody was singing, and he was eating a meal of many courses, and he sat back savouring a new mouth-watering dish that had been placed before him, and awoke like that, very gradually, with his mouth still watering.

He lay for some seconds trying to place where he was. He was very hungry. He was very cold. He knew he had been dreaming and that he was still between two worlds, and he lay screwing up his eyes in the bleak grey light anxiously trying to retain the best of both of them; a certain snugness about his lower quarters in one, a delicious sensation of food and singing in the other. He realized quite suddenly that the food and singing were common to both worlds and that the singing was screaming and sat up in alarm and saw where he was.

The girl was sleeping across his legs. The fire was out. They were alone in the cave. The piercing screams rang out one after the other.

He came up fast off the floor, shifting the girl from his legs, in such a panic that he scarcely knew what he was doing. His first thought was that the boy had impaled himself in some way; had gone foraging for food and had cooked it and had tried to return up the rope and had hurt himself, and was lying out there, screaming; and as the thought flashed through his head, found himself at the cave mouth, peering out.

He saw the boy immediately. He was lying a little below, on a projection of rock a yard or two to the right. He was lying on his stomach, gazing intently through the undergrowth. He was not screaming. Somebody else was screaming. The screams rang out with terrifying clarity punctuated by a gurgling intake of breath that was in a way more horrifying still. At the same time, Houston was aware of other voices; of somebody laughing and of a conversation going on. He could not see where this was taking place, his view of the track obscured by undergrowth.

The boy had got the rope looped round him. Houston tugged it, and saw him look up and motion him back into the cave; and a few moments later he appeared inside himself, trembling and quite grey in the face with fear.

'Sahib, the Chinese! They are right below us. They have got a woman. They are hurting her.'

Houston could hear that. He thought the screams would drive him out of his mind. He pulled the boy to the back of the cave to get as far away from them as he could and they stared at each other, so distracted by the ghastly row that they could not speak.

The boy said at last, 'They've put all their kit in a cave below us, sahib, just to the left. I missed it in the dark. They're cooking now. They're making the midday meal.'

'What are they doing to the woman?'

'They have got her feet in the fire. They say it's to stop her running away again. There are five of them with a jeep. Two helicopters went over earlier and landed on open ground, ahead. They must have come with it.'

'Where is the horse?'

'Five minutes away along the track. I took it up a hill last night and staked it behind a rock. You can't see it from below.'

They gazed at each other, horrifyingly aware of the danger of the horse making its presence known.

'Do they look as if they mean to stay?'

'Sahib, I can't tell. Come and see,' the boy said distractedly.

The screaming had mercifully stopped as they went out of the cave. The boy sat on the edge and lowered himself, and stepped sideways on to the rock, and turned to help Houston. His mouth was shaking and the narrow wrist trembling. Houston looked below through the frozen straggling bushes, and could see at first very little; a couple of bobbing caps, a steel rod swaying, the back of a jeep.

The boy had got down on his stomach and parted the vegetation, and Houston did the same. Two men were squatting over a fire prodding at food in a swinging pot. Another was sitting in the jeep fiddling with a wireless set; the rod was the aerial. He couldn't see anything else. The boy shook his arm, and he followed his glance and by craning could see, a little farther along the track, two more soldiers. He couldn't make out what they were doing. One seemed to be kneeling as if in prayer, and the other was standing watching him. As he watched, the kneeling man got up, and he saw what he had been doing. The woman was lying on the icy track with her clothes bundled about her head like a bag of rubbish. As one man got up, the other got down, and Houston turned away, afraid he was going to be sick.

The boy had caught his arm tightly, however, as he turned, and Houston saw that he was watching not the men along the track but the one in the jeep, who had now begun to speak into his microphone.

He was shaking so violently that even with the boy's help he could barely drag himself back into the cave. He lay just inside, sickened and infuriated, fighting down a savage desire to hurl himself among them; aware that for the first time in his life he wanted with his own hands to kill somebody.

That made it, of course, very much easier later on.

Every trail leading from the river had been blocked; where possible jeeps had been flown in to work back quickly along the tracks. The men below had found the track too narrow for their jeep to negotiate, and were asking for mule transport. They were told to remain where they were to rendezvous with a party now on its way to them.

There were several transmissions on the wireless set. The boy could not understand all that was said. But the girl could. The three of them sat, famished, in the grey, icy chill, listening to the soldiers eating, and to the transmissions.

The woman was raped four times more after lunch, and twice towards dark by the wireless operator, who had been missing his share. A wind had come up, and he dragged her back to the shelter of the cave to do so in comfort. As she passed below, the boy had for the first time seen her face. He was weeping as he returned to the cave.

Houston didn't ask him why, for he had already guessed. But the boy told him, all the same.

The expected party arrived after dark. It was a small party, consisting only of a man on a mule. He said that further transport could not be sent until the following afternoon, and that the jeep was to be returned immediately. The fire had to be stamped out before it could be manhandled round on the track; but within minutes, Houston saw it roaring away in low gear, headlights blazing. The four soldiers, the newly arrived visitor, and the woman remained. The fire was built up again. The visitor began to interrogate the woman.

He had been screening females in a near-by nomad encampment, he said, but had been checked by a peculiar difficulty...

Houston went back to the cave, for he had heard and seen enough; he held the girl in his arms and put his hands over her ears so that she should not hear.

There was no particular reason why anyone should have suspected the chief medical monk; and it was plain why the governor had not spotted him from his dossier. The man was not an easterner. He looked to be a full Tibetan. His voice came quite clear above the crackling of the fire.

'My sister, what is the use of resisting? Tell what is asked of you and the pain will stop.'

The pain did not stop. Within minutes, the screaming began again, even more agonized than before.

'My sister, learn wisdom. Shorten the Mother's journey and your own. She has no hope of escape. Describe her exactly and your troubles will be over.'

Alas, her troubles were not to be over so soon. Houston lay at the back of the cave, the girl's head pressed tight in his shoulder, and listened to her enduring them. Only two people in the world had known what the Mother looked like under her mask, and he did not think the one below would be telling. Little Daughter had given up her virginity, and, by the sound of it, almost her reason. But he didn't think that, apart from her life, she would be giving up anything else.

4

The boy thought he heard something above the screaming soon after nine o'clock, and came in to tell Houston so. Houston went out with him. They stood upon the projection of rock, listening. Fresh rhododendron wood had been piled on the fire, and it was hissing and singing as the ice melted. But Houston could hear it himself after a moment.

He said, 'It's the wind.'

'It isn't the wind, sahib.'

'The wind is blowing in that direction.'

'Yes, sahib. It can smell the food and hear them.'

'How long since it ate?'

'Not since yesterday at midday.'

'Can you get to it?'

'Not without going down.'

Houston looked up at the cliff above them; it shone with ice in the leaping ruddy light.

'You can't get to it from above,' the boy said watching him. 'You can't even see it. That's why I tied it there.'

But he went, without Houston telling him.

He was away for nearly two hours. He was blue with cold when he returned, lips and eyebrows frosted. He had not been able to get to the horse. He had worked to a point directly above it, and had let himself down on the rope. He had swung near enough to shoot it, but had been afraid to use his pistol. From the top of the cliff he had had an excellent view of the surrounding country, and all about him, as far as he could see, camp fires had gleamed; the soldiers were bivouacked in every tiny trail, and a considerable number seemed to be sited on the plain a few miles ahead. The horse had been kicking up such a din, however, and had so nearly bitten through its bridle, that in desperation the boy had tried other measures. He had collected rocks and, swinging on the rope in the freezing night, had tried to kill the horse that way. He had gone up and down on the rope for his rocks several times, and knew that he had caught it about the head and shoulders. But he had not killed it, or even quietened it. He was certain the horse would break free within hours.

Houston was so numb with cold and hunger and the strain of waiting that he could scarcely think.

'Is there no other way at all of getting at it?'

'None, sahib. I tried.'

'Couldn't you go beyond it on the clifftop and get down wherever you can and go up from the track?'

485

'Sahib, it might take all night. We haven't got all night,' the boy said. He was very frightened, his face again pointed and shrivelled like that of some small animal. 'We've got to leave here. We've got to leave as soon as possible.'

Houston thought at first he was offering the mad suggestion that they should all climb the cliff – for it was plain that the girl was not in a condition to climb anywhere. But Ringling was not suggesting that. He was half starved and half frozen, and shaking all over with fright; but the suggestion he had to offer was more fantastic still.

Houston thought he had taken leave of his senses.

'Sahib, it's our only hope.'

'Forget it.'

'Sahib, if we don't they'll get us. The horse will give us away.'

'They have to find us first.'

'They don't have to. They would starve us out. They will know we are here somewhere.'

'There are five of them below, you bloody young idiot!'

'Tomorrow there will be five hundred!' the boy said furiously. 'Sahib, we have only this chance. Two of them are asleep now. The monk and one more will turn in soon. Only one picket will stay up. We deal with him.'

'How?'

'With the knife.'

'Kill him?'

'All of them. It's the only thing.'

They looked at each other.

Houston found that he was trembling, too.

By midnight, two men were still awake, and it was still not time. Little Daughter had subsided, but she was still being worked upon. The medical monk had carried her out of the cave, and back in it, and was now outside with her again. He had tried arak and douches of icy water, and also the fire, which had been recently made up. None of these methods seemed to have worked and as Houston watched, the man took

486

a rest. He accepted a cigarette from the picket and sat by the fire with him, chatting, the naked body of Little Daughter alongside like some scarred stranded whale, the mule, heavily blanketed, dozing near by.

Distantly, against the wind, the horse was trumpeting: Houston heard it quite clearly, and he saw from the way the mule's ears twitched, that it could hear it, too. Beside him on the rock, the thin body trembled continuously. Ringling was to be the first one down the rope, and hence the one who would take on the picket.

They had worked out how it was to be done. They had worked it out in the cave. The boy had felt for Houston's heart under his jacket, and had traced it round to the back, and had measured with his fingers the distance from the spine where the knife must go. For the best part of an hour they had scuffled softly in the darkness, rehearsing it and the remainder of the night's work; for the men in the sleeping bags posed another kind of problem. It would be necessary to slit their throats; and each would have to be dispatched in his bag, silently and economically, before the next one was attended to. Writhing strongly against each other on the floor, they had developed a number of desperate refinements to facilitate this bloody and most odious operation: the gag made from a bundled glove; the sharp stab into the windpipe before the knife was turned in the wound and drawn across. They had practised so conscientiously that by now Houston could almost believe himself capable of it, and prayed only that he would be allowed to try before his resolve weakened.

The monk, however, seemed in no hurry to meet his fate. He smoked his cigarette. He chatted with the picket. He examined a boil in the picket's ear, and told him minutely what to do about it. He even got down on his knees again to recommence work on Little Daughter; but after flicking up an eyelid and shaking her chin, rose suddenly and stretched himself and went in the cave.

Houston and the boy looked at each other. The monk had said nothing further; no good nights had been offered.

Would he be reappearing to carry Little Daughter back into the cave, or to cover her up in the freezing night?

The guard seemed just as uncertain. He got up presently and looked into the cave, and stamped about on the track, and collected more wood and flung it on the fire. The horse trumpeted again in the night, much more clearly this time. The dozing mule came awake and tossed its head.

The boy eased himself gently up on the rock. Houston felt in his pockets for the stones. The idea was for him to throw the stones one at a time to the other side of the track to distract the guard while Ringling shinned down. At the bottom, he would still be out of sight of the picket, and Houston would tug the rope when the man was in position.

They waited a few minutes more, watching the cave.

But then something happened that indicated quite certainly that the picket was not expecting the monk out again, and that the stones would not be needed, either.

The man had been examining Little Daughter; and after another brief glimpse into the cave, seemed to have satisfied himself.

It was a moment or two before Houston saw what he was doing; and he felt then such rage and loathing that he would most willingly and with all his heart have gone down the rope himself.

But that was not in the plan.

'Now?' the boy said.

'Yes,' Houston said. 'Oh, yes. Now.'

Chapter 14

I

THERE was the barest rustle from the undergrowth as the boy went down. Houston stayed on one knee, ready to follow him and yet keeping his view of the track. Within seconds, he felt the faint tug in his hands, and returned it immediately, for the picket would never be in a better position and was quite distracted enough. But he stayed himself some seconds more, knowing he could not move as silently as the boy, and not daring to set up the ghost of a sound before he saw him at his goal. There was the faintest of movements below, a mere change in the quality of darkness, and the boy stepped out into the firelight. He held himself still for a moment, and then glided surely in like a cat. He came on the picket sideways, crooking an arm round his neck and plunging in the knife almost in one movement like a man scything.

Without fear suddenly, in a kind of drunken elation, Houston found himself swarming down the rope. He heard, as he did so, a gentle cough, the smallest of shuffles, as though a sleeper were turning over in some other room; and as he came on to the track, saw that the man was indeed trying to turn, his legs kicking feebly, shoulders arching. The boy bore down intently, and suddenly withdrew the knife and plunged it swiftly in again, leaning upon it with such grave concentration, his head turned a little to one side as he gazed at Houston that he was reminded fantastically of a mechanic turning some hidden screw.

The man expired like that, quite silently, with only the gentlest of shudders, and the boy lowered him to the body of Little Daughter, and pulled out his knife and wiped it on his back. He was panting as he raised himself. Houston realized he had been holding his breath. He grasped his arm and pressed

489

it. The boy nodded, no longer trembling, and inclined his head towards the cave, and began to move there.

Houston had been holding the knife in his hands for the best part of an hour, for the most part in utter terror, but now that the moment had come to use it, he felt nothing at all. He looked at it in utter disbelief, and his only thought was that he had used it last to cut his toenails and that it was too ludicrously familiar and domestic a little tool for the incredible tasks it would have to perform.

The cave was in complete blackness. They paused, just inside. They had decided in the interests of safety to deal first with the last man in, the monk. But the cave was evidently so much smaller than the one above, its low roof so muffled and flattened the snores of the sleepers that it was impossible in the darkness to tell their dispositions. The boy caught Houston's sleeve and moved on again, slowly; and suddenly stopped and drew back like a scalded cat. There was a grunt in the darkness, a shifting, a muttering. Houston realized he must have stepped on someone.

They stood perfectly still, not breathing, waiting for the sleeper to subside. The sleeper did not subside. He threshed restlessly, and coughed, and presently began to do something else. Houston couldn't tell what it was, but after a second felt the boy's hand withdrawn, and heard suddenly in the darkness a rasp and saw the cave leap horrifyingly into life as a flint sparked; and in the same moment, without thought, had thrown himself forward with the boy on to the barely-glimpsed figure of a man in the bag. He had an impression of a broad Asiatic face yawning and staring with absorption into a little brass lighter before the light was smothered. He did not see the man's expression change (or indeed anything else at all in the next extraordinary few minutes, retaining only the one dim visual memento of the experience like an imperfectly synchronized flashlight photograph). He doubted if the man ever saw them.

There was a nose under his hand, and he rammed the gag in below it and forced the man backwards; and felt through the

490

gag the single muffled hawk as if he was being sick. But the boy had struck too quickly and missed the windpipe, and the man writhed strongly so that he had to plunge again and again, forgetting the lessons they had learned, and hissing himself at the horrifying work; and as he did so another voice murmured in the darkness, someone else waking, and the boy shook him frantically with his other hand, and Houston found a glove in it, and took it and went mindlessly to deal with the next one himself.

He thought he had placed the murmur in the darkness, and was not wrong, for just as he leaned over the man spoke to him. He spoke directly into his face. Houston was driven so much into a panic by this simple but unexpected occurrence that he almost fell over backwards, but he held himself for a moment with the glove poised, and just as he spoke again rammed it down hard, and with horror felt the whole glove go into the open mouth and his knuckles with it, and stabbed with the knife.

The man leapt under the knife, his chest straining up out of the bag. Houston got his knee on it, and pressed with all his strength, and heard presently the muffled hawking and was almost sick himself. He thought the little blade was too short to complete the job, and tried to draw it out to stab harder, but blood had begun to run incredibly, and the knife was no longer in his hand. He searched frantically for it, and found it still there as the man thrummed below him, stuck in the throat, and grasped desperately, and found he had grasped a handful of what felt like hot raw liver, and in a paroxysm of horror got his fingers among it to feel the thin metal handle and sawed there and back to free it and felt the blade cutting as though through hosepipe.

He did not need to stab again when he got it out; and indeed could not for the life of him have done so. He kneeled on the chest for some moments longer, feeling cold sweat trickling over his eyebrows and down his face, so sickeningly nauseated that he hadn't the strength to stand. His hands were running with blood. The crumpled glove was soaked with blood. He hadn't in his darkest horrors expected so much blood. He had expected to be afraid, and he was not afraid. And he had expected a quick economical death; and it was not that, either. He had an impression of having fumbled inside a bag of blood and soft organs to sever tough cords; and it was the idea of the bag still spilling out over his hands and knees that, more than the boy's sudden gasped imprecations, brought him staggering to his feet in the darkness.

He knew then that the noise had been going on for a little while, and he lurched towards it, horribly afraid that he had already started to be sick. There was a sweet-sour stench of a butcher's shop as he moved, and he knew he was carrying it on his hands and couldn't bear to close them, and he realized with a certain refinement of horror that he was still carrying the glove also, holding it with a tea-table delicacy by one finger.

Bodies blundered against him in the darkness, and he couldn't tell which was which.

'Sahib, sahib, his head! Get his head!'

He clutched in the darkness and found a fur cap and knew the boy did not have one, and at once, vomiting over it, got both hands round underneath it. He found his wrist gripped suddenly in a pair of teeth, very hard, like a dog clamping on a bone. But he managed with the other hand to squelch down with the soggy glove, rubbing it blindly over nose and mouth and dragging backwards so hard that he tumbled underneath himself, the man's head on top of him. He held the head straining there for a second, and felt the sudden leap as the knife went in, and presently, under the oozing glove, the now-familiar hawk. The struggle continued for some seconds more, the man strong as an ox and fighting to twist away from the blade, and as he did so Houston released his wrist and pulled the head more cleanly backwards to present a better target for the knife, and felt it tugged this way and that as the boy worked the blade.

He had to get out from under the new-bleeding neck, and did so, vomiting painfully.

The boy was gasping beside him in the darkness 'Sahib,

sahib, don't be sick now ... There is one man more ... Help me, sahib.'

He was somehow on his knees again, and the glove was somehow in his hand again, and he levered himself up, hearing the boy fumbling for the one man more. He did not have to fumble long, for the man spoke suddenly in the darkness. It was the monk, who should have been first and was now last, and he spoke crisply – quite without fear, academically almost.

'*Trulku*? Do you hear me, *trulku*? You know it is not time for me to die? You know there is work before me?'

Houston did not speak, and nor did the boy, merely turning in the direction of the sound. The monk seemed to be sitting up in his bag, hands outstretched.

'*Trulku*, do not permit yourself to fall into error. It would be wrong. It would be a sin. You would lose merit. *Trulku*, allow me to embrace you ...'

Houston allowed the monk to embrace him, and felt for his face and automatically slapped on the glove and the man went backwards, still embracing him, his face wriggling this way and that under the disgusting gag. The boy's hand moved Houston to one side, and felt for the throat, and leaned wearily upon it. The knife slipped slowly in. The hawking went on longer than before, the boy not having the energy to make the cut across but merely turning the knife two or three times before pulling it out.

The monk did not struggle as the soldiers had struggled, but he took longer to die. They sat and heard him.

Houston was aware that the boy's hissing had not stopped.

'What is it?'

'Sahib, I'm hurt. Get a light.'

'Where is the light?'

'Bring wood from the fire.'

He collected himself up off the floor. He seemed to be doing it for some time. He was reeling in darkness. He was at the cave-mouth; and leaning against it and drawing in great draughts of the moving night air. He thought his eyes were playing him tricks. In the light of the fire, the dead picket seemed to be moving on the body of Little Daughter. He blundered past the man; but as he turned again with a flaring branch, saw that the picket was indeed moving, and watched him with horrified fascination. But the movement had come not from the picket but from Little Daughter; she was twisting below the corpse, groaning again.

He couldn't deal with this. He couldn't cope with it. He reeled back into the cave with the flaring torch and stood swaying with it over the boy, staring at the new complication.

The boy had a bayonet in his shoulder. It went in at one side and out at the other. He was sitting holding the shoulder and the bayonet, hissing. They gazed at each other dully.

'Sahib, what can be done?'

'I don't know.'

'Oh, sahib, what is for the best?'

He noticed suddenly that the boy was crying.

'It will have to come out.'

'Yes, out, out. Sahib, you do it. Take it out. I can't.'

There had been so much to cope with during this endlessly horrible night that Houston had given up thinking. He merely handed the boy the branch, put one fist on the shoulder and the other round the bayonet and pulled. He noticed while he was doing it that the light suddenly flared, and turning his head saw that the monk's bedding was on fire. The boy had passed out. He had dropped the branch.

Houston continued pulling out the bayonet. He dragged the boy out of the cave. He went back in, and put the fire out. He looked about him with the burning branch, and found a knapsack, and emptied it, and picked out a first-aid kit. There was a tin of field dressings, some tubes of ointment, a plastic envelope of powder. He could not read the Chinese lettering, but he opened the envelope and sniffed and thought it was sulphonamide. He went outside again. He bared the boy's shoulder and wiped away the blood and poured the powder on. Bandages. He had forgotten bandages. He went back in the cave again at a shambling trot and sorted through the knapsack. No bandages. Something else instead of bandages. He held up the branch and saw the four dead men grinning at him as they presented their torn throats for inspection, and without thinking, at once began to pull the monk out of his bag. He stripped his robe off and took it out and tore it and began binding the boy. The boy opened his eyes and watched him.

'How does it feel?'

'Thank you. Thank you, sahib.'

'Little Daughter is alive,' he said.

'There is a man on Little Daughter, sahib. Take him off.'

He took the man off.

'The Mother shouldn't see Little Daughter with a man on her.'

'All right, he's off now.'

'Help me, sahib.'

'What do you want?'

'We need the horse. We must have it.'

'All right, I'll get it.'

'I'll take it food. Give me the mule's food, sahib. There's a sack of it in there. I'll go with the mule. We haven't got very long.'

He got the food and put the boy on the mule. He didn't like the look of him. There was something wrong with his face. He had not quite answered any of his questions. It was almost as if he had not heard them. He seemed to be just holding himself in.

'Collect all the food, sahib, and the sleeping bags. Get it all together. And the Mother, and the bales.'

'Are you all right?'

'And the medical supplies, whatever they have. Don't waste time, sahib. We'll move right away.'

He knew he shouldn't let him go, but there was so much in this nightmare for him still to cope with that he did let him. He watched the slumped figure bob-bobbing along the track, and turned and went back up the rope to the cave. He let the abbess down, and one of the bales after her, and waited for her to untie it so that he could lower the other one. She didn't untie it, and he saw presently why. She was sitting by the camp fire cradling Little Daughter in her arms. He didn't disturb her, and she remained like that, silently cradling and kissing the large pallid face. Little Daughter must have died then, for when the boy came back she merely laid her down and passed a hand over her face, murmuring a prayer.

There was no time for dismemberment, but she would not leave without making the few obligatory mutilations; so Houston gave her his knife and turned his head while she made them, for he thought he had seen enough of mutilation for one night.

They left immediately after.

All this was on the night of 2/3 November. It was eight days after the party had left Yamdring, and two since Houston had gone over the cliff with the girl. He didn't know what had happened to the other members of the party, and was so dazed by his privations that he didn't care.

Something else happened before they left the camp. The girl left Houston's knife on the ground. It was the silver one with his name on it that he had carried since the age of 14. He forgot to ask her for it back, and it thus remained beside the body of Little Daughter until the Chinese found it when they brought up the mules. It was an oversight that Houston was later to pay for very dearly.

2

They kept going all night, the girl on the horse, the boy on the mule, Houston on his two flat feet. His sores came alive as he walked, and he greeted them like old friends, for they seemed to provide his only contact with reality. He could not believe that he had gone through the fantastic incidents in the cave. Somebody else seemed to have gone through them. He seemed to have been watching this other person, and he seemed to be still watching him, from a pace or two ahead, looking back and observing the flat-footed figure approaching him with the horse and the mule and the two sleeping riders. There was a connection between him and this dogged person, and he worked soberly to preserve it, checking off the regular signals that passed between them from thighs and neck and ankles.

The boy sat up suddenly after a couple of hours as if some internal alarm clock had gone off.

'What time is it, sahib?'

'Three o'clock.

'We're still on the track?'

'Yes.'

'Stop now, sahib. Stop.'

'What is it?'

'Help me down. We must muffle the hooves. We are coming to the nomad camp. The soldiers are there.'

He helped the boy down, and they muffled the hooves with strips torn from their clothing, and he helped him up again and trudged on.

What followed struck Houston in later years as in a way even less believable than the incidents in the cave, and indeed he often wondered if it had really happened, or if he had not himself fallen asleep as he walked and merely dreamed it.

The nomads were camped on an area the size of Salisbury Plain. They were camped with their tents and their cattle in a series of low-walled enclosures like sheep-pens; and the soldiers were camped with them. For miles on every side, the camp fires gleamed; the plain seemed to be populated as far as he could see. It was encircled entirely by mountains; a vast amphitheatre that shone in the light of the moon like some enormous stage set. Houston thought that he could see every detail of it as plainly as if it had been day: the clusters of tents, the pickets at their fires, cattle stirring behind walls, and even, standing by themselves, the two helicopters, like giant spiders upon the plain.

It seemed to Houston that he simply walked through the middle of this encampment. He had had an idea earlier that nothing could ever frighten him again; but he knew then it was wrong, for as he walked between the enclosures his hair stood on end. He had the fantastic notion that some spell had been cast on the men and animals who seemed to peer at them from both sides; that they had all of them petrified in the moonlight; or that he himself with his companions had been rendered invisible. He turned to see if the boy was aware of it, too, and saw, incredibly, that he was asleep again; and that the abbess was asleep, and that the horse and the mule seemed to be asleep also; and could not be sure in the drugging moonlight that he was not himself fast asleep.

Nobody checked them. No dog came to investigate. Like ghosts they passed silently through the camp, and by half past five had reached the mountain at the other side. The moon was still out. Houston kept on. The moon went half an hour later, but he still kept on; for he knew that if he stopped he would simply fall down. He had lost contact with his sores. He seemed to have lost contact with everything. There seemed to be no reason why he should not keep on in this way for ever.

He was aware that the boy was awake again.

'What time, sahib?'

'I can't see.'

'The moon has gone. How long since we left the plain?'

Houston didn't answer at all this time; for as he had feared, once stopped all his strength had gone. He found himself inexplicably grasping the horse's leg, and having to reach up to do so.

'Sahib, sahib, hold on. Don't sleep yet, sahib. I can't carry you.'

The boy was beside him, and he was smiling up into his face, telling him that he was far from being asleep, very far; and then he was asleep, and knew that he was, and tried to stop it buzzing for a moment to hear what the boy was saying. Something about his legs; that he should do something with his legs. But he couldn't find the legs, they had gone now, left him, positively would not be found; and he had to give up trying, had to open to the imperative buzzing, and he opened. and the buzz flew in, and sat upon his ear, and it buzzed.

*

It was day when he awoke. It was half past three. He looked at his watch and wound it. The abbess was there. The boy was there. The mule and the horse were there. All present. He tried to stir himself to get up, but could not stir himself. He was not sleepy; merely full of an immense lassitude. He looked about him and saw it was not a cave, but a big overhang; the first place the boy must have found. It was a dangerous place. It was too dangerous a place for them to stay. He fell asleep thinking how dangerous it was.

They stayed another day in this dangerous place. Neither the boy nor the horse would wake on the first. Houston tried, and couldn't wake them. He opened the boy's bandages and found the wound soft and yellow. He poured on another powder. That left two, for the soldiers had had four between them. They had also had a brick of tea and one of butter, a little sack of tsampa and another of rice, eighteen tablets of meat extract and four small wads of dried strip-meat.

Houston and the girl ate in the evening.

Later they slept again.

Ringling woke the second day, but the horse still slept. It slept lying down with its eyes closed. Houston tried kicking it for a few minutes.

'It's no good, sahib. The horse is sick.'

'What's to be done?'

'There's only one thing to be done,' the boy said in English, looking at the abbess.

'Can you walk?'

'I can walk. We could use the meat, sahib.'

'All right,' Houston said.

The boy killed the horse in the late afternoon while the abbess slept, and skinned it, and bound the meat under the lashings of the bales.

They left as soon as it was dark.

*

'Chao-li, the boy is in pain. He must have walked two hours. If he wishes, I will walk.'

'Are you in pain?' Houston said.

'No, sahib, no,' the boy said. He was hobbling stiffly on the icy path, holding his shoulder. 'With thanks to the Mother,' he said. He had not once looked at her, or addressed her directly.

'Does he know where we are?'

'Do you know where we are?'

'Ahead there is a place of wind devils.'

'Must he disturb the wind devils?'

'Is it necessary?' Houston said. He was tiring of his role as intermediary; but he knew it would be more tiring still to ignore it, for neither of them would speak to the other, except through him.

'There is a hermit hole there,' the boy said. 'We could rest in the hole, sahib.'

'Is the hermit known to us?'

'Do we know him?'

'The holy hermit is dead. He died two years ago. Ten of us were sent for from the nearest caravan to witness his funeral. The abbot himself directed the holy hermit's spirit.'

'Yes, I remember,' the girl said. 'I blessed that hermit. It is not wise, Chao-li, to disturb the spirit of the hermit, or the wind devils.'

'It isn't wise,' Houston said.

'Sahib, it lies in our path. No one would dare go there. From there it is only six hours to the pass into Chumbi. The pass will soon be blocked, sahib. We must get there quickly.'

'Is there no other way he knows, Chao-li?'

'What other route?' Houston said.

'Sahib, if we leave this track we must go over mountains. I don't know if we could do it. I don't know how long it would take. The place of wind devils is the wisest choice.'

'I must see the place,' the girl said.

It took several hours to reach. The track narrowed gradually, and suddenly narrowed still further, so that it was barely a track at all but rather a cleft in the mountains. The wind blew through it at their backs with extraordinary force like some pillow-covered engine shunting them along. It blew steadily, without gusts, in a single high-pitched note, peculiarly wearing on the nerves, and Houston, stumbling along in single file in utter blackness could well see how it might be taken for the malevolent voice of some devil.

He was quite unprepared, however, for the place of devils itself. The cleft had narrowed so sharply that, to enable the bales, which had jammed against the sides, to be swung round on top of the mule, the abbess had to dismount. She went ahead. A few minutes later they stopped again. The trail had stopped. It had come out to a little clearing, a depression, a mere space of bare rock and ice with a pillar of stones in the centre. The moon could penetrate here, and Houston was glad of it, for if he had not been able with his own eyes to see, he would have thought it full of wild animals. There was a fantastic roaring, a yowling, a moaning; the winds rushing and meeting from similar clefts in the surrounding rock. He thought he could distinguish with clarity the distinctive notes of a dozen mature cats in the row.

He could see the girl mouthing towards him, but her words were lost in the wind. There was no way round the mule or over it; he crawled on his hands and knees beneath.

'What is it?'

'Chao-li, the devils are angry!'

'Sahib, they are always angry.'

'Does he know where is the hole?'

'It is below the *chorten*, sahib – the pile of stones in the centre. The holy hermit's bones are in the *chorten*. The floor lifts up and there are steps down.'

'Has he ever heard the devils so angry?'

'Sahib, I have heard them only once. They were just as angry. See, they are not angry with the holy hermit. Not a stone has fallen.'

'The hermit has made his peace with them, Chao-li.'

'Only because the Mother allows, sahib. The holy hermit

lived here fifty years, and the Mother protected him from all harm. She can protect us also.'

'All right,' Houston said. He wished she would set about it. The tearing cold and the unearthly row had combined suddenly to reduce him again to a state of utter exhaustion.

The girl looked at him and turned away and walked out from the cleft. She was knocked down at once. Houston made to assist her, but was held back by the boy. She picked herself up, and was again knocked down, but raised herself in a doubled-over position, and went on. It could not have been more than fifty yards to the *chorten*, but it took her the best part of a minute to get to it, the wind hurling her this way and that, once spinning her round entirely. A few feet before the *chorten*, she stood suddenly upright, and Houston heard the boy gasping in his ear, but whether with pain or with astonishment at this manifestation of power over the wind, he could not tell. He had already calculated that since the pillar of stones was standing upright it must lie out of the wind; perhaps in the very eye of the turmoil. And such indeed proved to be the case, for when the abbess had bowed to the *chorten* and embraced it with her arms, she turned and beckoned to them, and after some bruising and suffocating seconds in the wind, Houston found that he too could stand upright. For a radius of some six feet around the *chorten*, the air was quite still; a dead freezing calm.

A large slab formed the doorway. The boy lowered it, and the abbess went in. A few moments later, they followed her.

3

The hermit hole of Bukhri-bo – such was the name of this abominable spot – was hewn out of solid rock, some ten feet below the ground. Its narrow approach passage led to a single large chamber, twenty feet by ten. The hermit's possessions had not been touched; they consisted of three wooden bowls, a small sack of tsampa, a lamp, and a kruse of cheap mustard oil to burn in it. The hermit had not used a blanket or a bed. He had not used the sunken fireplace, either, for there were no ashes in it. He had kept a calendar on the wall with a writing brush; it had stopped on the eighth day of the fourth month of Earth Mouse, two summers previously. The boy said he had been dead four months when found. The chamber smelt like it.

They heated snow over the reeking mustard oil lamp and made tea. They slept in their bags on the floor. The mule slept with them.

They left as soon as it was dark, and, as the boy had promised, took six hours to reach the pass. They turned round when they got there and came back again right away. The Chinese were camped on the pass.

The boy slept heavily for a day and a half on their return, and Houston let him. He had no more powders to put on the wound, and it was looking no better. The shoulder had puffed up like a football. He had sweated as he slept.

'Sahib,' the boy said when he awoke. 'I must go back to the pass. I will go alone, by day. It will be quicker.'

'What do you want to do?'

'The pass will soon be blocked. We must know how long the Chinese will stay.'

'How can you find that out?'

'They had porters with them. There must be a village near by. I will ask in the village.'

'What's the alternative if the pass does become blocked?'

'We must go over the mountains and find another.'

'I see,' Houston said. It was quite obvious to him that the boy would not be climbing any mountains for a long time. But he didn't see how he could tell him this; and he didn't see therefore how he could stop him from going.

He went out himself while the boy was away, to find wood. The boy had taken the only knife and he couldn't break the leathery branches that he found. He broke off little twigs and spent exhausting hours chasing them in the wind. But he filled a couple of knapsacks, and they had a fire that night.

The boy had not returned by morning, and Houston went to look for him. It was a couple of hours before he found him. He was simply sitting on the track. He had his back to the wind, and his face was screwed up with strain.

'Are you all right?'

'All right, sahib, all right.'

'What the hell are you sitting here for?'

'Having a rest, sahib. Just a short rest.'

'Does your arm hurt?'

'Yes, it hurts.'

This was the first time the boy had ever so much as admitted that his arm gave him the slightest irritation.

He didn't question him till he had eaten, and then he got off his bandages and had a look at the wound while listening to the story. It was not a very satisfactory story. The boy had found the village. He had found that the villagers were by no means opposed to the Chinese. The Chinese had brought them wrist-watches and clothes. They had hired their men at the highest rates. And they had promised that they would not be carrying burdens over the pass but merely going to and fro to the village for stores as required.

'Do they know what it's in aid of?'

'They know, sahib. They are bad people. The snow is late and it will be a hard winter for them. They hope the Chinese will stay a long time.'

'When do they expect the snow?'

'Not for ten days at least.'

'And how long are the men hired for?'

'By the day, sahib. As long as necessary.'

'Not so good, eh?'

'Not so good, sahib.'

The wound was not so good, either. It was yellow, and the tight swollen flesh around it was yellow. He couldn't tell if the dye had come off the monk's robe. The robe had not been very clean to begin with. He threw the bandage on the ashes and cleaned the wound with hot water. The boy sat hissing, his face tight and grey.

'Mei-Hua, do you know how to heal a wound? Do you know about herbs, leaves, anything of that sort?'

'No, Chao-li. It is not my function.'

'Sahib – if the Mother would permit,' the boy said in English. 'A piece of her robe – if she would bless a small piece. I don't know if it is possible for her.'

The girl didn't know, either. She considered the request, troubled.

'Mei-Hua, the boy is in pain.'

'Alas, Chao-li, it must be written for him.'

'Mei-Hua, it is a small thing that he asks. Give him the piece of robe.'

'Chao-li, it is a big thing.'

But she snipped off a piece and blessed it. Houston thought the boy's face cleared a bit as he bound him with this sanctified bandage.

They stayed in the hole for a week, voyaging out only to collect wood. It seemed to Houston that the boy grew more tottery every day. He seemed to cover the distance from the *chorten* to the track practically on his face, and he would no longer let Houston look at his wound. He bathed it secretively by himself in a corner of the chamber.

On the eighth day, he thought there were intimations of snow in the air.

'We better leave tonight, sahib. It's our last chance.'

Houston saw that his face was puffy and flushed and suspected that he was running a fever; but he made no inquiries for he knew the boy resented them; and as he had said, it was the last chance.

With the boy he had been eating his way through the horse, to leave the tea and tsampa for the abbess, who would not touch the meat. They had a large meal, and rested again after it. Towards midnight, they got going.

Houston hoped he had seen the last of Bukhri-bo. It struck

him then — as it was to strike him years later — as the vilest place on God's earth.

The snow began long before they got to the pass. It was early bitter snow like little sharp flints and it drove hard in their faces. They bent their heads, and it seemed to come up from the track. They turned their heads, and it whipped them in passing. There was no protection from it. The wind was so incredibly cold that it was simply not possible to face it for longer than minutes at a time. The abbess dismounted and they turned the mule broadside in the track and rested, gasping, behind it. Houston saw that the boy was scarcely able to stand.

He said, 'Ringling, we can't do it. We'll have to try again.'

'Sahib, no. It will stop. You'll see it will stop. It will be easier on the pass.'

Whether it was or not, they had no opportunity to learn. For it was iron grey dawn when they came to the pass, and it needed only one look to see that they would not be going through it. The Chinese were still there.

The abbess slept on the way back.

'Sahib,' the boy said, 'if the Mother should ask for a river, there is one before the village.'

'All right.'

'It is frozen and no one will be there. The water moves below the ice, sahib. It moves into the Tsangpo.'

'Why should she want a river?'

'If she does, sahib. Remember.'

4

Houston had not as then begun to keep a calendar, but by later calculation he made it 17 November when they had taken the last abortive trip to the pass, and the 27th when he and Ringling had gone back to the nomad encampment to buy curdled milk and garlic. The boy had been delirious for a couple of days, and in his delirium he had raved for the curdled milk and the garlic

506

– specifics which had cured him of many a childish ailment, and which alone would enable him to take them over the mountains. He was still hankering for them when he came to.

Because their food supplies were dwindling, and this would be an opportunity to renew them, Houston humoured him. He dragged him on his back across the place of wind devils and sat him on the mule, and they went.

It had been snowing hard for days, and the boy was sure the Chinese would no longer be billeted with the nomads. Houston went cautiously ahead to see.

He found that the Chinese had gone, and a considerable number of the nomads with them. A considerable number still remained.

He gave the boy what money they had managed to retain through their adventures – a sum of three hundred rupees in small notes – and helped him off the mule to transact the business.

They ran right away into unforeseen difficulty. The nomads would not take the money. The Chinese had told them it was worthless and would shortly be replaced by the yuan. They were prepared only to barter.

What would they accept as barter?

They would accept the mule.

The boy had by this time got his hands on the curdled milk and the garlic, and he agreed. Houston took him angrily on one side.

'What the hell is the point of getting rid of the mule? We need the mule. How can we move without it?'

'Sahib, how can we move if I am ill? The mule eats. It eats all day. What good is a mule that eats and has no work to do?'

His face was more flushed than ever, his eyes glittering, his voice far too loud.

'All right,' Houston said.

For the mule they got garlic, curdled milk, tsampa, dried meat, mustard oil, needle and thread, and four animal traps. They were offered also either a skinful of chang or a sled to drag the goods away with. Houston gave the boy no opportunity of deciding on this point. He began piling the goods in the sled.

The boy rode the latter part of the journey on the sled, and he ate garlic as he rode. He ate more when he got back, and he boiled up a head of it in curdled milk for his dinner. He crushed garlic in one of the holy hermit's bowls, and soaked his bandage in a solution of it. He stuffed as many cloves as he could into the wound. He was chewing garlic when he turned in and he was awake and still chewing when Houston turned out.

There were forty heads of garlic. The boy got through them in a week.

'Just wait, sahib,' he said. 'The garlic will work. We will be away soon.'

And indeed the garlic worked wonders. It cleared his fever. It reduced the watery yellow swellings. He had energy to move. Every day he accompanied Houston out of the hole to collect wood. He showed him how to set the traps, and how to skin their catch – two rat-hares and a fox, which they ate immediately to save the dried meat. But he tired quickly and had to be carried back on the sled.

'Just wait, sahib. Next week.'

Alas, the next week, which was the second one of December, the weather deteriorated into savage blizzards, which kept them in the hole, and the boy deteriorated with it. The flush came back to his face. The arm swelled up. The pain became unbearable.

Houston woke one night to hear screaming, and swiftly lit the lamp, and saw it was the abbess. The boy was threshing silently on the floor. He was stabbing at his shoulder with the knife.

Houston tore his bag getting out of it.

'Here, give me that, give me it!'

'Sahib, it's killing me! I can't stand it!'

'Come here, come here, stay still.'

'Sahib, stop it, oh, stop it! Take it away, sahib. Get it away from me.'

508

Houston took the knife and got him on his back and sat on the writhing chest and looked at the wound.

'Sahib, only stop it! Do anything! Cut it off. I can't stand it any more, sahib.'

'All right. Let's wash it first. Let's see what we've got.'

What they had got was something that all the garlic and all the curdled milk in the world would not cure. From shoulder to wrist, the arm was a puffy yellow mass. It spread under the armpit and over the shoulder. Blood and pus had streamed from the place where the boy had stabbed.

Houston's stomach turned over, and his heart failed him. For he saw that what the boy in his agony had prescribed was indeed the only remedy. The arm would have to come off. In a frenzy, because he could not stand the agonized bellowing, and because he knew he must stop it, he hit the boy hard on the head with a boot, and knocked him mercifully out, and held his own sweating head in his hands and thought what to do.

'The boy will die,' the girl said.

'No!'

'He will die, Chao-li. It is written for him.'

'Nothing is written!' Houston said savagely. 'I'll save him. I'll cut the arm off.'

But he didn't cut the arm off, and he didn't save him. Ringling died, as near as Houston could judge, on the 19th December – which was the date he gave his mother – and his death brought peace to them all, for he had bellowed continuously for three days.

Houston wept for him as he had not wept for his own brother. The girl remained composed.

'The boy was not a native of Tibet, Chao-li?'

'No, he came from Kalimpong, in India.'

'Then we will need a river,' she said.

Houston found the river, and as the boy had said, it was frozen and no one was there. He cut a small hole in the ice with the boy's knife, and dragged the stiff body off the sled.

The girl crouched beside it, shivering in the bitter wind.

'Where does the river flow, Chao-li?'

'Into the Tsangpo.'

'Very good. It will carry him home.'

She snipped a lock of the boy's hair, and murmured over it, and dropped it into the ice hole. Then she bent over the body and made two small incisions, above the eyes, and murmured again.

Houston remained looking into the ice hole. The hair was still there in the slow-moving water. It went just as the girl rose beside him.

'Is that all?'

'Yes. His spirit is now released. If it loses the way, the river will lead it home. For an outlander, it is very simple.'

'Yes,' Houston said. It had been very simple the first time, in the little stream, in the little wood, between Sikkim and India; a few drops of water, a posy of flowers.

'Good-bye,' he said into the hole.

Chapter 15

I

THEY left the boy on the ice. They left him naked to preclude the possibility of identification. They returned bleakly to the cave, and did not speak on the way. They turned in as soon as they had eaten.

The next day, Houston became very busy.

He slit two of the sleeping bags and sewed them together. He went out and began very methodically his immense collection of wood. He drew up his calendar on the wall with a bit of burnt stick.

In the week before the boy had died they had agreed upon a

rough plan. The plan was to stay in the hole for the winter and to make a quick dash for the pass as soon as the thaw set in. In this part of the country it set in very rapidly in the middle of April. In the space of three or four days the blizzards stopped and the sun shone. Unless the Chinese had left a party in the village – and it would be necessary to check on this – they could have as much as three days' start on any troops sent to cut them off. In three days they could be well into the Chumbi valley.

Houston drew out his calendar from December to May, and made a ring round 1 April when he thought he would make a reconnaissance of the village, and another round the 8th, for a final one.

The long-range planning struck him as utterly fantastic. The thought of April, in December, seemed to him as remote as the next century. But he clung to it doggedly, for there was nothing else to cling to. He even worked out for himself some refinements. The emeralds were heavy – the eight bags weighing each something like thirty pounds. With no one to help him, he thought he had better ferry them up to the pass a bit at a time. He thought he might make one trip on 8 April – when he would be going for his second look at the village – and another on the 10th. The rest could go with them when they left.

There were seventeen weeks from the end of December to the middle of April. Houston set himself to regulate them by a strict routine. They rose at seven, as they had done in the monastery, and washed and ate, and then while the girl, after setting their home to rights, embarked upon the ritual of prayer and mental exercise that had always made up her day, Houston went out on his wood-collecting and trap-setting labours.

He went out whatever the weather, and the weather in January was the most abominable he had ever encountered. The snow came continuously, and horizontally, and at tremendous velocity, driven by iron hard winds. He stood for a moment in the strange icy chillness beside the *chorten* and listened to the unbelievable howling, and took a deep breath before heading out into it.

He took the sled with him and collected his wood methodically, covering a different area every day and making a complete tour over a radius of some ten or twelve miles from the hermit hole every week. The traps provided at first almost nothing, but after a week or two he took to baiting them with what was left of the horse, and was soon picking up his dinner at least twice a week.

In the third week of January, when the weather grew suddenly worse, he found two rat-hares in the one trap; they had evidently gone for the same bit of food simultaneously. He took out the animals and rebaited the trap and moved on, and had no sooner turned his back than he heard the jaws go again. He looked round. Another rat-hare was in the trap.

Deducing that the worsening weather was bringing them down from the heights and that his remaining traps might be working just as hard, he gave up collecting wood (for a large pile was already drying in the hermit hole) and went straight away to inspect them. He was not disappointed.

For the following four days, in the vilest of blizzards, Houston went smiling from one trap to another. Some of the traps were buried deep in snow; but his little prey had smelt out the food, and they were waiting for him. He returned blue at the nose and chilled to the marrow; but by the end of five days he had returned with twenty-eight meat dinners.

Houston regarded this period, which was from the third week of January to the end of February, as one of the most rewarding of his life. The routine very quickly developed into a most regular and pleasing pattern. He would leave sharp on half past seven, punctual as some clerk going up to the city. He would climb the steps into the *chorten*, and pick up his sled, and nod familiarly to the bones of the holy hermit, and go out into it. The more horrible the weather, the greater his feeling of virtue. In all the seventeen weeks he did not come face to face with another soul; and for the first five of them was never happier.

He looked forward with the keenest relish to the evening. For it was dark when he left, and it would be dark again when he returned, hungry, half-frozen, with just energy enough to lug his tight-lashed haul across the place of wind devils. Smoke would be filtering out of the *chorten*, and the first breath of it would hit him as he removed the entrance stone. He would park the sled and clamber down in his bulky clothing – clamber down like Santa Claus descending a chimney, the warm scented air rushing deliriously up his body; and then it would all be there, waiting for him – a magnificent bombshell of light and heat, a treasure box of unfailing delight.

The cave was hot – gloriously, bakingly hot after the unremitting horrors of the frozen world above. The girl wore a light robe in it all day. Houston would strip, down to his singlet and trousers, and wash and eat, and then the evening was before him.

He taught her draughts, with bits of black and white stick, and noughts and crosses, and he drew pictures for her. On one wall he made a mural of Yamdring and on another of Bond Street. He drew for her also Trafalgar Square, and Fitzmaurice Mansions, and the living-room of number 62a (and at this period, too, on the back of her robe, the thirty sketches of her now in the Kastnerbank of Zürich). He told her about television and cinema and underground trains and ocean liners; and he tried to explain the basic political ideas of Western Europe. The political ideas bored her. But she was keen enough on religious ones, eagerly – sometimes scornfully – anticipating the theory underlying certain of the beliefs.

The instruction was not all on one side. For she explained to Houston many details of the life of the country that still baffled him. She taught him a number of mantras, religious chants, very useful for repulsing demons, and also for inducing, by repetition, a state of trance. Houston could not put himself into a trance by these means, but the girl could and very easily did, her pupils not responding to light nor her flesh to pain. She taught him also the rudiments of monastery dialectics, and engaged him in a number of simple arguments. Houston found the arguments fanciful and absurd, and the rules incomprehensible, but lying at ease in the crackling warmth with the gales howling above, he indulged her. He would have indulged her in anything.

He adored her. He could not look at her, or talk to her, or lie with her enough. Her hair had grown now, giving her a haunting waif-like appearance. He watched her by the hour, absorbing every nuance, every gesture as if it might be the last.

'Mei-Hua, do you love?'

'Chao-li, I must.'

'Above all others?'

'Chao-li, I must love all things. I am in harmony with all things.'

'But more in harmony with me.'

'Am I so, Chao-li?'

She eluded him. He thought he knew her every pore, her every molecule. He could trace the beginnings of every smile, and where the hair grew on her head, and where it had begun to sprout again on her body. He thought that physically he knew every inch of her; and not only physically, for she had no affectations, no reticences, no feminine wiles with him. Her nature was of the most unvarying, one of tideless affection. And yet there was something that he couldn't grasp – a feeling diffused through her of boundless good will for all creatures that he had to channel to himself alone.

Houston had never been particularly humble in love. He found himself now with the 18-year-old girl a suppliant.

He said, 'Mei-Hua, say you are more in harmony with me.'

'Very well, I will say it.'

'And that we will never be parted.'

'Oh, Chao-li, how can I say that? It isn't true.'

'Why can't it be?'

'Because some day we must die,' she said gaily.

She was leaning over him, rubbing her nose against his; so he said with a smile to match her own, 'The she-devil cannot die. You told me that. She only goes away and comes back.'

'Her soul, Chao-li. Her body must die. All seventeen of her

bodies have died. And so will this one. And so will yours. All bodies must.'

'Can't we stay together till they do?'

'Where will we stay?'

'Wherever you want.'

'Will we stay in heaven?'

'Mei-Hua, it isn't a joke.'

'Will we stay in the hermit hole?'

'I've been very happy in the hermit hole,' Houston said.

'I, too, Chao-li. Very happy with you.'

'Then be happy with me in Chumbi also.'

'In Chumbi I must be the abbess again. There will be nobles and lamas there. We could not live there as here. Besides, you would soon become bored with me.'

'Never,' Houston said.

'You would go away to paint your pictures.'

'I would paint you.'

'How often could you paint me?'

'Every day, until you're quite old.'

'No,' she said, nuzzling.

'Till you're *very* old. Till you're just an old, old body.'

'Alas, Chao-li, it isn't possible.'

'Why isn't it?'

'Because this body will not grow old. I must leave it young.'

'How do you know that?'

'I have always known. It is written for me.'

'You know when you will die?'

'The year and the month, Chao-li.'

'Then tell me.'

She drew back and looked at him with a wistful humour. 'Not now, Chao-li. Not ever, perhaps.'

Houston's heart sank as he saw how little it meant to her. But he persevered. He awoke one night to find her poring over his face in the firelight.

'What is it?'

'Nothing. I was just loving you. How beautiful you are, Chao-li!'

515

Houston drew her down with sleepy joy. It was some little way from the totality that he desired; but he thought he was making progress.

2

The first faint flaw in the gold appeared in the middle of February. The supply of animals dried up. It had started drying up within days of his last big haul. He thought he had worked out these particular areas, and shifted the traps. He had shifted them three times by 17 February, and his total catch for the period was two little rat-hares and one old diseased fox. He thought it was time to take stock of the larder.

He had for himself nine small hares, about a pound of dried strip-meat, six of the tablets of meat extract, and some unsavoury leftovers of horse. The girl had something over a stone of tsampa, several pounds of rice, about a pound of tea and two of butter.

Houston had been eaing one of the hares at a meal, with either a bowl of hare soup if he had boiled it, or of extract soup if he had not. He thought he had eaten rather well, and that it would be of no great hardship for him to cut down. If need be, he could manage for a month on what he had. That would take him, however, only to the middle of March. It would be the middle of April before they left.

The girl was in rather better case. At a pinch, her stocks would last the full period. She had already been rationing herself, and it seemed that she had had at the back of her mind the possibility that Houston might need to share her food.

'No,' Houston said. 'No, I shan't do that. The tea and tsampa are yours. Something will turn up.'

It was not until the very last day of the month, the 28th, that it was borne in on him that nothing was going to. He had finished that day a tour of all his traps. There was no sign of any animal. The traps sat in hard ice, the springs frozen solid, the bait frozen solid; no life, no life at all stirring.

He took his dinner with him the following day and also Ringling's sleeping bag; for he had come to a conclusion in the night. The animals had left the mountains. They had gone to seek food near humans. He would have to seek them there himself.

He went as near to the village as he dared, until he saw smoke. He baited his traps with meat that he could ill spare, and took himself back to a cave that he had marked on his way. He spent a miserable night in the cave, hungry and sleepless, a prey to morbid reflections. He had passed on his journey the hole in the frozen river. He had tried not to look. But he had seen something there; something; all that had been left by animals even hungrier than himself.

Because the country was unfamiliar to him, he had taken careful note of where he had left the traps. He was out early in the morning to find them. The first one wasn't there. He wasted half an hour checking to see that he was not mistaken before going on to the next. That wasn't there, either. He had got to the third spot before he saw the man. He was quite a long way off, trudging away from him with a mule towards the smoke.

Houston didn't bother to look any further. He went back to the hermit hole.

He had three rat-hares left and three tablets of meat extract. If he didn't exert himself too much he could make them last a fortnight. If he shared the girl's food they could both last another fortnight. There were six weeks to get through.

Houston lay in his sleeping bag and tried to face the situation. He would soon have no food. He had no traps to catch any food. How was he to live without food? To share the girl's was obviously no solution, for then the pair of them would starve. He had to get his own. Where was he to get it?

The nightmarish situation seemed to have been sprung upon him so suddenly that he couldn't all at once comprehend it. He was warm, well housed, comfortably bedded. He had three million pounds in emeralds and three hundred rupees in money.

There was a nomad camp on one side of him and a village full of people on the other. How was it possible, with all these assets, that he should die from lack of food?

He had not told the girl that his traps had gone, and he didn't therefore tell her what he planned to do about it. He thought she would object to the plan. He was not very keen on it himself. All the same, three days later Houston made another journey.

He travelled fast, recklessly spending energy for he meant to replace it before he returned. He took Ringling's pistol with him. His plan was to barter the pistol for food. It seemed to him that if the nomads wished to hand him over to the Chinese, they would not let him buy food first. If he bought food he was going to eat it, a lot of it, right away.

A group of them had been cooking when he was there last. They had been cooking a yak steak. They had hung a bowl beneath to catch the drips as it was basted over a fire, and they had dolloped the contents of this bowl over the steak before eating it.

Houston could smell it still. He felt his mouth dribbling as he smelt it. The thought that he would within a few hours be fastening his teeth into such a steak was so golden that it fairly lent him wings. With the wind pushing like a wall straight into his face and so light-headed with hunger that all his hesitations were dispersed, he made the journey in five hours flat.

He got to the plain at midday. It was not snowing. It was only slightly overcast. He could see for miles across it. He could see not a soul.

His shock and disappointment were so great that he felt his knees buckling underneath him.

The nomads had gone. It had simply not occurred to him that they could have gone. Where had they gone? Why had they gone?

They had gone because of the law promulgated in 1948 which forbade them to winter at the foot of the mountains. It was a taboo law, the only kind they obeyed, and they had gone as a matter of course as soon as the first heavy snows had set in. The Chinese, aware that they would do so, had not bothered to post among them the description of Houston that was now circulating in every village for a hundred miles. It was the only reason why he had not been apprehended earlier, when he had gone to buy food with the boy. He would otherwise most certainly have been; for there was a price on his head of a million old yuan (about £70, a fortune in money), and the Chinese were no longer enemies.

The fighting had finished in December, two months after the invasion and just a few weeks after Houston had taken up residence in Bukhri-bo. The ex-enemy was now treating quite amiably with 'ruling circles' exiled in Chumbi who were cautiously seeking ways in which they might without too much loss of face return to the comforts of life in Lhasa. One of these ways was by handing over certain specified 'criminal elements'. Houston was such an element.

He did not know this at the time. All that he was aware of as he looked across the plain was that there was some six feet of snow upon it, and that it was unlikely that the nomads would be returning to it for some time.

That seemed to leave him with only one alternative.

3

It was several days before he could screw himself up to it. His food, cut it as small as he would, was inexorably shrinking. His love for the girl was put nightly to an acid test as he watched her exercising a healthy appetite. He nerved himself to do what he must.

As reluctant as he had been to go to the nomad camp, he was still more reluctant to go to the village. He knew he dare not go during the day among people who had shown themselves so well disposed to the Chinese. He would have to go in the dark, and steal, with the gun as an ultimate persuader. The idea was so unattractive that he thought he had better try some others first.

He tried to eat wood and leaves. He boiled them to make a soup. The soup was bitter, bitter with the resin that enabled the wood and leaves to burn even when wet, and it merely made him vomit. He had to stop that quickly, for he could not afford to waste what he had already eaten.

He tried to fish. He nerved himself to return to the frozen river. But either the hook he fashioned from a buckle was unsatisfactory, or the bait unattractive, or the fish simply not there. For he found no trace of life.

There was no life anywhere. Nothing moved on land or water or in the air. The country was frozen hard, and there was nothing in it for him to eat.

By the 16th March, Houston saw that he could put it off no longer. He had a fragment of hare left and a few crumbs of meat extract. At the rate he was eating, there was enough for two days. He boiled them up, ate the solid parts that night, and in the morning set off with a cruse of the soup.

He had not been outside for a couple of days, and he realized right away that he was very much weaker. He had scarcely the strength to pull the sled. He thought he had better take a rest every hour.

After three hours an unpleasant suspicion began to dawn on him that he was not going to make it. He had a constant headache and there was a sensation of floating about his knees. He saw that he had run himself down too severely for such a journey, that he should either have made it days earlier, or have availed himself of the girl's food.

Houston tried to put the idea out of his mind for he realized that even at this juncture it would be all too easy to persuade himself against the mission. But once there, the idea grew. Why, after all, had he not shared her food? Could she survive if he starved? It was joint food. It was not only meat that he was after in the village. There was more likely to be tsampa there than meat. He would be getting food for both of them.

It was not yet time for Houston to have another rest, but he took one. He saw he had been foolish not to eat properly before attempting such a mission. By not eating he was jeopardizing them both. Unless he built himself up, the mission had no chance of success. He had much better go back and eat.

By half past ten, he had quite convinced himself, and he got up and went back. He carried the pistol in his hand as he walked, for he carried it with him now wherever he went. He had still not lost hope that some animal might be moving, and that Providence might set it in his path. And on that day, 17 March, at about eleven o'clock, Providence did.

Providence set the bear in Houston's path.

It was a very old bear, a hungry one. Houston calculated later that it had not eaten enough before hibernation, and had awakened early in the savage winter. It had blundered down the mountain looking for a meal.

At eleven o'clock it saw one.

Houston had not been using his goggles, but when his eyes began to ache with the snow glare, he put them on. The moment he did so, he was aware that he was being watched. He stood drunkenly on the track trying to comprehend this phenomenon. A couple of old men were watching him. They were watching him from the track fifteen yards ahead. They were bulkily clad in furs, leaning against each other. They were not only leaning against each other, but into each other, and then away again. He blinked and perceived that there was only one old man, and that he was not an old man but a bear.

Houston had never in his life seen a bear, except in a zoo. He had seen men dressed up as bears. This looked like a man dressed up as a bear. He knew all the same that it was not, and he felt in his pocket for the knife to increase his armoury.

The bear began to walk towards him, quite slowly, forepaws raised like a somnambulist, snout sniffing against the streaming wind. Houston couldn't fire the pistol with his glove on, so he took it off, and waited till the bear had covered half the distance, and then fired. He pressed the trigger four times. The gun did not fire on any of them.

Even at that moment, he could recall years later, he had not been in the least frightened of the bear. He thought he was too exhausted for fear. The bear came on slow painful pads. Its fur was stained with dried blood, and had fallen out in places. Its little eyes looked sightless, and were discharging, the teeth in its open mouth worn down to rounded stumps. Houston saw that an agile human would have no difficulty in evading it. He did not himself try to evade it. Dizzy and stupid with hunger, he stood swaying on the track, seeing intermittently one and then two bears, and his only thought was that so many hot meals were advancing towards him, and that if he kept them in focus he might have them.

The bear seemed to come upon him with love, whimpering a little, leaning its mangy, stinking old paws upon his shoulder and nuzzling his face, for all the world like some grandfather come to kiss him.

The bear was not trying to kiss him. It was trying to eat him, there, as he stood, too dazed and hungry to kill him first, taking his head in its mouth and mumbling ravenously.

Houston felt his cheek bruised and crushed as if in a pair of giant nutcrackers, and withdrew the knife he had plunged into its breast and stabbed upwards into its face. He found that he was on the ground. The bear was on the ground also, the pair of them too weak to stand and strive against each other. The blunt teeth had not penetrated Houston's furry balaclava, and the animal's wet pad of a nose snuffled round to find some more promising mouthful. There was an abominable reek on the bear's breath, an animal reek of excreta. It smelt the ungloved hand holding the gun and came gobbling hungrily at it.

Even in his reduced state of sensitivity, the pain of his frozen fingers being crushed was so agonizing that Houston cried out, and stabbed savagely, ignoring and tearing with the knife. The bear growled and released a paw and batted him with it, the claws viciously ripping the cap and scoring his face. Houston managed to release both arms in this moment. He got the one with the knife under the animal's throat and plunged it in, but could scarcely move the other with numbness, and the bear returned to it, ripping the sleeve with its paw, and grasping the whole arm.

Houston heard himself howling, howling like a dog with the insufferable agony of the hand and arm in the bear's mouth. He stabbed with all his strength, twisting and turning the knife in the bear's throat to make it stop. The bear, enraged, began to bite and shake his arm just as savagely, moving all the way up it to beyond the elbow.

The pain as his elbow was ground and crushed in the animal's jaws was such that Houston passed out.

The bear still had his arm in its mouth when he came to. It was still shaking it, but no longer biting. He realized after a moment that it was not only the bear's head that was shaking, but the whole bear. It was shuddering and coughing. Great gusts of the excreta smell was released as it coughed. Blood was running from its mouth, and from its throat. Its armpit and its breast were running with blood. The bear lay shuddering slightly, paws flexing and jerking as its life drained away. It did not gurgle from the wound in its throat as the Chinese soldiers had gurgled. It merely coughed, a slow tired cough, with several seconds in between, its whole body heaving like some great cat being sick, blindly and on its back.

Houston lay for over an hour with the bear's blood congealing on him. He could not somehow organize himself to move. He had withdrawn his injured arm from the dead bear's mouth, and with the sleeve torn back could see the bones sticking out.

He lay quietly, trying to work out how to pick it up. He thought that if he could do that, and hold it, he could get quickly back to the hermit hole. He could have it tied up and return with the girl, and between them they could get the bear on the sled. He could drag the bear home and eat it. He could eat it for weeks and weeks.

He drew the arm delicately towards him. The hand was not

unlike a bunch of hot-house grapes, purple and swollen. He took hold of the wrist. He saw that to pick up the arm he must roll over on his back, and he did so, and held it there above him, sickened at the sight of the bloody bone inches from his nose. He tried to sit up. He did not seem able to sit up. He fell into a mild panic at his inability to sit up; and in his panic, without thinking about it, began to rock himself up. He rocked as if he were lying on his back on a toy horse, rocking a little higher each time, until at last he made it and sat there, holding the arm and gasping.

He couldn't think what to do with the arm. He couldn't stand up while holding it. He saw that he would have to kneel first, and he placed it very carefully on his right knee, and got his left hand down on the ground and levered himself up. Then he picked up the arm and got on the other knee also, and knelt, holding the arm before him and plotting the next move.

Houston came up off the ground very slowly, holding the arm delicately before him like a contestant in an egg and spoon race. He stood bowed over it for a moment, and then began to move.

He had no recollection at all of the journey back. He remembered kicking with his boot at the entrance stone, and then coughing weakly in the blast of hot air, and then burping gently with an aftertaste of tea in his mouth.

'Oh, Chao-li, Chao-li, what have you done?'

He was sitting against the wall, on the sleeping bag. He was in his fur jacket still, and sweating. He wondered why he had the jacket on in the hot cave, and then saw the bones sticking out and saw why.

He was helping her to remove the jacket when he remembered suddenly that he mustn't remove it, that he had to go out again with it. He had begun telling her this, when he realized with alarm that everything had changed, that he was no longer sitting up but lying flat on his back, and that his jacket was off. One arm was tied to his chest with a strip of cloth. The girl was dabbing gently at his face with a wet rag.

'Lie still, Chao-li. Don't move yet.'

'Mei-Hua, I must go out. There is a bear.'

'There is no bear, Chao-li. You have been dreaming. You are safe now.'

'Mei-Hua, I'm not dreaming! There is a bear, a dead bear. I can eat it. It's food, Mei-Hua – '

'Yes, Chao-li, yes. See, there is tea and tsampa for you. Eat it and you will feel better.'

'Mei-Hua, I don't need your food. Keep your food!' he said desperately. 'I have my own food. I killed the bear. We must go and get it quickly – '

He saw that she had stepped swiftly back.

'Oh, Chao-li,' she said. 'It isn't true. Don't say that you have killed a bear!'

'I tell you I have!' he said, shouting almost above the hammering of his arm, and a peculiar swimming motion that had affected her head. 'I killed it, and I must eat quickly . . .'

'Oh, Chao-li, I cannot help with a bear.'

He saw that her head was not only swimming in circles but shaking slowly from side to side.

'Chao-li, I must protect all bears. It is a very great sin to have killed a bear.'

Houston went out again to the bear himself. He got into his jacket himself, and he staggered up into the *chosen* himself. The girl followed him while he did these things, weeping as she explained why she could not help him. Houston scarcely heard her. He was so feeble that he had room in his mind now for only one thing.

He imagined himself eating the bear.

He imagined himself eating it all the way there. He planned all the operations that would facilitate his eating it.

He would not be able to get the bear on the sled himself. He would have to cut it up first. He would have to cut off the limbs, and take them back and eat them, and then return for the body when he was stronger. He would have to hide the body meanwhile off the track.

It was quite dark when he came to the bear. It was frozen to

525

the track, with the sled and gun and knife frozen alongside. Houston booted the knife free of the ice and sat down on the bear and began to cut off a leg.

He started high, above the haunch, but the flesh had frozen into the consistency of toughened rubber, and he couldn't wait, and with his hand tore off a piece from the side of the incision. Holding it by the fur, he scraped off the meat with his teeth. There was very little taste that he could tell. But he felt it going down, and his stomach beginning to work again.

The wind dropped as he ate, as it usually did at this time of the evening, but the cold became suddenly more intense. He saw that he was not going to be able to sit about cutting off all the limbs, and that he had better take only one of them to be getting on with. The forepaw seemed the easiest, and he took that. He broke the bone with his knife and gun, and holding the limb down with his boot, finally wrenched off the paw up to the middle joint.

The paw was too big to go in his pocket, and too small for him to trust by itself on the sled. Houston walked home with it in his hand, in the darkness.

The bear tasted very little better than it smelt. But it lasted Houston. He ate several pounds of it every day. He ate it even when he was out of his mind. But a good half still remained when they left.

Chapter 16

THEY went through the pass on what Houston took to be 12 April, but which he later calculated must have been the 18th. Despite his tremendous calendaring, he had somehow lost six days – perhaps in delirium or unconsciousness. He had no recollection at all of the pass itself, and very little of the journey to it. It was not possible for the girl to have pulled him on the sled, for there were four bags of emeralds on it – over a hundredweight of them – so he reckoned that he must have been out on his feet; a state by no means unusual for him at the time.

He had passed through a month of unrelieved horror. The girl had not in any way helped to ease the pain in his arm, which she regarded as a penance for his sinful killing of the bear. Above all animals, the bear was sacrosanct, a mysterious creature of the mountains, who died each winter and lived again each spring. Not even to save life was it permissible to kill a bear; and the fact that Houston had done so during the period of its greatest mystery was so peculiarly abhorrent that she neither could, nor would, do anything to ease his sufferings. Some of Houston's most nightmarish memories were of trying to ease them for himself.

He had a confused impression of blackness and pain: of sleepless nights with the girl's tears trickling down his face; of a series of crazy, unreasonable acts. (He had tried, it seems, to set the arm, in a mess of bear fat; and later to freeze it; and then to unfreeze it. And he had wakened one night to find the girl gone, and had discovered her in the place of wind devils, quite naked, in a trance, trying to expiate his sin. Incredibly, she had come to no harm.)

But despite these vicissitudes, he had clung most doggedly to the plans he had made. He had staggered out of the hole on what he thought to be 1 April, and with the girl helping him had gone for his first look at the village. It was set in a hollow, on the banks of the same frozen river; and they had looked down on it for a couple of hours, seeing no Chinese.

They had made the journey again a week later, taking the sled with them this time and two sacks of emeralds. Houston had found a suitable cave for the emeralds, off the track, a cave whose curious ledged roof (the sacks were 'stuffed in the roof fabric – very laborious') he later sketched from memory. There were no Chinese in the village this time, either.

He had made one more emerald-ferrying trip a couple of days later; and it was on this trip, it seems, that he had knocked himself out for good. He had a recollection of clambering on to a rock with a sack on his shoulder; and then of finding himself in his sleeping bag, shouting aloud with the savage pain in his arm. He thought he must have fallen. He thought he had fallen on the arm.

After this, nothing was very clear.

It seemed to be colder in the hermit hole, the wood-pile shrinking.

It seemed to be darker.

It seemed to be stinking constantly, himself not in the big sleeping bag, but in Ringling's.

Vague impressions only came to him from the blur: of dragging up the smoky steps to the *chorten* and eating his meat raw; of crossing off days, the laborious upreaching effort worthwhile to record their final obliteration.

Of his own voice, drunken and slurred: 'No, no, you're wrong. It can't be. It's too early.'

'Chao-li, sit up. Please sit up.' An idea that his face was being washed. 'I tell you everything is melting. The sun is shining. I swear it.'

The sun indeed shining, the track wet, everything wet; the world running with glittering slushy water, and himself evidently tramping through it, boots turning an endless treadmill, some inevitable burden at his back, constant aching light in his eyes.

And then not light but dark, and everything gone but the sacks. Only the sacks left to look at in all the world; and he found himself looking at them very closely, and realized he was lying on them. He was lying on the sled. He was alone. It was night.

He came blundering up off the sacks in such distress of spirit that he heard himself wailing. She had left him. She had gone without telling him. Her time had come and she had gone. But then he remembered that it was only her spirit that went. It went and came back. Surely it could not yet have gone far; not beyond recall. He tried recalling her spirit, staggering about on the track in the dark. But it would not answer him, and he went weeping to look for her body that like all bodies had to be left; and saw it some time later, running towards him.

'Chao-li, be quiet, be quiet!'

'Why have you gone?'

'I was looking for the cave, for the other sacks. Chao-li, I can't find it. I can't remember it.'

'Oh, Mei-Hua, don't leave me.'

'Chao-li, keep your voice down, I implore you! We are at the pass!'

'Promise me.'

'Yes, I promise it. Chao-li, you must help me find the cave. There is little time.'

'How much time? Tell me, Mei-Hua. I must know.'

The unearthly conversation on the pass in the dark – was it a dream, a nightmare? – all that he could recall with any clarity; but that with much clarity, like the remarks of the surgeon as he was going under in the London Clinic some weeks later. No sense at the time of cross purpose, that the girl was intent on recovering the sacks before daylight, and he on reassurance that she would not leave him. He was obsessed with the idea that she would leave him soon, that she might have left him already and that it was some figment that he held.

'Oh, Chao-li, not for many years. I swear it!'

'Tell me. Tell me now.'

'I can't tell you. I mustn't.'

'You must. I won't let you go.'

'Chao-li, the sacks – we have only a few hours.'

'Tell me. Tell me the year and the month. You know them. Is it now? Is it now, Mei-Hua?'

'Oh, Chao-li, no. No, no. Not for a long time.'

'When, then? When?'

And was it then she had told him, or later; this side of the pass or the other? He couldn't remember. Nothing remained but the words, chasing there and back through his mind, slipping in and out of each other, but always there.

A pig with a curly tail, a tail that was six. A six pig, an earth pig. The six month of Earth Pig. It was a long way off, this pig. It was not yet a worrying pig. There would be time to deal with this pig.

'And then?' Oliphant had said. *'There must be something else that stands out. How did you come to be on the stretcher? Would that have been in Chumbi, or before? And what exactly is Chumbia – a village?'*

Not a village. A valley, a district. He had been in a little town, Yatung, and then somewhere else. But first? First, yes, a man with a rifle. And the girl in her heavy veil, suddenly. Just these two impressions: a man with a rifle, and the veil. *Then* the stretcher. A palanquin also, he thought. But whether for the girl or the Duke of Ganzing... Yes, the duke there, too. A distinct recollection of the duke seated amiably by his bedside.

'In a bit of a mess again, old chep. Never mind. Everything under control. They've got you a bottle of the Dalai Lama's urine – he's here in Yatung – marvellous specific in certain cases. Also a chep from Sikkim – very clever chep. He's set your arm. He'll have it as good as new.'

'Where is the abbess?' Houston said.

'Near by. Quite safe and well.'

'Can I see her?'

'Soon. When you're well enough to be moved. She sends to ask after your health every day.'

'Can she come here?'

'Not to Yatung, old chep. The Dalai Lama is here – a tricky problem of protocol.'

'Then I'll go there.'

'Certainly, old chep. In a few days. The snag is, there are rather – rather a lot of Chinese about at the moment. You left a knife lying about with your name on it. They've promised not to come into Yatung, but they tend to roam a bit outside, looking for you. Worrying.'

'I want to see her now.'

'Yerss. Drink this first. Do you good.'

Days lost drinking things to do him good; drugged days in which he thought of questions to ask when he was asleep and forgot them when he woke up; or was it the other way round? And then – when? – no butter lamps but stars, and a breeze on his face, and bumping up and down.

'Where – what – ?'

'Ssh. All under control, old chep. Going home now.'

'No. No! I won't – '

'Here. Time for your medicine. Have this.'

'I don't want it. I won't drink it. I'm not going home. I want the abbess. I tell you – '

'Quiet! *Quiet*, old chep. For God's sake – There are Chinese here. They're all over the place . . .'

'I'll shout to them. I'll wake the bloody dead – '

'Ssh. Ssh. For God's sake – Let me think' – and in Tibetan – 'How far to the Court of the Mother?'

'Four hours at least, Highness. It is not possible there and back before daylight.'

'Look, old chep, look, it just isn't *on*. It can't be done – '

'I tell you – '

'The Chinese are after you. If they get you they'll execute you. It's a matter of face for them.'

'I'm going to see her! I'm going to. She wants to see me.'

'She wants you to go. She's praying for it. Look, she's written to you. There's a letter and a gift in your baggage. It will bring her nothing but trouble and distress if the Chinese – '

'I know she wants to see me. I don't care what happens. Put me down. I tell you, I'm not going – '

More mumbled Tibetan.

'Very well. Now look. This is going to be a bumpy trip. You'll drink this.'

'I won't.'

'You will. We're going through the Chinese lines. I promise you'll see the abbess.'

'Do you swear it?'

'Honour *bright*, old chep!'

'All right.'

Blackness. Lurching, thunderous blackness again, with himself swimming in the middle of it, knowing the presence of soreness and pain but not in touch with them, and then swimming up into touch, re-establishing the old detested relationship. *Oh, God. Again.*

'Chao-li.'

'Oh, my love.'

She was lying on top of the covers. She was cold, her face shivering against his.

'Come inside,' Houston said.

She went away and came back, and was inside, on his left side, so that he could feel the cold length of her against him, their noses touching.

'You've cut your hair.'

'Yes.'

'I can't see – are you painted?'

'Only in Yamdring. When I go back.'

'Don't go back.'

She didn't say anything, merely looking at him.

He said, 'Don't go back, Mei-Hua. I love you.'

'I love you, Chao-li.'

'I can't live without you.'

'Yes. It will be very hard.'

Her mouth was open and he put his own to it and lay there, breathing lightly. He felt ill and weak. He said into her mouth, 'Mei-Hua, don't go back. Come with me. I couldn't bear to lose you.'

'You won't lose me. We are in the world together. I want you to live.'

'I love you more than life.'

'Yes, Chao-li. I, too. Don't talk now. Don't talk any more, my heart.'

Houston didn't think that they did talk any more then. He lay breathing shallowly into her mouth, and thought that he might have slept for a while. He was aware that she was sitting up, putting on her veil. Someone was knocking at the door.

'What is it?'

'Food, Chao-li. You should eat something.'

'I don't want anything.'

'Nor I.'

'Send them away.'

She called out, and took off her veil and lay down with him again; and for some hours then they merely gazed at each other. He had no idea how long he was there – a whole day, perhaps. There was knocking again.

'Yes?'

'Good Mother, it is time now. His Highness waits outside.'

'No,' Houston said.

'Chao-li – yes. You must go. Don't say anything.'

'No.'

'My own heart – I want you to be happy. You will always be in my mind. Always think of me. I have given you a half of my tears – '

'I don't want them.'

'Yes. Take them. They are yours. They are a half of me. When you look at them you will be looking at me. When you use them, it is I who will be nourishing you.'

'No. No, Mei-Hua, no. Come with me. Please come with me.'

'Oh, my love, don't make it harder. I want you to go and live. Don't say another word.'

He didn't say another word, sunk then in black desolation.

And black outside. And another drink to do him good, and all blackness then, welcome familiar blackness. And then leaving it, crashing out of it, falling. Voices were shouting, guns going off, coloured moons, a dozen of them, floating gaudily in the sky. Flares. Hands seemed to be lifting him, and he was back on the stretcher, jogging at a run. But his arm, *his arm*! Sheer blinding agony, flame-licked unbearable agony, rushing out of his mouth bellowing; and suffocating there as a hand clamped down on it. Searching desperately among the coloured

533

moons, and at last finding it – the welcome, the longed-for blackness; pain riding with him still, but detached once more.

It was mild grey morning when he came to, and he was lying on the ground. He was lying in a misty valley. He could hear eating and smell woodsmoke.

'*Trulku.*'

He knew the face above him. He couldn't place it.

'Safe now, *trulku*. In Sikkim now.'

He placed the man just as he spoke: it was the duke's major-domo from Ganzing. He tried to ask for the duke, but the words would not come.

'All well, *trulku*. They didn't get it. One man was hit and you fell from the stretcher, but the baggage is untouched. How is the arm?'

The arm was not good, and was to become a good deal worse. It was smashed again. They tried to get it looked at in two monasteries, but succeeded only in getting more stupefying drugs. Houston lay for two nights in the second of the monasteries, waiting for a doctor who had been sent for from Gangtok. The doctor didn't arrive, but just as they were preparing to leave again, an ambulance did. It was an old Rolls-Royce with a wicker-work body and a door at the rear. Houston lay full length in this impressive vehicle with his feet sticking out of the back; and so, still without his chitty but in some state, made his entry into the town he had tried so hard to reach many months before.

He saw little of it, for the surgeon at the Maharaja's hospital after one look at the arm gave him a shot of morphia, put him back in the Rolls-Royce, and pausing only to telephone a Mr Pant, the Indian diplomatic representative, sent him immediately off to Kalimpong.

There he was seen by an Indian medical officer of health who happened to be visiting the town, given another shot, and transferred to the Scottish mission hospital. He was booked in at 5 p.m. on 30 April 1951 – the first independently checkable date since he had booked out of the town rather more than a year before.

A few days later, at the urgent summons of the hospital authorities, Sheila Wolferston came up from Calcutta and officially took delivery of him and his baggage from the duke's bodyguard. They had refused, apparently on the duke's orders, to deliver him up to anybody else. They had been sleeping in his room, and eating, according to the mission's *Miscellany*, 'heartily'.

Houston knew nothing of this transaction, for in addition to his more spectacular ills he had contracted pneumonia. He was aware, without surprise, that Sheila Wolferston was with him, and also Michaelson. He didn't know which one of them told him what had happened to Hugh and the others. He did not seem able to grieve; he lay in a heavy stupor.

He lay there for three weeks (which might have been three hours or three years for all the sense of time he had) and was only vaguely aware one day that he was no longer there. He was in another place, a low-roofed, roaring sort of place.

'Are you awake, sport?'

He realized someone had been shaking him for some time.

'Where am I?'

'You're right. You're right, sport. We're flying to Calcutta. Look, seeing you're awake, there's things we ought to discuss – '

'Where's Sheila?'

'She's right. She's having a bit of shut-eye. Look, sport, she'll be awake soon, we haven't got long. I wanted to tell you what Da Costa is doing. He can definitely guarantee – '

'What Da Costa? I don't know who... Sheila!' Houston said.

'For Christ's sake, she's right! She's sleeping, I told you. Sure you know Da Costa. You like Da Costa. Strewth, I brought him to see you twice. All you need to do – '

'Sheila,' Houston said. 'Sheila!'

'Yes, Charles, yes, I'm here. Mr Michaelson, I particularly

535

asked you – you promised me you wouldn't worry him with this business.'

'He's got to worry about it some time.'

'What business? What is it?'

'Nothing. Nothing at all. Go to sleep again.'

'Da Costa?'

'Don't worry about it. Sleep now.'

He slept again, worried. Something worrying about Da Costa. A pale man, pale melon cheeks, dark eyes. A diamond flashing on Da Costa's finger as he talked. Who Da Costa? How did he know Da Costa? Da Costa had been met somewhere, worryingly.

He thought the doctor was Da Costa, but it was only an examination mirror flashing, and the cheeks were not plumply pale. Thin cheeks, Indian cheeks.

'Nor for some days, weeks perhaps. He is not strong enough. And in any case we would need authority. Who is the next of kin?'

'There isn't anyone. I've told you, doctor, I'm probably the nearest thing. But if you're certain it's got to be done, I would be ready to . . .'

'Mr Michaelson and Mr Da Costa – they are not related to him in any way?'

'Not at all. I'd be glad if you could keep them out, doctor. They worry him. It's a business matter he doesn't want to discuss just now.'

'Very well . . . In any case, he must be kept quiet. He needs a good deal of building up. Why was he moved?'

'A Chinese mission arrived in Kalimpong. His presence was considered a provocacion . . .'

Days of building up, of beautiful quiet, then. Sometimes he saw her there, reading, sometimes not. There was a row once near by, and he heard Michaelson's voice.

He said, 'Michaelson.'

'Hello. Did he wake you up? He's gone now.'

'What did he want?'

'Just to see how you are. How are you?'

He didn't know how he was, so he didn't tell her. He went away again. There was a fountain near by, and he often went into the fountain.

But it began to worry him over a period. At first he would forget it when he woke up, but then he began not to forget.

'Sheila.'

'Right here. Do you want to sit up?'

'There were some bags. There were two bags.'

'Yes. They're all right. I put them in your bank. I put them in Barclay's. I signed for them, and they'll only give them up on my signature. There were some drawings, too, on a piece of cloth, and a letter. They're all nice and safe, Charles. No need to worry.'

'A letter.'

'Just a letter. Nothing to worry about.'

'Can I see it?'

'It's in Tibetan. Can you read Tibetan?'

'Can we get it translated?'

'I got it translated – I'm sorry, Charles. I had to. There were one or two complications. All over now, though.'

'What did it say?'

'Do you really want to talk about it now?'

'From the abbess?'

'Yes. Just that she – she loves you and was making you a gift. You know. There was her official seal on it. That was why we had to get it translated and examined. The Chinese Embassy here claimed it was false, but of course it wasn't. Everything's all right now.'

'Can I have the letter?'

'Oh, I think better not, Charles. It's all locked up. Best to leave it where it is.'

'I want it.'

'Well. We'll see.'

'I want it.'

'All right. Rest now.'

*

But no rest after this, for he remembered it all, and had to have the letter, had to have it in his hand. Restless, sleepless nights.

'Hey – hey, sport, can I come in?'

'Have you got it?'

'What? Look, look, sport – keep it quiet, eh? It cost me a fortune to get in. I've got to talk to you.'

'I want the letter.'

'Yeah. Sure. Look, sport, if you don't like Da Costa, I can get another bloke. But we've got to be quick now. There's not a lot of time. They won't let you stay here, and you can't take the stones with you – that's for certain. Sheila doesn't understand. She doesn't get the situation at all. I *know* this bunch of bastards! They panic. They'll have you out of here in two twos if the Chinese get tough.'

'She's got to get the letter.'

'She doesn't need any flaming letter! All she's got to do is sign the form, and all you've got to do is instruct her. But for Christ's sake, you've got to be quick now. You've got to pull yourself together, sport.'

'What do you want of me? What is it?'

'Just two and a half per cent. Christ, it's bloody ridiculous! It's nothing at all. You'll still have half a million quid. Now, look – look, sport. I'm not getting any younger. You remember I helped you. I helped you a lot in Kalimpong. I've been there and back to Goa twice already. You don't like Da Costa, I can get you somebody else; But I tell you straight, you won't get better terms. He's offered forty million escudo. It's only half what the stuff is worth, but they have big risks. They've got to get it into Goa. And we can screw them up a bit. A bloke already offered me half in escudo and half guilders he was hedging it in Amsterdam. We can do better with Da Costa. He's got contacts in Belgium, Switzerland, America. Christ, sport – you can have it in the hardest currency you want. But you've got to be quick. You've got to shake yourself up. I tell you, the Chinese just signed a treaty with Tibet. They'll be signing one with the Indians next. And then you're cooked, mate. They'll have your guts for garters. You've got to get rid of that stuff now.'

'What stuff? What?'

'Christ, the emeralds. What else?'

'No!'

'Look, look, sport – quiet, eh?'

'No! No! Get out! Sheila! Sheila!'

Running and nurses and nightmares, then. He tried to hold on to the bags, face down on the sled, but they were talking him out of them. He wouldn't give them up. They were a half of her. He wouldn't.

'Charles, I'm desperately sorry – we've got to talk about it.'

'No. No.'

'Just let me talk, and you listen. Then say what you think. Charles, I've spoken to lots of people – dozens of them. It's quite right what Michaelson says. You won't be able to leave the country with the emeralds. There's a government regulation. They'll have to stay here. And it's almost certain then that they won't be able to resist the Chinese demand. The Chinese say that all monastery treasure belongs to the country, not to individuals, and that it couldn't belong to you in any case. Charles, dear, try and listen.'

'I don't want to hear. I don't care.'

'You want the emeralds, don't you?'

'They're a half of her.'

'The Chinese say they aren't. They want them back.'

'No. No.'

'Look dear, will you let me do what is best? I don't know what's happening at the moment. I don't know if they'll let you stay. You're not well enough to travel now, but they might make you. I'm trying to get the operation speeded up – they'd never dare to send you off then till you'd recovered. Please trust me.'

He didn't want to trust anybody. They kept coming at him. She was with them now, Michaelson, the dreaded Da Costa, guilders, francs, escudos. He cut himself off. He tried to remember the mantras, repeating them again and again for hours at a time.

'Charles, dear. They're going to operate on you tomorrow. Please, please trust me. It's for the best. There wasn't anything else to do.'

'Operate?'

'Tomorrow. I'll be with you. I'll stay with you.'

Operate. His arm, then. He must have expiated the sin by now. It was a hell of a long time, a lifetime since he had met the bear. He didn't want to think of the bear. He said a few mantras over and over to obliterate the bear. He said them for hours, but he didn't obliterate the bear.

'Just lie back, lie normally. You'll only feel a prick.'

He felt the prick, and then heard the bear. The bear began to shake him and roar. All shook and roared; a breathy in-and-out roaring, rhythmic, mantra-like. And then the rhythm broken. Confusion and argument, and his own voice muttering.

'Oh, God, he's coming to, doctor. Can't you please give him something?'

'It's very dangerous.'

'But this is monstrous – absolutely scandalous. I never heard of such a thing. How dare you – '

'Please Miss Wolferston, it is absolutely out of my hands. I can't interfere with a government order. A doctor and a trained nurse will sit beside him every minute until the aircraft – '

'Is it over?'

'All over now, Charles. Don't speak.'

'Is my arm – '

'You didn't have it. They'll operate later.'

Not have it? Why not have it? Not expiated? Sickness, then. Dreadful retching. Sitting up, her arms round him, leaning over bowl.

'Doctor, for pity's sake – you can see how he is.'

'Miss Wolferston, what can I say? I am very unhappy. I warned you – '

'At least let him stay till the plane is ready. What's the sense of lying in an ambulance?'

'Very well. I will allow that. I will answer for it. I will see the official myself now . . .'

'Do you want a drink of water?'

'Nothing.'

'Lie back, then. Lie still.'

Still. Nausea. Everything rolling, nothing to hold on to. People coming in and out.

'All right. But don't make a noise. He's sleeping now.'

'I give it in your charge then, Miss.'

'Thank you.'

'And it is with his approval I pay two and a half per cent to Mr Michaelson.'

'Yes. Yes.'

'You understand it is Mr Houston as vendor who pays this commission and not I? It is usual.'

'All right. I trust you.'

'You may trust me absolutely, Miss.'

'We're all trusing you, Da Costa.'

'Surely you have known me long enough.'

'Too right, mate.'

'You could have had cash, a bank pass book, anything you wanted, weeks ago. It is not my fault you must now at the last moment accept a promissory note.'

'It ain't my fault, either, sport.'

'Will you both go now? Thank you very much.'

'A pity he ain't awake. Tell him good-bye from me, eh?'

'Yes. Yes. Thank you. Thank you both very much. Good-bye.'

Queasy, shifting silence, then, which presently he could slow down to sleep in. To sleep in and roll in. Rolling, mmbling silence, in which he was being lifted; which was not silence at all.

'Four seats have been taken out. It is the best I can do.'

'You've not heard the last of this, I assure you.'

'Miss Wolferston, I have done everything I can. I am very busy.'

'It's the most callous, barbarous thing I ever heard of in my life.'

541

'I am sorry. Just one thing more. One of the passengers is a doctor. I have had a word with him and he will help you. He will give an injection, if necessary.'

'Thank you for that at least.'

'I am very sorry. Good-bye.'

Roaring. Deafening, lurching roaring, then. Roaring all the time. The bear roaring. The bear with his arm in its mouth. His arm! His arm!

'There we are, there now. You're all right old fellow. Drift off now. Go to sleep. Only landing.'

Landing and taking off and landing again. Fresh air and not fresh air and fresh air again. But all morphia sleep now; good familiar sleep, black solvent of all worry, events riding with him but no longer bothering him.

And so out again at last, with people streaming and engines revving, himself suspended in cool darkness on the stretcher. Large lit-up buildings and lights flashing, and one flashing very near, in his eyes.

'Oh, please. Please don't bother him. He's very ill.'

'Who is he? What name, please?'

'Why do you want to know?'

'Kemsley Newspapers. *Empire News* and *Sunday Graphic*.'

'His name is Houston,' she said.

Houston; and he was home; Saturday, 16 June 1961.

Epilogue

I

'*What I feel,*' confided T.L. in a memo dated February 1960, '*is that having committed ourselves so* hugely, *we shd leave no stone unt'd to (a) see that H. at least looks over our versn, (b) get a cast-iron decision on the copyrt position – further opins if nec, (c) get trustworthy indpt confmn of the facts. With regard to B-V, I never thought he wd. But take up his suggestns if you think fit.*'

This memo came to me attached to a letter from Professor Bourgès-Vallerin that I had sent through to him the previous day. I had invited the professor to edit and expand the Tibetan sections of the notebooks, reserving the right to delete to meet legal objections in London. He had declined this invitation on the grounds that his acceptable position with the communist authorities was dependent on his maintaining a strict neutrality in all his writings. He had offered, however, to supply a factual appendix – 'in no way implying that I express any opinion on the work or its author' – and had gone on to suggest that for the 'expansion' mentioned, one could not do better than apply to Dr Shankar Lal Roy, a useful source of Tibetan information and the chairman of the Calcutta branch of the India-Tibet Society. 'For the more singular parts of M. Houston's memoirs, I would myself have had recourse to Dr Roy. If anyone is able to confirm or deny them, it is he.'

There was a certain edge to this advice which I pondered, together with T.L.'s memo, somewhat gloomily.

I said, 'Miss Marks, when are you likely to be ready with

Underwood's stuff? I'll need time to study it before seeing Mr Oliphant.'

'Just finishing. You can have his comments now if you like.'

There were twenty-five pages of Underwood's comments. He had laboured for ten weeks at his task, and had kept back no crumb of evidence. He had been to see a divorced 'Glynis' at Swansea; 'Lister-Lawrence' at Wimbledon; 'Wister' in Yorkshire; and a Mr Blake-Winter at Abingdon. He had also written to, among others, 'Lesley', married, in Seattle; a widowed 'Mrs Michaelson' in West Australia; the niece of a deceased Mrs Meiklejohn in Arbroath; and the Duke of Ganzing in Delhi. Correspondence with them, and with a number of institutions in Kalimpong, Zürich, Auckland and Lisbon, were in another file, which Miss Marks was in process of sorting out.

Because I was seeing Mr Oliphant at four o'dock, his brightest time, and had to have lunch myself first with an agent, there was little opportunity to do more than skim through the material.

There had been very little luck with 'Sheila Wolferston'. The girl had married, it seemed a New Zealand journalist, in 1953, and had gone with him to Auckland the following year. In March 1955, the mother had sold her house in Godalming, and had flown out to join them. She had broken her journey on the way to see her husband's war grave in the Middle East, and had been run over by a bus and fatally injured in Cairo (just one of the maddening incidents that seemed to bedevil anyone connected with Houston's story). The girl had divorced her husband in 1958 on the grounds of drunkenness and infidelity, but had apparently stayed on in New Zealand; exactly where, and doing what, we had not been able to discover. Advertisements under box numbers in the Auckland *Star*, Wellington *Dominion* and Christchurch *Press* (booked, according to Underwood's notes, to run once a week until 31 March) had not so far brought any result.

Even more maddening was the fate of the only other living English person to have been involved in Houston's peculiar adventure. Underwood had seen 'Wister' in a mental home near Hull (where his wife worked as a secretary); he had gone for a walk in the grounds with the pair of them. Wister had worn a big trilby hat and a muffler, and had enjoyed himself for much of the time by sliding about on the icy paths. He was quite harmless, had been released by the Chinese at the same time as Sheila Wolferston (January 1951) and flown home immediately. He had nothing whatever to say. His wife said he would often have very talkative days, but had never to her knowledge, or that of his doctor, even so much as mentioned Tibet.

Sheila Wolferston had been to see him twice in his first year at the home, and another old colleague had visited him also. He hadn't recognized either of them. His wife was getting a small pension for him from the firm, and Underwood gathered that her principal interest in seeing him was a discreet curiosity to learn if any more money would be forthcoming. Miss Wolferston had, it seemed, mentioned that steps were being taken to coax the insurance company into making an *ex-gratia* payment. (It didn't, relying on the 'war' clause in the policy.)

She knew that Meiklejohn and Houston's brother had been killed 'while escaping', and that Houston himself had been badly injured. (Her impression was that he had been released at the same time as her husband.) Miss Wolferston had spoken very little of their dreadful experiences in Tibet, and she had not pressed her.

Nobody seemed to have pressed Miss Wolferston. Underwood had tracked down a married cousin in Beckenham, some tennis friends in Richmond, some work friends, even a couple of old school friends. Few of them had heard of Houston, and none of his curious role in the monastery or of the treasure.

All this had begun to acquire a somewhat sinister aspect. I went glumly off to lunch.

2

Mr Oliphant's main preoccupation of recent weeks had been the composition of a Founder's Statement for his bequest. He was still at it when I arrived, polishing away with all the lapidary zeal that had formerly gone into his primer. A good deal of buttering-up had been necessary lately to support his precarious spirits, and as soon as I opened the door and could see that he was actually conscious, I said vigorously, 'Well, Mr Oliphant! You're looking in splendid form today.'

'Am I, dear boy? It must be,' he said, writing busily, 'because I have arrived – one can only hope – at a definitive version. Listen to this.'

He read out his definitive version, in Latin and then English.

'The translation is a bit free, but it seems to me – I don't know – rather more succinct?'

'Very much more. Pithy.'

'And yet not without a touch of humour.'

'A strong touch. Mordant, I would say.'

'Mordant,' Mr Oliphant said, pleased. 'Yes. I'm glad it comes through. Sit down, my dear fellow. What is your special news?'

I sat down.

'I'm afraid it isn't very good. Bourgès-Vallerin won't take it on.'

'Oh,' Mr Oliphant said, heavily.

'His reasons seem fairly convincing.'

'What are they?'

I told him the professor's reasons.

'I've brought you a copy of the sum of our researches to date. You'll see there are still rather a lot of gaps in it.'

'There is still nothing from Miss Wolferston?'

'Nothing at all.'

'This is what I find the hardest to understand,' said Mr Oliphant. 'She is a most punctilious, *devoted* sort of girl. She was in and out of the flat constantly. She used to rub my chest!'

'Perhaps she hasn't seen the adverts. Not everyone reads them. She might have changed her name, too.'

'I think if you had phrased it differently. If you had suggested that Houston needed help.'

'Well. We can try it,' I said, and made a note. 'I had a letter from Scarborough, incidentally, last week – from the agent who sold him the house.'

'Scarborough?'

'Scarborough, Tobago. You'll remember Houston went there in 1958. Apparently he paid off his house staff several months ago and the place has been unoccupied ever since. It's in a spot called Rum Bay – a fine beach and nothing much else, one of the speculators' paradises out there. The agent has had no instructions to sell it.'

'What is his view?'

'He didn't offer one.'

It had taken me long enough to find him. I had written first to the Governor of Trinidad, who had passed my letter on to his Colonial Secretary, who had sent it to the Under-Secretary for Tobago. He had in turn put me on to a Mr Joshua Gundala, OBE, who apparently lived on the island and combined the function of publisher of the weekly *Tobago Times* with that of estate agent. It was Mr Gundala who had sold Houston the house. His letter-heading announced that he had several other choice lots to sell in Rum Bay.

'He has no theory at all?'

'Except that Houston must have left the island, no.'

'Then mine is almost certainly right,' said Mr Oliphant.

Mr Oliphant's theory was that Houston had bought a boat and gone off in it. He had done this once before without telling anybody, and had not returned for nine months. It seemed hard for him to settle. He had lived in Switzerland, Bermuda, Jamaica, Barbados, Trinidad, and now Tobago. Or was it now Tobago? It was because of this doubt that I was still advertising in the Trinidad *Guardian*, which circulated widely in the Caribbean.

Under the terms of his contract, Mr Oliphant had the right to approve our choice of writer, and he came up presently with a suggestion.

'The great thing is that we must not have either vulgarity or sensationalism. If you asked this Dr Roy something that called for a lengthy statement, you might be able to judge from his method and style how he would work out.'

'Yes. We might.' It was after five by this time, and we had not yet got to The List – a catalogue of queries that I had been systematically working through with him. He seemed alert enough, however. I decided to try a couple.

'I thought we might tackle this one about the monk – the chief medical monk. I've got here "Did Houston ever evince any theory why the man turned traitor?"'

'Traitor,' Mr Oliphant said. 'I suppose it depends which way you look at it. He was a doctor, quite a good one by all accounts, and I think the Chinese represented progress to him. He wasn't alone, you know, in that. The greater part of the intelligentsia wanted reforms of one sort or another, and they thought, mistakenly, that the Chinese would bring them... Perhaps it annoyed him to know that so much money was lying about in the form of useless emeralds when the country needed real hospitals and real equipment.'

'Yes. How could he have known how much money? You'll remember the governor told Houston that nobody knew this except the monastery council.'

'Ah. Well. I think the answer to that goes back to the time of the Seventeenth Body. You'll recall she was a lady of immoderate passions, and that the abbot had an unfortunate time with her one year. He had to be carried away and was delirious for a week. The monk looked after him for that week. I expect he let something slip... It doesn't seem to you convincing?' he said anxiously.

'Oh, yes. Yes, it does,' I said, scribbling. I suppose I must up to that time have read through the notebooks a couple of dozen times, but never, apparently. with the talmudic skill that Mr Oliphant had brought to bear. A supplementary had occurred to me while he was speaking.

'You'll remember Houston got half a million pounds for his two bags, and was told they were worth double. It would seem to give the eight bags a total value of four million pounds.'

'So why did the Tibetans value them at three, you mean?

I'm sure I don't know. Perhaps Houston was given wrong information. Perhaps the cost of living had gone up. I've never understood how they could have got them valued, anyway. Perhaps it was done simply by weight and they merely adjusted the value from time to time. No. Sorry . . .'

The agent had been fairly lavish with his wine and brandy at lunch and my head began to ache on the way back. Through Croydon there was the most enormous traffic jam, and hemmed in by Mac Fisheries vans and British Road Services lorries I had a sudden moment of panic. She-devils? Incarnations? Monastery treasure? What in God's name had I let the firm in for? There was no Houston, no Sheila Wolferston. The nurse Michaelson had married knew nothing, the bank in Zürich would say nothing. Portugal seemed to be full of men called Da Costa, none of whom seemed anxious to reply to our adverts. They were booked to run for weeks and weeks . . . It suddenly occurred to me with what ease, with what creative ease, Mr Oliphant had answered the question about the monk.

With sudden awful conviction I knew that from beginning to end the story was a phoney; that we were never going to hear anything more of Houston . . .

I had left a book at the office on which an opinion had been promised for the following day, so I had to go back to get it. Everyone had gone but I let myself in and went up. There was a letter on my desk with a note from Miss Marks. The postmark was Trinidad, and because the inquiries clerk had thought it another bill from the *Guardian* it had been sent in error to the accounts department. It wasn't a bill. The single sheet inside bore no name and no address. It said simply:

Dear Sir,
    If you're interested in the whereabouts of Mr Houston try asking Joshua Gundala, OBE, how his lunkies are doing lately. The Tobago Times won't tell you.

February and March are busy months in publishing offices and mercifully, in the press of work, there was little time to reflect on Houston and his problems. Beyond writing to Dr Shankar Lal Roy, and to Joshua Gundala, OBE (quoting my correspondent and his baffling lunkies – about which neither the *O.E.D.*, *Dictionary of Slang*, nor Colonial Office Press Section was very informative) I did nothing further about them. Paradoxically, things then began to happen.

The first was a reply from Dr Shankar Lal Roy, saying that he had himself started a dossier on the Yamdring treasure, on the basis of refugee reports obtained in 1951, and that he would be happy to help.

The second was from Joshua Gundala, OBE. He wrote:

I thank you for your letter of 27th February, the contents of which I note. It is great nonsense, and I think I know who has told you this. However, to cast light on the situation and get definite information for you about Mr Houston I will go myself personally to Rum Bay and will keep you fully informed.

The third, one of a batch of memos from T.L., who was in New York, was less good. I had not been keeping him in touch with our quest for *trustworthy indpt confmn of the facts*, and my heart sank as I read it.

TIBET BOOK. Harpers v. keen, will advance — dollars, sight unseen, also much foreign and paperback interest. No reason why we shd not agent this & collect the commission to offset costs. Pl. get O's agreement & advise by rtn.

The fourth was not good at all.

I said with mild panic, 'Miss Marks, get on to Worplesdon and say I'd like to come down this afternoon,' and watched while she did so. I was thus able to see her face change and to appreciate why.

I said, 'When was it?'

'Half past eight this morning. He never woke up.'

Father Harris took the service, and afterwards over a cup of tea I explained the position to him. He took it very calmly.

'My boy, you worry too much. I've noticed it before. Why not leave everything in God's hands?'

'I wish I could, Father. The snag is it's in ours at the moment. I'm in the unenviable position of being publisher, agent and trustee of a piece of literary property about which I entertain the gravest doubts.'

'Have your doubts increased since you began to look into the evidence?'

'They've certainly become more insistent.'

'Because you're worrying more about the unresolved ones this is all it is. As I understand it, there is ample evidence that this man went to Tibet, and that he came back from Tibet. All you're unable to check is what he did in between.'

'That's all.'

'Well. That doesn't seem to me,' said Father Harris with a sharp look, 'a good enough reason to doubt him. Every point you've been able to check shows that his account is a reliable one. If somebody had told you six months ago that an obscure schoolteacher had gone into Tibet and come out again with injuries that necessitated the loss of an arm, and with his material circumstances apparently greatly changed, wouldn't that have aroused your interest? It *did* arouse your interest.'

'Unfortunately.'

'Never mind about that,' said Father Harris. 'The trouble with you is you're getting blasé. You're dazzled by wonders. You want more and more of them. First things first. You were interested enough to want to publish the book. Why prevent this American publisher from doing the same?'

'Because we know a bit more about it now.'

'I'm sure you're doing this to annoy me,' Father Harris said. 'Well, I'm not going to be drawn. There is no point of scruple or conscience here. Quite the reverse . . . How many dollars did you say?'

I told him how many dollars.

'Heavens above!' said Father Harris mildly. 'What use couldn't I put that to? Never mind. The scholars will benefit. As your co-trustee, I say take the money. It's rather more than you put up, but then they're getting rather more for it by this time, aren't they?'

'What about my doubts?'

'Very obtuse ones,' said Father Harris firmly, 'which you are holding in the face of rather more numerous proofs than I am accustomed to considering. God and the logic of events will I am sure shortly set them at rest.'

Whether due to God, the logic of events, or Father Harris himself, my doubts began from that moment to disperse. A certain slap-happy hilarity set in. As publisher I had bought, as co-trustee sold, and as agent now began to collect commissions on, Mr Oliphant's notebooks; the two latter activities rapidly becoming extensive. Coincidently, and as though a portent of Father Harris's promised heavenly approval, confirmatory matter began to flow in.

From Portland Place, London, came a letter from the Chinese *Chargé d'Affaires*. He said briefly that he understood we had information relating to certain well-known valuables stolen from the Tibetan Autonomous Region during a period of 'separatist activities'. On the instructions of his 'Authorities in Peking' he had to point out that since our two governments were in friendly relations with each other, our correct course was to place this information at his disposal, and that any other course would be not only incorrect and unfriendly but would lay us open to the charge of compounding a felony.

'Hello. How did they get on to that?'

'Very rum,' Underwood said.

'I expect we'll find out in good time.'

We found out from Dr Skankar Lal Roy.

I write *(he wrote)* to advise you that you may hear from the Chinese Diplomatic Service – there is no need for alarm on this score. I am having to pursue inquiries with some of our people in Tibet. Some are 'doubles' working with the Chinese Intelligence Service, and to get information it is frequently necessary to give some – of a harmless and checkable kind. If you do hear it will be useful to confirm, without disclosing anything, that you have in fact some information relating to the Yamdring treasure ... I will write more fully later.

Dr Roy was as good as his word. An inundation of ten and twelve-page single-spaced letters began to arrive, which Underwood summarized as under:

Duke of Ganzing: left Tibet on ticket-of-leave at invitation of India Maha Bodhi Society which organized official world celebrations for 2,500th anniversary of the Buddha's enlightenment in 1956. Dalai Lama, heads of several monasteries, and hundreds of other lay figures also attended. No Yamdring dignitaries appeared, although invited. All religious figures returned, but 70 temporal ones did not. In 1957 these people offered amnesty by Chinese and also promised good jobs in government; almost all, including duke, then returned.

Very shorty after, situation worsened in Tibet. General Chang Kuo-bua, commander of Chinese Liberation Army, signed order of the day calling for 'constant vigilance against the subversive activities of imperialist elements and the rebellious activities of separatists'. His efforts approved by Peking Radio, which commented, 'The People's Liberation Army has the responsibility to suppress revolts and will certainly join hands with all patriotic Tibetan citizens in dealing firm and telling blows to rebellious elements.'

That blows not telling enough shown by subsequent widescale revolt. Tibetans set up revolutionary movement called *Mi Mang Tsong-Du* – People's Committee Against Chinese Communism. Chinese eventually lost patience, decided to drop puppet government and set up in its place Preparatory Committee for Proposed Tibetan Autonomous Region. Also moved in three million Chinese males and embarked upon policy of Pacification by Impregnation.

Every sizeable village billeted and forcible mating begun with all spinsters and women whose husbands taken away. Programme called 'Han-isation'. Apparently well organized and conducted on methodical lines, each 'district' or 'region' heavily garrisoned and patrols and pickets out on hilltops to keep area clear of 'bandit attacks' while operation completed. Army doctors followed up on schedule to make pregnancy tests, and when majority successful, troops moved on to next area. Tibetans fond of babies, anybody's babies, and in most areas plan seems to have worked very well.

By 28 March 1959 Peking announced rebellion over and 'Tibetan Autonomous Region in full exercise of its powers'. Few days before this, 17 March, Dalai Lama had fled to India. He reported to International Commission of Jurists that Chinese were sterilizing Tibetan males, had killed 65,000 of them and had destroyed 1,000 monasteries. Huge numbers of monks put on to road building work, in the proportion of (in English round figures) 15,300 to each 140-mile section. Several thousand miles of roads being built.

Policy, he said, to degrade religion as unifying force for Tibetans and humiliate religious leaders. Buddha himself described as 'reactionary element' in 'their vulgar propaganda'. Monastery treasure taken over by State or simply looted . . .

Governor of Hodzo: Chinese report that he was tried 1951, sentenced to 15 years. No information on wives, but children photographed in Chinese propaganda sheet 'happily joining hands with young comrades to build a steel smelter in the grounds of their Peking Academy.'

Abbot of Yamdring: 'died of over-eating' (Chinese report, April 1952 – evidently euphemism for poisoning); incarnation recognized January 1958 (*Mi Mang Tsong-Du* report, March 1959).

Abbess of Yamdring: no information. Dr Roy investigating.

Deputy Abbot and other dignitaries: no news, but monastery apparently still functioning (March 1959).

Yamdring Treasure: MMTD report, March 1959, 'Chinese operations still continuing to find residue of treasure, presumed to have been cached on route — to — .'

There was also a scholarly outline of the history and traditions of Yamdring with a detailed description of the ceremonies; no item of which departed in any way from Houston's own account. Since many of the details, particularly those concerning the Second Festival of the Monkey, had only recently, according to Dr Roy, come to light, this seemed to be a decided gain.

None of it, of course, was conclusive – but it certainly helped.

'It helps?' said Father Harris. 'I would describe you, Davidson, as a bit of a caution. Prepare your presses. Start writing some of those splendid advertisements. What are you waiting for?'

'For news of Sheila Wolferston, Da Costa and Houston . . . Unless we can shed light on – '

'News will come and light will be shed,' said Father Harris confidently. 'I have an instinct about it.'

That his instinct was justified was soon evident, but whether the news brought light or darkness was less easy to decide.

The first item came from Calcutta. Dr Roy wrote:

Abbess of Yamdring: still, I am afraid, nothing certain to add. *Mi Mang Tsong-Du* agents in the Chinese Foreign Section IV (a) – Movement Control, Transfer Section – report troop movements, evidently to quell disturbances, in Hodzo province last September (1959). Since Hodzo Dzong is itself garrisoned and apparently quiet (my letter 29 March) and the only other sizeable centre is Yamdring, we may conclude that trouble has broken out there. In this connexion it will be as well to cite an allegedly old prophecy that the Abbess would vacate her eighteenth body (i.e. die) in the sixth month of Earth-Pig (September 1959). Whether a disturbance broke out because the inhabitants were trying to avert this fate, or whether because it had actually occurred . . .

The next news came from Tobago. I had been having a bit of trouble with Joshua Gundala, o.b.e., who despite his promise to keep me informed, had not even replied to my two further letters. I had therefore shown the correspondence to Oliver Gooch, on whose advice I had written telling Mr Gundala that unless we heard from him by 30 April 1960, we would insert a displayed inquiry in the Trinidad *Guardian* putting forward all the information at our disposal including the anonymous letter whose contents had already been communicated to him.

Mr Gundala did not wait for 30 April. He wrote by return:

I thank you for your letter of 10 April but am unable to understand all the agitation. It is not as if Mr Houston was a man of normal habits. I hear he has gone away before for many months without warning. And with regard to lunkies, this is a piece of scandalous nonsense. No reliable witness has ever seen a shark of any kind near Rum Bay. If anywhere, they are at the other side of the island where unscrupulous rivals are jealous of my success. Rum Bay is a beautiful site, ideal for retired people – safer even than Montego Bay and far less spoilt. These stories of lunkies are put about by ignorant fishermen who do it only to get new nets from the government. Do you wonder that the *Tobago Times* will not publish such silly gossip

With regard to Mr Houston, the facts are as follows:

His houseboy states that last September he became very restless, walking about all night, etc. He went once to Scarborough (and perhaps while there bought himself a ticket either to Venezuela, Trinidad or the other islands – it is very easily done). One day Mr Houston gave a month's wages to the house staff, cook, gardener, and the boy himself, and the next morning was absent from breakfast. The boy found his shoes on the beach as if he bad gone for a bathe. This was unusual because with only one arm he would never bathe himself but always with the boy. The boy informed the police constable at Rum Bay D.C.

I saw the p.c.'s report, and in it the boy states he could not remember whether the shoes had been left on the beach from the previous day, which sometimes happened. The p.c. questioned the local taxi service, bus drivers, etc., but nobody remembered picking up Mr Houston either the previous night or in the morning. (In any case he could have walked to Wilmington, two miles away, where there is a choice of three buses to Scarborougb. The p.c. did not pursue his inquiries there, and by the time a reporter of the *Tobago Times* did so, nobody could remember. Nevertheless, I am confident this is what he must have done.)

Bearing in mind that Mr Houston never went bathing by himself, that no reports of drowning have come to light, that he paid off his house staff, and he has gone away in this way before, you will see it is very premature to jump to hasty conclusions.

As I have already promised to keep you informed and as I am quite sure that either I, as realtor, or our *Tobago Times* news service will be the first to hear anything, I hope you will not find it necessary to insert this inquiry in the Trinidad *Guardian* which will serve only to raise groundless fears and cast grave aspersions which might reluctantly have to be answered in other ways.

'What do you think?'

'I think the lunkies have been busy,' Oliver Gooch said. 'I wonder if Oliphant could have known this?'

'How could he?'

'I don't mean specifically the lunkies. But he might have worked out the Earth-Pig business and guessed something like this would happen. There was a funny sort of look about him when he told me the story first.'

'Well, what do you want to do about it?'

'You think Houston is definitely dead?'

'What do you think?'

'I think we've had it.'

'Yes.'

4

'You think we've what?' Father Harris said.

5

'To me,' T.L. said, 'the situation is completely crazy. You say Harris won't agree to pay back the advances and that as co-trustee he still means to try and get the book published — elsewhere if necessary. How can he do that?'

'He can't, without my approval.'

'So meanwhile the stuff lies here.'

'Yes. We're in a state of deadlock.'

'And your idea is what?'

'I haven't got one. Unless we could produce Houston we wouldn't have a leg to stand on in case of trouble. And to try and do the book without him would need so much fiddling we'd never get any reputable scholar to touch it. The fact is, we've simply got to get more material. We must turn up — in New Zealand and — in Portugal. We must also in view of the strong presumption of Houston's death try and get the bank in Zurich to play. Without all this we just don't have a book.'

'You don't think there will be a book?'

'No. I don't.'

'And meanwhile you have contracted with nine publishers including – I hesitate to mention it – ourselves, to produce one within a year.'

'Yes.'

'And should therefore tell them the situation and return the advances.'

'Quite.'

'Which your co-trustee won't agree to do.'

'That's the situation.'

'All right,' T.L. said. 'I've got it now.'

'Look,' he said, in the afternoon. 'Just sit down a minute. And don't blow your top. I've been having a word with Harris. I think there's something in his idea'

'Do you?'

'Yes. You didn't mention it to me.'

'Because it's simply preposterous. Can't you imagine the wild, rubbishy job a journalist would make of it?'

'There are journalists and journalists,' T.L. said mildly. 'And anyway, it will need fictionalizing a bit.'

'It's out of the question. Look, I've spent more time on this than anyone else, and I tell you the situation would be simply impossible.'

'It looks a good deal more possible to me than it has looked for some time. For one thing, the copyright headache seems to have vanished. You and Harris are now the sole arbiters of what is to be done with this. You've got to find some common ground. A great deal of money has already been spent, and I'm not disposed to drop it so easily. Besides, I quite like the story.'

'I gave certain promises to that old man Oliphant. I told him the job wouldn't be vulgarized or sensationalized in any way. I mean to keep those promises.'

'Fine. You'll be in an excellent position.'

'What do you mean?'

'You've been telling me how much time you've spent with it. I don't suppose anyone knows the material better than you.

558

Harris agrees with me. He now suggests that since you're publisher, agent and co-trustee, you might just as well be author into the bargain. For my part,' T.L. said, lighting up his pipe, 'you can set it up in type, too, if you want. So. Now you're the complete one-man band.'

6

That was in April 1960. It took some time to make up my mind, a bit longer for the other publishers to make up theirs, longer still to sort out, mentally and on paper, the enormous mass of notes and letters that had accumulated. I began writing in August, at week-ends and in the evenings; and it was July 1961, before the first complicated draft was finished.

Because there was still no definite news of 'Sheila Wolferston', 'Da Costa' or Houston himself (and still is not – the reader must formulate his own theories) and because these phantoms had been constantly in my mind as I wrote, denying this and underlining that, bringing injunctions and starting actions, in a way that made it impossible for me to assess the readability of the MSS, I sent it first to a couple of readers before showing it to T.L.

One of their comments I quote on the very first page of this book; for T.L.'s (which he gave me first on the telephone and then put in a memo) the reader will have to turn to page 233. He ended his memo:

> ... But if you feel so strongly do a little foreword explg the book and its backgd. Also it seems to need a bit of rounding-off...

A letter had come in from Dr Shankar Lal Roy in that morning's post, and I turned from the memo and read it again.

> I enclose *(he wrote)* the most recent issue of the *Shih Shih Shou Tse (Peking Current Affairs Handbook)* which, as you will see from the translation of the item on p. 22. seems to answer one more outstanding point.

The translation, headed *Bank Loans*, read:

AGRARIAN BANK: 700,000 New Yuan, interest-free, to the Commune of Yamdring (Tibetan Autonomous Region) for seeds, fertilizers and implements. This commune, established at the eager request of the citizens after they had dealt a firm rebuff to local separatists has been very rapidly converted into a lively community by the arrival of Volunteers from the Motherland. One thousand spinsters, formerly unable to find husbands due to reactionary customs and the gangster activities of separatists, are now joyfully married and raising a new generation to assist in the success of the Commune . . .

I had been smoking too much recently, and my mouth was sour. The thought of the lively Volunteers and the generating priestesses seemed to make it sourer still.

Miss Marks saw me shaking my head over the letter.

'Not very nice, is it?'

'Not very,' I said.

'But maybe it's all for the best.'

'Maybe it is.'

'It's hard to know how it could have continued in the old way. And anyway there wasn't anything very marvellous about that, was there?'

'They liked it.'

'Yes . . . It's an odd story, isn't it, all of it?'

'Very,' I said, as I had said once before, to Mr Oliphant.

'And this' – she nodded to the letter – 'seems to complete it somehow. I wonder if it's the rounding-off that T.L. asks for in his memo.'

'I wonder,' I said.

Miss Marks had provided, indirectly, the beginning. There was a sense of fitness that she should provide the end.